A QUARTER PAST

DANCING WITH DISASTER

LUKE MAUERMAN

BEEKMAN PLACE EDITIONS

Mauerman, Luke

A Quarter Past, Book I: Dancing with Disaster

First Edition

Library of Congress Control Number: 2021917531

ISBN 978-1-7330257-2-0 (paperback)

Published by Beekman Place Editions

Desert Hot Springs, California

Cover design - Peter Langdon, UK

Printed in the United States of America

Created with Vellum

PART I

2019 - SAN FRANCISCO

1

Thursday, October 17, 2019

If you could travel back in time, where would you go?" David sounds strained, intense. Not his usual self.

He's got nearly a tankard of Knob Creek going; the ice clanks in his glass. He offers me some as I stand in his kitchen. But I'm more of the scotch derivation myself, having grown tired of the pear notes in bourbon. All he has is Dewar's, but it'll do. He's never stingy with the portions.

I'm happy to answer his question. Sounds fun.

Yet I have come to his apartment tonight in specific and dire need of emotional support, a rare, slippery, doomed-to-fail grasp at empathy from him. All is not well in my personal life right now. But it appears he's off on some other direction this evening. And changing directions is not a thing David does lightly, no matter how much bourbon he's had. He's a scientist, through and through.

So I swallow my thoughts for now. I swallow scotch—it

burns nicely—and allow my mind to follow in this new direction instead.

I respond, "I assume you're speaking rhetorically, since time travel is inherently silly. But if I were given the chance, being a long-term San Franciscan, I'd have to go see this city in 1906. Before the earthquake and fire, to catalogue what was here, what was lost. And then to experience the quake, the fires—to watch how they coped.

"I'd want to enjoy the Castro in its gay heyday of the 1970s, before AIDS. Actually—the *Titanic*! I'd go on the *Titanic* so fast, I'd be like a compass near north.

"And I suppose I'd want to get a load of the London Blitz. See what really happened, since I lived there in the nineties."

"Yes, Mark, you remind me of it often."

It's a fun exercise, but as David says nothing further and is putting the finishing touches on dinner, I'm back to fussing about my own personal news; that which I've designated Problem Zero. It's so immediate that it isn't even Problem One. Problem One implies some distance from me, a thing I have to reach out to in order to touch. And that's not the case here. Problem Zero is, navigationally speaking, equivalent to my absolute coordinates: zero-point-zero. It resides within me, dragging me down, body and soul.

I'm inwardly near to screaming.

But David says, rather simply, "You'd need clothes suitable for the period. And old bank notes, which I guess you could order off eBay."

"Why are you telling me this?"

"Because I did it."

"Did what?"

"Time travel." He says it without irony—without even a hint of boastfulness. Which, frankly, serves as my first clue that he's pulling my leg.

The concept is beyond ludicrous. I can think of a million

and six reasons why time travel is impossible, and not a single one to indicate that it is. Plus, if it is true, he'd be so full of himself right now, so lit on fire—the fact that he's not makes me once again comfortable that he's just full of himself and being weird again. He's going off the rails—tonight, of all nights, just when I need him to be present and normal. For once. For me.

Well, friend or not, *present* and *normal* were never his strong suit. I figure it's best to just drop the whole thing.

"OK. So, other than that . . . did you manage to get your car fixed?"

"Mark, I'm serious. I did it."

His gaze is usually only this intense when he's about to climax in bed. It shocks me enough that I'm laser focused on him. It shocks me enough that I forget to take another sip of scotch.

"I spent four hours yesterday in the year 1950. I bought some stocks, had lunch at Tadich Grill, and smoked a cigarette at the table. My waiter lit it for me."

"But . . . you don't smoke."

He growls. "Mark? Focus?"

He goes to a drawer and pulls out a thin pile of stock certificates. They have an unmistakable mid-century look. Shares for AT&T, Dow Chemical, Johnson & Johnson and several to do with uranium mines. All dated February 3, 1950. It was a Friday. The certificates are franked, signed, and together worth about $5,000.

They are also brand new. I lift them to my nose and can smell the ink, a sharp blue tang. In running my finger across one I slightly smudge some print because it hasn't completely settled into the page yet.

David also produces an open pack of Lucky Strikes, in the old-style white and red wrapper. They, too, smell new and don't appear to be stale. I inhale the odor of damp, fresh tobacco leaves.

"Mark, it's real. I got it!"

He's allowing triumph to show, finally. It's beginning to ooze from his sizable frame.

But just then the rice cooker snaps off and he stops speaking as he gets dinner ready.

Things must be done in sequential order.

It's David.

This is Thursday. We always have dinner in his apartment at 18th and Danvers on Thursday; two bearded, middle-aged gay men, eating, drinking and watching TV together. Tonight he's making "Death by Garlic": Vietnamese chicken wings smothered in chopped garlic cloves over rice. My favorite.

But my little Problem Zero is going to have to simmer on low. Clearly. David's up to something, and when he gets like this, he won't hear a word I say. It'll have to wait. I know better than to try to help him in his own kitchen or to press him for further information right now. He'll only divulge what he wants, when he's ready. Because he is who he is.

And right now he ain't saying boo.

We seat ourselves at his kitchen table and begin attacking the pungent chicken wings, our tumblers of booze dripping with condensation. I try to focus instead on the enormity of what he's implying, wondering if it bears thinking about at all.

I don't believe him. But he's evidently convinced I should, for reasons unknown.

I force myself to switch gears to his harebrained idea about time travel and realize that it would thrill me. Yet I'm assigning only about an eight percent probability he's telling the truth.

I have travelled in time before. At least I think I have. A few times as a small child in the early 1970s I'd go into a seldom-used room at my grandparent's house, or into a nursing home, where everything was still the 1950s—even the very air. I'd seem to fall backwards in time. It would make me dizzy.

I once spent hours in the San Francisco Public Library

poring over historical photographs of the city. I got the images of how it used to look so firmly entrenched in my mind that, when I came out of the building, my brain saw the past and the present both at the exact same time and my mind reeled. It was almost an out-of-body experience.

That's the limit of my time travel thus far. I break our long silence to tell David this.

He was never bothered by talking with a mouthful of food —one of the traits I grappled with way back when I tried dating him. But in this case, it's welcome. I need for him to let something stupid slip so I know he's just having me on.

Still chewing, he begins: "You're describing déjà vu, and that's a common precursor to what I'm talking about. But only the very beginning essence of it."

His eating slows, his elbows rest against the edge of the table and he starts talking, stopping only to swallow more bourbon and pick an errant grain of rice out of his beard and pop it in his mouth.

"It wasn't a single process, a tiny simple breakthrough. I've spent thirteen years at this. I've burned every bridge, fried every brain cell, and even now I barely understand it myself. Only that it seems to work, and that I've managed to stabilize it into a viable thing."

"And just what sort of 'thing' is it?"

"I'd be more than happy to answer that, but it will take a long time."

His being a scientific, logical thinker means I'll have to be patient with David and let him progress on his terms, uninterrupted.

"I'll save most of it for tomorrow. Come to my lab at eleven and I'll give you the low-down. But, as a quick snapshot, picture time as a vast expanse of concurrent strands. It is not, as is commonly perceived, a linear progression. I've come to understand time as a vast field of interwoven tissue.

"Déjà vu was my first clue as to the simultaneous existence of all things. But that was a far cry from getting under the hood of it all.

"Our spirits don't always stay in the same place. They float. Memories, when properly focused, damn near constitute time travel in and of themselves. We only lack the physical properties to jump back and hold onto the appropriate past time strand in physical form.

"Take the rings of a sawed-off tree: Its entire past is still there, visible to us. Also visible are the strata of rocks in a geological formation. The past happened, we can see it. We just can't access it. Trees and rocks don't have appreciable memories. If they were sentient, we'd have a much clearer insight.

"Pick an early memory. Right now. Just grab an image from your early life."

I do. I remember being young—so young that my body was in constant pain, growing so fast, unbidden and unable to be expressed by words. I was sitting in the car with my mom, late at night. It was cold. We were in an empty parking lot in our Buick; she was wearing her navy-blue car coat—its oversized round buttons the same blue as the coat's wool. I was small enough that I couldn't see out the windows directly. The Universe of Car was confined to my views of the interior of the Buick itself. But I could look up. White mercury streetlamps buzzed loudly and showed nearly purple, especially when seen through the blue edge along the top of the windshield. It must have been January. Christmas decorations were hanging from light poles, unlit, bedraggled and forgotten.

And my mom was crying. I was too young to wonder why, just astonished that she would.

The image is within me, in every detail.

"You were almost back there, just then, weren't you?" David asks.

"Yeah."

"Well, that's the first part of the equation. Earlier times carry immense power. You must find them, harvest them, and create the ability to physically arrive there. Sounds pretty undoable, doesn't it?"

"Entirely."

"Well, I'm not one to leave well enough alone. Decades ago, I started looking into it. I'll tell you whole the story tomorrow. But the first thing you need to know, if you don't already, is that nature abhors a vacuum.

"She's not too keen on having her time filaments fucked around with, either. It takes quite a push to bump a body over the strands onto a different one, and, if you do manage it, Mother Nature responds immediately to throw you back in sync. Time's not supposed to be out of whack like that, and she is a harsh mistress. Until now, I don't think Mother Nature has ever been questioned out loud. She's finding me impertinent.

"I have no illusions that this sort of behavior poses a major mind-fuck to the universe. This is atomic, God-level shit. And humans are messy. I'm completely sure we shouldn't do it.

"As for the mechanics, though, it has been generally understood that the hard part is moving backward to another time filament—yet actually it happens more than you think. Again, consider the phenomenon of déjà vu.

"The real hard part is *staying* there, longer than a microsecond, and in physical form. Before being yanked back to your proper time strand by one seriously pissed off universe.

"The return mechanism is the default. Technology, thanks to yours truly, can now forestall this to keep one in the past. At first, I could only manage it for a few seconds, then minutes. I've gotten it up to three days now. When your time's up, you're rather unceremoniously flung forward to the moment you left. Nature is restored.

"Get what I'm saying?"

"Yes. I'm just not sure *why* . . ."

At least he smiles. He busies himself sucking a wing free of meat, with lips I've seen used in various ways before.

I swallow scotch. I watch his face for further signs that he's full of shit. My nagging personal problem is sliding away as my fascination, despite my higher-brain's efforts, is being pulled in.

He keeps going. "Mostly what I need you to know is how serious this is." He is looking at me intently, in a way I recognize as indeed quite serious after all. He's not faking his emotions. David doesn't know how to do that. He's sliding into awe—and actual fear. I've never seen this in him. Ever. It's starting to rattle me.

"I don't think we should use it more than a few times. This is potentially the most dangerous thing ever created. No one knows what will happen if you go banging around in the past changing things—assassinating Hitler or, in your case, turning the *Titanic* off to the right seven seconds too soon . . ."

"Left."

"Huh?"

"They turned left."

"Well. There ya go. Anyway, I can't profess to know the results. I can only admit that I've found a way to get there in real life, and to return home again. Even if you don't believe me —and I can kind of tell you don't—you must at least spot me the courtesy of telling no one. Ever."

The food's gone. I don't remember eating it. He gets up and starts clearing the dishes, stacking them on the counter.

I'm sitting at his table unable to think.

"I'll show it all to you tomorrow in my lab. I'm too liquored up and, frankly, too exhausted to do it tonight. But by tomorrow you will know."

"Can you go into the future?"

"Not so far as I can tell. There's nothing knowable to grab on to—it hasn't happened yet. I can't determine its properties.

Plus, I don't particularly want to see the future right now. Do you?"

"No. Not even a little bit." I shudder at the thought, and sit silent for a time before saying, "I want to believe you, but I need to be allowed to think you're full of shit for a while."

"Wouldn't be the first time."

"True dat."

We settle in the living room with our drinks, preparatory to switching on the TV. Normally by now attempts at conversation would be over. But the waves of body language coming out of him, not to mention the actual words, clearly tell me we're not done.

"Why do you only want to go to disaster sites?" he asks.

It takes me by surprise. Every place I'd mentioned visiting, something bad happened.

"I accept your question," I reply, "and I don't know. I guess, because, like any good child of the '70s, I was literally weaned on *The Poseidon Adventure* and *Towering Inferno.* The excitement, shock, and drama were enough to draw me in, at an age where nothing else really did. Why? Do you think I'm a drama queen?"

He laughs. "What do *you* think?" He is openly rolling his eyes at my expense. "Plus I happen to know you fall asleep most nights watching *Seconds from Disaster* on YouTube."

"Well . . . OK, you got me there. But I find people as a whole rather boring. I'm a lot like you, I guess, in that interpersonal drama, the who said what to whom . . . nope. Yawn."

"OK, in that sense, maybe you're not a drama queen," he admits. "Let me rephrase the question: When it comes to guys here in the Castro hooking up around you, and who's having *sex* with whom . . . Are you a drama queen?"

Pffffuck.

Yes.

Guys having sex and then telling everyone about it totally

wrecks me—despite playing no small role in it myself these past twenty years. I like secret connections. I have a romantic heart. I'm still looking for love out there in the dark.

David knows this. In fact, I still, begrudgingly, hold him responsible for a large percentage of my wounds.

"OK," I confess. "Yes. On that score, I am a drama queen."

"I'ma go a step further, Mark—and don't take this personally—but when it comes to the woes and arrows that affect you on the daily, how you respond, your propensity to fuss . . . you are a drama queen of the highest order."

I could slap his face in outrage, hence precisely proving his point. But our friendship is such that we can be that direct with each other and get away with it. A lot of water has passed under our collective bridge.

"Yes," I just respond meekly. "I'm a nellie fusspot. On the daily."

"Well, they say the first step is admitting you have a problem," he says, and we clink glasses—me, somewhat reluctantly.

Stating a return to the earlier question, though, I continue: "I think I'm drawn to disasters because they are drama on a distinctly higher level. It's in times of disaster that you really feel what's going on around you. Everyone remembers where they were, what they were doing, what was important. Disasters leave behind a single, crucial moment, forever frozen in time. A moment where everything becomes highly attenuated. Humans carry a forever snapshot of that instant, burned into them, and are marked by what they felt that day.

"Maybe I need to feel something real, and outside myself. Which is why, given this apparent reach of options you're dangling in front of me right now, I'm not drawn to, say, some quiet weekend in 1928 for the bucolic hell of it."

"So what's your deal with the *Titanic*, anyway?" he asks. "You know that one backwards and forwards. It's kinda creepy."

That stings a little, but I take another sip of Dewar's and answer the question.

"Mostly it's because if the *Titanic* had never sunk, the ship would have been worked for twenty years and then unceremoniously scrapped. Completely forgotten. But because something bad happened to it, we know everything: the food they ate, the music they played, everything.

"It gives us a precise, powerful glimpse into the past. It's as close to time travel as we can get. Plus it's just damned intriguing. I think it was Virginia Woolf who said, 'We can only note that the past is beautiful because one never realizes an emotion at the time. It expands later, and thus we don't have complete emotions about the present; only about the past.'

"I would argue that disasters are an exception to that. Disasters are intense punctuation marks in history. They are, excuse my French, the cum shot."

David snickers, and then says, "If you're going around quoting Virginia Woolf, your problems are beyond my scope of remedy."

He gets up off the couch and heads back to the kitchen. "You seem generally disappointed with San Francisco," he says from around the corner. "Maybe going to the past will be good for you."

He rejoins me on his sofa with fresh drinks in hand.

"If what you say is true, I think it might," I say. "I feel like I'm socially and economically drowning here." I take another sip, one tiny drop in the river of alcohol that flows through my life.

David replies, "Not only do you fuss too much, you either disregard men as completely boring, or you slavishly try to get into their pants—enjoying no discernible middle ground. You're uptight."

Ouch.

"Yeah, well . . . is your social life on any sort of trajectory?" I ask.

"No, but I don't particularly care about it one way or another. I can get laid whenever I want."

I feel slight horror at the image, and at the truth of what he's said.

I guess I'm still carrying somewhat of a torch for him after all. Despite all that happened between us.

David Meisenhoelder is a brilliant freak. The fact that he's so sexy only makes it harder on me. I first met him at the Lone Star Saloon in San Francisco in 2014. We hit it off right away and started going out. Sensuous voice, wonderful smile, built like a football player. Killer butt. Round, manly beard. A rocket scientist—literally—and an inventor. He spent years at CERN in Switzerland—a fact he never fails to lord over me.

But I dumped him because of his drinking—it only amplified my own drinking, which has frankly grown problematic these past few years—but more to the point, while going out with me David suddenly took on another boyfriend.

I was devastated. He was indifferent.

The other guy didn't last, but I could never quite trust David after that.

Yet he's my friend—I guess he's my only friend—even though he's off his rocker just enough that anything more serious could never work. He is fundamentally annoying. Strange sense of humor; a plodding, sequential thinker while I, myself, constantly spin through circles and gyres and emotional messes. David's always burying himself in his makeshift lab across town or burrowing under mounds of paperwork in his spartan, completely unadorned apartment, looking unbearably sexy but eternally unreachable.

"So what was it you said you had to tell me?" David asks—and with genuine concern, I'll grant you.

But be it the scotch or the enormity of what we're

discussing, I know that now is no longer the time. I swallow my thoughts. I swallow Problem Zero. I swallow more scotch.

I just tell him, "Never mind." I allow it to become a "later" thing.

I've absorbed more than enough to handle for one sitting. David seems to sense this and suggests we take a break, so we sit quietly and watch two episodes of *Feud*, the FX miniseries about Bette Davis and Joan Crawford. It's well-executed and soothing, just what I need right now.

Sometimes, even after all these years, we'll cuddle on the sofa. But not tonight. I don't trust him again, and I'm still too rattled to do anything so languid as to snuggle an ex-boyfriend on bad microfiber from Ikea.

When the shows are over, I'm in a funk again, resplendently amplified by scotch. I just rise and hug him goodnight and prepare to walk back to my apartment a few blocks away. My own secret is still locked deep inside me, feeling unreal and spiky.

David reminds me that I have promised to meet him at his lab at eleven o'clock tomorrow morning. I agree that I will and I'm down the stairs and out into the eternally chilly night air of San Francisco, buried deep into my thoughts.

§

My name is Mark Baldwin and I'm a freelance writer for a couple of unremarkable economics blogs. Underemployed. Barely hanging on in San Francisco, thanking God for rent control the first of every month. My career has nearly tanked. Somewhere along the line I think I just stopped trying.

Writing assignments—and income—won't come looking

for me. I have to be out there fighting for clients and recognition. I need "fire in the belly," presenting myself, guns blazing. I know all the tricks and tools to make this so.

But I don't. I just stick to my corner. Waiting for God-knows-what.

My specialty is economics in general, and cryptocurrencies specifically. Everyone always asks me if they should start getting into Bitcoin, and I smile when I politely tell them "only insomuch as you want to have fun with it."

A lot of my time is spent alone, writing articles, and reading enough to choke a mule. What does it say about me that I have a personal subscription to the *Economist*? Party dude.

Long story short, I guess I'm a bit of a loser. I'm not where I thought I'd be, not by a long shot. Career? Sinking. Love life? Cratered.

It's a short walk from David's apartment to mine. Downhill the whole way, with the roar of cars whizzing past on Market Street. The speed limit's 45 through here so the noise is constant and loud. But it's time enough for me to, unbidden and without formal consent, slide from the enormity of David's claims about time travel and into the microworld of my personal misery. Problem Zero.

It surges back to the fore, squeezing my stomach, even as I fight to keep it away.

Problem Zero is thus: I was expecting a casual visit at the doctor this past Monday, following a flurry of scans. I had the rest of my day planned, even what I was going to grab for lunch, and I was thinking a host of other things.

"We should start chemo right away" was not remotely on my to-do list. Dr. Tsieh had said it as if she were simply ordering a salad.

Non-Hodgkins Lymphoma, she told me. Type A, Stage II. Type A means it's not producing secondary physical symptoms yet, and Stage II indicates occurrences in multiple lymph nodes, not just one. It's small, but it is apparently spreading.

It was like her words caused the air in the room to become thin. I went from insouciant to shocked, all because of a human utterance. Just syllables. Gibberish. But the meaning changed the fabric of my existence.

Dr. Tsieh in her white coat, coils of stethoscope snaking up from her hip pocket, was apparently waiting for me to say something, to utter some syllables of language back at her.

I tried to read her face but couldn't. All I could think was that I wanted to leave.

The words "I maybe wanna think about it," came out my mouth. I heard them, even though they sounded as if they had come from someone else.

"Do. But Mark, just know the sooner we hit it, the better," she said, a little more insistently. Perhaps on the level of ordering a double vodka rocks.

I knew she didn't personally care which way I jumped. To her it's just another day at the office. I also knew I wanted nothing to do with chemo. I've seen what it does.

"What if I go palliative?" I'd asked. I think my voice squeaked when I said it but not much was registering.

She leaned back and sighed at that. Exasperation? Annoyance? Relief?

"That is, of course, your choice. We're here to fight cancer. It's all we do. If you want to fight, well, you know where to find us. Just know that, left untreated, the lymphoma will continue at its own pace—and that pace is different for everyone. You'll have a few years of peace and quiet, but if after that time you decide to turn and fight, by then you'll have a hell of a battle on your hands. Our goal is to nip it in the bud and stall it out."

"And that means chemo? Now?"

"Yes. We'll do a biopsy, but your PET scan lit up like a

Christmas tree. Chemo would be in conjunction with radiation and Rituxan—an oral medication."

She was staring me down at that point. All I could think to do was to remove myself from a painful stimulus. I wanted out of that room. I didn't want to look at her eyes or her white coat anymore. I wanted air and sunshine and time to take it all in.

She seemed to sense this. Not her first time at the rodeo.

"Tell you what," she said. "Let's make an appointment for you next week. Use this time to gather your thoughts, take it onboard, discuss it with your friends and family. Oh. And stay the hell off WebMD. You don't need to go down any rabbit holes right now."

I thanked her as she left to go ruin yet someone else's day and the nurse led me back out. The scheduling desk informed me the next available appointment wouldn't be until four weeks hence.

Well, I wanted time to think.

A friend of mine died of the same lymphoma. Three months—just ninety days—from diagnosis to the end. And I saw what chemo did to him. It was horrible. He was in agony, yet filled with stupid, useless hope and optimism as his lips and gums turned black and exploded and he just died anyway.

I've been sitting on this in silence for four days. Haven't told a soul—not even my mom back in Seattle.

Normally I'd be on the phone to her by the time I hit the sidewalk in front of 450 Sutter Street, but this time . . . no. Not yet.

Mom's good. We have an admirable relationship. She will be loving and supportive, and I know once I tell her I'll feel better. But it will be at the expense of her feelings. It's going to sting. And she just might try to jump on the first Alaska flight to SFO and, although I love her to bits, I seriously cannot handle that right now.

So I have held off.

Among other things, I guess I'm not used to being outside my comfort zone. Despite my ever-ready sass mouth, I have no truck with pain, risk, or anything that encroaches on my carefully manicured life. A quick look at my CV would make that abundantly clear.

Utter terror will eventually take me in its grasp. I don't even know what it will look like, or when it's liable to show up. Worry and fuss are my go-tos, my constant companions. Through them, I negotiate my woes and try to keep my life in an uneasy but serviceable balance, clear of external threats. But this is going to be a shock of devastating scale and, so far, I haven't heard a peep out of it. It's waiting for me. I just can't see it yet.

Back in the chilly Thursday night of now, I'm already home from David's as if I had walked in my sleep. I enter my apartment building, befuddled by garlic and scotch, with several universes of thought overwhelming my head.

Problem Zero is more than enough. Now David is seriously dangling time travel in front of my face? I'm still wont to dismiss it as some dim joke of his but for the intensity of his eyes and seriousness in his intent.

Once inside my apartment I'm not the least surprised to see that Rhoda has once again sprayed the dishwasher. She does it a lot.

I share my two-bedroom apartment with an aquatic turtle named Fluffy—I've had her twenty-five years now—and an adorably beautiful Ragdoll cat named Rhoda. Despite her stunning looks, Rhoda is a solitary, unwarm creature. She sprays the furniture multiple times a day. She even got on the counter and nailed the microwave once. Her vet assures me there's nothing physically wrong with her, it's purely behavioral.

I don't enjoy this about my cat. David says I should just "'crock-pot' the bitch."

But I don't go that way. It's not cool. And if I surrendered her to a shelter, she'd face a revolving door of frustrated owners, any one of whom might not be so forgiving and have her put to sleep anyway. I'll be damned if I'll let that happen. She deserves to lead a happy life and I'll just have to deal. I choose to love her. Furniture can be replaced, and I figure I kissed my security deposit goodbye a long time ago.

I just get out the Nature's Miracle deodorizing spray—always handy on the granite countertop—and clean it up the best I can.

I seldom have people over to my place. Another San Francisco gay guy whose book-filled apartment perennially smells of cat urine, I am thus relegated to type.

Too full of scotch and information to do anything useful, I head straight to bed. I don't even brush my teeth, a bad decision with all that garlic on deck. I climb under the sheets in my underwear and put the light out. Streetlights outside are bright, and the constant noise of traffic on Market has long been filtered out of my conscious awareness as part of the survival technique of living here.

Well. I wanted time to think. Here it is.

2

Friday, October 18, 2019

I'm sure you know the "morning switch": that precise moment when your brain, sweetly lulled by sleep and dreams, hands itself off to harsh current thoughts that flood your belly with an oozy shot of reality.

Add a scotch hangover, and it's quite lavish.

Not allowing for specific cogitation, I head straight for coffee. Strong enough to stop your heart and dark as Djimon Hounsou's left butt cheek.

I assume. Never had the pleasure.

It's 9:30. I veg on Facebook in my comfy chair, keeping all thoughts at bay—both lymphatic and temporal—as the coffee takes hold and restores my will to live.

At least I don't have any pressing work assignments right now. But that also means I don't have any pressing paychecks to cash, either.

I take it upon myself to finally, after four days, call my

mother and tell her of my diagnosis. I'm not nervous, mostly just sad that it will hurt her.

I just don't know. I feel emotionally disconnected from this whole idea of "lymphoma."

See? Even in my brain I do air quotes. Like it isn't real.

I call her and just lay it out. She has a catch in her voice, and says, "Mark, I'm so sorry."

We collectively say "wow" a lot as we talk through the ramifications. But Mom's ultimately pragmatic. Never turns from a challenge, and will always respond with "Let's begin immediately." Which she does here, too.

She makes no mention of flying down to see me—and I'm suddenly crushed that she doesn't. I lie only to the extent that I withhold Dr. Tsieh's wish that chemo be started right away. I tell Mom it's a possible course soon, that I might need a lymph node removed for biopsy first.

With the hard part over, we talk of general things, what my two older sisters and their grown children are up to, and it becomes normal.

We both agree we need time to process.

We each say, "I love you," and hang up.

And I know this news is now set to freely filter through the entire familial network. Everyone will know. It's just our dynamic.

I sit with my inert phone in my hand while Rhoda saunters by, stopping only to claw the hell out of my tattered sofa for good measure.

At eleven, freshly showered, I drive my Nissan Xterra, currently two payments behind, over to David's lab in the Mission District.

In the interim, I have slid into flat-out rejection of David's claims. My only intent now is to find out why he's going to such elaborate lengths to be an asshole. Whatever it is, he's playing it to the hilt and I really can't account for it.

His lab is an old, free-standing garage at 26th and Shotwell Streets. He rents it from this vegan hippie couple who own the house but don't drive. He's been in there for years. It's an ungodly mess of crap, none of which has ever made a lick of sense. I don't usually go there. It's confining and confusing, and I'm not often invited.

I luck out and find parking close by. He greets me excitedly and we hug.

"You think I'm full of shit, don't you?" he asks.

"Yes."

"Well. Get schooled."

He shows me what I've apparently come to see: The Machine. It's a large, Ridgid-brand plastic toolbox on wheels with a handle so you can cart it around, which is good because it looks like it weighs about seventy-five pounds. It contains a mass of bizarre equipment that makes no sense. It's plugged into two giant silver balls with tubes coiled madly around each other, like a nest of silver snakes.

Whatever it is, it's ugly and cruel.

"What's it run on?" I ask. "Souls of puppies and little orphan children?"

"Tried that. Didn't work."

And I'll never know whether he's kidding.

"I first tested it out on a cat," he continues.

He gives my pained, horrified look a dismissing wave with his hand.

"He's fine. The hippies have him and everyone's happy. Because one day, the idea occurred to me to try it on a cat, and just as the thought formed in my head, a mangy, scrawny cat popped into existence right before my eyes here on the bench. Alley cat, kinda hissy and bitey, but he showed no ill signs. I petted him and opened him a pouch of tuna. And then, mid-chomp, he disappeared again.

"Obviously, the cat had come from me. So it was then

incumbent upon me, later, to send a cat back to the earlier me. I felt plenty stupid going to the animal shelter to check out a cat, but once I got there, sitting in the third cage down was *the exact same cat*. That was probably the first time I got excited about this thing, because that's when I knew for certain that it works. I don't even remember what I put on the adoption questionnaire. Right below the eternal pledge to never have a cat declawed, there is a box about not using animals in experiments of any kind. I see the need for that, and I support it. But I lied."

David holds out a loose web of wires loaded up with electrodes. "A field is generated, contained within this web. This tells The Machine what item—or person—is meant to travel back. I designed it to accommodate a person and their clothing, otherwise you'd arrive naked. Which would be fun, but awkward. You'd want clothes and money suitable for the period, and I'd imagine an iPhone to capture your experiences. So it's all contained within this, and when you get to the past, you just take it off and throw it away. I have several, they're not that hard to make.

"Remember, going back in time is but one step, and the natural tendency of the universe will be to instantly spit you right back out again. That's why I've had to learn to bombard one's body with a timed decay element that slowly depletes until the universe takes over and throws you back. That's where the injection comes in."

"Injection?"

"Yeah. It just gets better and better, doesn't it? You have to inject the decay element into your veins. Goes great with Vicodin and gin. The concentration of the injection determines your length of stay. As it depletes, you begin to lose your battle with what nature considers the wrong timeframe. When its half-life is used up, you Snap Back. It's like a boomerang. It's built in.

"Among other things, it saves the need for any apparatus to get home. The Machine doesn't travel back in time with you, it stays in the present. And the thing runs on two car batteries. But I have to warn you . . ."

"*Now* a warning?" I say, parroting the line from the movie *Death Becomes Her*.

"We can probably only use this for a little while."

"What do you mean?" I ask.

"Well, think about it. If I can come up with this, it's only a matter of time before someone else does. And what do you think'll happen when ordinary assholes get their hands on this kind of technology? The effects could be worse than nuclear war.

"Look, I don't know what happens if you go back and change the timeline. There's an old riddle about, if you go back in time and kill your grandfather, you'd never have been born —therefore, it would be impossible to go back in time and kill your grandfather.

"It's all messy. We don't know what it'll do. So if you decide you want to use this—frankly, I think you're in desperate need to go on a fuckabout—go carefully. Don't screw anything up, and be ready for this to all be taken away. I'm sure it'll be found that humans aren't meant for it."

"Is it a health risk?"

"It's probably not *good*, no; soaking your DNA in greasy, quickly-decaying neutrinos is probably akin to streaking balls-naked around Reactor Four at Chernobyl."

"Awesome . . ."

"There's one other vitally important thing for you to know."

"Of course there is. I'd expect nothing less."

"It's a major distinction that you can't travel through time *and* space," David says. "That would be ridiculous, right? The ability to transport through space to another location would be teleportation, and that technology doesn't exist yet, and would be outside the purview of this.

"It is important to note that *where* you are doesn't change, only *when*. This will become clearer when—if—you decide to see The Machine in action.

"So know this: You can't be on a moving vehicle. Say your time came up while you were riding on a bus. The bus would instantly vanish from around you. You'd be roughly five feet off the ground, traveling thirty miles per hour, and would be unceremoniously chucked down onto the pavement and probably run over by a Prius. Do you understand?"

"Yes," I reply softly, picturing the scenario in graphic detail.

"Same thing for elevators. And don't even go there with airplanes."

More than queasy, I want to go away. The more I hear, the more gruesome the whole thing sounds. But he's doubling down. He means business.

I guess a wedge has started working its way into my cynicism. If he ain't lying, I'm going to want to be there.

I'm afraid of it, though. I actively consider dismissing it out of hand, as something unsuitable to my version of personal sanity . . . but I can't. I'm inexorably drawn to it in ways I cannot yet fathom.

"How could we try this thing out?" I eventually ask.

"Let's start simple. Where've you been the past few days?" he asks.

"Wednesday was my birthday. I was in my apartment all day, writing."

"Damn. I forgot about that. Sorry, I'll buy you dinner. But . . . during your day, didn't you want to be out with people?"

"Not really."

I never really went in for birthdays. Well . . . that's a lie. I go in for my birthday with all the glee of a little kid; it's just that no one around me seems to be willing to share in the magic. So I subdue my expectations. This one, my forty-ninth, I managed to go out for a few cocktails that night, saw a million acquaintances, and went home alone shortly thereafter to open my sole birthday present: a sweater from Mom. That was the extent of my celebrating.

"Was there something you'd rather have been doing that afternoon?" David asks.

"Well, this guy wanted me to meet him at Starbucks, and I didn't go, and I'm starting to feel guilty about it. I've kind of wanted to see if I'd like to go out with him. But I chickened out."

"OK, so what if you did both? Stayed home in your apartment and got work done, but also went to see that guy?"

"That would be the best of both worlds," I admit.

"OK, so let's do that."

I still wonder if he's setting me up to look silly.

"What about my iPhone?" I ask, looking for holes in his theory. "Assuming this thing actually works, and I pop into reality on Wednesday, there'd be two of the same phones on the network at the same time, with the same IMEI number. How would that work?"

"I dunno. I think it wouldn't work at all. One or both would probably lose signal."

"So what would I do?"

"Keep your phone on airplane mode, I guess, otherwise it'll mess up your phone at home. The other you. Could screw up a work call, and you don't need that. What time were you supposed to meet this guy?"

"Clarence. Four o'clock."

"OK, so let's send you back to Wednesday at three and have you Snap Back three hours later. Is that enough time?"

"I think so."

Am I really considering this? Like, right now? Is there some way for me to back out? If I chicken out, David wins, at whatever game he's playing.

The only word in my brain is *poff!* and I don't even think it's a real word.

"OK. I guess I'm in. Goddamn it, I'm in."

"It's 11:46 a.m. now, this is when you'll Snap Back to. You have to decide where you want to be when your time is up. Remember, you can't be on a moving vehicle, or in an elevator or anything that's not completely solid, or you'll die. Got it?"

"Yes. That's about the only part of this concept I do understand."

I still think he's nuts.

"You don't want to be in his apartment—even if you get lucky—because suddenly you'll reappear there two days later. It would be weird. So get back here or be on the sidewalk somewhere."

"What would happen if I went to my apartment?"

"There'd be two of you. One would be confused. Did you bring your car here?" he asks.

"Yes."

"Well, Wednesday it wasn't here so you'll have to take the J-Church streetcar. I wouldn't rely on your phone to get you a Lyft."

"You know damn well this is too much for me to resist. I still don't trust you. But . . . I give. Do your worst. Send me back. Prove to me you're not full of shit. And if I get laid by this man, upon your head be it."

David fiddles with The Machine and says, "Wednesday at three o'clock in the afternoon I was at home cooling off from my excursion to 1950. So the lights will be out, and I won't be here. When you get back, I will be."

I don't fully understand.

Next comes the fun part. He takes a syringe and injects

God-knows-what into a vein in my arm . . . which burns, by the way.

Maybe it's an hallucinogenic. So I'll just think I've traveled through time?

But that still doesn't answer the question as to *why*. I've known him a long time. I can't imagine anything he'd have to gain by doing this.

He hands me the web and directs me to put it on. It's nothing eccentric, just a black stretchy nylon weave, like the bungie netting I used to fasten stuff to the back of my motorcycle. Only it's human-sized and covered with electrodes. He has me stand close to The Machine and plugs the webbing into it.

I'm injected with drugs and hooked, by electric wires, to two car batteries. This just feels like a really bad idea.

"I've given you three hours. Use them wisely." He smiles.

He flips a switch and . . .

3

Wednesday, October 16, 2019

Everything changes. My insides feel like they're exploding. I have that feeling in my stomach like I'm on a roller coaster. Bright flashes of light come through my closed eyelids and a sharp zipping sensation rips through my head. I can hear the sound of it.

I fall and hit concrete.

The Machine is gone. David is gone. I'm in his lab. The lights are out, but sunlight is coming in the windows. The web is still around me, and I'm buzzing from electric shock.

I get to my feet and dust off, disentangling myself from the netting.

It's David's garage, just like it always is. The Machine is here; it's sitting on the work bench half-disassembled.

I look at my phone. It's getting a signal. It says it's 3:00 p.m. on October 16, two days ago, as advertised. Weird. I put it on airplane mode anyway, just to make sure. I was on some pretty important calls at home that afternoon. Which is now this afternoon. I guess . . .

I stand in confusion, in disbelief. Can this be real?

I'm starting to race through an impossible series of thoughts: *If this works, do you know what it could mean? I could go anywhere!* Titanic! *I could experience the earthquake and fire of 1906—No. More than that, I could see for myself what San Francisco was really like, before everything burned. I'd almost kill for that.*

Well, if it is real, I have an hour to get to Starbuck's at 18th and Castro. Just as David predicted, my Xterra is nowhere to be found—it must be at home in my garage and I'm in my apartment trying to write an article on European socialism.

I lock the lab door behind me as I leave. It's a schlepp to the J Church line and I work up a sweat as I walk. Everything looks completely normal on 26th Street. I pass people and they take no notice of me, as if I'm not actually the greatest freak that nature has ever had the temerity to let escape from her grasp.

I board the car, Markleyy Clipper card over the thing, and observe my fellow passengers almost with discomfort, with the overwhelming sensation that I'm not supposed to be here. We rattle our way up the Mission District, heading north into the Castro.

San Francisco's Castro District is the gay epicenter of the universe. I just walk out my front door and in three minutes I'm in the heart of it all. The little village is safely my own, my corner of the world. I know everyone, everyone knows me; we can spot gay tourists a mile away. They're usually the only ones holding hands and are often refreshingly good-looking.

It's my tiny village in a big city.

So that means I'm all hooked up and wildly popular and have loads of friends, right?

Ermp.

Something happens when you concentrate that many gay men in one place. It becomes cold and intimidating. So many strata of social standing: the A-list, muscle bears, tweakers, realtor bears, IT bears, all ranked by physical attractiveness and hours spent at the gym. Everyone is so agenda-driven, you can't so much as ask someone to accompany you to Costco because they'll think you're too clingy. People keep their distance. Everyone has their social aim, predicated on the type of person into whose pants they wish to ultimately get. And they will not be swayed from it or distracted by social niceties.

They also constantly move away. Everyone's getting priced out as tech-boomers and trust-fund Googlepersons pay cash and descend, like vultures, paying $3,895 for a one-bedroom/no parking. Everyone complains the city is losing its soul, and by all accounts this is true.

Before that, everyone around us died. Two decades of AIDS left deep wounds, empty hearts, an endless barrage of anemic estate sales, and the all-too-familiar experience of memorizing a man's most prized personal body part, only to recall that his parents chose to have him cremated. That buzzing, exuberant bit of human desire is but ash on a mantle somewhere.

Carry that realization forward for a second man . . . and keep counting. Once you're over a certain population of former sexual partners who have subsequently died, you start to feel generally untethered.

San Francisco teaches you to not trust people. It's a thing.

But it's my world. It is the pool in which I swim, and despite its foibles, I can't imagine being anyplace else.

At least I'm what I call Advanced-Placement Gay. I no longer question why I turned out they way I did, I accept it and know it is normal for me and for all them men I know. Our culture, as a whole, has a few monstrous drawbacks, but I'm in it for good.

I alight from the streetcar at Mission High School and walk

up 18th Street to the café, amazed that I am an aberrant time traveler, while all around me is completely banal.

Castro Starbucks is the nexus of the neighborhood. Where the elite meet. Always crowded, usually the same people, a daily visit for me. So why does this time feel so wrong? I'm overwhelmed with the sense that I oughtn't be here.

Clarence is already inside at a table with his coffee, and he gives me a friendly wave as I wait to order. He's very handsome. I get my usual grande quad latte, and my date and I hug it out and sit and talk for a while.

I see a copy of the *Chronicle* on the table, and sure enough, the date says Wednesday, October 16. "Car Ban for Market Street Gets Green Light," and "Blast Lifts Fireball over East Bay Cities."

I'd visited Clarence last week at his place at Casa Sanchez, the grotty apartment building where just about every gay man has lived at one time or another. We had sex for the first time. It was good. I could get used to it.

Clarence is deathly allergic to cats, though, which is odd. He's a strapping six-foot-three, 280-pounder with melty brown Eastern European eyes and a fun, hairy bod.

I wonder if he's someone I could like. I've been wondering that for a while now.

At forty-nine years old, I've never even had a steady boyfriend—at least not since college. And not counting David. All these years in San Francisco have been spent alone and it's starting to wear me down. My requirements aren't many. He must have facial hair—I don't know why I came out the way I did, but guys with no facial hair kind of freak me out. I'm like, *Dude—where's the rest of your face*?

I've long been in search of a kind man with passable good looks who's not an outright meth head. Apparently, I'm asking too much.

Clarence and I were supposed to go out together again last

Saturday, but he totally stood me up, with no explanation. I was pretty put out, and that's why I broke our coffee date today. Payback. But later I thought better of it. What's the point in holding grudges? I like this guy. The only downside I see is his allergy to cats. Everything else checks out: looks, job, body, sense of humor . . . not too annoying, so far as I can tell. It's very draining having someone in your personal space, and Clarence seems to resonate low on the harmonics scale. He's calming to be around. He deserves consideration.

Conversation is general, tediously so, so I start to angle in and ask about Saturday night.

"Oh," he says brightly. "I met this hot French-Canadian guy at the Eagle. We had sex all night in his hotel room. And in the morning, we went out for waffles."

"Oh."

"Yeah."

He's completely unconcerned that this might be an issue for me. My heart sinks.

I decide to let him twist the knife in a little deeper, to make sure I really feel it, and to make sure I remember to stay away from him in the future.

"So tell me about the French Canadian?" I ask, fake-brightly, bracing for hurt.

"Well, he's got a huge dick but he's all bottom. I came four times and fisted him. It was totally hot."

"Excellent."

Whatever happened to a little romance? Jesus Christ, I'm sick of this.

I always get this. Guys are so callous about sex . . . I'm just so tired of it.

I'm no stranger to having sex just for the hell of it, I do it all the time. But just once I'd like to meet someone who's willing to lay that all aside and be just with me for a while. I began to take it all personally quite some time ago, surely sinking my overall social standing.

Desperation is never a good look, and I know I must reek of it.

Well. It's over with this one. Clarence is just like all the rest. I erect my walls again, scratch him from the rolls, and try to begin moving forward in my mind. I put a fake smile back on my face. With my heart thoroughly disengaged, we linger and talk. I don't care what he says now, he's just another guy at the coffee shop. He tells me he has a date tonight with this really hot guy from San Diego.

I wish him luck.

He leaves to go get ready.

I've bombarded myself with greasy solar atoms and nuclear dross and this is my reward? I feel emptier than ever before.

Back on the street again, I decide to go to my apartment and see if I can see anything through the window. Probably not, but it'll be an interesting experiment.

Walking up 18th Street, I run into people I know and have delicate chats with them, acutely aware that I'm not really me. I'm a backup copy. The real me is in my apartment writing about French President Macron.

On my way, I think briefly on the two other times I almost did find love in this city. One guy named Doug professed his undying love for me about five years ago, right after David. But I ran him off. He was OK, everything looked great on paper. But I just didn't feel anything. It wasn't adding up. And by then he was starting to stick to the heel of my boot. He was becoming clingy and moving way too fast, so I cut him loose.

He went quickly on to find love with an absolute drip of a man and they live in Guerneville now.

The other one—the one I really liked—simply failed to divulge he already had a lover. When I casually mentioned something like, "I guess we've been seeing each other about five weeks now," he responded almost with a laugh.

"Mark, we haven't been seeing each other, we're just fuck buddies."

Welcome to San Francisco. Enjoy your stay.

I walk to my apartment building and stand staring from the far side of busy Market Street at Diamond. I see myself walking out of my office, past the window, through the living room to the kitchen. I must be getting another cup of coffee.

I capture the mental image of my own self. Alone on my birthday in my apartment, slogging my guts out on an article no one will ever read. For the briefest of moments, I see myself as others must see me: not terribly attractive, but not ugly either. Lonely, quiet, bookish. Always licking my wounds. It hurts a little, but I also feel defensive. I'm not so bad!

If I had to grade my looks—and I were frank—I'd give myself a C+. Crewcut, beard, five foot ten, 220 pounds, an endomorph with pernicious belly fat that won't go away. And not the sexy kind of fat, either. My hair is mousy brown, with ever-increasing gray in my beard and at my temples. Gray in my pubes, too. That was discouraging, the day I first discovered one of those.

A few therapists have all told me the same thing: I need to take more risks, make myself more emotionally available.

I have no idea what that means.

I just hide. Wondering why my life, love life and career don't ever seem to take off. I'm just treading water. It would be cheaper to live somewhere else, someplace where it isn't 58 degrees every *frikking* day of the year. But without the gay density of the Castro, where would that leave me? Alone in a duplex in San Ramon? No thank you.

Turning forty-nine isn't quite freaking me out, I find it more inconvenient than anything else. It's as if several years slipped through my grasp and I didn't get a chance to enjoy them.

We're fortunate that in today's gay circles being over forty-five isn't the death knell it used to be. There's a market for the over-forty now (although, being called "daddy" doesn't do a thing for me—or for anyone else I happen to know).

The older I get, the more I find solace in booze. Never in the daytime, but when six o'clock rolls around, I start. In it I find warmth, peace, and a break from loneliness. I can tell I'm definitely "on the spectrum," albeit the low end. I drink alone. I don't black out or anything—well, almost never—but most of my mornings are met with a hangover of some sort, and short-lived promises to never do it again.

I sometimes wonder if people can tell and discuss it amongst themselves. I don't know. It's possible. People talk.

It's also one of the many reasons David and I couldn't make it as a couple. He's quite the drinker, and when we hang out it always goes over the top. He brushes it off. "Hey. I know I drink like Larry Tate. I'm OK with it."

My self-viewing experiment over, I head back down the street. It's only five o'clock and I have another hour to kill. What should I do? I have just enough time to get some Thai food. It's almost dinner and I'm hungry enough. I go to Thai Chef and quickly order some panang chicken curry and the check right away. I guess I could Disappear without paying the bill, but they know me there. It would bespeak a rudeness unpalatable to me.

I'm weary of being in the right Castro at the wrong time. It's messing with my head and not working out at all like I'd hoped.

Well-fed but full of fuss, I head back down 18th Street toward Dolores Park and the J-Church streetcar line . . . screw that, I'll take a Lyft back to David's lab.

I stand and wait. Hopefully not getting mugged. I almost did one night in this corner of the park, when a gang started to converge on me but, for reasons unknown, decided to veer off.

The whole place used to be a cemetery and you know they didn't move all the bodies.

I wait more. Foolish rage begins to build. Some trick by David. I don't know how, but he's punking me. I'm about ready to turn tail and trudge back up the street and forget the whole thing when suddenly . . .

4

Friday, October 18, 2019

I Snap Back just at the edge of Dolores Park. One minute it's 6:00 p.m., October 16, 2019, and the next split second I feel like I'm dropping but I'm in the same spot on the grass. I fall over, splaying out in the raggedy lawn of the park.

I take my phone off airplane mode. It's 11:48 a.m., it is once again Friday. I call a Lyft: a seven-minute wait. *Grrr.* I just wander in circles at the edge of the grass until my ride shows up. Mission High School is across the street. The class bell rings twice, five minutes apart.

Finally, José pulls up in a Corolla and I climb in, grumpy but excited.

Whatever this thing is, it works. He ain't lyin' after all. My brain spins in far-flung circles of possibilities.

We get to David's garage. I see my Xterra in the street and David is inside. I give José five stars and a tip and send him on his way.

"How'd you do?" David gives me a big hug.

"Holy shit! It works!"

"Told you."

"It was Wednesday. The newspaper said October 16 and . . ."

". . . and you had sex. I can smell it."

"You can *not.* I had the opposite of sex. The guy turned out to be a loser. Treated me like you do."

"Whatever. Now you know the thing works. You need to think about where you'd like to go next."

"Everywhere!" I respond. "There's so much I'd like to see. I can really use it? "

"You can really use it. Decide where you'd like to go next and, with a little planning, we can make it happen."

"What about you? What are you going to use it for?" I ask.

"I'm not nearly so curious as you. I aim to use it for financial gain. Oops . . . just did." He shows me a great wad of cash. "Going back in time will be expensive. Crime costs."

"I'm dedicated to what I said to you last night. I want to experience the Castro in the seventies," I say. I'm sure I can handle it; it's close to home, after all.

"Then I want to go back to 1906 for the earthquake. And definitely I need to see the *Titanic.*"

"Done and done. Just put together some clothes to wear and get some money for the periods—you can only take what fits in your pockets, so plan accordingly."

And then he takes the time to tell me all about his invention, how it came to him. And, being David, it comes out in logical, sequential chunks. I want to go away to process, but he needs to do this, and I guess I owe it to him to listen. This is the greatest scientific breakthrough in history and no one can ever know about it. It must be killing him.

I thus set myself upon one of his work stools for what I'm certain will be a lengthy and orderly dissertation.

"I started out the old-school way. Lined my walls with rolls of butcher paper and proceeded to laboriously write down all the known sciences of earth. In long hand, in order, in great big rows that stretched around the room four times. Started with acanthochronology, the study of cactus spines, all the way through to zythology, the study of beer. I'd write off tangents on each I could, and it took me two months. I focused on things like chaology, the study of chaos; gravity; thermodynamics; nuclear dynamics; the theory of relativity, elementary physics and barology; quarks, mechanics, matter/anti-matter studies and neutrinos . . .

"In the end I had a working diagram of science. All of it.

"It was mad scientist time, *A Beautiful Mind* shit. If Man had come up with it, I transcribed it to my wall, omitting nothing.

"And then I spent two years trying to find connections between them, no matter how oblique.

"It was altogether informative, but not nearly enough. Wouldn't be, would it? Man has studied all these for generations, to no avail, save a Nobel Prize or two along the way. They don't add up into some new, over-reaching doorway into other worlds. If they did, we'd have found it long ago.

"It's like alchemy: creating gold from nothing but ordinary objects. It can't be done.

"That's when I knew I had to start fucking with the predominant paradigm. Come at it from crazy, insane, hypothetical and completely erratic angles. Think outside the box, nuke it from orbit, turn it inside out and pray upon the altar of insanity. I even spent a year and a half with the supernatural. Absolutism, mysticism, shamans. Peyote. Hypnosis, generational trauma, the Vatican Library, sweat lodges and *Star Trek* . . . "

"What finally gave it away? Aromatherapy?"

"*Psht*. Don't be cunty. It all came together when a Russian scientist I got to know while at CERN—we used to go out for a while, hung like a horse—discovered a bizarre, never-before-known bacteria in the Antarctic. Xavier Tsielkovskaya spotted it first and kept it close to his bosom. It's a microscopic, unremarkable bacterium but it does present one startlingly cogent behavioral characteristic. It's not temporally stable. It seems to shift in and out, back, and then forward again—only by milliseconds, but nevertheless, detectable. A result of some heretofore unknown chemical in the wee beastie's mitochondrial DNA. Which was quickly parsed out and replicated."

"You're shitting me."

"No. The Russians are all over it right now. No one's allowed to go anywhere near it. But because Xavier remembered me and liked my furry butt, I flew over and he gave me some DNA.

"He also gave me several specimens of the bacteria."

He smiles crookedly at his dirty little joke.

"Is it dangerous?" I ask.

"Not so far as anyone can tell. In fact, we can't determine a single purpose for it, except that it exists and multiplies, and has the uncanny ability to shift slightly in time to undo some bacteriological wrong it may have committed in the past and felt bad about.

"But to say it's the first of its kind is the understatement of the millennium. I'm able to grow it and have several samples. Put some in last night's chicken, if you're interested."

I gack visibly.

"Mark, I'm kidding!"

That's David.

"I just kept applying it in different ways," he continues. "I added it to Dr. Chin Xiao's work on energy's ability to transfer into kinetic force, which is pretty bleeding-edge shit right now. Plus Dr. Christine Basquiat's work on tetra quarks at CERN.

"You need a power source. You need coordinates—*time* coordinates—which are altogether different from spatial coordinates. You must first define an adjacent time strand to latch onto. That's hard enough, by god. It's still theoretically impossible.

"I cannot describe it to you, for, as of yet, I don't even understand how it works. It's layers upon layers of intense crap and even if I could tell you, I wouldn't. I don't want anyone to know. The results would be catastrophic. So I just need you to believe that it works—for now—and you're welcome to use it because I think you'd get off on it."

Annoying. Plodding. Eccentric. Often drunk. But damn it all if David isn't usually, on the whole, exactly right most of the time.

I can no longer allow that he's bullshitting me. It's real.

"Well, if it is as you say it is," I begin, "I can't ignore this and pretend I'm not interested. You got me hooked. Which I'm sure was your plan all along."

He smiles, probably in relief that he has finally been given leave to share his amazing discovery with another soul at last. And he knows about my love of history. It's become my true passion over the years.

While getting my degree in economics, quite a lot of financial learning dovetailed with the historical environment surrounding major fiscal events. And I suddenly found the history part to be far more nuanced and fascinating to me than the economics part. But I went on to get my degree and stay in the field, as it was where I'd already accumulated the bulk of my credits. That was a near catastrophe in and of itself. I do not have a brain for data sets and mathematics and algorithms; I scraped through those sections of my degree just this side of cheating and put the lot of it back out of my mind the minute my tests were handed in. It's really not my thing.

Economics was always supposed to pay much better. Well . . . the latter part didn't work out so well for me. Like most things don't.

So, yeah. History. Things that happened, how people felt, how they reacted, that they were just as real as we are. History is awkward and ungainly, disjointed and never makes sense at the time. Wars and depressions take years to spool by. Even amid unspeakable chaos, life still takes place: People fall in love and make babies and die of heart attacks.

There's a reason "Passenger Aircraft Lands Safely" is never a news headline. David can call me a drama queen if he wants, but such shocks and happenings are damned interesting.

Every person is shaped by history, whether they know it or not. It's deeply personal. I've often mused that major historical events can alter the world around you forever, but you'll probably most remember it as that day when your underwear was totally riding up your buttcrack.

My modern life in San Francisco is certainly at an impasse, and I've got nothing on the horizon to look forward to. History, right now, sounds like a highly unorthodox way out. I don't know exactly why; if history has already happened then there shouldn't be any actual surprises, right? So I don't know what I'll find. I only know it'll be a shit-ton more than I find here in my current life. I want it.

And I won't be able to tell a soul.

That's actually in the plus column for me. Maybe it'll do me some good to have experiences no one else can know about, like an immense rare diamond that I own but that no one else knows about. A secret love I carry in my heart.

For a moment I even wonder if David is doing this because he secretly still likes me after all this time. If he's just trying to get into my pants—which does still happen, by the way—he need hardly go to such lengths. So I reject that. He wants to make money and is already using his Machine to that effect.

I have to go home and decompress.

Back out into my Nissan and GAWVI is playing on the Bluetooth as I zip up and down the contours of Dolores Street, trying not to yell in excitement.

Maybe I just need to feel something. Anything. Excitement, urgency, *something* for once. Perhaps my little brush with

Problem Zero is slated to be my greatest disaster of all, but right now my brain is refusing to allocate it any disk space. I have something big enough to bump it from the headlines.

My drive home is complete, once again having taken place with me lost in a zombie land of tumultuous thought. I'm certain I observed all the rules of traffic and pedestrian right-of-ways, but I have no conscious remembrance of the trip. I just know that I'm safely in my own underground parking space, a luxury few San Franciscans enjoy. Street parking in this city is often like unto *The Hunger Games*.

Coffee, comfy chair, further processing: I'm timing out, losing ground, financially sinking, socially failed, romantically regressive and now my body clock is actually ticking.

I hug my arms around me. I sit and just feel my body breathing, living, yet knowing a bastard evil has taken root within. Maybe it's my friend? Maybe it will just complete the circle and do its job?

I want excitement. I want life. I want booze and sex and something to pull me away from all this. This is where David and his Machine can save me.

So that's it, then. Right there in my comfy chair, I slide my trust over to David Meisenhoelder, a phrase I never thought I'd utter. I'm going to give myself to the adventure and see what happens.

Maybe that's what that therapist was talking about? Taking risks, allowing myself to become vulnerable . . . probably way more than she had in mind, nevertheless, I'm in.

Let's do this bitch.

5

Saturday, October 26, 2019

I've decided to start small for my first true Incursion back in time.

San Francisco, 1979.

Zipping through the ages to some far-flung era sounds too overwhelming to me right now. I'm not about to hurl myself into Ancient Rome with a Latin grammar book as my only means of support. I want to stay close to my own back yard, and there's a lot to see right here in my own neighborhood. When the Castro was in flower, AIDS hadn't hit, yet the city was in plenty of turmoil and pain. It's no fairyland I'm planning to visit, but it is sure to be a kick to the system.

A trip to 1979 is just a run around the block. But it'll be cheap, tawdry, and super unrelentingly gay. Even I might get a little squeamish at how in-your-face gay it is liable to be. I'm probably going to get laid a lot.

And I'm so old I don't particularly care one way or the other.

David mostly seems to understand my choice of 1979 for my first trip to the past, although he does mutter something to the equivalent of, "You know that's going to plunk you down somewhere in between *Logan's Run* and *Xanadu*. You sure you can handle it?"

First, I have to get some clothes. This is major and excites me no end. Worn Out West, on Castro Street, would be my go-to place to get the most clever of vintage clothing, but wouldn't you know they went out of business just last year? Yet another casualty of skyrocketing rents and the further straightification of the Castro. But a little googling shows me a bevy of vintage clothing shops in the Haight.

Today I've ventured there. The girl in the shop is nice. I tell her it's for Halloween since that's coming up. I get a t-shirt that says "Studio 54" in that wiggy font like it's zooming at you. I procure a tight-ass pair of jeans, Wranglers that fit so snug I'm glad for a moment that I never plan to reproduce. I'm sure I'm doing genitals a turn. The legs flair out at the bottom and go *whip whip* when I walk in them, a long-forgotten sound.

Shoes. Platform shoes. Blue, if you must know. A good two-and-a-half inches high, lumbering, clunky, with laces up the front and shiny all the way down. It's hard to walk in them, although they're comfortable and fit surprisingly well for how weighted they feel.

I leave the vintage shop in a state of glee, somewhat poorer, but ready to do this.

Beards would be OK in 1979, but I decide to take it a step further. I shave myself down to a Fu Manchu moustache, leaving sideburns down either side of my face. I look perfectly ridiculous.

I buy some old twenty- and ten-dollar bills off eBay, having to wait for them to come in the mail, checking my mailbox like it's Christmas, hopping from foot to foot.

Finally, they come. I'm ready.

On the appointed day, October 26, 2019, David brings The Machine to my apartment. We're going to do it right here. It's about nine o'clock on a Saturday morning.

I say goodbye to Rhoda, who doesn't care in the slightest, and stand in the entry hall right next to the kitchen door where The Machine is set up. I've decided to leave from my apartment —but that just means I'll show up in the same spot in 1979. It'll be someone else's apartment, and here's me, Appearing out of thin air and possibly getting arrested.

I dial two o'clock, Friday, May 18, 1979, and I just have to hope that at that particular time, no one will be home.

Excited as hell I put on another web. He measures out my injection and administers it, with the admonition, "You're really going to have to learn to do this yourself, you know."

I give David a big hug, take a deep breath and press the button. It's like I'm falling.

And I do. I fall down.

PART II

1979 - SAN FRANCISCO

6

Friday, May 18, 1979

Landing in my apartment forty years earlier, I come to with an electrical charge in my hands and belly. I'm lying on the carpet, tangled in a fishing net.

David and The Machine are gone.

I cautiously, silently, regain my footing. Whoever's apartment I'm in right now is a slob. And they smoke cigarettes.

I see a dumpy couch covered in magazines; a papasan chair; and a tiny television sitting on a stand. The walls are white. A poster saying *Foxy Lady* in swirly brown and orange font is pinned to the wall with thumbtacks. A half-dead Boston fern hangs from a seriously overwrought macrame plant holder by the window, and god-awful green shag carpeting covers the floor. It hasn't been vacuumed—or raked—in a while.

I'm standing at my own front door, frozen, gazing at the scene in disbelief, waiting for signs that someone might be home and shoot me dead. Before I know it, I nearly jump out of my skin—shrill, horrible barking erupts as a small dog tears in from the bedroom, yelping like mad and heading straight for my shins.

I dive sideways through swinging half-doors (not there in my time) into the kitchen, giving myself some space and a second to think.

The dog, a terrier mix, has no problem coming after me under the doors. What was I thinking? He simply darts beneath them, his barks piercing the air. Frantic for a moment, I see dog treats in a box on the counter and dump a bunch out on the floor.

It helps. The dog munches down the treats and quits barking outright. But he's still growling, and chomping sideways, his fanged teeth showing. He keeps an eye on me as I tower above him.

I need to get out of here. I move to exit, all the while taking a mental picture of the changes to my kitchen. Cabinets, fridge, Formica . . . all turquoise and dumpy, and all long gone decades before I ever rented the place.

The front doorknob and locks are also different to me, and I tremble as I undo the deadbolt and pull the door open.

The apartment hallway is deserted.

I close the door behind me, locking the knob, but there's nothing I can do about the deadbolt. The person will just have to assume they forgot to lock it when they left this morning.

My heart is thumping wildly. That dog startled the shit out of me.

Safe in the hall, I take a moment to calm myself down. I also have to free myself of the net. I take it off and wad it up. It is simply a wad of black nylon coils, not appreciably bigger than a cantaloupe. I can drop it anywhere, it won't matter.

It smells different in here. It feels different. Yet I know it's my own building, just forty years in the past. It's the same . . .

but it's not. My higher brain knows what's going on, yet I'm utterly confused.

Everything is avocado green. I notice an ashtray bolted to the wall. The place had been remodeled in the early 2000s—all Tuscan and sienna—and none of that is here. It's original 1961 tile and carpeting, now seriously out of date.

Among my cascade of emotions lies a certain, nagging shame: My apartment building used to be totally ghetto.

I'd like to savor the moment, to drink in my surroundings, and to connect with the thrill of traveling through time, but actually I've just got to get the hell out of here.

I'm not ready to encounter another person while officially trespassing. So I swallow my confusion and head for the terrazzo stairs—which seem dizzyingly familiar—and leave the building quickly.

Cooler, fresh air swirls around me, as does the roar of traffic noise on Market.

The first thing I notice is the cars parked along the street. So different! But totally familiar, in an old, comfortable way. Lots of Volkswagen Beetles, Ford Pintos, Chevy Vegas, and older cars, too: a red 1971 Buick Le Sabre; a '66 Cadillac El Dorado in turkey-turd gold.

I begin walking down Market Street, immediately confronted by my platform shoes. I'm about to fall over. They're heavy and awkward and I'm walking funny. But I'm determined to not be viewed as an impostor, so I focus on my gait, picking my feet up enough to avoid shuffling or tripping—which not only makes me look like a weirdo, but a stoned one at that.

Cars are whizzing by and it sounds altogether different. No hybrids, Teslas, or modern Korean engines soften the noise. I think leaded gas is still available for those who want it.

I see a girl walking the same way, down the hill ahead of me. Like most gay men, I'm an extremely fast walker, so I slow down to remain behind her, unseen. I don't want to creep her out. It's just as well I'm in these abominable shoes.

I gradually get my footing and try to wrap my head around where I am and what I'm about to encounter.

I was alive at this moment in 1979, but only eight years old, living in a Seattle suburb. My memories of the time are vague, unformed. I was a nerdy, greasy-haired, emotionally over-sensitive kid, always picked on. I've been gay for as long as I've been self-aware. Although no child knows what it is, they just know they're different . . . that their journey must be borne in solitude, with no outside help.

The bullies at school knew. They always knew. I was hassled a lot, which only drove me deeper inside myself.

At this very moment, my eight-year-old self is six hundred miles away, blithely unaware of what "gay" is, what it could be, and that such a thing as the Castro District even exists.

I'm walking headlong into the gayest neighborhood in the world, at the gayest time in its history.

I take out my iPhone. Obviously, it has no signal. It still says it's 9:06 a.m. on Saturday, October 26, 2019. I rotate the dials to adjust the date and time to 2:06 p.m., Friday, May 18, 1979. The phone accepts this without throwing any errors. Apple is either more clever than we give them credit, or no one conceived it could ever be an issue.

I put the phone on airplane mode to save the battery and stick it back in my tight front pocket.

I'm now heading down Market Street like I do every day of my life.

It's the same hill, with the same cracks in the sidewalks—just forty years earlier. The buildings around me look pretty much unchanged. It looks like home.

I quickly arrive at Harvey Milk Plaza and the Muni station, only to come up short at the first visible difference. The station isn't done yet.

The sunken plaza's been bored out, its signature brown brickwork has already been laid. The escalator is installed but covered by a blue tarp and the whole site is fenced off. The Market Street Subway will come into use a year from now, in 1980.

As I approach, an orange and white Boeing-built Muni streetcar, brand new, follows the tracks into a huge concrete tunnel I've never seen before—it's in entirely the wrong place to my eyes.

By now I'm starting to see a lot of other people, so I stop at the railing over the station and wait. I need to get my bearings about the place before I tackle my bearings about the people.

The six-way intersection of Market, Castro and 17th Streets is much like today. On my right is the Bank of America building. Across the street is Twin Peaks Tavern, famous for being the first gay bar in the country with picture windows. Men were no longer willing to hide in a city where, only years earlier, it was illegal to serve alcohol to a homosexual.

At the Standard gas station beyond that, cars are lined up waiting for gas. Today is an "even" day; rationing is still going on. I spot an orange AMC Pacer station wagon with wood paneling. It is being fueled at the pump by a woman in business attire with broad lapels, high heels and feathered back Farrah Fawcett hair.

Gas is seventy-nine cents a gallon.

Lots and lots of men. My first takeaway, now that I'm daring to look, is of hair and track shorts.

I forgot about track shorts. Nearly everyone's wearing them: the high-cut polyester ones that have drawstrings, no useful pockets, and show everything.

As for hair, I'm seeing one or two crewcuts like mine, but a lot more men have the shoulder-length hair popular in the post-hippie era. Nearly everyone else has painstakingly blow-dried and feathered hair, parted in the middle, and I spot a number of Goody combs in the hip pockets of skin-tight, flair-legged jeans.

A lot of Tom Selleck mustaches. And a healthy smattering of beards. I'm pleased.

Loud polyester button-up shirts are worn open, with exceedingly wide lapels. Most guys are just wearing t-shirts, with Nike logos, Adidas logos, or political slogans. I see overalls. A few men are in business attire, polyester checked suits, but they're not lingering with the Castro crowd. They may belong here but seemingly have other places to go.

Men by the dozen are hanging out on the street doing nothing. At 2:10 on a Friday afternoon. Don't these people work?

Many of the men are Castro Clones, a somewhat derisive term used to describe a particular look: Levi's jeans, lumberjack shirts, black boots, mirrored sunglasses and close-cropped hair. Working men, yet rather cleverly cultivated. If you think Village People, you'll be forgiven. It's a popular look, and fairly sexy.

But there are people of all kinds here. Hippies and jocks, clones, stoners, cowboys, and disco queens—and lesbians, too. Now that I'm getting used to all the eye candy, I am indeed seeing many women. Straight housewives, still stubborn residents of a quickly changing Castro, but also loads of lesbians. Some butch ones dressed as clones, others as hippies, and many more handing out flyers on the corner. I see two nondescript, average women in their twenties, holding hands as they stroll across Market.

Not everyone quite belongs. I see secondary and tertiary eddies of the uncool, the hangers on, the lonely, the disenfranchised. Everyone's here trying to feel the magic.

People have come from all over the country to experience America's first gay neighborhood. To live, to hang out, to hang on, to find themselves.

Originally known as Eureka Valley, the Castro District has long been an average straight Irish and Italian-Catholic neighborhood, very blue collar and conservative. Starting in the early '70s, the area began to be overrun by hippies fleeing Haight-Ashbury, looking for cheap rent, and later by gay men looking to get away from the sleaze and crime of Polk Street.

First one gay bar opened. Then two. Soon the area began changing.

"Come out, come out, wherever you are!" The famous line from *The Wizard of Oz* is the unofficial motto of the new gay neighborhood, used by community leader Harvey Milk as a siren call to everyone who wasn't free to be themselves back home. Milk himself owned a camera shop on Castro Street, which was ground zero for politics and the not-so-secretly-gay Castro Village Association. Milk was later elected to the San Francisco Board of Supervisors, the first openly gay man elected in the country.

He was assassinated six months before my arrival here in 1979.

Many of the original businesses remain, while scores of straight families moved out in a huff. Rents have begun to skyrocket, and the neighborhood is booming.

I realize I'm stalling, standing here. Right now it's just a visual for me. It feels like, once I move from my perch, the actual act of time travel will begin. I'll be in it, an imposter, an observer, and bent into a new, never-before-seen reality. I finally peel myself from my vantage point and enter the fray, heading onto Castro Street itself.

It feels like it's happening for the first time. I'm inordinately concerned that I don't fit in; that I'll somehow blow it.

Greatly impeding the sidewalk is an endless row of newspaper boxes. Long-haired guys are sitting on them, some with their hands out. One asks me, "Got any bread, man?"

What I don't see are the legion of homeless who roam the neighborhood in my day. No crazy guy named Dane, no lady who sings, or that drooling, palsied beggar. Everyone in 1979 seems to belong to some extent, and, while I see stragglers to society, nothing like what we deal with in modern times.

That's when it hits me: I don't know anyone here. Not a soul.

I keep moving down the street, but suddenly I don't think I've ever felt so alone in my life. It's crushing. I see the same streets, even some of the same businesses, but I'm truly on my own, cut off by time.

It overpowers me for a moment, but I keep wending my way through the strangers around me. Spotting a guy's shark-tooth pendant, I'm reminded that I may have a friend after all: Peter.

Peter Groubert has lived in the Castro since 1968. My heart sings. Could I actually expect to find him? Hell, he wouldn't even know who I am. But right now the idea of seeing someone I know rocks me to my core. It becomes a slow obsession. Even if I don't find him, I feel much less alone as I walk forward into this world.

It's always grounding to me to get staples first. I have nothing but the clothes on my back and what I carry in my pockets. I'm going to be in 1979 for five days, so I'll need supplies. I make my way to the bottom of the hill, to 18th and Castro, and go into Star Pharmacy—what will someday become Walgreens.

Overhead fluorescents, tinny Muzak playing on speakers, straight women with big hair, old ladies, and lots of gay men are jostling through the narrow aisles. Not a lot of room to maneuver in here.

The prices slay me. Pennies on the dollar. I snatch up a toothbrush, yellow plastic with straight bristles and none of the mod-cons of a modern toothbrush; Aim toothpaste, and for good measure, a white, wedge-shaped tube of Pearl Drops tooth polish.

I quietly go *Ah!* when I see a brown and orange bottle of shampoo, *Gee Your Hair Smells Terrific*. My mom always used that. I pop the lid and smell a smell from childhood: floral, clean, a little bit plastic. I add it to my collection. I find some Ban Ultra roll-on antiperspirant in a glass bottle. It has the big round ball that I remember goes on wet and always manages to yank out armpit hairs.

Further on I encounter a plentiful number of Fleet enema bottles on display. No one's looking. I quickly grab one.

I line up to check out, feeling very conspicuous with my latest item. I try to hide it in my hands, and don't feel all that swell that an old woman is going to be my checker. Wearing '60s cat-eyeglasses on a chain, powder blue sweater, she doesn't even look up; she just crunches the keys on her register. All five items set me back $3.68. I pull a crumpled five-dollar bill out of my front pocket, and soon my items are hidden in a paper bag. It crackles under my grasp.

Back on the street. I think I deserve some beer. Toad Hall is the bar next door. I've heard about it for years, now I get to actually see it for myself. I approach the door, distracted by all the schmertzy brickwork on the face of it.

It's dark in the bar. They're playing, not surprisingly, disco music. *You Make Me Feel*, by Sylvester, a San Francisco local.

Cigarette smoke is everywhere . . . the place reeks of it. And of stale beer. The bar is not so empty as I would have thought. Rather than stand in the door like a rube, I head for the bar and get a bottle of Michelob for seventy-five cents.

I put my shopping bag on the counter and look at the strangers around me, my eyes adjusting to the darkness. A few sizable afros, two drag queens, clones; some men with long hair, some with feathered hair; hippies, men in Tom of Finland leather. Everyone has their look, be it disco, leather, or clone. You choose your tribe, and you cleave to it, barely tolerating the others.

Some things never change.

Most are painfully young, and here's me pushing fifty.

The only other men my age look like they're trying to be young again and it's a little sad. We still see it in our day, desperate attempts to cling to long-lost youth. But on the whole the people of 2019 aren't as drawn to false representations anymore. God love Baby Boomers getting old. I have hopes, as a member of Gen X, that we'll be able to keep it real.

I hardly notice my beer's empty. I've downed it in two gulps.

A guy in full leather—at 2:30 on a Friday afternoon?—seems to appreciate my looks. Like me, he also has a Fu Manchu moustache and sideburns. Tight-fitting, black leather pants, a leather vest with no shirt—not a lot of chest hair, and not a sculpted body by any means, but it's just fine and dandy. He does a lazy fly-by, making eye contact. I nod and smile. He looks to be in his late thirties.

He circles back and leans against the bar next to me.

"I'm Brian. You local?"

"Just visiting," I say. "Hoping to stay at Beck's Motor Lodge if they have room." I seem to be peeling my beer label with my thumbnail. I always do that when I'm nervous.

He winces and makes that sucking sound in through his back teeth.

"Gee, they might not have room for you. It's the weekend. But I tell you what . . ." He moves in much closer, hips first. "If they don't, I bet I can find a place to squeeze you in."

His eyes are warm. Brown and perhaps a little beady. The Fu Manchu moustache is working, though. Such a silly look on a man, but I'm digging it. He also fairly reeks of Hai Karate.

I smile. "I'm sure I'll get along somehow," I venture.

He leans in—up close he's quite a bit shorter than me—and plants a French kiss on my mouth, our silly seventies moustaches mashing and our spit tasting of beer. There's a joyous tickle to a good kiss, and it calms me down.

Maybe I won't be alone after all?

"Where you visiting from?" he asks, once he's done with the kiss.

"Seattle," I lie.

Brian goes, "Seattle, huh? I hear Capitol Hill is the place to be."

"It is," I answer, "but it doesn't compare to here."

"Hanging out with anyone while you're in town?" he asks.

"I might try looking up an old friend. Do you know Peter Groubert? Drives for Muni?"

"Hmmm. Name sounds familiar. Anyway, if you want to hang out that would be cool."

"I would." I'm smiling. A true smile that, a mere few minutes ago, I would have thought impossible to muster.

Brian leans up and gives me another kiss and grabs my crotch.

"I should see if I can get that room at Beck's," I say, pulling my mouth off his. "I'm Mark, by the way."

"Glad to know you, Mark. Mind if I tag along? If you get a room, we can make out. Otherwise we can just go back to my place over the hill. I have a waterbed."

"Sounds good."

I grab my paper bag and Brian holds my hand as we walk out of the bar and back into 1979. Well, that was quick. In and out in ten minutes, without the use of a single smartphone. Welcome to the seventies.

We walk holding hands, and the sidewalk is crowded with men. We have to wend our way through the increasing throngs. I see so many gorgeous guys, it's dizzying, and of course Brian knows them all. Kissing and hugging and introducing me to Bob and Steve and Mike and another Mike and at least three other guys named Mark.

AIDS is here, on these very streets, laying in slumber. The infection has already started. But no one knows yet. My doctor once described AIDS as a fairly slow-moving disease after all. It takes years to do its work, as opposed to the immediacy of something like Ebola. It's insidious. It hides, biding its time.

I feel dizzy with the horrible secret in my head as I look at the faces around me. Everyone's in a good mood. It's a party. It's a sunny weekend in the city.

I just focus on the feel of Brian's hand in mine as we dodge across 17th Street, avoiding another Boeing light rail vehicle.

We eventually get to Beck's Motor Lodge on Market Street, once a family-oriented '50s motel, now a well-known den of sin. Despite this, Brian and I instinctively let go of each other's hands as we approach the desk. Two gay men who look like Village People are trying to get a motel room together. We're hardly fooling anybody.

The woman at the desk doesn't care. She's dressed perhaps a little out of date: hair unfashionably done up with an oversized wooden barrette, and with ruffles and drawstring around the neck of her blouse.

I see AAA roadmaps and brochures from this other era and long to pore over them, but I must stick to the business at hand.

They just had a last-minute cancellation, so they have room for me after all. The woman gives me a registration card to fill out. "The rate is fourteen dollars per night; would you like to put it on your Master Charge?"

"I'll pay cash. I'll be here for four nights, if that's OK."

"Sure, I'll just need to see some ID."

Shit. The California driver's license in my back pocket has holograms on it and expires October 16, 2020. I panic for a moment. I look at Brian meekly. "I think I left mine in Seattle."

"Hmm," he says, not quite rolling his eyes. "Here. Use mine."

He pulls out his wallet and plops his license on the counter. I see it out of the corner of my eye, only enough to know that it looks vastly different from mine. But it does the trick. The woman looks it over and writes something down in a ledger book and hands it back to him.

We're all set. I'm given a key with a long, green, plastic diamond-shaped fob that says "208." Brian follows me up the outside steps and along the breezeway to my room.

As soon as the door closes, we get to work. I don't even have a chance to look at my new motel room; I've got Brian in my face. Which is fine. I close my eyes and hear traffic on Market Street, and the sound of us, two men breathing ragged through their noses.

"What would you like to do?" Brian asks.

"Everything . . . "

"We can do that," he giggles and slurps all at the same time.

Because he's been wearing leather all day, Brian is slippery with sweat and smells heavenly. We learn each other's bodies in that weird way when you're really just strangers to each other. We meld on the first of two beds and set about doing what humans do.

We're naked and out of breath a few moments later.

"Whew!" says Brian. "You're all right!"

"Thank you, my good man." I'm still smiling. I'm here and I'm OK and I'm smiling.

We lay there in each other's arms, staring at the dirty ceiling. Beck's is convenient, but seldom has it been called "nice."

"Where you from originally?" I ask.

"Pennsylvania," he says. "Wilkes-Barre."

"How long you been in San Francisco?"

"Since 1972."

"Did you know Harvey Milk?"

"Sure."

"I wish I could have met him," I say, putting my head in my hand, elbow bent.

"I volunteered against the Briggs Initiative," Brian says. "He was usually there. He was incredibly busy after becoming a City Supervisor. Harvey was an amazing man."

"Is his camera shop still open?"

"No, it's all boarded up. The space is for rent. I used to spend a lot of time in there. Sad to see it go. End of an era." He sighs.

Brian gets up off the bed and reaches over to collect his leather pants off the floor.

"You want a shower or anything?" I ask.

"Nah. I like the feeling of just having had sex. Why waste the water?"

"My thoughts exactly."

"Christ, there's nothing worse than putting on sweaty, wet leather pants," Brian laments as he sits on the bed and tries to work his legs back into them. "Shit, that's cold . . . you wanna go back to Toad Hall?" he asks, struggling and shimmying. "I could use another beer or three. I'll introduce you around. Later tonight a bunch of us are going to Trocadero Transfer."

"Wow, that would be great. Thanks!"

I hop up and get my clothes back on. My iPhone slithers out of my front pocket and plunks to the carpet. I pick it up quickly, but Brian is just now getting his leather britches around his hips so he can buckle the front and doesn't notice.

We gather our belongings and head for the door. I make doubly certain I have the key. A quick glance at room 208 shows a basic, seriously out-of-date motel room with unfortunate wood paneling, a bright orange low shag rug, two beds and a color TV. I'll want to watch some TV later. I'm sure it'll be wild.

We head out, down the steps in the sunshine and back toward Castro Street.

Despite the free, anything-goes atmosphere of the Castro, San Francisco is a deeply divided city right now. While it's famous for the Free Love movement and hippies of Haight-Ashbury in the late 1960s, and later the huge influx of gay men from across the country, forgotten are the normal straight residents who just want things to stay the same. To raise their children in a normal white culture. Conservative. Decent.

They openly despise what is happening to their city. City council meeting after city council meeting devolves into shouting matches. People are scared and furious.

Most homophobic among these are the San Francisco police. Even though it's estimated that almost twenty percent of San Francisco is now gay, the police continue to beat up fags. They raid gay bars without provocation, beating patrons to within an inch of their lives and then arresting them for good measure. During queer bashings the cops are useless—they've been known to sit back and place bets. People carry police whistles for their own protection; if you hear one, you come running because the cops won't.

The past November, 1978, was a month of hell for the people of San Francisco.

On the November ballot was the Briggs Initiative—statewide Proposition 6—that would call for the immediate firing of any schoolteacher accused of being gay. It was fully backed by Anita Bryant and conservatives across the country. Although it brought us the indelible episode of Mrs. Bryant getting a pie in the face on national television, it was a tense time, and the bill was expected to pass. It didn't; Prop 6 failed by 58 percent, to the great relief of the gay community.

Then, two weeks later, the Jonestown Massacre took place in Guyana. Reverend Jim Jones and his followers lined up to drink cyanide-laced Kool Aid in a bizarre suicide pact. Nearly all the 918 victims were from the Bay Area; his People's Temple operated nearby on Geary Street.

It shook the region to its core.

And only a week after that, on November 27, 1978, the city mayor and Supervisor Harvey Milk were assassinated at City Hall.

Former police officer and city supervisor Dan White entered the City Hall building at ten that morning through a window in the basement to avoid the metal detectors. He made his way to Mayor George Moscone's office to plead for his old job as supervisor back. A heated argument ensued, and, as Mayor Moscone lit a cigarette and made to fix cocktails for them, Dan White shot him in the chest twice, and then in the head twice at point blank range.

He then went to the office next door and shot Harvey Milk in the same way. White fled the building but later turned himself in to police.

Then-Supervisor Diane Feinstein found the bodies. She is famously remembered for making a brief statement for the television cameras: "As President of the Board of Supervisors, it's my duty to make this announcement: Both Mayor George Moscone and Supervisor Harvey Milk have been shot and killed. ("Jesus Christ!" yells a reporter.) The suspect is former Supervisor Dan White."

These people had lived through all that only six months ago.

Now I'm here in the 1970s sunshine to see how the city is getting along, and to get a handle on what it all meant.

Dan White's verdict is due in a few days. I need to be here to experience it.

It won't go well.

On the way to Toad Hall, I'm feeling very grounded and refreshed. The sex definitely helped, as it will tend to do. I notice more things around me. Louie's barbershop is still there, I go in all the time for my crewcut. Cliff's Hardware has been across the street since 1936, and the grand Castro Theatre with its signature marquee towers over the neighborhood. All achingly familiar landmarks to me, furthering my general confusion.

We get to Toad Hall and the crowd has picked up considerably in the short time we were gone. The music is substantially louder. Plenty of Michelob all around, and I meet many of Brian's friends, quickly getting lost in the shuffle.

"This is Barry. He has a big dick and loves three-ways," Brian yells over the music with a wink. I shake Barry's hand, which is sizable. Brian is definitely not lying about Barry.

I meet Silas and bearded Scott and clean-shaven Rick and another guy in a moustache whose name I can't remember.

Mostly they talk about sex and getting their rocks off; going to the cliffs at Land's End, where the gay men cruise even in our day, and Baker Beach, too. EST and Esselen, Fire Island. Laserium shows, a new Marantz receiver. Silas talks about some good Maui Wowie he had at an ashram in Sebastopol. Politics comes up, the Coors boycott and Anita Bryant.

I'm getting buzzed.

After several beers, the men decide to go to Welcome Home for dinner, and I'm beyond delighted that I'm invited to come with them.

Six of us head over to the café for a table. It's Friday night, but still early—only about five-thirty—so they have room for us in the smoking section, toward the back by the counter. We get seated. We're all served ice water in red plastic cups with straws and handed menus in clear vinyl. The table is covered with a red checkered plastic tablecloth, the kind with white felt underneath.

The walls and furnishings are cruddy and visually busy. Several banks of Boston ferns hang from the ceiling, fake brick wallpaper lines the walls below the picture rail, and the floor is a mottled linoleum made to look like red bricks. The menu is restrictive, too: chicken-fried steak, French Dip, hamburgers. No panini, no honey mustard dressing or edamame in sight. They probably haven't even heard of cilantro yet.

Five strangers are seated around me. I practice in my head: Brian, Barry, Silas, me, Scott and Rick. Whew.

Rick has a moustache and feathery blond hair and the oversized squarish, metal-rimmed eyeglasses of the day. He has a chipped front tooth; you can see it when he talks. Scott looks cute in his beard and thin, turtleneck polyester shirt. He has long, brown hair, rather greasy, that runs completely straight until it reaches the ends, which are curly. Silas has a sharp nose and quick eyes, and Barry, well, I notice the large ears, large nose and black hair parted sharply on the side and worn shoulder-length. Everyone has something around their neck—a pendant, a shark tooth, puka shells. They're all strangers from another time, but what I just shared with Brian makes feel less alone. Less like an intruder.

The waitress comes and we order two pitchers of Rainier and I get the French Dip.

"Salad?" she asks.

"Sure." I'm hungry. "Green Goddess dressing, please."

With the waitress gone, a few topics of the day come up. In my mind, I was ready for a little Patty Hearst, swine flu and the Bicentennial, but I'm a number of years too late for all that.

The Three Mile Island accident has just happened. Joking about the radiation leak, Rick says, "I dated a guy from the radiation zone. He had two dicks. A big one and a small one. We'd take turns."

Earlier this month in Iran, the U.S.-backed Shah has fled. What'll happen next? They want to set up a caliphate. It can't be good.

"How 'bout that Margaret Thatcher being prime minister?"

"She's a dyke. Hair Pat Nixon'd kill for."

"Could you see those two going at it?"

"Ew."

"*Tsk*. I'd rather rim Ernest Borgnine."

A heated discussion comes up about rent control for San Francisco. It's slated to be on the November ballot. I long to tell them it sure works for me, but I must say nothing.

I am shocked to learn that home mortgage rates are currently at 11 percent. Wow.

The president is Jimmy Carter, California's governor is Jerry Brown, and Diane Feinstein is now San Francisco's mayor.

Someone mentions a long-forgotten memory for me: In San Francisco, to know the correct time, you dial POP-CORN: "At the tone, the time will be . . ."

Various and sundry political topics are bandied about with no general aim, and somewhere in the restaurant a glass breaks loudly on the linoleum floor.

Barry says, "It's Sandy Duncan! 'Oh my eye!'"

We laugh.

They're pretty hooked up into politics—there's not a slouch among us. I'm glad for that.

But then some seriously raunchy Pollack jokes circle the table and I'm actually taken aback. They're mean as hell. I struggle to remember that's just how it was. The '80s was all about dead baby jokes. In the '90s it was blonde jokes. And now, in the '20s, we only have . . . dad jokes, I guess. Lest somebody get offended. I don't know from it.

I'm pretty lit, so defying the rules of polluting the timeline, I work into the dialogue the bit by Lily Tomlin and Jane Wagner from their show in 1981: "The 1950s was the most sexually frustrated decade ever. Ten years of foreplay. And the sixties? The sixties was like *coitus interruptus*. The only thing we didn't pull out of was Vietnam."

For a heartbeat there's nothing but stony silence, but suddenly the table erupts in deep raucous laughter. And I feel fine. I may be mousy and depressed, but I love making people laugh, even if I'm not the progenitor of the joke myself.

The food comes, and it is wholly unremarkable, as I recall most food of the '70s being. My salad is crudely chopped iceberg lettuce and one cherry tomato swimming in Green Goddess dressing with two saltine crackers in a cellophane wrapper on the side. The French Dip tastes . . . simple. Less chemical, industrial restaurant flavor, which I hate, and more like real food.

I try to listen, to dive in with something funny when I can. But I often feel like I don't socially belong, even in my time. Here, I'm a galaxy away. Floating. And still very much on my own.

Rick tells us a story: "So this friend of mine has to choose between three different men to date. One's a football hunk, dumb as dirt, great bod; one's rich and well-connected, maybe not as good looking; and the last one is a schoolteacher who's smart and creative and loves animals and nature. Which one should our man date?"

We all look at each other for answers.

Rick finally answers for us: "*Tsk.* The one with the biggest dick."

Everyone laughs.

Conversation picks back up, turns to the assassination, Jonestown, gets heated. I decide to ask questions.

"How could you handle the assassination? I mean, it was tough for us up in Seattle, but you guys must have been ripped apart."

"I've never cried so hard in my life," Brian says. "To actually know a man who has been murdered in cold blood! I was at work at the Flower Mart. They had a radio on in the office, and this straight dude named Gus told me and laughed it off. He thought it was funny. Harvey Milk was amazing. He really brought us together. Which is, I guess, why the establishment couldn't stand him.

"But I gotta say, the candlelight vigil was outta sight. Thirty-thousand people stretched from here all the way to City Hall—two miles—in complete silence, bearing lit candles. No one said a word. We just walked. It was so quiet! The only sound was the wind and people shuffling their feet on the pavement, and the occasional person crying. Traffic was stopped. No one hooted or got ugly. They wouldn't dare."

He's nearly choking up as he speaks. I feel the weight of it and remember videos of the vigil. All the tiny flames fighting to stay lit in the stiff ocean breeze. Tears on candle-lit faces.

"I was so upset!" Scott says. "I knew Harvey for four years. I used to hang out at the camera shop. I was working in the main post office sorting center in Oakland when I found out; I almost had to go home I was such a wreck."

"I was actually scared for my life," Rick adds. "If some psycho's going to gun down Harvey Milk in his own office, at city hall, how long is it before some yahoo comes into the Castro and starts shooting? We all know the police won't give a rat's ass."

"I just can't imagine it," I say. "The Briggs Initiative, Jonestown, Harvey Milk all at once."

"It was like we were losing our minds," says Scott with the beard. "It was surreal."

I can't help but picture how I'd hold up under such stress. Probably not well. And yet everyone here seems well-adjusted and doing pretty good.

"What's going on with the guy who killed them?" I ask.

There's a hesitation at the table. I immediately wish I hadn't brought it up.

"That sad fuck is on trial now," Barry explains. "They expedited his case. But the San Francisco police union has raised $100,000 to defend Dan White. He was always an absolute darling with the police union." I hear others at the table tut and scoff. "If he's not found guilty of Murder One, all hell's gonna break loose, I can promise you that."

I try to change the subject a little. "How many of you guys actually knew Harvey?" I ask.

Each man at the table nods or gives a wave of their hand.

"Hung like a horse. Rough in bed," says Silas. Everyone laughs.

Brian interjects, "Harvey Milk could walk into the Teamsters Hall in front of a hundred straight, white, Republican thugs, and in five minutes have them eating out if his hand. He just had that way about him. He was honest. Openly gay, he'd talk about it. He'd let them ask questions. *Any* questions. Most people had never actually met a gay person before. He'd completely disarm them. I've seen him do it. It was amazing."

I ask the assembled group, "OK. I've done all the touristy things here a million times. What else is there to do in San Francisco?"

"*Cruise!*" three of them say in unison with their beer glasses up. Everyone laughs again.

Barry leans in and quietly suggests he and Brian and I should go back to Beck's and have some fun together. All three of us.

Really? I almost don't want to.

I mean, it happens a lot more than you'd think here in the big city. We're all the same gender, and threesies can be totally amazing; yet I'm jaded enough that my initial reaction isn't one of excitement, but of dread—of an unnecessary overage of drama. They can fall apart horribly, on a dime, with shattered feelings and wrecked relationships in their wake.

The restaurant bill comes. Guys are pulling one-dollar bills and change out of the front pockets of their tight jeans and clinking of coins on the table. There isn't a twenty-dollar bill in sight.

On the street, we all part ways, Brian and Barry and I obviously going our own direction, the others smirking in smug appreciation. Except for Rick. He seems . . . sad and disappointed? I see him give one last, solemn look at Barry as we leave, and I see a world of hurt in that glance.

So these people do have feelings after all.

I'd begun to wonder: Did these people get hurt? Did they have feelings? Fall in love?

I couldn't live here. I'd be an emotional wreck, all the time.

But before long, I'm back in room 208 with the door shut and four hundred and thirty collective pounds of male human bodies to deal with.

Barry wastes no time revealing his trade secret. I was correct, he's packing serious heat.

They make their presence known, these two men. Instead of being some carnal freak show, there's a surprising comfort, an ease, to being with more than one man at a time. It can be very sweet.

After probably only a good twenty minutes, it's over. There's certainly no ceremony about it. Barry and Brian jump up to get their clothes back on before I can even catch my breath.

"Better take a disco nap," says Barry. "We'll be back to pick you up at nine-thirty to go to Trocadero Transfer."

"Thanks! That's great."

We take turns kissing one another goodbye, something that takes slightly longer when there are three of you.

Alone finally in my room, I climb onto the bed. It's a complete mess and I haven't even slept in it yet.

I get back up, though, to turn on the TV, an RCA ColorTrak with push-button channel selectors. It's 6:45 p.m. I would love to watch the evening news. But they're all done except Walter Cronkite giving the tail end of the national news—just now switching to sports—but on Channel 2 they're showing *Six Million Dollar Man*.

I lose myself in the commercials.

Ads for Vitalis, Shell No-Pest Strips, Miller Beer with the song, Alberto VO5, and a Bayshore car dealer selling a perfectly squared-off 1979 Chevy Malibu for $4,400. Then your actual O.J. Simpson running through the airport Hertz commercial comes on and I stare at it, open-mouthed.

I should sleep for a few hours if I can. So I turn the TV off and climb back under the covers. I'm tired and I'm drunk and I'm in 1979. I set my iPhone for a 9:00 p.m. alarm and remember I need to take my pills.

Back out of bed and filling the glass tumbler, wrapped in wax paper, with tap water from the spigot, I take my Truvada—a prophylactic HIV pill that won't be available until 2004.

How many men did I encounter tonight? How many of them are going to die of AIDS in the coming holocaust? Such a horrible way to die, emaciated, raving skeletons.

Thirty-three thousand gay men are going to shit themselves to death in this pretty, prissy little city in the coming years.

Before 1997, HIV was a death sentence. But we have the right drugs now. People with HIV lead perfectly normal and healthy lives. What was once a death sentence is now perhaps emotionally charged, but not overall more devastating, than developing Type II diabetes.

What happens if I, an HIV-negative man on PrEP, have sex with these people in 1979? Well, the same thing that happens nowadays: Nothing. I'm on modern medication (and brought plenty in my pocket), so I won't catch or spread the virus. That's just how it works in our day. It doesn't cure the virus, but it acts as a shield, preventing the spread of HIV.

It will come far too late for so many men. I can't even go there in my mind.

I finally get into this bed. I sleep. And dream of Swine Flu and, for reasons unknown, actor Robert Conrad in Marin County.

§

My iPhone alarm zips into its song and I shake my head and shut it off. It's 9:00 p.m. and dark out. The streetlights aren't apricot, they're blue and stark. I see all this coming through the window. The curtains have been open the whole time, providing quite an earlier show for anyone who wanted to look from the walkway outside the room. And at Beck's, I'm sure there were several.

Whatever. It's the '70s.

The room telephone rings just then. A loud, classic jangle from my childhood. I reach for the olive-green rotary phone next to an ashtray on the nightstand and pick up the receiver. The spiral cord is twisted and grimy.

"Hey. It's Brian. Just checking to make sure you're awake. We'll be there at 9:30 to pick you up and take you to the Troc."

"Thanks. I'll be ready."

I take a quick shower, washing those men right out of my hair, and put on my same clothes—they're all I have. I wonder how much money I'll want to spend on clothes for my brief 1979 experience. Probably not a lot, but I could use a few different shirts. I'm certainly going to ditch these heavy platform shoes the first chance I get.

Barry and Brian show up in the Beck's parking lot in a gold Plymouth Duster at about 9:35. I climb into the back seat—it's a two-door so Brian has to get out of the passenger seat to let me in—and I am immediately handed a lit joint. "Thanks!" I say.

I don't do well with marijuana; it just isn't my drug of choice. But when in Rome . . . I take a light toke and exaggerate my cough.

"If you don't cough, you don't take off!" Barry laughs. He's driving. From the backseat I'm fascinated by the rectangular speedometer on the dashboard, its glowing green light bathes Barry's face, at least what I can see of it. The instrument panel is covered in fake wood appliqué and has a fuzzy pink footprint stuck to it.

Wasting no time, Barry floors it and we lay a little rubber in the parking lot as he turns left directly onto Market. There's no median with palm trees in 1979. We head to South of Market. The backseat windows are high and make seeing out difficult. But Gerry Rafferty is singing "Baker Street" from the eight-track player in the dash, and I try to relax in.

Barry drives like a maniac, though. Any sense of Zen is wiped away as I struggle to find where to plug in my seatbelt.

Once at 4th and Bryant Street, we start the onerous task of finding a place to park. We circle forever. Finally, I'm able to pile out of the back of the Duster, Brian giving me a hand like I'm a grand dame.

Trocadero Transfer looks like nothing from the outside. It's in a grim industrial area. The surrounds are bleak and urban, a mere shadow of the 1.8 million-dollar condos yet to come. From the outside you wouldn't know it is San Francisco's hottest disco. It's just a dumpy, two-story brick warehouse. Yet people are lined up behind a velvet rope waiting to get in.

Shit. They're checking IDs. It must just be city liquor laws, or feeble attempts to find drugs.

I still can't show my driver's license to anyone, but I quickly come up with the only idea available to me. I fish out a $20 bill, palm it, and shake the long-haired guard's hand.

Thank God it does the trick. He says, "Thank you! Welcome to Trocadero Transfer!" And he actually winks at me, taking a quick look at my crotch for good measure.

Inside is an enormous space, a disco palace full of lights, mirror balls and a spiral staircase going up to a balcony on one side.

"This building used to be an old TV station," Barry yells over the din. "They had the sound system designed specifically for the space."

"I think it works," I yell, and I see, rather than hear, him laugh.

"Check out the DJ. That's Bobby Viteritti. Best in the world!" I see him up in his booth, working hard, unobtrusively doing blow.

The sound is enough to rend your ears. "Don't Stop till You Get Enough" by Michael Jackson is playing as we enter to strobes and lights and the pernicious wall of cigarette smoke, which I guess I'm getting used to. It was everywhere once, and we've forgotten that.

Rust-colored carpet going up the walls, trimmed with fake chrome piping. It was everywhere, I suddenly remember.

It's still early, only ten or so. Trocadero Transfer will be jam-packed all night long, a precious after-hours club that will run until the sun comes up the next day. I certainly hope we don't put that to the test.

We line up at the bar, and before I know it, Brian hands me an enormous bourbon on the rocks. Like I need any more alcohol at this point? Jayzuss.

Barry leads us to the spiral staircase off to the side, and we clamor up, hoping for a table. No such luck, but there's room for us to gaze down upon the scene below.

It's everything you think a disco should be, and more. This is one of the first. These folks pretty much wrote the book on it. People in bell-bottoms and all sorts of get-ups and evening wear are dancing on the floor of lighted squares. Some are gussied up in their disco finest: three-piece pantsuits, or yet more silk or polyester shirts open all the way down. Wide collars and lapels, all. Others, more practical, are in little more than gym-wear with headbands to soak up the sweat.

A series of mirror balls hovers over the dance floor, twelve of them, casting beams of light. We watch for a while; conversation is impossible. Once the culture shock wears off, I kind of get bored. This is not my normal milieu, but I appreciate it as a cultural reference point.

"Let's go dance," Brian finally yells over "Hot Stuff" by

Donna Summer. We go back down the stairs and make our way to the dance floor, the three of us. There's plenty of women, are they straight and posing? Looking for feminine rough trade? Lipstick lesbians? But mostly it's gay men, and some are really gorgeous. Brian and Barry continue to demonstrate they know everyone. I'm introduced to so many I couldn't keep them straight on a bet. The introductions and bourbons just flow until finally I'm just knackered.

It's been a long day.

I still have a hard time believing it's all real, that I'm actually in 1979. But the constant cigarette smoke is as good a reminder as anything that this honestly is the past.

"Heart of Glass" by Blondie; "Follow Me" by Amanda Lear; "Born to Be Alive," "Ring My Bell," "We Are Family," "I Will Survive," "In the Navy" . . . all the old disco songs of my youth are played, and so many more I don't remember hearing before.

After a while I'm by myself in the crowd, having lost Brian and Barry completely. I'm about to leave the dance floor and seek refuge at a table, assuming I can find one, when suddenly I'm faced by an enormous African-American individual. The man is garbed in impeccable women's disco attire: diamond headpiece, dripping in sequins, dress, heels. He's a commanding presence and he's resplendent in a red, feathered cape.

Sylvester! Holy shit! This is Queen of Disco himself!

The man now before me will leave an indelible mark on disco music. Some would say he literally wrote the book. "Do Ya Wanna Funk"; "You Make Me Feel (Mighty Real)"; "Dance (Disco Heat)" . . . not just anthems of gay disco, they *are* gay disco.

People are in awe as he takes to the dance floor in front of me. He shakes his groove thing in a posse of people; he's surrounded. He's astonishingly tall. Suddenly, though, he's dancing right in front of me and, since I'm fairly lit, I brave the step of gently taking his heavily ringed fingers in mine and kissing his hand. He gives me an enormous smile and winks.

I'm floored and laugh out loud. No one can hear.

We dance a moment, Sylvester and I, and despite being worn out and ready to bail, I manage to shake my groove thang like I've never shook it before. This is a moment for the ages. All eyes are on me—and I shouldn't even be here.

But, as with any magical moment, Sylvester gets perhaps a bit bored and turns to his other fans, dancing all the while, and is gone as suddenly as he appeared.

Brian is immediately at my side and gives me a pat on the shoulders and kisses my cheek, beaming.

Can't top that. I'm ready to leave. But I'm a guest of Brian and Barry, and they look like they're just getting started.

I make my way to a high-top table that is miraculously unoccupied and sit down on a stool, glad to get off my platforms—I wish I could take them off—but I am just glad to be finally sitting for a moment. I sneak a peek at my phone. It's 1:30 a.m.

I take a couple of pictures of the scene around me. The lights, the strobes, the lighted squares on the dance floor and the platform shoes stomping upon it.

No one notices, or if they do, they don't seem to care.

A woman in her thirties, a bit heavy-set, hair feathered back, wearing overalls, asks if she can share the table, which is littered with abandoned drink glasses of all sorts.

"Sure thing!" I say it loud.

"I'm Carla." She sits close enough that I can hear.

"Mark."

"I saw you dancing with Sylvester, that was amazing! I *love* disco; disco forever, baby!" She laughs and does a shimmy on her barstool. She's kinda butch; I doubt she's straight.

"Finding any hot people here tonight?" I ask.

"Oh, pretty much the usual. See that woman over there?"

She points to a blonde wearing a brown ensemble, swoopy around the breasts, wide-legged pants, clogs on her feet and gold chain glittering in the disco lights.

"Yeah. She's a knockout."

"Oh, but she is a cruel woman," Carla laments. "We went out a couple of times, just enough to drive me crazy."

"Huh. I thought only men did that."

Carla laughs. "The beautiful people get to call the shots, you ever notice that? We mere mortals can only stand in their good graces when we behave and don't try to pretend we're pretty."

"Oh, I know that one. We call them the A Group. A friend of mine in San Diego says just ignore the A Group. Head right to the top of the B Group and you'll never go wrong."

"Hey! You sayin' I ain't in the A Group?" She raps her knuckles playfully against my arm.

"Aw, you're way more A Group than I am! I've often wished I were better-looking. Then I would be nice to everyone, just to mess with their heads."

Carla laughs again and lights a cigarette. That woman, the blonde in brown, comes over and presents herself to Carla. Carla immediately stiffens up to attention.

"Give me a cigarette, woman," says the blonde. Carla promptly complies and lights it for her with her silver butane lighter.

"Vicki, this is Mark. Mark, Vicki." We politely shake hands —such a slender, fragile hand, surprisingly cold to the touch. Vicki has lovely eyes and shiny lip gloss. If I were to kiss her, I suddenly get the impression that it would be strawberry vanilla. My sister had that kind of gloss, I used to dab it on my finger and will never forget the taste.

I think I'm pretty drunk.

Vicki and Carla exchange pleasantries, seemingly careful to avoid anything substantive, whether for my benefit or because they simply don't know where to go from here given their shared history.

At one point a guy comes up and starts hitting on Vicki. Hard. Obviously straight, and he's coming on strong. Polyester disco suit, frizzy hair, turtleneck, gold chain, and platform shoes complete his look. He's right out of an old Montgomery Ward catalogue and seems to have no clue about how to talk to women.

Carla ends it handily. She moves between Vicki and the man and over the music I hear a long-forgotten admonition: "Kiss off, turkey!"

He sulks away but starts in on another woman almost immediately.

"Thanks, sweetie," Vicki says, and gives Carla a peck on the cheek. They hug, quickly at first, but then it becomes something more meaningful. I feel glad for Carla.

And at long last Brian and Barry seem ready to leave.

"Let's go to the Ritch Street Baths," Barry yells over the din, which, I swear, has gotten even louder. "It's right down the street."

Oh Lord Jesus I couldn't handle a bathhouse right now.

But, I argue quickly with myself, I'm only going to be here once. I wasn't even sure I had the strength to have sex again today, and I've already done it twice. I reluctantly agree to go with them. I bid a fond good evening to Vicki and Carla, and back up on my platforms, we walk into the chilly morning air and down Bryant toward 333 Ritch Street, Barry having pointed out it would be easier than trying to park again.

My ears are ringing in the sudden silence.

I'd heard of the Ritch Street Baths for years, but it was shut down during the AIDS crisis—they all were. Ritch Street was one of the most popular.

The purpose of a bathhouse is to get laid, as much as you can. It's a free-for-all in there, no boundaries, no rules—except no grabbing. If someone isn't interested, you have to respect that and move on, although not everyone honors that particular rule.

I remember being very offended at the idea of a bathhouse when I was first coming out. I wanted a Prince Charming/Cinderella scenario. Something as crass as a bathhouse would play no role in that, thank you. They were the lowest of the low and I resented the very idea of them. Until one night in Chicago in 1992, in a snowstorm, after I'd been an out-and-about gay bachelor for many years with nothing to show for it, I wandered into the Unicorn on Clark Street. My erotic self came to the fore, and it was actually pretty fantastic.

We pay our five dollars and go into yet more thumping music, dark environs and low ceilings. Room after room of men lounging around in towels, doors open, or wandering the corridors looking for their next shot at love. Lots of red lights and black-painted walls.

We only have the use of lockers; the cubicles were all booked. I leave my hosts in the changing room and head straight for the showers and the steam room. Glad, at this point, to know I'm guaranteed to be left alone. I'm too old, I'm too far outside the range.

One guy does try to hit on me but he's icky and I'm far too tired. I wave him off but throw him a hopefully genuine and kind smile.

Fortunately, a bathhouse remains true to its original purpose: a place to get some serious soak on. I pamper myself, going from shower to sauna to steam room, then sit on the benches and cool off and do it all over again. It's a mood elevator. It's good for the soul. And when you're full of bourbon, it just feels damn nice. I'm all about the soul. I feel above the sins of the flesh and ready to begin my quest as a higher being when suddenly—shit. I see him.

Look. Whatever your orientation, whatever your marital

status, no matter how many progeny you've spawned or what where your haughtiness lies, at some point you will see a human that knocks it all to hell.

And I see one such human here at the Ritch Street Baths at 4:30 a.m. in 1979 and I am thrown for a complete loop.

A man with a Super Mario moustache, Italian, muscular—but with just the right amount of body fat to reduce the harshness and formality of too many hours at the gym—hairy body, warm smile, built like a brick shit house . . . is strutting around without even a towel, showing everyone how God has graced him.

And God has graced him.

He looks like the porn star Bruno—if you remember him—only much taller and, unlike the porn star, actually standing five feet away. Which is rather in the plus column if you ask me.

The men around him all immediately fluff and primp, trying to get his attention. I don't have a shot in hell.

He's stomping down the hallway, beaming, looking from right to left, seeing nothing worth his while. And here's me, getting off my bench and willingly putting my forty-nine-year-old squingie body to the fore to be shot down in shame.

Ordinarily I wouldn't have the balls to even try this. I know my limits. They're pounded upon me on the daily back home. But maybe because I, personally, have just danced with Sylvester; that I have traveled through time; that I have seen a city in two eras in such a way that would make a normal man cry; and further, I've had bourbon.

I'm going for it.

Come to find out I'm a little unsteady on my pins as I stand up and head down the left hallway so I can hopefully pass him coming back the other way as he makes his circuit.

He smiles at me and nods as I stumble past. Wow. Didn't strike me as a patronizing smile, either.

Well. I'm committed to my walk of shame down the hall, so

I wander to the right. I see two guys going at it through an open door and I go back up the other hallway, past so many black-painted cubicles of men doing God knows what, so I can set about another fly-by.

I go weak in the knees. All this flesh here and he thinks I might be good enough to nod at?

He's gone into cubicle 157 and I pause for a sec, then approach the open door and rap on the wood. Even my knuckles make me sound gay. "Hey," I say. I have a catch in my throat from all the cigarette smoke and I have no right to be here. Seriously. I'm not worthy.

"Hey," he says. "C'mon in." His voice is gruff and warm. Not believing my good fortune, I step inside and close the door behind me.

Sounds emanate from other rooms. There's no ceiling, just cubicles, one after the other, held together with plywood, painted black. Base human sounds emanate over the thumping rhythm of the speakers in the ceiling.

The man is sitting on the cot wearing nothing. Suddenly I am given leave to touch, finger, peer at him in the dim light; for a few moments I have carte blanche to pore myself over the human of my dreams. He's built like a bull—in more ways than one. He's definitely the sort of man who likes to call the shots and I let him. It's fantastic. Even in my overly worn-out body, I find myself again.

You don't get to explore a man like this in real life very often. So I examine him, memorizing him, smelling him, the hair, the brawn, the muscles, the moles . . . everything. Before he disappears. Before he swats me away like an errant fly.

"What's yer name?" he asks as I caress him, tracing swirls of hair with the tips of my fingers. That's a good sign.

"Mark."

"Mine's Mitch. Good to know you." And he wraps an arm around me and pulls me to him and we lie, my head on his chest. I can hear his heart thumping even over the music. It's tender and wonderful.

"You live here?" I ask.

"Yep."

"I'm visiting from Seattle. Staying at Beck's."

"Cool. Now I know where to find you." He tousles my hair with his fingertips.

We lie there for a while until he releases me from his grip, my indication that it's time for me to go.

"What room are you staying in at Beck's?" he asks.

"208. Last name's Baldwin."

"Well, I might drop you a line, Mark Baldwin, room 208, Beck's Motor Lodge," Mitch says. Almost menacingly. But with a kind smile.

I grab my towel and plant him a big kiss and leave cubicle 157. I'll probably never see him again. I decide to call it good.

Fortunately, Brian and Barry are ready to leave. I find them in the locker room, Barry getting his bellbottom jeans back on, Brian once again fighting with his damp, cold leathers.

"How did you do?" I ask.

They both launch into tales of debauchery. It was a good night for both of them.

"What about you?" Barry asks.

"Just one. But it was . . . good," I say lightly. I don't want to share, it would dull the magic.

"Cool," Brian says. "Let's get out of here. My cocaine's wearing off."

The streets South of Market are dire regardless of century or time of day, but in the wee hours of this morning they seem particularly bleak. Dumpsters and trash and graffiti; it's deserted. I see one lone homeless man, looking like a stereotypical hobo, peeking into a garbage can.

We find the car and climb in. The windows are covered with dew. Barry has the stereo off and I'm glad for the silence.

We don't speak. When they drop me off at Beck's, the sun is just starting to come up from behind the East Bay hills.

I thank them profusely for a grand night out and off they go off in the gold Duster. No other cars are on the road, just gray concrete and the sound of the Plymouth growing dim.

I climb the outdoor concrete steps to my room laboriously. These platform shoes now feel like the ultimate form of torture. I want them gone. Pulling them off, I undress and get back under the covers and the bourgeoning daylight through the window doesn't bother me in the slightest.

I'm asleep before I know it.

7

Saturday, May 19, 1979

I wake up after 1:00 p.m. Surprisingly, I feel good. No hangover. I'm tired, but mostly hungry. I lie in bed a few moments and review all that had happened to me yesterday. It was a seriously long day.

Well. There's more to see. I get myself up and put my clothes back on, once again lacing those horrible blue platform shoes onto my feet. Today's the day they die. I know where I'm headed first: Orphan Andy's Café on 17th Street. They serve breakfast all day, and they're going to be my friend. Ham and eggs and lots of coffee sounds so good to me right now that my stomach is growling in anticipation.

Breakfast is very satisfying. I go through the pangs of not knowing anyone in there, of being a disconnected stranger in my own city. I find some boring parts of a leftover Sunday *San Francisco Chronicle*, nothing informationally rich. Orphan

Andy's itself looks much the same: posters, lots of James Dean and Marilyn Monroe, pink neon. In 1979, kitsch is hardly a thing yet, there's no irony to it, but there's ham and eggs and shockingly god-awful coffee, so I call it good.

Afterward I take the Muni streetcar to find some clothes. Instead of a new Boeing, I find myself on an old PCC streetcar, the traditional 1930s cars that now run as a moving museum along the F-Market line of today. The thing needs to be restored, I see a lot of rust. I sit on the green vinyl seat, feeling the springs poking my butt, and look out the windows as we head to Powell Street and Union Square.

Once again, the buildings are all the same, just the contents are different. But then I stare at the big Methodist church at 16th Street, surprisingly large and imposing. I've never seen its Spanish-style spire before. It burned down in 1987 and has been a vacant lot ever since. We pass Safeway at Church Street, the giant U.S. Mint sitting on the hill above, looking like a marble fortress. Further, passing under the sooty Central Freeway, Market Street between Van Ness and Powell appears quite seedy. I'm seeing homeless people now, and everything's dirty and covered in pigeon droppings. Graffiti, too. Billboards for Winston cigarettes and Rainier Beer and pool halls and loan companies.

I alight in front of the Emporium department store, and cross Market. Dodging a loud dancing group of Hare Krishnas next to a bank of pay phones, I go down into Hallidie Plaza, and to the entrance of the gleaming new BART station. The familiar sounds of a BART train, unspeakably modern, the tooting of the horn and whoosh of air, come from down below. It's completely familiar and serves to remind me that I am home, simply displaced in time.

The cable car turnaround holds a bit of a surprise: Normally tourists would be waiting in a great line snaking around the table, but instead, there are construction cones, a utility truck and open grates. There's not a cable car to be found, the whole length of Powell Street. The whole thing seems to be shut down for repairs.

But my aim is to go into Woolworths, and time travel once again smacks me upside the head. Fake wood-paneled cartouches set over orange-painted walls; I smell the popcorn and cigarettes, and a soft *ping ping* comes over the PA system and I quietly flip out a little inside.

I pick out a light windbreaker, a couple of t-shirts. One says "Keep on Truckin" and one says "California" in big, swoopy print. I find a package of Fruit of the Loom white underwear and happily stumble upon a pair of Converse sneakers that fit. The whole thing costs me a whopping $27.74, eating into a lot of my 1970s money. Overly eager to ditch the platforms, I put them in the Converse box, lace up the Converses and leave the box back down in Hallidie Plaza. Nearby, a man in a one-man band getup is playing the tambourine and harmonica and wearing a knitted pimp-daddy hat.

Maybe someone will find the shoes and love them to death. I never want to see them again.

Market and Powell are the same buildings, but with different businesses inside. Manning's Café, Florsheim Shoes. One Powell Street is a staid Bank of America with a huge stone clock over the door. It sports the old logo, the heavy "BA" letters depicting a bird. The branch looks yellowed inside under fluorescent lights, drop-down false ceilings and years of cigarette smoke; the place simply aches with boredom. It possesses none of the flash and come-hither glitz of a modern bank, but display signs depict a generous and much less predatory banking atmosphere: Simple savings accounts offer four percent interest, and I remember from school that charging more than eighteen percent on a credit card is an illegal practice in the U.S. right now.

Banks used to be boring but faithful. Nowadays, with usury

laws long swept aside, they're full of pizzazz. And robbing Americans blind.

And yet here's an ATM off to one side on Powell Street: a Bank of America Autoteller. It is a machine so rudimentary, no one pays it any attention. It has no visible screen, just a tiny digital readout and clunky aluminum buttons. Someone has hocked a loogie onto it.

Truly at a loss for what I should do and see for the next four days. I'm willing to call last night an exception. I have no intention of partying like that again.

The city is feeling large and unfriendly to me all of a sudden and I sense a need to be close to home. Even though it's not home to me just now. So I opt to go back to the Castro on another Muni streetcar, a Boeing this time. It even smells new.

Seats face each other in groups of four, very confrontational. I'm wedged in with three Chinese housewives heading back to the suburbs with their bags of bok choi and wearing bad polyester clothes. Unchanged throughout the ages. They cluck amongst themselves and don't know I can pick out a few words of their Canton dialect. They think I'm "one of those," and given how hard I'm struggling to fit in, I'll take it.

Back at Beck's, the message light is blinking on my phone. It would probably be Barry or Brian. I call the front desk to get the message.

The bored woman says, "You have a message from Mitch, please call him at 861-7138."

"Thank you!" I'm writing down the phone number and repeat it back to her, making sure I don't get it wrong.

I can't believe it. I stare at his number, quietly memorizing it and, just for giggles, put him in my iPhone—adding the 415 area code to make it real.

Come to think of it, I'll write down the number for Beck's Motor Lodge. I should have it so I can call and check for messages from a payphone while I'm out.

I'm not going to call Mitch right away. I don't want to appear desperate. But I definitely want to see him again. I cannot believe my luck.

§

It's Saturday. The fog is coming in over the hills, and no one here knows the fog will someday be named Karl, for reasons I've never understood. Nothing interesting is on the three television channels I get in the room, and I don't want to just go out and get drunk. It's 3:30 p.m. and I've got nothing to do.

So I walk the Castro. All of it. My brain can't possibly track all the changes. My favorite plant store is a liquor store; my Vietnamese restaurant is a book shop. Starbucks isn't around to hang at; it's a hair salon. My doctor's office is another bath house called Black Rock.

No need to go inside, I've already taken it up the ass in there. But that was by Aetna.

It seems that the only places to hang out in are bars.

I go to Harvey Milk's boarded up camera shop at the far end of the street. People are still waiting outside, for the man who will never return.

Suddenly, just as I'd hoped might happen, I pass my old friend Peter Groubert in the 500 block of Castro, walking with a friend. It's definitely him—only he's so young, it makes my head swim.

Without overthinking it, I just walk over and dive in, my hand out to shake.

"Peter! Hi, it's Mark. Mark Baldwin. We met at that party, y'know?"

"Hi, Mark" He looks confused—but not overly concerned.

Perhaps even amused. He doesn't miss a beat. "Good to see you again. Oh, this is Bob."

I shake Bob's hand, a tall, reedy man with long hair and a thin nose. But I'm drawn back to Peter, his brown eyes and soft brow line, long brown hair parted in the middle.

My mind is blowing out my skull as I keep staring at him.

"Nice to see you. I'm in town, staying at Beck's. I go back to Seattle on Tuesday."

"Seattle! That's right . . . "

"You going out tonight? Maybe I'll see you."

"We'll probably stop by Midnight Sun about six o'clock. I gotta work in the morning."

"You still driving for Muni?"

That clinches it. He knows I know him—he just doesn't know why.

"Yeah. I'm on the 5-McAllister line tomorrow."

"Cool. Maybe I'll see you later tonight?"

"Sure!"

"OK. Nice to meet you, Bob."

And just like that, a once and future friendship re-established. I decide I can stand a few beers after all.

Peter and I became friends in 1994. I was always fascinated by him. He'd lived in the Castro since before it was even officially the Castro, and, other than a two-year stint away in the Army, never left it. He knew more about its history than anyone. He'd seen it all.

I'll always remember one day when he went to a file cabinet and pulled out a yellowed article from the *San Francisco Chronicle* and handed it to me. It was from July of 1981. It talked about a mysterious new disease in gay men.

"I always knew this would be important," he'd told me, "so I saved it."

Peter had HIV as early as 1978. For some reason the Army

unfroze some of his old blood samples and checked for it. I never actually asked why they did it, but it happened, and yielded interesting information.

He always suffered from an ailment of some kind beyond his HIV diagnosis: diabetes, crippling peripheral neuropathy, heart stents, Bell's palsy . . . towards the end he didn't get around very much, but he was always a good friend.

He died in 2017.

I look back as he and Bob walk away, a young man with long hair and his life ahead of him. Full and round; yes, I look at his butt and it's fine and alluring. Just like the rest of us, Peter's looking for love, too. I know that, in his many years, he did find love along the way, but only in short increments. He was a bachelor more often than not, just like me. Sometimes I think there's no other way for it to be.

Well. The bars are calling. I wander from one to the other, not drinking much, watching hot men, and not so hot men, seeing the latter pluck up their courage only to get shot down. Snubs, cliques, posing and desperation. It's a microcosm.

Since I'm freshly laid, I carry the air of a man who's not bothered. And guys like that. Men can smell desperation. The more you need it, the more they stay away. I've long known this. I don't need it, thus I get more than a few glances, even at my comparatively advanced age. It's cool. I chat with a few guys. But most are looking for sex right away and I'm not.

Hey, I have Mitch's phone number. I never need to get laid again.

Finally, just before six, I encounter Peter, as promised, at The Midnight Sun. Conversation comes easily. I ask him questions I already know the answers to and tell him things about me which he doesn't know and can't remember why. He grew up in the Bronx and still has the accent. His brother Phil: Republican. Rolls his eyes. He becomes more comfortable with me, albeit confused. Whatever. He's not one to stress the small stuff, never was.

He introduces me to a couple of people. A few beers in, we're on equal footing again. It feels good. Peter has to work in the morning, so he calls it an early night.

It's about 7:30, so I go for Chinese food on 18th—where Thai Chef is now. It's called China Gate. I ate there twice a week in the '90s. An old woman who never smiled was always at the cash register, fanning herself. Tonight she's working the luncheon counter and she's young and . . . still not smiling. Imagine going your whole life never smiling. There's a lesson there, only I'm too drunk and too hungry to tell you what it is.

I order beef chow fun, like always. It's good. And it only costs $2.49 with a coke. My tip is mere change from my front pocket.

Back at Beck's, Brian has left a message for me, and his telephone number. I call him from the room. He and a bunch of guys are going back to the Ritch Street Baths again, would I like to come with? I am grateful for the invitation, but no, I don't really want to go. I tell him I'm getting a sore throat. "You dirty dog!" he says. We chat some more, and I thank him again for last night.

"Maybe we can hang out tomorrow?" I suggest hopefully.

"That'd be cool. I'll find out what we're doing and let you know."

"Cool. Thanks!"

"Bye." He hangs up.

I'll probably never see him again.

It's just before eight o'clock. I call Mitch from a pay phone, having deposited a dime from 2004. The phone rings. And it rings and rings. I remember the old days you were supposed to let it ring ten times and if no one answers they're not home.

There's no answer. He's probably back at Ritch Street. I get my dime back.

After that, it's 8:30 on a Saturday night in the Castro. The sidewalks are jammed with men holding hands, cruising, hanging out, smoking, smoking out. I feel much better in my windbreaker and sneakers. I cruise the length of Castro Street, both sides, just marveling at all the hot men. I'm in heaven.

I go back into Toad Hall for more beer. Chat up several guys, but none move me to tears. I'm grateful that people are so friendly here. Oh, there's plenty of attitude from the hot ones, but that's just a commonality to the universe I suppose, regardless of century. I try to catch up on local gossip. People are all talking about the Dan White murder charges. The verdict could come soon.

Stopping by a quickie mart next to Louie's Barbershop, I'm in the mood for a Tejava, but am quite out of luck on that. I get a Fanta and, what the hell—a red pack of Pall Malls, the kind with no filter. Book of matches, too. The pack of cigarettes costs eighty-one cents.

I'm back in bed for a good night's sleep, watching the evening news at eleven on KPIX Channel Five, with their jingle: "We light up the Bay!" Dave MacElhatton wows me in a light gray, three-piece suit, head nearly full of hair, earnestly describing the news with no spin, no smirk. Wayne Walker, sports, is looking fine with all that blond hair and big moustache. Their news set consists of one lone television screen mounted in the wall behind them. They don't seem to have teleprompters—they really are reading from their own pages.

Enjoying my Fanta, it has the old pull tab, the kind that if you dropped it back into the can it could supposedly choke you. And smoking in bed, I flick my ash into the ashtray next to the phone.

The news talks about the Dan White murder trial and other Bay Area news: a discouraging number of murders happened in the past day, all across the region. The weather map is little more than a colored sharpie on a drawing board. I tut and cluck and clamor across the bed to reach over and switch the Color-Trak off.

I get much needed sleep, the sound of traffic on Market Street my normal backdrop.

8

Sunday, May 20, 1979

At about nine o'clock I stir under the covers and I feel pretty good.

Not likely to go to church, I don't know what there is to do on a Sunday. So, before I can talk myself out of it, I call Mitch again. This time he answers.

"Hullo?" he asks.

Gulp.

"Hey. It's Mark from Ritch Street. I . . . uh . . . thought I'd call you back."

Wow, you are imbued with infinite grace there, Mark.

"Glad you did. Got any plans for the day?"

I feel myself brighten. My mood, my soul and my stomach start to clench in something, finally, besides fear and discomfort.

"I was thinking of renting a car and just tooling around the city. I know SF pretty well, but I just feel like going for a drive."

"Do you mind some company? I've got a car and I have the day off. I'd love to go for a drive."

It sounds heavenly.

"Sure! If you're positive I'm not pulling you away from anything."

"Aw, hell no. I'm supposed to be cleaning my garage, and I've been putting that off for three months now."

"Well, if you're game, I totally am."

"Cool. Want me to pick you up around eleven?"

"That'd be great."

"If I can find a place to park, I'll come to your room."

Upon close examination of my feelings on the subject, I realize that I am somewhat desirous that Mitch might find a place to park. I want him to park so damn good I nearly let out a yelp.

"If not, I'll just honk the horn. I'm in a yellow Datsun B-210."

"OK. See you then." I'm fighting to make my voice come out normal.

A day with Mitch: It just got interesting.

Failing anything else at my disposal, I wander down to the lobby of the motor lodge. They have an urn of Boyd's coffee percolating day and night. I'm encouraged, until I take a sip. Jesus, it's rank. But it is what it is. I fill a styrofoam cup—two, actually, and while I'm at it, I grab a few of those old AAA brochures too. I stumble back up the breezeway stairs to my room, my newfound leaflets under my elbow, and I'm careful not to spill the coffee, which is boiling hot. I have to set them down to unlock my room.

At 10:55, there's a knock at my door. It's Mitch. My God, he's resplendent! I'm so glad Beck's has no security guards to keep people out. I want this particular people here in my midst.

I'm still blown away by what greets me as I open the door to room 208.

"C'mon in," I say. I know I still sound lame when I talk.

He comes in. And we hug and share a long, probing, protracted kiss. I look into his melty brown eyes and my stomach does a sweet little flip. He's so cute, it reminds me of visiting koalas in Australia, that feeling when one actually wandered over to me to say hello. He's just that adorable.

He tousles my flat top.

"I love your hair," he says. "I like short hair on a man."

"I'm glad. That's probably in short supply these days. You wanna hit the road or visit for a while?"

"I got a place to park, so I'm happy to visit."

I melt in spiritual bliss, feeling a true connection to the universe.

He sits with me on the edge of my bed, and this time I can see him in full daylight. Instead of finding flaws, he drives me further toward the edge of oblivion. Mitch is exquisite.

And he finds things about my person to excite him. It's hardly a zero-sum game as I work to stir this mountain of a man. Quid pro quo. Oh, if they only knew back home. I'm very pleased to say I get him to trembling, and just when it would be kind for me to release him into surrender, I don't. I make him beg for it until he's practically barking.

We talk a little. He works at Security Pacific Bank as a loan officer, and in my mind, I can only picture the dot-matrix signs in the Muni underground when I first moved to San Francisco: "Security Pacific Bank—We want to be your bank for life."

Spent years waiting for trains watching that scroll by. Only SecPac died like all the others. I don't even remember if it's part of BofA or Wells Fargo now.

Mitch likes leather and dogs and lives in St. Francis Wood, which is pretty expensive and posh—it's also boring and straight.

Feeling warm and sticky, I follow Mitch out to his car. My legs are wobbly.

As advertised, he's driving a bright yellow B-210 with brown vinyl interior. When he puts the key in the ignition the familiar "ping-pong" alarm to fasten our seatbelts plays. It's a five-speed stick-shift, with a shiny brown knob.

"What do you want to see?" Mitch asks.

I tell Mitch I'd really like to drive the Embarcadero Freeway, because I've never been on it. It was torn down after the Loma Prietà earthquake of 1989.

He complies. We head down to the back side of North Beach and zoom along the upper deck of California Highway 480. It has amazing views, and I enjoy zipping past the Ferry Building on the left and the amazing, newly built Embarcadero Center on the right. Then we drive the Central Freeway. I've been on that in the old days, before it was torn down to become Octavia Boulevard.

"Why do you want to be on freeways? That's not where San Francisco is," he reminds me.

"Oh, I know." I look into his melty brown eyes. For whatever reason, they haven't lost interest in me yet. "I have my reasons."

"Lemme show you what," and he zips us up to Nob Hill and Pacific Heights. Everything looks the same, except the cars.

Then he takes me up to Twin Peaks, to the best lookout over San Francisco, the Bay Bridge, Oakland and Alameda. It's amazing. So many buildings aren't there right now: No Salesforce Tower, no giant condo building. My city looks small and almost rustic, but I am comforted by the vision of the TransAmerica pyramid, right where it should be.

Mitch stands close to me atop the lookout. I lean back into the solid mass that is himself. Not really believing he's choosing to be with me, with the vast city laid out below us and the tens of thousands of men; he's here with me. I don't get it. I just savor each moment until it's ripped away. For it shall do, either by time or circumstance. It's a given.

He announces his wish to treat me for pizza in West Portal

at an Italian place he knows. All my years in San Francisco, I've never taken a second glance at the West Portal neighborhood, where the trains come out of the tunnel and it's foggy all the time. Now I know I'll never forget it.

We have Budweisers and pepperoni with mushroom pizza.

That's when he drops the news: "I have a lover. Name's Richard. He's in Los Angeles this weekend. He flies back home tonight."

I'm not surprised. I've been waiting for something like this. It's all been too pat, too good. There had to be a catch. And here it is.

"I understand," I say as lightly as I can. "I go back to Seattle on Tuesday anyway."

"Do you have a lover?"

"Nope. Still single after all these years."

"Really? I find that hard to believe." He's looking at me kindly, but I sense bullshit.

He seems to really like my forty-nine-year-old self, and I don't know why. I wonder if this Richard doesn't maybe look a little like me after all. Squishy and older and, well, if that's Mitch's thing, so be it. Score one for me.

Lunch is over all too soon, and we're zipping around Laguna Honda Hospital dodging Pintos and Citations and a Chevy Luv pick-up. Before I know it, we're idling in front of Beck's, and it's time to say goodbye. I have a twisting, sad feeling in my stomach, the pizza now my enemy.

We French kiss in the Datsun. I take a final moment to savor this man. I trace my tongue over his teeth, the garlic from his pizza wafts over me and I feel satisfied that this lumbering hulk of a man, his pulse, his girth, his woolly black body hair and hopes and dreams are all hanging on my very tongue. It's the single most powerful kiss of my life thus far.

And I end it, pulling my mouth off his, breaking the circuit.

"Thank you," I say. "It's been great knowing you."

"You, too." He tousles my buzz cut one more time and, with nothing more to be said, I climb out of the B-210 and out of his life.

I force myself not to look back as he drives away. I simply let him go—an action heretofore unknown to me.

It's about 3:30 and it's over and done.

§

TRAVELING through time can kind of be a snoozefest. I've got nothing to do.

Maybe I could go see a movie? I grab my iPhone instinctively to check movie listings, forgetting that it won't work. Well, there's the Castro Theatre just down the street. I walk there to see what's playing: only a silent film and not for another hour and a half.

I have it in my mind to make a small trek down to 16th and Albion streets. A most heady time of my life was spent there, in San Francisco's firehouse number seven. I want to go see it.

Starting in 1990, brand new to the city, I found myself working part-time for a dirty magazine in that firehouse. The magazine was a black-and-white, in-your-face gay version of *Playboy*, lots of naked bearded men, extremely raunchy in style. Our tagline—honest to God—was "Naked Hairy Homo Smut." My time there was one of the more thrilling eras of my life, and, despite my average looks, I even managed to get to third base with more than a few of the porn stars that graced our pages.

It was eventually run into the ground by a meth-addled owner, as would happen with so many edgy gay businesses in the 1990s. It was all very exciting.

It's a twenty-minute walk through shabby, boring neighborhoods and dangerously close to Mission Street at 16th, a miniature Bed-Stuy of vice, crime and grime.

I arrive in the manner of the San Francisco pedestrian: lungs fully cycling, body unsure whether to sweat from the walk or shiver from the cool temperature. So it does both anyway.

In 1979 the firehouse is still in use as an actual San Francisco fire station. A wooden Victorian treasure, with slidey pole and horse stalls. Of course I can't go in the place, but I look at it and smell it. Red firetrucks of the 1970s variety are parked, gleaming.

I gaze up at the upstairs windows of my old boss' office, remembering my edgy times spent there, how it persistently challenged my comfort zones as a twenty-year-old back then. Eleven years from now.

A fireman looks at me suspiciously, like I'm a whacko or want to get something started. And Albion Alley was never a safe place to walk so I just turn tail and leave again. Not sure I got much from the experience, but there it all is: places, lasting through time. It's good.

Back at the Castro Theatre in time for the five o'clock showing of *He Who Gets Stabbed*. When I get there, I'm just in time to catch the organist playing, *San Francisco: Open your golden gate; you'll let no stranger wait, outside your door . . .* The sparse crowd is singing, clapping and stomping as the huge organ console descends back below the stage. Seems feeble now, but when the house is packed the effect is one of magic and extreme civic pride.

As I feared, the movie is no great shakes. From 1926, a silent, crime-story with a run-time of only fifty minutes. Wasn't much worth it, but the price was right and it was something to do.

Afterward, I go back to Toad Hall.

I wind up in a heavy deep and real discussion with a guy named Jeff. We're not really interested in each other sexually, but we fall to good conversation anyway, the kind that sometimes, if you're lucky, can happen in a bar. Aided in no small part by alcohol.

"So how is it possible to have a relationship around here?" I ask.

"Oh, it's easy," he laughs. "I'm having three of them as we speak." His eyes lose their twinkle, though, and his smile fades. "It's fucking murder," he says. "Any time you meet a hot guy, you have to assume he's already done all your friends, and they'll stop at nothing to tell you about it."

"Oh, yeah. I know that one," I say.

"Sometimes I think the only way to have a relationship is to leave all this behind, to move out of the city and to go hide in the suburbs."

"I know that one too. But do you know couples here in the city that manage to make it work?"

"I do," Jeff responds. "Quite a few. Usually they're wildly open and non-monogamous, 'anything goes' kinds of guys. Which is fine—if that's what you want. I know very few gay men in monogamous relationships who remain in the city. I don't know how they make it work."

"That's my big question, I guess," I say. "Is it possible to have a normal relationship and still stay in the city?"

"Well, it's possible, of course. Everything's possible. I think you just have to be really strong and really know what you want. And have a partner you can trust."

"That's the tough part, isn't it? I wouldn't trust anyone here in the candy shop. I'm not sure I'd even trust myself," I confess.

"It's true, there's always someone tastier right around the corner. It's like there's no upper limit to how hot they can be."

I think of Mitch and how supremely hot he is. I couldn't imagine finding anyone hotter, that person would have to be literally in flames.

Sometimes, in 2019, I feel like I'm finally getting a handle on life in San Francisco's gay dating pool. Hard lessons need to be learned, one by one, each an emotional trial by fire. My current realization is that you cannot make a man become interested in you if he's not. It can't be done. Having finally learned this, I can now sit back and watch others dance and wheedle and try to make the same mistake, glad to finally no longer be one of them. I've wasted a lot of years making a fool of myself along the way.

I mention this to Jeff. "You know the one about trying to get a guy to look at you who won't look at you?"

"Shit yeah. There's a few guys, I'll be introduced to them, I'm standing right in front of them, and they can literally not see me. They are visibly looking past, through and around me for someone hotter, like I'm in their way."

"Oh," I add, "how about when the same guy is introduced to you three times and he never remembers having met you before? That's my personal favorite."

"Right on, man. I swear one day I'm going to raise up my middle finger and fly some guy a big fat bird right between his bastard eyes. He *still* wouldn't see it . . . "

We laugh, but really we're not laughing.

I'm glad Jeff knows my pain. "I have actually considered trying that a time or two. Just to see what would happen.

"I met a guy at Ritch Street Baths the other night," I tell Jeff. "He was the hottest man I've ever seen. Ever. So hot. I would call him the upper limit. And he saw me. More than that, he felt me—I made sure of that. We spent today together before he told me he already has a lover. If I had a lover like that, I'd be a jealous hot mess."

"Hot mess? Hah. That's funny. Jealousy is the man-killer. You can't be around here and have a jealous—excuse the expression—bone in your body. You have to find a way to give that up."

"See," I say, "that's where I fall down. I do get jealous—real easy. Anytime you meet a hot guy, you have to realize that everyone else has already had sex with him."

"Yes, and that someone hotter is going to come along at any time and steal him away from you."

"So how do you live like that?" I ask again.

"You're not from around here, are you?" Jeff laughs.

"I live in Seattle," I say. "It doesn't have the gay density of San Francisco, so the problems are less. But it's still tough."

"Well, in a way, you're lucky. You don't have to live in this nexus. I do. And I'm still looking for love, and I aim to find it. I guess the lesson is you have to not get jealous and don't hang on too tight. When shit happens you just gotta let it roll off your back and keep on truckin'."

"I guess," I say. "You shoulda seen this guy I spent the day with: Italian, muscular, built like a brick shit house, looks like the porn star Bruno . . . "

"Oh. You must mean Mitch."

9

Monday May 21, 1979

There's not going to be anything to do today. It's Monday. Everyone's at work.

So, after breakfast at Orphan Andy's, I take the ferry to Sausalito. It really is the same, nothing's changed. The ferry rides are, as always, the most compelling part, being on the water, smelling the salt air and riding past Alcatraz. Commuters in suits, health nuts with their bicycles, a few cult types selling flowers looking for donations dodge the mounds of frumpy tourists. I hope I don't look like one myself. I'm a tourist all right, but no one knows my secret.

Once off the boat in Sausalito I have a lunch consisting of a wheat germ and alfalfa sprouts sandwich with carrot juice, and then wander the various art galleries, looking at how oil paintings have changed and how they have stayed the same. I'm biding my time and enjoying the sunny day.

San Francisco, as viewed from a ferry boat, is truly a

magical place. Sutro TV tower, high-rise buildings, cable cars, and so much drama. Oh, god, the drama. I can't smell Mitch anymore, he's washed away, slogging his guts out at Security Pacific Bank right now.

"We want to be your bank for life."

Back in the city, with the cable cars out of service, it's a long walk to a bus and then a streetcar back to the Castro. I sit for a while in my room at Beck's watching TV news. I'm not sure what time of day the Dan White jury comes back from deliberation. Come to find out it's in the early evening.

After fussing and waiting and getting restless, I'm back in Toad Hall with Brian when the news breaks. A guy comes in with a transistor radio in his hand, the antenna out and dragging behind him. He yells: "Dan White just got Manslaughter!"

What? People stare at each other in horror. Several people sigh, and visibly slump. The disco beats keep pumping, but the air feels thin.

Everyone assumes that a man who assassinates the mayor of a major U. S. city, along with a city supervisor, in cold blood, would get first-degree murder. In fact, the prosecution was asking for "special circumstances," which would open the door to the death penalty in California.

Dan White is found guilty of only voluntary manslaughter by reason of diminished capacity—not first-degree murder, as was expected. It is labeled "The Twinkie Defense." Since Dan White ate a lot of junk food, it is argued that Twinkies diminished his capacity and caused him to commit the murders.

And because Harvey Milk was "just a fag"—Voluntary Manslaughter? Five years in prison? It's a slap in the face.

This is why I decided to visit these people. To see this moment in time. I didn't strictly know I needed to feel anger—frankly, I have always avoided it.

But it's on deck. And it's palpable.

All of us pour out of the bar and into the street, and we're not alone. Word gets out differently in 1979. More slowly. There are no tweets. It's by word of mouth. Yet the news spreads with frightening speed. I see real anger in faces.

It's not quite dusk when people start to assemble in general foment.

Phone trees are pressed into service. Everyone has a list of five people to call when there's an emergency. With no voice-mail or answering machines, you've just got to call, call and call. It's generally effective, despite busy signals and crossed wires. People are lined up four deep at each pay phone, those on the phone gesticulating wildly and practically yelling, hanging up, inserting another dime and dialing once more. In a short time, approximately five hundred people are mobilized at 18th and Castro Streets, marching around the block.

We walk into the street, comparatively few in number for a while. I've somehow lost Brian, but I find myself holding hands between two women in a weak chain that nevertheless stops a 24-Divisadero bus dead in front of the donut shop. I see the driver, an African-American man in the brown uniform of Muni, honking the horn and waving his hands in exasperation. Someone comes up to the driver's side window of the bus and says something to him and what happens next surprises me. The driver sets the brakes with a hiss, pops the doors, and steps out into the street. I fear he may start swinging.

Instead, he joins hands with us as we continue to march.

I look back as the confused riders dismount from the bus to find alternative means of transport.

People come out of the bars and apartment buildings, the businesses of Castro Street, adding to the throng. Our numbers grow. There are bullhorns suddenly, and shouts of "Shame! Shame! Shame!" ring out. Around the block we go, blocking traffic completely. Soon the number of us is up to around 1,500. People are chanting and raising their fists in anger, faces twisted with rage.

Whistles. Dozens of police whistles. I'm in it. Around the block we go, from 17th Street to Noe, then back up 18th at Castro, only to find more people streaming from the buildings. The cars are hopelessly blocked now.

We chant: "Out of the bars and into the streets!"

After several orbits, the crowd gaining strength and momentum, we begin marching to City Hall, down Market Street, past Beck's Motor Lodge . . . and still our ranks are growing. I encounter Barry and Silas and we walk together, chanting, holding hands.

The crowd radiates an incredible energy. Thousands of people are united in outrage. By the time we reach City Hall two and a half miles away we are five thousand in number.

I'm keenly energized, and strangely unafraid. At least so far. It's obviously tense. Some bad shit's going go down, and I'm here to observe it, a fairly ballsy thing for me to do after all, but I've come this far. Wouldn't do to miss out. I've heard tales of this event for years.

Night has fallen. It's getting chilly and no one knows what's going to happen. This is uncharted territory. San Francisco police are waiting for us, three deep, in full riot gear. It's ominous to say the least. My stomach clenches.

San Francisco's city hall building is solid, sound and exquisite. It has served as a backdrop for countless movies and TV shows, a solid, capitol-like dome where everything is made of stone and copper filigree. It is also ordinarily a place of great tedium and bureaucracy. Tonight, surrounded by an angry mob and lines of riot squads, city hall looks more than capable of withstanding a little pressure. Some of the polish is likely to get dinged before the night is over.

At first there are chants and cries, but nothing more. We approach from the Van Ness side where hundreds of people are milling about. But Silas says he figures the action will be on the Polk Street side at Civic Center Plaza, so he drags Barry and me, our hands still locked even though we don't know why and it feels funny.

The opulent building is surrounded on all sides by angry protestors, and more police than I thought possible. So many. Nevertheless, they're hopelessly outnumbered by us.

I gaze up to the second floor of City Hall. Milk and Moscone's offices are just there. That's where they died. Two men shot through the head. And the man who did it is only getting a slap on the wrist.

Chants begin again. "Shame! Shame! Shame!"

"He got away with murder!"

"We want justice!"

"Kill Dan White!"

Sporadic violence erupts, then, nothing coordinated or particularly effective. People just suddenly decide to rush up and begin kicking in the glass doors to City Hall. Someone wrests an iron bar from one of the light poles and smashes windows. The police only respond in kind, beating back the vandals with clubs, sending them away covered in blood, and resuming their post guarding the building. Otherwise, they are not engaging.

A few people among us are pleading for calm, hands up, only to get knocked to the ground by livid protesters.

A Molotov cocktail is lobbed, trash cans are set on fire and rolled toward the building. People rush and smash, get beaten with nightsticks and shoved. They fall back and others come forth to do more damage; they're rebuffed by the police, but still the cops as a whole don't attack or work to disperse the crowd.

What are they waiting for?

I look up at the architecture of the building, hoping to find solace in its familiar beauty. But it doesn't help. What do you do when the very establishment, the system you rely on, fails?

You riot.

I get that now. Yet it unmoors me. I'm alone in a sea of rioters. I've lost track of Barry and Silas and civilization is breaking down around me.

I guess it needs to happen. But it's ugly. It hurts.

I'm shoved hard by an angry woman, her face twisted in rage, as she runs straight at the cops and starts pummeling one with her fists. The cop loses his cool. She's knocked to the ground, and he kicks her. She slinks back, arm out, finger pointed, yelling something.

"Kill Dan White!" The chant is repeated again, with fist bumps.

An enormous drag queen in an impossible wig keeps spraying Aqua Net over a lit lighter, shooting flames outward in a huge arc above the throng.

News teams are also here, camera lights shining bright, anchorpeople trying to do live coverage, but the scene is too chaotic. They have to fall back.

Twelve police squad cars are set on fire along Van Ness Avenue. Heat and flames erupt, ghoulish and strong, unsettling to see and feel. The powder blue Ford Torinos have their windows smashed and their interiors set ablaze. As they burn, their sirens wail into the night, each in turn a horrid, mournful sound of death and ruin that carries far and jangles everyone's nerves.

As the last squad car is set alight, I see the man with matches say to a reporter, "Make sure you put in your paper that I had too many Twinkies today!"

For three long hours I wander the periphery of the madness, wanting to be a part of something. I know that I must witness this.

I'm here for all the times I've been called a faggot from a moving car. For having to grow up entirely by myself, inside myself. I'm here for the horrible disease that's about to strike, knowing that 5,636 Americans will die before the bumbling president shall even bother to speak the term "AIDS" out loud.

I let it flow through me. I wasn't expecting this, but I feel powerful right now. More powerful than I've ever felt before. It surges. I'm not much on the destruction of property, but I get it now. I'm here to be angry. To have the right to be angry. I shout now, too. I pump my fist as well. I allow myself to yell my throat hoarse.

Sporadic damage continues, waves of clubbing, beating, bleeding. Cops gruffly snarling, "Get out of my way, you don't want to see me comin'!"

It all changes when the crowd collectively grows an intelligence.

A spontaneous sit-in begins to form from the madness. After three hours of chaos, people in their hundreds begin locking arms, sitting down. And singing. I join them.

It grows quiet. It becomes beautiful. Suddenly everyone sees it—the way forward. I savor the beautiful moment awhile. Because . . .

That's when the police strike. A sit-in would paralyze the city for days. It's the final straw.

The beautiful moment is shattered, and true violence erupts. Cops suddenly become activated, openly swinging nightsticks and snarling, grown men brought past the breaking point bring their anger and full strength to bear, clubbing people half to death. I see blood now. People are fighting back with anything they can get their hands on, but they are no match for the police.

Tear gas is deployed, choking us, driving us away.

Once the police attack it's over in fifteen minutes.

The spasm ends. The air is thick with choking gas and people are worn out, injured, moaning, crying, scurrying away.

Now I'm on Grove Street, trying to not blow chunks on the pavement. I'm out of breath and tear gas is clawing at my lungs.

I stand bent over, gasping for air, my hands on my knees, trying to rein in my stomach, looking at the tiny stones embedded in the concrete.

Our beautiful City Hall is smashed. Cop cars are burning, and people are still yelling, vowing revenge. Our handiwork. Our voice. But we're falling back in defeat, dispersing. Now that the tear gas is wafting away and the scene is safe, TV news crews finally converge, hungry for footage.

A young girl covered in blood is struggling to regain her footing. She's looking over her shoulder, waiting for further assault. I move to help her up. She says, "Thank you," and I steady her. Her forehead has a gash and there is a lot of blood.

"Do you want me to get you some help? An ambulance? A taxi?" I ask, feeling helpless. I don't know that any such things are available to us.

"I'll be all right," she says in the odd way where she's actually reassuring me. "I live just over on Franklin."

"You sure?"

"Yeah. Thanks." She gives me a sideways hug, keeping her blood off me as best she can, and careens off toward Van Ness and the direction of her apartment.

I just stand for some minutes now. The crowd is dispersing, the smoke clearing, the cop cars smoldering, and whatever this was, it is now over.

I turn and make my way back down Market amid a mass of people heading back to the Castro. Everyone is spent. It's like the crowd leaving a high-stakes football game where the favorite team has lost. It's a long walk. Somehow, the journey to City Hall, taken place with an angry mob, seemed far shorter.

After an hour of walking, I almost turn in to Beck's Motor Lodge as I pass by. But I'm not ready to go hide. Not yet. I want to be with people. I want scotch.

I continue walking until I'm at Elephant Walk, on the corner of 18th and Castro.

The Johnny Walker burns my stomach lovingly, the ice cubes clink in my glass. It's very safari-like in this bar, with bamboo fans swaying on rods, exotic posters, and instead of harsh red or blue lights, the place is lit warm and dim. It feels safe. It's cozy.

I gaze upon my fellow men, looking for guilt, exaltation, glee, triumph, shame, hurt. I see all of these, a bizarre mixture. Everyone is checking in with each other. What did you see? Are you all right?

And what music should be playing on the speakers? Sylvester.

I'm there over an hour when, with a loud crash, a sudden surge of San Francisco police officers converge on Elephant Walk, smashing the windows out. Nightclubs swinging, men being cracked over the head, bodies being thrown to the floor. I can barely register. It's happening so fast. I hear them hissing out phrases like "dirty cocksucker" and "sick faggot."

I'm toward the back by the kitchen, but the side door is blocked by two officers in riot gear. I'm trapped. And despite my weariness, I register that I have no viable ID on me. This could be bad.

I begin to feel more than sudden fear. It's different than I expected. Even though this is in the past, it is happening to me right now and a wooden club is a wooden club. I tense up and, with a bravery unknown to me, simply sidestep the carnage, bent on getting the hell out of there.

I watch men around me drop to the floor, truncheoned. I see yet more blood.

The police are already lining bleeding patrons up along the bar to arrest them. I hear the zip of handcuffs and the spoken charge: "blocking the sidewalk."

I've weaseled my way close to the gaping front window, and with no glass in the frame, I merely step through it and onto the sidewalk outside. Several other men follow suit.

Immediately I'm confronted by an enormous cop in riot gear. He shoves his nightstick lengthwise across my chest hard, nearly knocking me over backward. He growls at me to get back into the bar, but suddenly I'm beyond caring.

Seriously. I don't even belong here.

I don't know where these feelings are coming from. I just know that they are now in control. I look straight into the riot officer's eyes and say, "I'm going away now."

He must see something in me, a time-weary loneliness; a traveler who has been places he can't ever imagine.

I also do that thing we gay men sometimes do. I look him right in the eye with the cold, certain knowledge that, as a gay man who has unwrapped more pairs of jeans than he could ever dream of, I know all about his little cop body. With just a quick survey I know with complete certainty: he only has a small one. That it would curve up and have a little pointed head. His butt would be saggy, he has a pitiable lack of chest hair and droopy pale man tits too.

We gay men can size this up in a fraction of a second. I'm not saying it's right. It's certainly not polite. But know that we've got your number. We'll clock you. We have the knowledge.

Police riot man becomes keenly uncomfortable. He knows I know, and for a brief moment it's delicious. I simply move past him along the sidewalk. He looks at me slack-jawed and lets me pass, before turning his anger on someone else. I hear violence as I walk away.

I trudge across the street, away from the mêlée, and make it to Hibernia Bank without incident. There are squad cars everywhere, and cops roaming the street, looking to make trouble. I really should get back to my hotel, and struggle to think my way around this madness, when I'm jolted from my plans by none other than Peter Groubert. For a moment I'm confused. Why is he so young and handsome right now?

"Jesus, Mark, get away from here!" He seems to mean it. He

pulls at me and I follow quickly. "These motherfuckers are out of control. Are you OK?" he asks, and I find, for reasons unknown, that I am.

"Yeah. I guess I should get back to Beck's."

"No shit," he says, leading me across the intersection toward the donut shop.

We should have gone around. Down 18th to Noe Street—but we just aren't thinking clearly.

All too soon we realize our mistake. Our way is blocked by two cops, heading toward us coming down Castro. Two more move in behind us. We're trapped, right in front of the theatre. We are going to have to walk forward and just hope for the best. The cops get closer and we see that their badges are covered in black electrical tape and that they're wielding nightsticks.

My stomach squeezes again in that fear thing.

With the casualness of doffing his hat, one of the cops takes a half-hearted swing at my head with his club. While it's only a glancing blow, it hurts like hell. I see stars and my ears ring.

The other cop hits Peter hard, who has his hand up, and I hear the crack of breaking bones.

That's it; that's all they do. They just keep walking past like it's a normal day at work.

"Owww," Peter is hissing, cradling his right hand.

"Are you OK?"

"I think he broke my fucking hand! *Motherfucker!*" Peter yells at the retreating cops. They simply high-five each other and keep going.

"How far is it to your apartment?" I ask.

"It's just one block over. Let's get there before any of them come back."

We rush the rest of the way, at somewhere between a trot and an actual run. I feel relief that no police are visible to us, but I'm surfing a never-before-felt spike of energy. I feel attenuated, my senses strangely acute. We make our way quickly without encountering a soul. Word's out. People are staying indoors.

A block down Market and around the corner to Noe Street, we approach the first apartment building. Peter holds his right hand in a Frankenstein claw and says, "You'll need to get my keys out of my jeans pocket."

I fish them out. He's wearing skintight pants—we all are—and he uses his left hand to unlock the door. There are mirrors on the wall of the apartment lobby and I see that my head is bleeding quite a bit. It certainly hurts.

My "Keep on Truckin" t-shirt is soaked with blood.

Once in his apartment on the second floor, the two of us work in conjunction to make ice packs, one for my head, one for Peter's hand.

"We'll have to go to Davies Hospital in my car," Peter says. "Can you drive a stick?"

"Yeah."

Leaving right away, we go to the garage and get into his lime-green AMC Gremlin. I hurt, but I can't believe I get to drive a Gremlin—even if it's only for a few blocks.

"Go Your Own Way" by Fleetwood Mac blares loudly from the speakers the second I start the car. I turn it down and back us out. It's been ages since I've driven a stick-shift, and it shows. AMC products are not hale; I hope I'm not stripping any of the gears. It's a short ride, and of course, once we get to the hospital, there's absolutely no place to park. Eventually I clutch us into a spot on Waller Street.

The emergency room is full of gay men with battle wounds: black eyes, broken hands, gashes to the head. It's going to be a long wait. It's already well past midnight.

People are smoking in here. It's so hard to believe, smoking in a hospital.

It's hours of old magazines. Like, really old. There's a *Time* from 1976 talking about the Bicentennial. I wish I could take out my iPhone and play *Candy Crush,* but I know that's not a good idea.

That earlier energy shot, having done its work, leaves me feeling sapped and foggy as time slows to a crawl in that horrid waiting room.

Peter and I talk some, halfheartedly. I tell him what I saw at City Hall, how it felt, how the police activated themselves as if on a pre-arranged signal and ended it in bloodshed. Peter had a sense that things were going to go south, so he stayed in and watched it on TV. He ran out of his apartment when he heard the police were roughing people up in the Castro, although he's unclear as to what his actual plans were in doing so.

Finally, we're seen by a doctor. We go in together. Peter has broken bones in two fingers that have to be reset. He yowls in pain as the medics pull. They put him in a brace with bandages. I have only a bump and a small laceration, no signs of a concussion. They clean me up and tell me to watch out for blurred vision in the next couple of days.

We're released. I drive us back to Peter's in the Gremlin and he says I might as well spend the night. It's three in the morning at this point, so I heartily agree. We get into bed, bandaged and broken, and put out the lights.

I've had sex with Peter before, years from now, but my last memories of him are of him having progressed well into old age, frail, sallow, and needing a walker to get around. The man in my arms right now is young and super cute. He's not full of energy, just Darvocet. We lay side by side in his bed and let nature take its course.

Finally, we sleep.

10

Tuesday, May 22, 1979

I wake up in Peter's bed, his telephone is ringing in the hall. He hops up and shimmies, naked, to the phone. He has a protracted conversation with someone, telling them what happened to us last night and getting the latest news. Finally he hangs up and puts on some Folger's.

"That was Bob. About two hours in last night, Police Chief Gain finally came into the Castro and managed to disperse his cops. About twenty-five people were arrested at Elephant Walk for blocking the sidewalk. Not one of the cops has been hauled in or suspended. I doubt they will be.

"Tonight is Harvey Milk's forty-ninth birthday. There's going to be another march, a vigil. You wanna go?"

"Naw, I can't. My flight home is at two." But I'm struck that Harvey Milk and I are briefly the same age in this alternate universe.

"Oh, that's right. Seattle. Well, I hope tonight's thing is

peaceful. I think we've had about as much violence as we can take."

I want to reassure him that it will indeed be a very peaceful, moving affair. But I can't.

We have coffee in bed. It's hard because I'll never see Peter again. There were so many things I wanted to ask him, but I scramble now to remember what they are. A lot of them have to do with AIDS and it's not yet time for that.

So eventually I put my clothes back on and thank him for his hospitality. He gives me his phone number in case I ever get back to San Francisco. I don't give him mine. It would have to be a fake number and I just can't see doing that.

I look into his young, brown eyes and feel a catch in my throat. "See ya later, alligator."

And once again, Peter Groubert is gone from my life.

I go back to Beck's. It's ten o'clock. I've got four hours left and I just want to leave now. I wait the hour watching TV until checkout time. Then I just leave my unused items behind, turn in my key and go for a walk. Down Market to Church Street, I go into The Hideaway Café at Church Street Station and have a Reuben sandwich and iced tea, then I walk down Church to 18th, passing Mission High School. From here it's a modest uphill hike to my apartment.

I'm tired of feeling so alone. I want to go home. Which is weird; *This* is home. It's just that it's like a parallel universe. One that's frankly full of hurt and drama.

I'm to Disappear at two o'clock, Snapping Back to 2019. I walk slowly up the street. I figure on being on the sidewalk outside my building when the time comes—it should be safe. An unreasonable fear grips me that something will go wrong, or that it won't happen, and I'll be stuck here in this Castro of the wrong time.

I get to Market and Diamond Streets a few minutes early and stand and wait, not touching anything. A girl in overalls leaves my apartment building with a cigarette between her fingers and the terrier I met on Day One. It must be her apartment I Appeared in.

I mean, my apartment.

Several more minutes pass. It should have happened by now, right? I just start to fuss when the familiar ripping comes, which, rather than soothing me, makes me fuss more.

I fall in a blaze of light.

PART III

2019 - SAN FRANCISCO

11

Saturday, October 26, 2019

I hit the sidewalk outside my building. It's 9:00 a.m. Saturday, October 26. It's 2019 once again.

I feel woozy, groggy. I may finally throw up.

The first thing I see is a 2017 black Nissan Altima parked in front of me. It looks so normal I almost want to hug it.

I breathe deep, this air of 2019. It's Indian summer warm. I take stock of how I feel. My head wound is still there, a bump on my cranium that only hurts if I touch it. Hence it hurts a lot, as I can't seem to leave it alone. I fish my key out of the bottom of my pocket in my bellbottoms, which are pretty dirty by now. I enter my building and it's no longer ghetto, it no longer reeks of cigarette smoke. I'm willing to wager there isn't a macramé plant holder to be found.

I run up the steps and down the hall. David is there with my front door open, his Machine all packed up and ready to wheel away. I can't even catch my breath.

"Hey!" He actually seems surprised to see me, which is silly.

"This shit is so fucking intense!" I manage to stammer.

"You're alive, so I'm guessing it worked?"

"Yeah, it worked. Holy shit!"

I slam the door—my door—and feel the joy of coming home to my apartment in my century. My books are on the shelves, Rhoda's asleep on her chair. A "Foxy Lady" poster is not thumbtacked to my wall and the shag carpet is gone. It's back to the tongue and groove planking with the rug I got at Lowe's.

My kitchen is mine. My living room walls are now deep sage, not white. For some reason, just now my brain flashes back to David's reaction when I first showed my daring sage color choice to him.

"Ah," he'd said. "I think I recognize it. Ralph Lauren. From the 'What Were You Thinking' collection . . . "

Jesus, he can be an asshole.

But he's hugging me now, true and good. I've only been gone a few seconds from his perspective and holding onto his body seriously anchors me.

"Well. Out with it." David breaks the hug, leaves The Machine where it is by the door and moves to sit down with me in my boldly colored living room.

I splay out and tell him all. I'm emotional, I'm spent. I show him the bump on my head.

But David doesn't really seem to get it. These things don't move him. Nothing I could say would match the intensity of what I've just experienced. In fact, I flash in anger at him that he could be so dim as to not understand implicitly.

He has the brains to create a Machine like this but not the common sense to catch the nuance of the experience. He just wants to make money.

Eventually he leaves, and I'm alone and entirely unable to sit still.

After a shower I check in on Fluffy. She's happily paddling around in her tank. She lives with a supply of goldfish; she eats them, you see. It's not pretty but she lives a happy life.

I go back out into the neighborhood of now for brunch and groceries, once more sporting normal clothes and shoes. And wouldn't it figure? I run into virtually no one I recognize. The neighborhood feels lonely and foreign to me all over again. So many more chain stores have moved in: Elephant Walk is now Harvey's; Midnight Sun has moved around the corner and down; and what was Toad Hall now comprises the Walgreen's annex. The world's loneliest Pottery Barn sits up at the main intersection, their clever plans for a cornerstone location dashed when, at the end of the day no one dares be seen in the place.

Something about the cars of today bothers me I can't put my finger on, until I finally do.

We only get to pick cars in three lifeless colors, all of which are boring and suck: gray, blue-gray, or red. Who decided this? With my brain so out of balance I realize that it bothers me now on principle.

Once again back home I angle toward the emotional concept that I might think about sort of maybe doing a little work. To generate some income, even though my mind is reeling.

I do a search on the White Night Riots. Dianne Feinstein, appointed mayor after the slaying of George Moscone, had given police specific orders to stand down. That's why they didn't strike until the sit-in started to form. She has been both praised and excoriated for her decision for years.

I consider googling some of the men I met—in particular, Mitch. But I only now realize I came away without a single last name, which was either dumb, or the smartest thing I've ever done. Mitch would be around eighty years old now, if he's not dead to AIDS. It's all just as well.

As I lay my plans and get ready for my next journey, I make one additional discovery: I've come away absolutely rotten with 1970s crabs.

12

Tuesday, November 4, 2019

I've read a great deal about the 1906 San Francisco earthquake and fire. I'm about to live through it.

I love this city with all of my heart, but I need to see what it used to be—what it was supposed to be, as originally intended—before it was laid bare. Ruined. Interrupted. I am obsessed with seeing the bits and bobs, the epic buildings, the architectural trends, the history, the majesty for myself.

San Francisco is often described as one of the most beautiful cities in the world, and this is certainly true. But its original beauty, by all accounts far greater than what we see now, was ripped away. I am dying to see what was here before: the finials, the columns, the plinths, the newels, the stained glass. The opium dens, the whorehouses. Everything was made of plentiful redwood and no expense was spared to make San Francisco the leading metropolis of the West Coast. They put on serious airs, slavishly devoted to outclassing the monied splendors back east. And by all accounts, they were winning the battle.

Clothes and money: I could go right this instant but for clothes and money. I resort to eBay and order what seems to be a suitable costume for my journey. But then I have to wait for it all to arrive. Not my forte, waiting.

David and I talk about the validity of opening up a savings account in the past. Five dollars at 1906 value, compounded at a nominal savings rate over 113 years, would be somewhere in the vicinity of $2,900 today—basically free money. But during my visit this time, the banks will be decidedly out of service. And David declares that to be mere chump change compared to how he's planning on using his Machine for financial gain.

I decide to eschew specifics with him on that.

Currency in 1906 was stunningly beautiful, as everything was back then—from door hinges to toilet paper holders. Our modern one-dollar notes are a prime example of the style of that specific era. We rarely bother to actually look at them, but the U.S. greenback is an amazing, Neo-Classical thing of beauty, and perfectly representative of the period.

Go look at one. You'll see what I mean.

Now picture a whole city built to look like that. That's where I'm headed.

A 1906 dollar is worth thirty dollars today. And here I am, set loose on eBay with a budget, thanks to David, almost without limit. It becomes an obsession as I haunt various online auctions, always willing to buy just one more pre-Federal Reserve, First National Bank of Pittsburgh five-dollar bill with its vibrant red seal. Even when I pay far too much for it. Oh, to possess them! I keep forgetting I don't get to keep any of it. They'll be dumped back into the system in the past, only to be sold on eBay once more.

I find plenty of coinage as well, procuring several five-dollar coins whose nominal street value adjusted for inflation and minus the rabid speculation of eBay, is around $150 in today's money.

In stark, practical terms, I cannot go back to 1906 directly from my apartment. I'd suddenly Appear out of thin air on the third floor of a building that hasn't been built yet. I'd plummet twenty feet and break my legs.

David and I eventually decide on Portsmouth Square in Chinatown. It's centrally located to where I want to be and David says he doesn't mind lugging The Machine back and forth.

"I only hope there's parking," he grumbles. Big old queen. Sometimes, I swear . . .

I get dressed in my 1906 clothing, delivered by UPS. The wool pants, a medium gray with pinstriping, smell a little musty, but the cloth is soft to the touch as though it were to be worn as pajamas. The waistline feels like it comes up to just under my nipples. It's very odd and will take some getting used to. I have a linen striped shirt, and don a Scottish wool cap. I found a pair of old brown leather shoes, probably from the 1930s, that look like they'll do the trick. They aren't particularly comfortable but I'm hoping the leather will relax with use. I'll be doing a lot of walking.

This is a big one. I'm nervous. Even though I'll still essentially be on my home turf, I'm going to be in far over my head. It's a hell of a long way to travel on a hunch.

I'm bringing some 2019 money, my ATM card and a BART ticket in a separate folder in my trousers pocket. I assume I'll evacuate to Oakland or Berkeley after the disaster so that's where I'll Snap Back and will need to get home when it's all over.

I'm also bringing my iPhone. I plan on taking plenty of pictures. What the residents of 1906 will think if they catch me using it is anybody's guess, but I've got 128-gigabytes of room, and I intend to take full advantage of it. I hope they'll be too busy to care. It's easy enough to sneak a surreptitious shot with a phone. We've all done it.

We load The Machine into David's Honda Civic and zip through traffic, down Market Street, and loop around to head north on Kearny. Fortunately, we find a parking space in the garage under Portsmouth Square.

"I don't think there's been an open space in here since the Clinton Administration," David mutters as a Hyundai Santa Fe is just pulling out. We snag the spot. We haul The Machine out of the back of the Civic and lug it upstairs to the park.

It's a nice fall, sunny Thursday afternoon in October. David sets The Machine up on the pavement at the west side of the square and I watch him plug various things in and work the dials.

A few men playing chess observe us; old school Chinatown men in baseball caps all, God love 'em, impressed by nothing. A few homeless people are around with dogs camped out on the concrete who aren't paying us any attention. The usual collection of elders are performing Tai Chi in slow silence.

Suddenly, it's time to go. I put the web on, and David plugs it into the device. He readies my injection and unceremoniously rams it into a vein in my arm. I'm certainly not the first person to shoot up in this park.

I give him a big hug. "I'll see you in a week."

"And I'll see you in a few seconds," David replies, "unless you need a ride back from Oakland. Let me know."

PART IV

1906 - SAN FRANCISCO

13

Sunday, April 15, 1906

I Appear in Portsmouth Square, 113 years in the past. I'm getting used to the actual sensation of time travel. I don't fall down this time, although the dizziness is pronounced and my stomach doth to protest.

No one seems to take notice of the forty-nine-year-old homosexual from the year 2019 appearing out of thin air in the square. One second there's no one, and next, in what I can only hope is a devastating blaze of light, I am emerged. Standing on the grass in bad clothes, trussed up in an alien web.

It's eleven o'clock in the morning. It's spring. The air is warm and damp and full of promise. A promise the universe, in terms of San Francisco, will be unable to keep.

Across from me is the Hall of Justice on Kearny Street, gothic, imposing and resolute, with a spire going up. A U.S. flag waves a comparatively sparse number of stars.

I've only seen this building in pictures. It'll be utterly

destroyed in a few days' time, first damaged in the quake, then ravaged by fire. A much less opulent edifice will be rebuilt and used until the 1960s. But not only will it ultimately be torn down, in its place will rise perhaps one of the ugliest, "brutalist" buildings this city will ever know.

Portsmouth Square was originally the town square of San Francisco; now it's a footnote. They used to hang people here by the neck.

In 1906 it's mostly a grassy open space, with many trees growing, gently sloping down to Kearny. No concrete, no stairs, no playground equipment or parking garage. In our day, it's a vibrant part of Chinatown, festooned with banners and Chinese businesses. Right now, however, it's sedately Occidental. Brick multi-story buildings line the square in grand 1870s styles. Spires and cupolas, arched windows, and mansard roofs contribute to the beauty. The largest building has "Bella Union" spelled out in giant letters at its upper floor.

I realize, despite my excitement and nervousness, that I'm hungry more than anything else. Is there some reason I didn't stop at McDonalds before I left?

I extricate myself from the webbing, wad it up, and heading to the corner of the square at Washington Street, throw it in an ashcan.

Other people are around me, and they don't spare me a second glance. Which is good. I'm preoccupied with fitting in. I hope, at least from a distance, I do.

I buy a Sunday copy of the *San Francisco Morning Call* from a man in a wood kiosk. The newspaper is enormous; it costs three cents. Tucking it under my arm, I head bravely up Washington and hang a right on Dupont Street, entering a bizarre, wonderful inner world.

In 1906, Chinatown isn't a quaint tourist destination. It's a living, breathing civilization. People from Guangzhou Province haven't settled hereabouts to be cozy; they are forced to live in this tiny section of the city, decidedly unwelcome anyplace else. In 1906, people of Asian descent are legally barred from owning property. They're confined to this small district, which half the city wants emptied out and burnt to the ground.

I'd read for a while they seriously considered razing the district and putting in a baseball park.

A riot of color and smell swirls around me as I walk. It all has a dank, sinister feel to it. There are warrens and mazes and an entire culture not seen by the white man, a rat's nest of crime, drugs and actual human slavery. I'm not entirely welcome to go in. But I'm hungry and on a mission for a meal. I've trolled the back slums of Kowloon in the 1990s, let's see how I do here.

I'm now shoulder to shoulder with people hurrying about their day, and now I'm being given sideways glances. I'll not be able to know if it's because my clothes are wrong or simply because I'm not Chinese.

A few restaurants boldly display "Chop Suey" in English but I steer clear of those. I want something a little more authentic. At random I opt for a restaurant festooned with glazed ducks in the window. A man is in an open kitchen at the front fussing over pots and bamboo baskets. I choose to ignore concerns of cleanliness, I'm ready to do my best. I go in.

Not quite hostile, but a crude gesticulation by the man indicates I'm to be seated over on a hard wooden chair at the first table. A few other diners are further back. It's gloomy in there; they cease conversations and watch.

A hand-calligraphed menu in Chinese awaits me. I know the words for chicken and rice and beef and noodle and duck and tea. A woman with a pinched face waddles over in her apron, her outfit is rumpled, little more than a sack cloth robe.

I point to duck, rice and tea. She grunts. And waddles off.

All eyes are on me. Impassioned. Bored.

Well. I have this newspaper to get through, so I lay it open and begin reading in the dim light.

The Easter Sunday edition is one big fluff piece. Page after page of ads for corsets and garters and mourning clothes for women. Full-page articles like "Sure Cures for Every Woe of Body and Soul," and an article entitled "Cooking Without Fire," by Mabel Beeson.

I'm quite taken by the beauty of the newspaper. Scrolls and artistry, etchings, cartouches and even black and white photographs, amazingly clear. I'm sure it was all typeset, letter by letter, backwards and upside down, by experienced hands a few blocks away on Newspaper Row.

An etching of a rugged, shirtless man with a handlebar moustache holding a shovel gets my immediate attention. It's a flowery article about the California gold mines, and how they put this gracious, wholesome city on the map in 1849. It seems anxious to sidestep the truth about speculators, grifters, gamblers, murderous thugs and prostitutes—San Francisco's true heritage.

I'm interrupted by a steaming plate of duck. Hacked into slices, beak and eyes still attached but calcified. The dish is plunked down before me with an unceremonious thud, followed by a rice bowl. Two chopsticks of questionable cleanliness are fished out of the woman's apron pocket. There is no napkin.

I fold the newspaper back, and continue reading while I eat, all eyes apparently on me. If they're hoping I'll falter with the chopsticks, I am happy to disappoint.

The duck is chewy. Interesting spice. I pile the bones up along the edge of my plate and keep reading, waiting for my tea to cool.

I find an article on real estate prices in the city: Are they inflated? Is there room for them to soar higher? The article extolls the paradise that is San Francisco, with her fine harbor, her trade resources, and high-class corporate tenants. Nothing but praise for the future, which is looking bright.

The president is Theodore Roosevelt; the California Governor is George Pardee; Eugene Schmitz is the city mayor; and the economy is booming.

In general, the paper seems preoccupied with maintaining a glitzy, glamorous image of San Francisco. It's all about monied white people, high society and status, while completely ignoring the diversity of the city. No mention is made of the working class, the thousands of immigrants—the Chinese, whose sweat and tears made the whole thing possible.

The paper's writing is florid and meandering. It has its own sort of rhythm and requires a little patience to get through.

I stumble upon the comics section. "Bruno and Pietro," which features a black bear and his human friend, and "Little Ah Sid, The Chinese Kid," written in unflattering dialect. Not overtly racist so far as I can see, but I have no doubts it would turn unflattering should they ever hope to tell a joke.

Lunch costs me fifteen cents. I say thank you and goodbye to the owner in Cantonese. It seems to set him back quite a little bit. His mouth is open as I depart feeling, perhaps, a little bit smug.

And thus I am back on the street with my paper folded under my arm, ready to extricate myself from Chinatown and meet the city I love, at its peak.

I'm confidently strolling the streets of the Queen City of the Pacific, the New Orleans of the West. With a booming population of 410,000, San Francisco is the center of culture, finance, shipping and railroading for the entire west coast.

Los Angeles is less than half this size—a small town that, even now, is known for being self-conscious and for trying too hard. Bakersfield could totally take it in a fight.

San Francisco is the economic engine of California, home to the titans of industry, and wealth beyond compare.

It is also the most wicked, depraved city on Earth.

Can't wait to meet it.

I begin my journey on foot toward the Grand Palace Hotel on Market Street.

Everything as far as the eye can see will be burned out of existence. Fortunately, all the street names are the same, and in the same place. The city will be razed and rebuilt on the footprint of the old, with only nominal changes. That part's comforting, yet everything else is startlingly different. And that's precisely why I'm here.

The sidewalks are filled with people dressed in their Easter best, out for a stroll. As I'd hoped, no one seems to give me a second glance.

Noticeably fewer women than men are on the streets—the ratio of men to women, at the time San Francisco was founded, was quite literally 300 to 1. By 1906 there were significantly more women, but the city didn't reach actual gender parity until 1920. San Francisco is and always was a man's town.

And is it my imagination? Everyone seems a fair bit shorter to me.

The women of the age are welcome to wear whatever they should desire in public—just so long as it is a skirt or dress that fully reaches the ankle. Volume and quality vary by wealth. Among the plain Janes in thin, limp skirts, I see flowing, billowing dresses of the well-to-do, with collars ratcheted tight, or else subtly plunging necklines. Brocades, lace, corseted figures, trussed bodices, flouncy skirts that blossom off the hips, high-heeled boots. The women all sport bizarre, overwrought hat creations with broad planes piled high with birds, flowers or fruit.

I study what the men are wearing so I can buy the right clothes tomorrow. No one is bareheaded. Homburgs, bowlers and golf caps. Quite a few straw boaters, too. The men, almost all of them, are sporting facial hair of some sort, and I am in heaven.

The well-to-do men sport vests with watch chains, coats, black canes or furled umbrellas, handkerchiefs in their breast pockets. All outerwear and trousers seem to be lightweight wool in various forms. Lots of bowler hats that, to me, look slightly too small, perched high atop their heads and almost look silly. But everyone's doing it.

Less affluent men and women are also out enjoying the Spring air in simple work clothes. But still they have hats.

I examine the faces of the people passing by. They look normal and alive. Instead of that stuffy, vacant look you see in old black-and-white photographs, these people are real and three-dimensional. In color. I pass one handsome man in a black cloak, top hat, handlebar moustache and striped slacks and, instead of looking like a figure from a forgotten daguerreotype, he looks like his name would be Kevin and he'd work at Oracle.

The streets and sidewalks are covered with litter, dog shit and brown tobacco spit. Large sections of downtown San Francisco's main streets consist merely of packed dirt. Dust is constantly kicked up and whipping around at the slightest disturbance. There seems to be grit everywhere.

Gun shops and tobacco stores, corset shops and banks are all shuttered on this Easter Sunday, but I see innumerable businesses, storefronts, restaurants and cafés. The city is chaotic and busy, everything is ornate but nothing matches and the dust is a tarnish not only on the real estate but on my expectations as well.

Much of the available wall space is covered with billboards. For soap; Tacoma Beer, 5¢; insurance companies and haberdasheries. Quack cures.

A gun shop advertises itself as "'Frisco's Finest" and I come up short. We *never* call it 'Frisco. Maybe these people do? That's going to be a hard sell back home.

I also notice a large billboard advertising Everdry Underarm Deodorant. Huh. I guess I didn't know they had that.

I'm stopped at Montgomery and Market to drink it all in, to catalogue it. I want to retain this forever. The real reason I've come to 1906 is to see this city and its architecture—that which soon shall perish from the earth.

Gothic, Victorian, Beaux Arts, Classic, Neo-Classic, Federalist; trimmings and doodads and bunting and carvings; finials and spires, cupolas and pergolas, statuary and stained glass. These people took pride in building up their Paris of the West. They had money to spare and all the time in the world. They used their advantage well. The San Francisco I see here is exquisite.

My best friend back home in Seattle always claims Victorian architecture was specifically designed to frighten small children into submission. You can certainly see that here. The beauty is harsh, overwrought, formal. Yet what would be appropriate in the dank of England simply wouldn't mesh with the California sunshine. So they added whimsy and covered nearly everything in whitewash.

Starting four days from now it will never be seen again.

For the most part, the businesses of San Francisco survive the earthquake and fire. They hastily rebuild on the same location and get back up and running as quickly as they can. People will need fast, cheap and seismically stable—and fireproof—construction. All other concerns will become secondary. People won't want old-world charm. It's expensive to build, takes too much time, and it was only good for their grandmothers' day anyway.

As such, the San Francisco we've inherited is a cold reboot. The clock started again in 1907, severing any connections to the past.

While a few buildings are tall—one as high as twenty-one floors—overall this San Francisco skyline is much more low-slung and given to daylight. New brick construction sits next to the very old, original settlement houses, creating interesting contrasts. This lost San Francisco is beautiful—except when it's not. Next to prissy elegant I see dank clapboard, seedy wooden buildings, old and sagging.

Horses are still the predominant form of transportation in 1906. Hooves clop by in the streets, horses shit freely, an occasional man, often Chinese, will clean up after them with a bucket on a stick. A few livery stables are visible to me, but right next to them are auto garages and further down is a hardware store, and sitting in front is a primitive form of gasoline pump.

Automobiles are still little more than an expensive novelty. I see several specimens of cars, so rudimentary that they look like nothing more than horse drawn carriages with engines. Some are battery powered, others sputter and belch.

Steering wheels—and a few actual tillers—seem to mostly be on the right-hand side of the cars, like in England. The rest of the traffic consists of cable cars, horse drawn carts, buggies and new wooden electric street cars.

I'm surprised I don't see individual horses just being ridden, like in the old west. Maybe it's considered gauche, I don't know.

I'm close to my destination, the Palace Hotel at Market and Third Streets, but my brain is turning to mush. I'm going into complete overload and culture shock.

We're not built for this.

Intent on my destination, I pass a table set up outside The Union Trust Company at Montgomery and Market and am being hailed by someone.

"Sir!" A woman calls to me. "Can you spare a moment?"

Two women and two men are in plain-looking clothing, the men look positively funereal and the women prim with pinched mouths, hair in buns under plain blue bonnets that are the exact opposite of all the fashionable ladies flouncing past.

As a modern-day San Franciscan I'm more than able and likely to keep on walking, ignoring the calls and pleas of people on the street—for there are so many. You just keep walking. But I'm a guest here, and inexorably drawn.

"Good day, ma'am," I say, hearing my own voice in this alien landscape as if for the first time.

"We're from the Temperance League. Do you not agree, sir, that sin and vice are ruling over this fair city? We're calling on all citizens to put an end to lawlessness; to close the saloons and houses of sin, and to make San Francisco a dry city, once and for all."

Yeah, good luck with that, lady.

Yet I'm at the table. They have fliers that look like old western "wanted" posters but for the grotesque etchings depicting hellfire and anguish to those who succumb to drink. Writ large are garish demands to completely ban alcohol from San Francisco.

All four of them slightly converge toward me, in the way of Mormons closing in on a kill. They, for a brief moment, think they have found a kindred soul.

They most certainly have not. But I'm here for the experience.

"What's your plan?" I ask kindly.

She nearly peaks in a shudder of ecstasy that she has a listener at last. "We are calling on Mayor Schmitz to close the Barbary Coast, and to enact dry laws in the city." She leans in, handing me one of the fliers, ready to launch, her finger pointed to the print on the page. "The problem of spirits in the hands of men is well-known. But further have we ample evidence that this city is run on a bedrock of vice and graft. The policemen of San Francisco are paid puppets, turning a blind eye to sin and danger, and do you know what lies at the heart of it all?"

"No, but I have the feeling you're going to tell me."

"Spirits! Alcohol is responsible for all of it. We must end this scourge and make San Francisco safe for all her citizens!"

The others in her group are nodding their approval, half listening, half looking for other fish to spool in.

"It's a lot to consider. May I take this?" The flier would make an interesting keepsake.

"Certainly. Would you care to make a donation?"

I fish out a penny. To us it would be a hurled insult; she, instead, clasps it to her breast and utters a hearty, "God bless you, sir!"

As I walk away, I notice two beat cops strolling past, all buttons, hats and swinging sticks, and the disdain they show to their apparent nemesis is clear. They're laughing at the sight. Most of the police in 1906 are corrupt as hell—a good thing to keep in mind during my stay.

The Grand Palace Hotel, the most opulent in San Francisco, fills an entire block, from Third Street to New Montgomery. Its modern iteration is a simple, smooth-fronted building, but the original treasure is visually complex with bay windows, alcoves, cornices and columns. Built in 1875, it's actually considered an antique in 1906. And it's famous for being seismically stable. They had a hell of an earthquake back in 1868, far too long ago to be a modern concern. Piffle.

Crossing Market Street to reach The Palace is no easy task. There are no traffic signals, crosswalks, or any apparent right-of-ways. I trot around a horse-drawn milk truck and an electric streetcar, only to nearly be run down by a woman motorist squeezing her brass horn at me in anger. We make eye contact, her hat firmly tied atop her head by a scarf. She is peeved.

But I make it.

The hotel's ornate doors are opened for me by two

uniformed men who doff their caps. I'm not dressed well, nothing like the haughty Easter strollers out behind me. I feel like a country bumpkin. But this is San Francisco: There's no other place for culture for a thousand miles in any direction. The city must get its share of wide-eyed, wannabe dandies. It's my hope that, as long as you have money, no one particularly cares.

I walk into the hotel and approach the ornate, foreboding front desk.

Patrons are standing in line; I'll have to wait my turn. But it gives me a moment to collect my thoughts and calm my overloaded brain back down.

My eyes gaze at the carpets, up at the chandeliers, at enormous vases of flowers, burled wood Second Empire French furniture, and I drink in this world of excellence and cigar smoke and murmured conversation.

Tapestries. Loads and loads of heavy fabrics, bunting, tassels. All ready to burn.

Before me checking in are a man and woman, extremely well-dressed. He has a cane and has taken off his top hat, which he's holding in his hands.

It reminds me to snatch my own cap off my head real quick.

Men always remove their hats indoors; women don't.

The main clerk exudes a witheringly rude demeanor. A small man, near to seventy years old, with pinched lips, and spectacles festooned with a black ribbon are perched on his nose. He's persnickety. Punctilious. In charge of his domain.

By the time he beckons me to the desk I've psyched myself out completely. I stammer.

"Uh, hi. I just got into town, and, umm . . . do you have any vacancies?"

"Do you have a reservation?" he asks with disdain. He smells strongly of soft powder.

"I'm sorry, I don't. I was unable to telegraph ahead."

Oh, his gaze is withering. He could cut glass with his attitude.

"We happen to be fully booked just now." He says it with satisfaction and watches my expression with patent joy. I just huff myself up and decide to try a ballsier approach. I look him in the eye and give him the most genuine smile I can muster.

"I've so been hoping to stay here. Everyone on the Coast claims this hotel is simply the best—and is well known for its excellent staff."

It's such a load of horse shit I have to stifle a smirk. But it actually seems to work. He relents, ever so much. "I'll check the cancellation ledger; it may yield results. Please give me one moment."

He disappears behind a door for a second, and I fuss. But realize there are a million places to stay, all of them more affordable.

The man's demeanor has softened somewhat when he returns.

"Ah, it appears we do have a room available, if being on the second-floor would be to your liking."

"Certainly. That would be fine," I reply.

"Kindly sign in."

A large leather-bound book is swung around to face me.

I pick up the pen and begin scratching on the page, only to realize it needs to be dipped in ink first. I dab a little bit, gingerly, and as I start to scribble my name, a huge blotch oozes off the steel nib leaving a mess on the paper. But I surge on, writing, "Mark Baldwin, Berkeley, California."

My penmanship is starkly different to the other writing on the page. My handwriting looks barren, childish and completely without flourish, while everyone else's signature looks worthy of the Declaration of Independence.

"How many nights do you require?" the man asks.

"Umm, three."

I'll be in 1906 for four nights, but the Palace won't be available to me—or anyone else—after Wednesday.

"Can I settle my bill when I check out?"

"Certainly, if you have letters of reference." He says it with disarming lightness, as if it is no big deal. He has his hand out expectantly. My brain churns. I guess in these days a person would carry suitable documents in their breast pocket. Obviously, I have none. It's not like I brought my Capital One statement with me.

"I didn't bring them, so I reckon I'll pay cash."

"Certainly. That'll be $14.25."

Ouch. That's a chunk of money. I did, I really did; I had lavish visions of just charging everything to my room and simply taking a powder at the end. Rude as hell, but I figured it wouldn't matter. Billions in adjusted dollars are about to be wiped off the map. Any little foibles of mine could never be reconciled in the ruins.

But I'll have to pay up front.

I count out the money for Mr. Persnickety, quietly fuming. Now I'll have to be on a much tighter budget, with no back-up plan if something goes wrong.

I have no luggage—only the newspaper still folded under my arm—yet a bellboy insists on escorting me up to my room.

The elevator is a large "lifting room" with a settee, mirrors and a chandelier. It is seamlessly operated by another young man in a crisp hotel uniform.

"Did you get an eyeful of the Lieutenant Governor when he checked in?" my bellhop mutters to the elevator boy.

"I did! And an earful. He threw a complete snit about his accommodations. I thought Manning was going to pop a vein in his neck."

They laugh, and we're already out of the elevator on the second floor.

This young bellboy, not much older than eighteen, leads

me along a spacious, echoing corridor with high ceilings. It seems to go on forever in both directions.

"Your room will be 242. It's just along here." He opens the door for me, hefting a key on a massive iron fob. The door's brass plate is ornate and polished, the white porcelain knob looks cold to the touch.

My room is charming. A bit small, with a full-sized bed—it has curled, polished brass at the head and foot. The wallpaper is a gay, yellow pinstripe with white wood trim, high ceilings and crown molding. A large window looks out over Market Street, and I glance in the bathroom to see a tub, shower, sink and old-world toilet: wooden seat, tank up high with a long pull chain.

"The buzzer for guest services is here at the bed," the bellhop explains, and he points at the telephone: a deliciously arcane thing, brass and French and frilly. I rue that I have no one to call. "Local calls are three cents, long-distance calls to Oakland or the Peninsula start at fifty cents; the rates are listed on the card."

"Thank you, this will do nicely," I respond. But I get an idea as I fish out a nickel to tip him with. "Any good saloons in the area?"

He laughs. "Mister, in this town you can't spit without hitting a saloon. Although I would advise you to steer clear of the Midway just a few doors down. While they can quench your every thirst,"—he actually, lazily, glances down at my crotch when he says it—"it has a tendency to get a little rough. Watch your wallet if you go, and never let anyone buy you a drink."

Huh. OK. I'll have to figure that one out later.

I thank him, give him the nickel. He casually flips it up and catches it and drops it into his pocket. "Enjoy your stay with us," he calls over his shoulder and he's gone.

With the door closed I kind of want to do a high five. *I did it. I'm in. Whew!*

I put my newspaper on the bed, move to the window and sit on the tufted bench, only to realize that the view out my window is impeded by a riot of powerlines, telephone and telegraph wires. They are an ugly tangled mess, almost blotting out any hope of seeing the street below. The poles have six, sometimes eight crossbars, all stacked up and threaded with black wire.

But I can see enough, and it's amazing.

After a few moments, with a bit of a *tsk*, I notice my window can, in fact, open. So I slide the large heavy pane up in its sash. It's cleverly weighted to lift easily, and to stay where I want it. I'm now enjoying the spring air and the smell of horse manure.

A rush of sound greets me as well. Two main cable car lines run along the center of Market Street, a car going by every few seconds, bells clanging, people hopping on and off with careless ease. Outside that are horse-drawn trolleys, also on rails. It's a dizzying network of tracks, some branch in from side streets, and are further compounded by newer, electric trolleys crossing Market at angles amid the chaos.

Everything is moving at about nine miles an hour, top speed for a cable car. Horses move a little slower and cars can—and do—go faster, darting in and out of the horse traffic and cable cars, honking their little squeeze horns. It's complete madness, no one following any sort of lanes, just weaving to and fro, and pedestrians, taking their lives in their hands, brave the traffic seemingly without fear.

The cable car bells are the exact same bells they use to this day. It's such a familiar sound to me. Like music. Like home.

Across the street, I see "Tom Dillon, Hats for Men." To the left is the *San Francisco Chronicle* Building, in unusual rust-colored bricks and with a strange black gantry atop the roof. A large clock shows me it's twelve-thirty, and a deep resonant *bong* sounds once.

This is the heart of downtown, Newspaper Row. Montgomery Street, leading north from outside my window is called the Wall Street of the West.

Behind my hotel lays the South of Market neighborhood. I can't see it from here, but I know it as a seedy, industrial area with none of the flash and glamor of Market Street, teeming with smelters, factories and the clapboard-wood tenement buildings that only the newest of arrived immigrants dare to afford.

After a good thirty minutes of gazing out my window, during which loud bongs reverberate over the street from the *Chronicle* building, chiming the hours of twelve forty-five and one o'clock.

I decide on a quick nap. I think I've earned at least that much. I need to quiet my mind and try to peace out a little bit.

Next to the bed is a small, framed notice on the wall:

This Room Is Equipped With
Edison Electric Light.
Do not attempt to light with a match. Simply turn the key on the wall by the door.
The use of Electricity for lighting is in no way harmful to health, nor does it affect the soundness of sleep.

I DON'T GET under the covers, I just lay atop them, gazing at the ceiling so high up. I wouldn't call the mattress good, it's hard and sagging.

I should be too nervous and excited to sleep, but I do manage to doze. I'm just so overwhelmed. Cool puffs of air waft through the open window, almost enough to give me goosebumps but just warm enough not to. I get a good forty minutes.

A fairly standard-looking wind-up clock by the bed says it's after one thirty. I fish out my iPhone and set the time and date appropriately, again amazed that it works. I figure the time is only approximate here, that every clock will be slightly out of sync with one another.

I'm thirsty, looking for the hotel's four-dollar bottle of Dasani, then realize it's tap water or nothing. A glass sits on the shelf in the bathroom, again wrapped in paper.

I decide to wash my face and hands and come to grips with these people's interpretation of plumbing. It's stupid. For there is a hot spigot on the left, and a cold spigot on the right, and never the twain shall meet. I must juggle from hot to cold, alternately freezing and burning my hands. Whoever it was who finally realized we could put the two together should have won a Nobel Prize.

Now that I've secured myself a place to stay, I decide to take a walk, right back to Portsmouth Square. There's a little business I want to attend to. I'd planned on doing this and want to have the experience before this all goes wrong, or I get ripped away from 1906 in some unforeseen horror by David's Machine. Or in case someone steals my money—or any of the multitudinous things that my fusses remind me could go wrong.

I'm halfway to the lifting room and adjacent grand staircase before I realize I've forgotten my hat, an apparent necessity in this world. I run back and fetch it. And as I make my way along the corridor, I reach an interesting conclusion. Several doors have a "Do Not Disturb" sign out—which is in no way unusual. But the signs are placards, hanging by golden ropes. And suddenly I realize: A "Do Not Disturb" sign's original intent must have been to cover the keyhole from prying eyes. The holes are quite large. A body could get quite a juicy glimpse into the goings on of a hotel bedroom. And while it's clear that a person only need push the placard off to one side to peek in, by the time you're on bended knee in a public hallway, you're fairly committed either way.

Little things like that shall spur my mind to greatness someday. I'm convinced of it.

Hat safely atop my head, I make my way back into Chinatown. Not for a meal, but something much more sinister. My heart rate's up. I'm taking a pretty big risk.

Waverly Place is right where it should be, although it looks entirely different. A small back-alley of Chinatown, living quarters, squalor, chickens in cages far too small. After passing back and forth, I manage to find Duncombe Alley, an even smaller, dark lane. Overhead is covered by awnings, hanging laundry and Chinese advertisements. It's dark and foreboding, and crowded with people now openly eying me with suspicion. I don't belong here. True nervousness sets up in my belly. This could go bad.

I look at the signs and come upon a yellow door. I knock. A slit opens. Asiatic eyes peer out suspiciously. My knowledge of Cantonese is sparse, but I say, *"Lei ho ma. M'goy lei yapian."*

The slit snaps shut, and I wonder what will happen next. I hear the rather un-dulcet tones of a Cantonese conversation on the other side of the door. The slit snicks open again; a different pair of eyes. This time I have my money out and stick it up towards the slit—not so close that they could actually grab it—and it slams shut again.

The door opens. Two women in traditional garb and wooden sandals on their feet indicate I can come in with terse nods of the head, nothing approaching so much as a polite bow.

"Doh-tscheh lei," I say. "Thank you." And wonder why I'm trying to be so polite. I guess because I'm scared half to death.

The two women, after re-locking the yellow door, lead me down a long dark corridor with ceilings too low and steps going up and then down. There are doors leading to various rooms, and finally at the end of the hall, we go down more stairs.

I can't even catalogue the smells that assault my nose.

This is dangerous. People go missing in Chinatown all the time. They could take all my money, or there could be thugs waiting at the end of the hall to club me into submission. Shanghaiing still takes place; I could wake up on a clipper ship bound for the Orient with my legs in irons and one very sore bunghole.

My nervousness suddenly moves to a higher notch. Just as I start to turn tail and flee, my fears are allayed when they lead me to what I was hoping to find: a lounge with soft electric lamps, burning candles, day beds, and tapestries at the bottom of a half-run of stairs.

It's gaudy, lots of red and gold, and it doesn't seem particularly clean. Heavy odors of incense and cigar smoke and something dark and unidentifiable hang in the air. One of the women indicates a couch for me—three couches are already occupied. A businessman on one, and—shocking to me—a Caucasian mother/daughter pair on the two other divans, laying in stupor, ruffles and old shoes visible and limp.

"Five dollar," the other lady says and sticks out her hand. That's pretty steep. This had better be some good shit.

I hand her a gold five-dollar coin.

A young pretty girl comes in and cooks some opium for me in a spoon and readies to inject it into my arm. I squirm and immediately, visibly tense up: I was hoping to smoke it. Intravenous injection is a whole other thing and I'm instantly ill at ease, to say the least.

Well, I'm here. I'm queer. Let's do this.

I lay back and turn myself over to this young girl. I study her impassive celestial face, looking for signs of treachery, or of menacing glee. If anything, she's bored witless. Actually, she looks vaguely reminiscent of a younger Dr. Tsieh.

A tourniquet is applied to my right arm and pulled until it hurts. A blunt needle is shoved into a vein and I'm God's problem now.

Doesn't take long. It's heavenly! I just lay there—the lamps burning, the tapestries shimmering—surfing the feelings of ecstasy that wash over my soul.

I experience pure joy that I'm in Chinatown in 1906. I take a few pictures of the dark opium den—no one notices a thing—I take a few selfies, enjoying my slicked-back hair and looking really stoned.

An hour passes. I need to make sure I can maintain with my buzz on. Eventually I climb up the creaky stairs and one of the women appears instantly and escorts me back to the yellow door, and to freedom.

I really feel in command now. I got this.

I'm good. Happy. Centered. Brave. Time for more walking.

Since there's no Stockton Street tunnel yet, I double back to Kearny to avoid a steep hill. Crossing over California Street for the third time, watching the familiar cable cars that run along its length, I then angle over toward Union Square.

I figure the fastest way would be through Maiden Lane, a short narrow street that will lead unto Union Square and . . .

What the ever-loving fuck?

The sign denotes it as Morton Alley, and I'm not four steps down it before I'm beset with blatant prostitution and pimps, loud calliope music, spitting, broken beer bottles, and shouting and jeering at the new meat in their midst: Me. Even the opium doesn't cover my sudden shock.

It's a short, sick street. Women in bodices and mere slips, with weighty thighs and garish make-up are hanging out every available window, hooting and cajoling. These aren't merely soiled doves. They're rapacious, hungry hos. I'm having to fight off sleazy pimps thrusting calling cards at me and promising me "heavenly delights" in language that is in no way "heavenly" at all. It's completely carnal, and I'm in such shock I don't know if I should back out and retrace my steps or just trudge the short distance through to Stockton.

I'm more than halfway through it, so I trudge forth, not daring to think about the sorts of fluids my shoes are trudging upon, covering the cobblestones.

As I make my way clear of it, Stockton Street appears completely normal. There's no dividing line, nothing to demarcate the change. It's behind me now and everything is quiet again. It's as if the alley ought to have a vast curtain at each end, keeping its carnal secrets in the closet where they belong.

I think the last time I was down Maiden Lane, the offices of KKSF 103.7 were still there, back when they played Kenny G and Manheim Steamroller. Nowadays, it's dress shops and open cafés. No one knows it was bawdy enough to scare me—and I thought I'd seen it all. I'm almost shaken. But I let the opium come back to the fore and smooth my feelings over and regain my mellow.

Union Square surprises me with its verdancy. It is a lush park with the Dewey Monument towering in the middle of it. The Saint Francis Hotel is resolutely in place where it should be, looking exactly the same. Everything else, though, is suitably different. M. Friedman & Co Furniture & Carpets is in a huge Victorian building, next to Kast's Booterie. The City of Paris Department Store is at the lower corner. To the north are two towering stone and wood spires of an impressive synagogue.

I continue walking through the square and down Geary Street and rejoin Market at Mason. This stretch of Market is a less-dense mix of offices, saloons, cafés, theaters, laundries, dress shops and telegraph offices.

Dr. Jordan's Museum of Anatomy, at 7th and Market, creeps me right out: Human skulls and skeletons are strewn in the windows, with a banner proclaiming "Largest Anatomical

Museum in the World—Diseases of Men." So not only is it a museum of human parts, he also claims to be a functioning doctor. Charming. Maybe Aetna's not so bad after all.

Further along Market, drug stores are selling Coca-Cola at attended fountains. I consider getting some, but I think they removed the cocaine in like 1903. Or was it 1905? That would be my luck. Wouldn't mix with the opium to any great shakes anyway, so I take my time, savoring the late afternoon air—the weather is almost fine, but several clouds linger—getting lost in my thoughts.

But once again I get that bone-weary alone feeling. 1979 was nothing. I really am on my own here. Everyone's a stranger.

It's about four-thirty by the time I reach my intended destination: City Hall at Market, Grove and Hyde Streets—right where the San Francisco Public Library is for us.

Newly constructed at a cost of over six million dollars, City Hall is a proud, enduring monument to a proud, enduring city. Its gothic dome soars 335 feet into the sky and is touted as a marvel of modern, seismic stability.

Actually, it's going fall to complete bits on Wednesday.

Much of the six million dollars made its way into greedy hands up and down the construction chain, leaving it shoddily built, with hollow casements. They used plaster instead of stone.

Not only is San Francisco the richest, most gregarious city in the west, but it's also the most corrupt. And this failed City Hall will be a testament to it. Heads will eventually roll, but nothing can save this amazing building now before me. It is worthy of the Vatican with its columns, statues and filigree all about. I walk completely around it, surprised that the McCallister Street side is even more imposing than the front. The whole affair is like a confectioner's cake poured from stone.

It's unpopulated, being Sunday, so I'm alone and safe. But also I can't go in. I've never found any photos or depictions of the interior of this building. I might make a point of coming back later when it's open.

I get my fill of the exterior, snapping many pictures with my phone and checking out the ornate building to the east, connected by a colonnade: The Hall of Records. It's a round, stone, stoic building that looks like a mausoleum. It's ugly; it's beautiful.

In front is a tiny, tidy park with that big white Pioneer monument they've drug around this city for a century. It's sat at so many different places over the years, but right now it's here in this park, ignored by all, looking exactly the same as it ever shall.

From this odd, angled intersection at City Hall, I can see the famed Mechanic's Pavillion: "Roller Skating To-Night on The City's Largest All-Maple Floor;" The Majestic Theatre; The giant Rambler Bikorama and a bowling alley. Cable cars clang past; horses clop by, pulling wagons filled with goods, or broughams with people finely dressed, and a few motorcars sputter along, one emitting a huge cloud of steam and chugging quietly.

Around back, behind City Hall on McAllister Street, I see a saloon called Dunn Brothers. Not very elegant but not too dangerous-looking, either. I reckon functionaries and clerks from City Hall must frequent it all the time, so it can't be all that risky.

It's time I try to meet people.

Nervous, I pull the door open and enter the tavern and see dark wood walls, sawdust on the floor for men to spit their tobacco juice in—many spittoons are stationed about, but no one seems to be taking them seriously. Electric lighting is sparse, leaving an overall darkness inside. The air is moist, filled with cigar smoke and sweat. No music plays, just near silence. Not a lot of talking. This might not work.

I approach the barman and order a five-cent bottle of steam

beer. He doesn't so much as look in my direction. Several men, all wearing clothes made of wool in various strata of class and station, are seated at the bar.

I start, like a fool, with not only the nearest person to me, but who also seems to be the most attractive one in the room. A bearded bear of a man, looking very straight and rough, is at the bar eying me suspiciously. Handsome as hell, but he doesn't look very nice.

"Afternoon," I mutter, making sure not to stand particularly close to him or to make eye contact. He openly lets out with a *psht*. He snatches his beer and hat and stomps off to a stool along the opposite wall.

Ouch. Well, one down.

I see a kindlier-looking man further along the bar. He's also bearded, dressed plainly but moderately well; high collar and red necktie under rounded collar tabs. I'm still several feet away when I nod and say, "Good afternoon."

He looks up and smiles wanly.

"Happy Easter," he says softly with a tiny nod of his head, giving an ever so slight toast in my direction with his beer.

"Mind if I join you? I just got into town." I move over a little closer. Once again, I've forgotten to take off my hat. I do so now and put it on the bar next to the man's bowler.

He nods. Not in an unfriendly way, but he's being cautious.

"Name's Mark. Baldwin, from Berkeley." I stick out my hand, which, fortunately, the man accepts. We shake.

"I'm Ben J. Wade. Just moved here from Chicago a few months ago, so I'm more or less new here myself."

"Yeah? Nice place to be. How do you like it so far?"

"Costs a pretty penny, but it's good. Anything to get away from Illinois winter. I don't think people are meant to be huddled around a stove four months of the year."

"You came out to California on your own?"

"Yup." He's kind of willing to talk, I'm not sensing that he wants to bolt.

"How long did it take?"

"On the train? About six days."

"Ah. Sounds fascinating. I'd love to experience that someday. As for me, I'm from California, so I wouldn't know from an Illinois winter. I'm somewhat glad for that."

Ben looks to be about thirty-five years old, a little on the small side, with green eyes, close-cropped black hair, and a short black beard. Tiny nose and ears. I get a good feeling from him. He doesn't have a mean, gruff demeanor, full of defense mechanisms. Or an overage of testosterone.

"What sort of business you in?" I ask, hoping that, as in Europe, it's not considered rude to ask after a person's occupation in 1906.

"Banking."

"Good field. I reckon you're, what, vice president by now?" I say it in such a way that he knows I'm only playing with him.

He smiles, looking bashful.

"I'll be a regular full-fledged teller someday. Right now I'm a clerk. I spend my days buried in ledger books, mighty glad to have a job.

"Back home, outside Chicago—I'm actually from Berwyn—all the men in the area work in the stockyards. My brother Jason; my pop, too. I couldn't see slaughtering cows for a living, or even on a sizable bet. So I went to vocational school, apprenticed in bookkeeping."

He's making direct eye contact now, which is good.

"If nothing else, it allows me to be indoors instead of out in the weather. Bookkeeping isn't exactly a tonic for the soul, but it beats the ghoulish task of braining cows and pigs and hanging 'em on hooks."

"Congratulations on a fine choice," I reply, purposefully trying to not picture the activities of the men of Berwin.

I'm sensing Ben might not have very broad horizons under his belt. Cute though he is, and I'm sure he's clever at his job, I wonder how much of the world he's ever actually seen firsthand.

"Done much traveling in the world?" I ask.

"Oh, not really. Only around Chicago—and here. Unless you count a trip to southern Indiana to see relatives. How about you?"

I've hit the globe running during a few up-times in my career arc. When the money's good I'm always on a plane to Europe or Sydney, with one wild tour through Asia thrown in for good measure. But I sense it wouldn't be fair to gloat about this to Ben, so I decide to keep it on low. And it's been an embarrassingly long time since my arc has been in positive territory anyway. So I decide to lie.

"Just Northern California, born and raised. Say. Have you met any interesting people in the city so far?"

Ben's face does an odd thing just then. Ever so briefly a look of dismay clouds his features, and his eyes seem to momentarily go unfocused. He smiles immediately, then, but it looks just this side of forced. "Oh sure. Loads. Folks here all have fascinating jobs and there's so much culture and important business to talk about."

He's sidestepping. Apparently, no one is hanging out with him and I wonder why. He seems perfectly likable. Are these San Franciscans cruel? Mine sure can be.

"What about you? What do you do?" he asks, changing the subject.

I tell him I'm a writer. I keep it vague so I don't have to lie too much. I reveal to him the story I'd concocted ahead of time, should anyone actually ask: "I was living in a rooming house in Berkeley. On Shattuck. But I cashed in my chips. I'm now a resident of this lovely city, effective today. I got tired of looking at it from the outside. Saved enough money to get a room at the

Palace for a few days while I look for a permanent place to live. I'd appreciate any advice from a seasoned veteran," and I toast him slightly with my beer bottle.

His smile becomes more genuine at that. "The Palace, huh? Nice. I'm not too far from there. Rent a room at 5th and Folsom."

"How is it?"

Fake smile again, false cheer—like he's about to sell me an after-market car warranty. "Oh, fine. Perhaps a bit modest. There aren't a lot of vacancies in this town. I hope to move to an even better place when I get settled."

"What can I expect to pay for rent hereabouts, if you don't mind that I ask?"

"I pay four and two bits a week. You can find cheaper, but you might not like it."

Nineteen dollars a month for San Francisco rent. It's a world gone mad. I signal the barman and get us two more steam beers. Ben accepts his with a slight "cheers" motion with his bottle.

"Fifth and Folsom, that's quite a ways down. What has you over here?"

"Sunday's my day off. I pick other neighborhoods to walk through and explore. Saloons to maybe talk to people at. Enjoying what the city has to offer."

"Good plan. Have you been to the Barbary Coast?"

Ben looks slightly stricken. "Not yet. I'd want a posse with me if I ever do."

"I haven't braved it myself either. Perhaps if we did it together?"

"That would be interesting." He's intrigued but sounds cautious.

"Meanwhile, what is there to do here?"

"A lot of nickelodeons, vaudeville shows, movie cinemas, museums. Beaches, too, but they take all day and it's always chilly. Plenty of saloons. Mostly I work—and work hard. It's good for one, isn't it? To work hard. I don't have a lot of free time."

I decide to press a little harder. "You must have met a lot of people already."

"Sure. It's great."

This is 1906. People don't complain; they don't whine. They don't do drama. They are all about bravery and putting on a good face, even in dire circumstances.

But he lets his guard down just enough to say, "I'm sure it's just that the people of 'Frisco are probably just plenty busy with their own lives to worry about a newcomer."

There it is again: "'Frisco." I'm not sure I can get used to it.

Or maybe the people here are unfriendly to Ben because he insists on calling it "'Frisco." I need to get to the bottom of that.

Ben continues. "Every job that can be found under the sun is done in this city. Artists and playwrights and newspapermen and railroaders. It's all here. And the people who do these jobs are also here. I aim, eventually, to meet them. Then I'll be a regular swell."

That was a rousing speech. I want to see him get started right now. I wonder if I'm remotely able to give him a head start. Probably not, I'm more of an outsider than he is. But something has kept him from attaining social orbit here. It could be anything from a class/caste problem to some as-yet undiscovered weirdness in the man's personality. But as of right now, I see before me a genuinely nice guy. Earnest. Likable all the way through and not yet given a decent chance.

"I've been so busy decamping from Berkeley I haven't had a chance to glance at the paper. What's news these days?"

"Oh, not much. Things have been incomparably boring of late, I hope we're not saving up for something. The usual city graft; I don't think you can build a block of buildings or a streetcar line without it. Oh, and the Pompeii eruption in Italy. Sounds like it was a pretty big deal."

"Really?"

"Uh-huh. Last week it erupted for three days, lava flows and ash so deep it collapsed roofs. Everyone fled to Naples, which they say is still safe, except for the ash. Relief is pouring in; King of Italy is on hand to help out."

"King of Italy" is not a phrase one hears often.

"I got stopped by some temperance people earlier," I decide to mention. "They tried to hook me in. Didn't work." I take a swig of beer to emphasize my point.

Ben smiles. "I suppose I understand what they're all about, but they need to face reality. This city'd become dry the day the earth would open up. I don't suppose anyone is too keen on the current police situation, but those temperance people have it all wrong."

"They seemed a little peaked and hopeless. Thin spirits, thin ideals, thin minds."

"I was raised a good Christian, as I know you were as well," Ben says. "Yet here it is, Holy Easter, and I'm sitting in a bar drinking beer. But I hardly think I'm destined for hellfire and damnation."

He smiles and orders us two more.

We're getting along just fine, Ben and I. Connecting. It's good. I'm even starting to get the impression that Ben is somewhat like me. In a sense that could make my stay here far more intriguing than I'd ever hoped.

Meanwhile, I'm noticing that the asshole who wouldn't talk to me has been watching us with a disgusted leer on his face. He's been joined by another man and we seem to be the topic of their conversation. Ben seems oblivious, but I start to sense we'd better get out of here.

"I'm heading back to the Palace for dinner. I don't know a

soul here, obviously. You're welcome to accompany me. My treat."

Ben could recoil in horror at this. I'm really being bold, putting it on the line. But whether it's the beer or the loneliness or the fact that he's really a nice guy after all, he enthusiastically accepts.

We make to leave, and the assholes get up like they're going to follow us. Their body language is seriously unwell, I figure we might just be in for it. I try to not look back, and I say nothing to Ben.

It's gotten much darker out, yet City Hall is ablaze with light. Tiny incandescent bulbs trace the outline of the entire building. It's lovely; captivating. I'd be transfixed, but I'm much more concerned with the danger right behind us. I just guide Ben away, hoping for the best.

The men don't follow us beyond the front door of Dunn Brothers. They're just trying to scare us.

It's only when we wait for a cable car on Market that I realize I left my hat back in the bar.

I never wear hats back home, they look awful on me. I used to always joke that wearing a baseball cap makes me look like a chemo patient.

Well, I don't want to say that joke anymore. Not ever again.

I fuss ever so slightly about my hat, knowing I'm sure as shit not going back to Dunn Brothers to fetch it. I'll just buy a new one. I'm keen to try one of those too-small bowlers.

My head is buzzing from the beer and opium, and Ben seems nice. I'm suddenly not alone anymore and feeling good. Really good.

It costs three cents to ride the cable car and it's actually soothing to me. It's exactly the same—the vibrations and sounds are completely unchanged from my day. I get a jangle of feelings: being back home while being further from it than any man has ever been.

We stand along the running board and I see an enormous sign for Recreation Park, home of the San Francisco Seals, all lit up.

"Do you like baseball?" Ben asks.

"Not even a little bit."

"Me either." He smiles. "But I keep up enough to talk to the men at the bank. We lost to Seattle yesterday, five to four."

Ben points out sights he knows along Market, mostly penny arcades, nickelodeons, a few visibly second-rate vaudeville houses. They seem to comprise the basis of his knowledge of San Francisco.

Alighting at New Montgomery Street, Ben seems suitably impressed as we enter the hushed, rarified air of the Palace.

We head straight over to the Palm Court Restaurant and ask to be seated like a couple of swells.

It's the height of fabulous. The room in which we stand hasn't been seen by modern eyes: open all the way up to a glass ceiling high above, cavernous and echoing, yet the diners all seem to keep their voices low. Balconies and balustrades look down upon us from all eight floors above. The room is divided by white columns and gazebos, with palm trees and potted giant ferns placed amid sprays of Easter lilies to mark this special Sunday.

An orchestra is playing softly, and the room is crowded with exquisitely dressed diners. I see a sea of women's hats, bald-pated men and mutton chop sideburns everywhere.

We're seated next to a mirrored wall at a table for two. Our elderly waiter in uniform is diffident and experienced; he lays out our printed menus, which are florid works of art. Bread and water are deftly served, and I order a bottle of wine—French wine, for, in 1906 there are no California wines worth mentioning.

I ask Ben general questions about current events, more of what's in the news, in such a way that hopefully he doesn't suspect I don't know what the hell I'm talking about. I've only gotten partial glimpses of this world in my morning paper. It was too full of ads and lies about wholesome wealth.

"Do you like President Roosevelt?"

"I do! I think he's doing a bully job." Ben smiles. I think he's making a joke, but I don't get it. "I think it's a good thing, Roosevelt going after all those monopolies and trusts. Plus, he seems like a rugged man."

Yes, he is. Theodore Roosevelt is a stud, and apparently Ben thinks so, too. I take this as a good sign.

Ben goes on, though. "Being a Republican, Roosevelt is of course very pro-union, and I'm glad he is. The workers at my brother and father's stockyards are starting to organize and fight back. The younger kids were sent home from the slaughterhouses, told they couldn't reapply again until after they turn fourteen. Roosevelt's working to institute a national eight-hour workday. Could you imagine?" Ben is smiling.

"I'm certainly not unionized at the bank, hoh! My boss is an absolute tyrant by the name of Barney. He's very strict. He criticizes everything I do. I fantasize about Barney being run out of town on a rail. And about earning decent pay for once."

I reassure him. "I've had my fair share of bad bosses. Nightmares, actually. I can do my writing on my own, but, as you might have heard, writing is many things but rarely is it called lucrative."

"You seem to be doing all right," he waves around the dining room with a piece of bread in his hand, chewing.

I shrug it off. "Borrowed time. I'll have to pay the piper at some point."

But Ben continues: "So here we are in nineteen-six, a new century. We have telephones and motorcars and skyscrapers . . . not to mention aeroplanes now, too. Sometimes I think things all happen too fast, like everything is being sped up. You ever get that feeling?"

"Sure do."

"What I like about this city is that there's nothing for hundreds of miles in any direction. So San Francisco is like a magic island in the middle of nowhere. It's exciting. It has everything. It's scary, too; it can be a hard place to eke out a living. What are your plans for living here?" he asks me.

I keep it light. "I'd love to meet amazing people, make a million dollars, live on Nob Hill and drive one of those motorcars for myself."

Ben laughs, a kind of giggle.

"So you mentioned city graft," I say. "What do you suppose that's all about?"

"Cops, buildings, railroads, you name it." Ben leans in and speaks a bit more softly, as if it's dangerous to say these things aloud. "This city is propped up by very questionable dealings. Bribery, coercion, fake contracts; bending every law to keeping the resorts going."

I don't know what he means by "resorts."

"My horrible boss, Barney. I think he's up to no good. I have to make a favorable impression on him if I ever hope to move up at the bank. Meanwhile, he has me practically dancing upon the head of a pin, hoping for advancement and some acknowledgement from him. And he knows it. He gets a thrill from forcing me through hoops, and from smacking me back down any chance he can get. He is not a nice man, and I have no illusions that he would take a cut of flesh any chance he could get. Frankly, I don't know why his superiors don't see him for the crooked, nasty man he is. Unless the rot goes up a lot higher than I figure. In which case, well . . . " He shrugs. "Sometimes I worry there's no room in this city for a man who hopes to remain honest, upstanding and to simply work cleanly for a living. I wonder if people make fun of my values behind my back."

He takes a goodly draught of red wine.

And I suspect much of the wheels of this city are no doubt greased by graft and sleaze and have been for so long that someone like Ben would indeed be laughed at for having good, Christian, Midwest ethics.

He goes on, though, "What I'd really like would be to work for one of the railroads. I'm fascinated by trains, the big steam engines, intercontinental heavy rail—not just city streetcar lines. There will always be railroads and they will always make money, hand over fist. That's the industry to be in. But so far, I haven't so much as met someone who works at one. I'm sure I will at some point."

"I suspect you'll hit your stride. You seem like a nice fellow. I think your time will come."

He brightens visibly. "Might do. Someday. Thanks."

Changing the subject, I observe aloud, "It must have been difficult to just pack up and leave Chicago on your own."

"Nah. Piece of cake." His face starts doing that thing again. "Oh, sure, I miss my friends and my family."

"Well, I'm glad you're here," I decide to say.

"Thank you," he blushes a little but also makes some pretty startling eye-contact.

The elderly waiter interrupts to take our order. I go for the pot roast and potatoes, a good Easter Sunday meal, and Ben chooses likewise.

Once the waiter is gone, I decide to take a bit of a plunge. Quietly I ask, "So . . . you're not married?"

"Naw. Um . . ." he stammers. Not quite in alarm, but I instantly suspect there's a story there. I'll want the 411, but I don't want to corner him. "I was engaged in Chicago, but . . ." he turns crimson, and looks quite uncomfortable in his posh chair.

Given my take on him, that he's probably like me, I fill in the blanks quickly in my mind. He was most likely being rushed into marriage and it scared him. And he bolted.

Oscar Wilde once wrote, "It's an odd thing, but anyone who disappears is said to be seen at San Francisco." And here's Ben, locked in neutral in a new city literally ripe with potential, and probably not even cognitively in touch with what it is he's looking for.

"I've always been a bachelor," I decide to interject. "And I don't know that I aim to change that."

He looks up at me like I'm steadying him with my words. He seems to need to hear this.

If he really is like me, then Ben has no future. Even in a male-centric place like San Francisco, he'll either have to marry a woman and live a lie, or else exist in some strange bachelor half-life, lonely and always under suspicion. I don't know if he even realizes it. He has perhaps never allowed it to play out in his mind—it would probably throw him into a panic. He has no role models, no hint that what we call "gay" even exists.

Well. I'll be here for a few days. Maybe I can help show him a safe space along the way.

If he's willing. If my suspicions about him are correct.

"Do you enjoy museums?" OK, this is beyond lame, but it's the only thing I can think of to say right at the moment.

"Yeah, I've been to the De Young twice."

"I hope to see it. I studied art for a time—Raphael, Michelangelo. It's about the only time it's socially acceptable to see people naked. Although I did go to a naughty nickelodeon once."

Ben chokes on his wine and looks shocked. *"Really?"*

"Yes. It was tame, after all, but I suppose anything two people can do together can be photographed, which other people are then free to look at. Am I right?"

Ben laughs heartily and turns red.

I decide to make it worse. "People sing the praises of the female form divine, but I refuse to overlook the masculine form as well." I choose my words carefully, wondering if Ben will pick up on it. I've gone about as far as I can. He seems to be picturing naked men in his mind right now, ever so briefly, and with positive light. Good.

And further, he nods his assent. "I know what you mean," he says simply. He looks away, though, as he says it.

Our food arrives just then, breaking the moment. I watch him again lay his cloth napkin in his lap as if he's girding his loins, looking to hide the hand he's just subtly shown.

I was a lot hungrier than I thought, and the pot roast is really delicious in a way I can't put my finger on. Fresh and tender with no hint of that vile, modern restaurant seasoning, preservatives or chemicals. Untouched by corporate "metrics."

Ben suddenly asks, changing the subject, "I'm assuming you've spent loads of time here, since Berkeley is so close by. What all have you seen in San Francisco before?"

I'd be wholly inadequate to answering that question effectively, so I dodge the issue and simply say, "Oh, the usual things." I don't know what's here yet, in this Antebellum San Francisco, which is precisely why I've come to find out.

Ben muses: "It's strange. Once you live and work in a city, you no longer see its attractions. It just becomes home and work, with precious little time for anything else. My parents hope to come see me at the end of the summer, I'm greatly looking forward to that."

"Sounds lovely."

He asks me where I grew up, and Seattle, as my usual cover story, might not work. It was a small logging town in 1906—although, according to Ben, they're apparently big enough to have a professional baseball team, and one good enough to beat San Francisco yesterday.

I say I'm from Sacramento. I ascertain that Ben's never been there, and it seems safe.

I add, "I have two older sisters, and they have kids, but I

never had much truck with kids. I hope to do so eventually; they're great people. I'm just never around them enough."

"I've always wanted to have children," Ben declares. "But truth be told, I don't know that I actually ever will."

Our eyes meet and I slide further into the belief that I have really lucked out in finding a kindred spirit after all.

After dinner and wine, we are back in the main lobby, and I don't want to just send him on his way. And I get the impression he's not in a hurry to leave. He could panic out at any moment. I steel myself to the possibility, and I can't say I won't be heartbroken. He's cute. He's lonely. I'm lonely. There's so much we could do together, even if we don't "go there."

I don't always have to "go there."

I just dive in. "Would you like to see my room? I'm only on the second floor, but it's quite nice."

"I would! And thank you so much for dinner, that was very kind of you."

"The pleasure was all mine," I assure him.

We make our way to the front desk to get my heavy metal key.

"Gosh!" he gasps as I open the door to 242. "I've been in the Palmer Hotel in Chicago, but I never saw any of its rooms. I imagine them being quite like this. This is nice."

"Come see out the window," I say, and I throw open the sash and we sit on the window seat and gaze out. Same scene, just nighttime, beneath electric streetlamps that are way more ornate than the ones we have now.

We sit for a good long while, each with one leg crooked up. The *Chronicle* Building clock chimes the hour of seven, then the quarter hour.

We're near to each other, but not touching. I try to remind myself we may never touch, and I get all achy and blue inside. I would like it, but mostly I don't want to screw this up and make things uncomfortable for Ben.

He asks suddenly, completely breaking the spell, "How are the vaudeville houses out in Berkeley?"

Damned if I know. Hell.

"Not so good," I venture.

"Well, the Orpheum has a seven-thirty show, I bet we could make that. It's just around the corner."

"That's a great idea."

I still get to hang out with Ben, and that's a good thing.

Soon we're back out on the street, heavy metal room key safely at the front desk.

It is indeed a short walk. I've been by here thrice already, so I feel grand, full of wine and leading the way.

San Francisco's Orpheum Theatre will move four times in its life before eventually settling at Market and Hyde, happily charging people $480.00 apiece to see *Hamilton*.

In nineteen-six it costs a quarter.

The "O" in RKO Pictures stands for Orpheum. And it all started right here on O'Farrell Street in San Francisco.

We approach a mass of people on the sidewalk outside under the clear bulbs of the marquee. I'm amazed by how brightly lit everything is. Electricity is "in"; it's everywhere and being put to amazing use. I read somewhere that back in the day people were afraid of "electrickery" and had massive protests and campaigns, trying to stop its insidious spread.

Stupid is timeless.

Ben insists on paying, which is sweet of him, and we enter the grand hall. Opulent, finery, airs, proscenium arches and clamshell boxes and more curtains and tapestries surround us. The auditorium seats a good 3,500 people, and it's full tonight. People are smoking, talking, coughing and laughing.

We're angling for a seat near the orchestra—but so is everyone else. A near brawl breaks out as a cluster of men and women in old-fashioned garb nearly come to blows fighting for good seats.

Some things in San Francisco never change.

A lot of people leave their hats on, including the men. I suddenly find it insulting. But more crucially, the women's hats are totally blocking my view. It reeks of unfairness.

The immense show curtain is covered with delicate hand-painted ads, all scrolly and ornate: shoe shops, Santa Fe Railroad, "Latest Parisian Cleaning & Dyeing Works," "Try Bithinia Water!" "The Hub Hatters and Furnishers." All painted by hand, around an intricate and lovely scene of idyll. It's truly a work of art.

"Definitely better than Berkeley," I feel it's safe to observe. Ben smiles, proud of his new city that he gets to show me.

"I come here a lot, on my way home from work. It's a great way to pass the time."

I figure that would be true but would also contribute to his lack of finding friends. As far as Ben is concerned, we might be in a turn-of-the-century couch-potato situation here.

Finally the lights dim and . . . I realize I have no idea what to expect.

Ben leans over, his beard tickling my ear and giving me delightful goosebumps: "It always starts with the Dumb Show. A mime or other silent act. That way people can come in late."

And they are, loudly, crassly, catcalling one another as two mimes take to the stage and start doing their pre-Marcel Marceau act, generating a few giggles from the audience that serve to calm the madness and slowly draw the spectators' attention to the stage at long last.

Then the first true act takes the stage. An operetta. A young girl in a gown, lit by a surprisingly intense spotlight, her hair a cascade of ringlets, comes out and sings her heart out, her hands up in front of her heart, or reaching up, imploringly, to the audience.

There's no such thing as a microphone here. She must rely on her voice, which is formidable and masterfully fills the great hall. She trills and warbles in Italian. The orchestra is flawless and full of deep sound. I expect the audience to be disrespectful and continue to catcall, but instead they're listening intently. Some near to crying.

Once she's done, though, the Agoust Family of jugglers take the stage, with acrobats and hoops and drums. Brass music caterwauls, and heavy drums beat. The audience gets rowdy again, boots stomping on the carpeted, spit-laden and cigarette-burned floor.

Musical numbers, comedy sketches and popular songs alternate before us on the stage. A lively pre-jazz tap number with canes and hats and scantily clad women dance, festooned with ostrich feathers. Footlights throw brilliant illumination, feathers are flying off.

Then they do a variety sketch, some comedy of errors about a man asking a girl for her hand in marriage but who instead winds up kissing a live cow onstage.

They use jokes like a woman saying "Oh drat! I've lost my heel!"

"That's awright darlin'; you'll soon meet another one!"

Ben and the others around us laugh so hard they have tears in their eyes.

I was expecting a dog act, and don't have long to wait. Coleman's Dogs & Cats take the stage, a lot of jumping through hoops and walking on their hind legs to the roar of the crowd. I'm not even sure how they manage to get cats to perform tricks, but they do. Treats are clearly involved.

A comedy duo takes the stage then, two men in bowler hats, and one begins a story.

"Jackass Jill . . ."

"Huh?"

"Jackass Jill . . ."

"What are you implying, my good man?"

"Jack! Asked Jill! To climb the hill . . ."

The crowd goes wild.

Intermission comes, I'm after a drink at the concession stand.

"You can't," Ben tells me. "As few liquor laws as this city has, one of them is apparently that you can't serve spirits at concert and theatre venues. I think the crowds used to get out of hand."

Just as well then. I don't know that I'd want to be surrounded by 3,500 drunk 1906 San Franciscans. I shudder to think how many pistols are probably in this auditorium right now.

We settle in for the second half, which includes, among other things, a blackface number doing a cakewalk. People howl with laughter. I cringe. It's so un-PC it hurts.

After a while, it kind of seems to drag on. I think I remember hearing that the first half of a vaudeville show is where the money and talent goes, everything after that is considered second-rate. People begin to leave or talk loudly amongst themselves.

But suddenly a hush falls over the audience as the stage lights go dim, an immense white screen slides down and the Orpheum provides us with a short motion picture. The orchestra accompanies it flawlessly. *Esmeralda*, a French film by Alice Guy—a long-forgotten pioneer of filmmaking who, in 2019, is just being rediscovered and celebrated. I just saw a thing about her on Turner Classic Movies.

Then a few more second-rate acts wrap up the show and it's over. We shuffle out. People are already lined up on the sidewalk outside for the next performance. It'll go until two o'clock in the morning.

It's a real short walk back to the Palace. I've got to think of something quick to keep Ben from heading off to home. I don't want to be alone, and I'm finding I'd rather spend time with Ben in particular.

"Is it a long way to your place from here?" I ask as we

meander slowly, upsetting people behind us trying to walk like San Franciscans do—fast.

He seems to be lingering as well.

"Oh, about four blocks. But they're big blocks." His hands are deep in his front pockets, his shoulders slightly up. The April air is cool, and the evening fog pattern provides blasts of ocean air, ruining what could otherwise be a sultry evening.

"Come back to the Palace for a drink?"

"Surely!" He brightens up visibly at the prospect. His shoulders relax.

I'm elated.

For a moment I'm excited to be able to see the grand Maxfield Parrish painting in the Pied Piper, the hotel bar. I've been known to go out of my way just to gaze at it. Of course it's not there yet; won't be for decades. Maxfield is only about thirty-five years old right now somewhere, just hitting his artistic stride. As such the bar doesn't bear its signature name.

Yet it's just as posh as you'd expect, shrouded in cigar smoke and dark wood paneling. I order us two bourbons and I decide to just out with it. "Hey Ben. If you want, you're welcome to stay with me here for a few days. It could be fun." I pop a few peanuts in my mouth for something to do.

At any point, Ben could freak and bolt. He could be just some lonely guy looking for a friend, and here's me, over ten years his senior and nothing short of lecherous. I feel ugly, like I'm taking advantage of him.

No, I tell myself: I will not push Ben into anything he's not ready for. If he is willing to be friends, then I'll be the best one he's ever had. I wish for a lot more—it's true—but if that's not in the cards then I will be the perfect gentleman and Ben will never know. My task is to find his comfort level and remain within it. I shall match his energy and be above reproach.

I mean, he's seen the room. He knows there's only one bed, right?

And yet Ben agrees. "That's very kind of you, thank you. I could go directly to work from here, it's just a short ways. In fact, that would give me an extra twenty minutes' sleep at least. Thank you!"

We down the last of our drinks. Suddenly he seems to be in as big a hurry as I am. Along with feeling great relief, I find it adorable.

Instead of bothering with a lifting room, we climb the elegant, carpeted steps, laid down with gleaming brass runners. The staircase is broad and wide and with a very gentle rise, I'm certain to accommodate women in their heels and skirts without the risk of spilling their champagne cocktails.

Once in the room I'm determined more than ever to play it cool. It's not the 1970s anymore.

"I have to work at nine tomorrow," Ben says, going over to the brass alarm clock by the bed. "May I?"

"Certainly."

He picks it up and winds it and sets it for the time he wants.

Ben pulls off his brown wool jacket and kicks off his shoes. He's wearing suspenders, which are charming. He undoes the tie he's been wearing, takes his striped shirt off, undoing the collar which flaps wide open when he sets it on the table. With still no more ceremony than in a locker room he slithers out of his trousers.

I do likewise.

He's standing before me in a crude undershirt, dingy boxers and unsettling-looking garters to hold his stockings up. They have an orthopedic appearance, like I got Timmeh from *South Park* on up in here.

I put myself on automatic pilot. It'll do or it'll don't. Still, at this point, I want to keep him comfortable. That's my overriding concern.

He tries not to stare at my blue 2(x)ist boxer briefs.

Saying nothing, we slip under the covers in our skivvies and undershirts. I put out the overhead electric light and we're in the sheets, not touching. But the bed makes a jingle noise at the slightest movement and our breathing sounds loud in the room.

Plenty of light comes in from the street, baleful.

"Thank you for letting me be here. This is an unexpected treat."

"Sure . . . "

Risking everything, I gently pat his chest with my hand and leave it there. He doesn't flinch. I can smell him. Sweat and hair tonic and underarm odor, slightly perfumed. I guess that Everdry stuff doesn't work all that well—and I'm glad. I like a man to smell like a man.

Ordinarily I'd be too keyed up to sleep, but Christ, what have I been through this day? Not to mention your actual opium. It all catches up with me and I begin dozing, Ben begins dozing; cable car bells ring down below. Clopping of horse hooves on cobblestone.

14

Monday, April 16, 1906

The mechanical alarm clock jangles loudly at 7:30, and Ben and I are locked in embrace.

There's a thing, I don't know if you know it, where you fall asleep with someone—but forty-five minutes later you're awake, breathless and practically snarling with desire.

So it has been for Ben and me. All pretense is gone, all barriers dropped.

We are on the same page.

No words were spoken but we've come to understand a great many things between the two of us. More than relief, I feel honored to know Ben and the workings of his cute little body. He's a bit of a tiger, actually.

Well. 1906 or not, he's got to go to work.

A slight awkwardness is back. "Would you like breakfast?" I ask. "I just have to push the buzzer here."

"Please," he responds with a smile.

"Why don't you take a bath while I see to this? That way we won't scare the natives."

He laughs at this, a relaxed inside joke we now share.

I make use of the room buzzer, summoning a room attendant, and hiding behind the door, order breakfast for two and the day's paper as water sprays in the shower. Thank God he's not humming, although I'd find it funny. I order pastries and coffee and tomato juice. Ben is still in the bathroom when room service comes.

We eat. He puts on his same dirty clothes so he can get to work.

"What's the likelihood you can take the afternoon off?" I ask. "I'd like to see about renting an automobile."

"Oh, I'll ask Barney—I'd love to take you around to my place—but I don't think there's any such thing as 'renting' an automobile."

He could have a point.

"I'm going shopping meanwhile," I tell him. "Gonna get some nicer clothes. I left my hat at Dunn Brothers."

"That sounds fun. I wish I could join you. But duty calls."

We share a protracted goodbye with all the slobber befitting two men upon parting. He leaves, looking back repeatedly as he heads down that interminable hallway.

I try not to think that Ben could be falling in love. That won't do; for I can't stay here. I don't even let the thought form fully in my mind, instead setting about my own shower.

I like Ben a lot. If he lived in my time, would I date him? I think I would. I realize just then I'm not entirely certain the man has a sense of humor; so far, I've detected none. Can that be taught?

But I guess, because I know I'll only be here for five days, the whole thing is like a shipboard romance. There's an automatic kill-switch. It allows me to feel things I otherwise wouldn't allow myself to feel. At this point, in the San Francisco of 2019, I'd already be fussing about where this is going, what it means, and is he banging any of my friends?

This is refreshing and pure and removed from all that. I like it.

I take a shower, much like any other, but the handles are white porcelain knobs and the spray nozzle a bit anemic. A small bar of soap leaves a waxy film and smells like paste. There is no shampoo; the towel is scratchy, thin and far too small.

I only take a quick glance at the newspaper. The news does indeed seem very dry and boring. But in one article I see the term "resorts" used again, and in very unfavorable terms. They are the houses of sin: centered in the Barbary Coast, with others peppered throughout the cityscape. They seem desperate, depraved and wholly without redemption. The word "prostitution" isn't used directly, yet is writ large by carefully worded prose, leaving little doubt. There's a gawd-awful lot of it. Special attention is paid to the wretchedness of Morton Alley.

Out on the street with the mid-morning crowds I head for The Emporium to do some serious shopping for myself.

The department store is grand, epic and gothic, like everything else here. The Emporium will remain in business until 1996, but by then it was only a shadow of its 1906 glory.

As I walk in, a bizarre memory comes over me: One time, around 1992, I'd decided to try my hand at country and western dancing at the Rawhide. I'd picked out some used cowboy boots and was wearing them, badly, all over town. Clip clopping through the cosmetics department at The Emporium, just trying to find my way out, an old queen behind the Shiseido counter looks me up and down and snarls, "Something for *her*?"

I was devastated.

Now I'm here again, and all of me is a fraud.

The Emporium rotunda soars up six floors high. I gaze

upward to the enormous dome and skylight, the balconies and stairways, lush with ferns and potted palms. I could make an entire study of the light standards, richly ornate on squared wooden plinths sprouting globes, all dripping with carvings and cut crystal. Steps lead up to mezzanines and alcoves where massive carved wood cabinetry displays open drawers of lacy feminine bits or men's neckties.

Rich merchandise surrounds me in every direction. They seem to have everything. On my way to the haberdashery, I pass the floral department and take a moment to enjoy the array, color, and smells—good smells and that bitter, celery-like tang some flowers have.

Everyone is smoking in here, cigars, pipes, cigarillos, cigarettes; they even have spittoons strategically stationed about. As there is no sawdust on the floor, the men here seem more disposed to huck their wads actually into the cuspidors—but not at a hundred percent. Not if it's too far out of a man's way.

A kindly salesclerk named Horace helps me in the men's department. In his late fifties, he has a few strands of gray hair slicked over the dome of his head. His own clothes are expensive and on point, and his sharp moustache is visibly dyed black.

He initially seems to take pity on me. Up close, my clothes must look pretty sad to his experienced eye. But when you consider they had to go the long way to 2019 and back, I think they've held up remarkably well.

We have fun. He helps me pick out a pair of wool slacks, gray and soft, with a subtle stripe pattern. They fasten practically all the way up to my armpits, as all trousers seem to do right now.

I get two shirts. One casual; it's a striped button up. Even new, it's soft. It will age beautifully, and I love it. The other shirt is white and significantly more upscale, in case I should wish to go to the opera. Horace tries to sell me the latest word in formal wear, a starched white dress shirt that buttons up the back like a straitjacket. I eschew that. It looks uncomfortable and confining—I don't know how a person could expect to don it without having a manservant to hand—and then I look at the price. No thanks. I opt for the normal one.

Poor Horace is at wits end that he must show me how the collars work, because I simply have no idea. They are displayed in their own wooden drawer, sold separately, and must be attached with buttons.

I get a blue necktie, kind of a cross between a tie and a cravat. He assures me it goes well with my get up and I'll just have to take his word for it.

Suspenders—Horace calls them "braces"—that will button into the hemline of my trousers are added to the pile.

I need a new hat. Horace produces a black bowler that fits high and silly on my head, as the current fashion seems to dictate. I enjoy the texture of the fabric on my fingertips, and the shiny black ribbon around the brim, lovingly stitched into place.

And finally I select a coat, also gray wool, different from the trousers but in a way that works, with a handkerchief for my breast pocket. I'm starting to feel spruce.

"Would you like to look at shoes?" he asks kindly, having taken more than one surreptitious glance at what I'm wearing on my feet. My shoes are a fright, they're beat to hell. But I'm getting used to them and don't have all that much money after all, so I kindly decline.

He points out socks and garters, the socks look itchy and baggy. I decide to stick with my modern black nylon socks—I think I got them at Ross. They might get funky by Day Five, but I'm not of a mind to mess with garters and those sad, woeful-looking stockings.

It all comes to $8.68. Horace hungrily takes my money and thanks me profusely, issuing a polite bow, and a girl in uniform wordlessly packages up my purchases in perfect bundles, tied with twine.

Out on the street, carrying my bundles but wearing the hat and coat, I find a pharmacy and buy a toothbrush, some tooth powder, and oil for my hair, even though it's only marginally long enough to lie down flat.

I also discover a smoke shop and decide to buy a pipe, some burl-cut tobacco, and wood matches in a box. I linger over the snuff counter, looking at ornate and charming tin boxes of the stuff, wondering just what the hell it's supposed to do or be. I guess it's tobacco ground to a powder and . . . you snort it?

Christ these people are weird.

I lean up against the building to smoke my pipe and watch 1906 spool by. I have to take extra care to set my packages down in such a way that they don't get gooey with tobacco spit on the sidewalk, made muddy by street dust.

Across is the Powell and Market cable car turnaround, and the Flood Building. Instead of the sunken Hallidie Plaza that won't come for many a year, an entire three-story building sits in its place, lined with storefronts. It's visually very confusing to me. Pedestrians hurry along, and I marvel at their clothes and how hectic and important everyone seems to act. They've all got places to be. No one's even looking at the incredible beauty all around, unaware that it soon will be gone.

After pipe, which takes a good thirty minutes, I head back to the Palace with my packages, determined to ask the hotel about using a car for the afternoon. I quickly run upstairs and put on my new clothes, opting for the more casual shirt. They smell new. It's incongruous.

The hotel bell captain is at a desk adjacent to the check-in counter and I inquire if the hotel has automobiles for use.

"Normally we do," he assures me kindly. "I'm not altogether certain we have one today. Please allow me to check," and he picks up the handset of a seriously amazing wooden box and cranks a handle on one side. I can hear the other person through the earpiece, they're practically shouting to be heard through the current state of telephony. I interpret an affirmative on the other end of the line.

"Ah. You're in luck, sir. We do. Have you driven a motor car before?"

"Oh, yes, I have."

I omit that I have a 2016 Nissan Xterra back home, with Bluetooth and GPS.

"And I'm quite familiar with San Francisco geography . . . " I don't know why I feel compelled to add that. I guess I'm trying to reassure myself more than him.

"Splendid. Cash, it will be $11 deposit, $3 for the afternoon. If you have a letter of credit the deposit is $5." Gulp. "Do you anticipate needing it beyond this evening?"

"Oh, no, just a few hours'll do fine."

I have to hand all the money I own over to this man. If I bang up the car, I'll be in a world of hurt.

He has me sign another ledger with my address, which I make up on the spot with my scant knowledge of Shattuck Avenue in Berkeley. I'm also given an insurance form to fill out and sign. I try to give it a quick read, but its language is dense and officious, and I'll just have to not do anything stupid.

He bids me wait while he sends a boy to go get the car. And thus I fuss. Truly wondering how I'm going to operate the damn automobile once I get my hands on it.

My grandfather once told me how to drive a Model T Ford. I was spellbound. I wanted that information to stay with me for some reason, if I were ever given a chance to try it.

Well, here's my chance.

Soon I am escorted by the bell captain and boy to the New Montgomery Street entrance and over to a waiting horseless carriage, shimmying and sputtering. I become truly nervous then.

Before me stands a 1905 Taylor Aerocar. It looks brand new, which confuses my brain. It's old, right? It's painted dark blue with gold piping. The front seat consists of two clamshells of tufted black leather and the back seat is set much higher, obviously for the experience of being driven around in and seeing the sights—and of being seen. Its canopy is on, two sizable rods run up either side, leaving it a little dark inside. I'd kind of rather have the top down but am not about to kick about that at this point.

It has a crank start, gas-powered headlamps, wood-spoked wheels and a toolbox on the running board. The engine compartment is ornate, but I'm seeing it as essentially little more than a typical oil drum, turned on its side, mounted between the front wheels and firing microbursts of fuel with a general *putt putt* sound.

The car even has a license plate. I muse upon some department of motor vehicles office in its early inception.

These poor people. Netflix and antibiotics? They don't got. Antidepressants and therapists? They don't got. California DMV? They got. Seems pretty unfair.

The steering wheel is yet again on the British side of the car, and there's not even a door to protect the driver. It's just open. I wonder why. The other three doors are low-rise things that wouldn't protect anyone in a collision. Of course it has no seatbelts, the car is probably just designed to be thrown clear of.

I tip the bell captain a nickel and climb in. It rumbles with the effort of keeping its engine lit, but I discover I'm trembling, too.

Just as my grandfather had taught me, there are three pedals on the floor: brake on the right, clutch on the left, and reverse in the middle. No gas pedal, the throttle is a lever under the steering wheel. Plus a spark advance lever on the other side, which I don't know a thing about. I slide the throttle forward and back to get the feel of it and am frustrated to find that it's the complete opposite to what it should be. Pulling it back toward me gives the engine more gas—I strongly feel it should be the other way around. I guess I expect it should match the direction of a motorcycle throttle, which I drove exclusively for ten years.

With the bell captain and boy still watching—*why won't they go away?*—I put my feet on the brake and hold the clutch petal halfway off the floor, channeling my conversation with my grandfather so many years ago, so many years from now.

I unlatch the enormous brass handbrake to my right, which also engages the clutch. The car gives an ominous shimmy.

Fortunately, there are no vehicles immediately in front of me. It's a straight shot out into the street. Easing off the foot-brake and moving the clutch pedal down to the board, I pull the throttle back. The car lurches ahead. It does not die. I'm doing it! I give a quick wave to the men and make my way into the traffic of New Montgomery Street.

I'm ecstatic—even though I'm only going about four miles per hour. I nudge the throttle forward, thinking I'll go faster, but that instead cuts the gas and the engine almost stalls. I jab on the brake petal and keep the clutch on the floor, which is exactly the wrong thing to do. I give it more gas in confusion, also the wrong thing to do, and the car lurches and jerks, fighting me, the tiny engine whining in protest.

I'm trying to rev it in first gear with the brake on. Shit.

OK. Calm down. You can do this.

I release the foot brake, push the clutch down and give it some gas. The car moves forward gracefully once more.

Second gear happens when you take your left foot off the clutch completely. The Aerocar complains again—I don't have the right amount of throttle for it yet.

If all this weren't enough, I'm now a victim of the chaotic street scene. Horse drawn carts and other cars are zipping around me. I try to keep my place in the riot but I'm being cut off by every Tom, Dray and Hairy. The car jounces madly over the slightest bump and rut in the cobblestone street. New Montgomery has an electric trolley line, so I steer clear of the slippery tracks, fighting my way through the short distance to Mission Street so I can turn right, drive around the Palace and come back out on Market Street at Third. Someone cuts me off and I have to slam the clutch and brake pedals down, but the throttle is still open, causing the engine to race angrily until I remember to shove it forward.

Don't bang up the car! Don't bang up the car!

If Market Street had painted lines, it would be six lanes wide. But it doesn't. It's a free-for-all.

Turning left off Market Street onto Montgomery, I feel as though I may meet God: An onrush of cable cars, trolley cars, horse carts, and other automobiles are facing me ominously. And still pedestrians are dodging their way through all the traffic.

Finally I see a break in the chaos and take my shot, yanking the throttle arm back, dropping the clutch and hoping for the best . . .

Only to kill the engine completely.

The car jerks to a stop and, as such, I have to get out onto the street and crank.

A cable car is stopped just off my right hip. I can hear the whirring of the cable under the street, the car's grip man clanging his bell in anger. It no longer sounds musical.

It's well known that a car crank can kick back and break your arm. But the Aerocar's engine is warm and it lights with one good go. I quickly hop back in, now realizing why there's no door on the driver's side. Must happen a lot.

"Get a horse!" someone yells.

I complete my left-hand turn without further incident, squeezing around another cable car. An oncoming motorist lets me through this time, one of the first acts of kindness I've seen by the people of this San Francisco.

Montgomery Street, Banker's Row . . . this is where California's money lives. Suitable to that status, each building is staid with columns, rounded porticos, awnings and American flags. They have dull names like Union Bank, the Bank of Union Trust, and Crocker Bank. I peer while driving, trying to find Ben's building, which should be just up here on the right.

I find it right next to Montgomery Street Coffee House. I have no idea what the rules are for street parking, all I know is I'm grateful I can float safely to a stop in front of Ben's bank without having to try to figure out the reverse pedal. I leave the engine idling; the car doesn't even come with keys, so I figure it should be all right. Plus I don't want to have to crank start the engine any more times than I have to.

Montgomery Savings and Loan is grand, epic, gothic. As San Francisco commands it shall be. Beneath high, coffered ceilings stand electric brass candelabras, dripping with cut crystal. Everything is a study in fabulous: burled, buffed wood all carved with detail and artistry. It's stately, stuffy. People are speaking quietly which seems a bit silly, for hammering beneath the vast, cavernous marble ceilings are typewriters, banging away.

The teller's cages, at which people patiently wait in their heavy clothes, are in two types: Paying Teller and Receiving Teller. The employees are all men, all wearing arm garters and visors. I stop one such man passing by and ask to speak to Ben Wade. He seems displeased to have to go fetch a lowly co-worker for me, but he bids me to wait. For all I know he could be a vice president. He certainly seems irked enough at my request.

Ben comes out from behind the cages in his visor.

"Nice duds." True to the tone of the bank, he's speaking quietly, as if narrating a round of golf for ESPN.

"Thanks. I snagged a motor car from the hotel. Let's go for a drive."

"Mark, I can't . . . "

"You didn't ask for the afternoon off? C'mon, it'll be fun. Ask. What's the worst thing that could happen?"

"I could get fired?"

"Ask."

Ben gives a doubtful shrug and goes to his manager's desk and I see the individual he's been talking about, this Barney. Not a kind-looking man. Bald, sharp nose, *pince-nez* eyeglasses. He looks positively reptilian. I wait, and I also keep an eye out on the car at the curb.

Soon Ben comes back having pulled off his visor and bearing his cloak. "It worked. Let's get out of here!"

I take him out to the Aerocar still sputtering on the street. A beat cop looks like he wants to give me a parking ticket but when he sees us climb in and I pull the brake off, he shakes his head and puts his notebook back in his pocket.

"You sure you know how to operate this thing?" Ben asks, clearly impressed by the vehicle. His head is in motion as his eyes drink it all in.

"Totally. Piece of cake." I'm fibbing a little.

"How? When did you learn?"

"Ah. It's . . . complicated. Hey, let's go to your place and get some things you'll need to live at the Palace with me."

Ben smiles broadly at this, and I feel tickled I can make him happy.

So we drive the length of Montgomery Avenue (which will be renamed Columbus someday) and angle back through Chinatown.

I start to get the hang of driving the Aerocar. The wooden steering wheel is very stiff and high; not angled toward the driver in any ergonomic way. The throttle is temperamental, and the footbrake gives just the suggestion of stopping power. I wish I could say there's a rhythm to the traffic patterns, but there is none. You just have to move forward when you can, darting around everyone else, and watch out for pedestrians, street cars and carriages.

Having a car makes short work of the distance, but as soon as we're south of Mission Street we jounce off cobblestone and onto hardpacked dirt. Not to mention I'm driving south on what for me has always been a staunchly northbound one-way street. We reach Ben's place at Fifth and Folsom in just a few minutes. I find a spot to leave the car and cut the engine.

And I'm instantly horrified at my surroundings. It's bleak.

Ben's apartment is in a clapboard rooming house, visibly sagging. A mass of electric wires is strung overhead. Even though I'm only play-acting here, I have to remind myself that no, I don't really have to shop for an apartment in this San Francisco as I'd told Ben. The "four and two bits a week" deal is starting to come into focus.

All the buildings are about the same height and construction. Wood, cobbled together in one continuous block, with clotheslines strung everywhere. Dogs are barking and children are playing in the dirt in the street, stomping through a rivulet of filth in the middle of the road, dodging horse hooves and wagons and left to fend for themselves. Their young faces are covered in grime; they look forgotten and feral and one seems to be shouting in what I think is Yiddish. Or Ukranian.

I slide into culture shock.

Ben leads the way, bounding up the outdoor wooden stairs to the second floor of 894 Folsom Street—the building had been whitewashed at some point years ago but is mostly worn down to gray weathered wood—and taking me down a long, dark hallway to his apartment.

It's tiny. Like Ben's ears and nose. And dark. There's a single window, but it looks out into an air shaft.

A wood stove is next to a sink in the kitchen, open to the

main room. No water closet, Ben explains; there's a shared bath down the hall. The place has not much in the way of furniture, just a bed with a bookshelf over it, and a chair, piled with laundry. The walls are covered with faded and peeling Victorian wallpaper, and a single lightbulb hangs from a cord in the middle of the ceiling, with a cloth-covered extension cord connecting that to a rudimentary toaster on the table. Old gaslights are along the wall, prissy and pretty, but they don't look like they've been used for years. Cobwebs drip from the knobs. It's bleak, yet I suspect Morticia Addams would adore it.

Ben gathers some clothes, puts them in a leather valise and we get back to the automobile. I'm glad to leave.

I have to crank the car again, but it fires up quickly and I escape with no broken limbs.

Now we're clear and free to navigate.

The South of Market district was originally open marshland with rivers and, apparently, a lovely public beach where First Street is now. Ships could weigh anchor here, making it of prime importance to San Francisco's growth. But it quickly turned the area into a center for industry and filth. Factories, boiler works, smelters and depots sprang up close to the water at the east end. The marshland was quickly filled in. Mission Creek, running through the center of it all, served as the city's sewer for decades, earning it the nickname Shit Creek as far back as the 1870s. I can't picture those people using the word "shit," but some of their buildings still stand tall around us. New and old, brick and wood, hospitals, lumberyards and shanty towns are all jumbled into the area.

As the district began to reel under the weight of its own pollution, South of the Slot became an area of last resort for immigrants and the working class. Schools, churches, and community halls grew up alongside brothels, flop houses and open encampments. More of the waterways were filled in, the hills were graded down and the waterfront extended by several blocks.

It's all being held up by seventy-year-old wooden pilings—frames of abandoned sailing ships—rotting atop sand and silt. You can just imagine what happens to that in an earthquake.

I'm honored to have the chance to see South of the Slot in its last few days. It's not an attractive sight, and hasn't been witnessed for 113 years.

I glance at Ben, comfortably seated in the posh leather of the car. Because the steering wheel is on the wrong side, he's just off my left elbow. If I lean just so, I can feel him. It's good.

We drive around without any agenda . . . just to see. Some areas are downright scary. Downtrodden people sitting out on their front steps on a Monday afternoon, drinking beer, smoking cigarettes, and spitting into the dirt streets.

Up at the northeastern end of South of Market, it's a dense, busy mixture of industries, yet with a few fancy Victorian houses stubbornly remaining firm against the filth. Rail spurs and coal cars, furnaces, warehouses; a giant sign for Hills Bros Coffee; a few large piles of earth—the last remnants of Rincon Hill not yet pulled down to street level.

We come upon the Selby Shot Tower at First and Howard, a giant brick column where they drop hot lead to form bullets. It's over two-hundred feet tall, monolithic, and visible from all around.

I then find myself driving north on East Street South—which apparently people found so confusing they'll eventually rename the whole thing "the Embarcadero" and be done with it.

The Ferry Building at the foot of Market Street is the official gateway to San Francisco, the end of the line for the Trans-Continental Railroad.

The plaza is riddled with street cars and cable car turntables; the rails here form a giant circle so streetcars can turn around to restart their runs, snaking out all over the city. On the other side of the building, the water side, large steam ferry-boats nose up to the docks.

The Aerocar jounces over innumerable rail tracks, cobble-stones, and often just packed dirt. I continue us north on East Street North. Telegraph Hill, years before the arrival of Coit Tower, looms off to the left, amid yet more industry and a sizable brewery. Dozens of docks line East Street to our right. I can see masts and ships' smokestacks behind the buildings.

It's a quick drive around Telegraph Hill to Pier 39, your actual Fisherman's Wharf, busy with boats and nets and men who look like they have no sense of humor. Not a tourist in sight, and not a t-shirt to be found.

From here we can see Alcatraz, littered with small gray buildings I don't recognize. The Golden Gate is comprised of just hills and water. Nothing else.

Through North Beach, then back again, we chug up to the top of Nob Hill—the Aerocar can barely make it up California Street.

I long to see the grand mansions before their destruction. The Stanford House, the Hopkins, the Flood Mansion. The formidable stone Fairmont Hotel building rests at the edge of the hill, topped out but, as yet, unfinished—otherwise I'd suggest we go in for lunch.

It's hard to drive and simultaneously check out the scenery, so I circle around a few times, meandering through the streets until I've gotten a good look at some of the finest real estate in the country. True wealth and Victorian fierceness. Millions of dollars' worth, back when a million meant something.

"Could you imagine living up here?" Ben asks from my left. "I think this is how it ought to be."

"Right? It'd do nicely. We should look into it."

Ben smiles, dreamily.

I'd like to see my apartment in the Castro, even though my

building won't be built until 1961. I tell Ben that I want to look at Eureka Valley and Castro Street, that I might want to buy out that way someday when I become rich. He says sure. He's clearly loving the drive.

We motor down the dirt road that is Van Ness Avenue, past all sorts of stately manors. If the top of Nob Hill has the million-dollar houses, Van Ness is lined with the half- and three-quarter-million-dollar homes; the second tier of wealth. They're gingerbready and posh, set apart from each other on generous lots with gates and detached stables. The avenue is broad and open, yet with only a sparse amount of traffic.

Down toward Hayes Street we see the remarkable St. Ignatius Church, ornate, wooden and wonderful. It, too, hasn't long to live.

I enjoy the feeling of driving home 113 years ago.

Back on Market we're heading west now, into curiously different suburbs. This part won't burn, yet it looks nothing like I think it should. One-story businesses and houses, stand appearing bucolic in the cloudy daylight. No U.S. Mint or Safeway at Church Street, just giant, unexpected outcroppings of rock. A few amazing houses, crinkly and haunted looking.

Market Street ends at 17th Street and at a big, ornate, Victorian building with signs that say "Drugs. D.H. Wulzen Jr., Pharmacist" and "Post and Telegraph Office." This is where Bank of America should be—but not quite. The corner, I guess, will get eventually shaved off and set back, this beautiful Victorian razed and thrown away. Right now, there's a stand of ficus trees where Marcello's Pizza ought to be.

I'm slowing down, seeing that I have only two choices: 17th east or west, or to angle forward onto Castro.

I just chug through the uncontrolled dirt intersection, over to the 400 block of Castro Street . . .

I'm in shock. This should be Downtown Gay USA. Instead, amid several vacant lots, only a few wooden houses stand. No commercial enterprises operate here, certainly no theatre, hardware store or banks. Or bars.

There's nothing.

The only item of interest is a cable car line that runs from 18th Street over Castro to Noe Valley and back, the hill being too steep for horses.

My mind hurting with disconnect, I notice that Harvey's/The Elephant Walk is just a florist stand.

But I focus on operating the vehicle. I turn right and head up 18th Street to Diamond and park the car, engine running. I bid Ben to wait and I climb down to stand at what should be my apartment.

It's difficult to tell exactly where it should be. This whole block will eventually be bisected by the huge Market Street Extension, cutting a wide swath at an angle through all these vacant lots and tiny, low-end Victorians. I determine my apartment building should be this particular vacant lot.

It's completely bewildering. What would normally be a four-story building is completely empty.

Or so I think. Overly distracted by where my parking space should be, I walk around a large rock, fussing about the presence of this huge boulder. Only dynamite could take it out, and I'm picturing drills and TNT blasting when suddenly, with my focus down and brain lost in thought, I come face to face with a large goat.

He's gazing at me with suspicion, chewing on a clump of crabgrass. Those eyes! Goat eyes. Black slits within golden orbs. He starts toward me—whether to bite me or to have me scritch his beard, I cannot take the time to ascertain. I take a nervous step back.

"OK, Boomer," I tell him, trying to gauge his intent. I don't know from goats.

He simply resumes chomping on grass. His bell goes *plink*.

Many blocks out here are empty, but they're already platted.

Dirt roads form a complex grid but with only a smattering of houses here and there. Each lot will be twenty-five feet wide. It had all been planned in advance, so it is unusual to see single, narrow houses standing alone in open fields with sheep lumbering around. This section of town is like a big green bowl below Twin Peaks. Sutro TV Tower should be right about there.

Looking back at Ben sitting in the front seat of the Aerocar, I take a clear shot of him with my phone. He's not watching me. It's an adorable picture.

Finally, I jump back into the car and thank Ben for his indulgence. We drive past the gothic and lovely Clark Mansion at 19th and Caselli Streets—a friend of mine used to live in an apartment there in 2006. It stands alone.

We're in desperate need of lunch so I drive us down to Castro Street and park the car in front of 584 Castro street, at what for me would be the mailbox place and Worn Out West, before they folded last year. The building was always ever a standard two-unit Victorian house, but now it has people living in it and nothing else. "Downtown" Castro Street, such as it is, exists entirely on this block. A creamery, butcher, hardware store, candy store and fruit stand occupy the storefronts. There is a café restaurant though, about where Wells Fargo should be. It's called Weiler's and we have beer, minestrone soup and dark rye bread warm from the oven with fresh butter, which simply melts in our mouths.

"So you want to work for a railroad," I say to Ben as we down our beers, waiting for soup. "I think that would be a good idea."

"They occasionally post open positions in the want ads, and I apply to each one. Have not yet been granted an interview. I don't want to sound paranoid, but I wonder if Barney fields any potential callers and runs them off. It would be like him. Beyond Barney, I have no references in this city."

"Did you leave on good terms at your old place in Chicago?"

"Oh, yes. They were sad to see me go. Maybe the employment clerks don't want to go to the expense of long-distance telephoning on a hunch. Or maybe I just don't have the chops yet to qualify. But I sure aim to."

"Where I come from, they say it's all a matter of who you know."

"Yeah, that seems to be the consensus."

"We'll get you hooked up. Meeting people is easy once you get the hang of it. The secret is to not actually appear to want anything from them, but to be casual and off the cuff."

I got casual and off the cuff coming out of me in droves. My problem is, I can't seem to get beyond it to the next level.

"What are your parents like?" I ask.

"Typical American Christian family: devout, praying before every meal, not always a lot of food on the table so we were glad for what we had when we had it."

And I look around and for the first time realize that all the people I've encountered in 1906, with only one or two exceptions, are thin. Food isn't necessarily a given.

Ben dutifully asks about my family, and as always, I have to be vague and generalize. Father *in absentia,* wonderful mother. Two sisters, each with their grown kids.

Ben finally mentions that he has a younger sister named Charity. He seems uncomfortable bringing the subject up. His body language goes so tense suddenly I stop fiddling with melted butter and lean in and listen.

"When she was a baby, she came down with infantile paralysis."

Having said what he said, it is apparently incumbent upon me to offer something to soothe him, although I'm not entirely sure where this is going. I tell him I'm sorry.

"I was told to stay away from her, because the ailment is catching. Most of our neighbors don't even know about her, and amongst ourselves we don't speak of it."

This revelation is plainly hurtful. I'm getting waves of something deep inside him, it takes me a moment to add it all up in my head. Infantile paralysis must mean polio and Ben's primary emotion here is a deep, bruising shame.

"Does Charity attend school?" I try to keep it light.

"Oh good lord, no. It would be impossible. We keep her in a box in her room and my mother must feed her every day. At night I can hear her moaning. But I never go in there. We don't talk about it."

Despite my horror, I sense I must acknowledge that he's shared such a severe pain point with me.

Not giving a fig about protocol, I put my hand atop his from across the table. "Ben, I'm so sorry. Thank you for telling me. I'm sure it's a source of great pain for you and your family. Someday they'll find a cure for polio, I bet you a million dollars."

He appreciates this, and nods absently, his gaze distant.

Jesus. They keep her in a box?

With the overall tone of lunch pretty much shattered and there being literally nothing to see in this Castro, I feel let down. But we're well fed and relaxed, and I sense Ben is really enjoying an afternoon off on a Monday for a change. It's a bit of stolen time for him—and it certainly is for me.

Failing anything better to do, I head us back into town in the motor car. It cranks up just fine, and I manage a successful u-turn on Castro since there's no traffic to speak of.

By the time we get back into the traffic and chaos of downtown, back onto the cobblestones of Market Street, I'm feeling my oats with the car. I got this. Nevertheless, I'm more than happy to surrender it to the bell captain, delighted I didn't bang it up. I collect my deposit, minus the $3, grateful to have money back in my pocket.

Up to the room we take a nap together, continuing our sinful behavior from the night before. It works well. Ben is deft and responsive; he handles curves like a Ferrari and I somewhat chuckle in amusement, reflecting back on similar activities with David Meisenhoelder, who's pretty but drives like a Chevy Suburban and probably always will.

We sleep for quite a while. When we do stir, it's getting dark.

Ben sheepishly suggests Spreckle's Rotisserie Grill, on the 15th floor of the Call Building. It'll be expensive. It's the pinnacle of fine dining, literally on the roof of the world.

The twenty-one-story building, just a few steps down from the Palace, is the tallest on the West Coast. Gothic and fabulous, stone spires and cornices all the way up.

And it still exists today, horridly bastardized. They chopped off the top, removed all adornment and left it clad in liver-colored slab, neutered and sad, lost in a sea of gleaming glass buildings.

Tonight though, in 1906, it is the living end. A blaze of light and sculpted stone. At street level, windows show passers-by the printing presses of *The San Francisco Morning Call*, the machines thundering and men feverishly toiling, covered with ink in the basement.

Through the ornate rococo lobby, an elevator man delivers us to the 15th floor restaurant.

The eatery is a completely round room with windows facing every direction. It reeks of taste. People are sparse in number, being so early, but since we're so seriously underdressed, I'm glad for it. A string quartet is playing soft classical music and Ben and I are escorted to a table for two overlooking the east, toward the ferry building, far enough from the musicians that it's quiet, yet the music forms a charming background for us.

The maître d' tries to hide his scorn. The way we're dressed, I bet he wonders if we're going to dine and dash.

As I settle in, and before looking at the menu, I marvel that the east end of Market Street, in what nowadays would be a relentless jungle of fifteen- and twenty-story buildings, is quite low and open. It's littered with small wooden structures and billboards for cigars, beer, hardware, and guns, and gives that end of Market Street an entirely different, small town appearance.

We're in San Francisco's tallest building, on the highest public floor. Above us are six further stories, most assuredly given to executive offices of the newspaper. Those offices must be exquisite, with commanding views over all creation.

Our menus are hand-typed, listing "Specials for To-Day," and despite being exceedingly upscale, has prices that, for me, can't be beat.

We select a bottle of wine, and our conversation becomes surprisingly intense. The tables immediately adjacent to us are empty, being early on a Monday night.

I'm curious to know what happened to Ben in Chicago. Why he had to leave. So while we wait to order, chewing on some sourdough bread, I steer him around a little bit.

We have to lean in, and try to whisper, as this sort of conversation is not one to be undertaken lightly. Maybe it's not the right time and place, but we eventually get our tones, positions, and focus just right.

"Have you done this before?" I ask. Meaning sex, with a man.

"Yes. Back in Chicago. I grew up with a fellow named Charles. We were best friends from the time we were small. Once we became teenagers, we'd eventually get to roughhousing, playing around. Truth or dare."

I watch Ben grow softer as he speaks of this. He has a dreamy, far-off look in his eyes.

"One day during a snowstorm, we were in his parent's bedroom. We were fourteen, the windows were white, frosted over. The room was a blaze of white light. I looked at the naked form of another man in that light; it will always remain with me." He seems to shudder, and inhale sharply. "Charles showed me his, so I showed him mine. My heart was pounding so hard, I couldn't breathe. I thought my chest would burst open.

"And I touched it."

Ben leans back, takes a breath. Like it's long been some wonderful secret he thought he'd never share.

Of course, just then, a waiter in a black and white tuxedo approaches to take our order. We each get pork chops breaded in mushrooms, and he leaves again.

But Ben seems eager to continue, and I'm anxious to hear.

"It started slowly. We'd dare each other to do more, until it quickly became a ritual. Every Thursday when his mother was at the grange, we'd go into his parent's room, with his sister just down the hall. At first, we'd just touch. It was like we were each hoping the other would dare to do more." He's shocked to say it out loud. Like it's the sort of thing never undertaken before by two men in the history of the world.

"It sounds heavenly," I say. I'm certainly drawn in, and near to breathing heavily myself.

He notes my approval and says, "The touches became bolder, until soon it was like we expected it of each other. Demanded it. We became brave. Still, it was weeks before we let our guard down enough to . . ."

He looks around furtively. It's like he doesn't want to say it out loud. Not only because we're in a public place, but because he's talking about magic. To expose it to air would tarnish it.

I'm rapt. I also feel a sadness, because it's been so very long since I've found magic like that. For me sex became a familiar habit long ago.

"One day I kissed him on the mouth." His eyes look to burn just a little bit. "Charles didn't like that. He pulled away. Next Thursday, when I went to his house, his sister said he wasn't there, didn't know when he'd be back."

I can picture that deep pain.

"It was awkward for a good six months. Gradually we began to hang out again and it wasn't long before we were at it once more. But I learned not to try to glean another smooch from him. It was a boundary he couldn't cross, and it made me sad. But there was so much we could still do and did.

"Eventually we stopped. He began dating girls."

"Did you love him?" I dare to ask.

"Actually? No. I didn't. He was my best friend, sure, but no matter how exciting it was, it wasn't anything I've ever confused with love. I'm lucky, I guess. There wouldn't be anything sadder than me pining away after Charles as he moved on and, eventually, got married. I was best man at his wedding.

"I realize I'm lucky," Ben continues in a stronger, more confident voice. "He never made fun of me, he never made me feel like something was wrong with me, even though there clearly was. He understood how I felt about men and once told me he felt that way too a little, but that he thought about women a lot more."

Randy teenagers, looking for any place to stick it. I'm sure it's a common story. I wonder how many straight men have resorted to this in their youth, and how they might feel about it now. Some must be consumed with guilt and hate.

"So I wasn't in love with Charles, no. Yet standing there at the altar with him, watching their families all around and then as they left for their wedding night upstairs I became unbearably sad. I realized I'll never find a life like that. Because of how I am."

I can only imagine the strangling isolation he must feel.

Our pork chops arrive. It's a good moment to fall back to something as grounding as eating. The food's delicious; fresh, simple. Nothing drizzled and no shiitake reductions of any kind.

Ben continues, though. "The night of the wedding I slunk

off and roamed the area until all hours. I decided then that I would just have to face my situation head on and no sense kicking about it.

"But life has a way of being funny. I ran into Old Man Gustavsson. He's a farmer way down the road toward Berwyn. He's an old drunk and doesn't keep himself in very good stead, socially or physically. Yet he took me into his barn—it had to be two in the morning—and he had a bottle of rye and gave me swigs. Wasn't long before I figured out what he was after.

"I let him. It hurt. It . . . it took a long time. He was disgusting There were cows and horses in there; it smelled bad. He smelled bad. I felt so dirty. It was nothing like it was with Charles, but then I reckoned I'd never have the experience again. So I actually tried to savor it. I vowed I would treasure the gift that Gustavsson was giving me. I thanked him for it and left, knowing I would never be thus gifted again.

"I walked the long walk home and told myself to say goodbye to the idea of being with a man, ever. Life with another man? I knew it was never going to happen. How could it?

"So I worked hard at the savings and loan. And I eventually met Emily. Nice girl. Plain, perhaps—I know that shouldn't matter—but I look at what a girl is, and, for me, it just doesn't add up to something I would wish to utterly devour. Like I see when I look at another man."

"Trust me, Ben, I know *exactly* what you mean."

He's near tears again. "What's wrong with us? What is it that causes this hideous miscreation within us? It isn't right . . . "

"Ben," I begin, "I happen to know that it's perfectly natural. It can be found in all species and has been there since the beginning of time. Society doesn't get it? Well, to hell with society. You have to be the person you're meant to be."

"But what about God?" he asks.

Oh, shit.

"God made us this way," I reply. "End of story. Otherwise it wouldn't be."

"Do you think it's the devil? Like they say it is?"

"*Psht*. No, Ben it is not the devil." I look around quickly to ascertain no one is within in earshot. "Forty-five minutes ago I gazed into your eyes while we did what we did. You, also, were gazing into my eyes. Was Satan in the room with us in that moment? Is that how you feel?"

I'm pushing him. I doubt anyone in 1906 would talk to him like this, in San Francisco or anywhere else. I'm getting in his head and it might be inappropriate, but I have a plan. I want to get through to this person, because he won't have access to a perspective like this ever again. It will literally not be invented for another fifty years.

So I ask him again, softly: "Was the devil between you and me just now?"

His mouth is open. His brain is going places it's probably never been before. He shakes his head no, ever so slightly.

So I continue: "No. Satan was not in the room with us. I saw the look in your eyes, too. Even here right now, on the fifteenth floor . . . this is the exact opposite of the devil. It's beautiful. It's a wonderfully natural part of being human. Further, it doesn't hurt anyone else. Two people just loving each other—that's what God has chosen for us. There is no bad attached to it. It is pure good.

"Aw, Ben, if I were clever enough, I could almost remember the name of a doctor in Berlin who wrote a book about it. The Germans were discussing it openly as far back as the 1860s. I wish I could cite specifics, but it's out there. In it, the doctor described how men can be attracted to other men, women can be attracted to other women, and it's all perfectly natural. I believe it's part of God's plan, even if society as a whole hasn't caught on. Might be a while. But you're going to be fine. I know this."

Ben ponders that for a moment. The furrowing of his brow is less. Perhaps my words have found a place in his mind. I decide to let it ride; this is getting way too heavy.

"So what finally caused you to abandon Chicago? Did it have to do with . . . all this?"

"Yeah." He sounds glum again. I'm sure the subject does not bring happy thoughts.

"My marriage to Emily was all set. We'd picked a date, but I couldn't do it. I lost my nerve. I'd saved enough money that I could come to 'Frisco and start all over."

"I'm glad you did. Welcome!"

We toast with our wine glasses and each take a sip.

"By the way. Do people here really call it 'Frisco?"

"Sure. What else would they call it?"

"A'aight . . . "

Once we're out on the street again, Ben suggests we go to a show.

"We can start at the Alcazar," Ben says. "They're the best but might be sold out. All the theatres open their fresh material on Monday nights, so they're usually real busy."

The Alcazar is where the Apple Store is. They're showing *Are You A Mason?* which promises to be the "riotous farce of the year." But they're already sold out.

"No need for worry," Ben says, "we'll just try the Alhambra."

Eddy at Jones Streets is bit of a hike for us. *Queen of the Highbinders:* "A gigantic production of Theo Kramer's masterpiece!" They have seats. Ben pays.

Epic and grand, once again. We're seated on the main floor and the play is a well-costumed drama of an Englishwoman trekking through the wilderness of Albania. I'm not particularly drawn in, but for fifty cents I figure we're doing all right. Unlike the Orpheum, the audience is comparatively well-dressed and respectful.

Until they're not. Midway through the performance, rude

shouts emanate from the balcony behind and above us—more than once—greatly upsetting the entire house. A teenage boy is uttering profanities and barking and shouting with increasing frequency and it's getting seriously awkward. All patrons are getting rattled; so are the actors. The play goes on until a full eruption takes place in the balcony. A man, apparently having had enough, tries to scruff the boy out of the theatre, only to be set upon by dozens of angry youths. Suddenly everyone is on their feet, the actors have stopped, and a roiling raucous battle takes place up above.

"This is so rude," Ben says. We're standing, as is everyone else.

"Actually the poor kid probably just has Tourette's."

"What on earth is 'too retz'?" Ben asks.

"It's a diagnosed thing. People shout and beep and can't control it."

"Whatever it is, people like that shouldn't be out in public." He's glum and perturbed, and probably triggered right now.

I almost dislike Ben in that moment, my mind once again centering on Charity at home in a box. These are different times. Parts of the past are just ghoulish, and old prejudices will live mean and die hard. Society doesn't even begin to see the light of day on such matters as sexuality and empowerment for the disabled until, paradoxically, at the very time tact and chivalry disappear for good.

They are in no way mutually exclusive—I think society just missed a stitch. Someone should study that whole equation and put it right.

From what we can make out up in the balcony, the man, the ejector, becomes the one ejected—score one for Generation 1906—and the youth regain control of their section of the theatre. The apprehending man seems to have fled.

People take their seats once more amid a hubbub of musings and the play eventually resumes.

I find it decidedly weird. The play isn't particularly remarkable beyond the upset in the house.

We exit the theatre to find many of San Francisco's finest shoving teenage boys with nightsticks. The ruckus is clearly about to fire back up again, with Ejector Man leading the charge. Ben and I scurry away, free of the mess, happy to get distance from it.

Safely away with no further interference, I'm feeling fine and dandy. It's about 9:45. I suddenly get an idea.

"Maybe now's as good a time as any to try out the Barbary Coast."

Ben gulps. "I suppose so," he says casually, but I know he's feeling anything but cool at the idea.

"Shall we?" I ask again, just to make sure.

"All right." He sounds a little nervous, but I detect a certain determination in his voice. I feel excitement, and a little thrill of dread.

The Barbary Coast is lawless, evil and utterly without redemption. Murders take place almost nightly and the police don't even bother. It is dangerous, mob-run; a warren of sin and decadence. Saloons, dance halls, gambling, drugs and prostitution, a knot of city blocks spilling out in all directions from Pacific and Montgomery Streets.

I wouldn't dare go there alone. But having Ben with me makes me feel bolder. I have to see it.

As we head away from the Alhambra and make our way to the Forbidden Place, I ask Ben what he knows of the Barbary Coast, and what our risks are.

Ben speaks in clearer and stronger terms than I've ever heard him do. Frankly, I'd started to think of Ben as the tourist here and me the guide. In this following exchange, he briefly and firmly turns the tables as we walk.

"Never allow anyone access to your drink."

"I was told that. But why?"

"Patrons think the Barbary Coast exists solely to provide sinful pleasure and liquor to them. The actual reason the Barbary Coast exists is to separate said patrons from their money, by means both fair and foul. They'll dump any number of things into your drink to incapacitate and rob you—sometimes nothing more exotic than a drop of liquid nicotine that'll have you doubled-over and retching within seconds. And *pouf*. Your pockets'll be empty, and you'll be dumped out into a horse trough.

"Patrons go to the Coast thinking they're looking over a menu of delights. What they don't realize is that, in fact, *they* are the menu. How much money do you have with you right now?"

"I don't know; about seven dollars?"

"Put it in the bottom of your sock," Ben suggests, and we stop and each lean against a light standard and shuffle money into our shoes. I hate the sticky, clinky feeling of change under the pads of my feet. It's going to drive me crazy, but I consider it a worthy cause.

We press on, nearing the actual Barbary Coast of yore. This is dangerous. I'm psyched.

The buildings are much the same as all the rest in the vicinity; 1870s two-story brick structures with arched windows. But the district is ablaze with electric lightbulbs, and come-hither signs, promising all manner of devilish delights within.

It's all men. No women would be caught out on these streets at night. Oh, they're here. But they're all inside. Upstairs. Wads of them.

Liquor establishments of various types fill every storefront in the Coast. Saloons and beerhalls, one after another, each blaring discordant music played on calliopes or melodeon reed organs or even live bands. As it's only Monday night, it's not particularly populated, but the men we see in the area are a microcosm of San Francisco's sin-set, from the well-dressed and ready to pay to desperate wretches circling the boundaries of *delirium tremens*.

Ben leads me into the first establishment we come to. The Billy Goat, it's called, but we don't go much beyond the front door. It stinks inside and looks like what they call a "deadfall": wood planks laying atop beer barrels, sawdust on the floor, no music, serving only cheap beer and even cheaper wine, often tainted. It smells funky and seems menacing. An enormous woman, in striking contrast to the thinness of the age, is stomping about, obviously in command of the place.

Deadfalls serve those with hardly any money. As such they reek of desperation and danger. We see women in here, working the floor as waitresses, or trying to get men to buy them drinks. Given the condition of the place and status of the patrons, you can just imagine what these women look like. It's seriously unwell, and the many suspicious leers from the grizzled men inside cause us to do an immediate about-face and leave.

Further along Pacific Street, we see a bar called The Hippodrome and go in. Much better. A live band is playing ragtime, each musician smartly dressed. It's fairly well lit, and while there's still sawdust on the floor, it looks like it's been freshly laid. The men are dressed a little better and the beer looks legit. We order bottles, though, not draft. Safer.

Here we see more women of the Barbary Coast. Paid women, they're the main attraction, as barmaids, dancing partners, or what you will. The staircase going up the back of the hall is well traveled, people going up or down in heterosexual pairs.

Ben and I stand at the ornate wood bar, a huge, heavy affair, carved and fabulous. We try to look casual and blend in. I'm sure we look like complete targets.

A young woman comes over and tries to get with us. Her yellow dress is tight in the bodice, accentuating her rack. She's all bustles and cleavage, feathers, garish make-up and a big, silly hat.

"Good evening, gentlemen. Buy a girl a drink?" She's coquettish, and good at it. She don't know she's playing to the wrong audience. I'm actually kind of thrilled.

"That's a fabulous dress," I tell her and she recoils for a brief second—but then laughs and bats me lightly on the arm.

"I like you. What's yer name?"

"Mark. And this is Ben."

Ben is visibly squirming at this point. He looks like he wants to run away, fast.

"Well, boys, I'm Iris. Got plans for your evening?"

"We do," I say. I'm actually thrilled to be having an interaction like this. "We aim to get liquored up, then I'ma take Ben here back to the Palace Hotel and throw him a nice, juicy bone. He likes that. Dontcha, Ben?"

Iris, to her credit, doesn't miss a beat. She laughs loud, a sparkling, hooting laugh. Ben, however, has lost the will to live and is near to sinking to the floor in a puddle.

"Tell ya what, Iris. We'll buy you a drink if you can tell Ben some safe places in this city to meet quality men. He's a good kid. He just needs to meet the right people, know what I mean?"

"That he does, honey. I'll take a bourbon." Her hands are on her hips and her head is back in laughter and she looks righteous.

I buy her a drink for twenty-five cents, hoping Ben doesn't lose consciousness.

"Thank you, Mark," she says kindly, and tosses her bourbon back like a pro.

"Now," she begins, "The Dash, back on Pacific between Kearny and Stockton, is about the best place you can go in this town." She's explaining it to Ben, who's crimson and trying to heed the words from this fierce woman. "It just opened. I'm not saying you need to be an entertainer there—frankly, I think that's a bit out of your league. What you'll want to do is get to know the other patrons. San Francisco's a big town. You're cute. I bet you'll make out like a bandit. Just watch your back and keep your eyes open. You'll be all right."

"Thank you, ma'am," Ben responds, practically mumbles, I doubt he's making eye contact.

"Thank you, Iris," I say somewhat more brightly. "You've been a big help, and may I say you're looking particularly smart this evening."

She laughs again. She knows it's bullshit.

"Needs work, but I'll take it. See ya around, boys." Iris moves down the bar. She saunters over to a gaggle of her friends and is obviously telling them all about the new guys in the corner, waving her hand in our direction, talking fast. The other women glance over, mostly with intrigue and good humor. One looks at us with open disgust, but she's ugly and her mama dresses her funny.

I set about getting us more beer and risk a look at Ben. No longer crimson but white, he accepts his bottle and takes a good long draw. I don't think I need to muddy the waters with a lot of talk at this point. I just let him marinate. Hoping he's not pissed as hell right now.

The music's fun, if a bit loud, the saloon only somewhat occupied.

I'm looking the other way when, seemingly without notice, a man in heavy, turn-of-the-century business attire has sidled up to Ben and is handing him a calling card. Ben stiffens in quiet alarm; I lean in to hear what his angle is. Immediately my hackles are up.

"Finest girls on the Coast," I hear him saying. Ben timidly takes the card.

The man claps him on the back and turns to get him a drink.

Bad move.

I step closer and stick out my hand. It interrupts the man's focus enough that he grasps it, we shake hands, and I look into his eyes. I'm gazing into a dangerous, treacherous soul. But he's exuding calm confidence. He's smooth, whatever he is. He's also a great deal bigger than we are.

"How about you, my friend," he asks. "Would you like to meet some fine young ladies?"

"Actually, I think we'll be good on our own, but thank you."

"You're just being bashful. C'mon with me, both of you, I've got people for you to meet!" And he starts physically steering us to the door. He's strong. I resist, while also casting a glance at the bartender to see if he's hearing this. He's simply watching, wiping (rather than actually washing) dirty glasses. He's amused.

We're on our own. I'm unaccustomed to being put in a position such as this; I'm normally clever enough to avoid them completely. I feel fear. A sharp, unfamiliar feeling in my belly.

I wanted to go to the Barbary Coast. Is this the price of admittance?

While part of me wants to throw up or run away, an amazing surge pokes through my bourgeoning fear. I am unfamiliar with this. But I refuse to admit defeat so early in our adventure and by one of the oldest tricks in the book.

"Look, pal, we're not interested." I squirm out from around his arm, staring him down with forces heretofore never felt by myself. I'm surging. And from me, at least, he starts to back down. But he's still got a pretty good grip on Ben. Probably has a gun, too.

In a move that surprises the hell out of me, Ben whirls and gets in the man's face.

"Leave us be." He's staring the man down pretty good on his own and inwardly I'm like "Go, Ben!"

But instantly another man has moved in, even bigger than the first.

"You're not being very neighborly, pal," he says lightly, but with unmistakable menace.

We're kinda screwed. We're in a four-way stand-off. We have no idea what to do next. I'm afraid but also guttingly disappointed: We've only been on the Barbary Coast for five minutes and already we're licked. It just isn't fair.

Iris casually saunters over, with seductive walk and cheerful calm.

"Beat it, Milo. These boys are with me. How you holdin' up, Ben?"

"Fine, ma'am," he answers, apparently not noticing it was a rhetorical question.

"I thought Xeni told you to work the other end of the street," Iris continues. She's relaxed and commanding, keeping it very friendly on the surface. But she's evidently got some heft to what she's saying. "So why don't you just run along and take it back to Thalia's?"

She's a petite woman, but the men attend to what she says. They seem deflated. Not scared but perhaps a little bit bashful.

"You gentlemen have a nice evenin'," the one who started it all says to us in a humble way, doffing his bowler ever so slightly with the tip of an upraised thumb.

They slink out. Whoever Xeni is, they're afraid of him.

"Iris, you're a sweetheart," I say, flooded with relief and admiration.

She bats my arm again. "Aw, listen. You'll get the hang of it around here. But how's about another round for old time's sake?"

I'm more than happy to oblige. I get three bourbons, and the bartender pours one for himself, too. We toast, and knock 'em back. In the presence of Iris, I feel no alarm over an open drink.

"We might shuffle along," I muse, to no one in particular.

"I hope you'll come back. I could teach you boys a thing or two." Iris looks seductive again, her hips forward in her bodice and tongue just ever so slightly at her red-painted lips.

I want to give her a hug, but I'm sure that's not done. So I doff my bowler and give her a slight bow, and Ben does likewise.

"Hope you have a nice evening, ma'am," Ben manages to stammer, and we retreat from the hall.

Out on the street we don't see any sign of the two men, which is good.

We pass another deadfall only to find two roughish individuals beating the hell out of another, smaller man. Others on the street stop to watch in amusement, albeit from a distance. We're the fools who walked right into the scene unknowingly. The two men pick the third one up and throw him directly at us—we dart sideways to avoid getting knocked down, and the small fellow skids, face-first, across dirty cobblestones. I'm thinking running away would be good, but Ben, bless his heart, reaches down and actually helps the little man back up.

The victim nods a quick "thanks" and then puts his bloodied head down and runs back over to his assailants like a battering ram and headbutts them, hard. They grab him by his oily hair, yank his head back savagely, and haul him back into the deadfall, hugging each other, and suddenly they're all roaring with laughter.

Ben has blood on his hand, which, failing anything else, he simply wipes on his trousers.

We keep going. Finally I ask, "Do you want to look at the place Iris told us about?"

"I guess so," he says. He starts trudging down the street in that direction. And I do mean trudging. He looks like he's going to the gallows and is in a hurry to get it done.

The Dash looks the same as the others from the outside.

But inside the doors, we come upon quite a shock, even for my road-weary sensibilities.

Drag queens. Female impersonators. Flouncing around, they look like a damned good approximation of Iris herself. A calliope is playing a dirge-like air, it isn't a good quality apparatus; it frankly looks like it has seen better days and happier environs. The place is cheap and sparse and there aren't too many men in there: The ratio of performers to patrons is sadly disproportionate. I lean into Ben, allowing physical touch in public for the first time. I want him to know everything will be all right.

He's horrified. But I think he realizes, slowly, as disgusted as he might be, he's finally found a place where he could meet men who like men. He now sees a hole in the fabric of society, one into which he might slip and find connections. It will be dangerous. He could fall to sin and drugs and even drag, selling himself just to find love.

Well, it is what it is. He's found home. I brought him to it. I opened a new pathway for him.

The Dash will probably not survive the week, but now Ben knows such places exist. There will always be one or another such establishment in the future. There always are somewhere.

Ben doesn't want to stay, and I don't blame him. So I walk him far from the place at a good, steady clip.

"Always remember what Iris said," I say quietly, still leaning in close. "It's the other patrons. That's who you want to meet."

"I know," he says glumly. His shoulders are up again.

We need drinks. Further on, we decide we're up to facing the Bella Union, the one visible on Portsmouth Square. It's huge, and disappointingly sleazy. A hoochie can-can dance roars on the stage and all the tables are walled off from each other, much in the fashion of the cubicles at Ritch Street Baths. It's loud. The goings-on there are sure to be deeply unsavory and unsettlingly heterosexual, but we're ensconced at a table in our stall watching the show.

Taking no risks, we order our own bottle of rye and two glasses. Hours pass as we get drunk, beaten down by noise and catcalls and flashes of well-lit cooter.

It's the Barbary Coast. We're in one of the most venerable of its institutions, and I wanted to say I'd been there.

We'd have left long ago but feel it's our duty to finish off the booze.

By the time I pour the last of the whiskey into Ben's glass, I'm wobbling, slurring and feel that the universe owes me significantly more alcohol *tout de suite*. That's how I get. More begets more. But even in my emplasticated state I realize I'm in a dangerous place with a man in tow who seems to be my responsibility now.

I grab hold of Ben, who's in no better shape than I am, and we stagger free of the Bella Union, unharrassed, the experience ultimately a success.

I'm hammered; Ben's hammered; but here we are sloshily wending our way through this San Francisco I've wanted my whole life to see. Once again down Kearny to the hotel, it's all become my personal stomping ground and I experience pure joy.

Back to the Palace we get into bed and put out the Edison light, but I need to make sure he's OK after the culture shock I threw his way tonight.

"You doing all right?"

"Yeah. Just a lot to take in all at once."

"I know."

"Don't you want to be with me?" he asks.

"Huh?" I'm thrown by the question.

"You spent a lot of this evening trying to pawn me off onto other people. Don't you want me around?"

"Oh, Ben . . ." Shit. This could get ugly. "Sure I do. But I won't always be here. I might have to go to Los Angeles soon, about a writing assignment."

"Yeah?"

"Yeah. I mean, do you want to settle down right away? Fall in love? I'm assuming you've come to a place like San Francisco to build up friends, to have some fun. You need to get it wet. Dip your wick."

"It's true. I have had sex with three men now. I want more."

"And you shall have it. You're a fine, decent man, Ben. We just gotta get you into a decent crowd."

I'm frankly surprised and a little let down that Ben doesn't profess mad love for me on the spot. Oh, it would be extremely incommodious, to say the least. But it would have been good for my drunken ego right now.

I'm feeling chuffed enough, actually, that I haul out my iPhone. Ben is near to passing out, so I put the EarPods into his own cute, adorable ears and queue up my two current favorite songs: "My My My!" and "Fight for Me."

He listens. I feel goosebumps form on his arms as he's wrapped in full, rich music, completely alien to him.

"They sound negro!" he yells out from under his EarPods.

But he's in bliss. I can feel it. These two particular songs are my everything right now, and they are fierce. And I get to share this with Ben in 1906 against all the rules and it's good.

After that we snuggle under the covers. I find comfort in Ben, and he in me.

15

Tuesday, April 17, 1906

Ben gets up early and heads to work. It's only our second day together but it already feels like habit. Comfortable. We don't say much, just sigh a lot and take turns in the bathroom.

Ben decides to get his own breakfast on his way. I'm willing to bet he's feeling awkward about how I'm always throwing my money around.

I linger in bed before I decide to do more walking. I press the room buzzer and order breakfast and a paper from the man who appears at my door; I climb back in bed with a copy of *The Morning Call* and eat my eggs and ham.

This whole trip feels like I've been traveling the same tracks back and forth, Kearny and Market Streets, and this morning shall be no different. I decide I owe it to myself to get an inside look at these peoples' city hall building. It won't be around much longer—this will be my only chance, after being closed on Sunday.

First, I stop by the Opera House at Fourth and Mission, having to hook round back of the hotel and down a bit. It's a surprisingly squat brick building, fairly old, nothing elegant or showy, with the ubiquitous arched windows and heavy black iron marquee. A kindly gentleman at the box office informs me that I can, indeed, get two of the last tickets to tonight's show: Enrico Caruso performing Don José in Bizet's *Carmen*. "They're not the best seats," he admits, "but you're in luck. All of San Francisco will be here tonight."

This morning's newspaper was all about last night's opera. It was the season-opening performance of *The Queen of Sheba*. It filled the front page of the paper and gave a complete roster of all who were in attendance, along with some quite catty remarks about how some of the women were dressed.

The name of every single human in attendance at tonight's opera will likewise be printed in the newspaper. If I go tonight, my name will appear in tomorrow's news and I worry about that for a sec, until I remember that there shall be no tomorrow's paper.

Well, that's not true: It will have been entirely written, type-set, run off and stacked in bails of fifty, ready for distribution, when fire shall take it. Plates and all.

On that score, at least, I have nothing to worry about.

With my handwritten billets safely in my breast pocket, I head down south, into the cacophony that is Howard Street, two-blocks parallel to Market, unpaved and industrial, looking in shop windows. This is more of a wholesale district. Every-one's got their shingle out: bakeries, undertakers, doctors—who have little to no actual training—seamstresses, cobblers, saloons, public bathhouses (running water is sporadic, even now; people by the thousands have to go public to bathe once a week), social organizations and meeting halls. People live above their shops. I spy an optometrist shingle, a single great eye in a Teddy Roosevelt monocle that gives me the willies.

It's about 10:30 when I angle back up to City Hall, past the Pioneer Monument once more. All is as resolute as it was the other day, only now there are men everywhere. All in wool suits with hats, looking important and busy. I see virtually no women, save for some frumpish turn-of-the-century secretarial types, and a few society women dressed to the nines, in voluminous skirts of crushed velvet in every color, mincing in and out of the Municipal Water Office or City Planning Department, visions of newly added gazebos and breakfast nooks dancing in their heads.

I just walk into the place like I own it. In some measure, as a citizen, I do.

It has me bewildered.

It's the living end. Terrazzo floors and carved would-be stone arch over me as I walk to the center of the floor and gaze up the three hundred feet to the top of the dome. It's grand and enormous, streaming with daylight, not unlike standing under the capitol dome in Washington, DC, or the current SF city hall dome.

But different. The proportions seem vaguely wrong. This is taller and thinner. And for some reason I'm reminded of how men's personal assets are all essentially the same, yet still unique to one another. This dome would feel great. It quite literally thrusts skyward.

I openly use my phone for pictures and, as I figured, nobody cares—to these people it looks like a little black notebook like everyone carries in some or another pocket.

I ascend the steps and wander hallways, under transoms and through archways and despite the glamor, there's only so much informational richness to be found in the office of the Department of Sanitation.

It's just a shame the place is toast. A goddamn shame.

Ben and I had decided to splurge and meet at the Poodle Dog restaurant for lunch at Mason and Eddy Streets, so I hop a cable car—they run so frequently—and sit inside, scooting heavily along the tracks back toward the little downtown nexus that is my new home.

He meets me exactly on time, on the sidewalk outside the restaurant.

I show him the opera tickets.

"That's great," he says. "Just *great!*"

The Poodle Dog has been there since 1856. It has pricey French food and, most importantly, is known to be the haunt of the two most powerful men in the city: Stunningly handsome Mayor Eugene Schmitz and the man who actually runs San Francisco, City Boss and municipal thief, Abe Ruef.

Abe Ruef is a lawyer and politician. He got Schmitz, a violinist and amateur composer, to run for Mayor on the Union Labor Party ticket. Schmitz became Ruef's puppet and was elected Mayor in 1902.

Ruef will later be indicted on more than sixty counts of bribery and coercion. He winds up in San Quentin Prison, and Mayor Eugene Schmitz is removed from office following years of corruption.

The Poodle Dog is where they hang out. I want to see them.

I tip extra to be seated upstairs in the second-floor dining room. Ben steals anxious looks at the men as they hold court at what must be their usual table, many city dignitaries joining them, alcohol flowing freely.

The whole cabal would later be dubbed "the paint eaters." They're so rapacious and greedy, it's said they'd eat the paint off a house.

Ben and I are at a two-top table in the corner hearing conversations on taxes, permits, slush funds and liquor licenses. The city officials are so drunk and loud it's impossible not to listen. These men have nothing to worry about. They've got a strong, epic city sewn up tight and haven't a care in the world. Other than the occasional state regulations officer showing up unannounced, what's the worst that could happen?

Ben and I enjoy a lunch of rabbit in white cherry sauce, with a bottle and a half of wine. We eat mostly in silence, as we monitor our little floorshow.

Having gotten myself tipsy, as I leave, I decide to shake their hands: Eugene Schmitz and Abe Ruef. Ben pleads that I don't, but I wander off and barge over to the most powerful table of men on the West Coast. Probably weaving as I walk, surprised at my newly found balls, practically clanking as I go, "Apologies, Mr. Mayor, may I shake your hand?"

A few of the gentlemen around him seem startled, and I wouldn't be surprised if more than one hand reached for the butt of a gun under the table. "Handsome Jim" Eugene Schmitz beams and stands and sticks out a meaty paw. I grasp it. He's tall. I gaze into his smiling brown eyes under heavy brows for a moment. I'm transfixed. He looks good.

"Mr. Ruef?" I turn to the man, the weasel. He remains seated and doesn't make eye contact as I shake his thin sweaty hand.

"Thank you for all you're doing for the city," I say and take my leave.

We're halfway down the stairs before Ben hisses, "I can't believe you just did that!"

Ben goes back to work, worried he'll be in trouble with Barney for such a long lunch and being a little tipsy.

I go back to the Palace and take a nap. Then I go for just one more walk around the neighborhood. I need to soak it all up, hungrily cataloguing it. I openly take pictures now. Wandering to the northeast, Sansome and Battery Streets, I stare into a bustling café with tall ceilings and people wearing garters and high hats. A sign reads: "Reserved Seating for Ladies."

Someday it'll be a Planet Fitness. Women in Spandex is a

jarring image to me normally, and in particular to me right now.

All roads pretty much lead to San Francisco's Ferry Building so that's where I currently find myself.

The last miles of the nation's mighty railroad networks must humbly downgrade to ferryboats for the final stretch to reach San Francisco. While some may consider it a frustrating geographical hiccup, it seems to me a most suitable and genial effect. After nine days on a train from Boston's Back Bay Station, a person would spend their last three-and-a-half miles gliding on a calm green bay, arriving to this crisp proud building. It must seem like entering a magical land.

For, on either side, are the boat slips that can take one straight onward, over the Pacific to the Orient.

San Francisco is the hub. It's the farthest west; the only city to the north and south; it's nestled in beauty and apparently has the most beautiful hookers the world has ever known.

I hook to the left to get back to Market and the Ferry Building. Situated right where Market Street ends is a wide plaza, which will save the terminal from the fires. If I'm right, we'll be evacuating the city by ferry boat tomorrow or the next day. I pass through the building to look at the boats. Surprisingly large steam ferries with paddle wheels and slatted white wood and hatted folk heading to Oakland. Smaller steamboats audibly chug around doing whatever it is they need to do. The water is green and the whole place smells of creosote.

I turn and look up Market. I'm standing dead center, in the heart of it all. It's a straight shot, all the way back to the basin of the Castro District, nestled in the hills.

I feel grand. The original San Francisco is starting to feel normal to me, and that's what I really, really wanted—more than anything.

San Francisco in 1906: A fast-paced, hard-working town, preoccupied with the business of the day. It is jangled and messy, chaotic, class-divided and sometimes it smells bad. A city concerned with fashion and the Dow Jones, which has recently reached the remarkable milestone of one hundred points.

Average life expectancy is fifty-five years, meaning I'd almost be at the jumping off place myself about now.

My brain tries to remind me that actually, I *am* at the jumping off place when I get back home. I manage to tell said brain to put a sock in it. I will not spoil my moment.

It works. For now. Once again.

Some day that mechanism will stop working and the emotional dam will burst, but it hasn't happened yet, and I've managed a more thorough set of distractions than any human alive so far. I aim to keep at it. If it ain't broken . . .

A fire wagon gallops past just then, a cartoonish affair drawn by four horses, clanging a bell. Red-painted water tank sloshes, flaccid hoses coiled, and hatted men bent toward their emergency with all the authority and importance that is their due.

It would be appropriate for me to start feeling anxious about what's to be unleashed on these people tomorrow, but for some reason, I'm not. Not yet anyway. The same brain device that's refusing to let me ponder Problem Zero is also blocking my feelings about this city's impending doom. It is a crude and indiscriminate mechanism.

My plan is to take Ben to Union Square tomorrow morning for the earthquakes. It will be an open space, away from falling walls and breaking glass. It should be safe for us. The trick will be goading him out of bed at 4:30 a.m. He's a heavy morning sleeper. I'll just have to tell him I have a big surprise waiting for him. Which is true. He's just not going to like it much.

At ten past six he's at my hotel room door and I let him in, and it feels damn nice and cozy, like we live here now. A stolen escapade.

"I had a pretty interesting afternoon at work today after all," he tells me. "Barney has, for the first time, entrusted me with a very important task. It's a major responsibility and I'm very excited about it."

"Well? What is it?"

"I'm not going to tell you. It's confidential, bank business." He clearly loves being able to utter that phrase, so I quell my curiosity and allow him his moment. "I need to get to the opera early," he declares. But beyond that he doesn't wish to elucidate.

Ben can and does bump up his wardrobe quite a little bit. I work myself into my dress shirt and futz with the collar; Ben helps me. With the tie in place, I feel like I can't breathe. He seems to be fumbling with something in his pocket and is throwing off strange vibes.

We grab an early dinner in the Palm Garden again—lamb with mint sauce. I notice Ben just orders the same things I do, like a puppy.

To the opera we go. The performance is at eight, but by half past seven, long before we get near the place, we see fancy horse-drawn carriages and a few automobiles lining up to discharge their passengers on the red carpet of the Grand Opera House. Its heavy queue extends all the way back to Market Street.

"I have to greet a patron personally," Ben explains. "So why don't you go in and I'll be with you in a moment." He's playing it to the hilt. I know it's part of his assignment, and I'm pleased to keep quiet and let him bask in his important task.

I hand him his ticket, and as I turn to be admitted see Ben trot off after a motorcar still waiting in line for the red carpet.

A uniformed man takes half my ticket and I find myself alone in a sea of overly dressed people in the Grand Lobby of the Grand Opera House.

What a dump. I think it was grand at one time, but this

building is quite old now. I spy worn carpets and bits of plaster badly patched, or flat-out missing. I overhear a circle of patrons discussing a brand new civic opera house, to be opened in 1909. As I wander off, I hope they haven't already paid their architect.

The men are all in black tails and tuxedos, top hats. The women are an array, anything you can think of as long as it's 1906: lines, bunting, feathers, diamonds, taffeta. Tiaras, chokers and stomachers. Everyone looks like they're in a Renoir painting.

Except for me. I almost feel as if I ought to check my heels for the presence of horse shit.

Finally Ben makes his entrance, looking chuffed and a damn sight better-dressed than me.

"Everything work out all right?" I ask.

"Like clockwork. Thank you, Mark, for this evening . . . for everything!" He's feeling good about life right now.

Soon another uniformed man is walking around on the red carpet with an ornate glockenspiel, pinging out notes, sweetly signaling we should take our seats.

Despite its age and modest curb appeal, I must say the Opera House is a thing of beauty. Most striking is the auditorium itself: It is round. Makes for a byzantine seating plan, but the acoustics are sure to be a thrill.

Ben and I hoof it up the carpeted stairs to the third balcony. Everyone's crammed in up here and it's a long way to the stage. An unadorned red velvet curtain hangs beneath the ornate proscenium and the orchestra is warming up the way they do, discordant and at low volume.

The ceiling is also a circle, with a giant plaster rosette and an immense, menacing chandelier hanging over the main floor. Guess what that's going to be doing tomorrow morning at a quarter past five?

We're given programs, fabulous to peruse. Scenes I, II, Intermission, III and IV. Pianos by Weber. Ads for oyster bars and dress shops (no prices even mentioned). An exciting opera season is planned in the coming weeks, which, regrettably, isn't going to happen.

The electric house lights dim, floodlights and footlights come up, bathing the stage in brilliance. The conductor comes forth and bows to the applause, turns himself to the orchestra and . . .

The sound issuing forth blows my ever-loving mind. *I know this song!* Every note of it!

If you had asked me if it were the overture of the opera *Carmen,* I would have looked at you like you were high. But the utter familiarity, on a cellular level, of this music, being delivered to me 113 years off-kilter is exquisite and bizarre. It is an indelible part of my childhood, here, in an alien place.

My mom always listened to it in her '79 Ford Thunderbird.

I'm so overjoyed and surprised I must be positively squirming in my seat. Ben leans over to me and whispers into my ear, "Whatever is wrong with you?"

I just turn to him beaming from ear to ear.

It's a lovely, lively piece. And Caruso, of course, is magnificent. A towering figure on stage. Superb singer. Kinda cute, with a button nose. I follow the story the best I can, marveling at the sets and costumes and pure talent on the stage before us. These people can sing! The sheer power of the unaided voices knocks me for a loop. A wall of sound, coming from well-heeled throats, can fill such a space so utterly that I feel it in my chest.

More than a few of the tunes are somewhat familiar to me, which helps ease me into the thing. Still, it gets boring at times.

Thankfully there's an intermission and we go to the lobby again to gawk at the clothes. A reporter is making his way through the well-dressed throng, taking names and making notes. He heads toward Ben and me with obvious intent, but once he gets a good glance at our attire, he visibly loses any wish to deal with the likes of us. He moves quickly past, in search of more worthy prey.

I consider a run to the men's room but don't.

Back in our seats for Scene III, it all starts to seem to go on too long. I begin to daydream and look around at the other opera goers, secretly reading more in my program. Everyone seems mesmerized, including Ben, who has a far-off look on his face.

Actually, I need to pee.

And it is here, captive and pinned down in a dense, heavily clad crowd, that true nervousness begins. I keep looking at that chandelier. At the beauty around me. The ornate carvings, the tapestries. Plaster and wood and cloth.

In ten hours it will be an inferno.

I start to squirm. Now I *really* have to pee, and there's clearly no way out without upsetting a mass of people.

I fight my battles, both imaginary and urinary, but manage to return my focus to the opera. Carmen's a capricious bitch, and I am ultimately drawn back into the story by the time Caruso shanks her with a knife (I hope I didn't just ruin it for you), and . . . that's it. The opera's over and I make a beeline for the Gents'.

Whew. As always, things look appreciably better once that's done.

But now I can't find Ben again. I just stand amid the elegant throng with no one to speak to, just wondering if Ben will come back at all. I really don't know what he's got going on.

Just as concern begins to mount, Ben finally emerges from an alcove in the lobby, looking like always. So we stand at the portico and watch people get into their carriages and automobiles at the red carpet.

After that we decide to go carousing along the Market Street saloons.

I want to soak up as much as I can. This city, both charming and dangerous, only has a few hours left.

Still, we do all right. We meet people of all sorts, have a long conversation with a couple from Potrero Hill named Hugh and Betsy. I make sure to draw Ben into the conversation—he is, ultimately, rather shy—and who knows? Perhaps he'll stay in contact with this Hugh and Betsy when things get back to normal. Ben needs friends. More importantly, he needs to learn *how* to make friends. And suddenly I find it ironic: I'm the one who's lonely and alone in my San Francisco, but as I slosh through my gallons of beer, I realize bar conversations and casual acquaintances were never a problem for me. It's something deeper that I have always lacked.

A nondescript gentleman at a tavern on Fremont Street strikes up a conversation, and we're delighted to learn that he works for the Southern Pacific Railroad. This is Ben's big chance. The man, Oliver Jacobs, only works in the switchyards, but he knows the ropes on how to get in touch with the employment office. He gives Ben a few pointers and the name of a contact. Ben's overjoyed. He writes it down with a tiny pencil and little leather-bound notebook he carries in his breast pocket, and eagerly accepts yet more beer, his spirits visibly soaring.

It's probably the best augur of success, the clearest glimmer of hope Ben has received in his five months of living here. I'm delighted I could help make it happen.

We have a little bit of trauma to get through first. I hope Oliver Jacobs survives, and that Ben survives, and that I survive, and they can stay in contact when things get back to normal.

It's time to draw the evening to a close. Liquored up and overtaxed, fear and sadness begin to overwhelm me. 'Tis not just the evening that must draw to a close, but this entire place.

Damned glad to have made its acquaintance.

It's with growing sadness that I stagger Ben back to the Palace to rest up and mentally prepare for the morning.

But then it all starts to fall apart.

Ben's drunk and is belligerently refusing to come back to the Palace. He wants to go home.

Huh? No! He can't! His neighborhood is going to collapse and burn in a heap.

"Ben, don't. Come with me." I'm forcing myself to sound gentle and calm, but inwardly I'm anything but.

He shakes me off.

"Naw, lemme go . . ." He's not being an obedient puppy now. He's surprisingly strong. I've not known him long, but I've certainly never seen him act this way. Tonight of all nights.

I'm horrified. This wasn't what I'd planned at all. He could be killed! How do I convince him to stay?

He wants to go.

When no one's looking he gives me a boozy kiss and says, "I'll see you tomorrow."

"Ben. I really think you should stay with me at the Palace tonight. It's important."

"Naw, I want to be in my house. I still like you; I just need to be in my apartment. I'll ring you on the telephone. We'll have lunsh and take a nap."

And he's gone.

I'm in shock, feeling abandoned and worried, standing alone on Market Street.

What the hell was that?

I head dejectedly back to the Palace. Nervousness is now edging toward heavy fuss, and, again, I have to pee.

I'd already set up for 4:30 a.m. coffee and breakfast for two. I'd had to cause a bit of a stir to arrange service that early, but the fifty-cent coin I produced from my pocket finally led the manager to promise he'd see what he could do.

Alone again, trying to figure out what the hell is up with Ben, I try to sleep, but by now I'm straight up scared.

Hell is only a few hours away, and I'm supposed to sleep?

I can't get Ben out of my mind, passed out in his dry-rotted wood boarding house atop ship masts and old shit.

South of Market is a deathtrap. It only has a few hours left.

16

Wednesday, April 18, 1906

The earthquakes will happen at 5:12 a.m.—two of them in rapid succession, the first one lighter, a pre-tremor; but the second no less than devastating. Things that had been knocked loose by the first will crash to Earth by the second.

I feel like I've just finally fallen asleep when my iPhone loudly launches into song, a jagged rip away from the inner peace of slumber.

I switch on the overhead light.

Just then I hear a knock at the door. "Room service." It's 4:30 a.m., pretty much on the nose.

A bellboy rolls in a trolley all covered in white linen with a gleaming silver coffee pot, and I can smell the coffee even though I have a pounding headache. I thank him for the earliness of the hour and tip him another fifty cents—"Thank you, sir!"—and hope he doesn't die in the next forty-five minutes.

I have coffee and pastries and a slice of melon. The coffee and food help revive me. I eat as much as I can and shove the rest of the pastries crudely into the pockets of my cloak, along with an apple that sticks out and looks silly. We'll want them later.

Now I have to decide whether to still go to Union Square for the earthquakes or ride them out here. The Palace Hotel was famously overbuilt to be seismically stable, and it will hold together with little damage this morning. Before the fires come.

I dress, get my shoes on, put my bowler on, and make sure I have all I expect to carry in my pockets.

I choose to stay in my room. I'm much closer to Ben's place here—that's what ultimately helps me decide.

Dawn has yet to break. It's plenty dark, even with the streetlights on.

I check my phone. 5:10. Two minutes to go.

I wait, breathlessly. Nervous. I sit at the window, trembling. My heart is thumping so loud I can hear it in my ears.

Suddenly, a jolt snaps through the building. It isn't much, just a P-wave of the smaller, first quake.

Then the small earthquake begins. It rumbles for a few seconds, I feel a slight sway in the building. Almost gentle, in a way. Then it stops.

Twenty seconds . . . here it comes.

The hotel simply, with no preamble, jerks savagely three feet to the north like it's been kicked hard. I almost fall over with my arms out. Then the havoc of the earthquake seizes complete control of the region. Man's most beloved accomplishments suddenly mean nothing. We're now in the grip of raw force. Scale: planetary.

The room sways like mad, plaster popping and glass breaking, back and forth, devoid of any pattern or rhythm. My brain dimly reflects that that's the problem with earthquakes: they've got no rhythm. They in no way allow you to maintain your dignity.

The earth shakes generally from north to south, in waves up and down. The sound of it is ungodly, and still there's no pattern to the savagery, no opportunity for man or masonry to acclimate to any specific direction or form of movement. It just jumbles and tears indiscriminately, constantly finding new directions, halting back, surging differently and never in the same way twice. It is chaos, for a hundred miles in all directions.

This earthquake is a 7.9, epicentered just off the Golden Gate. It's shallow and it's close. The downtowns of Santa Rosa and San Jose will completely collapse in the cataclysm, and they're fifty-four and forty-eight miles away, respectively.

Foreknowledge doesn't help me. My heart is pounding in my chest. I am in fear, holding on for dear life. I thought I'd try to film it with my phone, but that quickly becomes not only physically impossible, but emotionally impossible as well. It's too overwhelming to allow for YouTube right now. My hands are trembling to the point of wobbling. I'm so scared I can hardly catch my breath, and when I do it's choked with dust.

Forty-six seconds of heaving and roaring elapse, and around us, the shattering of glass and raining down of bricks, clanging church bells and the unholy roar from the Earth itself fills the air. Wood snaps. Walls buckle. Church steeples fall. Many of San Francisco's buildings have ornate cornices or gargoyles and they all come tumbling down. People begin staggering and lurching into the streets at Third and Market—the early risers; newspaper people. Soon it will be a sea of humanity, fleeing the snapping buildings.

I try to stand up, to see all I can see, out the window that I have open. It breaks. I move away from the angry shards of non-safety glass. All the lights have been out since right after the shaking started. I think. I'm really not certain.

Forty-six seconds is a long time.

I'd read avidly of the damage that would be taking place at this moment: giant fissures opening up. Streetcar rails bending and snapping. Many old wooden buildings will be collapsing now, the Valencia Hotel will topple, killing more than twenty people; San Francisco City Fire Chief Dennis Sullivan is being crushed under a wall of bricks in his own bed at his fire station —he'll later die from his injuries.

Floors are buckling, beds careening across rooms, like being on a ship at sea.

South of Market will virtually collapse. That's why I didn't want Ben to go back there. Water mains are breaking, gas lines rupturing, chimneys falling, the streets sagging and bowing. People are being buried in their beds, or unable to get through doors that are now bent and won't open.

Finally, the rumbling ceases.

My heart is pounding wildly. My ears are ringing in the sudden silence. For several more seconds, nothing happens. But soon I hear slamming doors and excited voices in the hallway. Everyone is evacuating the hotel.

Ben! Where is he right now? Is he all right?

I can't know these things. I only know that my primitive brain is directing me to leave this place at once. I calm myself enough to do an ultra-fast survey of my room. The mattress has half slithered off; windows broken; fancy old telephone on the floor, silent. I take a few flash pictures of the room, but I don't think they'll ever be anything but blurred blotches, given my current condition.

I dash to my room door, which opens appropriately, only to find myself in a pitch-black hallway. Not a single filament of Northern California's brand-new electric grid remains connected right now and I can't see a thing. So I feel my way along the corridor. All this and I never bothered to look at where the exits were? How stupid am I? But the main stairway is right across from the lifting rooms and I know the general way. I hug the wall as I move thus, joined by ever-increasing numbers of other bodies in the hall. No one's uttering a word or seeing a thing; just coughing up dust and drawing ragged breaths.

The staircase is a broad, graceful open space—precisely what you don't want to experience in utter darkness. Crowds of people are snarled up, grasping for handrails and gingerly stepping down one by one. I suppose. I can see none of it. I can only sense what the general trend seems to be.

I find myself in a mass of humanity, all savagely grasping one another, be they bare arms or some form of nightclothes. We're stumbling down the steps blindly in a large human clump. I have rich fabric in my grasp—the person seems to be large, corpulent and patently sweaty—and I dare not let go. Similarly, I feel two different people grabbing my jacket from behind, tugging it awkwardly as their gaits are halting and out of sync with each other and with mine.

We move as one and pour out into Market Street.

A bit of daylight has begun, just enough to show me that the sidewalk is a nearly impassable litter of debris and broken glass, and that the night shirt onto which I'd been clasping is being worn by none other than Enrico Caruso.

He turns to me and snatches me into a massive, odiferous hug. He kisses the top of my head and moans "*Mio dio, questo è orribile! Stai al sicuro, mio buon uomo*!" and wanders off, gingerly avoiding bricks in his slippers, still babbling, seemingly intent on going away to some other place right now.

I can only decipher that he said, "My god, this is horrible," and called me a good man.

More people are still fleeing the immense hotel, so I move down the street to help clear the way and to begin my trek towards Ben.

The ground is treacherous with bricks and crowded with

frightened citizens. People are talking volubly now, sharing their experiences, some are just moaning and crying. The result is a loud human sound, confused and outraged.

Ben is at Fifth and Folsom—that's two streets over and two streets down. But they're long blocks. I tear off in that direction, my pace slowed by stones, wires and confused persons.

The damage is startlingly random in the growing, cloudy dawn. Ruined buildings are right next to buildings that have no apparent damage at all. Many buildings stand askew, many look fine; yet virtually all windows are broken. It doesn't make any sense. Some buildings' façades have crumbled, leaving bedrooms, parlors and offices open to the morning air. I come upon many buildings that have collapsed completely, twisted, slid or otherwise pancaked.

It gets worse the further I go into South of Market. The streets themselves are pitted and flexed, having sunk several feet in places.

Telephone and telegraph poles are down, their wires sparking, tangled masses; several fissures have opened up in Folsom Street. Gas lines and water lines are busted, and from the gas lines you can hear a sharp hiss and, in many places, they jet savage flames into the broken wooden buildings.

People are pleading for help and I should stop—but I'm determined to make sure Ben is all right. I keep moving, reassuring myself that there is no shortage of personnel in the streets. Help is all around.

At each collapsed building knots of people form to pull wreckage aside and to free trapped victims, more often than not finding mangled corpses. People help where they can. Boards are shimmied and levered, bricks stacked and cribbed, time and again, amid the ambient horror I hear cries of joy, of reunion and salvation. But those not so much.

I press on, running full speed down Folsom from Fourth and stop in dread. Ben's apartment building has collapsed.

It's the second tenement from the corner. The outermost building, fronting on Fifth, has completely corkscrewed into the street and is on fire. The ground floor of Ben's building has buckled in on itself, leaving the second story only a few feet up off the sidewalk.

People are standing outside shrieking and crying. I don't see Ben among them.

"*Ben!*" I yell, several times, my hands around my mouth like at a football game. But I don't hear his voice. Fires are close; one from the left and another one is visible from behind. The air is a chaos of disjointed sounds and smoke.

Ben's apartment is halfway back in the building on an airshaft, in the direction of that fire. He might not even still be in there. He could be out and around the corner on 5th Street—I take the few seconds to dash that direction, hoping to see Ben somewhere on Fifth but I don't. I'm not seeing him. Only the corkscrewed wreckage, thirty-year-old rotted drywood, rapidly catching fire.

Which means Ben is probably still inside.

While my body is screaming for me to run away, my brain, clouded by sudden fear, fights in conflict. If there's a chance he's still in there, I have to go in and check. I'm back at the collapsed front of Ben's building and no one else is to hand. They've moved away from the flames and I can't do that yet. It doesn't seem to be an option.

It actually comes down to me? A human life? I'm not used to making a difference—back home I can't even take a stand on which restaurant we choose—yet I know I'm on deck.

I have to do this. And it may be for nothing. He could be wandering up Fifth Street in a daze right now but I cannot escape my duty to check.

I feel entirely unequal to the task, facing raw, unchecked fire. The smoke makes me heave. But what I never knew before is how *loud* fire is. And now I need to willingly get much closer than any sane person could reasonably expect.

Also unknown to me is that fire creates a fierce gale of superheated wind. A torrent of air is ripping into this broken window, dashing in to feed the conflagration. It whooshes past, eager to get in on the action.

Fight or flight? Jesus. They never mentioned *fucking freeze*—which is all I seem capable of doing. For I am locked in place. The situation is worsening by the second, acrid smoke offends my senses, and I'm looking down at the dirt and shards of glass and beyond the smell of that horrid smoke, a visceral memory of some other smell wafts into my mind with intoxicating power.

It is the heady smell of the most vulnerable, dangling participles of Ben's person.

He could be in there right now with the flames coming and suddenly I'll be goddamned if I'll let them lick Ben as I have licked Ben. I won't share him with the tongues of Hades. Only *I* get to do that.

For the first time in my life, I seem to get a mental rope around raging panic and lasso it into fear, and somehow go a step further into the unknown: I harness it all into direct action. It's a delicious process I never thought myself capable of, but neither am I controlling it. I feel my entire body surging but my brain has gone elsewhere.

I throw one leg up into the broken window frame, amazed that my higher, imperious, over-functioning brain is no longer functioning at all.

A new me, pure instinct, is only dimly aware that I've banged my head hard. I'm in someone's front parlor. It's a twisted wreck. An upright piano has slid down the canting floor, smashing all the furnishings to the lower side of the room. The floor is at a crazy angle, my shoes are slippery and it's tough going across to a snapped door and the hallway beyond.

The choking smoke is overpowering.

The hallway is twisted sideways somehow, and is apparently all that's holding the upper floors in place—and only barely. I'm saved from having to operate in total darkness by the very flames I'm trying to avoid. I see them at the far end of the corridor oozing from the other side of the wedged door, which serves as a momentary fire break. It's not going to last long.

Ben's apartment door is ajar, bent in the frame on the downhill side. I jump on it and crash through and slide down the floor right into his bed.

He's there. He's breathing, he's still warm. I think the bookshelf must have knocked him out. It's lying atop him.

The pungent smell of smoke is somewhat less in here just now, but that won't last.

"Ben!" I yell shaking him hard. He groans. Waves me away.

"C'mon, Ben, work with me here!" I give him some light slaps to the cheek and shake him again.

He's awake now. "Whoa. Wha' happenin'?"

"There's been an earthquake and fire's coming. You gotta move, *now!*"

He stirs then but is still in a daze.

"Waaaaaiiiiit. I can't find my shoooooeeeeees!"

"If there's anything you wanna grab you gotta grab it now. *C'mon!*"

He's still dressed from last night, and, unable to find his shoes, he makes hasty, flailing grabs at a few things and snatches his coat and follows me, barefoot, out into the hall.

I'm eager to get the hell out of here, my tempting of fate having been accomplished. It's time to go and the loudness of the fire is all consuming—except for some other sound. I'm tempted to disregard it, for I've done what I needed to and we're free to leave, and leave we must.

Yet within the space of half a heartbeat it becomes plain that the alien sound is human. Infant human. Baby infant human.

Helpless baby infant human. *Fuckitty fuck fuck! We don't have time for this*!

Ben hears it too and seems to be on a slightly lower fear profile than me. As such, he seems more casual as he makes a full stop in the smoky hall and quickly isolates the sound to a door on the opposite wall. It's uphill to us, and the sound is now unmistakable.

I want to get out of here! But we have to do this. It's not a question.

Ben gives me a boost up toward the uphill door. I manage to get the apartment door open. There's a baby crying in a crib on the downhill side and no one else in the room. Why is there no one else here? Did they flee, leaving a baby?

I climb up with great difficulty and peer into the crib. A swaddled infant is crying in senseless confusion. I unceremoniously snatch it and hand the baby down to Ben. I spare the briefest of moments to peer further into the apartment. Dim, smoke-addled daylight is coming in only because the building has broken open where it oughtn't, and a woman is visible in her bed. A beam has fallen upon her. She is dead.

Flames are roaring along the hallway ceiling now, tendrils of fire like a clawing hand looking for purchase. The heat is withering and the smoke insufferable. We've got to go, no matter who we find next.

We skid through the sloped piano room and back out to the window. Flames follow us. The upper story is fully involved. I'm no longer even aware of my actions. I just basically shove Ben headfirst out the broken window and wish him luck because, holding a fighting baby, I've got flames, withering heat, smoke, shards of glass and a three-foot drop to contend with.

I toss the baby out blindly—I can't see—and tackle the opening feet first.

The exact moment my shoes hit dirt, a rush of fire blasts out from the window and up my back. Metal strings in the piano sproing sickly in the blistering heat.

We dash forward into a surge of people who escort us away from the conflagration. I hand the baby to a woman as we walk. Ben, with calm normality, reaches down and presents me with my bowler from a sea of broken glass on the ground. There's nothing for me to do but to put it back on my head unthinkingly. It must have rolled a fair distance when I banged my head climbing in the window.

The woman now holding the baby says she knows who it is—where's its mother?

"She's dead," I tell her, more brusquely than I intend to.

The woman nearly faints; she crosses herself with her free hand and kisses her knuckles. The baby's still crying, and the fire is getting hotter. We move further from it. Ben hasn't any shoes. Miraculously, his feet seem thus far uninjured. I inspect my hands. They have a few light cuts from the window frame, and I pluck a few shards of glass out. It stings more than hurts. There's not a lot of blood. I am lucky.

"Does anyone have extra shoes?" Ben asks. "Size eight?"

"I have some shoes," a chubby man in nightclothes with an accent answers, ducking into his intact house across the street as we move away from the conflagration. Ben's building is fully involved in flames, an intense hellfire. The flames are reaching tall, belching smoke and radiating heat. The third building in, the one to our right, looks normal, but smoke is starting to seep out its glassless windows.

The man comes back with some shoes for Ben. They're pretty beat up and a size and a half too large but anything's better than going barefoot with all the broken glass about. Ben thanks him profusely, but the man just runs back into his house.

We move quickly to the east, away from the burning buildings, away from the dazed people, the old woman still holding the now-orphaned baby.

"This is incredible," Ben whimpers, looking around at the devastation in the growing daylight.

Amid rubble and choking smoke, Ben safely by my side once more, I get a wave of dizziness and feel for a moment like I'm going to pass out. I'm able to catalogue it as the tail-end of an adrenaline spike. I don't think I've ever had one before. It slithers through me, clouding my mind, yet my body is still accelerated and surging. This mismatch has me very sketched out as I stomp down the street with Ben, altogether unsettled and—I don't know why I know this—permanently bent into a slightly different version of myself.

I just interfered in the past. Big time. No one else was going to fish Ben out of his burning building. I did that. And don't get me started on the baby. I don't want credit for it—quite the opposite. I hope no one finds out.

Perhaps this is the real danger of time travel. For it would not have been possible for me to not perform these acts, scared though I was. It would be inhuman.

Yet I seem to still exist. We've turned north and I'm still walking up a ruined 4th Street with Ben.

My life, which began in 1970, continued appropriately enough that I should encounter David and the phenomenon of time travel and come back to 1906. I haven't vanished into nothingness. So whatever I did 113 years ago had no impact on my birth sixty-four years later, rippling back 113 years as some sort of whiplash. The world, as a whole, probably moved forward OK.

So I just try to put my mind at ease. This is complicated.

Being on a wider boulevard somehow makes me feel more

at ease. The piles of debris are further apart, there's room to move and to breathe. It's become full daylight, but smoke blots out most of the cloudy sky.

I always imagined this day being completely sunny. It's not.

Doesn't matter either way, as most of the sky is a snarl of smoke and ash. A pronounced roar and snapping sound fills the air from burning areas all around.

"Where should we go?" asks Ben.

It was always my plan to go back to City Hall to get pictures of the pre-fire devastation. There aren't many. And now that we're free of South of Market, I'm regaining my feelings of mastery over the surrounding misery. I pretty much know what's safe and what's not.

"I don't know," I answer. "City Hall?"

"That's good," Ben says, "Maybe they'll tell us what to do."

I know what we'll find there but I don't say anything to Ben about it.

My brain is so shorted out that I start to fuss on the ridiculous nature of my time spent in San Francisco of 1906. Instead of making grand circles around the city, seeing the most of everything in the allotted time, I've been trudging to and fro over the exact same territory; up and down Kearny, back and forth over Market . . . It is imprecise and silly, and a very odd thing to be concerned about right now. But as much as it's bothering me, I acknowledge that David Meisenheolder would be spitting nails at the inefficiency of it. Right now I just find it simply wry.

Fifteen arduous minutes later, we near our destination, having passed scenes of devastation all remarkably similar but no less horrific.

Ben stops in his tracks and groans loudly upon his first sight of City Hall in the distance.

The shattered dome, so high up, is denuded of stone. Hanging at disgusting and bent angles are iron lattices and twisted steel. The golden statue remains at her imperious station, but at a vulgar, sickening angle. Columns, so resolute-looking before, are now laying in the street like so many fallen logs. I've known of this image since I was old enough to look at picture books. But to Ben it is a visceral punch to the gut. He nearly crumples in defeat. I put my arm around him and guide him the long distance toward the ruined monument.

We're surrounded by others, streaming in from all sides, converging on the seat of the city's power, only to find that it has been knocked down as if it were a plaything.

Every face shows a person completely untethered and hopeless.

I thought I would freely walk around the building, but actually I can't get near it. With so much rubble everywhere, I could easily twist my ankle, so I abandon the idea. I take a few quick, unobserved pictures with my phone. The Hall of Records building looks intact, but it and all the documents within shall burn in a few hours: birth certificates, building deeds, plans of the city's water mains—which have just shattered and bled completely dry.

A mass of people has gathered in the tiny park in front. No one has the vaguest clue as to what to do. I stand close to Ben, remembering the apple and crumbly pastries I'd crammed into my pockets earlier. I give them to him unobtrusively, in this sea of unfed people. He hungrily accepts them.

A vague sense of purpose starts to build around the Mechanic's Pavilion at Larkin Street. It's the size of an entire city block. Beneath its signs—still boasting the largest all-maple roller-skating floor in the city—corpses are being taken inside. It's now a makeshift hospital. Word's already getting out; wagon after wagon pulls up and people on stretchers are carried into the pavilion. Dozens of injured are hobbling inside on their own power, seeking aid.

Ben keeps checking his watch. "I should be at my bank. Do you think it's safe?"

Even I, with some foreknowledge of the catastrophe, don't have an answer for Ben. I know only roughly what will burn, and when.

The fires that consume San Francisco don't proceed in an orderly fashion. Several different fires converge throughout the course of the day. The South of Market fires, eleven different ones, will converge and roar over Market Street at Newspaper Row from Third Street, and tear into the Financial District around noon.

The "Ham and Eggs Fire" will begin at 9:00 a.m. A woman returns to her house determined to fix breakfast at Hayes and Gough Streets, only to realize her chimney is faulty. This fire will burn to the south, through Hayes Valley, overtaking City Hall, and jumping Market Street at 9th. The Mechanic's Pavilion right in front of us, where so many dead and injured have been taken, will soon be abandoned in panic, the last people getting out just as flames engulf the building. The impressive structure will succumb in a mere twenty minutes, the dead left to the inferno.

Nob Hill will be consumed by a blaze that breaks out at 8:00 p.m. tonight in the Alcazar Theatre. It is believed to be, if you can stand it, arson.

Throughout the city the fire hydrants are dry. There is no water with which to fight. Fire wagons and trucks, still horse-drawn, can't even get out of their own collapsed fire houses.

With no other recourse at their disposal, the fire department and Army Corps of Engineers begin dynamiting buildings all over town. It is believed that demolishing buildings in the line of fire will create breaks and stop the spread of the flames. It's completely useless. It only stokes the flames, creates more fuel that burns hotter and more efficiently. But they doggedly continue blasting until they run out of dynamite, only to eventually turn tail and flee in defeat.

There are only two options for the tens of thousands of people standing around in the streets. First, make their way west to the undeveloped sand dunes around Golden Gate Park, or, second, to leave the city—south, by foot, or northeast via boats from the Ferry Terminal. Thousands make their way to the east end of the city, to the awaiting boats while Market Street, at least so far, is free of the inferno. That will change.

People, even in the non-burn areas, are afraid to reenter their houses, except in quick dashes to gather belongs. Some are shot by the police, mistaken for looters. Residents start piling their belongings in the streets. Stories circulate of folks moving their tables and chairs outside and having breakfast on the sidewalk.

We make haste back once more to Montgomery Street, to Ben's bank. It takes a good twenty minutes, and we meet all manner of humanity in the street, most are heading the same direction we are—northeast to the Ferry Terminal. People have meagre possessions with them and are scantily dressed.

Drays and hacks and cars are pressed into service to haul money and jewels and personal possessions out of the city towards the south. Some banks work to empty their vaults as quickly as they can. For those that can't, it will take ten days for the safes to cool down enough to open them again. Most often the contents are reduced to ash.

At the Montgomery Savings and Loan, they're hurriedly emptying the vault and clearing out ledgers, loading the contents into a waiting dray. The team of four horses is clearly rattled, with ears back and stomping feet. Several men stand in attendance with guns cocked. No one's going to mess with the money.

Ben has some sort of heated conversation with Barney, I'm not within hearing range or possessing of the desire to particularly care, but it appears to be intense. Barney, looking even less pleasant up close, storms over to me. Ben and I are enlisted with the task of carrying ledgers and files. We do so, hauling items to the wagon. Barney yells at me about something stupid and I nearly tell him to get stuffed. He reeks of being a prick.

Eventually the wagon drives off, the horses visibly glad to be on the move. They head north, probably hoping to skirt the fires. Barney and the armed men are riding atop the dray.

It's only 7:30 a.m.

Chunks of ash are coming down from the clouds above.

Ben starts trudging up Montgomery, seemingly with strong purpose. Then he stops, looks around, takes me up against a building and produces a leather pouch from his pocket.

"I need to show you something," he says.

"The reason I didn't stay with you last night is this." He opens the pouch and therein are jewels—a monstrous diamond necklace with rubies, all curled together in a dazzling heap.

"These belong to one of our clients. She wanted them to wear at the opera last night. When Barney found out I was going to be there with you, he handed me the responsibility of providing these to her when she arrived at the theatre. I was excited. He's finally trusting me with something genuine." His eyes search mine, possibly expecting to see enthusiasm in my face. I'm more slack-jawed, wondering where this is going.

"She wore them at the opera, made sure she was seen and admired, that the news reporters saw her, and I was charged with collecting them afterward and putting them back in her safe deposit box at the bank this morning. I . . ."

Looking into Ben's honest, earnest eyes, my brain completely spins out.

I have questions. At least fifty.

"Ben, you carried these around *all last night*?" I finally manage to stammer.

"Yeah. I figured they'd be safer with me."

It is literally the dumbest thing I have ever heard.

"Ben . . ."

I am flabbergasted. I suddenly want to bop his nose with a rolled-up newspaper.

But among other things, I sense we should be on the move. Even I don't know why at this point, my mind is still reeling.

"Ben . . ."

Nope. Words are not coming out my mouth. I'm incapable of forming them.

We just start walking again. My brain twirls, trying to align itself with Ben's line of thinking on this and coming up exceedingly short.

I have questions.

"You might have put them in the Palace safe," I say only after several deep breaths and in a soothing HR voice.

Ordinarily I wouldn't care one way or the other, but I feel protective of Ben. Like he's suddenly my responsibility. I am unused to the sensation, and frankly, right now he's not making it easy.

He's trudging in the direction of Nob Hill. It looks as it should in its pre-fire beauty, nothing seems out of place. Until I peer more closely and spot pockets of wrecked wood and plenty of broken windows.

"I just didn't think it was a good idea," Ben finally responds. "The Palace safe was robbed at gunpoint about a month ago. It was in the paper."

Well, that's at least some of the equation. I'm just about to launch into more interrogatives, trying to not openly scream, but I decide to stay mum for a while.

"I think this whole city's going to burn," Ben says.

A modest puff of Pacific sea breeze rustles past my ears and I answer, "I think you're right."

Finally I'm calm enough to be able to form the relevant

question. “Ben, why didn’t you put those items in the dray with the rest of the bank’s assets?”

He doesn’t respond right away. He just keeps walking.

Finally, he answers. “I don’t trust them, Mark. Remember what I said about Barney? He’s not right. That wagon could wind up anywhere. I’ve always thought they were damned crooks. I want to make a good impression, beyond the realm of Barney, so I made an executive decision to personally get them back into their owners’ hands.”

OK, right now I’m thinking the words “executive decision” and “Ben’s brain” do not belong in the same sentence, but I choose to let that go for now.

But Ben's wound up. He keeps speaking, breathlessly: “There could be a promotion in it for me. But not only that . . . don’t you see? The owners are rich and will be so grateful they may express their thanks directly.”

“To me” is not said by him but is clearly his operational goal. Ben's got his eyes on a prize. His face is lit with something akin to glee. He has already shifted his paradigm and is using the disaster to his direct advantage. It's a pretty risky, cagy move; it's not the direction I would have taken, but that realization hardly matters. This is our path now.

“Do you know where she lives?”

“She’s up on Nob Hill. Dorothy Sprinkles, Taylor Street at Washington.”

“So we should go there and give her the . . . stuff?”

“Yes. I want to personally place them back in her hands where they belong. It’s a long walk and these shoes are killing my feet, but the sooner we get it done the better for all concerned. I’m certain she will be very thankful.” Hope is evident in his voice.

I voice but one of the concerns swirling in my head. “How do you know they haven’t already fled?”

“I don’t. But Nob Hill’s fine. See? Look. I bet someone’s

there. Someone will hang back to mind the place, keep potential looters out, even if the Sprinkles' themselves have gone."

That, at least, is not an entirely unreasonable line of thinking. Ben does have a brain, I decide, even though he's using it in ways different than I would.

"Well, there's no time like the present. Let's do this."

But I quickly sense something's wrong. Among the varied and harried pedestrians, we've now come parallel with two men who have been half-lounging at a light standard, dressed shabbily, watching the unloading of the bank and the driving away of the dray from a distance. I was aware of them but didn't consciously think about it.

After we pass their position, they begin following us. They have an intensity that I can feel on a base level. Their sole focus is us, and they look nearly rabid.

I take Ben's arm in mine and propel us forward quickly.

"We're being followed," I whisper to him.

Ben looks back. I cringe—I'd hoped he wouldn't do that. He quickens his pace even more. I do too. The men behind us pick up their pace as well.

We're in for it.

The two men make to move in on us. They come up from behind, knives out.

We're in broad daylight on a busy street, but no one's paying us any attention. Everyone has too much on their mind. We're on our own.

They dive in front of us and, using knives to make their point, one growls, "Up against the building. Now."

We comply. I seem to be shocked more than I am concerned —yet. We find ourselves backed up to a doorway with no glass and no escape, arms instinctively up.

For the second time in as many hours I'm sliding back into fear's arms and I don't like it.

"Just empty your pockets and no one gets hurt, see?" one of them growls.

"Not gonna happen," I say, unworried that he might not get my dialect. I'm staring him down, doing my Knowing Gay Stare into his eyes . . . only to immediately realize that's not going to work. He's clearly more well-appointed than my flabby cop in 1979. In fact, he's kind of hot, in a dirty, scary way. Which not only lessens the effect of the stare, it turns it into a serious liability, and damned quick.

He senses it and becomes slightly agitated. Now, more than a mugging, he's now got an apparent couple of pansies on his hands and the stakes have just shot way up. Complete backfire.

Neither Ben nor I move to comply. I don't know if we're both in shock; I think for me I'm just curious to see if these guys have the guts to take this all the way. I think they're in over their heads. And for the briefest of moments, they seem almost ready to back down. But in the fraction of a second, somehow goading each other by body language alone, they rally to their goal in unison and come at us, one each.

They don't lead with their knives after all—which is what I would do—they're leading with their fists in spite of having knives. As if still too scared for the art of deliberate bloodshed, they're holding the knives the wrong way in their hands and simply pummeling us with fists.

They ain't pros. They're just lowlifes who want a shot at some free loot.

But being struck in the face with a fist isn't sitting well with me. Before I know it, my adrenaline is back and I dive at my attacker. I know that Ben also fights his, but I can't spare the bandwidth to see how well he's doing. I don't know anything about fighting, I just have a desperate male human intent on invading my personal space. It's rapid and messy with hands striking and darting and, somewhere in there, the blade of a knife ready to do damage. While I'm expecting to learn what it is to be stabbed once and for all, suddenly the whole thing devolves until we're practically just slapping one another.

We all suck at this. And it's going nowhere—until I have both hands around the knife-wielding wrist of my assailant. Somehow I manage to swivel and shove, fairly ninja-like, impaling the man's wrist on a shard of glass still clinging to the door frame.

He goes *"Oow!"* and drops his knife. Everything freezes for a moment.

Just then the sweet sound of a police whistle is heard, and suddenly there are six of us and we're all indiscriminately beaten with nightsticks about the head and shoulders. Not just our attackers, but Ben and me, too.

"Awright! Break it up, the lot of you!" a policeman barks. The two large cops have the four of us pulled apart from each other. We're heaving and snarling.

"What the hell is going on here?" the other policeman asks, hatted, dark blue uniform, buttons proudly going up his ample chest.

"These . . . *whew* . . . these guys just tried to mug us," I say, wiping my chin with the back of my hand. There's blood coming from my mouth. My heart is pounding, and my face has encountered its first-ever true fisticuffs. Which really hurt by the way . . .

"No, sir!" One of the thieves pleads, cradling his arm, which I guess I've just impaled on a piece of glass.

"They tried to jump us, they tried to take our knives away."

"Horseshit." That's me, I think. Maybe it's Ben. I really don't know. I can't catch my breath.

The cop's not buying it either. "I don't care who did what to who, you're street fighting during a civil emergency. Probably on account of something you're not too keen on sharing amongst yourselves. We'll find out what it is, and anything else that takes our fancy." He grabs Bad Guy Number One gruffly and pats him down, as his associate goes after Bad Guy Number Two. To their credit, the hoods don't fight back. Coming away satisfied with only knives, one in hand and one on the pavement, a cop then holds Ben in a lock while the other one claws my arm with one hand and uses his other to go through my pockets. He finds my BART ticket, my California driver's license, my ATM card and my iPhone.

"What's this?" He's only interested in the phone and lets go of me in disbelief.

"It's my good luck charm," I say meekly.

He moves it enough that it lights up and my stomach sinks.

"I've never seen the like," he says, looking at the vivid beach scene on the screen. It's scanning his face, trying to unlock.

"It's a new type of photograph. I'm an inventor," which I know immediately to be the weakest phrase I have ever uttered out of nearly fifty years of speech.

"Unh." He examines it again, the screen comes on again. He turns it around in his hand a few more times, like a caveman seeing something he cannot comprehend, and suddenly hands it back to me.

I melt in relief.

But now he rifles through Ben's pockets and immediately finds the leather pouch. His eyes bulge when he sees what's inside.

"Hoh-hoh, what have we here?" There's awe in his voice. The jewels must be worth hundreds of thousands of their powerful 1906 dollars.

"Those belong to my client. I work at Montgomery Savings and Loan," Bed says rapidly, breathlessly.

Cop One leans in savagely. "We just watched that dray drive away with all the bank's assets, and you somehow forgot about these? What's more likely is that you decided to keep them for yourself."

"But I didn't!" Ben is starting to panic. "They belong to Dorothy Sprinkles on Taylor Street."

"I don't doubt they do. You know we're authorized to shoot looters on sight?" He's practically got a hard-on, up in Ben's face now, snarling; his formidable frame is fighting a desire to shoot Ben right here and now.

His body screams, "Try me!"

This is no casual event. I think the cop is seeing stars, or a medal of honor: His historic deed on this historic day.

Supremely screwed, have we become.

"All of you are coming with us. Now!" The other cop barks.

They both have their clubs out and start steering us along.

Suddenly our two assailants make a break for it and dash up Montgomery Street at top speed, heading for the Barbary Coast. Even in my shock I'm surprised at how quickly they move. They're gone.

That just leaves Ben and me. The cops are livid. "All right. March it!"

After all this, Ben calmly bends over and hands me my hat. Again. It goes back on my head; maybe it'll help keep what remains of my thoughts inside my cranium where they belong.

The cops prod us brusquely onward to the Hall of Justice nearby, the ornate building at Kearny and Washington Streets, right at Portsmouth Square where I first Appeared.

It's just after eight in the morning, and, to be frank, I'm having a really bad day.

The building has suffered obvious damage. Some columns are broken, windows are out, and the flagpole up top is at a rakish tilt.

Just then the famous aftershock comes—it's a big one, it scares half the city to death—and as we're approaching the Hall of Justice an immense stone cornice comes down and smashes to the street, killing two horses. The cops are rattled. So is Ben. I am, too, but for a different reason: By about 1:00 p.m., this entire place will become an inferno. And unless a miracle happens, we're going to be locked up inside it.

Despite the damage to the steeple and all the glass knocked out of the windows, the Hall of Justice is doing a bang-up business, as a morgue, a jail, and a makeshift hospital. The building is overrun with excited personnel, criminals, cops, volunteers.

We're led to a booking desk and our names taken. We're processed and interviewed by a detective. Ben is righteously sticking to his story. For being true, it sounds entirely pathetic.

Ben repeatedly pleads with them to call Dorothy Sprinkles on a telephone.

"Well, young man, you may well know there isn't a telephone that works in this city right now, and we're not about to spare a man to go chasing down some spurious claims."

"Then let us go!" I say, trying to be all *CSI-Miami.*

Doesn't work. Didn't think it would. My throat is closing up in disgusted dread.

"Please, sir," Ben says. "Please just have someone send for Dorothy Sprinkles. Or my boss, Barnard Decoursey. This can be straightened out in mere moments, I swear."

The desk sergeant sighs. Looks annoyed. Looks at Ben, and probably sees what I see in Ben: He's not got a wily bone in his body. He's incredibly earnest in all things, and damned cute, too.

He relents, a very tiny bit. "All right. If we can spare a man, we'll send 'im. But don't count on it. You're not going anyplace soon."

We're patted down again. They keep the jewels, of course. And it sickens me to surrender my phone, my BART ticket, ATM card and driver's license. The men don't even look at them, they're just thrust into a metal box and slotted into a drawer. The police are very distracted this morning, about the only thing going in our favor.

We're escorted down one floor and locked into a large

holding cell. Surrounded by metal bars and scary-ass men of every kind—thieves and murderers—I know we must look prissy and way in over our heads. Ben and I simply sit on the floor. The benches are all taken.

Time may be passing very quickly all around this jangled city, but in this cell, it has completely ground to a halt.

We wait. Trapped.

Outside you can hear the occasional booms of dynamite as the city foolishly tries to blast itself free of fire.

I figure it's about a twenty-minute walk to Taylor Street and a twenty-minute walk back, assuming the police bother to send anyone at all. And further assuming anyone's still at the Sprinkles Mansion. If they had a lick of sense, they would have long ago fled south in a richly appointed—and carefully packed—motor car.

I'm well past that latest adrenaline spike. I slump down in utter fatigue and resignation. I have plenty of time to fuss and fret. But finally, after perhaps an hour of looking inward, as is my usual want, I finally manage to turn my thoughts toward Ben.

He's clamming up, out of fear and post-adrenaline too. Probably with cold realization that his little plan for doing an end-run on Barney was not well considered. Surely by now it must start to coalesce. I'd be consumed with shame if it were me, but I don't know if he realizes yet how many missteps he's made in that cute little head of his.

I feel bad for him. He did what he could in his mind and I'm not going to punish him—with a rolled-up newspaper or in words spoken harshly. He had his reasons, faulty though they may have been, and he must eventually come to recognize them with nauseating clarity.

So I leave him be. I just sit near him and breathe and consider our predicament.

When the fire comes, they'll evacuate us from here, surely.

The history books didn't say anything about letting prisoners burn. But then again, history books have been known to look the other way every now and then.

Hours pass. Sustained hours, experienced as if we were rats in a trap. A lone, open toilet is in the corner, and, disconcertingly close to it is a rudimentary water fountain. I try it once. No water comes out.

Still, we wait. It's two-and-a-half hours before we hear: "Fire's coming this way!"

We get a whiff of it in the holding cell—not of fire, but of fear.

The men in the cell become agitated. Everyone's up, pacing, either rubbing their hands or hugging their arms, their shoulders hunched. The air becomes rank with tension and a unique, primal sweat I've never encountered before.

Finally, police officers start marshaling the prisoners out. Not us first, of course. They start further down in the building and we have to watch, still trapped, as manacled men are being led to wagons up at street level and driven away in groups, probably to the Presidio.

I want us to be saved, but I also need my money and phone back.

Confusion mounts. A flurry of activity across the building, you can feel it as people begin to move things around, grab files, leave.

Then we hear the sound we thought we'd never hear: "Wade and Baldwin!"

Oh, holy Jesus!

We're let out of the cage. Everyone else who must remain, if their stares were but bullets, they would have shot upon our hearts. But whatever. We're free. Only now I smell the smoke. A lot of it. Strong, acrid. Things are burning that aren't supposed to burn. It is hideous.

We're taken three flights up to an inspector's office. Smoke is clouding the air now and people are scurrying about like the Feds are coming. In the inspector's office sits a beautiful woman in an aubergine bodice, tufted shoulders, corseted to within an inch of her life, grey wool skirts and startlingly purple hat with stuffed birds on it.

"My dear Mr. Wade, I cannot thank you enough," the woman says as we're led into the room. She rises and puts her gloved hand out.

"And Mr. Baldwin. I am Dorothy Sprinkles," she pronounces her first name like "Darrithy." "It's an honor to meet you." She gives me a light, ladylike handshake.

"Thank you for coming for us," says Ben sheepishly.

We hear an excited pronouncement: "Ladies and gentlemen, the fire is approaching. Kindly remove yourselves from the premises quickly."

"I have my motor car outside, do come with me," Dorothy says calmly.

We're handed back our belongings, my iPhone included, and are led out of the building. Fire is consuming the southwest side of Portsmouth square, two buildings down from this very spot and I'm really over the sight, smell and sound of them. I'm gripped with fear and revulsion.

The air is doing that thing again, whooshing past us to join in the orgy of fire.

We clamor up into an open car with a chauffeur and are seated in the back with this woman. Fire is licking all around, heading our way. People are scrambling from the Hall of Justice behind us. More prisoners are being led out. I hold Ben's hand unobtrusively in the backseat of the car as our motorman pulls his lever, and the car lurches up Kearny toward Jackson; we jounce away, dodging piles of debris in the street.

"Please come to my home and rest for a moment," Dorothy is saying, loud enough for the chauffeur to hear. "I insist. We've had a bit of damage this morning but everything is going to be all right." She says it with calm assurance.

"We'd be honored," I say.

The driver takes us to Washington and Taylor Streets, just below the top of Nob Hill. A circular drive in front of a Victorian style house, very grand—perhaps not quite the highest tier of wealth, but charmingly close enough. The house is stunning. It'll certainly do. Woodwork, devastating in scale and elegance; squared mahogany columns, atrium; grand foyer, Victorian furnishings, fronded palms, gold spittoons. Colored skylights play with the available sunlight, somewhat bastardized by smoke.

We're led through to the main parlor, where we can see an enormous expanse of glassless windows and a panoramic view of the city.

The sight is horrifying. South of Market is a smoldering ruin, the flames now racing across Market Street. I can see Newspaper Row, at Third, Market and Montgomery, right at the Palace Hotel. This is the pinnacle of communication and press, the Wall Street of the West, engulfed in flames that roar hundreds of feet into the air.

Dorothy insists on having us served cold sandwiches and lemonade, something we're very grateful for—we're starving, and dying of thirst. A maid brings them in on a silver tray. She's visibly trembling, the items on the tray are clattering. She clearly wants to get out of here but is compelled by her mistress to remain.

We sit on the settee, very proper, pinkies out, as Mrs. Sprinkles tries to engage us in appropriate social intercourse.

"I cannot tell you how sorry I am you went through all this Mr. Wade; Mr. Baldwin."

"That's all right, ma'am," Ben says, chewing on his sandwich. "We were jumped by some men on Montgomery Street. It was touch and go there for a moment."

"Jumped? Oh, how perfectly dreadful! Those jewels have been in my family for a hundred years. They have a long and storied history. I knew they'd be in favorable hands with Mr. Decoursey, and, of course, I was right."

Ben's face falls, ever so slightly. Despite all his heroic efforts, credit is falling to Barney after all. It must be his worst nightmare—present crisis excepted. I feel keenly sorry for him.

"Oh, we had an awful upset this morning but now that's all over and done with, we can move ahead again. I do wish they'd hurry with that dynamite and get this wretched fire under control. You see, we have an especially crucial dinner party here this evening—you must come! Both of you! I won't take no for an answer!"

I listen to her go on. I look around at this splendid house, forty years old if it's a day, knowing that after 9:00 p.m. it's going to become a smoldering ruin.

How will Lady Sprinkles adapt?

True to her class, she'll come out on top. Her sort always does.

I listen to her pratter away about this evening's dinner party that'll never happen, and I wonder about the poor baby we pulled from the wreckage this morning. Where was its father? Does it even have a father? I suddenly realize I don't even know if the baby was a girl or a boy. Whatever. The people of Folsom Street aren't going to pull through all right.

I know, by grace of time travel, that speeding across the continent on every train are all the supplies and loaves of bread available. People from Key West to Ketchikan are baking pies, donating clothes, blankets and emergency supplies. The U.S. Army orders every tent in the nation to the city, but it will take several days. Until then, San Francisco is on her own.

We stay at the Sprinkles' House just as long as is appropriate but no longer. We take our leave of Darrithy, promising to be back at eight.

"Gosh, that's amazing!" Ben says as we make our way up Washington Street. "We'll be a couple of swells at that party!"

"Mmmm," is all I can manage to say.

We go to the Clay Street water tank, an outcropping from whence you can see in all directions. I watch in sadness as the beautiful Call Building dies, becoming the greatest Roman candle the world has ever seen. The black huff of smudge to the left of it would be the Palace Hotel, burned out.

I'm unsure of how to proceed. We should make our way west of Van Ness Avenue, but Ben can't get far in those shoes. He's not one to complain, yet I'll be very surprised if his feet aren't bloody by now.

The most workable option would be Lafayette Park at Washington and Octavia Streets. That part, according to what I've read, never burns.

But what if history is wrong?

Lafayette Park: It has a history in my own life. It's the first park I ever cruised men. Eighty-eight years from now. A man in gray sweatpants, walking his springer spaniel . . .

Now we will sleep there on the ground there. If we're lucky.

We head that way, in no hurry at this point. The flames, for now, are well behind us. We're surrounded by posh homes that don't know they're about to die, raving beauties all. Complex and stunning architecture that will never be recreated because no one will want it anymore.

A large crowd is converging on the park; it's almost to overflowing already. They're just at the point of turning people away, sending them further west, but Ben and I manage to slip in.

The people with us are not the glitz and glamor of the immediate area. Those people are still safely in their homes, sweeping up glass and planning to move forward, thinking the worst is over. No, we're surrounded by poorer refugees from other parts of the city. The Army has already begun setting up a relief station in the park. They have jugs of water for the thirsty and chunks of bread are being handed out. They immediately begin constructing and assigning tents in any available space, doling out blankets. With so many women and children, so many elderly people, Ben and I agree to forego the tents. We sit on the grass and try to stay out of everyone's way.

It's about three-thirty and there's nothing at all to do.

After resting, I'm about to suggest we see if we can help, but Ben takes his shoes off and it's worse than I thought. With no socks for protection, his feet are nearly shredded with blisters. He's not going anywhere.

So we remain, waiting.

"Say. I have a question," I begin.

"Yes?"

"Why doesn't Dorothy Sprinkles keep her jewels in her own house? Place like that ought to have a safe bigger'n your apartment."

Ben looks uncomfortable, like he doesn't want to spill. He leans in. It's a secret.

"According to Barney, Elron Sprinkles has been known to get himself liquored up and break into the family safe and lose everything at the poker tables. So his wife keeps her valuables with us. I reckon she's lucky she still has those jewels at all."

Ah. Unraveling a little more of what possessed Ben to act the way he did. Dorothy has a head on her shoulders. And a nice juicy skeleton in her closet, too. I'm pleased.

We're surrounded by people. It would be like a concert on the grass at Dolores Park, except the only music is a distant dull roar of flames and flash-bang of dynamite. The women of the era have voluminous layers of dresses, regardless of class, so they're almost comfortable. It's like a blanket for them. The men are less fortunate, with only thin wool trousers. Babies are held in arms, fussing, and younglings run around playing, their terror this morning already forgotten.

We are landlocked amid the crowd, hearing tales of woe. Everyone is talking about where they were, what it was like; rumors are it was the eruption of Mount Shasta. Others are saying Los Angeles is down, too. There's no way to get news in or out, so no one has a complete picture of the devastation.

Soon darkness will fall, but even in daylight there's no mistaking the hideous orange glow—somewhat to the east, but far more menacingly down the hill to the south. It reaches into the glowering sky, smoke so vast I'm certain it would be visible from orbit.

More bread and coffee are announced. I wait in line, leaving Ben on the grass. Bread and coffee do not make a satisfying meal—caffeine just leaves you hungry again. But it is what it is.

As evening falls, it becomes much cooler. No open fires are allowed, so there's no light, no warmth. It becomes uncomfortable.

Plenty of light without, though. A ghastly glow.

The people around us get bored and want to talk. We're surrounded by several families, a few of whom don't seem to speak English. They take their cues from the voices and expressions around them. But others, a family from Harrison Street, and two women from South Park—I wonder if they're lesbian —tell us their tale. Another family from Hayes Valley talks about how what will later be known as the Ham and Eggs fire started a mere two doors down from where they live. They had mere seconds to grab a few precious belongings and run away.

The most common theme is the horror of the temblor and scores killed outright when buildings, both brick and wood, fell to bits at 5:12 that morning. Frantic dashing around, looking for loved ones, not knowing, even now, that they've made the right choice on where to flee.

Rampant speculation that we could all have to flee again at any moment, even now.

A little girl walks purposefully up to me on the grass. Since

I'm sitting on the ground, we're facing each other at eye level. She asks me, "Do you have a chicken?"

"Penny!" The mother, in a mass of woolen long skirts, admonishes her daughter and looks over to me in an apologetic fashion.

But Penny's gazing at me with a bright face. "I have a chicken named Pecky, but Mum says she has to move away. We're going to get a new house."

"I bet Pecky will like her new house," I volunteer.

"Do you have a house?" Penny seems intrigued that I may.

"I'm afraid I don't. Not anymore."

"Mum says our new house will have a telephone. You could ring me and say, 'How do you do.'"

"I think that would be lovely. I shall indeed."

The girl smiles broadly and canters off to tell more people about Pecky and her new telephone.

Conversation ebbs and flows. We're on the periphery of most of it. For a while, songs are sung among us on the grass, tunes I don't know, but Ben does. Ditties and shanties and "My Darlin' Clementine" among others. It actually seems to help.

After a while Ben and I fall to private conversation, just the two of us.

"Mark, I owe you my life." Ben's looking at me with intensity, in all earnest, and it would be easier for me to break eye contact and to gaze off in the distance, but I guess I have to pay my dues.

I've never saved a life before—hell, I can't even save my own. I choke on bitterness.

"You'da done the same for me," I say simply and half pat, half spank his lower thigh in a manly, jocular way.

"Well, Mark, nevertheless, thank you. I mean that."

Now would be a good time to smooch it out, but obviously that's not an option here, so we just sit in pregnant silence. I hope he's not seeing me as some sort of dashing hero. I consider myself just this side of a smashing train wreck.

I change the subject. “What do you think you might do when all this is over? I gather you don’t want to go back to Chicago.”

“I really do not know. I’ve just lost everything, not that it was much. I could go anywhere. Who can say? Will they even rebuild here? For all I know San Francisco might be abandoned, a modern-day Pompeii.”

“I’m sure they’ll rebuild. There’s money here. These people have a lot of spirit.”

“I hope so. I don’t want to go someplace else, but it looks like I’ll be starting all over again no matter where I wind up. I’m back at square one.”

“I guess it was a bad idea to give up my boarding house in Berkeley when I did,” I say, more to dispel any ideas Ben might be getting of him and me living together in cozy sin in Alameda County any time soon.

It is after eight when news comes that a new fire has taken hold below Union Square. This would be the arson case, the one that didn’t need to happen. But it does. Nob Hill is now under a deathwatch.

A low-grade panic fills Lafayette Park. And even I, with a foreknowledge of events, am not immune to this panic. I feel it in my gut. We might need to flee, fast.

Sure enough, a brighter orange begins behind the hill and we watch helplessly as it spreads and grows. There’s nothing to stop it. Fire likes to go uphill and there’s an awful lot to burn.

By eleven o’clock, open flames are roaring atop Nob Hill, consuming those precious, irreplaceable homes; the stained glass, arched windows, cupolas and turrets are all destroyed, closing the door on the most splendid era in human architecture.

We sit in silence, hearing the crackling roar and watching

the proud district go up in flames. It's a fierce, all-encompassing inferno, impossibly large and close and heading this way. The sheer size of it defies the imagination. Several times I feel a sense of panic, like I need to get up and run. What's to keep the flames from overtaking us? I'm all over in a feeling of disgust, and as rattled as everyone else around me.

People make a good show of settling in for the night, but no one really believes it. Everyone lies down but with one eye open, ready, at any time, to be woken and told to run. Low grade fear oozes in my belly, and try as I might, I can't get myself to unclench. The savageness of the inferno at Ben's won't leave my thoughts. I don't care what history says, we're in a great deal of danger here. I lie, tensed up, waiting for the word to be given.

No such warnings come, however. The fires don't pass Van Ness Avenue except in pockets.

17

Thursday, April 19, 1906

It's still early when we awake the next morning, cold, stiff and sore. Everything and everyone is covered in dew.

It is bitter. We ache all over.

Anxious glances reveal complete devastation just to the east of us. Everyone in the park must be having the same reaction: wonderment that the fires came so close to us, and disgust at the complete ruination left behind. There is palpable relief, but also a profound, communal sorrow.

People stir from the tents, those who are lucky enough to have them, and begin waiting in line for coffee and bread. I queue up with everyone else, secure some and bring them back to Ben on the grass. Afterward I return the cups to be used, unwashed, by others.

I'm to Disappear in a while. I get to leave all this and go home. To comfort, warmth, cleanliness and wi-fi; yet I'm not about to leave Ben sitting in the dirt on his own. I want him safe.

His home is destroyed, his job is destroyed. I'm going to have to break his friendship, and in only a couple of hours' time. I don't know how he'll take it, and I wish it weren't so. I suddenly feel sad and dirty. I think he likes me and has come to rely on me. I am unused to this and gutted by the knowledge that it must end abruptly.

Maybe I should have kept to myself this whole time, instead of creating a bond that will have to be savagely broken? It was built in, our parting; There was never going to be any other way about that. I recognize that my entire experience of this San Francisco would have been dull and disconnected had we never crossed paths. Ben brought the experience to life. He made it real for me and I think, I hope, I gave him a few days of excitement and intrigue. I like him. I want him to be well, to find love, to find connection with his tribe, wherever he might find it.

"We should leave San Francisco," I say. "It would be less walking if we got out by boat, to Oakland. Do you think you can get as far as the Ferry Building?"

"Sure. Piece of cake."

"It's going to be a good two miles. But I don't know what else we can do."

"No, I understand," Ben replies.

He's lying. But it's the best overall solution. Fires will continue to ravage the city for another two days. There's neither food nor water. It's not a good place to be.

"Well, we should do that, whenever you feel you're ready."

We harumpf up off the ground, our bed for the night, stiff and sore and powerful cold, and set out for the Ferry Terminal. I get a few steps before realizing I have, once again, forgotten my hat. I snatch it off the ground and put it back on.

Part of my brain revolts at the concept of deliberately

walking into this scene of destruction, but it must be done. To go around it would take a day, and Ben's feet would become hobbled and useless.

Our bodies quickly warm up. The stiff soreness of sleeping on the ground eventually shakes itself loose and we begin making fairly good time, despite what must be agony for Ben in his ill-fitting shoes.

Down the hill toward Van Ness, the first part of our walk seems normal. The houses this side of the avenue didn't burn, although many chimneys are down and windows broken. Once we get to Van Ness and step into the burn area, I go numb.

The brain can't catalogue the sheer scope of the devastation. More confusing than that, though, is how everything has been completely flattened. Except for a few random brick walls or chimneys, it's an uninterrupted view of ruin. It's startling because there are no reference points. It's black and empty. Everything is ash. You can see for miles, and the burned world around us still gives off incredible heat . . . and a choking stench.

The streets are surprisingly clear and passable. The wood houses just immolated and collapsed in on themselves, leaving an open grid of empty roads, with only occasional piles of debris, dead horses, blackened automobiles, burned out cages of cable cars.

We skirt the steepest parts of Nob Hill, making our way toward what I can only assume is Sutter Street—I simply have no way to tell. We hold handkerchiefs to our mouths, trying to filter out the ash. The only saving grace, if you can call it that, is we are far from alone. A steady stream of people is making its way through the empty streets with us, leaving. What few police and soldiers we see just watch in helpless resignation. Occasionally, they'll shoo people along, as if they're still in charge, but mostly everyone ignores them, their faces down.

There's nothing to steal.

I periodically check in with Ben, on how his feet are doing. He must be in agony, but he won't let on. Stoic and brave: That's how people are in 1906.

Empty blocks are behind us, the wooden buildings that simply vanished. Now we're coming into the brick areas which still stand, completely charred. Many are several stories tall, teetering, menacing, blocking out the daylight with their burned hulks. Any one of them could come crashing down upon us.

But once on Market Street, the end of our journey is in sight in the far-off distance, the gray, untouched tower of the Ferry Terminal straight ahead.

By now we're in a crowd. A bizarre Easter Parade of refugees, dazedly heading to the Ferry Terminal, shuffling, limping, jaws clamped shut. Suitcases lugged, children carried. The only sound is the scuffing of feet and an occasional cough.

My phone's battery is sure to be dead, but I have to know how much longer before I Disappear. I cannot be on a boat when it happens: I'd splash into the Bay alone and drown.

I subtly fish my phone out. The battery is at 3 percent and the hour is 9:05, give or take.

We're running out of distance to the Ferry Building, and I'm running out of time.

Passing the Grand Palace Hotel, the structure's roof and interior floors have completely vanished. The windows thus leave a checkerboard of sunny spots on rubble in the morning light.

We arrive at the Ferry Terminal to the disheartening realization that it's going to be hours waiting for a boat. Tens of thousands of people converge, hungry, thirsty, covered in soot, coughing and hacking untold hazardous materials up their lungs. There's no single, discrete line to wait in, no semblance of organization, just a general surge oozing into the building and to the boats lining up on the other side of it.

I'll never make it.

I ascertain that Ben is in the right place, he's where he needs to be to find safety.

This is it. I gotta cut him.

"Ben," I begin, turning to face him. "I'm . . . I'm not going to get on a boat."

"What?" He looks confused, but quickly attempts to change gears. "Where are we going?"

"We aren't going anywhere. You are going to get on a boat and go to Oakland. I'm not."

He's starting to protest, but I cut him off. "I'm a writer, Ben. Well, here's my story. I can't leave it." I indicate the city behind us. "But you need to get out of here. It's not safe for you to stay. Your feet are trashed and there won't be a lick of food over here for quite some time."

I brave a glance into his eyes and instantly regret it. True hurt. Confusion.

"Mark, I don't understand."

We're in a sea of people standing; no one's moving, we're just packed in. Anyone could hear us and, among other things, I wish this wasn't so.

I've just to rip the band-aid off. The quicker the better. Whatever Ben's feelings for me may ultimately be, it's time to go away forever.

"You're a good man. I know you'll find someone. Someone who can make you feel complete. I've just got to stay."

Among other things, I have to lie my ass off to him. My stomach is clenched with emotional hurt. "I'll get my story and take it to Los Angeles where it can be published. I assume I'll just camp out there a while until things here get settled."

"Let me come with you!"

"No." I put my hand on his chest. He deflates a little.

"I don't like this," he says, his voice choking back tears.

"Me either. Ben, you're really a good man. Getting to know

you has been completely amazing. You'll do well once you get back up on your feet again. I know you will."

"Mark, I don't want to lose you." He says it low, looking at the ground, but with pain enough in his voice that it breaks my heart.

Ben grabs me in a giant bear hug. People are starting to notice.

"I know." I say it softly in his ear and we stand, locked in a smoky, woolen embrace. "I don't want to leave you, but I have to, Ben. I really do."

"How will I ever find you again? I don't have any address now."

"You can't. But I'll be back in San Francisco someday. We'll find each other."

It's a lie and I want to throw up.

"Here." He breaks his hold on me and fishes his tiny pencil and notebook out of his pocket. He's trembling so bad he can hardly write.

"This is my parents' address in Chicago. Write me there!"

Oh, it's so sad.

But I take the piece of paper, my hand wrapping around the scratchy warmth of his own and holding it just so. For a moment. I once more gaze into his soft eyes and see his pain.

"Promise me you'll get on a boat here today?"

"I promise I will." And I believe him.

"Goodbye, Ben."

"Goodbye, Mark." He turns away rubbing his nose and I walk off.

I have to push my way through the throngs, and I don't look back.

I'm crying.

A man has moved me to tears. This hasn't happened since San Francisco pounded it out of me a decade ago.

I'm disgusted at a cellular level at what I've just done, yet surprised I could do it at all.

I look at this ruined city: How many years have I wasted in it trying to find love and meaning and attachment? And now, amid this end of the world, I manage to find it? I'm obviously missing some point, although at this time I'm not empowered to know just quite what that point is, other than it seems some form of cruel joke.

Well, true emotion for another man is still in me after all. Frankly, I thought I'd lost the capacity. So maybe I'll find it again someday?

What's more, I feel certain Ben will find it again. He just needed a little shove. And while I've just kicked him in the pants, maybe it'll get him out of his shell and ready to meet the others he so richly deserves?

Maybe I opened a door for him. He sure the hell opened one for me.

I head back down ruined Market Street, away from the Ferry Building, crowds pushing past. I'm the only one going the wrong way, back into the destruction, gazing in shock at what I see before me.

The beating heart of California has stopped, the West Coast suddenly decapitated.

Over three thousand are dead.

Hundreds of square blocks of brick and charred lumber—people's lives, vital documents, cash, clothes, pets, photographs, art, architecture and entire cultures—are incinerated. Now only to be hauled away as trash. It's everywhere. It's simply too much to understand. Where do you even begin?

Off in the distance I see the Call Building, the city's biggest and most beautiful. It's a twenty-one story, burnt-out wreck. It is the largest single ruin I've ever faced, sickening to behold.

San Francisco will start rebuilding within four days. They'll sweep this whole event under the rug and pretend it never happened. They will rewrite history to downplay the earthquake—it's bad PR—and for generations simply refer to all this as "The Fire."

Los Angeles, meanwhile, eagerly stands ready to scale up and assume the mantle as the Queen City of the West.

San Francisco will never be number one again.

PART V

2019 - SAN FRANCISCO

18

Tuesday, November 4, 2019

It comes. I Reappear in 2019 in Portsmouth Square, scaring the shit out of this Chinese girl in her twenties. She almost drops her phone and apparently thinks I'm some sort of rapist.

I'm still wearing my long black coat and bowler hat and beard and woolen slacks, and ash comes up to my knees. I'm a mess. I know I must stink.

David is a few feet away, packing up The Machine. I go up to him. "Hey."

"Oh, wow," he responds. "You made it."

Big hug. "Sorry if I reek," I say. "It was a pretty wild ride."

"You smell like smoke," David says.

"There was a lot of it."

"You look a little worse for wear. Nice outfit. How was it?"

"Intense! I stayed at the Palace, went clothes shopping, met a boy named Ben. We spent all our time together. Managed to see Caruso—and Abe Ruef and Eugene Schmitz."

"I'm impressed. What was the earthquake like?"

"You really couldn't stand up, it was just like they said. But there was a hell of a lot more damage by the quake than you'd think. Nearly every building had something busted. People pretty much kept their cool, though. Saw a lot of dead bodies."

"Well, let's get you back to the car. I got this," he says, wheeling the toolbox behind him.

It feels odd putting a seatbelt on over my heavy cloak. I have to have the window down. I don't know why, I only know that I need air. I hold my bowler in my lap and we drive through the San Francisco I know so well.

Everything seems so solid and normal . . . and mind-numbingly bland.

"Do you want to stop at my place? Maybe take a bath?" He's clearly hinting that I need one.

"Yes, please. Plus I'm starving. And dying of thirst."

"Here." He hands me a partially drunk bottle of water from the cup holder, and I greedily suck on it. I've already had his germs. Beyond caring.

"I'll fill the tub when we get to my place. Get you something to eat and drink, too."

"Thanks."

"Did you get many pictures?"

"Quite a few."

"Can't wait to see."

We drive through the city and I relax in the plush seat enjoying the view. No horses, no smoldering ruins. We get to David's apartment at 18th and Danvers; he, too, has a garage spot. We leave The Machine in the Civic and go upstairs and he draws me a bath. While he's doing that, I fix myself a sandwich and a hefty helping of scotch and splay out on his sofa.

I plug my phone into one of David's cables and do a quick Google of Ben J. Wade.

He died in San Francisco in 1937, a retired senior accountant for the Southern Pacific Railroad.

Never married.

David comes back in and sits down next to me. I hand my phone to him. He starts going through my pictures, and lets out a long, appreciative whistle.

"Nice! Is that Ben?" He shows me the picture in the car outside what is once again my apartment.

"Yeah."

"Cute. You should find out whatever happened to him."

"Just did. He died in 1937."

"Sucks."

"Yeah. But he got the job he wanted. It was grand getting to know him . . . " I feel myself choking up again.

Oblivious to that, David says, "You can borrow some sweats to wear home if you don't want to get back into those clothes after your bath. Mine'll be way too big for you, but whatev."

"Thanks."

I finish my food and take my drink into the bath with me. Once fed and scotched I give David a peck on the cheek and carry my clothes and hat the few blocks home on Diamond Street. David's sweatpants nearly slide down to my ankles twice, I'm eventually walking with the waistband wadded up in one fist.

Rhoda is unimpressed as I grab and hug her. She wants me to set her back down. So I do.

I climb into my bed and curl up, safe and fed and unsooty, in a city rebuilt from the ashes. Can't sleep and don't know why, until it occurs to me: I go to my 1906 pants and pull out a crumpled-up piece of paper, still new, written on with trembling hand. It reads:

Ben J. Wade

in care of Jason & Ursula Wade Sr.
2304 Elmwood Ave
Berwyn ILL

I smooth it flat on my comforter. I think of Ben and begin to cry.

19

Thursday, November 14, 2019

Settling back into a normal life afterward has not gone particularly well.

I've earlier intimated that I don't find people particularly interesting. It's a crushing thing to admit as true, but now I'm able to refine it a little, and somewhat more to my favor: I find the people of 2019 singularly uninteresting. It's like everyone has their head up it, worrying about little things that don't matter in the slightest. I find it ever-increasingly difficult to have meaningful conversations with anyone.

The time has come for me to return to 450 Sutter Street, San Francisco's famed art-deco medical building, and place myself once again face-to-face with Dr. Tammi Tsieh, MD, Oncology.

I walk back into the Burn Zone for the first time in 113 years. Although it looks normal and as it should, I'm keenly aware now of what was here before. The St. Francis Hotel is essentially unchanged; the cable cars look and sound the same on

Powell Street. But I miss that amazing synagogue where my medical building is now.

My heart rate is up when "Tammi" walks in, same stethoscope in her pocket.

"Hi, Mark." She shakes my hand and sits at her computer screen. I can only see the back of it, the little "hp" in a circle. "Have you come to any conclusions?"

I certainly have. Despite my best efforts at keeping the entire reality out of my mind, no thought can be banished completely. It has circled back on me countless times, its sting never anything less than a stab to the gut.

"Doctor Tsieh, it's going to be really hard to explain, but for now, I'd like to hold off on chemo."

I'm feeling strong enough to stare her down when I say it. As before, I know it doesn't particularly or personally matter to her in the slightest. Her job is to provide options.

Nevertheless, I detect a note of disappointment—even sadness—in her voice that's almost enough to trigger a rethink.

"I understand, Mark. I know it's a lot to consider. It's a personal decision and I have no doubt that you've poured a lot of yourself into making it.

"But, again, it's my responsibility to remind you that you have options. The earlier we hit it the more likely we are to have success. Your window for effective treatment will only get smaller from here."

"I know. I truly understand. I'm . . . working on a project right now that's taking all of my concentration. I'm really pouring my heart into it, to the point that I don't want anything to take it away from me yet."

She looks at me curiously, but kindly.

I go on: "You may well find me here begging for your help soon enough. But not yet. Not now. I got stuff I need to do. It's important."

More eye contact.

She relents.

"I understand. We've got your information here; we will move forward on your say so. I would suggest, however, that we do another PET scan in ninety days. It will show us if there's any progression in the lymphoma. It could remain the same, or in some cases even reverse a little bit. Would you be willing to agree to another scan in ninety days?"

"Certainly. Thanks. And please don't think I'm trying to blow this off, I'm not. I hear you, and rest assured, my mind has been full. I'm just on a certain path right now."

With the hard part over, we go over any potential secondary symptoms, night-sweats, body aches, changes in weight or appetite, sores and a host of other danger signals.

I have none.

The mood is lighter when we shake hands again and she leaves.

Whatever I'm doing, I'm free to keep doing it for now, and that's all I wanted.

If I can only convince my brain to get with the program.

§

THE OTHER PROBLEM IS DAVID. Still haven't told him.

Being a pragmatist and scientist, he won't understand my decision at all. He's liable to get very arch with me. But I'm unwilling to take advantage of his amazing gift of time travel while simultaneously keeping such an intense personal secret from him. It wouldn't be right.

The disclosure takes place tonight at our usual Thursday night supper at his place.

Since he hasn't developed any further inventions that

threaten to rend the universe apart, David has been pretty smug and quiet of late. He's used The Machine a few times for financial gain and refuses to disclose much about it. But I can't help but notice the enormous new 4K HDTV in his living room. Televisions are getting large enough to trend toward being silly.

With booze flowing as freely as ever and over a vat of homemade chili, I affect the change within his mind that comes with the revelation of Problem Zero.

"So, I have some news. Beyond all this time travel shit. It's pretty important." I keep it light and unthreatening. A display of emotion would only detract.

"Nothing bad, I hope."

"It is." I seem to have his attention.

I lay it out. No emotional perceptions or embellishments, they won't impress him. Just the facts.

"They want me to start chemo right away. But I'm not sure I want to go there."

"Well, first and foremost, Mark, I am truly sorry." And he means it. His brown eyes meet mine and a brief, rich moment is shared between us. "And you're determined to go palliative?"

"For now. You saw what happened to Jeff. And he just died anyway. Doctor says I can float along for a few years on my own. Her professional advice is full treatment, but it's her job—and probably her legal responsibility—to say that."

"Maybe you should lay off with The Machine for a while."

I stare him down in umbrage.

"Don't you dare! I swear. I got stuff I need to figure out. The San Francisco of now doesn't seem to hold any answers for me. It never did. Not to get 'kumbaya' on your ass, but I suspect going back in time seems to actualize me in a way I can't describe. I don't understand it yet. But I want to keep going, and taking it away would not help. I can promise you that."

"Hmm. Hell, maybe the neutrino bombardments will have

the ancillary benefit of shrinking your tumors." He issues the nasal-snort of the half giggle.

"Nah. Life's ironic, but not *that* ironic."

"Well. If you need anything along the way, Mark, I'm here for you. I mean that."

And I see that he does. This is rare. And welcome. It seems the message has been delivered and received and is now properly filed.

Tonight we watch *Chernobyl* on HBO and, amid much alcohol, snuggle.

20

Sunday, December 1, 2019

So far, I've traveled back in time, but I've stayed safely on my home turf of San Francisco, which helped ground me, despite the overwhelming nature of the thing. Through it all I knew I was just an electronic bend and snap from being back home where I belong.

That's over now.

My next two Incursions will take place in London. Hence, I shall embark on a journey of time and space, as I'll no longer be safely tethered to home. I know London pretty well, but still . . . the stakes—and my resulting emotional tension—key upward several notches.

David lets me splurge on an open-ended round-trip business class ticket on British Airways. We ship The Machine ahead of time, so it'll be waiting for me.

At first, I was going to stay at the St. Pancras Hotel, my favorite building in London. But I did some research: Between

1935 and 1980, it was used as railway offices. September the 4th, 1940, is a Wednesday, so I'd Appear in an office full of people. Sounds unworkable. If I Appear at night, the doors will be locked. No push-bars back then, I'd be barricaded in all night and have a lot of explaining to do the next morning.

Still, a hotel is overall the best place from which to launch this thing. I put a think on it.

The Ritz? It's here now, it was there then. And fabulous at any point in time. Might as well go for style, right?

A few days ago, I broached the idea with David, expecting him to protest. Instead he said nothing, and merely looked down and fiddled with his phone. I figured he dismissed the idea entirely and had already moved on to something else in his mind. Yet after mere movements of his thumb, he turned his phone around and showed me my booked reservation.

At the Ritz.

Despite his mountain of flaws, David is a pretty righteous dude.

Today he's dropping me off at SFO and we hug goodbye in the awkward sideways manner that occurs in the front seat of a Honda.

I'm excited. I'm fussed, of course. But mostly excited.

Despite being in Business Class, on the upper deck of an Airbus 380 no less, I decide to go cazh. I'm wearing jeans and Nikes and my black Burlington Northern Santa Fe polo shirt.

The super jumbo rotates and takes to the air in a heavy, lazy manner. The only sensation is a slight shudder when the enormous gear retracts and tucks itself away.

Inflight service begins with a hot towel, and I enjoy much champagne and a delicious meal. I watch *The Girl on the Train* and it's good, but then I try to sleep.

Jetlag flying east is a bitch.

21

Monday, December 2, 2019

When I get to Heathrow, insufficiently rested, it is of course the next morning, on account of the whole planet being round and burdened with time zones. I breeze through Customs and Immigration. Brexit just happened, so it's still a little uncertain and chaotic, but luckily done in a flash.

I have to pick up The Machine from a cargo facility somewhat removed from the airport, so I get a taxi in front of Terminal Five. But when the driver finds out he's been queued up for two hours only to go a mile and back, he throws a near fit. He drives savagely, taking a corner on two wheels—a stunt I never thought a heavy London taxi was capable of.

I could hire him all the way into London, but he's being so whiny about it I just collect The Machine and demand to be taken to the Heathrow Express train terminal instead. I'd rather lug it and my garment bags than give him the satisfaction.

He roars off, livid.

Welcome to England.

Now I'm aboard the highspeed rail from Heathrow Airport to Paddington Station. We're traveling 130 mph with video screens, all screamingly high tech.

London in 2019 is an odd place. For a country that spent the last century so stodgy and traditional, they're now opting for ultra modern, at unsafe speeds. The classic red phone boxes are long gone, of course. Brilliant and bizarre (and in many cases unfortunate-looking) skyscrapers are shooting up all over the city. And don't get me started with their newest London bus design. I can't even go there.

Once at Paddington, since I've got so much heavy stuff, I decide on another taxi to the Ritz.

The lobby is exceedingly elegant and refined. Bright white. Columns and gold and enormous sprays of flowers in vases. I feel underdressed checking in, wearing American street clothes and in desperate need of a shower. The Macedonian man at reception is efficient but not overly friendly, which is what I've come to expect in London. Friendliness can be in short supply. A bellman helps me wheel The Machine and my garment bags to room 422.

The room is quite nice. Small, but that's normal for London hotels. Spotlessly clean, painted white. Comfy pillow-top mattress and luxurious white duvet have me, in my jetlagged state, ready to dive in. The room comes with an enormous flatscreen TV; with the bellman gone I grab the remote and put on the news.

"A Clapham man has been charged with indecent exposure . . ."

I turn it back off.

I can go back in time whenever I want, but the truth is I'm not looking forward to this Incursion. It's going to be the most uncomfortable one by a mile, I'll be far from home and actually in a fair amount of danger.

So I decide to stay the night here in 2019 first. I've got to catch my sleep back up, so a nap would be in order. It's only 11:30 in the morning, and I've been awake for twenty-nine hours. I take a shower and climb into that gorgeous bed. I set my alarm for six this evening, and fall fast asleep.

§

IT'S ALMOST impossible to wake up. I force myself. I need breakfast. But it's nighttime here, which, for me, usually means Indian food. I forage around the neighborhood and find what I seek: lamb khorma with pilau rice and garlic naan bread, with lots and lots of beer. Breakfast of champions.

I head over on Tube to The King's Arms in Poland Street, just below Oxford Circus. It's a kindly gay bar, and even though it's only a Monday night, packed with evening commuters, straggling and mingling before taking their trains back home alone. I see some nice-looking blokes.

Then I walk the byzantine streets of SoHo to the Duke of Wellington, also a good gay bar. It, too, is packed. I make English Eye Contact with a few guys.

In England, unlike in the U.S., it does you no good to stare 'em down. They don't like it. You have to look, then look away, then move to another location, and then look again. If they've followed you, you're in. If not, better luck next time.

That's how I meet Nigel. He's a squat, bearded, furry little Englishman with dashing features (read: crooked) and lovely blue eyes. He's got a gravelly East London accent and a chipped front tooth. We get to talking, "What brings you to England," that sort of thing. He lives in Lewisham, works in tech and, after thirty minutes of conversation, we decide to come back to the Ritz.

Fe Fi Fo Fum; I smell the blood of an Englishman.

That's actually true. There's something about the way Englishmen smell. It's distinct and it's good. Earthy, with Boots' brand body wash spray and something reminiscent of freshly baked bread.

Nigel thanks me for giving him an audience at the Ritz, he's never been inside it before, and we exchange numbers. I wouldn't mind seeing him again.

He leaves and I'm wide awake.

22

Tuesday, December 3, 2019

It's 1:00 a.m. in London and 5:00 p.m. back home. Maybe I'll just go now? I'm a little drunk, but that hardly matters.

Part of me doesn't want to do this. It's going to be a bitch—and scary.

I'm going back to the London Blitzkrieg. To the day when everything changed. When World War II finally came to the shores of England.

I have a lovely little interactive app on my phone that shows every bomb strike in London, but that won't work in 1940. No cell network, no GPS. So I'm just as much in the dark as anyone when it comes to where the bombs will fall. For there are so many. There's no way I could remember them all.

I could be killed on this one. Twenty-thousand Londoners are.

For no reason in particular, I've elected to stay near Sloane Square. It's a nice, upper-class neighborhood, not too far away, nothing remarkable, nothing terrifying. I've done what I can to memorize the bomb locations, and I've chosen a ten-day journey back in time. Four days before the Blitz, and six during. That way I can see both Londons of the period. I'll be going back from September 4, 1940, to September 13.

I get dressed in my late-1930s suit, the best I could approximate—a light gray double-breasted thing with a striped shirt and matching trousers—they have two-inch leg cuffs—and again have a pants line that comes up way past my bellybutton. What *is* it about old pants anyway? They make it sufficiently difficult to check out a man's backside. I've got modern black dress shoes this time. Men's shoes are pretty much unchanged for a century, and I have my comfort to consider.

I'm bringing my iPhone, although I don't see using it much. There are plenty of pictures already. In my pockets, I have some late 1930s English currency.

The money in England before 1971 is like performing calculus. Twenty shillings are in a pound, twelve pennies to a shilling, with guineas, crowns and farthings to boot. Prices are listed to three decimal places. I write a quick summary of it on a little piece of paper and keep it in my pocket.

A single, 1940s-era pound sterling is equal to twenty-eight U.S. dollars of the exact same 1940. That valuation differential is striking.

Am I really going to do this?

With a lump in my throat, I set up The Machine, put the Do Not Disturb sign on my room door, and get ready. I don my webbing, measure out the correct portion of David's ungodly fluid that will allow me to remain in the past for ten days. I inject it into my body and, before I can change my mind, flip the switch.

PART VI

1940 - LONDON

23

Wednesday, September 4, 1940

A hotel room is least likely to be occupied at noon, so that is when I choose to arrive. At worst I might encounter a cleaning lady in there.

I'm fortunate. I appear in room 422 in 1940 and the room is vacant and clean.

It's almost shabby. Years of Depression have taken their toll on the venerable Ritz. It was probably last decorated in about 1927. Of course the pillowtop mattress and comfy duvet, the HDTV, are all gone; there's only a hulking, art deco-style radio on a sad, scratched desk. The carpet is a little worn, and the place reeks of stale cigarette smoke.

The light fixtures are rather fussy and elegant, though, and the room is spotlessly clean.

I extricate myself from my webbing and sit on the bed for a long while, aware I'm wrinkling the freshly made bed. But I just want to take a moment.

My grandmother had this same bedspread: white with funny pill-like threaded nodules all over it. I run my hand over the texture, remembering my childhood.

I'm still a little drunk on beer from the Duke of Wellington. I can even smell Nigel in my moustache. I wonder what he'd think if he knew his essence was being savored in 1940.

I reset my phone to 12:02, September 4, 1940. The phone accepts the preposterous date without complaint.

Ten days is a long time.

England is at war with Germany—has been since September 3, 1939, when, unprovoked, Germany invaded Poland. At the declaration of war, over a million women and children were evacuated from London. But fighting didn't actually materialize for several tense months. Many of the refugees began to trickle back. Since nothing happened, people began calling it the "Phoney War," the "Bore War"—and even by the Germans, in a rare moment of humor, the *Sitzkrieg*.

Tensions were tremendously heightened, yet nothing actually happened. For a while.

Then the Nazis stormed into Western Europe. Holland, Belgium and finally France submitted to the humiliation of brutal German rule.

Hitler's formidable military machine is now poised twenty miles off the south coast of England. The Nazis are doing their best to starve Britain into submission. Their U-Boats are the terror of the seas, sinking everything in sight—passengers and all.

England is isolated and alone. Food supplies have begun to run low.

German bombing raids over England have intensified. Each side had been bombing the other's factories at night—that's just what you do when there's a war on. But someone, somewhere, started to get cocky. At an unknown juncture during the summer of 1940, civilian casualties suddenly started showing up on the balance sheets. And when they did, the established rules of warfare quietly went out the window. England and Germany each claim the other side started bombing innocent people first—and as late as 2019, I still can't officially find out who did—but now both are doing it as a matter of strategy. It's a new type of horror, devolving rapidly into never-before-seen High Ugly.

To speed things along, Hitler has made it clear he intends to invade England next month, in October of 1940.

And here I am. Smart, huh?

Plucking up my courage, I leave room 422—once I'm out, I'm out and can't get back in again—and head into the hallway. Sure enough, the maids and their carts are there, cleaning rooms. They don't seem to pay me any mind as I ditch my webbing in a hamper and head to the lifts.

Still grand, the lobby is largely unchanged, the style of the Ritz being timeless after all. Despite the shortages, flowers are everywhere.

Once out on the street, I'm surprised that . . . I'm not surprised. I have seen so many movies and photographs of 1940 that I'm not nearly as unsettled as I thought I'd be, except that everything is in color.

Bright red double-decker buses chug by in clouds of gray exhaust, festooned with dazzling ads for Lucozade and Kodak. Black taxis roar past, and gorgeous 1930s cars in all manner of hues try to outpace one another on Piccadilly Street.

The skies are blue and free of clouds.

I hang a left and head for Piccadilly Circus, a major crossroads, shopping and entertainment hub. From there I can catch the Tube to anywhere in this city of 6.6 million people.

All the neon signs of Piccadilly are sparkling. Bovril; Guinness; Jacob's Cream Crackers; Wills's Goldflake Cigarettes. Countless theatre marquees are visible down all the branching streets, everything shining gaily in the afternoon sun. Each will turn completely dark at sundown. Because that's when the bombers are likely to come.

It would all seen completely normal, but for massive barrage balloons hovering over the city. Large gray torpedo shaped blimps, cabled by tethers, float high in the air, designed to snare enemy aircraft. They're filled with hydrogen, which will explode on contact.

It seems unlikely the English don't know this, but these barrage balloons seem far too low to be useful against modern air assault. They were designed for the last war. They'll be useless now, won't they?

Pedestrians stride by, each seemingly in a hurry, despite having a war on. Heading to tea, to work, or to go have an affair. A higher-than-normal number of people are in military garb, the olive green of the English Expeditionary Forces, and policemen, still unarmed even now, are wearing steel helmets.

The civilian men are quite nattily dressed in double-breasted suits like mine, with broad lapels and long dress jackets, ties . . . and, of course, hats. The women are dashing in flounce and frill, proud hats, clutch purses, thick, high heels, and the beginning of shoulder pads. I even see a few black lines up the backs of nylons.

Vavoom.

Unfortunately we have now arrived at the point in fashion where men do not have facial hair. I'm the only one. In fact, a few people seem to stare, shocked, at my beard, like I'm some sort of beatnik. Or a Marxist. Definitely on account of my being the only person without a hat. I suddenly feel conspicuous and gauche.

It seems natural for me to begin, like always, with lunch. There's no vegetable biriyani or lamb khorma this time of century, so I amble around looking for a standard pub. I find one in Haymarket that looks like it will serve my purposes. I order fish and chips that come wrapped in newspaper and spare a few points against my liver to down another beer. It's good beer, nut brown in color and served at root-cellar temperature.

I don't have a lot of money on this excursion, plus with rationing I won't find a lot to buy. But here I am now, having to transact in this bizarre currency. The barman's in no mood, he's in a hurry, and demands six shillings. I feel like a little kid counting out my coins: I give him a crown and a shilling. I guess I get it right, for he sends me on my way with a slight "ta," which elates me.

It being a most agreeable day, I elect to walk in the direction of Sloane Square.

Fifteen minutes later I'm sorry I did. It's a normal jaunt back the way I came, down Piccadilly past the Ritz and on through Hyde Park, easy enough and truly lovely. But the closer I get to Belgravia, it all goes to cock. I've made a wrong turn and I'm in danger of getting hopelessly lost.

London streets are nothing if not a hot mess in the best of circumstances. But now, many street signs have been taken down or painted over. Should the Nazis invade the capital, we'll want them to become stymied and disoriented.

It's working. I'm toast.

I stop outside Belgrave Square Garden to rest, take a breather, and try to orient myself, fishing my arcane brain for geographic memories.

Oh! Could it be? I fish out my iPhone and tap on Google Maps, just on a wild hunch that . . .

Nope. The last thing I was looking at was this area of London. I was hoping it would still be loaded in cache, but it's not. It just swirls, looking for a signal.

Back on my feet, I amble in a southerly direction. I'll just have to try my best.

The cars, which at first were simply charming to me, now seem like angry machines, dashing around with impunity, while I'm stuck on foot without the advantages of a clue. I can't spare the cash for a taxi.

Fortunately, central Belgravia, for whatever reason, is more conventionally grid-like than most of *Londinium*. I sift through streets, mostly at right angles to one another, until I get to Eaton Square, which I remember from my maps as leading down into Sloan Square, my destination.

Whew. I make it.

It's now 2:30. I'm tired, frustrated, alone, empty-handed and with no place to stay. I'm feeling pretty low at this point. Everything feels ugly and alien and there are Nazi divisions less than a hundred miles away from where I stand.

Why did I come here?

First things first, I need a place to stay. And thus start on what I identify as King's Road. I know that no bombs fell on that street, so I happily set about looking for accommodations —only to find none. I'm going to have to cut deeper into the neighborhood, onto streets whose fate I'm much less sure of.

I'm walking in circles. I pass the same cobbler three times—he's starting to notice and look at me like I'm some bearded Nazi saboteur. I feel keenly self-conscious. And more alone than ever before in my life.

Finally, I spot a rooming house on Symons Road—the street sign has been spray-painted over in dull gray, but the lettering is of the older kind, slightly raised, so I can still make it out in the sunlight.

My hopes are up—but they have no openings in the house.

Hopes slam shut.

Another sad-looking house on Holbein Place has my hopes up again but . . . no. They claim not to have a vacancy either. Actually I suspect the wizened old man does have a room, he just seems to not like the cut of my beard.

Hopes slam shut again. An unhappy emotional slide begins to formulate an attack on my person. I can feel it.

Striking out towards the southwest, I stumble upon an epic stone building set back on punctilious acreage. It's decidedly posh and bucolic, but it's eating up a lot of valuable real estate that could otherwise house a person like me. Nevertheless, I allow my curiosity to the fore and wander through the campus. It takes fifteen minutes to walk all the way through, accomplishing nothing, but I emerge somewhat refreshed—except for the number of olive drab anti-air gun emplacements scattered about, determined to remind me of the stakes in my new little game.

Down at the bottom of the parkland, then, finding nothing so much as a hotel, I loop up to the north, my spirits crumbling.

It's after four, I'm exhausted and, frankly, starting to freak.

I figure on spiraling in toward Sloane Square one more time to find food and drink and maybe ask in a pub. Before turning in, though, I decide to try one more street. I'm able once again to discern the raised letters: Sloane Gardens, SW1.

It's a nice quiet lane, a straight shot down to the end. Fledgling chestnut trees are planted along, small and frail. The houses are kind of interesting. It's the brick: a bright rust color. All of it. Like most houses in London, they're all connected to each other in a huge, unbroken row, each one identical. In this block they're fairly ornate. I see finials and spires and excellent brickwork, so I'm not thinking I'll find a rooming house here.

But at the very end of the lane, at the last possible house, number 36, is a sign: "Nutley House. Furnished Rooms to Let."

As cranky as I am, I still muse at the "To Let" signs the English use everywhere. Just scribble an "i" in there and they all say "toilet" and that's some funny shit when you got jetlag.

But right now I ain't laughing.

Don't much care for the name, Nutley House. Sounds awful. The place looks pretty beat up, amid these lovely homes.

I climb the six marble steps under the curved archway and to the door with a window in it, curtained. I see a knob that's obviously meant to be a doorbell, but how does it work? I push it; nothing. Twist it; nothing. So finally I give it a yank and a mournful chime fairly wheezes from out of some mechanism inside.

After an interminable wait, a snaggletoothed woman answers the door, dishtowel in hand. She's got a crooked nose, crooked teeth; crooked head, from what I can tell.

But she has kind blue eyes and appears to be near to her seventies.

"Yes, dear?" she asks.

"I'm looking for a room to rent for a few days. Do you have a vacancy?"

"Oh. You're an American! It so happens we do. Please, step in."

If she's uncomfortable about my beard, she's gracious enough not to show it.

She stands aside to let me pass and closes the door. She's wearing a frumpy tartan wool skirt, well past her knees, stiff clean white shirt buttoned at the throat with a cameo broach, and a smart vest that matches her dress. Her gray hair is in a bun, her feet in sensible shoes.

As I step inside, I take a quick initial survey: Stairs go straight up from the foyer, living room to the left, hallway with a mini desk set in an alcove, which seems to serve as a tiny office. It's got a guest registry and an array of keys hanging on hooks. The house is musty but clean. I'm sure it was lovingly decorated at one point, but that was long ago. Burgundy wallpaper, striped, wainscoting and chair rails and threadbare carpeting give it an altogether gloomy appearance.

It's perfect.

"How long do you anticipate staying with us, Mr. . . . ?"

"Baldwin. Mark Baldwin. Ten days, if you have it; I've been roaming the neighborhood for the better part of the afternoon, so if you have any days at all I shall be glad to take it."

"Ten days will be fine. And Baldwin is a good English name. So much the better! It's sixteen shillings a week. Have you any luggage?"

"No, none. I should like to go shopping at some point."

"Oh, wouldn't we all?" Her eyes are sweet and sparkly. I can tell she's a kind woman, and I find myself relaxing ever so much.

"I'm Mrs. Spettegue," she adds. She goes over to the alcove and grabs a key. "Number Five is available; that's on the third floor across from Mr. Bill Markley." She lowers her voice to a conspiratorial whisper: "He speaks *German*!"

It is the custom in England to go look at the room first, so this Mrs. Spettegue begins hoofing it up the creaking wooden staircase. I admire the mahogany bannister, leading me up two flights to Number Five. She seems spry. Meanwhile, am I out of breath? I decide it must be the smoke from all the fires and in no way a reflection of my absence from the gym.

Number Five is, as I expect it to be, a bit of a dump. Sagging brass bed, tired wallpaper. Picture rail, a few framed prints on the wall. Bath towel, porte manteau, armoire. But because number 36 is the last in a row of houses, all the rooms have side windows, a major bonus. Number 5 is a corner room with windows on two sides, making it bright and airy. Although they all look directly at the neighboring, identical houses along the way, it affords daylight, something not many Londoners are privileged to have. A glance out and down shows me that I'm in the rear of the house, with a view of a sizable back garden.

I assure Mrs. Spettegue it will be fine, and I feel myself beginning to relax. If that's allowed . . . I don't know yet.

She walks me back downstairs and over to the alcove and I sign the registry. Once again, I have to dip the pen in ink first, and I use my actual address in San Francisco. No reason not to, so far as I can tell.

"Kindly leave the key when you go out during the day. I

don't allow smoking in the house. I'm not on the telephone, but there's a phone box at the top of the lane. Tea's at six, I only serve it once, so you'll want to be on time." She has clearly recited this many times.

I must have a completely dazed look on my face as I try to compute ten days' rate at sixteen shillings a week. Hoping for the best, I give her a guinea, a half-crown and a shilling, which, if I understand correctly, is £1.3s.6d. It should cover my rent with a little left over.

Apparently I do all right. She slips the coins into the fabric of her vest. They clink in her pocket.

"If you need anything further, Mr. Baldwin, I'll be in the kitchen downstairs."

I thank her and she hooks around, down the staircase behind the main one, much smaller, going to the kitchen level in the basement of the house.

Back up to my new room I spread out on the creaking, lumpy bed and look up at the ceiling. The plaster is cracked in several places and I immediately think of earthquakes. Well, there won't be any of those, only something far worse. Man made. A tool of war. Deliberate, and far more effective at destruction than a mere shaking of the Earth.

It's four o'clock, and dinner isn't until six. I take a brief nap, setting my phone alarm. I'm well within the grips of jetlag, I've spent over three hours walking and I'm worn out.

I don't know yet exactly what my expectations are for being here, but I feel dull and terribly far from home. Excruciatingly alone. I spend some time feeling thus displaced, but sleep does come to me.

When I wake to my bleating phone, hating it, hating life, it's 5:30 p.m. I was really out. Damn, I was asleep. All sweaty . . .

I go down to the lounge on the main floor. It's also rather dumpy. Like the Ritz, it might have looked good in the late 1920s, but it's wear-worn and fussy and not very shipshape now.

The walls are a dark blue wallpaper with florets and flowers. Spindle furniture, and yet a lot of daylight coming through the netting over the windows. This time of year the sun doesn't set until nearly 8 p.m.; I remember that from growing up in Seattle. It's just a thing about the northern latitudes.

An older man is in there listening to the wireless, a seriously out-of-date wooden radio nearly the size of a juke box.

"Oh, hullo," the man says, kindly enough. He stands and snaps off the radio.

"Hello. I've just checked in. Name's Mark Baldwin."

"Oh. You're an American! I'm Rodger Devereaux." He extends his hand, and we shake.

"What part of America?"

"San Francisco."

"Ah, grand place, San Francisco!"

Rodger is in his sixties, much shorter than me, bald with a few wisps of hair over the top of his head. He has a craggily kind face, crooked ears, and I suddenly find myself wondering if everyone in England is crooked? I'm of primarily English stock myself. I know my brain, at least, is deeply twisted . . .

Rodger has a three-day stubble over what would be a clean-shaven face. He's wearing bib overalls and a work shirt. We make small talk for a moment or two, Rodger says he's never been further afield than France. (I wonder if in World War I, but don't ask.) He says he'd love to see California, he hears it's lovely.

"Well, I should get ready for tea. Please make yourself comfortable, and welcome to Nutley House. We've got a full roster here now, and I think you'll find the other guests to your liking." He heads up the stairs, leaving me alone in the lounge.

I sit on the hard settee.

Still shaking off the vestiges of my nap I pick up a magazine, *Britannia and Eve*, anxious to see what's going on in this England.

At first, I fear the magazine will be useless to that effect. The main headings are "Fashions," "Everything's Under Control," and "Knitting."

But as I dive into it, I realize they are talking about some serious things. They use sentences like, "It was the fag-end of a cloudy spring day at the aerodrome," and print story after story about Royal Air Force readiness; skirmishes and actual strafings over London.

Last week a lone German plane flew over an undisclosed area and opened machine gun fire on a bunch of women and children coming out of a shopping center, killing several.

Wow, that's a dick move.

The lounge leads to the dining room just behind, through double pocket doors, slightly ajar. I can hear Mrs. Spettegue setting the table for tea, but no one else is there and I don't want to be the first, so I nose into a longish story in the magazine entitled "Heart of British Oak."

In the story of a British ship *The Lancashire Maid*, Captain Jasper Hannay captures Lt. Kessel of the Luftwaffe, a bomber picked up at sea. I get the impression they practically have sex together, drinking every night in the captain's quarters, toasting each other's honor and bravery. But they ultimately turn the tables on each other, and the German's rescue U-Boat, briefly poised to sink *The Lancashire Maid*, itself gets sunk by the British. The men part friends even after all that. It's a silly story, but politeness mixed with treachery is quite intriguing. It repeatedly mentions getting word to the German Admiralty, in direct contact—like, actually calling them on the telephone and getting word through to the German sailor's parents in Bremerhaven. It blows my mind. I didn't know they could do that.

The magazine displays ads like:

If you are working 7 days a week, you need Sanatogen Nerve-Tonic!

You can't buy a new car—but you can give new vitality to your present car by fitting a new set of LODGE spark plugs.

Reading through the articles I'm shocked to see how deadly accurate German intelligence is. They seem to know everything: which British ships are sailing, who is in command, what the cargos and itineraries are. All of it. That's kind of unnerving. They can just line their U-Boats up, like shooting ducks in a pond. Someone's feeding information to them. How do they get it? And who would do that?

Another article states:

"Up to the time of this writing, there are no signs that the Government intend to commandeer our motor cars for military use." It goes on to describe how to permanently disable your vehicle in an invasion to prevent its use by Nazi troops.

And readers might also consider this:

Trousers the Rage for Women:
Seasonable Garb for the Shelter

More of Britain's women are wearing trousers than ever before in history. Factories are turning out thousands of pairs per day. Hitler is responsible!

An adorable, lifelike drawing of a Labrador retriever's face on yet another advertisement:

For Air Raid Shock & Fear, Bob Martin's Fit and Hysteria Powders—a safe, speedy sedative for your dog or cat. Cartons 6d, from chemists and seedsmen.

Then I read something that causes me to come up short:

There may be circumstances in which people are caught in the open during an air raid, with no chance of reaching a public shelter. If bombs, splinters, machine gun bullets—spent or otherwise—

are falling, don't attempt to race to a shelter, unless it is close at hand. Keep calm, make use of the best protection near at hand; and, above all, lie flat on the ground. In a built-up area, partial protection from flying splinters and debris—remember that such fragments may be thrown half a mile by a bursting bomb—can be found in archways, doorways and against stout walls. Failing all this, the gutter gives some safety. Lie flat, face downwards, supporting the head on folded arms, keeping the chest just off the ground, to avoid the earth shock of an explosion. In a field or open space, find a ditch or fold in the earth and "stay put" until danger has passed. You should keep the mouth slightly open, and this can best be done by gripping a piece of soft wood or a handkerchief or a piece of India rubber between the teeth. Don't run out of your home to a public shelter intended for people caught in the street. Stay where you are!

And finally, one article closes with the simple reassurance: "But the kettle stays put!"

I'm startled from this at the sound of the front door opening. In walk two men, engaged in conversation. I stand to meet them.

I am introduced to Robert Montague and Cecil Hayden. Mr. Montague replies, "Oh. You're an American!"

Robert Montague is in his late fifties, puffy and heart-attacky, balding with a paunch, in business attire: ample suitcoat and heavy spectacles.

Cecil Hayden introduces himself as an actor and looks it. Dashingly handsome with a pencil moustache. He has blond, slicked-back hair and alert green eyes. Cheekbones, clever chin. Handsome, perhaps a little plasticky. He, too, is in a double-breasted suit with a garish tie.

Nevertheless, they are cheerful, and the older one, Mr. Montague, asks me how long I've been in London.

"Just got up from Southampton today," I say. "Wandered for quite a while trying to find a place to stay, so I feel privileged to be here. Say . . . what's that great building on the parkland just to the west of us? Looks impressive."

"It's the Duke of York Headquarters," Cecil tells me. "It's been commandeered for the duration. You'll see quite a few searchlights coming up from the grounds during a nighttime alert."

"Ah . . . "

"Mrs. Jarvis about?" Cecil asks me.

Of course I have no idea who that is. I'm putting together a picture in my mind of a librarian-type in her sixties who'd have several cats.

What suddenly bounds down the stairs leaves me in shock.

Pamela Jarvis is a blond bombshell. She's about twenty-four, and she has a figure like Jayne Mansfield. She's wearing a simple blue sun dress and light espadrille shoes and . . . is nine months pregnant.

I mean, like, completely pregnant.

Without even knowing it, I find myself moving to the stairs to help her down, my hand out.

"Hello. I'm Mark Baldwin. I just checked in."

"Oh. You're an American!" She takes my hand, and we shake, gingerly.

"Yes, yes, I am. From San Francisco."

"Oh, I've always dreamed of going to San Francisco. Is it beautiful?"

"It is. You should definitely go when you get the chance."

I look into her blue eyes and can't look away. She's fascinating. I don't remember when I've seen a more charming face. Her hair is long and luscious, piled in curls atop her head but sharply pulled back on either side, then curling under behind her. It's all golden waves.

She'd give Veronica Lake a run for her money.

I can't think of a single thing to say, the four of us now standing awkwardly in the hall. Fortunately Mrs. Spettegue announces tea and we all pile into the dining room just behind the lounge. Lots of dark wood furniture, an oriental rug that's ratty and worn, sideboard, dumbwaiter, woodwork and yet more fussy, out-of-date wallpaper.

We sit. An extra place is set for my new neighbor, Bill Markley in Number 4, who comes rushing in at the last second. "I'm so terribly sorry I'm late."

"We were just welcoming Mr. Mark Baldwin," Pamela Jarvis says.

I stand and reach across the table so we can shake hands. William Markley is about thirty, slender, brown hair, also slicked back—it's the current fashion. Pinched face, altogether somewhat creepy and hulking. He's wearing a sharp, double-breasted wool business suit, again with the wide lapels and a dashing tie of red and orange. He has a twitch in his face, ever so slight. He doesn't make much eye contact.

"Nice to meet you, I'm sure," I say.

"Oh. You're an American!" I just nod by now.

Rodger joins us and Mrs. Spettegue begins to operate the dumbwaiter from the kitchen below, turning a metal crank. She produces a pot of watery chicken soup in a white porcelain tureen, and gray bread with margarine. The bread's nasty, some wartime staple, but Mrs. Spettegue has warmed it up in the oven, which helps a little. The margarine is greasy and bland, white more than yellow. Yes, I can believe it's not butter. Served with radishes, sliced on a plate, and apples in a similar fashion. Everyone is given a tiny salad with vinegar and oil.

"The salad," Mrs. Spettegue announces, ostensibly for my edification, "comes from our garden. I hope you enjoy it."

"Thank you, it looks lovely," I say.

We eat heartily as we can. I wonder if this will be the entire meal; I sure hope not.

"How do you come to be in England, Mr. Baldwin?" asks Mrs. Spettegue of me, passing a plate of sliced apples.

"I work for a small newspaper in Northern California. I'm here to cover the war. Landed at Southampton just this morning, came up on the train."

Pamela Jarvis interrupts. "Weren't you afraid of U-boats?"

"As a matter of fact, I was terrified."

I'm lying of course, cleaving to the story I'd engineered for just such a conversation as this.

"I came over on the *SS America*. The ship was mostly empty. Not a lot of people seem to want to test the waters around Britain these days without a good reason."

"I'd be petrified," says Pamela. Her eyes are wide-set, very open and bright.

I keep laying it on, as I'd practiced: "We had to be full blackout at night, not so much as a lit cigarette on deck. During daylight hours we zig-zagged in our course to present a more confusing target. Strictly speaking, the Germans have no right to fire upon an American vessel, but as we've seen of late, they're becoming a little indiscriminate."

Truth is, I don't like lying. But in my present line of work, I seem to be doing an awful lot of it. I think it's ultimately worthwhile, even though I don't strictly approve of it.

"Those blasted U-Boats are a hideous creation," says Cecil Hayden. I notice that Pamela beams when he speaks. "It's completely shameless the way they operate, utterly without dignity. Torpedoing merchant vessels as well as military. They're trying to starve us."

Rodger butts in. "Navy's giving them hell, though. We sank two of them only yesterday, according to the Home Service."

"Have you had many bombings on London itself?" I ask.

Robert answers this. "We were in the shelter six separate times on Saturday. The Nazis fly over the Channel and into our airspace, so our planes scramble to meet them. Pamela can tell you about that; her husband is a flyer. Mostly we've encountered single planes, few in number. Bombs have been dropped on London, but mainly in the east end; the Germans are primarily gunning for the aerodromes. But on Saturday they came over London looking to clip barrage balloons."

"I was noticing those. Do they do any good?"

"Yes," Robert continues. "You see, the Germans fly low on their bombing runs, as low as they can. That puts them very much on the level with the balloons. And further, to avoid them, they find themselves corralled into a narrow alleyway where our surface guns can concentrate their fire. On Saturday, the Luftwaffe tried using machine guns to snap the cables. Wasn't effective for them. We shot a couple down; the pilots bailed out and were taken into custody. The planes crashed, obviously, as planes will do. That damages property and endangers lives, but it's certainly better than the alternative."

"Is it true that Hitler's planning an invasion?" I ask.

"That's what he says," interjects Cecil.

I'm noticing Bill Markley has remained completely silent.

Cecil explains, "I don't think he actually will. We're dug in from Portsmouth all the way to Hull, I think we're impenetrable. They'd never get past the beaches and they know it. And every time they start to amass troops and landing craft in Calais, our boys go in and scatter them."

"If Hitler tries to invade England, we'll give him hell!" This from Rodger, seemingly already well into his brandy.

"Here here!" says Mrs. Spettegue. "I'll take up my broom if I have to."

Pamela says to me. "As Robert says, my husband Edgar is in the Air Force a few miles down the road. They bloody well won't even let him loose to be with me."

"Now, dear," Mrs. Spettegue pats Pamela's hand, "you're hardly on your own. You have all of us. And please don't use that word at the supper table."

"Yet you've chosen to remain in London? Is it safe?" I ask her, once again simply drawn to her in wonder.

"I've been living with Mrs. Spettegue for a year now. I can't quite see going someplace else. I'd like to be close to my husband; he's stationed nearby. Foolishly, I thought that would mean I'd see him more often. Hasn't been the case at all."

"When are you due?" I ask, hoping it's not an impolite question.

"September 15th. Less than a fortnight away."

"Well, congratulations. It must be a very exciting time." She smiles, but in a distracted way. She's obviously got a lot on her mind.

I don't envy her position, about to give birth and her husband unavailable to lend a hand and in constant, unspeakable danger.

Conversation naturally returns to the war.

Bill Markley finally pipes up: "This is all uncharted territory for me, since I've spent so much time in Germany. I speak the language really well. The people there have always been a little neurotic and overly organized, but they're good people as a rule. They've suffered mightily since the armistice of the Great War. It's only natural for them to reassert themselves at long last. Only, they do seem to have taken it a step further than was anticipated."

Rodger cuts in, almost sharply: "It was *highly* anticipated, and by a great many people . . . "

"Where in Germany were you, Mr. Markley?" I interrupt, hoping to sluice through any tension.

He does a little face twitch again; his gaze seems to be focused on my chin. "Oh, call me Bill, please. I was all over, but I spent most of my time in Berlin—I'm in insurance—with occasional forays into Frankfurt. Berlin is a wild, crazy city. At least it was."

I get the feeling that Bill is gay. He's not really my type, which is just as well. There's something off-putting about him.

Bill continues: "I've listened to some of Hitler's speeches on the wireless. He's an amazing orator, full of vim and fire. He's definitely got his way of stating things . . . "

"'Old Nasty,' they call him on *It's That Man Again* . . . " Pamela interjects, with almost—but not quite—a giggle.

Rodger says, "I cannot believe how they managed to just roll over France like that. The French army was considered the most powerful in Europe, and . . . *pouf*. And then Rotterdam—they completely leveled that city from the air, just to make a point. Now with Belgium and Holland out, the Germans are knocking at our front door. It's unimaginable."

I decide to venture, "I've heard in occupied territories you have no choice, you have to join the Nazi Party or you'll lose your job, your house and your family. They have a complete lock on their people. You can do nothing to speak out against the Party."

"It's true," says Robert. "The Gestapo has neighbor pitted against neighbor. Any sight or sound of treason, or even of listening to the wireless, and you'll be dobbed in and sent to a labor camp. They ask no questions, they simply take you—and your family, too, for good measure. It's an entire network of paranoia. They keep files on everybody."

"That's no way to live. It's not right," says Pamela.

"It's because they know they're no good. They're nothing but thugs, and now, they're taking it to the world at large," Rodger grumbles.

"I've had it with all this talk about Germany," Pamela says poutily.

"Well, know your enemy," Cecil says. "If I'm any judge, they're going to fight like hell."

"Then so are we," says Mrs. Spettegue.

"Here here!" echoes Rodger.

Mrs. Spettegue turns to me. "I had Rodger put an Anderson shelter in the back yard. It's a bit late tonight. I'll show it to you in the morning. You should become familiar with it. I doubt we'll go long without further alerts."

I thank her.

We eventually talk of other things. It doesn't take long for the meagre supper to be eaten. We're just sitting around at this point, all drinking tea and brandy. I think they're remaining at the table and being polite for my sake, the newcomer.

I learn their various stories, in abbreviated fashion: Pamela is on maternity leave from a munitions factory. Robert Montague has a job for the gas works in an office down the road, his wife and children were evacuated to the countryside and he misses them terribly. Cecil Hayden is an out-of-work play actor in the West End, and Bill Markley is in insurance. Rodger is official handyman to Mrs. Spettegue.

We break from our sad, inadequate dinner and everyone heads to the lounge to listen to the wireless, which, when they turn it on, spews sprightly music. Mrs. Spettegue is darning socks and Pamela's fairly pacing to and fro. It's still plenty daylight, and I want to be outside. We're going to be cooped up soon enough for days on end and the weather is quite nice.

I ask Pamela if she'd like to take a walk. I get the sense the assembled guests seem to find it an impertinent suggestion; it feels like a serious lead balloon moment.

But Pamela says she'd love to. "I've had it with this blinking house," she says. In her clipped Estuary accent she drops all her H's, so she says it like, "Oy've 'ad it wiv viss blinkin' 'ouse." She grabs a sweater, pulls a darling hat off the peg and dons it, and we go out the door.

At 7:15 p.m. we're in the long twilight of summer in England. Soon it will be dark, unlike any darkness I've ever known.

All the British Isles, including Ireland, are in complete blackout at night, and have been for a year now. There is to be no light, period. Every window must be shuttered or blanketed, all the streetlights are out, the brilliant neon of Piccadilly

Circus and West End theatres is extinguished. Car headlamps are just a narrow slit, as are brake lights—causing countless traffic accidents. People get lost mere steps from their own front doors. They often wander into the streets and are killed by cars. People avoid going out at night at all, it just depends on the moon and the stars, which, under Britain's notorious cloudy skies usually means dire blackness. If you work a day job, your only moments of free time will be spent indoors, in curtained darkness.

For six long years.

White objects are about the only thing you can see in the dark, so pedestrians are recommended to carry newspapers or to wear white gloves to be more visible to motorists.

But Pamela and I have a comfortable margin of twilight remaining for us to go walkies. We take a sharp turn just past number 36. Sloane Gardens makes a right angle just at Nutley House and leads to Lower Sloane Street. We then head north, up to the Square.

"Are you married?" she asks.

"Oh, no; ever the bachelor."

"Me mum says I got married too early, but with the war on it seemed to make sense. We're in love, Edgar and I. Very much."

"I'm glad," I say. "What's he like?"

"Oh, tall, blond and devastatingly handsome."

He's English. I wonder which part of him is crooked.

"Incredibly smart," she says. "Smartest bloke I know. That's how come he's a pilot—they only take the best, you know—plus he's funny. He makes me laugh. So why aren't you married, Mr. Baldwin?"

"Please, call me Mark. Well, let's just say I haven't found the right girl yet," I say in response.

"Have you ever been in love?"

"A few crushes. But no, I've never been in absolute love."

"I think that's a bleeding shame."

"Me too."

I really like this girl.

"I think Bill Markley's a spy for the Germans," she says. "He speaks the bloody language and is always saying what fine people they are—and every night he disappears."

"Disappears? Does he say where he goes?"

"Out walking, is all he'll tell us. Which, during the blackouts, is completely ridiculous."

"Hmmm," I say, pondering her observations. I suspect he's probably out "cottaging," which is British slang for cruising men.

Before reading the evening's newspaper, I would have scoffed at the idea Bill Markley would be a spy for the Germans. But after seeing the wealth of knowledge the German Admiralty has on all things related to British shipping, I'm not so sure. Can someone who works in insurance get a working knowledge of exports and the movement of manufactured goods? Ostensibly, I suppose he could.

Still. I think of that man at the supper table, the homosexual, the facial-twitch guy. Doesn't add up.

Not to mention *why* would someone help the Nazis. Nazis are bad.

"Oh, I doubt he's a spy," I say. "He could be out looking for love."

Pamela laughs.

"I'm thinking I should volunteer for Air Raid Precaution services while I'm here, just in case," I muse.

"I'm sure the ARP would be glad for your help."

"Swell."

"How did you wind up choosing the Nut House as a place to stay?" Pamela asks.

"The Nut House?" I laugh. "That's funny. It was the first

place I found that had any rooms available in this neighborhood. I think I'm glad I'm there."

"I'm glad you're with us," Pamela says.

We walk for a while further, entering Sloane Square proper, mincing across the traffic to the square. No trees, but a small fountain, bubbling sweetly, shops, banks, businesses all 'round. A theatre. The Tube station.

"Have you ever thought of what you'd look like without a beard?" she asks.

God I *hate* that question.

"Yes. Have you ever thought of what you'd look like without a moustache?" And immediately I come up short. It's usually funny when I say it, but I have no idea how this'll go over with her.

"Oh!" She nearly shrieks, and bats playfully at my arm. "You!"

"I've always had a beard. It pleases me. I think men without facial hair look sort of silly. Like they need another ten minutes in the oven."

"If Edgar were in Africa, they'd probably let him have a beard. I just know it would come in all blond. I reckon I'd like that."

I'm certainly enjoying the image.

"How are you feeling, overall?" I ask, subtly indicating her condition.

"Tremendously excited. This is my first, obviously. I'm also scared, I've heard it hurts like bleeding hell. But then I'll have someone to look after. Someone who's my own little person, do you know what I mean?"

"I can imagine."

"I've got two younger brothers. I always had to look after them. Little brats, if you ask me. I'm hoping for a girl. I'd like to think I can teach her right from wrong, and, what's more, all that's fun and interesting in the world."

"I hope you get your wish."

"Thank you! You know, you're very kind. Not like so many blokes." By which she probably means I'm not immediately trying make a move on her. She must get hit on incessantly.

"Well, thank *you*. Too many unkind people in this world already."

"Too right! I don't think the Germans are kind people."

"Right now, no. They're not."

I think of the horrors being perpetrated, a mere four hundred miles away, and I shiver with dread. It's going on *now*. The extent won't be known for another five years. Then the world will know that the Germans were not kind at all.

Across the Square we go a little further to Holy Trinity Church just north on Sloane Street, but we don't go in. We just collectively, without saying anything, turn around and head back. We're passed by a couple who smiles and nods knowingly at us in the deepening twilight. They obviously assume I'm the father, a weird sensation to say the least.

"Never been in love . . . " Pamela muses.

"It's not too late. I still have hope."

"Well, that's good. The minute you shut the door on hope, it all turns inward and you become an old wreck like Mrs. Spettegue. Oh, I shouldn't say that, she's an absolute dear. We've become quite close.

"Did you know she was only married for six months? Years ago when she was young. Sometime before the turn of the century. Her husband was killed and she never remarried. I think it's sad." She puts her hand on her belly. "I lay awake at night terrified that Edgar could be killed at any time. It's horrifying. I make myself sick with fear, the idea that he might never come home." Her voice chokes a little and her head is slightly turned away from me, so that a stranger might not suffer the keen embarrassment of seeing emotion on her face.

I want to put my arm around her but wouldn't want it misconstrued. I barely know her.

"Where did you grow up?" I ask, changing the subject to avoid feelings, in what I hope is a suitably English fashion.

"In Essex. Came up to London to work. That's when I met Edgar. I was selling cosmetics at Selfridges, and he kept wandering by my counter. Of course I assumed he was after lippy and rouge for a lady friend of his, yet I was painfully distracted. Took him three days before he finally got up the nerve to speak to me. I was so relieved there was no lady friend; he merely wanted to ask me for tea. That's the sort of chap he is. His mind is always working, he always surveys a situation before making his move. We married after only three weeks' time. I know his proposal was carefully considered, and of course I said 'yes.' I just knew he was the one."

"That's very sweet."

"Then the war came up and they carted him off," she says. "First to West Malling, then to Biggin Hill. And then it was bombed. Bombed! It's so dangerous! I only saw him a few times after that."

"When's the last you've seen him?"

"Just two weeks ago." She pats her stomach again. "We write each other nearly every day. He can't say much about his life—the mail's censored, you know—but he's working bloody hard. He's an interceptor. It's his job to fly into gobs of enemy planes to see they don't get as far as London."

"Why haven't you gone home to Essex to have the baby?"

"My mother and my father! They're a nightmare, honestly. They were against my marriage to Edgar in the first place, saying it was too soon, that I was too young, which is silly; I'm twenty-three. My mother is extremely overbearing. I couldn't wait to get out from under her. She's the reason I came to London. She's a mare. She'd be haunting me and the baby, and

I don't want my child growing up around that sort of negativity." Pamela's getting a little wound up.

"What about Edgar's parents?"

"Bleedin' hell, you're just like the rest of them!" she says angrily.

I put my hands up in the growing dim and step back half a pace. "Sorry! I didn't mean to offend. I only want you to be in a safe space for the big day."

"Just because a woman wants to be on her own don't half upset people, is all. I've always been very independent. If Edgar can't be here, then I'll do this on my own. Everybody's after me to go home, or to be with Edgar's parents, and I just don't want to."

"Then you shouldn't."

"Thank you."

"I must say you have an admirable quality about you," I say, and I mean it. I think there's a bit of awe in my voice.

We've gotten back to Number 36 and Nutley House. I open the latch and push the door open for Pamela. A blackout curtain that wasn't there before is now hanging just inside the door. She ducks behind the curtain and I follow.

"Ta for the nice walk. It's time for me to retire for the evening," she says sweetly and heads up one floor to her room.

In the lounge are Mrs. Spettegue and Rodger, intent on the radio. It's about eight o'clock, and the BBC Orchestra is playing.

"Figgy pudding?" Mrs. Spettegue asks me.

"Do what now?" I answer.

"I have a tin of figgy pudding. Would you care for some, Mr. Baldwin?"

"Oh. Yes. Please." I'm still so hungry from dinner that anything sounds good—even tinned figgy pudding, whatever it is. Rodger and I file back into the dining room, the windows of which have been transformed in my short absence. Blackout curtains are now drawn, completely. It makes the air in the room feel dull, and the sound of our voices thuds against them flatly.

Rodger and I are served something like mincemeat pie from a can on darling little dessert plates. It's not bad actually.

"I suppose I need to learn how to follow blackout procedures."

Rodger answers. "They publish the blackout times in the newspaper. Tonight it's at 8:15. We simply must make certain all windows are completely covered if we hope to put a light on."

"What sort of writing do you do?" Mrs. Spettegue asks.

"Largely human interest," I respond. "I'm here to see what the conflict is like from the British perspective. War of nerves, that sort of thing."

"Well, our nerves are shot!" says Mrs. Spettegue.

They're shot now? You're in for one hell of a disappointment.

"Well, we'll see if Hitler tries to invade," I say.

"Won't that leave you rather stuck here if he does?" asks Rodger.

"I'm willing to face a little adversity for a good story," I respond.

"What other sorts of stories have you written," asks Mrs. Spettegue—like I've got troves to draw from. I haven't.

"Oh, things that would bore you," I say. "Mostly economics. I'm looking to branch out. Although your rationing is, from an economic standpoint, quite interesting."

"Interesting! It's a pain in our sides. Oh, we all know how important it is, but eight ounces of bacon a week, why, it's substandard. How's a person to subsist on that? You may as well know, Mr. Baldwin, that I ask all my guests to lend their rations to the house as a whole. Have you a coupon booklet yet? You'll get one, and I'll feed you mornings and evenings with help of everyone's coupons. Otherwise I wouldn't have a prayer. You can still do well eating in restaurants for lunch. It's expensive but they aren't rationed so far."

English rationing will become severe, eventually down to the unthinkable level of one egg per person, every two weeks. It will reach its zenith in 1947, two years after the ceasing of hostilities. As an economics major, I'm fascinated at the phenomenon.

"I understand. I'm not sure how to go about getting a ration book myself. I'm here as a sort of freelancer, an interloper. I'm not English, so I don't know if I'm even allowed to have one. But I am quite interested in participating in the Air Raid Precautions, if they'll take me."

"Why, they'd be lucky to have you!" says Mrs. Spettegue, her teacup up at her lips, holding it with both hands, elbows on the table.

"I don't know where to ask."

"The local ARP office is right in Sloane Square. Just next to the green grocers."

Meanwhile there's a bit of brandy left in the bottle and we each take a dram or two. OK, three.

"Are you married?" Mrs. Spettegue asks.

"No, ma'am. I'm afraid I'm a confirmed bachelor."

"Well, perhaps you'll meet a nice English girl whilst you're here," she says, with a wistful sparkle in her eyes. She seems to really mean it.

"That would be lovely," I respond.

Rodger finally speaks. "Well, it's nearly nine o'clock," and Mrs. Spettegue jumps up and we file back into the lounge. At nine the news comes on the radio. I'm curious how many stations they get. Turns out they get precisely one: the BBC Home Service.

We gather around the radio and I'm once again impressed by the size of it, a wooden walnut cabinet, three feet tall on legs, and it looks like it would weigh a metric ton. It has tiny black controls up at the top center, without even an illuminated dial.

My last radio was the size of a box of Tic Tacs and is somewhere in the bottom of a drawer, a completely bygone technology.

"This is BBC Home Service; and now over to the news."

Bong.

John Snagge is the BBC presenter. Everyone on the radio speaks in clipped, proper Received Pronunciation, or RP for short. You have to go to school to learn how to speak that way. It doesn't occur naturally in the wild.

The evening's broadcast is led by the news that an air skirmish took place over England's southeast coast this afternoon. A large German air armada was turned back by English Spitfire and Hurricane aeroplanes and by ground anti-aircraft emplacements.

British Bomber Command scored several hits last night in nighttime raids to a Bosch plant in Stuttgart, to oil installations at Frankfurt, and a key railway junction in Genoa, Italy.

A British aircraft carrier, along with its battleship, cruiser, and destroyer were attacked in the Mediterranean, and the news reads the official Italian published account: that the aircraft carrier was attacked amidships and left to founder.

Fifty aged-out destroyers are being donated by the U.S. Navy to Britain, to be crewed by English sailors. The first eight are in Boston and will be handed over to British crewmen on Friday.

American Isolationists are claiming that Franklin Roosevelt is becoming America's first dictator, that the destroyer gift to Great Britain is wholly unconstitutional and was done in utmost contempt of the democratic process. They fear it is likely to bring America one step closer to war.

After twenty minutes of rapid-fire reporting on dark and unfortunate news items, one after another and each more depressing than the last, suddenly the news is finished. It's 9:20 and time for *Tonight's Talk*. A lengthy discussion on freezing consumer prices for the duration of the war is hosted with a panel of guests. Voices become strident, advocates for and against the freeze.

As an economics major, I'm all up inside it, but my jetlag has me in way over my head. I'm losing the battle. I'm falling asleep. I announce to the little group, "If you don't mind, I think it's time I got a little shut-eye. It's been a long day. Please excuse me."

"Certainly, Mr. Baldwin. Pleasant dreams," says Mrs. Spettegue.

I head up to my sad little room and feel a little better. I'm worried about the coming lightning war, but am pleased to have met a small band of people who seem to have taken me in.

And Pamela! She's amazing.

The hallway is mahogany paneling with excellent fiddly bits and struts; people spent a lot of time, money and energy creating paneling like this. It's exceedingly labor intensive, and the payoff well worth it. I picture myself in Dracula's castle, it almost has that sort of feel. The floor creaks when you walk across it.

In Number Five, I find the light switch and snap it on, the little black plastic tab that, like all the light switches in England, is wrong: Down is on and up is off. What were they thinking? In a leisurely fashion, I take off my suit coat and drape it over a chair and start in on my tie before I realize with a start that it's supposed to be blackout and I've got the lights blazing.

Idiot!

I dive for the switch, flick it up, plunging the room back into complete darkness. Feeling stupid, I use the screen of my phone to survey the situation, only to find that the blackout curtains are, in fact, closed. Rodger or Mrs. Spettegue must've come in and done that while I was walking with Pamela. I'll have to make sure I know how they work so I don't put them to any trouble.

With my phone back off, I pull one curtain aside and look down into the garden in the back of the house. In my brain not only do I expect to see streetlights, but modern apricot-colored ones.

Of course I don't. It's utterly dark.

I reattach the curtain and reach down to turn on the 1920s headboard reading lamp over my bed—you remember them, the foot-long shade all pink with flowers painted on it and a little dangly chain. We don't have those anymore and we should. A decanter of water sits next to the bed, with a single drinking glass.

Peeling off my shirt and the rest of my suit, and letting it all just crumple to the floor, I climb under the covers wearing nothing but my modern-day underwear. I try to get comfortable on the sagging mattress. The bedsprings creak with the slightest movement; there'd be no such thing as having a wank under these circumstances. Not that I have anything to wank to. Maybe Cecil Hayden, in a pretty-boy sort of way.

My brain is fried and failing. I fall asleep almost immediately.

24

Thursday, September 5, 1940

I awaken at some unknown time, amid complete and utter darkness. I fumble for my phone to check the time: 3:50 a.m. *Pfft.* Damned jetlag. The brandy didn't help either.

It's completely silent except for a wind-up clock next to the bed, the travel kind with its own brown leather case. The kind where, if you're not careful, the lid will snap shut and pinch your finger. Its ticking is faint but driving me nuts. I close the case, which only marginally muffles the sound.

I've always joked that I have a blackbelt in overthink, and there, in the darkness, wide awake, I do to fuss mightily. This whole time-travel thing, the people I've just met, Hitler rolling over Europe like he did, the horrors that are taking place . . .

Finally I manage to fall back into a deep slumber—if I had to guess I'd say at about 5:30—only to be woken at seven by Mrs. Spettegue politely rapping on my door.

"Breakfast, Mr. Baldwin. It'll be done and put away by 7:30. If you'd like some tea best come down while it's still hot."

"Thank you, Mrs. Spettegue," I say through the door as sweetly as I can muster, which I assume must have come out sounding just shy of a snarl.

Ugh. I put on my same clothes and make my way to the bathroom at the middle of the hall to the tiny water closet I share with Bill Markley. I fantasize about leaving behind a copy of *Drummer* magazine just to mess with him.

Down in the dining room are Pamela and Cecil Hayden, involved in conversation, newspapers spread about on the floral tablecloth. The curtains and blackout shades are pulled aside, the room is streaming with sunlight, but the view is merely that of the façades of the houses across the lane in the same, rust-colored brick. The sun filters through Pamela's golden hair in a delicious way. She's wearing a simple blouse and Cecil is wearing a fresh, light suit. In this day and age, casual wear is not really a thing. I'm noticing the men always wear their suit jackets, even indoors. So I guess I should, too.

"Good morning, Mark." Pamela and Cecil both say cheerfully. I'm still groggy as hell, but I do my best to smile and bid them good morning. They resume a quiet conversation.

"Good morning, Mr. Baldwin," says Mrs. Spettegue as she bustles in, dressed identically to how she was yesterday, lifting a plate of sad pastries from the dumb waiter.

I help myself to tea at the sideboard and sit down. I'd like a crack at the newspaper, but my fellow breakfasters are totally bogarting it for now.

The tea helps. I drink it black, trying to pretend it's a quad latte. I drink several cups until I feel myself getting wired.

It would appear Pamela is quite taken with Cecil. She looks at him hungrily and blushes when he speaks. The bloke doesn't seem to care or, being an actor, is quite used to it.

Poor Mrs. Jarvis: Her hormones must be off the charts right now.

I decide to interrupt their conversation. "I thought I might look after getting some more clothes, at least pajamas. But I don't have a ration book."

"Oh, you don't need rations for clothes," Pamela says.

"Any decent second-hand shops hereabout?"

They both look stricken. "Oh, no, you wouldn't want to do *that* . . ." Pamela says quickly.

"Why not?"

"See here," says Cecil. "There may be a war on but that's no need to act uncivilized. Second-hand clothes hardly befit one's class."

Huh. I guess it's not the 1960s yet.

"You'll do well at Selfridges on Oxford," Pamela says, warmly after Cecil's rebuke. "Of course, I'm biased 'cause I used to work there. But any shops along the way will do a right job. I wish I could go with you, but I have to stay close and help Mrs. Spettegue."

"Thank you. I don't suppose I'm in a hurry. Glad to know they're not rationed. Maybe I'll try Whiteley's."

"Ooh, that's expensive, but it's a lovely place to shop. Me mum took me there when I was little just to gawk. It's delish," Pamela says.

"I spent a summer at Queensway and Bayswater when I was young," I explain. "I might like to go back up that way and see the old neighborhood."

I omit that I'm going there only to see how many buildings did or didn't get blown up.

In London, every time you see a 1950s, '60s or '70s building in the middle of what would otherwise be classic old-world block of buildings, that's your indication that something's been bombed out and filled back in. There are a lot of them.

My housemates' conversation continues, leaving me flat out of it.

"I didn't get the part of King Lear," Cecil is telling Pamela, "but I wound up being an understudy for a great part at the Royal. Living as an understudy is only a half-life, it's almost unfair."

Pamela's fascinated. Meanwhile it seems I have no hope of getting my hands on the newspaper, or of getting to enjoy conversation with either of them. I feel slighted.

We all wish each other a pleasant morning and I head back upstairs—only now I must face the bathtub. It's on the floor below Bill and I, in a larger bathroom shared by Robert Montague and Pamela. There's no hot water, see, not as such. Amid a tangle of blackened and cruddy pipes there's a metal box, which serves as an in-line, gaslit water heater. You have to light it. A giant book of "The Church Bell" matches, "made in Sweden," in a bright red box, sits on the counter. I have to light the damn thing, hoping it doesn't result in a miniature explosion.

I twist the gas knob on, evidently for far too long. When I stick the lit match in, the whole thing goes *WHUPP* into my face, singeing my beard. I can smell burnt hair. But eventually a trickle of warm water comes out the tap and I'm able to get it done. Then back into my same sad, tired clothes once more.

Number 36 is a large house, but feels quite empty, even with Pamela, Mrs. Spettegue and Rodger, Cecil and I puttering around in various locales; lots of empty room between the empty spaces, with surprisingly little noise. It's quiet. For now. Once more I hear birds happily chirping outside. I'm glad it's summer. England is so frightfully dark and gray in wintertime.

I take a few pictures 'round the house with my phone. The stairs, the lounge, my room. No one sees me. Pamela is in the lounge knitting. She knits like mad—I always wished I had a handicraft to rely on for emotional support—she's currently working on a magnificent sweater for Edgar. She's already knitted tiny booties and hats for the baby which, before I can stop her, she proudly goes up to her room on the second floor and brings down to show me. They're darling. Edgar's sweater is going to be an opus; it's an amazing gray pullover in a luxuriously soft-looking wool, and Pamela is no slouch at the craft. It looks patently professional.

Well. It's time for me to head back out into this world, on my own, excited at being out into this London, seeing what I can see. As long as we don't get an air raid, I still haven't decided what my feelings will be at the prospect.

I put my key on the peg at the desk and walk out onto the street.

Amazing cars are parked along the street: a Ford Prefect, a Morris, and so many others I could never hope to recognize. They're almost all black and look taller and narrower than American cars of the period. Petrol is increasingly hard to get, and some of these cars look like they've been parked quite a while. Every slot is full; every car a masterpiece of 1930s English roadsmanship.

It's a short walk to Sloane Square Station, and I enter the underground network.

The station, serving District and Circle Line trains, is a "trench bore," meaning they just carved out a ditch one story below street level and laid tracks in it, way back around 1870. Sloane Square Station, as I see it in 1940, has a large glass roof over the tracks, spanning the length of the station. The roof is dirty, and covered in pigeon droppings, but it lets daylight in.

Sixpence buys me a paper ticket, torn just so by an old man in uniform at the gate.

As much time as I've spent in London, I still have to look at the reader board to get my bearings and learn which track I need. It's a confusing network, particularly anything involving the District Line, which ultimately goes in five different directions.

Despite the wafting of cigar and cigarette smoke, and the differences in time, the London Underground smells exactly the same. Creosote and dampness and steel dust.

I stand on the platform waiting for the next train. It kind of all looks the same, until the District Line Service clatters up to the platform. It's made of wood, painted a dull red. Handholds that go *sproing* hang from the ceiling, and a wooden floor with grooves in it is littered with cigarette butts. Interesting advertisements for 1940s products, among strident calls to buy war bonds, are pasted to nearly available spot along the walls. The train carriages are old and dark with blackout curtains ready to be pulled down at nighttime.

The only lights in the carriage are blue to comply with blackout rules, as many trains run above ground at some point on their lines. It would be quite impossible to read so much as a newspaper in that light. Fortunately the curtains are up, being daylight as it is, but most of the journey is spent in an eerie darkness. It's disconcerting and glum.

I change at Notting Hill Gate to the Central Line, which is a different type of system. Three separate wooden escalators deliver me down into the deep-core depths of London's Underground. The trains down here are smaller, made by competing rail companies back in the late 1800s. So the size and technologies differ, and the air is measurably colder and more damp.

This is where people will shelter by the hundreds of thousands starting soon, in these deep-bore stations.

Out on the street, Queensway is, indeed, quite different. No trees, for one thing. None of the modern buildings are there yet. This is pre-Blitz and I'm surprised that the uninterrupted rows of old buildings are still intact. In the 1990s, it would be a riot of shish-kabob restaurants and hookah parlors and souvenir shops, Starbucks, fat women in burkas waddling and getting out of black Maybachs. In 1940, it's traditionally English with green grocers, chemists, appliance repair stores, and a few pubs. A notions shop. It's quaint.

At the top of Queensway, just before Bishop's Bridge Road, is the grand Whiteley's Building. In 2019, it's being converted to condos, like everything else of value. But in 1940 it's a gorgeous, high-end department store. I go in and wander the shopping aisles. It's beautiful. It has an enormous atrium and a swooping marble staircase, bifurcated, like at Twelve Oaks Plantation.

This building is so beautiful, in fact, that Hitler has ordered it not to be bombed: He wants it for his headquarters once England has submitted to the Third Reich.

Pamela's right, they're much too expensive. I never was much of a shopper, yet I fairly drool over the selection. Even with a war on, textiles are still aplenty. People are still managing to worry about fashion to some extent.

Realizing Whiteley's won't serve my needs, I wander behind, onto Westbourne Grove, and find a natty shop in which to do my shopping. Much cheaper. Salesgirl named Jane —at first she tries the distant, diffident, detached demeanor of an English shop keeper, but I eventually get her to cut loose and we have fun. She has me try on an array of shirts and trousers, pajamas, and a few pairs of boxer shorts, which frankly I never cared for—I don't like my bits to just hang unsupported like that. Two undershirts, two dress shirts, and two ties. It comes to £1.8s. I also find a heavier wool coat that comes down to my knees for another one and sixpence. I'll need it for the air raid shelters, for they are bound to be chilly, even though the days are still fine.

I need a hat. Jane recommends I go further on to a shop that sells those. I find a gray fedora to match the light gray of my suit, and I feel complete.

I need to go to the chemist for a toothbrush, toothpaste, and butch wax for my hair. I select my goods and am feeling chuffed, only to stall out at the register. I haven't got a ration booklet, so I can't buy them, the woman behind the counter explains. She looks at me like I'm an idiot—a damned unpatriotic one to boot.

"Oh. I'm an American."

"Well, maybe you are, but nevertheless . . . perhaps you can borrow one? Next?"

By this time, I'm getting cross, so I go to a pub on Queensway for beer and steak and kidney pie.

I don't eat the kidney parts. I just sort of kick them to the side with my fork.

And here I find a copy of *The London Guardian*, which I'm free to take my time and read.

Tensions in Romania, cabinet resigned, Transylvania ceded to Hungary, Iron Guard and pro-Axis groups all convening around Europe, throwing in with Germany for a shot of fame and glory. It all sounds like a frightful mess, and I fear it won't get any easier as time goes by.

Hitler promises invasion: "We will come; Britain will be broken," he declares, assuredly barking in German, jerking his hands as if seized with fit.

Another RAF attack on Berlin last night blew out power stations and an arms factory was bombed.

Several Luftwaffe raids in England's Southeast yesterday focused on aerodromes. The Capital (us) was ready and on the alert, should the Germans venture too far north. But our boys managed to scare them off.

Liverpool and Birmingham docks and industry were badly hit in bombing raids.

A minesweeper has been sunk in the Aegean; sailors' families being notified.

"What local bomb damage actually amounts to is not disclosed because making it known would convey to the enemy information the military authorities wish to withhold," the paper states. That's a disconcerting concept, but I guess it makes every bit of sense.

While I'm sitting there avoiding the kidney bits, I suddenly find myself reading a lengthy speech by Adolf Hitler. I've never done this before. I've never wanted to. "Old Nasty" actually has the balls to play the victim in this article. He decries the mean old British trying to starve the continent, calling the English "virtual pirates of the seas."

The Fuhrer claims that "no one country should ride roughshod over another." And, at that, I nearly gack out loud.

Jesus. Gaslight much?

Hitler ends his missive by saying that the British are cowards, bombing Germany only at night; they know they'd be beaten soundly if they were brave enough to strike in broad daylight.

Well. I've certainly read enough of that. I fold the paper back for someone else to enjoy those fruitful words and head back out onto the street.

I wear the coat and hat back to Sloane Square so I don't have to carry them, but soon I'm too warm and take them off again anyway, sweat beaded upon my brow.

Cecil is alone in the lounge, reading and listening to Sydney Lipton and His Band on the wireless. It's around two o'clock. I say hello to him and head up to my room. A nap is in order. Mrs. Spettegue has made my bed, something I'm surprised to see. I mess it up again, getting into my new pajamas and climbing under the covers.

I have a right good sleep until nearly four.

Upon waking, I ask Mrs. Spettegue to acquaint me with her Anderson shelter.

I find her down in her kitchen, on the very bottom floor. The kitchen is bright and white and clean, getting plenty of light from the area at the front, through the railings up above at street level. Stove, ice box, sink, large butcher table. She clearly spends a lot of time here, she's set up for everything, even though there's not much food to be had. Someday there will be again.

Mrs. Spettegue's basement bedroom is at the back of the house. It does have a window, but small and up high. It's a little sad, this bedroom of a seventy-year-old widow. I try not to look, but what I do catch out of the corner of my eye is a glum disappointment as I follow past. I wish better for her, such a sweet woman.

We go up some stone steps and into the bright backyard.

London housing is universally bleak. Stone, cramped—yet the majority of houses and flats do have a tiny backyard. They needed a place to put their outhouses in the pre-plumbing days. London would be insufferable without them. Yet it's rather like being in a fishbowl. You're surrounded by the backs of all the other houses, divvied up by fences and clothes lines, and all those windows looking down would be Gladys Kravitz's wet dream.

In an unusual turn, number 36 has an enormous backyard. Instead of houses behind, it's a double length plot of land ending in a high stone wall of the same orange brick. Mrs. Spettegue mentions that just behind it is Lower Sloane Street.

Her garden is flourishing and includes a great apple tree. I'd love to sit under it and read in the sunshine.

It's all lovely until we get to the goal of our visit. A hideous pile of sandbags in a mound, and hidden behind yet more sandbags is a small, gray, metal door.

Such shelters, invented by an Englishman named Anderson—hence the name, obviously—can accommodate six people under normal circumstances. The essential design is corrugated iron sheeting in an arch formation, buried and covered by several feet of sandbags. The fact that it is arched saves countless lives by deflecting the blow of the bombs. But to actually be in one, night after night . . . Water seeps in. They are hideously confining and, being made of metal, they serve to only amplify the sounds of the bombings outside. They are not built for comfort.

Mrs. Spettegue's is set up for the full six. She leads the way proudly. Down the steps, through the tiny metal door. There's barely any room to move or breathe—I can't even stand upright, although Mrs. Spettegue is short enough to not have any problem. Four bunks, two on each side, take up the bulk of the space, with barely room for two old cast-off dining room chairs. An old oriental rug is placed in the middle of the floor. She pridefully shows me the electric lightbulb Rodger has installed in the ceiling, with an extension cord running from the house.

The shelter is excruciatingly small: about six feet by five—not appreciably bigger than a queen-sized mattress. For six people!

I'm ill-at ease, to say the least. It's tiny and cramped and looks like a deathtrap. There won't be room to move, to breathe. I feel disconcerted just thinking about it.

One of the most enduring images of bombing raids is perhaps the thousands of people crowding and sheltering in the deep tunnels of the London Underground. In the coming years, 170,000 people will find shelter there night after night. But that doesn't happen the first couple of weeks of attack. While I'm here in 1940, the Tube doors will actually be locked shut the minute an air raid begins. The Home Office is worried about people crowding into the Tubes and interfering with daytime service and the rapid, mass deployment of troops. Thus the Tube station at Sloane Square will be a no-go during my stay. And being the shallow kind means the station would be next to useless anyway.

Mrs. Spettegue's shelter can hold six. I'm the latest arrival, I make number seven. So how will this even work? I can only assume I need to go it alone somehow. It's unsettling. They must have a public shelter up at the square. I guess I'll need to check it out. Soon.

Mrs. Spettegue closes the door to the shelter and takes me on a tour of her garden like nothing's wrong. She guiltily admits to planting some delphinium and salvia instead of devoting the entire Victory garden to growing vegetables, as everyone else is doing. Hers includes green beans, radishes, corn, leeks, tomatoes, potatoes, zucchini, green beans, onions, carrots and lettuce.

I compliment her on the loveliness of her garden. With rationing on, it must be a boon to have fresh produce on demand.

But as we head back indoors, I'm somewhat in a state of fuss about room in that shelter for me.

Grabbing my new hat from the peg on the wall behind the door and, saying nothing to Mrs. Spettegue about it, I walk back up to Sloane Square to look at the public shelter. It may be my only hope. The signs point the way to a locked door, to what will certainly be stairs heading to the basement of a hardware store. "Street Communal Shelter," it says in bold letters. Judging from what I read in the papers, it is primarily designed for motorists and passers-by to duck in at the last minute when caught out in a bombing.

I read the notices pasted to the stone walls, rules for shelter behavior and the admonition, "Absolutely No Pets."

Well. It is what it is. Glumly I turn and walk back home in time for tea, feeling pretty low for the task I've set before me—perhaps my lowest yet. This is not, nor was it ever going to be, a walk in the park.

We're all present for tea, save Bill Markley. No one knows where he is. In fact, his absence is barely noted. A place is set for him, but nothing said. And everyone seems a little more at ease because of it. There doesn't seem to be anything specifically wrong with the man. He's just an odd duck and not particularly pleasant.

We have a supper of franks and beans, with that industrial gray bread and margarine, and more apples and radishes, salad, and brandy. Rodger seems to have a limitless supply of the latter. I've never been much of a brandy drinker, but I must say it helps. They kind of hid it from me my first night, but now the brakes are off and Rodger eggs me on, assuring me there's plenty more where that came from and, after all, there's a war on.

Mrs. Spettegue is prim and proper, but she'll knock back brandy like a pro. Atta girl.

Again, the meal isn't much, but we sit around the large table and talk.

I tell my tale of shopping, but of not being able to buy a toothbrush and toothpaste. Cecil says I can use his ration book for it. There's a chemist just at the top of the Square.

"I got a letter from the children," Robert Montgomery is beaming. "Oh, they're moping and moaning, they want to come back in like most of their friends already have, but I won't allow it. They're in a good place; I aim to keep them there until I know this whole kerfuffle is finally over."

Cecil shares about his life, growing up in Nottingham, and working to hide his accent. He always knew he wanted to be an actor, and his dying wish is that he could break into motion pictures. He recounts a few tales, of his mates long gone to the military, blokes he misses dearly and still keeps in touch with through the mail. He tells a modestly raunchy joke, and we all laugh unduly, save Mrs. Spettegue who merely goes tut-tut. Pamela turns crimson in mirth and continues to look longingly at Cecil.

Rodger, uncharacteristically, tells meandering tales of his years as a train driver for the Great Western Railway. He has endless stories to draw on, my favorite being about some Karen hurling abuse at him through his cab window one night in a blinding rainstorm, all because her train was delayed.

"And suddenly my lights all went to green and I was completely free to signal the doors and drive on once more, leaving the poor wretch soaking on the platform. She was mad as a wet cat, and I can't remember ever being happier. It must have taken her hours to finally get home." He says it lightly and we all giggle.

After Pamela helps clear the dishes, we take a walk again in the evening air. I was hoping we could all day. Once again, it's pre-dusk, about 7:15.

We walk south this time, toward an enormous hospital, and what Pamela declares to be the Chelsea Barracks and verdant parkland. It's lovely. But the hospital and barracks shall be targets, shall they not? They're so close by. I feel a new sense of unease.

The hospital reminds me more of a haunted sanitarium than a place to get well. It's macabre and hideous and industrial-looking. Several searchlights are set up on the grounds, and Pamela describes what she knows of the place; that Christopher Wren designed some of the buildings, which go back as far as the 1600s. The barracks themselves aren't particularly impressive: two-story brick buildings with a few gothic square towers with flags on to brighten it up. More green grass everywhere. It's tranquil, despite the name.

From here it's not that far of a walk south to the River Thames at Chelsea Bridge. We amble in that direction. Lower Sloane Street becomes Chelsea Bridge Road, and, even with petrol rationing, too many cars roar past, making conversation difficult. We say little as we walk along the path toward the river.

Chelsea Bridge was only just completed in 1937, so it is a brand new, lovely suspension bridge leading to Battersea Park across the Thames. In normal times it would be all lit up at night. As such, in this late wartime evening, it looks new but joyless and austere.

Another ugly, temporary bridge is right next to it. "They just put that in this spring," Pamela mentions to me. "It's for tank movements, should the main bridge be blown up."

Charming.

But my attention is taken by a huge industrial building on the opposite shore with four great smokestacks. It looks vaguely familiar to me. I ask Pamela what it is.

"That's the Battersea Power Station. Dreadful thing, I shouldn't wonder it wouldn't be the first to be taken out by the Luftwaffe."

I gaze at it, wondering why I've seen it before. Then it clicks: Pink Floyd used it on an album cover. As ugly as it is, it apparently survives the war just fine. Bodes well for me, I decide just then.

We find a grassy, park-like area near the riverbank, away from the noise of the traffic, and sit on a bench, anxious to get off our feet. Pamela is wearing perhaps the shoes of the day, but they're ugly clunky things that look like agony on a stick.

"Do you have a doctor? Who's going to deliver the baby?" I ask her.

"Doctor Kelso, he lives just two streets over. He's on high alert, just a phone call away. Mrs. Spettegue almost had a telephone put in for when I go into labor, but I talked her out of it. They're terribly expensive, and I don't want to be a fuss."

"Hmm. Well, if you ever need me to go and fetch Dr. Kelso, just teach me where he lives and I'll get him in a flash. That's a promise."

Pamela laughs. "The neighbors next door have a telephone, and they've given us permission to use it whatever time of day or night it may be. But thank you."

"You're certainly welcome."

We sit for a while.

"Have you been in love? Before Edgar?" I ask.

"Oh, blokes have been cracking onto me my whole life."

I believe her. Pamela is, strictly speaking, a regulation hottie.

"I've had to learn how to fend off advances ever since I was a girl. In Chelmsford, before I came up to London, I was a secretary for an undertaker—ghoulish business with horrid people—and one of the embalmers was really laying it on thick with me. For a brief while I tried to like him but just couldn't, could I? I'll tell you a secret, if you promise you won't let on?" she says.

"Sure. I promise," I say.

"I'm inordinately distracted by Cecil Hayden. I think he's a dream. And then I feel awful about it. I know I'm in love with Edgar and all, and I am—I really am. But there's something about Cecil that's driving me absolutely starkers."

"Does he know?" I ask, not wishing to indicate that it's painfully obvious.

"No, heavens no. I'd die if he knew."

"Well, he certainly won't hear it from me."

"Do you think I'm a wretched person for thinking like that?"

"No, not at all. I'd say under the circumstances it's perfectly natural. You're 'nesting.' It's built into the system. No shame in that."

"I suppose you're right. It's not as if I'm in a position to do anything about it."

"Well, technically you are. But I agree it might not be prudent."

"At nine months up the duff? You must be mad!"

"No, it's still a going concern. Don't ask me how I know, but I know."

"I will most certainly ask. How do you know?"

"A friend of mine had six children," I say, "and he was rather frank about it. He told me tales that would really set you back. Suffice it to say, it's perfectly acceptable. In fact, it's one way to . . . " I pause.

"To what?"

"Never mind, it would be too much information."

"Now you have to tell me!" Pamela demands.

"Well, all right. It's one way to stimulate birth contractions."

"My *word*! I had no idea . . . "

"Sorry. I didn't mean to shock you."

"I'm not shocked. I feel comfortable talking with you."

"I'm glad," I say.

I marvel at what Pamela doesn't seem to know about pregnancy. She's just a young girl, half my age. I can't believe that I, as a gay man, seem to know so much more about it than she does.

It's getting darker, but we're content on our bench. We should head back soon, but I'm enjoying the calm idyll away from all the motorcars, even with that evil-looking power station towering over us in the growing gloom. It certainly won't be lit up tonight. I bet it looks positively monstrous in the dark.

"So Edgar's the one, huh?"

"Oh, yes. A thousand times yes. I simply adore him. At school, there was a boy named Charles. We dated, rather seriously," she tells me. "He made all sorts of promises, but he really just wanted into my knickers. Once I let my guard down, he bolted. I was devastated."

"I think I know the sort of man you mean," I say, picturing Clarence Kovacs.

"Why are men such prigs?" she asks.

"I think it comes from men being rather singular in their needs, whereas women are much more complex creatures, not so tied up with the . . . main event." I hope it's OK to say that.

"Oh I'm quite a fan of the main event," Pamela giggles. "I

just don't think you need to lie about it and cheat because of it. Have you ever lied to a girl to get into her knickers?"

"I'd have to think about that. I'd say no. Where I come from, people are a little more direct about what they want."

"Just because you live in San Francisco?"

"Well, not just that, but there are cultural differences."

"So, are you saying the women of San Francisco don't say no?" Pamela asks incredulously.

"Well, it's difficult to describe, but suffice it to say, there are significant differences in my world."

"What sort of differences? Just what world do you live in?"

Shit. I kinda walked right into that one.

I wasn't really prepared to reveal myself to Pamela. This is a different time. Such things are not spoken of; in fact, it's completely illegal—and eagerly prosecuted—in England, all the way up to the 1960s. But I like her so much. I want us to be on the same page, frank with each other. She's so fundamentally cool in all things I can't imagine her "throwin' an epi," as they say, about it.

I gaze off at the power station. It could turn all kinds of horrible at my next words.

"It wouldn't be easy for me to tell you . . . "

"Well you'll have to. I can't read yer blinking mind."

"I'm . . . different . . . from most men, I suppose you could put it." My heart is pounding. I could just lie to her, but I don't want to. Chances are—fifty-fifty—that she'll freak. If she does, I suppose I'll have to decamp from the Nut House and go somewhere else. That would be a shame. I'm starting to warm up to these people. Certainly to Pamela.

"Go on," Pamela says.

"I prefer men," I say simply.

Silence. Seems to take forever, but in reality, that's probably just my imagination.

For Pamela does respond, and after only a heartbeat or two.

"Oh is *that* it? Golly! Well. Right. I understand now. That wasn't so hard, was it?"

"It's not something I tell a lot of people . . . "

"I'm glad you did, Mark. Really. I'm not all that fussed about it. My youngest brother's the same way. He doesn't know I know, but I could always tell."

She takes my arm in hers and we stand up and resume walking back toward home. Suddenly, I'm elated. I heave a huge sigh of relief and say: "So your child is going to have an auntie."

Pamela bursts into laughter.

"He or she will be one lucky bugger," she says. "Oh! Mrs. Spettegue would be devastated!" Still laughing, "She's determined to find you a bird of your own."

We head back north, in the direction of Sloane Gardens, back to the roar of traffic.

"Someday, I'll want you to tell me the bits about your friend that will set me back," Pamela declares.

And I just may do it, before the baby comes. There's so much she doesn't seem to know. I hope I'm here for the birth. I'll be heartbroken if my ten days are up before the baby arrives.

"So anyway," she continues, "thank you for telling me what you told me about yourself, but I'm still saddened that you've not found love."

I laugh bitterly. "Me too. Just before I left San Francisco I had coffee with a man I really like; he was meant to spend an evening with me but totally blew me off—sorry, stood me up—so he could go out with some French-Canadian guy instead. In no way did he apologize for his behavior, in fact, he told me all about it in graphic detail, like he was proud of it. I was really hurt."

"The nerve!"

"Right? You see, where I live, people are so fond of the

main event that they're really callous about it. It drives me crazy. Like you, I'm fond of the main event just fine, I've done my share of catting around. But I still have feelings. In your world, you pick one person and that's it for life. In mine, it's a free-for-all, and there's no stability. It feels like there's no love."

"That sounds sad. I often think the normal way of one person for life is a bit silly. But this is all talk. I couldn't go through with cheating on Edgar, I just couldn't."

"Nor should you."

"But I wonder what I shall do if Edgar doesn't come home?"

"He'll come back. I'm sure of it. But in the worst-case scenario, nobody would think less of you if you found love again. Look at Mrs. Spettegue. I don't know the story, but it seems she made her choice when her husband died . . . "

"I'd say her face made the choice for her," Pamela interjects and we both laugh like school children.

"But I won't countenance the idea that your husband won't come home," I say. "He will. And soon. They must give him leave when the baby comes?"

"They say they will, but you have to go through channels. English bureaucracy is the envy of the bleeding world. I daresay they won't set him free until I produce a placenta in triplicate and fill in a form."

"What type of flying does he do?"

"He's pilot on a Defiant, in the 141st. Biggin Hill. The Defiant is an experimental aeroplane; they're just trying them out. Edgar's an interceptor—he doesn't drop bombs. His job is to provide air cover for Bombing Command, shooting down enemy planes. He's the one actually flying the thing, while a gunner sits just behind him. Actual aerial dog fights. I'm . . . " she looks around almost furtively, "I'm not supposed to know such things, but Edgar tells me they've determined the Defiant has a much better safety record doing nighttime sorties, as opposed to operating in the daylight. I'm not sure why that is . . .

"But the upshot is, every time darkness falls," she sort of sweeps her arm out helplessly at the glowing darkness, "he's in the air. Right at this very moment, Edgar has surely just finished his tea and is suiting up as we speak. He's only a mere twenty miles away, fighting it all out there in the dark. I honestly don't know if I like that better or not." She's getting a little choked up. I'm suddenly very glad she's taken my arm. She's holding me tightly.

"Biggin Hill aerodrome was badly bombed a fortnight ago. He wasn't there yet, they moved the 141st in just after that and got the base operational again in double time. Married quarters were available, I could have almost been there—it would have been lovely—but they ended the program just after the attack. So it's just as well."

"I'm glad you're safe here," I say.

I look around in the darkening air, the barracks, the trees.

The western sky, deep azure as the sun has finally set.

In 2019 that sky would be a god-awful crisscross of pollution. Contrails in and out of Heathrow, one of the busiest airports in the world. But now it's a clear, deep blue—and completely empty. The residents of Hounslow live in a sleepy, quiet English village, in no way associated with aviation. No triple-window-glazing to keep the jet noise out, no frozen stowaways dropping out the nosegear of 777s in from Nairobi. Just a quiet English suburb.

So much is about to change for these people . . . not all of it good.

"You must be quite proud of your husband, though. I understand your unease, but he sounds fierce."

"Oh, he is. He's a brave fighter, very patriotic, at a time when we must all rally 'round God and country."

"Yeah. God save the queen, and all that . . . "

"The *queen*?" She's frankly shocked.

"Oops. King. I was thinking of Victoria. Sorry."

Damn. Who's the king right now? The one who stutters? Bb-bb-ertie?

"What do you think of Princess Elizabeth?" I ask.

"Oh, she's a bit cheeky and precocious. But I can only hope my daughter, if it's a girl, will be as clever. Elizabeth may be queen someday."

"She may at that."

We've reached the end of our walk just as darkness has fallen and we duck through the curtains at the front door.

"Thank you for a most productive walk, Mrs. Jarvis," I say pompously in a Received Pronunciation accent.

"The pleasure was strictly all mine, Mr. Baldwin, truly it was," she says in Heightened RP, which, even in 1940, is only heard in stage plays and by the King and Queen.

I'm still on cloud nine that I told Pamela the truth and finally have what feels like a powerful ally in this strange universe I've plunked myself down into.

"Figgy pudding!" Mrs. Spettegue is all up in her treasured dessert. We go in and have some of it with sherry, and I'm really glad. It's a nice distraction from the hunger left over from the franks and beans. Pamela slinks upstairs to rest.

Then it's on to the wireless for the nine o'clock news. More on the American delivery of fifty destroyers, air raids over the southeast, RAF bombings over Germany and Calais. As horrifying as it all is, it's virtually unchanged from the day before.

I excuse myself afterward and go up to read. I'm in the middle of Neil Gaiman's latest book on my iPhone. I'm torn between reading like a fiend and wanting to save the phone's battery life. The distraction of the story helps ease the growing dis-ease in my belly. Am I getting nervous? I suppose if I had a lick of sense I would.

Mostly I resort to my long-held habit of low-level fuss. I try to remember a quote I heard: "People with anxiety frequently choose to worry instead of relaxing to avoid large jumps in anxiety when something bad actually happens." That's me to a tee. I hope I don't have a large jump in anxiety. I'm not particularly good at it, as was taught to me the hard way a couple of weeks ago in 1906.

I read with the screen on its lowest setting in the dark until my eyes begin to give out.

Jet lag mostly gone, and despite the damn jiggling of the bedsprings, I manage a gentle wank anyway, thinking of blond Edgar in his blond beard, only maybe a good fifteen years older, Edgar being English and probably crooked, with some meat on his bones, in his uniform, blond, somewhere out in the Dardanelles . . .

25

Friday, September 6, 1940

Today is England's last normal day for the next ten years. The Blitz that will kill 44,000 Britons and define a generation will begin tomorrow afternoon. Their lives will never be the same.

They know it's coming. They just don't know when, or how bad it'll get.

Early, just after brekkies, I go to the ARP office and sign up as a volunteer. They ask after my qualifications and I tell them I am classically trained in first aid and in San Francisco's Neighborhood Emergency Response Team for earthquake rescue. Even though it won't exist until the 1990s, I nevertheless carry a dim memory of all that training. They seem pleased to welcome me to their ranks.

My choice of duties as an untrained visitor are few: rescue services, first aid, stretcher duty, ambulance driver and messenger. I quickly learn usually only kids under eighteen are messengers, and driving ambulances is strictly the purview of the womenfolk.

Being an actual warden is a full-time job and serious business—not for a dilettante like me, so I am glad I don't cockily enquire after it. They'd find me impertinent.

So light rescue and first aid it is.

I'm given a metal hat and shockingly blue cotton overalls and a badge that says "ARP" on it. And a handbook. It's pink. It is entitled *Rescue Parties and Clearance of Debris*, issued by the Home Office, only nine pages long. I somehow feel the coping skills needed to get through World War II should take more than nine pages. But it's all I'll get. Taking a moment to flip through the booklet my eyes fall upon a line that reads, "A casualty due to flying glass is gory and spectacular, but rarely fatal."

And thus I am comforted. Not.

I'm there just in time for a brief orientation, as luck would have it.

In a group of four other men in a rank basement beneath the green grocer's, we're sat down in front of an ancient blackboard. An older, frankly icky man named Rand is our instructor. He's got excruciatingly bad teeth, crooked features, and dandruff. Rand has got a fiercely strong accent, and despite a depressing, monotone beginning, eventually turns out to have a wicked sense of humor.

"You won't be fire brigade or heavy rescue, if you don't mind; you'll serve as able-bodied men in a pinch. It won't always be easy. Wish I could tell you otherwise. You'll be out in the night, during the air raids, and you're likely to see many uncomfortable scenes. Well. Everyone's got to help out. If you don't mind, I'll start with . . . "

Rand has obviously done this many times before. He opens with the nature of normal exploding bombs; delayed-reaction time bombs, which are designed to detonate either a few seconds after impact or substantially later; and some other bombs are designed to detonate twice. Once initially, then again after rescuers—us—have rushed to the scene, to inflict maximum injury.

I find it offensive in the extreme.

And yet there's always the likelihood of a dud. Each unexploded bomb must be treated as a live issue, in which case, our job is to stay back and keep others from approaching at all costs.

Certain materials and structures cushion blasts in varying ways. When a bomb goes off, there's an initial shockwave. But several seconds after that, chunks of debris and broken glass will come raining down and can seriously injure one.

Rand draws pictures on the blackboard of happy bombs with swastikas and tits on them and the men chuckle, so I chuckle too. Heh heh. Boobies. Heh.

Then he goes on to explain why we're here: to assist the heavy rescue as a back-up. Hauling bricks and, occasionally, sweeping a darkened room to search for survivors if called to do so.

"You'll want to sweep in a counter-clock direction, if you don't mind, always in teams, ensuring the scene is safe. Your team leader will serve as anchor at the door. I'm a team leader." He beams a wide, crooked smile. "So you lot get to go in and face the danger, while I wait at the door enjoying a nice fag until you get back. If you *do* get back." He sounds simply bored at the prospect. Another round of nervous laughter.

"Truth be told, I won't be smoking a fag, and neither will any of you. I don't care how fond of them you may be, each damaged building has to be treated as a live gas leak until proven otherwise. Do not attempt to light up until you're well clear. Ever.

"Given your experience level, it's rare that you will be the senior man on a scene with no one to advise you, but if you should find yourself thus and lives are in imminent danger, remember the following . . . "

It's all getting really serious. My stomach knots up.

He lectures and draws pictures with chalk on the board, teaching us how to look for survivors, how to leverage and crib rubble, and how to make a stretcher out of a blanket and two broomsticks.

Then he speaks of triage. How to segregate and divide victims into minor, serious, critical and deceased categories, with nothing more elegant than a strip of tape and marker across their foreheads.

Rand breaks the tension like a pro: "Stick by the critical ones; you might cop yourself a nice dose of morphine. They'll be your best bet."

The men giggle.

The group breaks. My brain is fried.

On my way back home, juggling my ARP supplies, I finally stop by the chemist, armed with Cecil's ration book, to get Euthymol Tooth-Paste and a standard white toothbrush. Still have to go home first to drop off my hardhat and coveralls, booklet, and supplies.

It is hence noon. I aim to explore London this afternoon. I catch the District Line Tube and head to the Embankment to look out over the river. The tide is low, the water brackish. Broad promenade, iron and copper light poles dripping in formed leaves and rings aged green. Stone steps go down to the river at various places, and giant metal rings for tying up boats look too heavy to lift.

I stare a good long while at Tower Bridge off to the east, one of London's most beautiful and iconic landmarks; that which looks like a castle, and the Tower of London, looking squat beside it.

The Houses of Parliament and Big Ben are just behind me. I hear Big Ben strike one-thirty, and I drink in the scenery of

Parliament, and for reasons I can't describe, decide to go a few steps hence to Westminster Abbey. Within the silent and dark confines of the grand cathedral, I just wander from alcove to alcove, basking in light from the stained glass. Walking gingerly over to the Poet's Corner, I gaze at the stone markers for Chaucer, Charles Dickens, Rudyard Kipling and so many others.

I allow the magnificence to wash over me. I even quietly say a prayer in the cathedral; precisely to whom, I do not know, but I tender it with genuine awe, and hope that it is heard.

I then head on foot to Covent Garden. Bookshops can always be found there, and I will have plenty of time to read. I go into one at random and find a copy of *Wuthering Heights*. It should, at least, get me started.

Lunch is at around 2:30, in a pub on Lower Regent Street. I ask for the roast chicken with potatoes, only to be told it's not available, what with the war on. I'm downgraded to liverwurst sandwich on sad bread for 3s2d and a cup of tea for sixpence. I start in on my new book, dense English prose from an earlier age. It's going to be a ripsnorter, I can tell already.

Then back to the Nut House, completely wiped. All in all, a nice day out. It's tiring, in its way. I'm fighting another nap.

Yet Pamela is clearly going stir crazy in the house under Mrs. Spettegue. I ponder for a moment and then suggest we take in a film at that movie house just up at the square. She's thrilled at the idea. Grabbing our hats and leaving our keys, we head up to the New Court Theatre at the top of the lane, just past the entrance to the Underground. We don't even check to see what's playing, we just go to the guichet and pay our fee. We only have to wait a short moment for a four o'clock screening.

It's *The Blue Bird*, starring Shirley Temple. Of course the theatre is nearly deserted. It's weird going to a movie in a war, in England, in 1940. Such a banal thing to do. The movie house is spartan and modern, with plain carpets and bare walls and doesn't even have a concessions stand.

The presentation starts with black and white ads exhorting us to buy stamps and war bonds.

Then the newsreel begins, labeled with Pathé Gazette and the little chicken logo. Suddenly a bit about the RAF comes on and Pamela grabs at me tightly. But it's all song and praises and she relaxes so we can enjoy the film.

Awful movie. They obviously wanted it to be another *Wizard of Oz,* but . . . *awful.*

We go for tea after—or at least try to. I've forgotten my hat again. I dash back to the theatre and explain myself to the manager and am let back into the auditorium to fetch it.

Finally we're ensconced in a café at the square. It's all very warm and gracious, tea in thick white ceramic cups with saucers and each with a decadent slice of lemon cake.

"Yummity cakes!" Pamela fairly squeals. "Oh, how I miss *food*! Real food you can sink your teeff into, dja know wot I mean?"

She dumps an awful lot of strong black tea into her system while preggers; well, it's not for me to go there.

"Did you enjoy the film?" I ask Pamela graciously.

"No."

"Me neither."

We both laugh.

"I imagine, with a child on the way, you're going to have to develop a taste for all things childlike, and in a hurry. Keeping a young one entertained is going to draw upon all your forces."

"And here I've just been fairly aching to get back to work. I wonder if I can do both—have a child and work at the same time? I think people will frown on that and accuse me of being a terrible mother. But to hell with them. I've been known to do as I please. I know with absolute certainty that being a mother shall please me. But I'll also want to work."

"Mmm," I muse, "I think that might be a thing. At least some day."

A heavyset, mid-fifties-aged woman has rushed up to Pamela with her arms full out, gushing, beaming. She's near to stumbling into Pamela full-force, overridden with glee. "Oh, my dear, when are you expecting?"

"In a fortnight," Pamela answers proudly. She likes the attention, and I don't blame her. But the woman obviously thinks I'm the father. I play the part, grab Pamela's hand, and we make kissy noises.

And giggle, as the woman teeters off, her own heart in a state of joy and good grace—she's feeling grand at two young lovers in a café, and bless her heart for that.

"Let's follow Bill tonight," Pamela says to me over the table. "I want to find out where he gets off to."

"Are you sure we should?" This is something I would normally never dream of undertaking. People generally don't interest me enough to bother going out of my way like this, doing something nosey and flaunting the rules of propriety. But somehow the temerity of time travel is making the idea of spying on a creepy dude just an amusing distraction.

It sounds, in short, like fun.

"Probably not," she laughs. "But that's what makes it interesting. Hell, aren't you curious? I want to know where he goes."

"All right. But we'll have to be careful. We don't want him to suspect we're onto him. He might alter his behavior or do something weird."

We meander back to the Nut House. I wash my hands and face. There's only a single tap in the water closet Bill and I share on our floor, and the water's as cold as a mountain lake. The sliver of bar soap only becomes a filmy residue on my hands, and I detest that feeling of water running up my arm and getting the insides of my sleeves wet.

At teatime we're served fish, green beans from the garden,

tomatoes and rice with salad. Almost a perfectly normal meal, except for the size of the portions: small. Robert is away, dining with friends. So it's just Bill, me, Pamela, Mrs. Spettegue, Cecil and Rodger. We try to chat Bill up, Pamela and I, goading him. Pamela making fun of him just a little bit.

"Reckon you might have a stroll later?" she asks, passing him the rice.

"I might," he replies, tight-lipped and twitchy.

"What I think is that you've got a bird on the side and you're afraid to show us."

"It's not that."

I'm watching Pamela skewer Bill. She's clearly enjoying it, although I can't imagine what's she's after. It's not my style, but I have to admit it's kind of fun.

"She must be a real looker then, your hiding her from us and everything," she says lightly. Not in an unkind way, she's just making him squirm for the hell of it. He turns a bit red in the face.

He responds, "I just like to be out with friends is all."

"Good for you. Everyone needs friends, isn't that right, Mark?"

"Sure," I say, ill-equipped to get a handle on where Pamela is going with all this.

"Call yourself amid good friends in this world, and you'd scarcely ever need flinch an eye."

Bill's face twitches; I glance at Pamela . . . and she meant it, all right. I'm shocked.

Cecil, meanwhile, has turned beet red, eyes squeezed shut, fighting tears of mirth. He's near to gyrating in his seat, trying to keep from laughing, his napkin covering his mouth. No one else seems to have caught on—least of all Bill.

Rodger, too, isn't getting any of this. He downs some brandy and picks his fork back up, and feels it his duty to talk of the war. "We blew up a lot of oil refineries in the Black Forest last night. Sneaky of the Jerries to hide their tanks under trees. But by God, we rooted 'em out. Blew the Potsdam railway station to hell as well. Only lost three aircraft."

Pamela shudders ever so slightly.

"Rodger, I've told you! Not at the table!" I've never heard Mrs. Spettegue so arch.

"Oh, Edgar'll be all right," Pamela says lightly, but with a twinge of fear. "I just have to get used to it. It's the way of things now."

I simply gaze at Pamela in wonderment, at everything she must be going through. Edgar sounds like a dreamboat and he could be killed at any moment. She's pregnant with his child, and she's cool and wonderful and I honestly don't know how she's managing to hold herself together. How can she stand to look at a paper or listen to the news? It's seriously blowing my mind.

Conversation becomes, if anything, overly genteel at that point. Talk of the neighbors and something about someone who owns a shop at the top of the lane and business problems and price controls.

As usual, Bill makes to leave around eight. He bids us good evening and puts on his hat and a houndstooth coat and out he goes into the growing blackness.

This time we follow. We announce that we're taking a walk, which causes a bit of a stir, as blackout is in just a few minutes (the newspaper tonight it said is to be at 8:12).

We have to follow perilously close, keeping Bill's houndstooth in sight at all times. If he'd been wearing dark colors, we'd never find him. There's an ever-so-slight headwind most of the way, so if we make any noise, he won't hear us.

He doesn't look back. If he did, he'd instantly recognize Pamela in her condition. We keep several paces behind him, ready to duck into a doorway or up some steps at a moment's notice. We put his silhouette into our memories and follow him up one street and down another. I'm quite lost by now, but Pamela seems to know the streets well.

He goes into a flat in a nondescript road some distance away and we watch the windows for any signs of a light being switched on. With blackout curtains it's nearly impossible, but if you're looking closely you can tell from around the edges. We're certainly paying attention. The front basement light comes on, barely visible. The gate to the "area," the little patio underneath the front stairs, is off the latch, but it squeaks loudly when I pull it open. We freeze. Blackout curtains work both ways. If he's in there he can't see us any better than we can see him.

But he could hear the squeaking of the gate.

There's a tiny pinprick of light coming through the shroud, enough to bring an ARP warden running with a strong admonition and possible fine, but for our purposes it's a Godsend. We creep down the stairs into the area and I glue my eyeball to the tiny hole in the curtain. Light is coming through; I can peer in.

What I see shocks me. I lean back, and Pamela takes a peek as well, having to stand on her tiptoes. She's unable to lean in because she's so pregnant.

Bill Markley is sitting at a shortwave wireless radio with headphones. In a kitchen. The place seems otherwise dilapidated and deserted.

We hear the whine of the wireless and static and beeps and streaks of sound. I shoo Pamela back, which is perhaps rude, but I'm dying to suss out what the hell he's up to and put my eye back to the peephole. Soon Bill starts speaking.

In German.

Komm 'reim. "Come in . . . "

Bist du's? Wie gehts? Wirst du gut behandelt?

We can't hear the answer, for he's wearing headphones.

I know very little German. But having had to fight my way

through unknown languages before, I know the trick is to not get hung up on some word you don't understand. Your mind will want to seize upon it and try to decipher it, by which time you've completely lost the following words forever. You just got to let it wash over you and, if you're lucky, general meaning eventually comes through. I relax my mind and try it here, to some useful effect. More than that, though, the general tone of the conversation is apparent. It is not harsh or militaristic. It's soft; cajoling.

Ja, ich vermisse dich sehr!

Alles ruhig hier. Es sind noch keine Bomben gefallen . . .

Ja.

Morgen Nachmittag?

Ja. Ich werde bereit sein. Ich verspreche, das ich anfpasse.

Verspreche!

Wie geht es deinem schönen großen schwanz?

(Did he really just say what I think he just said?)

Ich vermisse Ihm, und kann es kaum erwarten euch beide wiederzuschem . . .

Wo geht's demm als nächstes hin?

Paris? Wunderbar!

Ich hoffe das es für dich nicht gefährlich ist!

Ich werde dich morgen anrufen . . .

Ja.

Du hör mal—Ich liebe dich!

I understand what he said at the end, and it sure as shit wasn't "Heil Hitler."

Bill takes his headset off and powers down the machine. I make ready to bolt but he calmly goes to a cabinet and pours himself a glass of liquor and pours it into a coffee cup. He lights a cigarette.

Pamela hisses in a whisper: "I bleeding knew it!"

"Shshshsh!" I admonish.

We've got to get the hell out of here.

I pull Pamela with me, back out of the area and onto the street once more. The gate squeaks again. After looking through that chink of light I'm completely blinded in one eye. I have Pamela take my arm and we set off toward the Nut house like that, holding one another.

Pamela is fit to be tied.

"I knew it!" She says again as we make our way back.

"Hold your horses, Pamela, it's not what you think."

"I think he's a bloody German spy, that's what I think."

"Do you understand any German?"

"Of course I don't. Filthy language."

"Well, tonight, my dear, it is." I stop and take both her hands in mine and lean in, so we're practically forehead to forehead. It's so dark I can't make out her face.

"Bill Markley," I begin, "is very much in love. That was a love message, nothing more."

"It could have been in code!" she retorts.

"That's a possibility, but I really don't think so. We heard his voice. It's love."

Pamela doesn't seem to know what to say. I let go of her hands, but she takes my arm in hers and we continue walking the way we'd come. She doesn't say anything for quite a while.

I fumble a little myself, thinking, *Was it in code?* I heard the tone in his voice, and it wasn't furtive or gloating. It was pleading. Clandestine, yes. But very personal. Even though I barely speak the (filthy) language, I heard actual components of Bill's personality just now, in defiance of my suspicion that the man has no personality at all. His last words were "I love you."

"You're certain?" she finally asks.

"I am," I respond. I decide to go ahead and tell her the truth: "He was asking after his lover's giant prick. Wondering when he gets to see it again."

If she's blushing, I can't tell in the dark.

"Oh," she says finally.

"Oughtn't we at least to tell someone?" she asks after another moment of silence.

"Aw, live and let live. The war won't last forever, no matter who wins, there will always be love. Besides, the man he's talking to is committing a crime. Homosexuality is completely illegal in the Third Reich. But unauthorized radio transmissions? That's straight-up firing-squad material. So whoever Bill's radioing to is taking one hell of a risk. I say let it go. Mystery solved."

"Still, I don't half wonder if we shouldn't dob the bastard in."

"It would ruin him. He'd probably be arrested as a spy, and you know what they do with those."

The War Office has made it known that several German spies have already been captured in Britain, interrogated, and given the option to either turn spy against the Third Reich—or be put to death. Quite a few spies have chosen the latter option and been executed. At English hands.

Bill Markley doesn't have the guts.

We try to make our way back to Nutley House in the utter darkness, but after a while it's plain that we're lost. We make several wrong turns, but Pamela doesn't seem fussed. She's talking loudly, in normal tones.

"Aren't we supposed to be quiet?" I ask.

"No, silly. We're supposed to be *dark*. The Germans can't hear us." And she lets out with a loud, sing-song utterance: "Oi! Old Nasty! Try and fiiiiiind us!"

We laugh. Somewhere a dog barks, wanting to join the fun.

And shortly thereafter Pamela declares: "Ah. Holbein Place! We're just 'round the corner from Sloane Gardens."

We go in the front door and take turns dashing around the curtain.

It's well after nine. *Tonight's Talk* is all about victory gardens,

Mrs. Spettegue is rapt, but Rodger is nodding off in the lounge, a magazine near to sliding off his lap.

I kiss Pamela goodnight on the forehead—that much seems appropriate now—and tell her good night and happy knitting, which she's sure to do until all hours.

Nothing for me to do but go to bed. Tomorrow is September 7, 1940.

Bill said it on his radio set: Tomorrow, it's coming.

He knows about it, too.

26

Saturday, September 7, 1940

The birds are singing, the sun is shining, and it's a beautiful day. Great visibility. A lovely day for an airplane ride.

Well, Britain's got nearly a thousand bombers on the way and their views of the topography will be unimpeded.

We have breakfast with cups of tea, and I ask Rodger and Robert Montague their plans for the day. I know Mrs. Spettegue will fritter around, doing laundry by hand and hanging it on the line in the backyard. Rodger is to be on the roof cleaning the gutters, and Robert says he must travel out to his main office in Twickenham for a few hours of meetings. Pamela is nearly done with Edgar's sweater. It's a beautiful gray wool pullover. She's just about ready to stitch the pieces together.

I'm nervous. Can't sit still. Don't know when it's going to begin or how bad it's going to get.

I pace. It's hard to picture this city under aerial assault. The few spits of bombs thus far have been nothing compared to what shall be unleashed today. I walk around the neighborhood. It really is an extraordinarily gorgeous day, and this'll be my last chance to wander around unfettered.

What will we hear first—the droning of the planes or the wailing of the sirens?

I don't dare venture far, though; I don't want to be somewhere across town when it comes.

The day's temperature is near 90°, which is odd for England. I've always found it confusing when London gets hot enough to smell like New York City in shimmering heat.

I begin to fuss and fret with a little more basis in fact. I've become so agitated that Mrs. Spettegue finally asks, "Is there anything wrong, dear?"

I assure her there's not a thing.

Try to read but can't.

Finally I go out back and help Rodger pull weeds. I feel cool English soil beneath my fingertips, get it under my fingernails; I place a snail back upon a rock so he can keep going, his little dealie-bobs search the air for meaning. I keep a nervous eye on the shelter and the pile of sandbags hiding the door.

At 3:30, Pamela bounds out into the garden in a sundress and flouncy hat and pronounces her wish to go for another walk. A quick look at Rodger and he shrugs *go ahead.*

Pamela wants to go back down toward the hospital and barracks, but I want to stay close, and I don't particularly wish to perambulate next to an aerial target. So we stick to Sloane Square. People are out, enjoying the fine day. Ice cream vendors are doing well, and a few children ride in push prams or are out waddling the way kids do, with their arms flailing.

"So tell me of your friend with six children. What was it you couldn't say the other night?"

It's my turn to be embarrassed. "I'm not sure I should . . . "

"Oh, but you must! I'm about to live through this, I need to know all I can. Besides, you brought it up."

"Well, the tale he told, if I can believe it, is that his wife was at her due date and they were making love. They must have been fond of it, with five children and a sixth due any minute . . . "

"Go on, you . . . "

"According to him he . . . entered her and could feel the baby's head inside with his . . . thing. It broke her water, I expect, because the contractions started immediately and, this being her sixth child, the baby was born at home before the doctor could even get there. It practically rolled out of its own accord."

"Good God."

"Told you it was quite a tale. So. Anyway, he delivered the child himself. He'd had lots of practice by then. It was a girl. She's nearly twenty years old now."

"I couldn't imagine! But in a way I can . . . it's got my insides positively squirming." She's clearly picturing the entirety of the scene.

We walk for a spell, saying nothing. Not much can top that.

"Have you never been with a woman?"

"Nope. I'm what we call Gold Status: Never been there."

"Haven't you ever wanted to?"

"Not really. Women are lovely, truly beautiful creatures. And I'm told the parts fit together well, but it just isn't on my to-do list."

"What do blokes do?"

"Same as heterosexuals, only better." I smile. She smiles back shyly.

I hope she's not actually picturing it in her mind. It's not for the uninitiated.

"What sort of men do you like?" she asks.

"Well, I have a strange preoccupation with facial hair. I

don't tend to notice a man if he hasn't got at least a moustache—where I live, lots of men have beards. And I like a stocky build and a hairy man."

"The men of England must be a frightful bore to you then."

"Oh, your men do have your moments. Meanwhile, you like blonds . . . I can tell."

"How?"

"Well you say Edgar's a blond, and Cecil Hayden is a blond. You're two for two."

"Two for two?"

"Perfect batting average. I suspect a pattern. What, is your father blond?"

"Yes, he is! How did you know that?"

"Just a good hunch. Little girls are ultimately attracted to their fathers, tell me it's not true . . . "

"Except my father's a ruddy arsehole," Pamela says. "That's why I love Edgar so much. He's a kind man."

We continue for a while before Pamela comes up short. "Wait, you say your friend has delivered babies before. You don't mean they've actually allowed him into the delivery room?"

"Of course."

Oops. Out of bounds.

"I've never heard of such a thing."

"Oh, it's becoming a new fad, at least in California. Men want to be there for the delivery. They say it's very healthy."

"San Francisco sounds like such an interesting place. Not like here."

"It's quite unique." I don't mention the eighty-year time differential.

"I hear San Francisco's beautiful."

"It is. Despite the fire, which destroyed everything that *was* beautiful, they've managed to make a very lovely city once more. The weather is always mild, the new bridges are stunning—they lend a kind of fairy tale feel to the place."

"What year were you born?" Pamela asks.

Oh shit. I'm terrible at quick math. I'm 49 in 1940 so that would mean . . .

"Eighteen ninety-one," I answer triumphantly.

"So were you in San Francisco for the great fire?" Pamela asks.

"I was growing up in Seattle, Washington. I'm rather glad I missed it."

I hate lying, and long to tell her the truth: But my story would gush out in torrents of excitement, probably complete with bubbling snot. I lived through that hellscape a mere month ago. It is still very fresh in my mind and heart, and it was horrible.

Pamela asks me about Seattle, and I describe it in general terms: It's a pretty exciting place now, but in 1940 it was a small, out-of-the-way city. So I describe it thus. The weather is mostly terrible. Worse, sometimes than England.

§

THE *SITZKRIEG* ENDS AT 4:12 p.m.

The precise moment true war finally comes to England, Pamela and I are in Sloane Square sitting on a bench. I'm begrudgingly admiring her brown, clunky shoes with clasps and heavy straps. I've got her talking about the first time she had sex with Edgar. We're leaning in, practically whispering, when a wailing sound begins somewhere in the distance.

A hand-cranked air raid siren is being wound up.

"Probably another ruddy drill. You get used to them,"

Pamela says casually and resumes her discussion of Edgar's hand on her breast in the front seat of a Vauxhall.

But it's not just one hand-cranked siren. It's three. Then four. Suddenly the square is filled with a plaintive, mournful sound. Each siren is slightly out of pitch with the others. It's a jarring, horrid noise—it was never meant to be anything else—and it's getting exponentially louder, spreading like a virus over the 600 square miles of London. Within seconds the air is filled with it.

With little ceremony we get up off our bench and start back toward Nutley House, walking quickly, but apart from the noise, it's still so normal out that we don't actually hurry. Others begin making their way home too at a normal pace, but even from far away you can see the look on their faces. Concern, but not panic.

It's all still just the realm of theoretical possibility, nothing more.

I glance up at the sky. What looks at first like a black cloud moving in from the south, and another from the northwest, is in fact a sea of tiny dots. My stomach runs cold when I realize what I'm looking at with my own eyes. Mile after mile, hundreds of them, very high up, in a formation so precise that it disgusts me. It's well-practiced and deliberate.

Suddenly my body is rent by a sound I have never known in life: anti-aircraft artillery, from practically right where we're standing. Pamela grabs me, shrieking. We nearly fall down with the shock of it.

And now it begins. My heart rate shoots up, about on par with the earthquake. Which is by no means inconsequential.

I see things streaking up into the sky from the elegant streets of Chelsea: tracers. Coming from just to our right—probably from York HQ.

The booming guns pound relentlessly. It's all the inspiration we need to get the hell out of there. We dash down Sloane

Gardens to number 36, through the main floor hallway and down the rear steps, out the back door and across the garden to the closed door of the shelter.

It's when we cross the yard that we hear another sound, also heretofore unknown to me: the whistle of an incoming *spreng-bombe cylindrisch funf-und-swanzig*. The Germans are surely instructed to focus on strategic targets, but there's no mistaking the percussion of bombs raining down upon us. Why us? Left-overs, dick moves, boredom, over-excited bomb pilots—whatever the reason, we're obviously not free from destruction, even in our harmless housing district.

My fear response needle jumps toward the *Seriously Unwell* zone as Pamela and I leap down into the shelter at top speed, into what seems to be utter darkness, and slam the door shut behind us.

So much is happening in so few seconds that one part of my brain simply takes it all down calmly, so another part can parse it out later:

- The whistle of a descending bomb really does sound like a *Road Runner* cartoon.

- An explosion is ringing out very nearby. So loud, I feel the percussion in the air, and I'm wondering if it's all over for us before it ever began.

- It's dark in here. There is no room, no air, yet I sense the bodies of other people.

- I smell dank earth, radishes, human breath and wool.

- I see light in the shelter after all. The tiny lamp, thanks to Rodger and his extension cord, is on, it's just that I'm so blinded by daylight I couldn't adjust at first.

- Mrs. Spettegue and Rodger are sitting calmly, shoulders down, hands in their lap, with their mouths open.

- Robert's not here, nor are Cecil or Bill.

- The explosion must not have been as close as I thought because we're still here, we're not blown up.

- The sirens have stopped. The cranks are abandoned after one minute, each siren winding down of its own accord.

- I'm thinking of burning cop cars in 1979 because it's exactly the same noise.

- A new sound: The droning of propeller aircraft is filling the air outside.

§

"WE WERE IN THE SQUARE," Pamela is saying as she moves to embrace Mrs. Spettegue gingerly.

"Oh, my dear, take the chair, please!" says Rodger, surrendering his wobbly dining room seat for her, making way for her and me by moving deeper into the shelter, to the bunks. He takes one.

"Thank you, Rodger," she says. "We turned right back, but when the ack-ack started we nearly lost our nerve!"

"Ack-ack?" I ask, wedging myself into a lower bunk across from Rodger; I don't seem to have a choice but to lay down. There's no room for anything else.

"Anti-aircraft artillery," Rodger explains, from the bunk opposite. "There are emplacements all over the city, usually in private gardens and courtyards. They used to test them. It's a God-awful ruckus."

The ack-ack guns are still going strong. Somewhat muffled here in the shelter, but by no means a mere background noise. It's unrelenting.

"They've got several over at York HQ, with more down the Barracks. Don't know what chances they have, but anything they can dish out, I'm sure the Germans deserve, and more."

I wonder two things: what happens when the shells don't

reach their aircraft targets? Doesn't that mean they just fall to earth and explode on someone's car? And, if the emplacements are spewing fire, doesn't that make them prime targets? York HQ is just one street over.

We're in the middle of an outgoing fusillade. This just isn't good.

I'm getting scared. For in my mind just now is the concept of carpet bombing. Later in World War II planes will lazily set up a grid-like network of ordnance and napalm and, from a safe, high altitude, unimpeded, simply wipe entire districts off the map in a matter of minutes.

We did it to Tokyo in the spring of '45, killing a quarter of a million people. From high above, in the space of two hours, without even breaking a sweat.

Roger. Returning to base.

True fear builds within me, but my higher brain manages to take over.

The Germans don't know this yet. Carpet bombing does not exist.

I need to get a grip. This is only a low-tech air raid.

I focus on what I can see around me. I'm lying in death position, hands folded across my chest as if a lily were already there for my internment. That's what it feels like, because just over my nose, painfully close, are the rusted springs and coils of the bunk above. Mattress ticking, wool blankets folded in neat corners, awaiting the inevitable. Rodger's right beside me, if I wanted to, I could reach over and touch him. In the closeness of the shelter, I can hear his breathing, even over the ack-ack guns. Mrs. Spettegue and Pamela are whispering a quiet discussion amongst themselves.

But I'm hearing more explosions now. Not nearly as close as the first, but they're happening nearby. It may not be carpet bombing, but I suddenly come to realize these bombs are happening *to me*. And I've put myself in the middle of it.

I came here on purpose.

With that upper bunk seeming to press in and deprive me of air, knowing how small that shelter is and that bombs are going off and ack-ack fire unrelenting all around . . .

I snap.

Are you fucking kidding me? I almost leap out of my own skin.

GET ME THE FUCK OUT OF HERE!

§

I'VE HEARD of panic attacks, we all have by now. The concept always seemed simple enough, and reserved for those with unsteadfastness of thought.

Suddenly I am host to it. Raw, ridiculous panic is starting to ooze out of me and I have no idea what to do.

The first swipe at me, like a cat's paw striking lighting quick, full force, yet with claws still sheathed; one warning shot, fast across my cheek, begins a new dance. One I have never known before.

I always thought I knew what real fear was, until I had to climb into a burning building to look for Ben. That was a fairly concentrated wake-up call, but apparently, I didn't deal with it or its after-effects, because now I'm faced with something entirely worse: being buried alive in a dirt coffin.

I have mistaken fuss and worry for true fear my whole life, never knowing the merest fragment of what it really means to be scared. Physically scared and in serious immediate danger.

Still, I'm focusing my brain and trying to fight my fear, assuming it'll be an even fight.

I'm just in a confined space and I don't like it. *Calm the fuck down!*

And it almost works, too.

But the universe, calmly, with deft, delicious delicacy, takes this moment to finish me off for good.

By the way: You're also dying of cancer, you useless piece of . . .

There it is.

I always wondered when it would come around. That it should choose to do so during an air raid in World War II is, apparently, just Nature's way of finally introducing me to her parents.

Raw, inescapable terror takes a complete hold of me. Without making a sound, locked in rigor and darkness, I lose my ever-loving shit.

I phase out of existence. I am gone in panic I never knew possible.

It's psychologically delicious, I'm sure. It would make a fascinating paper. But in that moment my spirit leaves my body. I squelch out into madness, far beyond rational thought or psychological awareness.

I've never known such horror in my life. I've rolled over into a ball on my side away from Rodger, facing the cold, damp corrugated metal, and I only seem dimly aware that I'm not actually screaming. For my body to emit sound would be impertinent. My own body wishes me dead, and now so does the Luftwaffe.

I'd wet myself if I thought it would matter. But of course it doesn't. Nothing I could do will ever matter again. I may escape this coffin, this here and now, but I'm still going to die young. Horribly. Just like my friend Jeff—he liked it when I brought him chocolate shakes from McDonalds even though he threw every one of them back up.

A bomb goes off one street over. I hear it, I feel it—Christ, I can smell it. I jolt in cowering shock.

Silently raving in panic, unable to speak or get enough air or even to whimper, I now grasp the cold reality that I am going die. If not today, then sometime in the next couple of years.

All my stoic bravery, thinking I had my diagnosis under complete emotional control, in no small way nudged by the co-morbidity of having to climb into Ben's burning building, are all now laughing their ass off because—get this—I then went on to willingly set myself right down in the middle of a world war, without a clue as to what it would do to me.

The only cogent part of my brain is shrieking at me in derisive laughter. All else is reduced to static and shorted electrical sparks.

I'm out. I fight to keep the bile down, to breathe the air that's available to us through that tiny vent; it's not going to be enough. It's not . . . I'm huffing . . .

It rolls me around in the existential mud for a good twenty minutes. I'm a quiet victim of lunacy, uttering not the merest sound. I freeze into position and fight to get enough air.

All my years of overly rational thought have just melted away. I can no longer reach it. I'm pure id, out of control and sinking.

Longest twenty minutes of my life.

Eventually—probably because it is simply too exhausting to remain in such a state of psychological agony for any appreciable span of time—a glimmer of sanity tries to reassert. My overly cognitive brain is asking, politely, to once more be given the reins. I try to push the panic aside. It takes several attempts. All my newfound hellions swirl and cackle.

But suddenly a clear, concise message lights up on an auxiliary control screen in my brain. A simple, dimly helpful set of words: *Separate Your Hazards.*

They taught me this when I took advanced motorcycle lessons. They taught me this the two times I could afford to take flying school, too.

"Separate your hazards."

I say it out loud, not caring that anyone may hear.

In an emergency—or crash, or skid, or stall—you have to regain control of your vehicle immediately. You must right yourself first. Then you inventory the scope of your emergency, breaking each bit of the crisis into manageable pieces. You prioritize them, and deal with them in order of importance.

And right now, to right my ship, to prevent a skid or a crash, I recognize Job One is to remain quietly right where I am, in this box, with these people, until the bell rings.

That is my only task.

This is supposed to go on all night. So here it is. Right now, I don't even know if I can successfully complete Job One without combusting into screaming, gelatinous goo. But my immediate task is at least clear to me.

Just exist. Breathe. Cry if you need, but simply breathe.

Anyone can do that, right? Literally all I have to do right now is to continue breathing. Can I do that?

I'm working on it . . . I am breathing, after all. Actually, I finally notice that I've been hyperventilating the whole time. I have far too much oxygen going on, and that's part of my problem.

I try to slow it down.

Even that seems too much, until I suddenly decide it is of the utmost importance that I leave London immediately. That would be Job Two: I have to go. I have to leave. I can go, right? No reason I have to stay. None. Only one other human even knows I'm here and that's David and shit, I'm getting so used to lying now, I could tell him whatever the hell I want.

Out. I gotta get out. I've got to run away.

Panic begins to ebb—by virtue of formulating a plan, no matter how feeble and dripping with shame—but having a direction slowly does the trick. Very incrementally, in waves, back and forth. Whatever's got a grip on me is finally beginning to waver.

Yet I'm not going to pop the hatch right here and now. Much as I want to do that, I don't want to die, and I'm not so far gone that I wish to jeopardize the lives of the people in my midst.

Ultimately, I'm fairly protected in this shelter. The chances of an exact bomb strike are low, and the thing is designed to take a hit. I just don't like it. OK. We'll deal with that further down the chain.

Panic is still laughing its ass off at me but is starting to withdraw its tendrils from my chest.

Ultimately? I don't have to do any of this. I can go away, anytime, anywhere.

There won't be any getting out of London tonight. I'm sure all the trains are stopped. So first things first: I'm here for the night. I'm safer in the Anderson shelter than I would be anyplace else, so there's no viable place for me to be other than right where I am right now.

Will this go on all night? What if I have to pee? Oh Jesus, I don't want to pee in front of Mrs. Spettegue.

I'm going to be all right, I tell myself, still curled into the fetal position on my bunk. *I'm going to be fine. They haven't invented carpet bombing yet.*

Slowly I start to calm down.

Overhead, the Germans have an actual right to be pissed. They've finally had enough of the English bombing their factories, missing, and hitting innocent German civilians. It's all just coming to blows.

Right now, some uncircumcised German dude named Henreid is flying in his plane, 15,000 feet up over London. I wonder if he likes having his nipples played with. When was the last time he had sex? What did he eat for dinner? Did he just fart in his canvas ejector seat? Is he scared, too?

Edgar Jarvis is up, doing the same thing, right now. Fighting to protect us. Cuts both ways. It's war.

It's all so fucking stupid. San Francisco didn't deserve to die, but at least it wasn't deliberately ruined in battle. It suddenly strikes me as the height of human idiocy: all wrecking each other's shit. And here's me, caught in the literal middle, by my own foolish choosing.

My cute little fascination with disasters is going to have to bear scrutiny at such time when my brain, or what's left of it, begins to function again.

I can't publish any of this. No memoirs or gripping observations can ever be shared.

I can't even talk to a therapist, now or ever. I'm truly on my own here. Just now I realize this: I put myself here and it hurts. It's cutting me, I'm emotionally bruising. There's no support group for this, there never will be. It's all a secret I must carry to my grave. I could die here and no one at home would ever know where I went or what happened to me.

OK. So. Say it's tomorrow morning. The hatch opens. The sun is shining, and we're not blown up. I can leave then, can't I?

First order of business is survival. That's what I'll do. I'll survive. I'll leave London, go out into the country and sit under a tree in a field that nobody named Klaus or Hans would ever think of dropping a bomb on, whether he likes his nipples flicked or not, and just wait until my time is up and I can go back home and tell David whatever the hell I want.

I'll go to Cornwall and eat apples and it'll be cold at night but . . .

"Mark, you OK?"

It's Pamela. Sweet, pregnant Pamela. Her voice sounds dull in the confines of the metal shelter yet so wonderful to me just now . . .

I roll over, away from my cold wall, so I can see her.

"Sure. Piece of cake," I manage to say. I hear my own voice

as if for the first time, and it strikes me as nasally and weak. "How about you?"

Pamela is looking radiant in the light. And damn if she doesn't seem to be perfectly composed and content.

"I'm not particularly fond of this," she says. "But there's nothing for it I'm afraid."

"Don't suppose there is," I answer.

Rodger has an actual twinkle in his eyes in the dim light as he looks across at me. "It's your first one. I can tell."

My immediate instinct is one of pure outrage.

But he quickly reaches his arm out and clasps my bicep in a firm, warm, steadying grip.

"You'll get used to it, m'boy. I can promise you that. It's not pleasant. Wasn't ever meant to be; it's just what it is. Hold fast."

Pamela and Mrs. Spettegue have been muttering quietly between themselves throughout the entire time. I haven't been particularly curious to know about what. Seems maddeningly banal, like trying to read a copy of *People* magazine while your airplane is spiraling into the ground.

The assembled group is dealing with it better than me. Which threatens to throw me into another shame loop, but I manage to remember: This isn't their first time at it. They've all had practice.

It is mine, though, and that's when I begin to feel true shame. Am I really that sad? By whatever device, I'm here now. Am I really going to cop out?

They sit and talk. Now that I've realized I can run away as soon as the coast is clear, I'm marginally more calm.

Meanwhile, they're prattling away about what the neighbors have been up to, names of people I don't know and never will.

I feel practically post-coital. I've just been emotionally flayed by the universe without anesthesia. I'm drained and spent and in a puddle of ooze that is only just now starting to reassemble itself into constituent bits.

While I lay in exhaustion, taking psychic inventory, an odd sound pulls me from my woes.

Those air raid sirens, the ones that started the whole thing, are firing back up. But instead of wailing up and down, they all spool up to their highest voice and ring loud, clear, disjointed and steady for nigh unto two minutes.

The All Clear?

There must be some mistake—I thought we'd be at this all night. That's what it said in all the books . . . It's a trap!

Seriously. That's what I think for a moment. I surreptitiously pull out my phone and . . . It's only been *ninety minutes*?

Fuck me . . .

And I signed up for six more days of this.

Everyone scrambles out of the shelter, bright daylight streaming through the door, and at the last moment I don't want to come out. See? First I didn't want to be in there, now I'm too scared to come back out.

Nevertheless, knowing I have an audience, I extricate myself from that bunk and stoop toward the doorway and breathe the fresh clean air of Mrs. Spettegue's garden. I step out into freedom. It's still a lovely day. The incongruity of it would rattle me if I had anything left to rattle.

I turn to look at the tiny hole in the ground from which we have just emerged. It looks the same, but in that bunker, I have left an indelible part of my own self—certainly a good part of my psyche. I should wonder that splatters of my flung mental state do not yet remain, spewed across its walls, slowly dripping and drying like blood.

Wow. I just lost my shit. I've never done that before.

I also know that, next time I go back down in there, it will all be waiting for me once again. I'm free for now but immediately doomed to face the same horrors once more.

No visible damage appears around us, but a riot of angry squiggles litter the sky: puffs and streaks, aftereffects of the manmade crud of battle. It was clearly a fierce aerial fight—some of it undoubtedly Edgar's.

We trek back into the house, nobody saying a word. I'm decidedly wobbly, adrenaline still coursing out of me like sparks, making it difficult to see straight.

Everyone else is dashing to the wireless, expecting frantic, rapid-fire reports. I follow, hungry for news.

BBC Home Service is calmly playing *Stuff & Nonsense* with Wilfred Pickles and Violet Carson.

It's astonishing. *We've just been attacked, for God's sake!* Yet coming from the radio we hear genial audience laughter and applause.

Rodger makes to get the gas back on—the valve needs to be shut off each time there's a raid going—and to relight both Mrs. Spettegue's sink and stove, which only takes a moment. He's had plenty of practice already.

Mrs. Spettegue says she'll get tea on and disappears downstairs into her realm.

Rodger is determined to go to the roof to check for damage, and I opt go with him. I'm reasserting, somehow. I need to present as normal to these people, and specific activity will be the best remedy. I'm trembling, but I follow Rodger.

The roof is accessed via a small ladder at the top of the house, through a hatch in the ceiling. Rodger's bedroom is here on the fourth floor, his domain. Smells like him.

At first I'm petrified, stepping out onto that roof top, yet I reel it in fairly quickly. The attack is over. The Germans will be back soon, but they're not here right now, so take a fucking pill.

I thought the roof would be steeply pitched, that's how it looks from street level. But, in fact, it is a broad, flat expanse covered in tarpaper.

It's high up; five floors. What a sight! Chimneys—thousands, in all directions.

A few bomb hits are visible in the immediate vicinity to us, crumpled masonry in pockets all around, with heavy smoke, or ambient clouds of dust.

But our attention is immediately drawn to the eastern skies. The East London docks, Isle of Dogs and Thames River Estuary have been hit bad. There is a great deal of industry in that area, and, most strategically, shipping.

It's where our food comes from and it's on fire.

A wall of flames, an all-to-familiar vision to me in my new life, roars some four miles away. An entire district is burning, throwing up angry pillars of smoke, thousands of feet into the sky.

Saint Paul's Cathedral is visible from here, the fires a visceral backdrop to it. Battersea Power Station, with its enormous four smokestacks still standing proudly in the late summer daylight, behind me and to the southwest.

London is in silence. Approximately 6.6 million people—minus a few hundred now, I muse glumly—are reckoning with what's just happened to them. Assessing.

Having ascertained that the structure at 36 is sound, and no danger is in the immediate area, Rodger and I get back down the stairs in time for the six o'clock news broadcast. They may have something to say by now.

John Snagge wastes no time. Immediately after the *"bong,"* he begins speaking rapidly in a strained, monotone voice:

- The raid lasted 98 minutes. It came in four waves, two from the south and two from the northwest, the bombers at a nominal 15,000 altitude but zooming much lower on their bombing runs. They were focused on industrial targets, but with many civilians, particularly in the east end, hit. English

> fighters, including Czech and Polish volunteer units, were dispatched in aerial combat. Anti-aircraft gun emplacements across the city responded in kind. Sixty-five German aircraft were downed, compared to eighteen of ours.

(Pamela puts her hands over her face. Mrs. Spettegue moves to hug her.)

- The Government have sent a strong dispatch to Berlin, decrying the outrage.
- Buses continued to run; casualties are certain; everyone is being brave.
- Further raids are expected; they could come back at any time. Be prepared. Be brave.
- England prevails.

Snagge makes a special report on incendiary bombs, apparently being used by the Germans, describing them as white hot phosphorous canisters designed to start rooftop fires. You have a chance to stop them if you're quick with blankets and sand. He recommends people guard their roofs at all times during an alert to put out the fires immediately.

It begins a practice that officially starts today and will last for many years.

Rodger immediately pipes up, "Well, then that's what we'll do."

"But it's so dangerous up there!" Mrs. Spettegue says. "You'll be exposed to Good Lord knows what . . . "

"Well. That may be. We'll start by gathering as many blankets as we can. We ought to be able to bring up buckets of dirt from the garden—plenty of soil left over from the construction of the Anderson—I'll get a few now and several more tomorrow."

Robert Montague then bursts through the front door looking white and haggard.

"I was stuck on the train from Twickenham," he explains, removing his hat and coat. "Richmond Railway Bridge . . . they just stopped us cold mid-span and there we sat for nearly two hours, exposed, on a bridge, in broad daylight! Hell of a place to stop a train. We saw several bombs land in Putney. Finally we began moving again towards Richmond station at the All Clear. The Richmond Line Tube was back running again, fortunately for me. I'm sure glad to be home."

So, all this, and the trains are up and running. Just like that.

Should I leave? Tonight? Am I really going to do it?

"Good Lord," says Rodger, drawing my focus back to the conversation. "I can't think of a more dangerous place to stop a train during an air raid than on a bridge. You should write and complain. I certainly would. If I put my mind to it, I'm sure I can dredge up the specific bloke you should write."

By now, tea's ready. Mrs. Spettegue had been roasting a rare-found chicken for hours, only slightly delayed by the gas cut off. With that margarine, it's not so good, but she parts the bird deftly with a huge knife; tiny portions, meted out gingerly. A tiny few mouthfuls are all I'm capable of right now. My stomach can't handle much.

I'm upset. My hands are trembling.

Rodger pours the brandy freely. I feel conspicuous in the amount I serve myself, but it helps brace my nerves. Nerves I never before knew I had. They're as fragile as an old spinster's now.

If I get out of this mess, will I ever be normal again? Normal enough to die of cancer with dignity?

Separate your hazards, dude. Leave your lymphoma for a later time. You got to stay present in the past, or else there will be no past to aid you in your future.

§

I THINK my brain's not working.

As we eat, we attempt to listen to the wireless program, *Saturday Spotlight*, a magazine program. It is so lacking in intensity that listening to it feels wrong and banal. Everyone's too rattled. Rodger switches it off, and what would have been an awkward silence seems appreciated by all.

Shortly after that, Cecil Hayden comes in. It's around eight; it's nearly dark outside now. He'd been assisting at a West End play backstage, something unemployed actors would do to keep their hand in, so long as they steered clear of the unions. He tells us they sheltered in the basement of the theatre and still expect the curtain to rise at eight. But he didn't want to stay.

"Wasn't much for me to do tonight, besides, everyone thinks the Krauts'll be back."

I suspect he's right. And I have feelings about that.

Mrs. Spettegue fetches Cecil a plate of food. In no way would she chastise him for being late for tea now. He thanks her and eats.

Pamela wants to go for a quick walk up and down Sloane Gardens, but it's immediately clear that it's not going to happen. We can't see much. By now it's 8:10, time for blackout, so we settle for sitting on the front steps of number 36. It's still warm and agreeable out, which just confuses me. We've been attacked, with more on the way. How can it be so pleasant and sultry? Has the evening no sense of propriety?

"I bet the Germans will be back in a while," I say.

We'll be in the shelter for nine more hours tonight; I know that as historical fact. I'm beyond dreading it, I'm inwardly raving.

I panic that I'll panic again—which, if you don't happen to know, is the worst sort of panic to have.

"Bloody hell." Pamela's clearly not in the mood, either. "They've been promising it for months," she says. "But maybe I secretly started to hope it wouldn't really happen . . . d'ya know what I mean? Blast! I guess it's come."

We sit for a while, not saying anything. I'm fussing mightily.

I can't leave London now, I have to wait. I will stay tonight, then think about it—particularly as it's a given that I won't spend the night sleeping. None of us will.

Then I feel disgusted with myself at the idea of abandoning Pamela. I fundamentally suck.

Bill comes wandering up the street, looming in the darkness, startling the wits out of me sitting on the front step.

"Hullo, Bill. You 'right?" Pamela asks.

"Oh, fine," he murmurs. "I was in a public shelter at Victoria. I don't know that I think much of this." And saying nothing more he shuffles up the treads, his shoes make that sound dress shoes make on stone steps, and into the house. I'm sure Mrs. Spettegue will feed him too if he needs, but there won't be any chicken left.

I still feel the oils from the fat of it in my mouth.

But with Bill back in the house . . . now that means that all seven of us are here, and there's only room in the bomb shelter for six.

See? Shit.

Oh. Rodger's announced he going to be on the roof all night watching for incendiaries, so technically yes, there will be room for me in the shelter. But do I want to go back in there?

I think the minute I climb back down inside it, I'm just going to panic out again.

Some strange semblance of a plan begins to form in me. An idiotic one, but the more I consider it, the better it makes me feel. Soon, I've come to believe that I'm going to act upon it.

We follow Bill inside, the lights are still on in the hall and lounge, and as such we take extra care taking turns ducking behind the curtain over the door. A pile of old blankets has been collected and lies on the floor, along with three buckets of dirt.

"Well, I'll get these to the roof, then." Rodger is saying, fairly firm about it.

No matter what, he'll need help with that, so I move to gather as many as I can carry, again in the knowledge that doing something—anything—helps my mental state.

"Thank you, Mark," he says kindly. "I'll probably need you to hand them up the ladder for me to chuck out onto the rooftop."

And here's where my new plan comes to fruition. Like I said, it's 600 square miles of city, and I constitute just one homosexual-sized dot. What are my chances, really?

I'm going with Rodger. I don't want to be in that hole in the ground another moment, and I don't care how crazy that sounds.

I need air. I need to see what's happening. I might die, but technically I'm dead already. It's just a matter of form and duration. A bomb blast would beat six months of wasting away in agony, and I suddenly see a way out for me.

Roof. Out amid it all. Not trapped, able to breathe. Able to see it coming, if tonight it should deign to come. I'm good for it.

Ever since I started using David's Machine, I'm finding out that there's fuss, which I have always mistaken for actual fear. Now I know actual fear. I'm also acquainted with adrenaline and pure panic. They're all different from one another, and to that array, I now add this new outlier: Flying into action in spite of myself. None of it seems to line up right in my head right now, but I acknowledge, in my current state, nothing will.

The sirens go again at 8:31, just as loud as before, and my stomach immediately clenches back up. Everyone but Rodger and I hurries to the shelter. He stops to turn the gas valve off and shows me how it works.

I don my ARP helmet, which is perhaps silly; I probably look like a dork.

By the time the sirens stop wailing I'm out on the roof breathing the evening air, with six or seven blankets at my feet. Silence falls. The sun is down. The Dockland fires are still a going concern, in fact they look ever more fierce and frightening in the dark. London burns just like San Francisco burns. Harsh light and dastardly smoke continue to fill the air in the east, altogether pink in hue.

So far, I hear no droning planes, no ack-ack, no bombs falling. Could all this be some giant false alarm even now? It's not likely, but I wonder.

Then I hear a dull buzzing. Incoming aircraft. High up, in formation. They've gotten pretty close to us without having been scattered by Edgar and the rest of the RAF. I'm a little offended.

I feel a combination of fear and exaltation. I'm soaringly glad to be free of the shelter. The night air is crisp and clean and limitless.

What are the chances of a direct strike? Astronomically low. I feel glad to be of use.

The crusty switches in my brain start flipping, one by one, to "ON." Action. Visibility. Service to others. These priorities shall be my way through this hellscape into which I've thus decided myself to plunk.

It's a clear night but for the enormous pall of smoke in the east, reflecting firelight all over the city from the earlier bombings.

"See the fires?" Rodger asks. I nod. "That's right where they'll head, I guarantee you. The still-burning scars from the first wave will serve as a beacon for the second." He almost spits, he's so disgusted.

I practice in my mind what I'll do if an incendiary should land anywhere on the roof and prepare myself for a long night of it.

Now that it's night, and in contravention of all the blackout orders, London is once again ablaze with light. Only it's all wrong. Each window is still dark, the streets invisible chasms of blackness, but the sky is ablaze. Tracers going up, an endless cavalcade of them, and searchlights are out, dozens, piercing the night sky, looking for enemy targets. It's like some theatre opening, only entirely wrong and evil.

Rodger narrates: "The German planes are in five types. Messerschmitts, Henkels, Dorniers, Junckers and Stukas. You don't want them so near that you're able to tell them apart. You wouldn't find it to your liking.

"What's always been galling to me is that the Kraut aircraft are all painted bright yellow on the nose. While it makes them easier to distinguish, it's utter indignation. Rather an imperious thumb to one's snout. It's like they're proud as a peacock. The Germans are an arrogant lot. What crust!"

Crump crump crump is the noise the bombs make when they hit, even from this great distance away. How far is it? Half the sky seems to be on fire—originally toward the east, but now the city seems ringed with fire in all directions as the attack becomes less tightly focused. So many German planes are in the air now, they can drop their ordnance wherever they please. Their specified targets are already saturated with air traffic, so tonight, for the first time ever, they have been given leave to let destruction fly wherever they please.

Bombs occasionally hit nearby. A German plane—its motors a low, droning sound—will almost lazily leave the chaos of the industrial areas and fly slowly and directly over our residential section of the city to drop a few bombs. Out of boredom or for pure sport, I'll never know.

Rodger and I become quite adept at detecting the sound and hitting the deck.

New waves of planes are zooming overhead every two minutes. Their motors seem to grind rather than roar, and to have an angry pulsation to them. Two dozen incendiaries go off in our neighborhood. It all happens in a jagged instant, too fast for the eye to even register. Their aftermath, burning goo, flashes brightly, sending off sparks of gold, which quickly simmers down to white pinpoints of light.

The individual dots get beaten down by the roof monitors except for the occasional bit developing an orange flame that leaps up in the center of the heat. That is true fire, taking hold.

Everything overhead is pink. Smoke is pink, the sky is pink. Flashes of light, anti-aircraft shells exploding, too many to count, illuminate the hellscape in random strobes. The sounds loudly echo our way seconds later. There is so much of it you cannot possibly attribute which boom belongs to what flash.

It goes on for a great while. We're just standing there Rodger and I, only intermittently diving for cover. Even that becomes less as we become more attuned to the sounds, directions, and bearing of the assaults. We're becoming selectively cautious.

Meanwhile, everyone has at least one lookout on the roof. It becomes a world of its own. Everyone was glued to their wireless earlier, so everyone now knows that roof duty will become a way of life for years on end. We call to each other, learn each other's names and drink toasts with whiskey, brandy or tea.

After that, though, Rodger and I just stand in silence for the longest time. We can see toward the east where the docks are on fire. It's a huge and unnatural glow.

"So what's actually happening here?" I ask.

"Well, obviously, you have the German planes, nominally at 15,000 feet, but they'll scream down and dive in as they begin their bombing runs. Meanwhile, our boys in Hurricanes, Spitfires, and Defiants are swarming all over the skies, trying to shoot the Germans down and attempting to corral them into narrow areas where the ground guns can take their shots.

"We have over three hundred ack-ack guns already mounted all over London, and the Army Air Corps assures us that that number will be trebled within a few days.

"Ack-ack guns operate by a new system that uses an electronic computer. It's the latest thing. They are actually connected by telephone lines. To correctly fire one, you must have range, distance, bearing, and ceiling—one bloke doing the calculating and another one doing the aiming and firing. I'm told some of them are now equipped with radar. But that might just be a rumor from the Ministry of Information."

I watch the tracers go up from the ground guns and feel a surge of pride, to be honest. We're giving Jerry hell. Rodger tells me, "AA shells detonating all around, they call that 'flak.' Sometimes it's enough to just explode one in the path of an enemy plane. He flies into it and his propellers bang all to cock. Can be enough to bring him down."

Sure enough, far off, we see a plane plummet to the earth, or, in this case, a heavily populated section of Bermondsey—or Elephant and Castle. Can't see from here if the pilot has ejected or not. The plane tumbles down into death and is no more.

Further, we don't know from here if it was one of theirs—or one of ours. Could've been Edgar himself.

I decide it's not.

The action is in two arenas: The dropping of bombs and air-to-air combat. This is where Edgar Jarvis is sure to be in his Defiant, performing epic plane-to-plane battle maneuvers. Planes are zooming and fighting, twirling and firing, an insane knot of carnage. I can't fathom how afraid each man must be in his little cockpit up there. I know from old movies that the planes aren't pressurized or heated. Each and every pilot is working in subzero temperatures and there's no such thing as a potty break.

I ask Rodger, "What happens to the anti-aircraft shells? Don't they just crash down again? Isn't that a problem?"

"Can't you see them exploding?"

"Oh yeah . . . "

"They're designed to explode midair. Part of the firing computation is setting the fuse to the right time. I suppose some are duds, and aye, down they'll come. But it's all got to be organized. Our fliers have to hold back so the guns can come into play and not get shot down by their own anti-aircraft fire.

"About the only thing working in our favor here is that the Germans, who have taken off from airfields in France, can only remain aloft for 90 minutes. They burn half their fuel to get here, have only a few moment of action, then must flee back over the channel to refuel and rearm. Each man will make up to six sorties a night."

I check my phone, it's only eleven o'clock. We're already three hours into the attack. And I'm just standing there watching it in the altogether like a nutter.

But I feel better.

Eventually we decide to sit down. I make myself a small nest in the blankets.

So many planes are overhead, yet there is a pattern to it. High up they're not a direct problem. They're focusing on their targets in the east. If one zooms low or close, that's when we get worried, and Rodger and I will hit the deck when the approaching sound is just wrong enough to warrant it. It's probably a useless gesture, but try *not* hitting the deck when you see a Messerschmitt 109 coming at you.

After another hour of the fireworks of war, no one side seems to be gaining the upper hand. It's just battle, back and forth, loud and messy, terrorizing the city cowering beneath it all.

27

Sunday, September 8, 1940

Long about midnight, I eventually ask Rodger to tell me a bit about himself. I wonder if he'll even answer, but he does.

He was born in 1880, married in 1902. His wife died six years ago of a heart attack.

"Worst day of my life. Found Florence in the kitchen at the sink with the water still running. It was the greatest shock. It was terrible. I'm still not recovered from it. We were married thirty-two years. I was away driving for the railway and came home from work—and there she was."

"I'm so terribly sorry." I can't think of anything else to say.

"Thank you, my boy. So I moved into the Nutley House that very day; I wouldn't stay in our flat in Edgware Road another minute. Never slept in that bed again. I didn't even stay to collect my things. My world ended, and that was that.

"I eventually lost my job at the railway—I became useless

and drank to excess. Mrs. Spettegue took me on as a handyman, and I'm damned grateful she did. I like being useful."

He's silent for a while, then speaks: "This bombing is a nasty business. I fought the Germans in the War of '14, and here we are all over again. I wonder if there isn't something inherently wrong with the Germans?"

"What did you do in the War?" I ask.

"I was a trench soldier. It was bloody, horrifying work. I was at the Somme, Yprès, Verdun. Month after month, rotting in those trenches . . . mustard gas, night raids, barbed wire. Everything you hear about it was true. My best mate, Colin French, was shot right beside me. Had to leave him where he was and scramble back under the wires alone. They left him to rot in the rain, I could see him through the field glasses for two weeks. Until we were sent to another area.

"Sorry. Didn't mean to be so blunt."

"It's fine," I assure him.

"The last war was useless and bloody. It served no true purpose, had no appreciable outcome. Everyone just went insane for four years and, upon the blowing of a whistle, stopped and picked up the pieces.

"This is a whole different thing yet again. I have no doubt the Germans—and the Japanese—aim to conquer the world and divide the spoils for themselves, enslaving all of us under a new version of government that ought never to have been invented. None of it is any bleeding good. The Germans have vast military power at their disposal. It's as if they're obsessed with it. This is a war machine, carefully and secretly built over the past few years, and it frightens me.

"I find myself blaming the Germans, but really, the problem is mankind itself. Every adult alive today lived through that last war. Each and every last one of us personally witnessed how utterly horrific and useless it was back then. We spent years with no food, no heat, no semblance of purpose but to huddle in terror until it was all over.

"No sane person, possessing those ghastly memories, would ever dream of deliberately firing it all back up again. There's simply no excuse for it. I can only conclude that we are flawed beings. Perhaps we deserve what we get."

The man sounds near tears.

I'm surprised that the quiet and unassuming Rodger has spent time thinking such profound thoughts. Further, being English, and born in the late 1800s, I must recognize that what he just shared with me would be considered a brazen outburst of emotion. It's not done. He's bent out of shape and hurting, as his city is attacked before his eyes.

I decide to ease him back from his pain. I say nothing for a while, out of respect. Yet before it becomes an awkward silence I admit, "I'm scared, too. I must say, I'm not fond of this," I sweep my arm out, indicating the East London fires. "How hard was it to resume a normal life when the war was over?" I finally ask, wondering if there are clues to my predicament and probably growing PTSD.

"Oh . . . " Roger has recovered from his outburst and his voice is normal once more. "You just go about your business." He says it firmly—as he would, I muse. In 1918, when Rodger was at the height of his post-war trauma, open discussion of it would probably have been vilified. In England, in 1918, there would be no such thing as emotional support. They didn't even have Prozac—only armagnac.

Yet Rodger drops his guard with me. He speaks softly. "It wasn't easy. I had nightmares for years. And they've come back now. It's all starting up again." He's staring off into nothingness.

That's his generations' equivalent of weeping on my shoulder. I feel honored that Rodger would be so frank with me. And I say nothing, as I'm sure it would be appropriate to do.

We sit atop Nutley House with only blankets for protection

against enemy aircraft. I've long believed in the subtle magical powers of the blanket, but this is quite insane when you get down to it.

"I liked being married," Rodger says suddenly after perhaps three quarters of an hour of silence between the two of us. "There's a comfort to it; an ease."

I get the feeling he's going to chastise me over my apparent bachelorhood.

"I don't know how I could settle for just one woman," I say carefully.

"I settled for Florence, it's true, and that part becomes a bit long in the tooth. But you don't want to miss out on that. It's the natural way of things."

If he's scolding me, I cannot tell.

I reply, "I always saw myself as being married. It's a tough pill to swallow, being forty-nine and still a bachelor. I assumed I'd be long married by now. Nothing ever stuck."

"Well, you're still somewhat young," he says. "It's never too late. I sense you're a far more reasonable man than our young Mr. Hayden. All wind and piss, that one. And being a bachelor, I'm sure has its advantages." Rodger has a sparkle in his voice. "I assume you take the opportunity to find happiness along the way?"

"Fortunately, yes. That doesn't seem to be in short supply," I assure him.

"Good man. Myself, I was always faithful to Florence. Except once. During the war. Me mates and I got into trouble one night on leave in Paris, oh, this would have been in '16. After too much champagne, I was led to a brothel and met a girl. She was brand new, an absolute jewel. I'll never forget that night. I was her first; she was terribly nervous and shocked but most of all she seemed deeply sad. I'd never had it off just for the sake of having it off. I never knew it could be like that."

A flurry of incendiary canisters showers down three blocks

away, lighting two roofs on fire; in the light we can see their roof watchmen, silhouetted in the white-hot flames, battling the fledgling infernos with blankets. They seem to be winning.

"I'll always remember the color pink," Rodger continues, watching. "The room was pink, and the curtains were pink, and the girl was pink, and it spirited me away. Fabrice was her name. I was as kind as I could be, I drew her out. She was so much more afraid than I was. She spoke no English, and I no French. Shy, unwilling at first . . . in the end we had it off three times. We wound up locked in passionate embrace. She called after me as I was escorted out. In a way she was the love of my life. I've never stopped thinking about her, Fabrice. I wonder if she'd even recognize me at this late stage, but I remember everything about her.

"I've never told anyone this before," he says, looking down. "But it was exquisite."

"I'm glad you told me." I'm very surprised that Rodger is opening up to me. I'm honored.

"Of course, I was wracked with guilt when I came home to Florence. We never spoke of it; she never asked, and I certainly never volunteered any information. But I had a bit more passion about it for a while at home. I think I surprised the hell out of Florence, but she didn't complain. Have you never been in love?" Rodger asks.

"I've loved a few women, but they didn't love me back."

"Ah. That's always the way, isn't it? Still." He pats me firmly on the leg while struggling to stand back up. "Don't hang it up. Perhaps your time will come yet."

Rodger climbs back in the hatch into his attic hallway, ostensibly to go relieve himself in the dark and silent house beneath us, saying he might make do with a cup of cold tea, since the gas is off.

I'm alone on a roof with only a helmet to protect me as

London burns. Again, I'm struck by the ridiculousness of the situation I've put myself in.

The Luftwaffe circles loudly, imperiously overhead. Arc light beams continue to swing through the air, looking for targets. I'm seeing aerial battles now, RAF against Luftwaffe, Spitfires against Messerschmitts. They do far more good than the blasted ack-ack guns. I wish they'd just go away.

The ground guns go strangely silent for long periods, then begin firing again. Range, bearing, distance; lorries scrambling all over London's empty streets to keep the guns fed with shells.

I've never particularly valued silence, but now I crave being away from those awful guns.

Am I still going to run away?

I'm altogether less certain now. I don't want to leave Pamela. Being out of that wretched shelter helps. I like the roof. This is just so god-awful dumb. What was I thinking by coming here?

When Rodger returns, I suspect he's been at the brandy and I don't blame him. I wouldn't mind a gallon or two myself. He spends a few long minutes gazing out at the rooftops of London, seeing that nothing has changed.

We take turns napping in the blankets under the wartime sky.

All told we spend nine hours up on that roof, once again in complete alignment with the history books. When the All Clear comes at 5:22, it's still quite dark. The Germans want to get some distance away before daylight returns.

London has just had her first night of a new reality.

The Nazi plan, thought up by Old Nasty himself, is that, starting last night, the English will be so demoralized, the streets so choked with panicked and fleeing refugees—and further, the government and monarchy will collapse in terror—that Germany will stage a smooth invasion and fulfill their master plan.

As I climb down off Mrs. Spettegue's roof, I'm plenty traumatized, but I'm also happy to report that, although sorely bruised and bent out of shape, the British shall hold fast. No street becomes choked. No monarch flees their palace. The British double-down and call the Germans' bluff.

Standing safely at the top of the stairs of number 36 Sloane Gardens, I suddenly acknowledge that any sane person would choose to travel here to celebrate victory at the end. But for reasons unknown to me, I decided to be here at the opening of a generational trauma. I can't focus on anything beyond that right now; I'll have to figure it out at some later point.

Here in Britain, the next two-and-a-half months shall be an experiment in terror. The Germans will throw everything they have, raining down all the fires of hell night after night. But the English won't budge an inch. The coming December weather shall eat away at German air effectiveness, and the bombings will become fewer and more random. They don't stop—they never stop—for five more years. But Germany's grand plan collapses when faced with the famed, bulldog-like stubbornness of the British.

Spoiler alert: By 1945, carpet bombing will definitely become a thing. The nations of the world will pull together and show the Germans what clogged streets and panicked citizens really look like, once and for all, as Berlin gets blown completely off the map.

§

ALL AROUND THE city people emerge from their shelters and go back into their houses. Rail lines are being inspected so the trains can get back on schedule, buses firing up in sheds, ready to dodge craters in the streets. Shops reopen, thems what can.

I try to take stock of my anxiety during yesterday's first attack. I multiply what I felt—times six million persons also engaged in the exact same degree of pleading—I picture that volume of human emotion, shooting skyward from every heart in London.

And it didn't matter. The universe didn't give a damn. It leaves me humbled and deflated.

I can't believe anyone is able to walk in a straight line, much less drive the number 27 bus to Chalk Farm. But they're out there. All of them. As if nothing happened.

I have no work, obviously. Only my precious injurious thoughts for companionship as I get into that bed. I'm not in a well space, but I need sleep. I decide on two hours, from six to eight. I need to check in at the ARP.

My alarm has me jaggedly awake, back up and at it. Unbathed, I stumble downstairs. Mrs. Spettegue provides tea and a few hard biscuits. The morning *Telegraph* has somehow arrived despite the hazards, but I only take a casual look at it, save the headline: "500 BOMBERS RAID LONDON." Big headlines, small, hastily typed articles, general damage, times. Dispatch to Germans decrying the outrage. Four hundred are believed killed, with 1,300 serious injuries. King Bertie is calling for a National Day of Prayer, today, this Sunday.

Bleary-eyed, I don my blue coveralls and report to the ARP office in Sloane Square. I melt in gratitude when they tell me they have all the volunteers they need. The man thanks me and lets me go, but kind of looks at me like I'm an idiot: I'm needed *during* an attack. Not on a sunny Sunday morning after it's all over and I've had a nice gay lie down.

Behind the gentleman's smile is an oozing of contempt.

Feeling like a daft prick, I walk back to Nutley House and fall into my lumpy bed for sleep. A true zizz this time.

Except there's another attack at 12:29. At the sirens I grab my book and coat and bound down the stairs, joined by Pamela,

Mrs. Spettegue and Robert Montague in our haste to the Anderson shelter. Rodger's once again on the roof with Cecil Hayden. As per usual, we don't know where Bill is or when he'll be back.

To the sounds of the sirens and far-off anti-aircraft artillery, our companion emplacements are silent just now; I don't know why. The planes overhead seem to be ours. Few in number, and somehow, they don't sound so hatey. It's slightly more cloudy today, but that's going to work in the Germans' favor. They have everything plotted out ahead of time and it's our boys on the ack-ack guns who have to fire blindly through the blotting cloud cover.

Diving back into the hole in the ground, the scene of yesterday's horror, I gingerly take to my same bunk. My emotional splatters did not cover the walls with their muck. It looks normal. I'm mightily ill at ease, but so far not tending back toward yesterday's panic. Maybe it's like throwing up . . . you just gotta do it and get it out of your system. But the memory lingers, like a smell.

I haven't run away yet. Why have I not run away? I'm somehow being compelled to stay in the role I've assigned myself. Writer, time traveler, friend to Pamela Jarvis. I seem to be gaining some semblance of a backbone. I don't know how or why. I only recognize that it is a process not without great pain.

Running would be the ugliest thing of all. I'm disgusted that I even considered it.

You can be in a bomb shelter, huddling for dear life, and still manage to hate your own guts. I'm learning this now. And it is bitter.

Wuthering Heights, as I expected, is impossible to focus on. I couldn't handle so much as a coloring book right now, even if I had decent light.

Pamela, having finished Edgar's sweater, is feverishly going to town on some new project—an off-white baby jumper with plush soft wool. I watch her deftly clatter her needles, not sure how she's able to make sense of it all.

Since the sounds of war are significantly less than yesterday, the mood is lighter, and Mrs. Spettegue is speaking, talking about her husband Edward. Slowly, begrudgingly, I let go of my self-preoccupation as she describes the heartbreak of her marriage. It's enough to draw me out of my misery and into her story. Which was, as I had suspected, one of misery, too.

"I was twenty-two and very much in love," she says. She describes how they met, their courtship, and how scary it was to get married to a man. It was 1896. She speaks of their wedding night, how she was told nothing of the facts of life, had no idea what to expect—she thought something must be terribly wrong, that she was being inappropriately used by him, while all around her kept giving her knowing winks and smiles. But then she describes the joys and challenges she faced as a young homemaker. The thrill of learning, after only three months, that she was pregnant.

"How did Edward die?" Pamela asks, putting her hand on Mrs. Spettegue's arm.

"He worked for a quarry in Cambridgeshire and was driving a cart loaded with slate. They told me one of the oxen was acting up. He got down to look and the creatures bolted; he was caught beneath the wheel. He didn't die right away, I was able to see him one last time." She begins to tear up. "It was ghastly. But I'm forever glad I got to see him before he died. He told me he loved me from the first time he laid eyes on me." She blots at her eyes with a handkerchief.

"The baby miscarried four weeks after that."

Jesus.

"I was disconsolate," she continues. "I'd moved back home with my mum, hadn't even come to grips with the loss of Edward when the baby died. It was a horrid time. I don't suppose I'll ever completely recover from it. One doesn't; not really."

"Oh, my dear," Pamela says, nearly crying.

"I haven't spoken of it," Mrs. Spettegue says to Pamela, "because, particularly with your Edgar away, I didn't want you to upset yourself."

"I'm all right." Pamela gives Mrs. Spettegue a hug. "Whatever happens, we're in this together."

They fall silent. I lay back on the bunk with my arm over my eyes and listen to the occasional booming of far-off placement guns and the droning of aircraft.

Fuss comes back to me in waves, then subsides. I realize I'm fighting a battle, in some ways bigger than the one outside: how to stay sane in this tiny shelter for the next six days. I still want to laugh; I signed up for this! It's horrible!

After a quarter of an hour or so, with the four of us just sitting and staring in silence without speaking, I decide to distract myself enough to ask Mrs. Spettegue: "How long have you run Nutley House? Where does the name Nutley come from?"

We hear an explosion not too far away, a dull thud and we feel the earth shake just a little. My heart flutters and my hands begin to shake. But it's just the one hit. Mrs. Spettegue says nothing for a great long while, then answers.

"Nutley was my uncle's name. He ran the place until he became too infirm to keep going. I worked under him here since 1900; it's always easy to remember which year it was. I was twenty-six. My word, I've been doing this for forty years! Mind you, I've seen a lot of people come and go over that time."

"Who was your longest tenant?" I ask. Conversation seems to distract me from my panic. It gives me focus. It seems to be the only tool available to me right now.

"Oh, without a doubt Mr. Donald Anderson. He was here from aught-two until he died in 1936. He died in your very room, Mr. Baldwin. Although I assure you, I've certainly changed out the bedding."

Terrific. An old man has died in my room. I picture the room full of his junk. I wonder how long it was before he was found. I shiver. It just makes the air raid shelter feel smaller and hotter. I tug at my collar.

"Are your parents alive, Mark?" Pamela asks of me.

"My mom and I are quite close," I reply. "She lives in Seattle, Washington State, in the Pacific Northwest. I don't know about my dad. I assume he's still alive."

"But you don't know for sure?" Mrs. Spettegue asks, somewhat shocked.

"No. He and my mother divorced when I was seventeen. He took a new wife and is raising her children as his own. He cut my two older sisters and me out of his life."

"My word, that's sad," Pamela says. "Was he unkind?"

"No, he wasn't. It never felt like he was phoning it in—sorry, I mean to say, his affection seemed real enough—until just suddenly he wasn't there anymore. It's too bad because my sisters and I are good people. We don't deserve to be just cut off like that, but the decision was his to make. If I passed him on the street, I don't know that I'd recognize him."

It's been some time, in fact, since we've heard any noise from without; no ack-ack, no explosions . . . nothing.

The All-Clear sounds just after I realize this. We trundle back into the house. It's 1:24. There's this thing now where you take a quick survey and see everything is normal and so you simply go about your business.

Can I get into this groove? It's real; it's not going away. And apparently neither am I, as I've made no further attempts to effectuate some sort of escape from the city.

Mrs. Spettegue invites Pamela and I for liverwurst sandwiches. This isn't included in our room rate—it is a gift of Mrs. Spettegue. It's sweet of her.

While I was happily sleeping this morning, Rodger had taken it upon himself to bring huge piles of dirt, bucket by bucket, up to the roof, with a shovel and more buckets full, ready to go. I would really have liked to have helped him with that, but there I was, sleeping like a log.

Yet more shame.

Bill Markley comes in, saying he went somewhere. "At friends'," is all he'll say. He goes into his room.

The afternoon is spent shoveling more dirt from the garden. Rodger assures me he has all he needs and manages to say it without making me feel ashamed. But Mrs. Spettegue's vegetable patch has taken quite a hit and I'm determined to stack the earth back into reasonable rows and replant that which had been so unceremoniously ripped out. A good dousing from the hose makes me feel confident no real damage has been done.

Tea, at six, is somewhat different, in that the doors to the lounge are wide open and the radio is broadcasting news from the Home Service. While we feast on bread and carefully limited portions of corned beef with cabbage, we listen.

"Today's attack proved to be of a minor character," says John Snagge The Radio Man. No planes made it all the way to London; they approached in waves over Dover and were chased away by the RAF.

Last night's raid took place from 8:26 to 5:22. Eighty-nine German bombers were downed compared to 22 English machines lost. Pamela shudders. The BBC reads information, "according to the official German news agency."

They can get that?

I guess they can. Sounds odd to me, getting news from the enemy, even though it's certain to be riddled with lies and half-truths.

- Many bombs fell wide, causing considerable

damage to private property and casualties to persons. Two unnamed hospitals were bombed, but fortunately had been evacuated. At one location a falling bomb managed to pop straight down an airshaft somewhere in East London, exploding inside a crowded shelter, bringing great loss of life.

- A passenger train was raked with machine gun fire from a passing aeroplane, at an altitude of sixty feet.
- A viaduct at Waterloo Station was obliterated, causing rail disruption.
- The attacks are being directed by field marshal Goering from the North of France, who declares them reprisals for RAF attacks on Berlin.

Because I'm tired and have jetlag and am in over my head, I observe in my fellow residents as the news tumbles from the speakers. Everyone around me is doing the same thing: mouths open, eyes glazed over, each listening or lost in their own thoughts. It's fairly zombie-like. No wonder people decried radio's initial introduction into the home. It turned vital people into what looked like lifeless, slack-jawed idiots, drooling and not interacting. Taken at face value, it sounds patently unhealthy.

But the information we are receiving is life-altering. No one can hear it and not be changed, regardless of facial expression.

I'm shaken from my observations by a burst of big band music coming now from the radio. We all just kind of look up at each other, our focus back, shoulders down, mouths open.

Conversation is nil. No one apparently has anything to say. We finish our meal in silence, and I help Pamela clear the plates to the dumbwaiter.

Pamela and I opt for the bare minimum of a walk, just around the block, and I realize that, although we're each participating in a conversation, we're not really talking about the same subject. Neither is listening to the other or responding in kind.

The nighttime raid begins at eight o'clock. Sirens, but no ack-ack at first.

I'm taking roof duty again, this time with Robert Montague. I feel like I'm slowly getting a handle on all this. Roof is definitely better than shelter. I need to see what's happening all around, even if that means standing in a hail of shrapnel like a damn fool. I'm still, in general, nervous and trembly, easily startled at any loud sound, but for whatever reason, I'm not the psychological puddle I was just a while ago.

Robert and I discuss what's likely to happen around us and we review what to do should an incendiary come down upon our roof. We take stock of the dirt buckets, shovels and blankets. If an actual bomb should arrive in our midst, there won't be anything to do but enjoy the flash-bang and the brief second of having our lives pass quickly before our individual eyes.

There's nothing to do but wait for something bad to happen, which may or may not come. Most planes are high overhead, at altitude, which is good. That's where we want them to be.

"What do you do for the gasworks?" I ask Robert.

"I'm in procurement, that's been my occupation for many a year. It's good, steady work. Perhaps not very exciting, but you reach a point in life where excitement no longer appeals. Like all this," he tilts his head over toward the fight. "I could do without it."

Robert, too, seems fascinated by my status as a bachelor. Asks the same questions as everyone else. "How can a man your age have no wife?" he asks.

It's a blunt question. But there seems to be no malice in it.

"Well, it isn't for lack of trying." I weary of the same constant scrutiny.

"As long as you still fancy birds," he says, perhaps with a tinge of acrimony.

Hadn't occurred to me he might not like me being "one of those people." But he seems content to drop the subject. I doubt he'd be any more comfortable about it than I would. On the whole, he's been respectable and relaxed around me, so I just leave it as is.

"I'm too old to be called up for the army, plus, being a procurement manager for the gasworks means I'm in a protected position . . . which is just as well. I was in the navy in the last war. I don't want to live through that again."

"What did you do in the war?"

"I had a desk job, thank God. Procurement then, as well. If you really want to know about life in the trenches, you should talk to Rodger. He was there."

"I have. It sounds awful."

"It was. I worked for a hospital ward. It was like a meat factory. It really was the war to end all wars, and now we're back in the same ruddy predicament all over again." He shakes his head. "This is a new form of warfare, though this time it's different," Robert says, gesturing to the skies above. "Bombing innocent civilians. It just isn't cricket."

"How did you wind up at Nutley House?" I inquire.

"Much the same as you: I wandered in. I wanted to be close by in case they split the offices up, which, of course, eventually they did. You see, rather than having the offices at the gasworks, which is a prime target of the bombers, all offices and administration bits are split into smaller bits, distributed into various houses around London. That way if any one location is bombed, it doesn't create havoc to the system as a whole. Rather ingenious, actually."

I admit that it is.

"My division is in charge of parts and equipment. We have

doubles of everything, so if a bomb hits, we can reassemble quickly and keep going."

It strikes me again how prepared England has been. They seem to have thought of everything. Except how to use the Tubes for shelter, and that'll start in a few weeks' time.

"What do you enjoy doing in your spare time?" I ask him.

"Fishing and playing poker."

"Maybe we should get a poker game going."

"Mrs. Spettegue wouldn't half bust a gut! Rodger and I talked about it one night at dinner and she wasn't having it. I was surprised at her ardor, the poor dear."

"That's too bad. I wonder if she draws the line at bridge; I wouldn't mind picking that up again, I barely have the basics so far."

It's midnight, and I seem to have exhausted all conversation with Mr. Montague.

28

Monday, September 9, 1940

The rest of the night with Robert Montague passes without incident.

For a time I stand alone at the parapet, lost in my thoughts.

I watched San Francisco die. London is facing attempted murder, but she will survive her injuries, somewhat scarred. Overhead, men are trying to kill me. It's hard not to take it personally. Rather than fear, though, I try going over to anger, perhaps for the first time. It is a strong tonic. It's the opposite of fear, refreshingly so; I'll have to look into it further. I don't get very far with it before returning to my general confused state.

I look out at London under attack and think back to my earlier thoughts about just exactly what a city is. It is a collection of buildings, and now we know even that can be taken away. So what am I missing?

People. It is and always was all about the people. Yet, I've never managed to make that gel. What's wrong with me? Maybe it's a good thing that I'm going to die, by Messerschmitt or Problem Zero, because thus far, I seem to have completely missed the boat.

I'm trapped back home in the San Francisco of 2019 just as effectively as I'm trapped on a roof in an air raid.

I'm going to go ahead and assume I'll get through this and be given leave to survive and get to go back to San Francisco. But to what? Even if I ignore Problem Zero—which I'm only just now understanding how effective at that I truly am—how am I going to make it all work? Love, career, friendships . . . I guess I needed stimulation to nudge me out from under my rock.

Well, be careful what you wish for. I now got stimulation coming out my ass and, apparently, I can't even remotely handle it.

So what's the answer? How do I survive? How do I find meaning and purpose in the city of San Francisco, when I've already exhausted my dating pool and played my career hand to no avail?

A German plane flies by us, low and slow, lazy, with none of the diving whine or blazing of guns. I'm unafraid. He's just having a good look, as if wanting to ask a passer-by how to get to the British Museum. Surely he must know the thousands of souls huddled in the dark buildings below him and he's just out for a Sunday drive.

Humans hunting humans for sport. Blowing up their lives. Tiny cogs in a huge machine of war from which will emerge no prize but the ruination of cultures and the deaths of millions.

And I need San Francisco to make sense to me?

Up on that rooftop, as that particular Messerschmitt guns his throttle and banks up to rejoin the hostilities, I decide that maybe there was never meant to be any sense of it at all.

Robert and I don't seem to have much in common. So the

night is long and silent. We take turns napping in the blankets. Few bombs fall near to us, but quite a few more incendiaries and the ack-ack guns roar the whole night through until the 5:00 a.m. The All Clear sounds, long before the sun begins making itself known along the smoky eastern horizon.

§

ALL OF LONDON will report to work on-time and dressed properly. If the rail lines have been blown up, then we suggest you find alternative means of transport. People will hitch rides, take unfamiliar buses or walk.

But they won't be late.

I don't know how they do it. I picture Robert working all day, having only napped sporadically all night. It's disgusting. The man might not sleep again for years.

Mrs. Spettegue, too, doesn't miss a step. The minute the All Clear sounds and the gas is back, she's down in the kitchen getting the kettle on, making tea and providing meals.

I happily tuck into my breakfast of tea, toast and porridge, glad for the daylight and calm.

Then a nap. Radio at one o'clock describes times and durations of last night's attacks, and that another 400 were killed. His Majesty the King went to East London in the day to survey the damage personally and pronounced "Everybody wonderfully brave."

Not likely to leave the house, am I? So what do I do all day?

I help Mrs. Spettegue fuss in the newly reassembled garden. Pamela helps for a time but her back's been hurting.

I study my pink handbook a little more . . .

An air raid happens from 5:10 p.m. to 6:27. I take to the shelter with everyone else. My fuss is less, a familiar, almost ease is taking tentative root within me. It just remains a vague abstraction in the back of my mind and I wait to get really afraid again. The only thing I know for sure is that it will happen once more.

I sense a pattern that the Germans do a small daylight raid followed by an all-nighter. So I chance that this will hold true, and I sit and talk with Pamela in the shelter. This time, I'm in my bunk, she in Rodger's. Her back still hurts. Probably a combination of nerves and carting around the weight of the child within. We whisper to each other in half phrases and in code words that have already sprung up between us, about boys and girls and what makes them so different. How we both prefer boys, and why, giggling.

Not much happens as we wait. We hear a few hits: a crunching sound nearby and everything rattles. We feel it as much as hear it. I find myself mostly calm.

An hour passes and the All Clear comes. Mrs. Spettegue immediately sets about getting us tea—eggs on toast, late, owing to the alert. I'm hungry. It's a good sign that I'm beginning to normalize under this self-selected strain.

Tea at table includes a discussion about the change in bombing intensity. The Germans are clearly serious about things now, it's ramping up, aggravated and definite. War is now upon England in the way promised, but not before seen up close.

We help Mrs. Spettegue clear the table. I take it Pamela wants to go for one of our walks and yet she dithers. Something's up; she can't seem to sit still.

Instead of walking, she sits and tries to read a magazine. That doesn't work, so she stomps up to her room, only to return ten minutes later.

Finally, after eight, she proclaims her wish to go for a walk with me.

"I've got to get out of here for a while."

"Should we? It's after blackout. There's going to be another attack . . . "

"I don't care."

I've never heard her sound like this before. She seems determined to go out and, if anything, I can't let her go alone. So despite my misgivings, I grab my heavy coat and hat and out we go.

It's dark. Yet Pamela is determined to keep walking. She's trudging, saying nothing. We go much further than normal and are walking fast—she's practically marching, determined to crack onward to some unknown destination. We've passed Sloane Square and have headed west down King's Road. It's one road I remember that doesn't get bombed, so I feel pretty good about going so far, with another air raid surely only minutes away.

"Where are you going?" I finally ask.

"I don't know. I just need to move. It's all that feels good to me right now."

I decide to try to get a conversation going, anything that comes to mind.

"What are you hoping to become after the war?" I finally ask.

"Well, I hope I'm not a Nazi housewife. I can't imagine England being under German rule, it's too terrible to think about. Do the Nazis let women have careers? I suppose I'll have to learn German."

"I think we'll win the war. I think good eventually triumphs over evil. I bet the Americans will finally get involved."

"I hope so. The Americans don't seem too keen on anything that doesn't involve them directly. No offense."

"None taken."

"Either way the war turns out, I still want a career."

Having a conversation, even a dull one such as this, seems to be working. Pamela is slowing down her pace, beginning to amble more akin to our normal habit.

"It'll be hard, being a working mother, but I worked before and I don't want to only stay home with children. I want more. I have too much to offer. Ouff. I just wish my stomach would settle down."

By now we've gone as far along King's Road as we dare before turning back. It's dark.

I hope her sudden stomach pains don't mean what I think they mean. We're a good twenty-minute walk from Nutley House, and my fear is coming back around.

"Ouff!" Pamela barks it out loud again and doubles over with one hand on her spine.

"Pamela, are you in labor?"

"No, I'm a bleeding Tory. Of course I'm in labor!"

Just then the air raid sirens go. I knew they would; I cannot for the life of me understand why we are in this current predicament. It's like she planned it.

It's 8:40, eighteen minutes past blackout and even the Germans are running late tonight. We're way down King's Road with a long dark walk ahead of us. And now she's having contractions.

We hear planes, and not just out east. They're here. Some bombs go off quite near, which is strange and completely alarming. Yet another anti-aircraft emplacement is close by, seemingly just over the wall to our left. We are being rent by sound and percussion. We see streaks of the tracer bullets arcing up from the booming guns.

I start to panic again. Or maybe not actual panic, just normal fear for life and limb. Thank God, I'm beginning to learn how to differentiate them enough to still function. I put my arm around Pamela and begin guiding her in the direction of home, still in shock at the ridiculousness of our situation.

Bombs are falling quite close and we're out in the open. Where can we take shelter? Also, why are they bombing Sloane Square right now? Turds.

After ten minutes, we get back to the square and the Underground station, only to find the gates padlocked, as expected.

Pamela doubles over again.

Her water breaks.

"How much farther can you walk?" I ask.

"Not far. I need to sit down."

I look dully at the shut gate of Sloane Square Station. We're so close to home! This is so stupid!

"Do you want to go into the public shelter just over there?"

"No, Mark. I do not."

"Well, just what exactly do you propose?" I say it kind of whiny. Don't mean to, but here we are, exposed and dilating. None of this is any good.

Pamela can't seem to walk any further. I'm holding her and realize she's more frightened than I am and that snaps me out of it.

I need to grow a pair. Right now.

I pull against the metal gates of the Tube station, finding them as solid as expected. I'm probably going to have to go against her wishes and haul her pregnant ass to the public shelter anyway. Either that or get us down to Nutley House. But I'm altogether uncertain she can make the walk.

I rattle the gate hard again in frustration.

One side where it attaches to the wood doorframe has a slight give to it. The gate's solid as ever, but the wood to which it is attached is old and soft. I examine the hasp, screwed into the board. It's loose, the screws stripped with dry rot.

I use a farthing to unturn one of them, and it comes out quite easily.

Pamela is moaning occasionally, leaning on me, so I quickly go after another screw.

It works. After four of them, painstakingly pulled loose by my tiny coin, which I drop twice, I reach through with my hand in a tight claw shape and go after the four screws the other side of the metal. The wood there is even softer. The gate now has enough give at the upper corner that I can yank it back and squeeze us through. Barely.

I reflect that, if it's going to happen, it might be better here than in that tiny, crowded Anderson shelter where Pamela will have no privacy. It's so cramped, with at least four or five other adults and no room to get out of the way. It would be horribly awkward and embarrassing.

Maybe this is better after all? It's not much protection, not like the other deep bore stations of the Underground network, but it's here and bombs are coming down nearby.

I shimmy over the badly angled metal and, bending it down hard, help Pamela inside.

The Tube station is deserted and black as night.

I have no choice but to get out my iPhone and use the flashlight. Pamela's beyond caring.

"Let's get you underground," I say.

Just as we have crossed the main floor and have headed down the stairs to the tracks, the whistle of a falling bomb can be heard and a building down the road dissolves in a riot of bricks, blown to dust. Flames roar forth.

I'm holding Pamela and carrying her purse. A third of the way down the stairs, we hear yet more explosions from the street above—my closest ones yet. The concussion is terrifying. We grab each other and fling ourselves against the wall of the stairwell. I can feel the wall quake with the force of it.

Pamela has another contraction—a bad one. She remains against the wall, waiting for the pain to pass. The percussive force of an exploding bomb, seemingly just on the other side of the staircase wall, jars my organs and squeezes my stomach into acute pain. It's surely doing the same to Pamela, and to her child within. It is so close to us, I conclude it must be a direct hit on the New Court Theatre. It has probably just been blown to dust.

As the explosion subsides, we dash down to the platform, the lowest part of the station. Shining my iPhone around, I'm startled to find a train parked on the opposite track. It's dark. Its doors are open and the whole thing deathly silent, and only just hastily abandoned. A large piece of equipment, nearly two hundred feet long, looks utterly ghoulish and macabre in the dark. Red paint looks flat and black. I walk up and down the platform, looking in each carriage, my flashlight reflecting harshly back at me by all the windows of the train. I'm desperate to find a fellow human, but they're gone. When the air raid came, they must have parked the train, opened the doors, cut the power and headed to the public shelter. They must've only just left; the air has that feeling of temporary, like they've only gone for tea.

I lay my coat down on the platform for Pamela—so glad I brought it—and she sits and reclines against the wall of the station and I sit beside her, under a giant ad for Guinness. The floor is of macadam and none too clean, littered with cigarette butts, wads of gum and rat droppings.

It's not completely dark in here, for there's a fire practically next door—a big one. The fire brigade and ARP are already on site; water is being sprayed. It splashes on the glass roof in huge, loud sheets, startling us. There are people out there, fighting the fires, and they don't know we're here, hiding, and in no way safe.

"The raid shouldn't last too long," I try to reassure her. "And then we'll get you back to the Nut House."

She has another contraction then, worse than before. "I don't want to go back there," she declares.

"What?"

"I did this on purpose. I couldn't possibly stand doing this in that ruddy shelter. In . . . *whew, whew* . . . in front of Cecil! I'd die!"

"What on earth did you have in mind?" I'm stunned. She must not be thinking clearly.

"I don't know. I only know I don't want to be back there, not right now. I feel safer with you."

I take her hand in mine. It's all so bizarre . . . I'm touched, but scared shitless. Fear, once again. My new friend.

I hold her and stare at the dead train and just quietly freak.

The contractions are coming quicker and harder each time. No further explosions seem to be happening upstairs. I somehow feel that the longer we go without another one, the more likely we're going to be safe. But then I realize that's purely irrational. I don't know what to think.

Apparently, it falls to me to do the thinking for the both of us.

I figure it's best to encourage her. "You're coming along fine. Most women take more than a day to have their first baby, so we'll be safest here if we can just wait it out."

"Bloody brilliant," Pamela snaps. "I can't believe you know so much about childbirth for someone as bent as you."

"Well, I can't believe you know so little about it, frankly." I'm surprised I've said it out loud, but it has truly had me at a loss for some time.

"There's no way in bleedin' hell I could ever have such a conversation with my wretched mother. And I knew Mrs. Spettegue had something horrible happen to her in the past, so I never brought it up."

She hunches over with another contraction.

"Listen, I don't know all that much. I've been nearby for friends' and sisters' births," I say.

Pamela is breathing hard and rapid. I have no idea what to

expect. I keep hoping for the All Clear so we can head for home, but frankly I'm not even sure she could make the walk in her condition. No, it's just not good.

Any idea of propriety gone, she raises her knees and spreads them.

29

Tuesday September 10, 1940

I'm an idiot. I haven't been timing the contractions. We should do that."

I set my phone on the platform. The green of the timer button is warm to look at, yet it's bathed in the hellish light of the fire above. More water from firehoses gushes over the glass roof, startling us.

She informs me that a contraction has begun. It lasts almost a minute, and then subsides. I watch the clock. We don't say anything, we just quietly wait for the next one. It comes in only four minutes.

"According to that, you're quite far along after all." I guess I'm amazed. "It may have to happen here."

"In a ruddy tube station?!" she sounds aghast.

"Unless you have any better ideas.?"

"*Whew. Whew. Whew*," is her only response.

I ponder our situation. Of course, I've never been in a

delivery room before, I just know what I know from watching TV. It's a natural event, there shouldn't be much for me to do except to say "push" and catch the baby. Assuming nothing goes wrong. If it does . . .

For a moment I banish those thoughts from my mind. And then, suddenly, I realize that I will do no such thing. I have to fish those thoughts back out and deal with them squarely. Now. If something does go wrong, I'll have to abandon Pamela to go get help. For the first time, my concern isn't for me dashing down Holbein Place in search of Doctor Kelso, but of leaving poor Pamela alone in a cold station with fires all around and death raining from the sky.

We're just not going to feature that, I decide firmly.

We hear the dull thud of bombs exploding in the streets far away—not close, but a bomb is a bomb and they're still out there. The Blitz is still a going concern. We have to stay put then, there's nothing for it.

"So you're hoping for a girl?"

"At this point I'm hoping for a doctor."

"You're in no shape to walk, and we got no place else to be. What do you know about giving birth?"

"Next to nothing. It hurts! I'm learning that. Which is bloody useless information for me right now. Is this really happening?" she asks me in a pleading, almost childish way, reminding me once again how young she really is.

"'Fraid so. It's really happening. The only question is when, and that's up to the baby by now."

"Fuck," she says plainly, wincing with another contraction and breathing heavily through pursed lips.

Hours pass. Waves of contractions with nothing in between. We talk in between contractions. Edgar, parenthood . . . I try to take her mind off her pain.

Failing anything else, I tell her a story. *Mrs. Frisby and the Rats of NIMH*, my favorite book as a child. About a mama mouse living in a cinder block with her three baby mice, and they need help and go to the rats that live under the rosebush. Turns out the rats have a highly technological society in there, complete with electricity, air conditioning and amazing tales of their escape from a laboratory, where they were gifted with great intelligence.

I get into it, and by gosh, it seems to help. It gives us focus. Takes our minds off the discomfort of sitting on pavement, and what can only be keen agony for Pamela.

Contractions. Closer and closer together. Gathering to their inevitable crescendo.

I'm holding her tight, one arm around her. Clasping one another's hands, hers so very cold to my touch, we just wait. Listening to the bombs overhead, ack-ack guns pounding the night air, and angry snarling aircraft.

Timing more contractions.

It's chilly and my coat is under Pamela. I doubt it'll ever be used again. I look at the giant clock over the platform. In the light of searchlights above and ragged remains of the fire below, I can make out that it's 1:00 a.m., and outside, the Germans are showing no signs of letting up. Tonight they're not focusing on the east end; they're up to something here in the west. The hospital? York HQ? Buckingham Palace?

The contractions are coming faster. She's unable to track conversation so I just babble on about anything that comes to mind; nonsense, poems, bits of stories, *Return of the Jedi* . . . the only thing I know is that talking helps her. It's the only help I can give.

Suddenly, after another hour, the time has come. Pamela pulls off her soaking knickers and throws them down the platform and is now bearing down, her face a rictus of pain.

"Breathe," I keep saying; it's the only thing I know to say. "Breathe."

"*Shut it, you git!*" she snarls through gritted teeth.

Pamela is legs up, wearing a skirt, and with my wool coat beneath her. She slumps and starts bearing down.

"I think it's happening," she says.

"Right."

It's time for me to take up position as midwife.

I disentangle myself from our hours-long embrace and crawl down between Pamela's legs—a place I never in my wildest dreams thought I'd be. I shine my iPhone upon the situation, and it's a little tough on me, but this is real and she needs my help. I banish my embarrassment and steel myself for my new role.

"You're doing fine. When the time comes just push, real hard."

"Oh my God, it's happening!"

A major contraction comes, and she bears down. I see the crown of the baby's head and I tell her so. She stops and catches her breath for a moment. But the moment doesn't last long and soon she's bearing down again, screaming.

Thrice more she does this, and soon the head is out. The shoulders are another significant hurdle; after that, the whole packet shoots out with a squish into my hands, warm and slippery.

It's a girl.

The baby starts crying immediately, drawing air into her tiny lungs. This is good. Her cries echo sharply in the station. I shine the light up to Pamela's face, which is drenched in sweat, her hair matted, and she looks deathly pale. I hope she's all right. The umbilical cord is still attached and coming out of Pamela. It's blue.

I'm holding a fifteen-second-old human in my hands. She's so tiny! And, yes, covered in goo. I put the baby on Pamela's chest and get up—my knees are hurting on the concrete—and I move down to retrieve Pamela's knickers to wipe up the baby a little bit. It helps. Pamela has her sweater three-quarters off, and we use that to swaddle the baby.

"I've got to cut the cord. What have you got in your purse that will help?"

"Mrs. Spettegue put in a sewing kit for emergencies," Pamela said weakly. "Thank God for that, now I know why. She didn't actually tell me."

So with her permission I empty out the contents onto the platform and among a compact and stick of lippy, I find a leather pouch containing small scissors and spools of thread. Again, I've only seen it done on TV. Tie it tight in two segments, close to the baby's belly, grab the scissors and cut. The baby cries in the dark, empty station.

I look at the clock again: 2:33.

"She was born at 2:33 a.m. in Sloane Square Tube Station," I say. "What are you going to name her?"

"Oh." Pamela is winded and speaks slowly, through ragged breaths. "We'd fought over a few girl's names; Claire, Isabelle . . . but . . . " she pauses several long moments, "right now I'm of a mind to . . . to call her . . . Sloane."

Sloane! Oh my God, it's brilliant!

"I'm glad we weren't at Goodge Street Station," I laugh. Pamela smiles wanly.

"Hello, Sloane, I'm your Auntie Mark," I say, shining my light on mother and child.

Pamela undoes her blouse and Sloane immediately begins to feed; I hand Pamela a handkerchief from my back pocket and let her use it to wipe her sweaty face and more from the baby.

Contractions continue afterward for a while, and I don't attend to what I'm sure will happen next—the afterbirth. It's all there on my coat, and there it shall remain.

I'm beaming with pride, and overcome with relief that nothing, apparently, went wrong after all. I sit back down next to Pamela and put my arm back around her.

It's incredible.

We're cold and hungry, except for the baby, who's eating a feast at Pamela's expense.

Pamela and Sloane doze, and I take several pictures of the sleeping mother and child. They're precious, like a marble statue at the Vatican, set beneath an ad for Guinness.

The fire above is long since beaten down, taking with it any semblance of light and the perception of warmth, if not warmth itself. Which just leaves us cold and shivering. I wrap Pamela in my arms the best I can, and we three just exist, once again reduced to waiting for the air raid to end.

We doze. All three of us. And seem to sleep.

§

THE WAILING of the All Clear comes at 5:03 and wakes us.

I'm not rested. I'm terribly uncomfortable. But then I think of how Pamela must be feeling, and I'm overcome with shame. It's not about me.

"Can you walk?" I ask her.

"I think so. Probably not very well, though. Blast, we have all those bloody stairs to climb," she fairly wails.

"We have two options: wait here another couple of hours or get ourselves out of here and over to the Nut House on our own."

"I don't want to wait another minute in this bloody station. I'm freezing!"

"OK. We'll take it in small stages. Let's get you to your feet. Do you think you can do that?"

"I think so. I'll try."

Agonizingly slowly I get Pamela up, holding Sloane to her chest. I manage to get her standing, holding on to the station wall.

"Whew. I feel woozy," she says.

"Take all the time you need."

We begin walking slowly. I wad my coat up and throw it into a trash bin. No sign remains on the platform of the miracle that has just taken place. Only chewing gum and cigarette butts. I carry her smart clutch like a football and lean in to support her as best I can.

We make our way along the platform, back toward the stairs. We rest at the bottom, Pamela holding Sloane to her breast and slowly we climb—ever so slowly, one step at a time.

"How bad does it hurt?" I ask.

"Better all the time. That last push nearly saw me black out, it was so bad. Men will never experience anything like the pain of childbirth," she breathes. "I think the world would be a better place if you lot did."

It takes us ten minutes to climb the steps. I stay behind her to ensure she doesn't fall.

"Are you bleeding?"

"Bleedin' wot?"

"Down there. Many women require stitches."

"I don't think so. I just hurt all over." Pamela shivers again, and I rue the fact that I can provide no comfort, other than to just get her the hell home as fast as I can.

We're in the ticket lobby and have made it to the warped metal gap we used to break our way in.

We entered as two people and are leaving as three people. I cannot wrap my brain around this arcane fact.

What awaits us outside is the aftermath of an inferno. As I suspected, the New Court Theater next door is bombed completely out, the fire mostly extinguished and the action steadily winding down. Ambulances and the fire brigade are there, in small contingent, and we're in need for someone to help us.

Pamela's getting heavy and falling to bits. The walk up the stairs took her all, there's no way she'll be able to walk to the Nut House from here.

I finally get two ARP volunteers to stop for us.

"We've just had a baby and I don't think she can walk. Can you help us?"

"Oi! Congratulations, mate!" They run, double-time, and produce a stretcher—two brooms and a blanket. They set the stretcher down and Pamela lies back on it, still cradling Sloane. I explain the situation and we get her the short distance to Nutley House. The men are in good spirits as they drop us off, wishing us well and hurrying back up to the dead slag at the top of the lane.

§

We come spilling into the house and Mrs. Spettegue nearly faints, but her need to dash, headlong, toward Sloane and Pamela overrides her need to pass out. They all come running from the dining room—everyone's there, even Bill—and we're instantly surrounded.

"Where in heaven's name were you?" moaned Mrs. Spettegue. "We thought the worst!"

"We broke into the tube station and sheltered underground," I say. "That's where this happened," and I gesture to Pamela and Sloane.

Pamela, although utterly tired and wobbly, is beaming with pride. "Everybody, please say hello to Sloane Claire Jarvis."

There's nearly a stampede as all five adults rush Pamela and the baby. Much oohing and ahhing. Sloane, only three hours old, yawns, her face crunched up in fatigue and confusion.

"Oh, she's a beaut!" says Rodger.

"Darling!" says Robert.

Cecil and Bill are obviously pleased but holding back a bit.

Mrs. Spettegue is weeping openly, begging to hold the baby. Pamela seems reluctant to hand her over but does do, and Mrs. Spettegue sweeps Sloane into her arms and rocks her side to side. Sloane gives a hic and a cough and every one of us goes "*awwwww.*"

"I can't believe you came while I was away," Mrs. Spettegue says in a baby voice. "How naughty of you! I was meant to be there!"

"She came as a surprise to us all," I say.

"Mark was wonderful!" Pamela declares. "He delivered the baby at 2:30 in the morning, right on the train platform. He was very brave. I couldn't have done it without him."

"Oh, it's *too* exciting!" Mrs. Spettegue gushes. "We must get you off your feet, you poor thing! Can you manage the stairs, dear? We must get word to your husband, right away! We'll go to the telegraph office this minute and wire for Mr. Jarvis. Oh, but first you must be famished! No . . . a *bath*, you'll want a bath!"

We men all smile among ourselves; we've never seen Mrs. Spettegue this animated before.

"I do think I should lie down," Pamela says helpfully, taking Sloane back from her patroness. Sloane hasn't made a fuss in quite a while, she's been sleepy and quiet.

Mrs. Spettegue helps Pamela upstairs to her room on the second floor. They draw a bath for Pamela and Sloane—I hear the striking of a match to light the heater—and get her ready for bed.

I feel somewhat slighted as Mrs. Spettegue takes over. My part is done. I'm just the auntie now.

Rodger runs next door and telephones for Dr. Kelso who's out helping bombing victims. He leaves a message for him to come when he can.

More than anything, I rather need to wash my hands. Down in the kitchen, the sink there has its own hot water, so I do a refreshing surgeon's handwash, luxuriating in the warm suds. I find a piece of cold toast on the kitchen counter, pop it in my mouth and head for bed.

Still in the bathtub, Sloane is loudly crying behind the closed bathroom door. It's not an easy sound, but I think it's a good omen: the sounds of a baby crying in such a dumpy old house full of disjointed, lonely adults.

I go to sleep, climbing into that rickety bed some old man named Anderson probably kacked in.

So long as there's no air raid siren, the world can go to hell.

I don't feel fear. I feel marvelous.

§

I SLEEP from six to ten. I'm starving, but the first thing I want is a bath. I deserve that much at least. Pamela's door is closed and it's just as well. She needs her privissy.

Dr. Kelso stops by at about 11:00 a.m. and pronounces mother and baby in excellent health. He weighs the baby, she's a fine six pounds, nine ounces. Dr. Kelso's clearly not slept all night and doesn't stay long.

Somber gray today, threatening rain. It's much cooler now, and I no longer have a coat.

By lunchtime the sirens still haven't gone, and I'm so thankful. Pamela and Sloane need quiet and bed rest. But the Germans will be back. Mother and daughter are going to have to take to the shelter at any point, which sickens me. Mrs. Spettegue delivers lunch to Pamela and then joins me in the dining room with Rodger. Egg sandwiches on that sad, gray bread.

Rodger tells us of the dogfight we missed over the Houses of Parliament last night. About what it was like on the roof with bombs coming so close this time, a few plinks came down on the roof of number 36, eventually harmless, but a lot more incendiaries were strewn nearby. Watching stuff as close as Sloane Square getting blown up was probably very triggering to Rodger, although he wouldn't admit to it.

I finally broach the question: "How do we handle an air raid with a newborn baby? They can't stay in the house, but a shelter is no place for someone only a few hours old."

Mrs. Spettegue has a ready answer, though. "I know. It's a ghastly situation. But it must be done. We'll have her well swaddled; I have a sufficiency of cotton bud, which we can place in her ears. Hopefully, it should protect her from the noise. Other than that, the poor lamb is in the same boat as the rest of us."

"All right. I guess you gotta do what you gotta do."

In the afternoon I read the *Telegraph*, but it doesn't have anything new to say. More attacks, locations not disclosed, dogfights, AA strikes, downed planes.

I keep an eye out now for the words "Biggin Hill," "Defiant," "141st Division," and "Edgar Jarvis." I am relieved when I see none of the above mentioned.

I manage a brief visit with Pamela and Sloane in the afternoon, which is comprised of me standing in the doorway like an embarrassed gentleman caller. I guess I'm a little nervous around her now. I don't know from a one-day-old baby in the least.

But I'm relieved to see that mother and daughter are doing

fine. Pamela's appetite is good and her coloring much better. By god, she was pale this morning . . .

We manage the whole day without an air raid. It's marvelous. But it only means they'll be back at night, doubly angry, doubly German, and loud as ever.

Pamela and the baby don't join us at table for tea at six; Mrs. Spettegue brings it up to them.

Tonight's my night for ARP duty, and there's sure to be an attack. Sure enough, the sirens go at 8:43 and I'm off at a brisk trot to the ARP office in the square, wearing my overalls and tin hat. I'm there before the sirens quit wailing.

Rand meets me there. If anything, his dandruff is even worse, sprinkling his shoulders out from under his helmet. If you don't mind.

I experience my normal nervousness. Which is good. It is situationally appropriate.

Many of us wait in the basement under bland incandescent light bulbs. So far, we're not hearing much, just waiting for a tinkle on the telephone or a message runner to come in. I'm not hearing any ack-ack . . . in fact I'm not hearing much of anything. I brought *Wuthering Heights* to read but don't get far along before I start to fuss, and then the fear starts to come back.

Roof sounds safe. Whatever I'm liable to face tonight will not be. Now I'll deliberately be walking into destruction and ruin, and my brain flashes back to Ben's apartment and how I went in there, wondering how I managed that at all. It messed me up. And I've elected to reinsert myself into the same scenario once more. I become more and more frightened the longer I sit. Even though nothing is happening right now.

For the first time, I have the option of direct action against the onslaught. It makes me almost giddy. I get to do something, even if it's as menial as clearing bricks. It's something. I get to put something in that the universe is trying to take out.

I hate war now on a much more personal level. I hate it bad.

It's quiet in the basement. I'm left stewing alone with my fear hormones until after 11:00 p.m. Everything begins to change at that time, when local AA fire begins booming nearby. We can't hear planes in the basement but it's a sure thing that things are going bad for our district.

It's not long before we get a call to Chester Row, a few streets over, which has taken a hit. By the time we scramble up to the street, it's just gone midnight.

30

Wednesday, September 11, 1940

Two heavy lorries are waiting for us upstairs in the dark street, jury-rigged with every imaginable piece of heavy equipment: axes, poles, ladders, crowbars, blankets, and brushes. We look like mad chimneysweeps. The headlights of the trucks are taped over, forming but a narrow slit to let a useless amount of light through. I'm just piled in the back with a bunch of seriously formidable equipment, all those crude tools, and several other tin-hatted men. We bump and grind our way over to Chester Row to find the fire brigade already there, but I can't see much in the way of flames.

A German bomb has fallen through the roof and exploded midway through the house, blasting outward and down. The street is choked with brick and debris.

It is ascertained from the neighbors that the family of four had no Anderson shelter, braving it alone in their dining room. People would do that: Thousands of Londoners had no choice but to hide under furniture with blankets to protect against shrapnel and glass, clinging to hope.

The entire scene doesn't look promising.

Jesus. Last night I greeted a new life into this world, and now I could be presiding over the exit of four others from the self-same world.

Nevertheless, I choose to be optimistic as we begin. Fear tries to close my throat, but I get the better of it, set my body into mindless action, and start upon the pile. A surging, honest desire to help make things better spurs me to perform my designated task. I know not from whence it comes. I am unused to this sensation, but I can use it to my advantage.

It's impossible to walk over such debris, you can only clamber. Instead of a normal house façade, it's just a pile of brick rubble. There won't be any room searching—we're going to have to climb up to the very top and start digging down.

Directed by Rand, nine other men and I start a sort of chain gang, quickly handing down bits of rubble and stacking it on the sidewalk. It is backbreaking work, and difficult in the night's darkness. I don't have gloves and wish I did. More than once, a man gives his ankle a nasty turn climbing on the pile of bricks. I don't feel much hope, the house is completely caved in. We worry about the walls collapsing in upon us, as Rand occasionally has us stop while he reconnoiters the scene with his torch, but since all the houses are attached masonry, it seems fairly stable after all.

Hours pass. Fingers are shredded by jagged stone.

Planes roar overhead, but nothing much in our sector. Nothing much more, that is. They've done plenty of damage already. Searchlights swirl, incendiaries drop, but nothing upon us, which is a godsend in its way.

Finally, at about two in the morning, we reach what is obviously the dining room, finding a shattered sideboard and broken dishes. We clear all the way down to a mattress on the collapsed dining room table, and then the table itself is lifted out and the horror becomes visible in the light of hand-held torches.

The family of four is crushed beneath it: a man, a woman and two young girls. Plus a small dog.

I'm all over crying as I picture this young family so ensconced, making a game of it for the children, feeding the dog scraps. Telling ghost stories with their flashlights, playing cards, singing songs.

At least it was over in an instant. Had to be.

Due to being in the wrong place at the wrong time, it becomes my job to help carry the remains out to a waiting coroner's van.

I quietly begin to lose it. My eyes are welling up and my stomach threatens to heave in disgust. But, after a series of deep breaths, made difficult by the choking particles in the air, I manage to rein myself in enough to step up to the task.

I just get it done. "Doing the farm thing," my sister calls it: a duty that befalls you that just has to be done and there's nothing more to be said. Still, I'm repulsed, shocked, angry, and deeply offended by it all. Fucking war. It has got to be the most useless of Man's inventions.

Using blankets and tarps, we deliver the remains to the van. It takes more than one trip.

Rand, while not actually helping, is near to hand and offers words of encouragement. Tells us we're doing a man's job, and that he's proud to see us holding up, of "being British."

When the ungodly task is completed, he produces a metal bucket with a small amount of petroleum in it and a few rags. For me to use to wash my hands and arms. They need it.

He then clamps an arm around my shoulder. "We'll mop up here, if you don't mind. See about going onto another site on Eaton Terrace. It's just 'round the corner." He promises me I'll find a much more palatable scene. "Oi!" He calls after me.

"After your little petrol bath, I wouldn't suggest trying to light a fag, at least not until you get your hands on some water, if you don't mind!"

I nod with a knowing smile I in no way actually feel, and then I trot off in the prescribed direction.

I'm more relieved than I thought possible. In fact, tears of a new sort come, unbidden, to my eyes. Relief to be away from that scene.

At Eaton Terrace, as advertised, the news is much better. Although the entire row of houses has fallen in, the families were all in Anderson shelters in their back yards and have been miraculously accounted for.

The entire façades of three houses in a row are caved in and lying in the street. A crater is formed by the impact of the bomb, cars blown all to hell and the houses are still burning a little. They're made of brick, like all the houses of London, but the floors and contents are quite vulnerable to flame. The fire brigade is spraying water. I subconsciously put my gasoline-soaked hands in the pockets of my overalls. I'm sure the vapors have dissipated by now, but I don't want to take any chances.

Some man unknown to me is in charge here, essentially taking notes, cataloguing the damage for vital statistics, issuing various orders to the men.

I shine my flashlight up on the surreal scene of wallpaper and pictures hanging on the wall fifteen feet up, family photos dangling crookedly from their wires.

Not much need to stay present at this scene; the fire's almost completely out, but after talking to some neighbors, we are informed there's a cat missing. Sparkles. Lives in the middle flat and was refusing to be scruffed down into the shelter with its family.

A man named Dennis and I decide to go in looking for the blasted animal. We're told not to stay long, to watch for falling masonry, and to consider our safety above all else; yet here we go.

I consider it in the plus column. After the horrors of mere moments ago, I get the chance to make someone happy, and I'm all up in that.

And yet I'm faced with going into yet another destroyed building in the dead of night, with bits falling down, setting out on what some would consider a fool's errand. Most of the ARP men are already packing up and moving on to the next call, but Dennis and I climb up the mound of debris, torches in hand, last of the water being sprayed by the fire brigade. I catch the edge of one jet from a fire hose, clearing some of the remaining petrol from my hands, and feel better for it.

Strangely enough, once we're in the house where the cat purportedly lives, it's almost normal. I have a combination of weird feelings: being in someone's house, in darkness, with a flashlight, seeing personal possessions studded by shrapnel and sopping in water from the fire hoses.

Half the staircase from the ground floor is a broken jumble, but it is still passable by hugging the wall, the ambient light just enough to lend a glimpse at the wallpaper. It looks agonizingly English and boring.

Dennis and I take turns eking up the staircase to where the bedrooms are, half wrecked. Dennis finds the cat cowering behind a toilet. I hear his shout and scramble over to him. Wet from the fire hoses and thoroughly disgusted with the whole proceedings, Sparkles hisses mightily and seems determined to put up a fight. But Dennis takes the upper hand. He gets the beast in a good grip, and while the cat's still having none of it, I follow Dennis and puss back to safety, glad for something positive in all this. We climb quickly back out to the street. Dennis chucks the cat into the cab of a lorry, and I, careful not to let it out, climb into the passenger seat and clack the door shut.

It's quiet in here. The air close. Just for a moment, I need to sit down. I need to interface with Sparkles, for I know it will make me feel slightly better about life in general. At first the cat has nothing to say to the likes of me, but after a few minutes he cautiously approaches, sniffs my fingers, the fumes of gasoline cause his nose to wrinkle in disgust, yet he rubs his muzzle along them. He then gives me a moment of love the way cats do, bussing my hand and turning circles on my lap. I give 'im a few butt smacks.

He likes that. I knew he would.

A Stuka races low overhead, causing everyone to duck. I see it close, out the window of the truck, yellow nose reflected in distant firelight. But Klaus, the *deutscher Jagdflieger* at the Stuka's controls, apparently doesn't choose to do anything stupid upon us. It's probably time for his break.

I've been hearing ack-ack the whole time. Who would know that I could ever just filter it out as mere background noise? For now, that's exactly what it has become. They're on our side, after all.

Sparkles' family, roused from their shelter by the bombing, is finally brought the long way around the block to reunite their little girl with her cat, tears flowing freely from her and perhaps from a few from us although we'd never admit to it. Rand suddenly appears on the scene and tells me I can go. I'm sent back to the office and told to take messages from the runners and to come get him if anything else comes through.

The rest of the team moves on to another scene without me.

I walk the streets of London by myself, alone, in darkness, in the middle of a German bombing attack. And I feel fine.

It's a ten-minute walk back to Sloane Square and the ARP station office, and I feel exultant, as if nothing can hurt me.

Which is stupid. I could get whacked from the air at any second.

But you really get used to the sounds of the planes. Overhead and high, you're good. Zooming in and low, you're bad;

whistling of a bomb, you're done. A diving/zooming plane is still traveling at over 150 miles an hour, so by the time you're even aware of him he's already gotten past Maida Vale.

It's what he drops that concerns you: a bomb, which whistles, or incendiaries that whoosh and crackle.

No such whistles or crackles dampen my walk back to the square.

I always feel better when I'm alone. Even in an air raid. Someday I may take the time to figure out why that is.

My book is right on the chair where I left it. I try to read but can't. Wish I could sleep but can't. Nothing happens. I sit and stare. I'm trembling again. Fear seems to be in abeyance, but I'm hardly composed. I've really fixed things for myself, haven't I?

My survival will depend on erecting steel walls in my brain to block that family of four with their little dog from ever coming to the fore again. I don't want it in my world, or in my mind. Good happened yesterday: Sloane was born. That magic has just been subtracted by a factor of four: one in, four out, leaving me in negative territory and trembling all over. I try to think of Sloane but can't. So I think of Sparkles and focus on that. Studiously.

The All Clear comes at 4:45 a.m. and I'm released to go home and get some sleep.

Walking home in near complete darkness—searchlights are extinguished, and the attack is over for now—I can't help but reflect that this morning is September 11th.

This isn't that dissimilar, only it's a protracted anguish, an attack that takes months instead of hours. And it isn't such a gutting shock. The events of 2001 were completely out of the blue for us. Oh, there were always those imperious few who'd say we should have seen it coming. But we didn't. The pain cut us deep.

These people have been ready for bombings for a year now

and they are determined. They've also got another four years of this on the horizon.

I get home to Nutley House. Everyone having just now extricated themselves from the shelter or roof duty, is just settling into bed to get some much-needed sleep.

I strip out of my shirt—it's toast—and make do with top and tails in the lavatory sink on my floor. Soap and cold water only, I'm too tired to go find warm water elsewhere in the house. I away to bed.

My brain is overloading. I conspicuously avoid thinking about the bad things and do a pretty good job because sleep comes and is so heavy, I shift beyond the universe. I don't know that I've ever slept so deeply before, but my dreams are tinged, weighted, by unspeakable horror just out of reach.

§

It's 10:30 when I stumble downstairs.

Mrs. Spettegue has some rare and precious bacon for me, with a glass of milk, and eggs on toast. This is lavish. We're alone in the dining room. It's gray and cloudy. And quiet. Oh, how I value quiet now.

"Mr. Baldwin," Mrs. Spettegue says, "I just wanted to say how happy I am you're with us. Your help with Pamela the other night is a most wonderful stroke of good fortune. Why, I dare say, she couldn't have been in better hands. I'm further quite impressed with your willingness to help the ARP."

"Oh," I say, trying to dry swallow a piece of toast. I feel awkward.

Mrs. Spettegue doesn't know what a coward I've been. She

doesn't know how close I came to running away, willing to use her seventy-year-old body as a shield.

"I was just the only person available. In the right place at the right time, all that."

Being English, she says nothing more. For which I am eternally grateful.

§

THE GRAY DAY is spent in and out of the Anderson shelter in the manner of some sick, revolving door.

Three air raids in a row. It's not even remotely funny.

The first one comes, and I help Pamela and Sloane, and she is swaddled to within an inch of her life—I can't even see her under her wrappings. But I take in Pamela hungrily with my eyes—her glow has returned, her fierceness is back, seemingly mildly peeved at the gall of an air raid. We don't say anything, though.

I take to my bunk wondering what, if anything, is going to happen next. Wondering where my fear is. Right now I can't find it, which makes me suspicious. I know it is still there, and I know that I cannot control when it will choose to pounce on me again.

We don't hear any sounds of battle. It's quiet. Then the All Clear comes.

So we go in the house, and turn the gas back on.

Air Raid sirens go again a short while later, I turn the gas back off and we tumble back into the shelter. Don't hear anything. All Clear comes. Back in the house.

After a while it's just getting ridiculous. My new-found adrenal glands are sputtering and spiking at all the wrong times. One moment I'm completely calm in the deathtrap of the Anderson shelter under direct threat of death, and forty-five minutes later I start to panic for no reason alone in my room—while an attack isn't even underway.

Having a baby to worry about just increases the stakes. I'm entirely focused on begging the universe to keep Sloane clear from harm, even while knowing the universe takes a particular delight in obliterating the most vulnerable. Sloane somehow becomes an anchor in all this—the pinnacle of fragility. She is the opposite of war, yet the most susceptible to it. A wrongness that twists my mind ever further.

We don't say much while in the shelter anymore. No one's in the mood. We're all just waiting for it to go away. We huddle around one another, locked in our own thoughts, taking comfort in each other's presence, taking turns holding the baby.

Sloane, obviously, has no idea what's going on, she just looks up at us in unfocused confusion, ears perennially stuffed with cotton.

The radio later says that most of today's alerts are due to air skirmishes in the southeast, nothing that approaches London airspace.

I go upstairs to visit Pamela and Sloane. I'm invited into her bedroom for the first time. It's also a corner room, with windows on two sides. It is done in sunny colors, far better than mine. Mrs. Spettegue has obviously been pampering Pamela in any way she can. I'm surprised to see a full layette: crib, changing table and supplies. She must have been scrounging for months. I say so.

"Oh, yes. All of this," she says, "is second hand. Mrs. Spettegue put the word out on the lane and nearly everyone had something to chip in. I even have a push pram."

"I'm glad," I tell her. "How are you feeling?"

"Almost normal. Can't wait to go walking again. I hope we can resume together soon. Aside from these blasted air raids."

Sloane is fussing in her crib. She cries sometimes—not a lot, not like some babies that never give it a rest—which is good. Mostly she gurgles in an experimental way that's charming and encouraging.

We forego our walk then, and just visit in Pamela's room. I sit in a chair next to the bed.

"That night, when Sloane was born?" Pamela says, "When I was pushing, I kept thinking of what you told me about your friend and his wife. It helped, somehow. I knew I wasn't alone, isn't that silly? I thought of that wife and I realized just about every woman in history has gone through this. And I knew I'd be all right. I even thought of the main event, to see if that would help. Not sure that bit did."

"I'm very glad I could be of help. Have you heard from Edgar?"

"Oh, yes!" Pamela responds. "We've exchanged half a dozen telegrams. He's thrilled it's a girl and says he laughed out loud at the name Sloane. He loves it!"

I'm picturing LOL on a telegram. No emojis. Stop.

"Does he say when he'll be here?"

"'Soon' is all he can say." Pamela becomes fussy. "Damned Air Force! Surely they can spare him for a couple of days. He's only just down the road after all."

I realize I'm uncomfortable at meeting Edgar. What must he think, some strange man giving birth to his own child when he should have been there?

"I wonder what your husband's reaction to me will be?" I ask. "After all, I was . . . there . . . for you where I had no business being."

"Oh, it was an emergency," she says. "He'll be fab, really. He's not the sort to act jealous or petty. Not in the least."

"Well, if it helps, and if he's the kind of man who can

handle it, you're certainly welcome to tell him I'm 'bent'? Is that what you called it?"

Pamela laughs. "Thank you, Mark; I'll keep that in reserve, but I really don't expect him to."

Sloane has beautiful blue eyes and wisps of blond hair. She looks a bit like Pamela. She must look a lot like Edgar. I ask if this is true.

"She does," Pamela returns. "She has his chin and his nose. Isn't it simply miraculous that two people can create a baby human, a combination of themselves? I marvel at it."

I go down to read the *Telegraph*. Last night held only the one attack on London itself, from 8:43; they focused primarily on the outskirts until 11:00 p.m., when several high-intensity bombs were dropped in Central London—including a time bomb that was dropped directly upon Buckingham Palace. It apparently blew up in one of the state rooms.

On Tuesday, Saint Paul's Cathedral was cordoned off as a large, unexploded time bomb had been discovered on the grounds.

In the newspaper, the name Biggin Hill jumps out at me and my heart does a little flip. Biggin Hill aerodrome was approached yesterday in one of the late afternoon raids, but the Germans were driven off by Spitfires. No damage to the station.

We won't say anything to Pamela about that. I hope she's too distracted with Sloane to read the paper. It would be best.

Again I picture Edgar, suiting up, taking off, zooming around, facing near certain death, now knowing his baby daughter is alive and well and so utterly anxious to meet her. Not only can he not be here, he could die at any moment. I picture a man I've never met shaking his head and forcing his attention back to the controls of his fighter plane.

I can't handle it. He must be in agony.

It helps me match energy levels with my newfound fear. We've all got it, and here's a prime example of someone who's got a shit ton more on the line than I do. And I've never even met the man.

Tea tonight is bubble and squeak, a mixture of cabbage and fried potatoes. We listen to the radio as we eat at six; Pamela joins us for the first time, Sloane is sleeping peacefully on a cot in the dining room. The news is pretty much the same yet again: general horrors, met with the proud resolution of British blood.

Tonight they air Winston Churchill's speech from today in the House of Commons. I stop eating my bread and salad and simply listen to the man speak.

Actual chills. I allow myself the thrill of knowing I'm hearing from the Old Man himself. He drinks. You can hear that. He smokes, too; but Winston Churchill is often considered one of the world's greatest orators. I feel honored that I can hear him on a tinny wireless amid the very storms of war that, through my direct idiocy, have now become my own personal problem.

Since I clearly won't be walking with Pamela this evening, I instead help Mrs. Spettegue clear the dishes via the dumbwaiter and wash them in the sink for her downstairs. The warm, soapy water soothes me.

Air raid sirens go at 8:37; the Bloody Jerries are fine tuning their arrival to coincide with blackout, showing their requisite German efficiency. Everyone drops what they're doing and rushes back to the shelter.

This time it's me and Cecil on the roof with the sand, and making no bones about it, Cecil brings an enormous bottle of whiskey and two glasses. I gladly partake.

We observe the scene, gazing out over the vastness of London. I'm getting used to it; he has yet to have had the experience and seems a bit rattled. The specific wall of fire in the east is gone, now it's scatty, all over, random, and seemingly, much more personal.

I show him the blankets and sand like I'm the old pro at this and we settle in for a long night of keeping watch. We make nests for ourselves in the blankets and sit. And wait.

I seem to be getting better at this. It's only been a few days, but this is blowing any conception of stress I've previously held all to cock. Writing deadlines? Behind on my car payments? A crush making out with someone else at the Lone Star?

Has my life been so devoid of stimulus so far as to make my forty-nine years thus far a complete waste of time?

Apparently so. I'm only just now getting a glimpse of how long I've had my head up my own ass, and while it shames me to think, I also feel somewhat more energized. I don't think I'm going to be like that moving forward, regardless of the amount of time allotted to me.

"Aren't you at risk of being drafted into the military?" I eventually ask Cecil.

"Good gods yes!" he responds. "All of my mates have either volunteered or been called up; I don't know why I haven't. It's only a matter of time and I'm petrified. One of my best mates was killed in the Navy six months ago, his destroyer took a hit. The ship didn't sink but it was badly damaged. It's horrifying. Look at me, I'm cut out for the stage, not a bloody bunker on a hill. Still, I'm an actor, I can play the part when my number comes up. I'll bloody have to."

We drink more whiskey.

"Tell me about San Francisco," he says.

I describe the city and my life there as best I can, but it's difficult. I have to lie a lot. No wife, just the occasional dalliances.

"I've never been married either," he says. "I've had plenty of offers, women quite frankly flock to me . . . "

A bomb comes loudly whistling down a few streets away and we, even though it won't help in the slightest, hit the deck and cover our heads. It comes down in the middle section of a row of houses and goes off in a shower of brick and mortar. This is followed by a heavy dusting of incendiaries, sparkling down onto rooftops in the area to the east. We can hear the sizzle and crackle, like fireworks. As before, we watch the local roof guardians leap into action, beating down the flames with blankets and sand.

"Bleedin' Christ, this is nasty business," Cecil says in a fearful sort of awe. Our conversation is forgotten as we stand and watch. One of the incendiaries gets the upper hand and a row of flats begins to burn in earnest. We watch—for hours, it seems—as jets from fire hoses can be seen arcing through the air at the burning homes. The fire is bright. It will attract more bombs from on high. Their local ARP wardens and search parties will be there, doing what they can to mitigate the damage and rescue people. I don't envy them their task. We just sit in silence watching, wondering if we'll be next. A sea of rooftops and chimneys is silhouetted in the flames.

The sun has long since set and it's overcast. It's very dark, save for the firelight. It's approaching midnight.

31

Thursday, September 12, 1940

After a while, Cecil and I resume talking upon the darkened roof.

"How close to getting married have you come?" I ask.

And Cecil responds: "Pretty damned close. I actually left a woman at the altar two years ago."

"No," I say, unable to help myself.

"Oh, yes. A girl named Gemma. I couldn't go through with it. For one thing there was Nancy. I was still having it off with Nancy the whole time I was with Gemma and I knew it wasn't right. I couldn't do that to her. I know it was cruel of me. I was all dressed and ready to go to the church . . . but the daylight beckoned. I jumped into my friend's roadster and drove all the way to Brighton. I didn't stop until I saw the sea. Then I just sat on a rock in my smoking suit, wondering if I'd done the worst thing imaginable . . . or maybe the right thing after all."

"Did you ever see her again?"

"Yes. We met so she could give me the ring back—it's my grandmother's—and she walked up and gave me a right slap across the kisser. I just stood there and let her do it; I couldn't blame her. I let her vent . . . how humiliated she was, how utterly despicable I was. I just let her say what she needed to say. 'I'm sorry' are some pretty uninspiring words in a case like that. But nevertheless, I did apologize wholeheartedly to her. She wouldn't hear it. I didn't expect her to.

"I felt like a heel, but in the end, I think I did her a favor. Sticky bit of it is, Nancy, when she heard what I'd done, ended it with me right then and there as well. I went from juggling two women to being stuck on my own, and I was alone for a good long while. I felt like what they call 'box office poison.' People knew what happened. They all gossiped, and it got around."

"Must have been awful," I say.

"Do you know how it is? If you're fairly gagging for it, women can sense it and they stay away in droves. The minute you decide you don't give a toss they come running. Those eight months were pretty damned dark. I was doing a run of *Julius Caesar* at the Regal. Thank God I had the play to keep me going.

"For me, it's always about women. I love them, what can I say?"

"I know the feeling," I respond, although I'm thinking about men instead and how Cecil is right: If you're desperate and in need, men can somehow sense it, and give you a wide berth.

I decide to ask a rather brave question: "How have you managed to comport yourself around Pamela without getting . . . distracted?"

It's really none of my business, yet I'm keen to know.

"Wasn't easy, mate! At first, I was a fright every time I had to be around her, bumping chairs and dropping teacups. But then

I grew to like her; nay, to respect her. I've gotten to know Edgar as well. He's a fine, upstanding chap. I like Pamela too much now to try anything stupid."

We drink heavily of the whiskey and watch the row of houses burn about a quarter of a mile away. That whole street is now in danger of burning down. Whatever the Germans are using is savage enough to burn brick.

"What's the closest you've ever come to getting married?" he asks me.

"Closest I've ever got was a fourth date," I say. "I've been very unlucky in love. I blame myself, but I also blame San Francisco. It's a cauldron of rampant advantages, too much so. People there don't settle down."

"Like me, then," Cecil mutters. He's a little drunk by now, getting maudlin.

"Well, yes, frankly. No disrespect."

"None taken."

"I'm forty-nine years old, and I've never had a steady girlfriend. Well, I take that back. There was a girl in college, we went out for about a year and a half. But that was over twenty years ago. It doesn't sound good, saying I haven't had a girlfriend since the . . . " I do the quick calculation in my head backwards from 1940. " . . . since the Harding Administration. Sometimes I think I should get a girlfriend just for the sake of having one so I can say I've got one. You know, just grabbing the next girl I see and making it work for a while. Just to see what it's like. Raise my estimation in the eyes of others. 'Street cred,' they call it back home. But then I realize it wouldn't be fair to her.

"Oh, mind you, there are plenty that I'd be thrilled to have as a girlfriend, but, of course, they're completely uninterested in me. Do you have that problem?"

"Hell, mate, they're all interested in me. I'm the fabulous Cecil Hayden!" He says it smilingly but then his smile quickly fades. "Of course I have that problem. I'm known as a bounder, a cad, a scoundrel. So I attract loose women, and they aren't girlfriend material. Good girls don't like scoundrels."

"I find that hard to believe. Women love a little Rhett Butler in a man."

"Oh. *Gone with the Wind*. Yes. I saw that last month. Well, Rhett Butler had charm and money, two things I completely lack. No, most of the women I run with, you pretty much have to watch your wallet when you're around them. Respectable girls are hard to come by."

I giggle at the reference; I can't help myself. Cecil doesn't seem to get it.

"Tell me about some of the girls you like but who aren't interested in you. What are they like? What makes them so unobtainable?"

"Well, they're brilliant, handsome women and they know I exist, they just don't care. I'd gladly get serious with any of them, but it's not in the cards."

Cecil helps himself to more whiskey.

"I love the female sex!" he says loosely and loudly. "I haven't had it off in three months. I'm going starkers."

"Nobody on the horizon, eh?" I ask.

"There is this bird, Pauline, I've got my eye on her. Tits out to here," he makes the motion with his hands, "and a waistline like Lana Turner. Heaven!"

"Does she know you exist?" I ask.

"Aye, she does. She was a costumer on my last show, and we know all the same people. We've been introduced, but since Mrs. Spettegue isn't on the telephone I haven't been able to give her my number, and I've been too embarrassed to ask for hers. Everyone is under tremendous strain right now and, strangely enough, I don't want to add to hers."

"So it's been three months since you've had it off?"

"Three months almost to the day. A woman named Lucy.

She ended it because I wouldn't get serious with her. Hell, why do they always want you to get serious with them?" Cecil laments.

"Beats me. I wish I could find one who would."

Cecil's drunk.

"Good looking bloke such as yourself ought to make out like a bandit," he says.

"Why, thank you . . . "

"What size yer plates?"

"Huh?"

"Your feet. What size yer bats?"

"Oh. Eleven and a half."

"Good sign. Women know to look at the size of a man's plates. I wear only a nine and a half, but don't let that fool you. I can play the strithers real buona."

He's losing me in slang.

"When's the last time you've had it off then, mate?" Cecil asks of me.

It's only been a couple of days. Nigel. At the Ritz.

"Oh, not long. Nigella. Girl I met here in London."

"Wot'dja do?" Cecil asks.

"Put it to her right nice, I did," I say in a Cockney accent.

Cecil roars with laughter and claps me on the back.

Another low-flying squadron zooms over, ack-ack guns going loudly, and we hit the deck once more. But whatever the target is, it's not us. They're heading over towards Ealing. To which I, giggling, launch into:

There once was a lady from Ealing;
who had a peculiar feeling;
so she laid on her back,
and opened her crack,
and pissed all over the ceiling.

It's a modern composition but seems suitable. Cecil loves it.

"Speaking of, I've got to have a wizz," he announces.

“Me too. Should we flip for who goes in first?”

“Bollocks to that!” he says. “I aim to let it fly right off the flipping roof, like I’m pissing on bloody Jerries!”

I’ve had just enough whiskey that it sounds like a capital idea.

The two of us walk to the edge of the roof facing the southern bend of the street and Cecil steps up upon the parapet. *Jesus!* He’s very unsteady in his inebriated state. I try to reach up but can only grab him at butt level. So among other things, it becomes readily apparent that I have to climb up too, if only to make sure he doesn’t tumble off.

“C’mon, dude. Not a good idea.” I try, but it’s not having any effect. He shows no signs of climbing back down. I, in fact, hear his zipper go.

I don’t want to do this! But I have to be there to steady him . . . I step up onto the rim of the roof.

Even drunk, I am shocked and awed. Can’t even see the street below, it is shrouded in darkness and a very long way down—five stories. I move closer to Cecil, almost in a hug, to make sure that he doesn’t tumble off the edge. It’s horrifying. I’m staring at instant death.

But we’re quite close in the dark.

I do have to pee—bad—so I unzip my fly too and Cecil starts first, letting go off the roof and I’m right there with him.

And there we are, pissing off the fifth story of a house in the middle of an air raid with German bombers growling overhead.

It’s surreal.

“Fuck you, Fritz!” Cecil roars, splaying widely side to side. I laugh.

Our streams arc high in the air and out to the street below. There's sure to be no one out there in the middle of an air raid, and if they are, too bad for them.

Cecil, without warning, reaches over and puts his left hand on my junk. I nearly jump out of my skin—a dangerous thing to do on the edge of a roof. He holds me as the few remaining drops splatter out. His hand feels nice. Failing any reason not to, I reach out with my right hand and grab him in the same way. He's English, so he has that little extra bit at the end that I do not. We're standing side by side with each other's manhood in our hands and I've felt plenty of them in my day, but something tells me this is special.

He has to go a lot more than I do. It's still flying out of him and he whistles a tune like he's at a urinal in Victoria Station. I can feel the scratchy hairs and the warm, soft testicular epidermis, the slight buzzing sensation of the stream coming out of him. I'm not sure what to do with my hand. Do I pleasure him? It's really up to him. His hand starts tracing mine, which, since I'm only human, is starting to respond. That sets him off and he starts to stir as well.

And thus we stand, pleasuring each other with our hands on the brink of a roof in the middle of an air raid. If we fell, they'd find us with our dicks out.

OK, it's not funny anymore.

After just a few moments of touch, Cecil takes his hand away and hops back as casual as anything. That's it. I'm a little saddened. But remembering my training on how to recruit straight men (kidding!), I follow his initiative and pull up my zipper.

I smell my fingers, though. The scent is intoxicating.

That's it.

We don't say much after that. He's wobbly. The whiskey is almost gone, I am going to seriously regret this in the morning. I suggest we take turns sleeping in the blankets. It's by no means comfortable, but it'll do. I recommend Cecil go first. He's drunkest. So he's out quickly, asleep on the pile. The ack-ack guns don't seem to bother him in the slightest and I sniff my fingers once again.

No bombs land near us for the rest of that night. I have to

pee more and don't need to repeat the roof nonsense, so I quickly nip down the ladder and down the stairs, leaving Cecil snoring to the skies.

The All Clear comes just before five, so we weave back downstairs to our respective beds.

He says nothing about the evening's frivolity, and I know better than to ever bring it up.

§

I AWAKEN at about 11:30 a.m. I have a pounding headache from the whiskey. "Spun out," I call it—the dizzy, shaky, dry, achy feeling after too much drink.

I know it well.

I take lunch at a pub in Sloane Square. New Court Theatre is already half cleared; bricks stacked, tarps up, pedestrians trudging by, scarcely giving it a second glance.

The pub is very crowded and loud. People are glad to be out and about, making up for lost time and hours spent huddling in either boredom or horror. I'm not sure I should have beer with such a hangover on deck but decide to go with it anyway. It helps with the trembling. God, I had a lot of whiskey last night. Still, if I have to be on roof duty, it's a good way to go about it.

I read a spare copy of *The Daily Mirror* while I eat a sad, ration-era approximation of shepherd's pie.

A lot happened September the 11th, 1940. It becomes known that Hitler had indeed planned to invade England yesterday. It was to be called Operation Sea Lion, and it seriously almost happened. But a combination of factors foiled his plans: weather, and delays in staging such a massive force. And now the weather is deteriorating, so it looks like we've squeaked by.

According to the paper, during yesterday's morning raid, the king and queen were in southeast London and had to shelter in a police station, where they were served biscuits and tea. It was one of the raids where none of the enemy machines made it up to London, so a genial moment was shared by all. I picture Bertie and the Queen Mum, young and crisp and having tea and bikkies and how thrilled everyone must have been.

There were three daytime raids on London yesterday that were "disastrous to the Germans. They have not yet got the mastery of their daylight raids and it is costing them dearly."

During the second alert, an exceptionally large armada of German planes was turned back by British fighters. East London suburbs became witness to a massive aerial dog fight. Some bombs were dropped at the beginning, but then they left that off and turned to a classic plane-to-plane combat. Waves of German bombers tried to break through the snarl to London but were repulsed. Two Messerschmitts were downed, they "yowled in a funny noise, smoke streaming from them," as they spiraled into houses somewhere in the southeast.

After lunch I go back to the Nut House and Pamela asks me to come to her room. She holds up Edgar's sweater to me. It's finished. It's radiant. She nailed it.

"It's gorgeous!" I say. "Edgar's going to be thrilled."

"It's for you, silly," she says.

"Oh, Pamela, I couldn't!"

"Well, you're going to. Oh, Mark!" She rushes over and locks me in a huge hug. "I was so scared. I'm so glad you were there! Thank you, Mark." She kisses my cheek, twice. "Thank you!"

I'm floored and embarrassed. I have tears welling up and a sting at the base of my sinuses, and I hug the sweater to my chest and trudge up to my room, clearing my throat repeatedly.

§

An afternoon air raid comes, and I take the shelter this time. It's at 4:41 p.m. Me, Mrs. Spettegue, Pamela and Sloane, and Cecil. Rodger is up on the roof alone. He seems doggedly determined to be up there as much as he can, and we let him. It's like it's his purview, his burden, perhaps making up for having survived the trenches in the last war when so many did not.

Thus the shelter is crowded with the four adults and a baby, and my panic bubbles up a little more again. The more crowded it is, the more claustrophobic I get. Makes sense, but still hurts.

More than that, though, I'm sullen. It's my last day and night with these people. It's been an unusual ten days, to say the least. When it's my turn, I hold Sloane for all I'm worth, she seems so precious to me, so tiny, so vulnerable. She never cries in my arms, when I hold her to my chest, feeling her warmth against my bosom.

I wish I could tell everyone I'm leaving, but I'm planning to ghost. I figure it'll cause less of a ripple than awkward goodbyes and forwarding addresses that'll have to be fake. I can't find any other way to do it.

And that just makes me feel worse.

Pamela has news: "Edgar's coming home! Saturday! Oh, Mark, I can't believe it, they're letting him free to see Sloane. I can't wait for you to meet him."

"Great news!" Great indeed. I'll be gone. Well, it saves the embarrassment of having to meet the man. I'd continued to worry about that.

Pamela babbles on about all the things we'll do, the four of us, when Edgar's back. She seems to be forgetting there's a war on. Their time together will probably be spent in this very shelter, not rowing boats on the Serpentine. But I, of course, let her think what she wants and wouldn't dare disappoint her.

After the All Clear at 5:42 p.m., we dash into the house to use the loo and get something to eat.

Tea is watery chicken soup, with gray bread and salad, and we have the wireless on. John Snagge speaks of the almost-launched invasion yesterday, actual barges and troopships gathering to march upon English soil, scattered by the RAF and foiled by weather.

So it's about 7:15 that evening when Pamela and I take our walk. I doubt we have much time, the bombings seem to start at about eight or eight-thirty every night. We agree to not go far—not like the night Sloane was born. That was on purpose and silly.

This will be our last walk together, Pamela and me. I'm going to miss her to pieces. Something about her touches my heart, a spark. I can't put my finger on it, but I've enjoyed it just the same.

In a way, I realize I'm in love with her. I have been ever since I first laid eyes on her.

We leave Sloane in the good care of Mrs. Spettegue and head up to the Square. Pamela still looks largely pregnant and we're passed by several people who again smile knowingly at us. I'm getting used to it.

The sun is below the buildings but evidently just over the horizon. Golden summer light streams below the gray clouds, on gray buildings; nothing knows if it wants to be in light or darkness, so everything just sort of dapples. Such a bizarre contrast to the darkness of these nights.

"Do you think you'll have more children?" I ask.

"Right now, I couldn't imagine, but I suppose I might."

"You'll have to go back to the munitions factory, when you're all better."

"Probably. They have day care centers for the children, but I'd rather leave her with Mrs. Spettegue. She was denied her own child; that's probably why she takes such an interest in Sloane and me. And I don't mind. Good for her, if you ask me."

"I think you're right. My God, the woman has known tragedy."

"It will be right sad, having to leave Sloane and go back to work. But in its own way, it'll be good to get out of that blasted house. I've been cooped up for so long. I'd have gone mad if it weren't for you, Mark. I'm so glad you're here."

It's like a slug to the gut, but I say thank you to her and we walk some more.

"How long will you be with us?" she asks.

"Not for much longer, I'm afraid."

"Oh. Blast."

"I need to get back to San Francisco."

"To your bearded men who don't love you?"

She certainly calls a spade a spade.

"To my bearded men who don't love me, yes."

"So why were you here?" Pamela asks.

"Like I said: To see the war from the British perspective. On the ground. Up close and personal."

"How did we do?"

"You people are amazing. I hope all of this comes to an end soon. It's hard to imagine it going on and on."

"Well if it does, we'll be ready. I'll be goddamned if I'm going to wind up speaking German and making that silly salute."

§

This evening's air raid starts at 9:13 and has me and Bill Markley on the roof in total darkness. We check in, review sand and incendiary procedures.

Conversation doesn't come for hours. Only the occasional facial twitch, barely discernible in the dark.

It's after midnight when at least some discussion begins.

32

Friday, September 13, 1940

Just when I expect nothing by way of conversive arts from the man, resigned to a night of abject silence, he ups and pops the same question they all do: How come I'm not married.

"Frankly? The same reason you're not."

"Oh," he says. "I thought so."

Twitch.

"Pamela and I followed you. We know about the radio. You must be crazy, taking a chance like that."

Bill is stunned. "Oh," he says again.

"Who is he?"

"His name is Dieter. We met in Berlin in 1938. I'm madly in love with him."

"I understand. It can't be easy for you."

"I had to leave Germany once I knew Chamberlain was going to declare war. Dieter was already in the army, but he'd get leave occasionally, and come back to Berlin so we could be together. He went into France with the rest of the German Army and has been there ever since.

"Mark, I don't know if you know what it is to be completely in love."

"Sadly, I don't," I respond. "At least, not from personal experience."

"It's an exquisite form of torture. Now that our two countries are at war, I don't know what's going to happen. He could be killed. But right now, he's safe. He's in Paris."

Occupying Nazi scum, is he being an asshole to the Parisians? Abusive and shouting orders and humiliating the French? The occupation of Paris is a scorching shame upon the French. They broke ranks and let the Germans pass in order to save their beloved Paris from the scars of war. The Germans are plucking Jews, Gypsies, resistance fighters, communists and homosexuals out of French society and shipping them on trains to concentration camps for extermination. Or simply shooting them against the wall. France is being forced to pay hundreds of millions of francs per month for the honor of hosting German troops.

Our dear Dieter is part of that sickening machinery.

"How do you survive the . . . political differences?" A polite way of putting it, if I do say so myself.

"Oh, he doesn't really believe in all that. No one does—you have to go along to survive. It's a different world today. If not Hitler, it would be someone else. It's just how things are now. Mussolini, Stalin, Franco, Roosevelt, Churchill; it's all the same. Maybe it's time for totalitarianism; democracy is on the run. It hasn't worked."

I have a hard time listening to these words.

"Do you really believe democracy is finished?"

"I do. It's time to try something else. Look at Italy: Mussolini has done an amazing job. He's raised the standard of living, created great civic projects. Right now even Italian trains are running on time.

"It's the same with Hitler. Although he is disagreeable on some points, he has raised Germany from a battered, hungry nation into a proud force to be reckoned with."

"But fascism won't let you openly be yourself!"

"I've never been open to be myself. What's changed?"

"I just can't condone fascism, if that's what you're talking about. It's too radical. It's the ultimate in corruption and cruelty. What about the Jews and the concentration camps? How can you support that?"

"I don't believe all the tales. So some people are removed from society . . . "

A flurry of incendiaries come down to the north—a shower of them—in the area of Kensington High Street.

"What about all this?" I say, my voice rising, sweeping out with my arm at the incendiary bombs.

"And what about Churchill bombing the cities in Germany?" he replies. "Civilians, too. It's happening on both sides. I don't subscribe to war, I hate it and wish it were over. Germany will provide iron stability to the people of Britain when the end comes and they finally give up. The English are only prolonging their own agony."

I've never hated someone more.

The words coming out of Bill's mouth make me seethe. I don't know how a gay man—or any man—can think like that. It's like someone shooting himself in the foot.

"Where do you go at night?" I inquire, trying to think different thoughts.

"To be with people who think like I do. Friends. Mostly we drink and talk politics."

"And read *Mein Kampf*?" I can't help myself. My blood is boiling.

"*Mein Kampf* is a deeply flawed work. But he touches on some interesting points."

"Such as?" I practically snarl.

"To serve the body politic, the weak should be winnowed out, lest they become a drag on society as a whole."

"So mentally retarded people and blind people should be put to death?"

"Not to death, no, but if they aren't serving society, what good are they? We're moving into a streamlined world of mass efficiencies. The automobile assembly line, high-speed trains that go a hundred miles an hour, aircraft that can fly you from your own San Francisco to Honolulu in a mere nine hours. Everything is sleek and new. It's time for our thinking to become streamlined as well. It's the future."

A hornet's nest of German bombers zooms by at low altitude, at a lazy, slow, assholish speed, dusting us with incendiary bombs. One lands on our roof at number 36, and several neighboring roofs as well. It just splays out in a jagged spew, as if it were some white-hot gel jetting out from a paint gun by a passing car.

We leap to action, my hatred fueling my efficiency. It's a sticky glop and it's burning, damned hot. We work together, Bill with the dirt and I with the blankets, following the trail of burning phosphorous, blotting it out as quickly as we can. The hot goo melts tar instantly; it's very effective in a diabolical way. I'm determined. I scramble around the roof, beating the material with blankets, and Bill tossing dirt. Neither is particularly effective on its own, but in conjunction we make progress.

We trace the phosphorous and work together putting it out. We get it all.

This all takes place in the space of a minute and a half. Our breathing is ragged, and we're sweating heavily. Soon it's all out, leaving black scars and melted tar paper. My hands almost got burnt, but like with the broken glass in the window of Ben's apartment in San Francisco a few weeks ago, I'm lucky. They'll be sore for a few days, but I'll be all right.

My relationship to Bill Markley, however, has just burnt to the ground and won't ever be rebuilt.

We spend the rest of the night in stony silence.

Or would do, except, as I lay upon the fire-stench of burned blankets, trying to lure myself to sleep, my old friend, my time of the month, a visit from my overly emotional Aunt Flow decides to pop round for tea: I slither into another delicious, *grand mal* panic attack, not appreciably less than the one I had before. Only this one has a lot more weight added to it. The horrors of Chester Row, the vulnerability of Sloane, the wretched goings-on in the mind of Bill Markley . . . Problem Zero, San Francisco, trapped.

No matter what I do, I'm going to die early without ever understanding what it is I cannot seem to understand.

It goes for a long while, the waves of savage, baseless fear. I try to remember what I know about panic attacks. Now that it's not my first, I at least have experience to draw upon; the knowledge that panic has nothing to teach me, it isn't a lesson to be learned. It is merely a symptom of having been cut too deeply, leaving the brain no other recourse than to flip the fuck out. Which it does, deliciously. So I do that for about fifteen minutes, and afterward I'm so wiped out I have no choice but to fall asleep.

Panic attacks are a sustained vomiting of the soul and they take complete, overriding control. Although it never feels like it at the time, they will always pass, and empty you out.

§

THE ALL CLEAR sounds just after five o'clock in the morning. I'd managed to sleep fitfully on the burned blankets for some of the night, flipping in and out of a fear state, and any time I was awake, I'd think of Bill and his brains and how poorly they functioned.

I don't trust Bill anymore. He disgusts me.

I go down to room Number Five to take a nap. I set that old portable alarm clock by the bed for roughly 11:00 a.m.; my iPhone battery is now stone dead. I spent too much juice reading my book.

I fuss mightily about whether to tell Pamela about Bill or not. I've always had a non-gossip policy in life—again, normally finding people too excruciatingly dull to merit the breath. The only exception is if someone is actively creepy or a stalker, then I'll blab. So it's a judgement call with Bill Markley. Is he dangerous? I don't think so. Not on his own. He's entitled to his opinion, warped as it is.

But then I realize I solidly don't want him hanging around Pamela or Sloane.

So I guess I should tell her.

§

NO NEED FOR THE ALARM. The Air Raid sirens go off at 10:50 a.m., and it's back to the Anderson shelter. It's only Pamela, Sloane, Mrs. Spettegue, and I. Rodger and Cecil are on the roof and Bill and Robert are, as always, at work. I'm hungry. There was no chance for breakfast.

I'm to Snap Back at noon on this day, Friday the 13th, the day of bad luck. Just over an hour from now.

Already this attack feels vastly different. The Germans are

really going at it. Close by, too. It's somehow more serious. More personal.

It's fully overcast, threatening rain, stymying our anti-aircraft guns.

My plan is to feign a panic attack—which will come quite naturally to me—and declare I'm going to go into the house to use the loo and for a nip of brandy.

Unlike my other incursions, Disappearing from this one makes me sick. I'm just going to bail on these people. I'm going to walk out of their world without a word said. It's rude as hell. It's a horrible way to repay their kindness at letting me play a part in their lives.

Nevertheless, by 11:45, I need to be out of that shelter and safely on the street.

So I only have fifty minutes left in this world with these people, and suddenly I don't want to go. Ain't it sick?

It's like, I'm not happy there, I'm not happy here. I'm just not ever happy.

I need to tell Pamela about Bill but can't find a way. There's no such thing as having a discrete conversation in an Anderson shelter. I'm not ready for Mrs. Spettegue to hear it—she's liable to bounce the man out on his ear.

With a dead phone in my pocket, I don't know what time it is, and timing is crucial. Mrs. Spettegue has a little old lady watch, a brooch kind of thing on her lapel, upside down so she can flip it up and read it.

Just when I think it's beyond time, I ask the hour and learn it's only 11:34.

So I must sit and wait.

And wait.

Finally, I move over to kiss Sloane on the forehead and whisper *I promise I'll find you* to her and hand her back to Pamela. I look into Pamela's lovely eyes and want to say, "Thank you for being a part of my life."

But I must say nothing.

German activity is clearly focused in our area though. The AA guns are going mad and the zooming of planes is particularly angry.

Whatever. This is it. I gotta go.

"This might not be proper, but I need to get out of here for a mo; I'm going in to use the loo and have a nip of brandy. I need air."

"Oh, Mark, ought you, though?" Pamela asks, holding Sloane, and her concern melts my heart. Her eyes mesmerize me as they've always done.

"Oh, I'll be all right. Need me to bring anything back from the house?"

"No, dear," answers Mrs. Spettegue absently. Pamela simply shakes her head no and looks back down at Sloane, breaking eye contact with me for the last time.

Tears are once more in my eyes as I open the door to the shelter and let myself out into the gray daylight, closing the door quickly behind me. Up the steps, around the sandbags, I go through the house.

And take a moment of stolen time. The house really is empty just now. After ten days it feels like it's a segment of my life. Its fiddly bits and bad wallpaper are in me now, a part of my story. This is why I'm here . . . to make it real. The past has the power to stretch me beyond the boundaries of my own little life back home, and I think it's the only thing that would have power enough to do so.

But it's time to go back. To my men who don't love me.

It's only when I get to the front door I realize with a shock: Pamela's sweater! I run up to my room and put it on and put my suit jacket over it.

I'd never forgive myself if I'd left without it.

The sweater's a bit large. Edgar must be strapping. Good for him.

I hear the planes while still in the house. There are so many of them. Their droning is as maddening as the bombs, yet I have to consciously remind myself I'm still hearing all the ack-ack too. Those guns, originally so frightening to me, have been long filtered out as background.

I know I'll never hear a propeller plane the same way again. What was once a quaint sound now means death and despair and war.

Opening the door, I cross the vacant street and wait under a chestnut tree at a black Morris, long-parked there, covered with grit and leaves, waiting for petrol to become available again. Planes are zooming overhead. I'm seeing the bright yellow noses and ugly gray underbellies of large German bombers, flying low, and I hear the whistles of several bombs.

Why now? Why Chelsea?

Arschlöcher . . .

As I wait beneath the tree, one of the whistling bombs gets closer and closer. And closer.

Are you shitting me?

I drop down to the pavement and half slide under the Morris and put my hands over my ears, remembering, at the last second to lift my chest off the ground like they said, to not have the shock break my sternum.

This could be it. Instead of fear, I swear I almost chuckle, as if it's completely ludicrous after all.

A fierce explosion rips overhead. My ears pop savagely, and I feel the concussion in my bones.

Chunks of masonry, glass and burning boards fly all around me, clattering to the cement in a cruelly musical sound. I feel the heat of the blast. I'm struck by many shards of brick, as only a small part of me could actually fit beneath the Morris.

I wait; it falls silent. I wait a moment more and then scramble back up, covered in debris, smudgy with leaves and glass, but I stand and . . .

Nutley House has taken a direct hit.

Just like the house on Chester Lane, a bomb has cleanly pierced through the roof but exploded in the upper floors and down through the house, blowing out the windows and some of the walls. Yet the building, as a whole, is still intact.

Cecil and Rodger are on the roof!

As the explosion subsides, only dimly aware of a fierce ringing in my ears, I'm instantly on my feet, running back to number 36. Most of the roof appears to be in place: The bomb popped through it before it exploded. And I hope to God that Cecil and Rodger are all right. But don't see how it could be true.

The interior of the house is a complete wreck. A fire is burning. I can see through the carnage to the rear walls of the house—it's still whole, so nothing will have fallen backward onto the Anderson shelter. Everyone inside there should be safe. I stand there helplessly watching the place burn. I see Sloane's crib roll from the bright yellow room down the canted floor through a hole into the lounge below.

I long to run in but my time is almost up. I cannot be caught between floors in a burning building when I Disappear. I have to be in the open street.

Shaking my head, with tears in my eyes, I walk back behind my tree and wait and stare dully at the ruins of Number 36.

They will forever believe I was killed in the house.

PART VII

2019 - LONDON

33

Tuesday, December 3, 2019

I Reappear in 2019, to bright lights and utter silence.

It's sometime after 1:30 a.m. Streetlights are burning like brazen sin. A few apartment windows are lit without a care in the world. The city around me is clean, sedate, and altogether properly assembled once more. The tiny chestnut tree is huge and gnarled; it looks to have been trimmed back many times in its long life.

I still have bits of glass in my hair and face, probably a cut as well. But all seems to be in complete silence—a fierce ringing in my ears bespeaks potential hearing loss. Hopefully only temporary.

I turn back to Number 36 Sloane Gardens and find it perfectly restored, as if nothing had ever happened to it. It's an apartment building now, six door buzzers are lit with round blue LED lights. The house is still oldie-worldie with spires and finials, and it matches the other houses to a tee. Mrs. Spettegue must have had enough money stashed away to have it rebuilt to its original state. It would be like her, to have tons of cash in reserve. I don't think insurance companies pay for wartime damage.

It looks quaint and clean.

I stand and stare at the building for a good long while. All the lights are out, the residents happily asleep in their house that once was bombed. I wonder if they ever think about it. Probably not. If there's one thing I've learned in my journeys through disaster, it's that people don't like to dwell on unpleasantness.

Except for me. I seem to excel at it.

It's cold. I've just popped from September to December and my heavy coat was lost.

The District Line is shut down for the evening, and I'm not in the mood for a night bus. I have no money for a taxi; my iPhone battery is dead so I can't call an Uber. I'll have to walk in the cold all the way back to the Ritz.

Modern cars are parked everywhere, Audis and Fords and Toyotas, shining under the streetlamps. I'm still in my gray suit and fedora. And Edgar's sweater, which helps against the chill.

I'm starving. I haven't had breakfast—or a decent meal of any kind—in ten days and I know I must positively reek of body odor and baby spit.

I walk up to Sloane Square. It's unrecognizable. The trees are enormous, blotting out the night sky and view of the buildings around the square. It's still the wee hours of Tuesday morning—I wonder if Nigel has even gotten to bed in Lewisham yet.

The Tube station is locked. Still have that farthing, I bet I could find a way in. But it looks totally different, all brushed steel and cladding: the newest version of TfL.gov.uk.

The few people I encounter on the streets seem preoccupied and concerned with their daily lives, climbing out of automobiles that look like elegantly advanced, alien, scientific works of art. These people have no idea what concern and stress actually are. It's funny what you get used to, how stress piles up and starts to feel like a new sort of normal.

I'm out from under all that. I feel free as a bird. I'm safe.

It's a long walk. Well-lit, at least. No diving planes or heavy ordnance. But even though I have that going for me, I'm demoralized, trudging through the streets of London looking like God's last hipster. It takes a good thirty-five minutes before I finally close in on the Ritz, eventually working up a sweat under Edgar's bulky sweater.

Bit of an upset at the hotel—I didn't think to bring my key card with me, and I don't have any ID. It's in my room. So security has to let me upstairs to check my passport, which I left on the desk.

The guard seems irritable and nasty. He's clearly not into me and my get-up, so I'm all too happy to flash him my passport and to prove that I really am me. He looks at it, he looks at me, and savoring his moment of power, looks at the passport again just to be sure.

"Thank you, Mr. Baldwin. Have a nice night," he snarls.

By now it's well after 2:30 a.m. and even room service is shut for the night. My stomach is growling, so I attack the mini bar. I eat a Mars bar and Pringles and get into the scotch. I try not to think about the price.

My jetlag is gone, but I'm sleepy after so many air raids and nights spent on the roof. Still, I pull out my laptop and plug in my phone, which just flashes a red battery on the screen for like a minute and a half before finally powering up. I have pictures of Pamela and Sloane. I copy them to my desktop and save them to Dropbox, too. I never want to lose those pictures.

Finally I close my laptop, peel off that dreaded suit for the last time, gently fold Pamela's sweater into a drawer. I sniff it first; it still carries the smells of her, of that house. The very air molecules in its weave are from eighty years ago.

After a long, luxurious bath in the tub I get under the crisp white covers and find a dull, dreamless sleep.

34

Wednesday, December 4, 2019

I awake in 2019 London to a beautiful December day and order breakfast and coffee in bed from room service. I bang on my MacBook, writing all I can into Scrivener by the time breakfast arrives.

It's heavenly. God, I missed coffee! I salivate thinking of my afternoon trip to Starbucks for a quad latte.

I'm nervous, but I Google for Sloane Claire Jarvis.

I find only one potential match: Sloane Jarvis Norbury in Walnut Creek, California. She'd be eighty this year, and all I can picture is this tiny ball of goo being birthed into my hands on a Tube platform. And Walnut Creek is just twenty miles from my apartment.

Mind: blown.

I Google Cecil Hayden, actor, and can't find anything. He may well have been killed. I don't know. I think of our escapade on the roof and am overcome with sadness. And Rodger; what was his last name? Devereaux. Unsure of the exact spelling, I can't find any entries for him, either.

I feel very alone. I decide I need a day off in London, in December 2019. I need a rest. This isn't fun anymore.

But I came all this way and I have one more incursion to make. It should be easy and restful and it's the one I've most been looking forward to.

I saved the best for last.

I spend the day in bed. Finally I call David Meisenhoelder when I know he'll be awake in the morning in California. It's six o'clock in the evening here.

"I just got back from ten days in the Blitz."

"How was it?"

"Blitzy. The place I was staying at got bombed just as I left. I met some good people, two of them may very well have been killed, I don't know."

"That's sad. I'm sorry," says David.

"I had something happen on this one."

"Yeah? What?"

"I actually birthed a baby, right on an empty Underground platform during an air raid. She was born right in front of me. It was incredible."

"No shit?"

"No shit," I reply. "Plenty of blood and goo though. I've never even seen a woman's business before, much less one with a baby coming out of it. Her mother, Pamela, is this fierce girl. I'm practically in love. But they all think I died when the house blew up. This one left me feeling wrung out and sad."

"Sounds like it. How did The Machine do?"

"Perfect. It really works."

"I should hope so," David says. "When you get home let me use it. I need to go back and buy some more stocks. I might want to watch Lincoln get assassinated, too. Maybe. You're getting a lot more use out of it than I am."

"Is that OK?"

"Sure. Like I said, I built it to make money. You're using it to become a different person."

"That I am," I agreed. "This was a cold, hungry, miserable trip back. But I wouldn't have traded it for the world."

"That's good. I'm glad you're getting good use out of it. How much longer you going to be?"

"I've just got one more incursion, which I'll do tomorrow, and then I'll ship The Machine back to you and fly home."

"That'd be great. I hope you take some time off when you get back."

"Hells yeah. But my last trip should be a breeze. A little boat ride then a few days in 1912 Ireland and a few more in London."

"You going for ten days?"

"Yes. Meanwhile I might come up with ideas for other trips back. I kind of want to do the *Hindenburg*. If I spoke Latin, I could go to Ancient Rome, but I only know a couple of words; they'd brand me as an idiot the moment I Appeared. They'd probably think I'm a moron."

"Well, you don't look like a moron to me. Awwww, there there."

"Gee, thanks."

"OK, well, I don't really need The Machine right away, so have a nice restful journey to 1912. Call me when you get back."

"All right, I will. Thanks ever so much. For The Machine, for everything!"

"You're welcome. Enjoy your trip," David hangs up.

Once again, I go to the King's Arms and Duke of Wellington. I don't meet anyone, just enjoy my Kronenbourg 1664s and feel normal again. I see some of the same blokes as I did the night before—even though that was ten days ago from my standpoint. I see one guy that looks a lot like Cecil Hayden.

Life is good. I'm showered. Fed. Slept. Clean clothes, *normal* clean clothes, with pants that fit properly.

Sometimes it's the small things in life.

The next day is cold and raining but, completely free of jet lag now, I do touristy things. I go through Churchill's war rooms exhibit, getting mildly triggered, and then walk to the Tower of London—even though I've been to each before.

35

Thursday, December 5, 2019

I'm rested up and restless, both. Time to think about my next incursion. It should be my favorite. Easy, gentle, and kind. I need the calm relaxation it shall provide. I need to feel normal again, if that is even possible.

I'm sailing on the *Titanic*—but only overnight, first to Cherbourg, France, and then getting off at Queenstown, Ireland, the next day, saving that nasty bit at the end. For we all know the *Titanic* sinks on her very first voyage at sea.

When David first mentioned time travel, *this* was the apex experience. The others were just a warm-up.

I've always loved ocean liners, and the old Atlantic steamship liners in particular: *Mauretania*, *Titanic*, *Aquitania*, *Imperator*, *The Queen Mary*, the *Normandie* and *Europa*. So I've chosen the grandaddy of them all, even if just for a quick overnight. To be able to say I was there aboard her, that I've walked her decks and eaten her food—this is the stuff of dreams.

I'm a complete and utter *Titanic* geek. I've studied everything about it and come into it with a lot of knowledge aforehand. I'm incredibly excited.

So much so that, originally, I was going to stay in Ireland a few days in 1912 and then make my way back to London. But I've decided on a far better idea: I still want the experience of a trans-Atlantic crossing on an ocean liner at the peak of the period, so when I get off in Queenstown, I plan to find another one leaving Ireland right away so I can sail to New York in style —maybe on the *Aquitania*. A full trans-Atlantic crossing on a grand dame of a ship. It will be the height of luxury and a well-deserved rest.

I might even catch a glimpse of *Titanic's* Captain, E.J. Smith, all bearded and handsome. There will be some very august personages in that little first-class section of the boat. If properly executed, I'll be rubbing elbows with some serious money and power. They will probably be polite but not accept me among their ranks. I'm not going to ask them to. I just want the experience of checking them out.

For this I must go back to April 9, 1912, and make my way to Southampton, England. I wait until about 5:00 p.m., when excitement takes over and I just can't stand it anymore.

Every time I approach The Machine, I get nervous. Fears I've never imagined try to squeeze my belly. This whole thing is messing with me on a base level. I'm hungry for more, remembering what David had said about this only being good for a little while, that it can't go on forever and I understand that completely.

But I want it until I can't take it any longer.

A first-class ticket on the *Titanic* does not come at an inconsequential price; it's freakishly expensive. To help me out, David has gifted me with a superb gold pocket watch, laden with rubies. He assures me it will cover my bases. When I get to 1912, I'll simply have to sell it.

I put on the clothes I brought for the experience: Some well-tailored, formal gentleman's wear, black morning cut-away coat with tails, white shirt, white suspenders, a white waistcoat, some modern black leather shoes, with a white tie and my 1906 bowler hat. I have my money, my gold watch, my phone, my pipe, my credit cards, and my modern-day U.S. passport. I almost don't take the passport; I have no earthly reason to burden myself with such an important document, about which I must constantly worry and keep track. My goal is to enter New York in 1912, before passports were a thing, but something compels me to put it in my pocket anyway. Life is just weird enough, you never know.

I dial up The Machine, checking the batteries—they're getting low but still have enough charge—and set my destination. I inject my veins with the appropriate amount of goo for ten days (hit a nerve this time, it's acutely painful) and hide the syringe in a drawer so housekeeping doesn't think I'm some sort of user. I don my net, plug it in and triple check that I have the appropriate date.

It's go time.

PART VIII

1912 - NORTH ATLANTIC

36

Tuesday, April 9, 1912

I Appear in room 422 at the Ritz Hotel at five in the morning.

To my horror, this time the room is occupied. Much screaming . . .

A woman in foundation garments and a silly nightcap is yelling her head off in French from the bed.

"*Excusez-moi, madame! Je me suis trompé de chambre!*" I attempt to placate her. It's not working.

Still screaming . . .

She appears to be alone, no *gros brut* named Gaston is around to bean me over the head, or worse. I bolt out the door and hurry down the hall as other room doors open and people check to see what's the matter. I feel like a pervert, still covered in my webbing; and as far as these people are concerned, that's exactly what I am. I force myself to walk quickly, but naturally to the stairs—no way am I going to try to mess with an elevator. I've got to get out of here.

I'm thoroughly freaked out as I exit the Ritz, anxious to get as far away as fast as I can. Thank God they don't have phones and walkie-talkies, or I'd be in a heap of trouble.

Once on the dark street, I try to calm myself down and mix in with the few early morning pedestrians. I finally have the chance to snatch my weave off and toss it into a trashcan.

The cars and buses of the period are crude, and not significantly improved from 1906. I'm astonished to even see horses pulling carts, although not as many as there would have been six years ago.

The further I get from the hotel the safer I feel, but I keep expecting the large hand of an angry cop to clamp down upon my shoulder.

Nothing happens. I'm three streets away toward Piccadilly Circus. I'm lost in a crowd, all men, all wearing black coats and bowler hats, and I'm starting to blend in as we head to the Underground. Daylight is not yet breaking; the air is heavy with a night of rain, and streets still sopping and splashing.

I'm safe. *Whew*. That was nasty. I feel dirty. Further so, for now I must go to a pawn shop and hawk my watch.

Learning my lesson from 1940, I have many screenshots of local street maps in my phone, so I won't so easily get lost. I head to a likely area around Carnaby Street and do, happily, come upon a pawn broker at Loundes Court.

Two things become immediately clear: It is a complete dump, and it is closed. The sign says they won't open until nine a.m. That's three hours to kill. I fuss accordingly, but then decide to do what Londoners would do, I guess: set about finding breakfast and a copy of the paper. It's only just now becoming gray daylight, threatening rain, but traffic and pedestrians are picking up. It's a Tuesday morning full of commuters, glum and darkly clad, cloaks and hats, many men with elegant walking sticks, a spring in their step, hoisting their canes ahead sharply and down, stepping to the rhythm of the walking British man.

It does start to rain. I don't have a brollie of my own, and I don't feel like buying one, so here I am in my 1906 bowler doing my best against the elements, wandering for a place to break my fast. Despite the gray gloom, several cafés and tea houses are crowded and glowing with warm light from within, their windows fogged over with wet bodies and pots of tea, and, hopefully, warm breakfasty buns and cakes.

To the west, at Regent Street, I select one called Bailey's Fine Teahouse and go in, quickly realizing it's more Bailey's than Fine. It's crowded, but I find an open seat at a table with a few gravelly looking sorts of working-class Londoners. No newspapers are in evidence. I'm woolen-elbow to woolen-elbow with a certain strata of London citizenry, entirely neck and neck with true London and cockney scrags. "Ow" is used as freely as "like" is used today. We're all crammed in, the tables are shared and mostly joined, and it becomes clear most of these blokes know each other.

The only women in the place are serving in white, almost nurse-like, uniforms, and it bothers me. I'd rather have at least one of them seated beside me, tapping on her iPad, quietly talking into her Bluetooth about raising the offer to "a million-five and text me when you hear back."

I'm given tea in a heavy, white porcelain cup and saucer, along with milk and sugar cubes in a pile and some manner of raisin bun. I mostly stare into space, still sleepy and shaken by the rudeness of my arrival this morning, greatly in a fuss about getting decent money for my watch, and being successfully on my way.

Why the fuss? Well . . . because I always do. Can't get arrested for passing off a phony watch, it's as real as I am. I guess my fear is that it somehow won't work, that I won't garner enough money to go on the ship—my whole reason for being here in the first place. Without any resources to do otherwise, I'll have to wait my time out here in 1912 in abject poverty for ten full days. More likely, I'll get enough for my watch for only a third-class ticket. Which would still be righteous, but not a fraction of the experience I'm hoping to have.

"Oi, mate," a doughy, red-faced man—with a crooked nose and crooked head (no cup of tea in sight, he's straight-up drinking a pint of Fuller's lager)—addresses me in a harsh London voice from across my table. "What's a bloke like you doing 'ere dressed like that? Fancy dress ball?" A few of his mates chuckle, yet alarmingly free of actual mirth.

I'm momentarily stunned. My clothes are certain to be all wrong. I dressed for the *Titanic* to the best of my 2019 ability, which was only ever going to be a bad approximation to the real thing. I guess it shows, especially in a place such as this.

"Shop mannequin," I issue brightly. I strike a ridiculous pose and freeze that way, cheeks sucked in and vacant look on my face.

Some of the old blokes guffaw heartily; a few look uncomfortable at me as being potentially fey and in their midst. But the overall mood is jocular.

"Stay clear of 'Arrod's, guv, you'll likely find yourself with a metal rod up your arse."

Open laughter now.

"Fortunately, they can't afford me," I offer.

They hoot. Any lingering tension passes. They seem content to leave me alone now. I have naught to do but just look up at the badly stained, peeling ceiling and catch snippets of their conversations: the coalminers' strike, minimum wage, job sites, woes with "the missus" and the collective merits of "birds."

Finished, and dropping my three pence on the table, I make

my way free—rain has already abated—and decide not to look back or attempt further levity.

So I'm back out on the still-wet street with ever more daylight, traffic snarling with greater intensity. I sneak a peek at my phone, it's only seven. Two more hours.

I walk. Not much else for it, right? Outside Sothebys, Hanover Square; the gray and tumultuous skies are keeping further rain to themselves, but I could use the cardio anyway.

There is a sameness to the streets of London pre-WWII. The buildings all match each other, as they were intended to do. I just wander through lane and mews and close and road, killing time, lost in thoughts that have become without form.

I seem to have a new intellectual state of null and void. I'm spending an awful lot of time there lately.

By the time nine rolls around, I've angled back to Carnaby Street, and a few bedraggled individuals are queued up for the pawn broker's lights to switch on and shades to be pulled up.

The door goes *ping*, and we few souls shuffle in.

There's nothing posh about a pawn shop and there never will be.

First in line is an elderly man, shabbily dressed, apparently late-stage alcoholic (and I remind myself that I may have my own issues, but I do not want to end up like him). He's wielding three leather-bound books and a silver picture frame. I don't listen in to his wheedling at the man in the wooden cage. I spend my time looking at the goods in the pawn shop. Amid no small amount of dross, I see stunning pieces of silver, candelabra, violins and banjos, figurines and bits of Victorian furniture that I would, frankly, kill to have.

The man leaves, the look on his face is relieved—for at least the time being—and a woman in a heavy, tattered cloak and bedraggled hat begins her transaction. To it, I likewise listen not.

Finally, it's my turn. The man in the cage looks perennially bored, not liable to be impressed, and in no way apt to be friendly. I produce the watch, and try to gauge his expression. He seems to be attempting to hide being impressed while suppressing a measure of glee.

"Have you a receipt for this?"

Shit.

"No, it's been in my family for years."

As "off" as my clothes might be, they are of a certain status and quality. At least I hope so. I'm neither desperate nor furtive. But truth be told, I'm nervous as hell and I doubt this goes unnoticed by the man.

"Have you any idea of its origin?"

"My grandfather brought it from Prussia; he always claimed it was in 1850. Friedrich Roetig, German makers. If the stones aren't rubies, then we've never heard otherwise."

The door *pings* behind me. Others are ambling in, but I don't look.

The man grabs a loupe and cranes in, one eye scrunched.

"They're rubies, all right. Except that last one; I suspect it was a garnet. They'd use that for good luck. This would be during the reign of Frederick William the Fourth. I'm tempted to try to act bored by it, but it's actually a lovely piece."

"I'm sad to part with it, but my time in England is at a close. I'm being called back to Philadelphia."

Jesus, I'm turning into a liar with ease.

"I have a fondness for watches of this era; more to the point, so does my father. This'll quite bleedin' kill 'im."

This cranky old man is now speaking in a much different tone. It's hushed, reverent. He's actually somewhat moved. David picked me up a damned decent OK watch.

"I can give you thirty-five pounds, and frankly hope you'll never return from Philadelphia to reclaim it."

"Thirty-five pounds would be acceptable," I say calmly.

Inwardly I'm going, *Yass! Score!*

"The only sticky bit is, I won't be able to meet your price until after lunch. I'll need to make a few arrangements. Would you be willing to come back at two?"

"Yes, I would."

"All right. Kindly fill in this form. You will, of course, retain the watch, and we'll see you this afternoon."

I dip the pen in ink and scratchingly fill in a green card, *Name*: Mark Baldwin. *Address*: I confidently use 36 Sloane Gardens, SW1; I also add *Address in Philadelphia*: and make one up, somewhere near my friend Bill's apartment, 10th and Locust Streets. I've woken up there a morning or two, and feel I can appropriately claim it. Certainly worked hard for it back in the day. He was borderline painful.

"Very well, Mr. Baldwin," says the shop owner. "I'll see you later this afternoon."

I emerge victorious. I don't spare a look at the others who had wandered into the pawn shop, just glad when the door goes *ping* again that I'm on the other side of it.

Yet more hours to kill.

The weather remains perfectly normal, which, for London, means patchy gray and angrily threatening yet more rain. I have few options with the cash I currently have on hand; a bath house, a cinema . . . Doubt either would interest me. I walk aimlessly, suddenly feeling conspicuous with the watch on my person. It wouldn't do to have it pickpocketed. Wouldn't do at all.

Sloane Square? Do I really want to go there?

I do, but I don't. Actually, it's patently ridiculous. Why would I trek halfway across town in the rain to see a place *before* anything happened to it? Where nothing will have changed and it'll be the same as when I saw it in 1940?

But maybe I'm missing Pamela right about now. And Mrs. Spettegue.

Ah! Mrs. Spettegue was there from 1900, she said. So if I

went to number 36 and rang the bell, I would meet the woman twenty-eight years in her past. Do I want to do that? Can I stand it?

I think I can.

Suddenly glad to have a place to go, I head forth. To a before-time that's actually far in the future.

The Tubes of 1912 are a shock. They smell the same, they sound the same, and cost less. But the carriages are flimsy wooden affairs, covered in grime. No blackout lights are installed, but the bulbs are so frail and faint, and so many are burnt out, the effect is eerily similar. Old, tattered ads are plastered to the walls, most everything is painted gray or black with some white tile, long coated in soot. They used to run steam engines below ground, and I'm wondering if it's ever been cleaned since.

Just a short ride along the District and Circle, I'm so overly blessed with free time, I ride through Sloane Square station, eyes glued to the window to see the exact spot where Sloane will come into existence, and continue to South Kensington. I figure I'm good for a stroll back eastward and into the greater Sloane Square neighborhood.

It's not a lovely walk. If I were south along the riverbank it would be charming, but this is just the usual warren of loud, busy London streets. Every building is five stories tall, hence one is like a rat in a maze. That's just how London has always been. I make my way down Sloane Road. I decide to angle to the right a bit first to see the Duke of York Headquarters grounds, still verdant and looking spiff without anti-aircraft gun emplacements mucking the place up. By then, I know the way like the back of my hand, and my thoughts turn to Pamela.

Darling Pamela. In 1912 she would be . . . minus five years old. Parents probably haven't even met yet.

How long since I've seen her? Day and a half? She's as much in my mind as if it were yesterday—for it practically was, the last time I was with her. She was cradling Sloane, her eyes down, advising me not to slip back into the house as I ignored her advice and disappeared.

And, as far as she knows, was killed for it.

Maybe I shouldn't have come. Lower Sloane Street is before me and whether I want to or not, I'm looking at the high stone wall, that rust brick, hiding the back garden to Number 36.

During my walk I'd developed a plan, and I have to force myself to stick to it now, because most of me just wants to get the hell back out of here.

Around the corner and up those steps, those marble steps, to the front door.

Nutley House. Rooms To(i)let.

I draw on the wheezy old bell pull, and the door is opened much sooner than I expect by a wizened old man.

You can never politely or openly suggest someone is overweight. You can never politely or openly suggest someone isn't very bright. You can never politely or openly suggest someone isn't very attractive.

But with old people, we still have one out: "He really is . . . rather elderly."

This rather elderly man at the door must be eighty-five at least, at a time when eighty-five was a graciously advanced age. What hair remains on his head is in white fluffs, and he's stooped with his head forging forward, so he looks at me with his head tilted up to one side, focusing with one eye.

"May I help you, my good man?" he asks. His voice is craggy and yet kind. And professional.

Sticking to my latest lie, I greet him.

"Hello, I'll be staying in the neighborhood for a few days. I'm almost certainly promised a room up at the Square but won't know for sure until later this afternoon. I'm here to see if you have any openings, should my first plan not come to fruition."

"Certainly, certainly. We do. Please step inside."

He moves off to one side and allows me to enter and the . . . *sameness* . . . of the place makes me dizzy.

It is the same.

Everything is new and clean and un-scuffed. Better wallpaper, in a clean and bright parchment pinstripe.

"Our Number 3 is available. Would you care to inspect it?"

Suddenly I feel horrible at the imposition. I don't want this poor old man to needlessly walk me up even one flight of stairs. He looks like he could break a hip just putting his shoes on.

"Well, I'd hate to be a bother, especially since I'm not even sure I'll actually need it."

"Nonsense. You'll have a nice look-see. For all you know you might find us a much better accommodation after all. It'll certainly be far more quiet than up at the Square." He says it with a wink and a genuine smile.

He waddles to the desk alcove, grabs the key to Number 3—which will be Pamela's room—and, in a move that takes me by surprise, grabs an old walking cane and bangs it sharply on the wooden floor four times.

I'm not certain what to do or say before I hear footsteps coming up the back staircase, the one from the kitchen. Before I know it, I am face to face with a spry, late-thirties Mrs. Spettegue with auburn hair pulled back, those same kind blue eyes and crooked head.

"Good morning," she says brightly. Her voice is the same, but without the catch of age that carries in the throat in later years. As will be the case twenty-eight years from now, she has a dishtowel in her hands and is wiping her fingers absently with it.

"Good morning. As I was just explaining to Mr. Nutley," (Oops . . . I'm not supposed to know his name) "that, while I'm virtually guaranteed a room up at the Square, I thought it wise to have a contingency plan in place."

"That's clever of you. Certainly no harm in looking. I'll be happy to show you our best room. It's all windows, and at the end of the row. You might quite fancy it."

Old Man Nutley hands her a giant fob to Number 3 and he shuffles off into the lounge. There'd be no radio in there, I wouldn't begin to presume to know what one does with one's time alone in a room in 1912.

"Thank you, Niles," Mrs. Spettegue says sweetly in the old man's wake.

With an agility that warms my heart, the young Mrs. Spettegue boldly marches up the familiar staircase—some of the deeper scratches and notches that I never consciously noticed in the woodwork are here yet again in 1912—and she recites her spiel once more for me, in a younger, clearer voice.

"Rent is two shillings a week. Kindly leave the key when you go out during the day. I don't allow smoking in the house; I'm not on the telephone but there's a public phone in the post office at top of the lane. Tea's at six. I only serve it once, so you'll want to be on time."

She proudly opens the door to Pamela's room, and I drink it in with interest. She's correct, being all windows, and without the burden of blackout curtains, it's charming. Only now the walls are a light ochre instead of yellow. There is no crib or changing table; no sound of Sloane crying. A fairly standard room after all, but the windows are a keen selling point.

I'm standing upon a wooden floor that shall one day be blown up by a bomb.

"It's quite nice, thank you."

"Certainly, Mr . . . ?" Her eyebrows raise in polite curiosity for my name.

"Baldwin. Mark Baldwin."

No way she'd remember such a common name nearly thirty years later.

"Ah. A nice English name for an American. Good for you."

She shows me the WC and bath, mentions a few things about the house and how quiet it is, with a sizable garden out back, and I express my appreciation for it.

"Thank you for showing it to me." I make my way back out the door and toward the stairs. She follows, locking the door to Number 3.

"How long do you plan on being in London, Mr. Baldwin?"

"Just three or four days." Lie.

"Well, the weather may not be very sportsman-like over the next week, but I'm sure you'll find plenty to do."

"Thank you very much for your kindness, ma'am." We're back at the blackout-curtainless front door, and I've doffed my cap for her. I take the briefest moment to look into her kind blue eyes once more, clear of age, free from worry, and feel a consistency to the universe that warms my soul.

I'm suddenly very glad I came.

The now-quite-familiar walk up Sloane Gardens to the Tube is refreshing and clean and newly rained-upon. There are no trees planted along the street; the cars, of course, are hulking early machines and far fewer in number, leaving plenty of extra places to park.

The Square itself is also much the same as I left it—only younger. The New Court Theatre is an entirely different enterprise and hasn't itself yet been blown to bits.

It's close enough to two o'clock that I don't need to waste time walking all the way back to "Saff Ken," but simply enter Sloane Square station as I've done so many times. Another man tears my tiny paper ticket, and down on the platform I just stand near the birth site, knowing that it exists. Knowing that nothing significant will take place there until nearly thirty years from now. It's just a dirty train platform, being trodden unthinkingly upon by thousands every day. That sacred site is occasionally spat upon while I wait.

I take lunch in a pub, shepherd's pie and a pint. The price is a joke, and by then it's time to return to my pawn broker.

Again in a fuss. What if he changes his mind?

Seriously. I fuss at the drop of a hat. Maybe I could learn to just not do that anymore? What would that be like? To be . . . fussless?

The pawnbroker's shop is free of clients when I *ping* in and the man is waiting for me and smiles.

"Nice to see you again, Mr. Baldwin. I think we'll have everything we need to transact."

He has my green card out and an envelope and I produce the watch.

"May I?" He needs to see it again, to reassure himself I didn't swap it out with a fake. I dislike that he doesn't trust me and feel sad to live in a world where people actually pull crap like that.

"Certainly." I hand him the watch. I'll be sorry to see it go. Just having something so rich and elegant in your pocket makes you feel better about the world, I think.

"Ah, yes. Thirty-five pounds, I believe we said." He counts out the cash from the envelope, puts the green card back in front of me, and I dip the pen and fill in the lower portion, signing for the cash. I retain the bottom section, should I return to reclaim the watch. I can't imagine any circumstance in which this would be likely, but I've seen too much to completely discount the possibility. I put it in my pocket.

"Have a nice trip to Philadelphia," he says in a normal, genuine tone. Based on what I saw here this morning, I'm sure he enjoys having a more civil transaction now and again.

"Thank you very much. Ta," I say, doffing my hat and heading back out to freedom.

Ping.

Now I'm energized. I'm on my way!

With no hesitation I beat feet straight to Oceanic House,

just below Trafalgar Square. It is the head London office for The White Star Line. I made sure to look it up before I left.

It's in Cockspur Street. Nice name. *Heh heh. Cock. I like it when cocks purr. Heh.*

Anyway . . .

As I approach the elegant building, I can see your actual British Admiralty right across the road. It's all situated just below the famed Pall Mall, a nice neighborhood to say the least.

Oceanic House, headquarters of one of the grandest shipping companies in the world, would be full-on ornate and stately, and in this I am certainly correct. I instantly feel underdressed as I enter the grand lobby with stone floors, vaulted ceilings, subdued torchieres, offices and posters and ship models under glass. To the left is the ticket office, just rotten with scrolled brass ticket counters, staff dressed to the nines, and a hushed, reverent tone throughout the place.

This is literally the dream of a lifetime. I approach the first-class ticket window and a man with a monocle and natty black clothes greets me unctuously.

"How may I assist you, sir?"

"Good afternoon. I'd like a stateroom on *Titanic* for tomorrow, if possible."

The ship won't be full on its maiden voyage—I checked—but still, here comes the fuss, wondering if they'll have room for me.

"Certainly, sir. Will this be one way or excursion?"

"Just one way, thank you."

Bitch, please. Ain't gonna be no round-trip . . .

The man produces a chart of still-available first-class staterooms and their relative costs. There's a bit of an array; I see one as high as £97 and one as low as £18. I choose for middle-lower, and select a £23 one with my index finger.

"Certainly. Kindly fill out an embarkation card," he hands

me a slip to fill out and there's yet another ink pen sitting in its black well. I put my true information on the card (no reason not to) and count out the £23.

It's a ticket all the way through to New York. I didn't think they'd sell me a ticket just to Queenstown Ireland, and I don't want to raise any red flags.

The man, with a lovely, enviable flourish of handwriting, fills out a ticket with my name on it.

RMS *Titanic*. First class. Mark Baldwin.

"How many pieces of luggage shall we expect?"

"Actually, none. This is terribly last minute for me. Will there be a haberdasher aboard?"

"Normally yes, but as this is the maiden voyage, I'm not altogether certain it will be fully appointed. Shall I enquire?"

"Oh, no sense bothering; I'll manage to pick up a few things this afternoon. I also wonder if you can recommend accommodation for me tonight here in London?"

"Certainly. Our company-sponsored hotel, the Metropole, is at Whitehall Place, just a few steps along the high street. I shall ring them on your behalf. They'll be expecting you."

I'm awash in the excellence of the service. Despite what Hollywood tells us, the English rarely bother—at least if you're below a certain wealth-set. But when they do, it's simply the best. For a brief moment, I'm in the club.

Next, he kindly explains to me the Boat Train. First-class passengers shall leave from Waterloo Station at 7:30 promptly upon the morrow, on a special chartered train, all the way to quayside in Southampton. The *Titanic* sets sail at noon.

I thank him for his kindness and take my leave.

Ticket safely tucked in my breast pocket, I follow his instructions, out from Oceanic House, across the road and to the left, past the Admiralty.

The Metropole Hotel forms a seven-story, narrow triangle where two streets meet at a sharp angle. I enter the main doors to find it just as posh and grand as one would expect. Yet the lobby is in chaos. I see piles of steamer trunks getting carted to various storage rooms by smartly costumed bellboys. The valises and trunks are each a study in fabulous; fine leathers and straps, yet with garish travel stickers slapped on Louis Vuitton luggage that would cost thous. People gussied up to the hilt are milling about, being served drinks, waiting impatiently to be checked in. Women are wearing fur and men are smoking cigars.

It's three-quarters of an hour before I finally get a room key and beg the bellhop off.

My room is small and unassuming but certainly adequate. Nearly everything is white and it's spanking clean.

Messing around with my iPhone, using some screenshots and my calculator, I am able to convert £23 in 1912 to today's U.S. dollars and am gobsmacked to realize I just spent $3,300 on my ticket.

And it won't even make it all the way to New York.

At the window to my room I can see toward the north. I gaze up at the gray sky. There are no aircraft to be seen anywhere. The skies are free of machines. The only way to travel is by ship, which is why they are so luxurious and obsessed with speed. In the days before the steam engine, it could take two months on ships not appreciably larger than two city buses cobbled together. And people would die by the half-dozen along the way.

Now an Atlantic crossing only takes five days, and one can only barely ascertain one is at sea at all.

I have this evening to myself. I'm rich. So I'll buy some clothes, that's what I'll do. London is many things, but it is also a relatively well-appointed city. I ought to do well.

I don't stray far from the Metropole, but I find a men's clothier in Pall Mall and purchase a much nicer black coat with tails and truly luxurious, golden silk lining. I also procure a decent hat; black, mostly a derby but with a dash of early fedora mixed in to give it a devilishly rakish look. I quite like it.

The hotel books a play for me in the evening, the latest and greatest farce in the West End just now. I happily hoof it over to the theatre district to attend *Better Not Enquire* at the Prince of Wales's Theatre. It's very clever and drôle, in the way of a turn-of-the-century English parlor comedy. I don't catch all the jokes, or more importantly, they don't strike me as particularly funny. But I've spent a few times in my recent incarnations enjoying formal operas and playhouses, losing myself in the surprising intensity of the stage lights, the makeup, and costumes. The audience falls headlong for the deadpan butler who deftly runs his patrons in circles.

When the play lets out, I wander Covent Garden and Leicester Square, watching the other theatergoers in their finery and jewels. It very nearly threatens rain again, but none actually comes until after I go into a pub for a few pints.

A steady drizzle is coming down as I, full of beer, emerge and emotionally prepare myself for a long walk to the Metropole in the rain.

To my amazement, a black, sputtering taxicab, not much removed from a horseless carriage, has pulled to the curb for me. The driver sits in the open air getting wet, which strikes me as unfair, but I am happily clacked safe and dry into the cabin behind him. I feel rather silly. The cab is somewhat cruddy, the engine barely manages to stay lit. But the window's open and I choose to have a bit of fun with the driver, asking after The Knowledge.

"Of course I have it, sir. Wouldn't be here if I didn't."

The Knowledge, which requires memorizing of all of London's streets, is one of the most grueling exams on Earth. Men have been known to wet themselves and even pass out in the face of it. My cabby informs me he only had to take the test twice himself. Only one in five eventually pass.

Just to have fun with him I ask where Clennam Street is, and he goes "Psht. You'll have to do better than that, mate."

"Well good for you. I have a lot of geography in my head, on somewhat of a global scale. I've always admired you lot." He seems pleased.

It's not a long drive to the Metropole but since I've had a sufficiency of beer, I ponder the odd reality that the English drive on the other side of the road from us. According to what I read, the English method is, technically, correct: When on horseback, approaching a stranger whose intents are unclear, one should be able to quickly draw one's sword with one's right hand. Which would necessitate passing to the left.

Further, while driving carts and carriages in towns, the man drives seated to the right. That way, should someone unexpectedly slosh the contents of their tosspot out a second-story window, the man, rather than the lady, should chivalrously bear the brunt of it.

Stuff like that fascinates me.

I'm almost ready to ponder that at least humans have evolved far enough to no longer hurl our feces but still have small matters such as World War II to contend with, but my driver deftly delivers me to the Metropole and I tip him extra. He says, "Ta, guv."

I hang close to the hotel after that. Get some serious scotch on in the bar, and people around me are murmuring about their voyage tomorrow on *Titanic.* But I hold back and don't talk to anyone. Normally I'd be on my phone, slumped over the bar with my chin in one hand, glued to Scruff or Facebook. Tonight I got nothing. I don't want to mix with these people. I don't know why, I just don't belong here, and they're going to die.

Well, not the rich women.

Finally it's time to go to sleep in my room, which I do. I'm endlessly excited.

37

Wednesday, April 10, 1912

I take an uncomfortably early breakfast in the hotel. I'm delighted to see they have coffee, but it is bitter and a rather half-hearted attempt, focusing mainly on tea as the English will do. Pastries and cheese and an excellent marmalade round out my morning meal.

It is a woefully gray day in England, just how they like it. Multi-gray clouds hang in round and fluffy variances of gloom, with patches of blue sky. Occasional gusts of wind huff past, each from a differing vector and it doesn't seem that rain will be far off. It'll be a mixture of everything, if I'm any judge.

The White Star Line springs for a taxi. Actually a great line of them are waiting for a sudden outflow from the Metropole. So I, with no luggage, bundle into yet another virtual horseless carriage. It's a straight shot down The Strand and over the river at Waterloo Bridge. Waterloo Station is just there to our right, a hive of activity.

It is not an attractive place. It's a jumble of worn-down brick, unadorned and visually confusing.

"Looks a little hard-pressed," I mention to the cabby, not wanting to be rude but a little taken aback.

"Oi. Just shows to go ya. This here station was only ever meant to be a mere stop on the line. They planned to make a grand terminal in the City across the Thames. But as it happens, they never quite got 'round to it. What you see now is the beginning of a whole new remake. Should be quite nice in a few years' time. Mind yer 'ead." We've come to the curb and I'm lighting out. I flip him a shilling which he seems to quite appreciate.

Inside there's nothing modern at all: no WH Smith, Boots, Nero Caffè, Vodafone stands or brilliant LED screens proclaiming Lancôme and showing some color close-up of a woman's navel. Just a low roar of crowds going about their Wednesdays, commuters and children on school trips and heavy clothes everywhere. Clouds of cigar and cigarette smoke. Occasional whistles being blown, a chug or two as a steam train harumpfs itself begrudgingly into motion one more time, heaving untold carcinogens up toward the girders and glass panes over the barn.

I purchase a newspaper and sit and wait on an unforgivingly hard wooden bench, alternately reading the paper and checking out my surroundings.

The special train, the White Star Line Boat Train for first-class passengers, leaves at 7:30 from platform 10.

Finally my train is called. Not by Tannoy—that won't come for decades. Slat boards with slide-out cards list destinations, times, and numbers. Various station attendants stand around with clipboards and call out track numbers, trains, and times every dozen yards or so apart from each other, most in a bored, over-practiced, singsong fashion.

I go down track platform 10 and get to the correct car

according to my ticket. Each compartment has its own door that swings out. "Slammers" they used to call them. The train is a wooden carriage, some of it well-varnished teak. It has a gently arched roof and fussy wooden steps up from the platform into my intended compartment. There's no corridor in this type of train; we have a door on either side and that's it. A small, enclosed compartment seats six, and that's your lot.

It means there shall be no tea trolley—and no toilet either. One must be British and suffer.

Two middle-aged businessmen and a lone woman in a black-velvet, long dress with a high collar and black hat—I assume she's in mourning—are in my compartment. Since this is a chartered train, they shall also be my traveling companions on the *Titanic*. Small valises and cases are hand-carried; they'll probably have massive amounts of luggage being carted to the ship in the baggage carriage.

We all nod and say good morning and no further conversation seems necessary. I'm glad. It's too early in the morning for, "Oh, you're an American." With three across seating and only four of us, everyone has an empty seat next to them in the middle.

Antimacassars on all the headrests have the White Star Line logo on them, the brick-red flag with a white star in it. This is a London-Southwest Railroad train, running on LSWR track but chartered by the shipping company for us to get to *Titanic* with ease and grace.

The windows are large, and I can tell the one in the door can be opened and raised or lowered. A beat-up, leather strap hangs down with notches in it.

A few hand whistles are blown along the platform and the train lurches into motion. I can hear the chug from the steam engine, the creak of the wheels and clunk of the clamps, and imagine the great wheels and gears coming to life.

Soon we're going about thirty miles an hour—it's quite

smooth—and I'm watching the ugly industrial buildings of South London spool by. Not long after that, we're going much faster . . . yet we slow down, shunting through the hot mess that is Clapham Junction. We reduce speed but don't stop. This is an express train after all. We pick up our pace again, the buildings are becoming more sparse, and I'm getting glimpses of open spaces, pastures, sheep, and horses.

We top out at about seventy. I'm pretty excited. The engine fairly chugs, and occasionally blows that high-toot whistle of English trains. A storm squall causes sheets of rain to streak down my window, running aft in rivulets. I can hear the drops smattering hard on the roof of the carriage.

Don't you adore England?

I'm riding backwards, which I don't like. And I'd rather look out the window than read my newspaper, but after about half an hour, I'm able to pull myself away from the view and glance at the news.

The front is a full-page ad for girdles. Inside are articles about Prime Minister Asquith, which devolve into discussions about what's happening with the national coal strike. England has been paralyzed by the strike; factories shut down, rail service cancelled, people unable to heat their homes for weeks. The strike ended on April 6th, four days ago, but it's going to take weeks to get coal back out and into circulation. Several steamships have had to delay their departures.

A few sizable stations fly by out my window: Woking, Basingstoke. The train roars through each imperiously. I see flashes of faces of people standing on the platforms, living their 1912 lives in heavy clothes, bored with their day, and here we come, *whoosh*. We don't stop. We're important. And rich. We're going places.

Only the train does stop dead for a while, in the middle of nowhere. Out the windows are heather and heaths and a few piles of hay, a broken, early form of tractor rusting out in the open. No announcement is made. It's silent, the air close. We sit quietly for quite a few minutes, then a few minutes more. My stomach churns menacingly. That coffee I had at the hotel . . . I start to fuss mightily, as is my wont. Why would they build trains with no toilets? Furthermore, why didn't I go at Waterloo?

Water. Loo . . .

I banish these thoughts from my mind. I close my eyes and select a different panic: I don't want to miss the sailing.

But everyone on this train is headed for the thing, and they're first-class people, too. They'll wait for us, obviously. According to history we get there on time, so I need to just chill out.

I squirm in my seat and my innards manage to pressure-compensate and the moment passes. Shortly after that we lurch, once again, into motion.

It's open countryside until we chug through Southampton itself, past a Queen's Park, and we slither through on our dedicated track, directly onto Berth 44: The White Star line. Because I'm facing the back of the train and on the wrong side, I can't see what's ahead. I can't see the smokestacks of *Titanic.*

If I could I'd practically be licking the glass.

A great hiss is heard from the engine and brakes, and wooden doors start opening all along the train. People step off onto the platform in their heavy shoes even while the train is still coming to a stop.

I jump out of the train, using the opposite door than the one we climbed in, to find us in a drafty, cold, industrial building. I'm a little dismayed with my surroundings until I happen to look up. And with an actual thrill in my belly, through the high square warped windows of this building, I am seeing the upper superstructure of the RMS *Titanic* with my own eyes.

It's actually kind of small.

Huh. I'm used to the *Queen Mary* in Long Beach, roughly a third larger, visited countless times.

Yet we're talking substantial, nonetheless. Just shy of four 747s in length, three football fields long, *Titanic* is the largest moving object on Earth this day. Solid, already getting dirty and rusty, she'll never reach old age and it's a damned shame.

After an interminable wait in the terminal building, elegantly dressed dozens queueing up impatiently, finally a door is slid open and we proceed out onto the quay. I'm approaching the behemoth. It's a solid wall of portholes and rivets—millions of rivets. I crane my neck up and only see the outer hull from this close; black, looming. A few heads peer down from the upper railings. I surmise I won't get an accurate and all-encompassing external view of *Titanic* until I leave tomorrow afternoon in Ireland. I plan on watching this thing sail away. I won't want to move from my spot until she is over the horizon and back into the history books.

But right now she's mine—all mine. She's real and this is now. *Thank you, David!*

A canvas-covered wooden gangplank leads to the ship's steel doors, steeply sloping up, with wooden runners placed at inconvenient intervals.

The women of the period are all about clothes, especially those of first class. Massive hats are still the style of the day, each one is a creation unto itself, each well past the circumference of the woman's skirts. I'm not looking up any dresses, but can see ankle (I know, right?) and the shoes they are forced to wear. That's why boarding takes so long: The women can barely walk in their tight, high-heeled shoes, laced all the way up.

It's finally my turn. I glance over and down at the narrow space between the dock and the ship, see gap between the ship and the pier, a small jet of effluvium running off from the great ship into the water.

A rather small gangway door is open for us, next to it a sign that reads, "STOOP! Mind Your Head."

Through the hatch stooping, I board the RMS *Titanic.*

The actual dream of a lifetime.

It smells brand new. The tang of enamel paint, linseed oil, carpet glue and the smell of coal dust fills the air, the latter being a sulfuric, gasoline-like smell.

The entrance lobby is on D-Deck, port side, just forward of the grand staircase. I note the feeling when you are finally aboard in a tightly enclosed space with unnatural lighting and ceilings that just feel a trifle too low. Sound is muffled. It's exquisitely luxurious, but it's still a ship. A machine. A world unto itself.

Ahead of me is the elevator lobby, solid oak paneling, and three lifts. To my right is an expansive lobby. The walls and low ceilings are white, yet the carpet is red with rosettes in it that somehow combine to make the lounge look altogether pink in hue. A few potted palms, tables and chairs are stationed about. I'm sort of stumbling over that way with my mouth open, already I can see that just past this is the first-class Dining Saloon and drinking it in, realize once more how large the ship actually is . . . only to be brought up short.

A uniformed steward suddenly blocks my way, clipboard in hand, asking me for my name and ticket. I fish my boarding card out of my breast pocket and hand it over. He marks it with a pencil and ticks my name off on his clipboard. They must have telephoned or telegraphed my name down since yesterday.

I'm assigned stateroom A-15. Nice, solid number.

"Would it be all right if I retained my ticket? As a souvenir?"

"Certainly, sir," he coos sweetly in a way that lets me know in no uncertain terms that he finds me crass and impertinent. He nevertheless hands it back over to me. I'll want to keep it forever.

"Where do I get the key to my stateroom?"

Open horror now. "We don't give out keys, sir. Any valuables in your possession can be locked in the purser's safe. If you find you do require to have your cabin locked, why, you can arrange that with your deck steward." He looks repulsed. Like I'm a criminal, or some kind of perverted sex maniac.

"Oh, no, thank you. I just wasn't sure how it worked."

He snaps his fingers, and a young cabin boy is quickly front and center to take me to my stateroom. Do not want.

"I'd rather find it on my own, if it's all the same . . . "

That's it. They look at me like I practically took a dump on the carpet. Tacky American. If they roll their eyes, they do it away from me and I do not see. Fortunately, people are streaming in behind me and they move off to help the more civilized passengers under their care.

I'm also free to walk to those stairs. The famed Grand Staircase, made of solid English oak, is instantly recognizable, with the carvings of cupids on it, chandeliers and light standards. I simply stare and mourn its impending loss.

The RMS *Olympic*, the *Titanic's* identical twin sister, already in service eleven months, will sail the seas many years successfully. It has the exact same staircase, but in the 1920s, someone will get the harebrained idea to stain it all green. Honest to God: green.

I can't imagine. Such a shame.

The white-tiled floor with black fleurettes has kind of a rubbery feel to it.

I watch the stairs, and people's reaction to them. Without exception, everyone sort of fluffs themselves and puffs up like vain, tropical birds. They're smiling and putting on airs as they make their way up or down the staircase, burdened by their clothes, hobbled by their footwear, but exalted by the opulence of their new surroundings.

On its plinth at the foot of the stairs is one of the famed

cupid statues, meant to look angelic, but up close, its face is nearly a grimace. Yet I can't help but reach out my finger and trace its tiny cheek. A lady wearing a hat like a birthday cake sees me do it and looks at me disapprovingly.

I'm anxious to see my cabin, so I climb the steps three levels to A-Deck and make my way forward to A-15. It's along the corridor on the starboard side.

The companionway is white on white, beveled trim, more sedate rubber tiling on the floor, and quite confining.

My door is unlocked, sure enough. I step into A-15 and here it is: A tiny, windowless room in pitch blackness. Fortunately, a wall switch is right where it should be, and I flick the light on. A high-up single bed is to my left and a gorgeous marble washstand to my right. I also have a wardrobe, into which I have nothing to put. A White Star Line bath towel hangs from a rod. Wanna steal that right now . . .

There's no toilet. Even in first class, only the most expensive staterooms have their own bathrooms. To pee you have to go to the Gentlemen's Lavatory, forward down the hall and around the corner. I go there now, ultimately needing to relieve myself, and to wash the newspaper ink and train soot off my hands. A men's room like any other, porcelain urinals that say *Armitage Shanks* on them like a thin blue tattoo, three wood stalls, sinks with framed mirrors above them.

Across the hall I notice two bath closets, doors ajar, each with a claw-foot tub and racks of never-before-used white towels. A framed sign tells me to contact my deck steward for bathing appointments.

Back in the cabin I hop up to my raised bed and give it a try. It really only fits one person, with natural oak spindle railings, ostensibly to keep you from rolling out of it in high seas. It's just a flat, unyielding mattress with crisp white linens with the little red flag and White Star Line logo. I kick off my shoes and lounge for a few minutes, taking a few pictures and selfies that I'll never be able to show another soul.

Could have paid a little extra for a port hole, but then again, I'll only be here for twenty-four hours. This won't be where I'll be spending my time.

There isn't much point in just sitting in my tiny windowless cabin all alone. I need to explore.

It feels weird, not locking my cabin door, not coming away with a little plastic keycard extolling the virtues of Hilton Honors™ on the back of it.

No question that I should get myself up to the Boat Deck, post haste. To watch people board, to take the air, to see the grandeur of this greatest ship afloat. It's only one more flight up, out the lobby and the aft-facing oak doors, inset with glass panels, and *oops*: There's the door sill, the five-inch wood waterbar over which people are forever stumbling their first few days at sea. But for the grace of God I remember in time and don't make the classic mistake myself.

I'm out on the highest deck on the grandest ship and all is revealed under the gun-gray sky.

Huge funnels: four of them, painted an irrepressible golden yellow with black bands along the top. Each one is big enough to accommodate a train locomotive inside. They're plunked down into the deck housing at a rakish, back-swept angle, held snugly in place by steel cables all the way around. Secure. Immovable. Permanent. They're everything. They firmly demonstrate to the mind how large this ship actually is.

Even higher than these monstrosities, running from the spires of foremast to aftermast, are the Marconi wires, which will keep the ship in telegraphic contact throughout its voyage. And during its demise as well.

An apparent earlier rain squall has cleared, it's still wet. I approach the portside rail to find huge droplets of rainwater coalesced on the varnished wood. I swish them aside with my hands so I can lean my heavily wool-clad forearms upon it. I'm looking out over the city of Southampton. Church spires, trees, Victorian buildings and chimneys everywhere. Looks like a nice place. I smell the salt air.

I start to relax. This is going to be great!

We still have an hour and a half before sailing, so I steal throughout the first-class accommodations of the ship. I walk from the Dining Saloon to the Smoking Lounge on the A-Deck, first-class Lounge, through corridor after corridor, made difficult for they are quite narrow, and people are still boarding, laden with their cabin bags. It's awkward. I bide my time, drinking it all in.

Having made the circuit twice, we still have plenty of time before departure and I don't have anything specific in mind.

Finally, I go back up to the Boat Deck to wait. Quite nearby I notice a startlingly handsome man in a derby hat and bushy black handlebar moustache stride over to the port rail on my right. He smokes a cigar and nods and we each say "hello."

"Grand day for a sailing, eh what?" he says.

"I'm quite excited to be here," I admit.

He proffers his meaty hand. "Jake Slocombe, Sheffield."

"Mark Baldwin, San Francisco. Good to meet you." We shake.

"Oh. You're an American. San Francisco! You don't say? How's life in San Francisco after the fires?"

"The city lost part of its soul a few years back. They're making up for it by building like mad."

"You didn't happen to be there for the big event, did ye?" He has an English Midlands accent, one that I've always found unbearably sexy.

"I most certainly was. It was quite a catastrophe. A very difficult few days."

"What had you in England?" Jake Slocombe asks.

"Business dealings for my father," I lie. "We're in lumber."

"Good field. I'm in tobacco, meself," Jake says, holding his cigar between thumb and forefinger, suddenly examining it proudly. I decide to relight my pipe.

Shortly we are met by a woman in an enormous hat, yellow dress with all the trimmings, opera-length white gloves, and a parasol, tightly wrapped; she uses it as a walking stick.

"This is my wife, Letitia. Letitia, this is Mark Baldwin, San Francisco."

"How do you do, Mr. Baldwin," she says, proffering her gloved hand for me to shake gingerly, which I do. "It's thrilling to meet you." Her accent is several pegs above that of her husband. I wonder how well that goes over in society. But Slocombe is such a rugged, handsome man that I'm sure it makes up for many a social shortcoming.

"Very pleased to meet you, Mrs. Slocombe."

I inwardly suppress a giggle—it comes out of nowhere in my brain, a sudden remembrance of Mrs. Slocombe from *Are You Being Served?* on TV in the 1970s.

Captain Peacock: Can you peer through the letterbox and see my pussy?

Just then the ship's whistles blow, so loud and sharp, we all jump. The whistles are not very far from where we stand, high up on the front smokestack. A violent spewing of steam signals their use.

The tone of the *Titanic's* horn surprises me in that it's higher, more baritone than I expect. Throaty. But so, very, loud. It takes my breath away.

"My nerve!" utters Mrs. Slocombe, hand to her heart.

"All ashore who's going ashore!" cries a steward, clearing the decks of visitors, of which there seem to be many. Reporters too.

We watch the last of the passengers board; first and second class through the forward gangway to D-Deck, and another one further aft for the steerage-class passengers. Cranes load cargo, cars, and trunks.

It is time for *Titanic* to depart. She's all lined up, pointing south, downriver. It'll be a straight shot to the open sea. People line the rails of the port side to wave, and confetti is passed around by the stewards. This is an event. The newest and biggest ship afloat, on her maiden voyage, and it's thrilling. A musical band is playing down on the dock, far below us.

The lines are cast off, and I move forward along the port side. I want to get a glimpse of Captain E.J. Smith, and I do! I see him on the bridge wing. He's famous. And handsome, all up in his white beard. Next to him is a nondescript man in a completely different uniform, who must be Southampton pilot master Bowyer.

Smith's busy and in his element as lines are cast loose. Ropes as big around as my arm are slaked off, splashing in the salt water and getting reeled up into the ship by unseen hands.

The whistles go again; it is a powerful utterance. It's as if we can see the noise of it ricochet off buildings and spires and chimneys, only to be thrown back at us in a thousand different shards of sound. Three blasts.

Soon we are sliding forward under our own power. You can't feel the ship's engines from the Boat Deck, moving ahead Dead Slow. Black coal smoke belches from the first three funnels as the ship builds up its own steam. I hear a deep hiss from the stacks. We begin pulling away from the pier, the distance between the rail and the dock begins to slowly widen. We are moving. We begin heading down into Southampton Water, away from the city. The shoreline on either side begins making its way past. Other ships at various piers toot their horns and whistles as we inch along, using a mere whisper of the ship's true power.

I excuse myself from the Slocombes and head away from the rail. I have to force myself away. I'd love to stay and watch but I have a little experiment to run. For this, I will need to be at the back rail of the *Titanic*.

The after deck, your actual "poop deck" of yore, is technically third-class territory, but at departure time no one seems to protest my being there. After a hasty few minutes' walk, I'm now at the very back end of the ship, happily once again able to see out and catch the views of all the action. It's crowded with third-class passengers and we haven't traveled very far. Several tugboats, each huffing mountains of steam from their stacks escort us.

We pass Berth 28 and I see a smaller, older steamer, the *New York*, already heaving dangerously against her mooring lines as we pass. Even at Dead Slow, the *Titanic's* propellers are creating turbulent havoc in the water.

Suddenly, just as was told in the history books, the *New York* breaks free from her moorings. A loud *snap* like the report of a gun is the sound of her metal hawsers, three inches thick, snapping. Her gangplanks plop straight down, and the ship quickly begins to drift, back-end, toward the *Titanic*, now inexorably drawn by the wake created by the superliner's engines.

Having read ahead I know that Captain Smith (or would it be Harbormaster Bowyer?) orders *Titanic*'s port engine into full reverse in an attempt to propel the *New York* away. It's all happening right in front of me and my heart rate goes up as the *New York* continues to move toward us, stern first. *Titanic*'s left engine is grumbling as hard as it can just below me, a savage froth and silt of whipped water jetting out in a wide angry swath, in an attempt to repel the other ship.

Tugboats huff in to intervene at full speed, but it becomes a race to see what will happen first. The *New York* gets so near to us that I can easily look down onto her decks and see the upturned faces of startled crew members, their mouths all in a silent "O," and I can clearly make out the woodgrain of the *New*

York's deck planking . . . and it's all happening, literally, right in front of me.

The *New York* doesn't even remotely have enough time to fire up its own engines in defense . . .

Eight feet.

That's how close the two ships come to colliding. Everything almost changed in that moment. But by blasting the port engine of the *Titanic*, along with heroic tug efforts, the *New York* is saved, and what would have been a disaster to these people is avoided.

We are now free and clear to sail off into history, straight into the hands of what a real disaster looks like.

In truth, they probably should have just let the ships ram into each other. But that just isn't how it works.

Titanic, meanwhile, is now at a dead stop. People are confused and excited, chattering to each other in any number of languages. We sit idle for almost an hour. The huge superliner remains at rest in the middle of Southampton Water as reports are made, nervous brows wiped, other ships' hawsers made double fast. The *New York* is obediently led back to her berth and retied to her dock.

The excitement over, people wander away to explore the new ship. A potential further rain squall looks like it wants to move in.

I go back to my original place on the Boat Deck, surprised and happy to see the Slocombes still there. I tell them of the goings on aft. They're suitably impressed and Letitia once again exclaims, "My word!"

After a great long while, with no signal other than the feeling beneath our feet, the *Titanic* huffs back to life, engines begin turning over, screws rotating on their shafts once more, and we begin to move forward in earnest.

Wind becomes stronger, the shore gets further away, and blue water surrounds us. We enter the greater channel and then, eventually, the Solent. The Isle of Wight is to our right on the starboard side, the village of Cowes just there, busy with tiny boats. I mention to the Slocombes that the only thing left to see will be when the harbormaster, who I don't specifically name as Bowyer because I don't wish to appear to be a geek, gets dropped off into his tender and heads back to Southampton.

We watch it take place; nothing intrinsically interesting, a man deftly springs down a rope ladder and into an awaiting craft. He salutes Captain E.J. Smith who returns the salute from the bridge wing with a smile on his face. Bowyer heads back up the channel, surely to a nice cup of tea and with a peace of mind that will shatter on the morning of April 15th.

That kindly, jaunty salute will most likely haunt him to the end of his days.

We're on the move again, picking up speed, picking up wind. I'm starting to feel the cool Atlantic breeze on my face as the Isle of Wight moves behind us and *Titanic* takes to the open seas.

I smell the salt sea air. Seagulls dive and dart playfully around us, squawking.

With nothing more to see, the Slocombes mention they'd reserved a table in the à la carte restaurant on B-Deck and I'm welcome to join them. I am surprised, honored and delighted to oblige. So much better than just trudging about the ship by my lonesome.

Yet I do worry about conversation. Can I hold my end of a discussion? Also, it costs extra. I immediately fuss about protocol.

We parade past the Café Parisien and all its trellises; at the à la carte entrance we're met with a welcome desk and 6s3d are demanded of us up front by a dour English maître d'. Definitely not his first sailing aboard a ship, he's neither impressed by his surroundings nor by us—until I detect a certain stiffening of interest when he gets a load of Jake.

Old queen.

Fortunately, I have the coins in my pocket and can surreptitiously pay my own way before the Slocombs try to offer. I'd feel better if they didn't.

The restaurant is warmly appointed with wood paneling, lots of pink, and flowers on the tables. Doing a bang-up business as well, with waiters scurrying about.

We are seated at a four-top, take our hats off (except Letitia), and peruse the menu. Fois gras, chilled cucumber soup, roast duck, lamb, chicken à la king, salad Niçoise. It all looks so good.

We order and settle in, coffee all around, and sit pleasantly, waiting for some semblance of a conversation to begin.

Fortunately, Letitia is a well-bred Englishwoman, and she's not going to drop the ball. She kindly asks after my time in England, my life in San Francisco.

"Have you a family?"

I answer in general terms and politely. She's a master at being a Lady, and a Lady always makes those around her feel at ease. That's the actual old-school definition. Same goes for a Gentleman, too, by the way. We could stand to bring some of the old ways back.

I ask about their plans in New York, with a sick feeling in my stomach. I've studied passenger lists till I was blue in the face, and while I hardly committed any to actual memory, I don't recall seeing any Slocombes among the survivors.

Jake describes his tobacco business, and the opportunity to purchase a small tobacco company in Brooklyn. We talk of general sightseeing in New York. I wish I could recommend things for the Slocombes to do in New York, but in terms of 1912, I'm of precious little help.

Then I remember that they might never get there anyway and my stomach drops.

Conversation naturally lags as we enjoy eating our lunch. Sitting in my stalwart chair, gazing at the woodwork and flowers and graceful tables comes the first of many waves in my belly at how horrid and ridiculous this whole thing is about to become. It all seems so sad. This, at the bottom of the Atlantic? It is surreal. *Titanic* is far too big to just go away. All the dishes and silverware and glasses and linens—the salt and pepper shakers—the carpets and flowers . . . all of it.

And the people, too. But somehow, I can't process that in my mind. The loss of human life *en masse* is something I can't bring myself to understand. I unwittingly remember the complete carnage on Chester Row in Chelsea, that young family I had to clear out, but this is different. That was bloody. This will be hypothermia and surrendering to utter cold. Not just four people and a dog, but one thousand, five hundred of them. I can't grasp it.

I only seem to grasp the ruination of the salt and pepper shakers in my rapidly devolving brain.

I've really developed a sick-ass hobby for myself. I don't know how much longer I can keep this all up. I find myself trembling at odd moments, ducking against loud noises, shrieking every time I see fire and cowering when I see a Ryanair 737. Granted, most people cringe when they see Ryanair, but this discomfort is more acutely felt and bespeaks more deeply held emotional scars.

I'm fine. I'm just fine. Thank you for asking.

But I pull myself back to the present and observe the Slocombes.

We have a genial conversation then, about the weather mostly, generally what they can expect in New York, how the streets are laid out in a grid, their new subway and elevated trains, and how in-your-face the people can be.

Our delicious meal concluded, I thank the Slocombes profusely for sharing lunch with me; it truly is a delightful and unexpected treat. We're assured we'll see each other again at dinner tonight in the first-class Dining Saloon.

I wouldn't mind playing a card game or two with Jake afterward. He's something.

After lunch I wander the ship, all over once more. I need to see every last inch of it. I decide to start at the bottom. I check out the swimming pool and Turkish baths down below on F Deck, close to the waterline. I look down a crew companionway, a brightly white-painted metal staircase leading to the lower decks and what I understand to be the mail hold, unseen by passengers.

Right about here is where the unstoppable sea water will first rush in.

Back topside I sneak a peek at the gymnasium on the Boat Deck, reading the posted sign about times of use: Mornings for men, mid-day for children, and women from two to four. I wander the elegant Reading and Writing Room, first-class Lounge, Smoke Room and Verandah Court, all on A-Deck. I even go to back to Steerage and look around. It's very crowded, but quite an improvement over older ships of the day.

I'd like to take pictures with my phone but I'm never alone; someone's always around. I'll have to wait till night when everyone's been drinking.

All told, I expect I've walked a good two miles at least. The ship is that big.

By now it's 3:30 p.m., and I've luncheoned and toured all there is to see. Over the railings there's naught but gray ocean under gray skies to look at.

I am now tired enough that I can envisage a nap in my cabin. Once there I strip down and sleep, feeling the pulse of the reciprocating engines two city blocks away and seven decks below. It's quiet, but you can hear a definite powerful and rhythmic chugging of the steam engines. A spanking new, well-oiled machine, humming along nicely. Instead of the low rumble I'd been expecting, *Titanic* makes more of a *pockitty pockitty* sound. Before I left home, I looked up how the two main engines worked, and was surprised that each is a simple four-cylinder engine—only they happen to be the size of a KFC.

The ship is crossing the English Channel to Cherbourg, France, where we'll take on more passengers this evening. Then we'll double back overnight to Queenstown, Ireland, for yet more passengers. *Titanic* leaves Queenstown for New York at 1:30 tomorrow afternoon, and that's when I shall take my leave of her.

I suspect I may be overcome with emotion to see this proud and beautiful liner—and all who sail upon her—move off into the great blue sea, never to return. I can tell you now I won't move from my spot until she is well and truly out of sight.

I sleep. For a bit, despite my excitement. I start to relax. This is supposed to be fun. I've got nothing but luxury to look forward to. Changing ships to another westbound steamer might be a bore, and there's a good chance I won't be able to afford first class, but hopefully at least second class. Either way, I'm going to be in the lap of luxury for several days and it is good.

Some naps make me cranky, but this one's fine. I'm excited enough, I bound to my feet, get my shoes on, checking the time. I decide to pretty much leave the lights on all the time; it's so dark otherwise, it simply doesn't suit one.

By now, it's about six o'clock, so to the A-Deck Promenade I go to watch us drop anchor at Cherbourg. I'm just in time. *Titanic's* engines are once again at full stop. I assume some ungodly large anchor has dropped to hold us at station keeping. The April daylight is nearly gone. I see the lights of the French village and watch the tender coming alongside. Ship's lights are shown down to the boats and crewmen help people up a box to an open gangway door. The *Titanic* swallows them up.

It's about 6:30, and while I've been watching, it has become full night. Yet the ship is brilliantly lit, all over. It reflects upon the darkening sea.

Titanic's horn once again blasts three times, and now it's time for dinner.

I've been dreading this.

A veritable cavalcade of famous people is going to be in that dining room. The Astors, the Guggenheims, Margaret Brown, Lady Duff Gordon, the Strauses. And here's me, an underemployed writer with no name, no money, no place in society, 107 years off-axis from these people. I do not belong. And my clothes are patently unsuitable.

But maybe I'll see Jake Slocombe again, that'll be fine. I'm hoping to see Captain Smith up close, too.

Down that grand staircase, to D-Deck, reception room, diners are already lining up, surprisingly underdressed. Not casual—by today's standards that would never be allowed—but I was expecting bejeweled and pretentious and I don't see it. Then I remember: On the first night at sea, it is acceptable to underdress. Ones' maids and valets are still unpacking trunks in staterooms all over the ship.

So I have the distinction of being improperly dressed, after I'd worked so hard to fit in. It furthers my discomfort.

The seatings begin.

Tables are assigned and shared, in a hierarchy of social standing, radiating out from the Captain's Table in the middle of the room. I'm sure I'll be at a table with six strangers, as far from the center of attraction as possible, as I'm led in by a steward.

There must be a mistake: I'm on a cheap-ass ticket, but I'm escorted to a three-top table just next to the Captain's table. I can see everyone from my vantage point. Although Captain

Smith isn't here, I can see his place at the table and the assemblage of guests already being seated.

I'm resigned to dining conspicuously alone and have my napkin in my lap and have already had a sip of water, trying to suss out the dizzying array of cutlery at my place setting. I count fourteen knives, spoons and forks—wondering how I can sneak some away in my pocket—when the dining steward ushers another man to my table.

Major Archibald Butt? I remember him!

This man made an impression on me as a wee lad. I must have been about ten years old when I saw his picture in a book about the *Titanic* and—after first giggling myself purple over the ridiculousness of his last name—the truth is, I sort of fell in love with him. In the pure and charming way of a ten-year-old. I'd look at that handsome face, feeling strange feels, exponentially magnified by the knowledge that this young and attractive man died before his time.

I quickly stand up as the steward leaves and my brain stutters. He's an indelible image from my childhood, yet now he's right in front of me, eyes and face smiling, reaching his hand out.

I'm in shock.

"I'm . . . I'm Mark Baldwin. From San Francisco." I feel relief I'm able to stammer it out at all.

"Archibald Butt. Pleasure's all mine, Mr. Baldwin." He has a high yet resonant voice.

We shake hands firmly and both sit. His hand is warm and soft. I struggle to regain my composure.

Stealing another quick glance at the man: Archibald Butt isn't the looming rugged warrior I'd always imagined. I almost laugh; I'd built him up as a towering figure, astride a cavalry horse brandishing a sword. Instead, he isn't any bigger than I am. He's got strawberry blond hair, parted in the middle and slicked back on either side, like a kid in *Our Gang*. It borders on the ridiculous. His round, babyish face is punctuated by a darling blondish-red moustache and deeply dimpled chin. His ears sit rather low on his head; his bright green eyes are set rather close together, and curve down at the outside—but they arch up over his nose, giving him an alert, quizzical look.

It's just this side of freaking adorable.

He's younger than me. That, too, is a strange sensation. He's only about forty-five.

He settles himself down, scooches his chair in, splays his napkin on his lap, and takes a casual, frowning look at the dinner menu. He's dressed exceedingly well in a pinstripe mohair suit, smelling vaguely of ambergris, slate and cigars.

I don't want to be too chatty, but I'll be damned if we're just going to sit here in stony silence. I take a deep breath, purposefully slowing my pace and mannerisms down, trying to act casual.

"How are you finding the *Titanic*?" I ask as casually as I can.

"Oh, it's splendid," he responds in a distracted way, still studying his menu. "I have a rather odd stateroom, but it's perfectly adequate."

He doesn't look up. I'm noticing a bit of Southern twang. Although he speaks in an economical, officious way, it is tempered by an apparent Georgia accent.

"I, for one, am delighted to be here." I say taking another sip of water. He looks up from his menu and our eyes meet and I feel myself blushing. He's got a frank look, like he's staring me down. Sizing me up. He is a powerful man. I doubt he fears much in this world, he has that way about him.

"What had you in England?" he asks, his earlier detachment slightly in abeyance. He seems marginally more interested now.

But I must lie again. "I was doing some work in London for my father. We're in the lumber business."

"I see," he says. "What sort of work in London?"

Uh . . . *really*?

He's looking at me directly, his manner crisp and efficient; he's something big in the U.S. Government, and here I am, just a gushing queen, lying my ass off.

"We're looking to export California redwood. We've found some demand for it in England right now, as it's such an unusual wood."

Whew. It sounds plausible, even though it is complete and utter bullshit.

"I see. Well, I hope your trip was a successful one," he says, not dismissively, and it seems my answer satisfied him.

"It was, thank you."

"I would ordinarily endeavor to just have salad," he volunteers. "I'm so tired of rich food. It's all I eat. But perhaps not tonight. Not yet." He smiles, putting his menu down.

"What had you in Europe, Major?" I ask.

"I've been vacationing. President's orders," he says sheepishly. "Those around me ganged up and prevailed upon me to get some much-needed rest. We're looking at a rather busy year ahead, what with the election. I drive myself like a steam engine and feel tired all the time, I suppose it was starting to show. Several times I tried to cancel out of it, but the President finally put his foot down and growled at me to get out of his sight."

Ten million questions are forming in my head, but we're suddenly interrupted. People are still filing into the dining room and several of them stop by to shake Major Butt's hand; and by proxy, and somewhat reluctantly, me.

As if I weren't sufficiently gobsmacked thus far, suddenly I'm face to face with Benjamin Guggenheim, a major titan of 1912, and his female companion. She is introduced to me as Léontine Aubart. She's a knockout. Guggenheim is somewhat handsome, in a doughy kind of way. I shake their hands and don't even attempt small talk—my brain is fried, although my new dining companion seems quite off the cuff and makes droll pleasantries.

"Give my regards to the President," Guggenheim says. "Let him know the New York situation shouldn't be a bother to him any further now that Pinchot is out of the way."

"I will, sir. It's a pleasure to see you. Ma'am?"

They saunter to their table.

We sit and Archie very quietly volunteers that "Mrs. Guggenheim isn't here right now, but our dear Léontine is Benjamin's special traveling companion." He says it in such a way that I immediately catch his drift.

I try to formulate another angle of conversation with this man, but we're interrupted again. Aw, hell, who is it this time?

Only Colonel Jack: John Jacob Astor the Fourth—arguably the richest man in the world—and his wife, Madeleine. Again we stand. Again Archie introduces me. I keep my mouth shut, shake hands, but smile lamely. Astor also tenders his greetings to the President of the United States by way of my new tablemate.

We're barely seated once more when the Slocombes stop by. I proudly introduce them to the Major. The Slocombes are being escorted to some far-off table and yet Major Butt greets them warmly.

I'm certainly getting tired of standing up, shaking hands and sitting down again, having been introduced to a couple called the Wideners, an exceedingly well-off couple from Philadelphia, just opening the highly anticipated Ritz Hotel there.

Even Margaret Brown saunters over and greets Archie as if he's an old friend. Margaret Brown sizes me up frankly. She's middle-aged, perhaps just this side of portly, talks out the side of her mouth, and seems to be a real kick in the pants.

I was in her house once, in Denver, in 2004. It's a museum now.

By the time traffic settles back down I think we've stood and greeted no less than six times. It is frankly obnoxious.

"You know all these people?" I ask.

"More to the point, they know me. I've been dreading this crossing for weeks. Everyone on this ship will do their damnedest to pump me for dirt, get some shred of inside information from me, and try to guess my take on the goings on. I'm just not up to it in general."

"Ah. Then I promise to find you insufferably dull."

His eyes dart up to mine to see if I'm being serious, and of course I'm not. A mere cloud of fuss passes over his countenance, but then he beams into the smile I had been hoping for.

"Thank you. It would be a relief."

"Further, if you need me to run interference, just gimme the word. I'll bore 'em to death so you can run the other way."

He chuckles.

I ask, "Where in Europe were you?"

"Primarily Rome, visiting friends. I was in no mind to do any actual sight-seeing. It was gratifying to stay in one place, no frantic schedules, nothing to do with yet another blasted train ride to nowhere. The Mediterranean climate is quite restorative. So different from Washington, which, even in April, can still be icy and unforgiving."

"Ah. I hear Italy's a wonderful place."

"Despite my best efforts at relaxation, I did make a swing through to our embassies in Berlin and Paris before meeting up with my brother in London. That part was best, getting to see family again."

A roar of laughter erupts from the guests at the Captain's Table, distracting us for a moment. "Actually, I can't wait to see Captain Smith," I say homosexually.

"That'll have to wait, I'm afraid. Captains on English ships never dine with passengers the first night at sea. Old tradition, I suppose, to make it look like he's terribly clever and important.

Or more to the point, so he can drink like a sailor and not be found out."

Damn. This is my only night here, an opportunity lost. Still, I did get to see Captain Smith with my own eyes earlier on the bridge wing. I'll have to call it good.

Meanwhile, it's apparent that no one else is going to be assigned to our table. It's just a childhood hero and me.

A white-jacketed English steward takes our orders. The Major selects escargots, turtle soup, roast pork and a beet salad. I'd like to order the same, but I can't handle snails—they're just slugs with real estate—and I have a pet turtle at home. So I order pâté fois gras, tomato soup, roast pork, and beet salad.

"Would you care to share a bottle of wine?" I ask, still unable to believe this is all happening.

"Excellent idea. We'll have the '98 Margaux," he tells the steward off-handedly.

"You're a Major; obviously that denotes military, and successfully so."

"Ah, well. Rank is no guarantee of success, or even of common sense. I was U.S. Army from 1900 to 1908, it's very much a part of who I am. Oh. By the way: while my full name may be Major Archibald Willingham DeGraffenreid Clarendon Butt, everyone calls me Archie. I hope you will, too."

I practically melt. All Southern twang 'n shit . . .

"Thank you. Please, call me Mark. Your last name—it's perhaps a bit unusual."

"Ah, yes. Don't for one moment suppose it's easy growing up with the last name 'Butt.' I learned early to fight. Don't like to, but kids'd call after me and mock me. Come to find out, a 'butt' is a unit of measure: some number of 'hogsheads,' all equaling an ungodly quantity of wine. So I carry the mantle with pride, and do my best to drink like a Butt."

Seriously, how charming could this man be?

As if to punctuate his statement, the steward appears with

the wine just then, makes a show of uncorking the bottle and pouring a taste for the Major. He pronounces it good, and our glasses are filled.

"Cheers." We toast each other. The wine is silky, smoky, and dank. It totally works.

"So I take it you live right in D.C.?"

"Yes. I just moved into a lovely home on G Street. Only a few blocks from the White House, which is perfectly convenient. Where do you live in San Francisco?" he asks.

"I'm at the far end of Market Street in a neighborhood called Eureka Valley. Have you been to San Francisco?"

"Many times, yes. But usually only in passing. I haven't been there since the fire; I rather don't want to see it. I'm afraid I'll find it bland and hastily uninspired."

"Ah, well, on that score, you needn't worry. I can safely state that they've done a bang-up job rebuilding. Some character was lost, of course, but San Franciscans are, frankly, rather vain about their city. It's not so slap-dash as it could have been."

Our first course arrives, and we start eating. I can smell the garlic from Major Butt's snails, but I'm glad I'm not eating them. My pâté is delicious, crusty little bits of bread and a tiny silver knife like I am born to this.

"Were you there?" He's taking an interest. "For the earthquake and fire?"

"Hoh, yes. It was quite something; the quakes first, then multiple fires, all over town. It was a day of chaos, very painful to observe."

"Well I'm glad you made it out in one piece. Meanwhile, here's to San Francisco." He hoists his glass of wine and we clink them together once more.

Still fishing for things to say, despite having to lie in general, I decide to speak an emotional truth to this man. "I have a tendency toward overthink. As I looked at the devastation in San Francisco, it really took me by surprise." I guess I'm talking nervously now, prattling on. "What constitutes a city? I've been thinking about that a lot. We tend to think of a city as its famous buildings. Well, now we know those buildings can be taken away in an instant. So that, clearly, isn't it. A city is something more. I'm impressed by what I can only assume is human spirit; the willingness to overcome. Someday I aim to figure it out for myself."

He's looking at me funny, with his mouth open. I guess that was an overshare. I really am nervous talking to him.

"I must admit," he says slowly, "that's a fascinating observation."

I'm elated. I feel a surge of pride that I can hold his attention; that I can impart, to an historical figure, direct, personal experience of another historical event... *because I was there.*

I add: "In practical terms, the amount of loss in San Francisco immediately after the fire was staggering to the imagination. I couldn't get past the sheer volume of rubble that had to be cleared. And the logistics of keeping people fed and sheltered until help could arrive."

"Ah. That's my bailiwick!" He smiles.

"Hmm?"

"I'm in the Quartermaster Service for the Army. That sort of thing is what I do. Organization, supplies . . . or did do, until I fell into this sort of half-life where I am now."

"Where exactly are you now? Is it all right if I ask that much?"

"President's personal aide," he says lightly, finishing his chewing and dabbing his wee moustache with his napkin. "Originally to Theodore Roosevelt for the last ten months of his term, but I stayed on with Will Taft. Not where I saw myself being, but thus I am ensconced, and have a ringside seat to some pretty serious goings on in the capital."

"While not wanting to fall into the camp of 'pumping you for dirt,' I'd love to hear about it."

He smiles. Fortunately. I don't seem to be boring him. Yet.

"Well, the long and short of it is, I handle the President's schedule, organize official meetings, White House dinners and guests. Change clothes five and six times a day. Silently observe all functions. I spend half my life worrying about seating arrangements and the other half keeping the house staff from bothering Mrs. Taft. I'm part bulldog. I must fend off everyone, from ambassadors, rapacious society women and the press, to unwanted Democrats.

"I will say that working for President Taft is a different animal to that of his predecessor. My ten months with Roosevelt were a complete whirlwind . . . but then again, I was so new that everything took me by surprise. But I was thoroughly bonded with the Roosevelts in a way that remains with me to this day."

Our soup course is expertly swooped in before us, and I grab what I hope is the appropriate spoon.

"Roosevelt put me in charge of his horses. Do you share my passion for horse flesh?"

"Horse flesh? You mean like . . . food?"

Archie blanches. "Good god, no! Riding! Whatever is the matter with you?"

I feel my face turn red. "Ah. Sorry. I don't think I've ever heard that term before. I quite like horses, yes, but have only gone riding a few times. Enough to not fall off, at least. Managed a full gallop once and am proud to say I didn't lose my hat."

I decide not to mention how a poorly trained rental horse had completely bolted on me. I lost my Starbucks thermos and, when I finally got the beast to a halt, I jumped off and threw a complete hissy and walked the rest of the way. Now is not the time.

"Roosevelt didn't have a motor car, state or otherwise, but Taft prefers automobiles. He's the first president to have one—

but I'm honored that I'm still able to keep my gelding Larry at the White House stables. I can visit him when I want and take him riding when I find the time."

"So, you're, like, actually in the White House?"

"Well that's where they put my desk, so I'd look rather foolish if I've gotten it wrong all these years. Rarely in before seven a.m. but often until after midnight most days."

"Ah," I reply. "Well, that's all well and good, but I can ride my local streetcar without paying because I know the conductor. I bet we're very much alike, you and I."

I cower for a moment, wondering after his response.

He laughs, heartily. "Mark," he says, "you've got to slow yourself down, or you'll wear yourself out like me."

Archie kind of turns pink when he laughs, and looks at me with appreciation and amusement, like he's wondering where the hell I come from.

The wine is hitting me. I feel the slight motion of the ship, feel the whooshing and knocking of the engines. I look around at the shiny white enamel paint on the ceiling. White linens. It's nighttime beyond the opaque windows of the Dining Saloon, and the surprisingly bland overhead lighting gives the place a soft, cozy feel. The diners are hushed, yet some raucous laughter suddenly erupts from the captain's table again.

I seem to be "in." Archie's talking to me. I'm getting him to laugh. A warmth spreads in my belly, the rare kind when you feel connected.

I quickly struggle to remember any bits of history from this era, of the Taft presidency, and the only thing that comes to mind is a vague rumor that the 350-pound president got stuck in a bathtub once.

"Is he a good man, Taft?" I decide it's safe to venture.

"Oh, yes!" Archie answers it emphatically. He clearly means it.

"He is the kindest, calmest, most deliberate, level-headed

decision-maker I've ever encountered. No detail will escape his attention. On the whole, I'd say he's done more against the trusts even than Roosevelt. And that's saying something. And as of yesterday, Taft has over 500 delegates for the convention. He's clearly the front runner on the Republican ticket.

"But, as you well know, now we have Theodore Roosevelt back, stirring up trouble. He wants a shot at a third term. Both men would be excellent presidents. I can say this with absolute clarity, having worked closely with both. And both men have reached out to me for support."

For the first time I see the light in Archie's eyes fade. He looks suddenly wan and tired, unfocused, just barely, around the edges. If Archie worked for—and clearly admires—both men, it must be a source of difficulty for him.

I just know that both men will lose to Democrat Woodrow Wilson.

And that Archie Butt will die in four days.

I refill the Major's wine glass and he smiles at me. Some of the glow is back, but it's clearly troubled. I don't want my childhood hero to be troubled.

Our main course comes. Roast pork, potatoes and blanched carrots. Without even asking, I signal to the waiter for a second bottle of wine.

"So that's why everyone wants my opinion, my take, any inside information on the whole thing, and it's not in my manner to divulge. I'm sorry, Mark. It's rude of me to bore you with my personal woes."

"Archie, I find it keenly interesting. My regret is, I have nothing interesting to tell you. It won't be long before you figure out how frightfully dull I actually am."

He smiles kindly. "Don't say that. The fact that you aren't motivated by anything is, I find, quite refreshing. It's good to be with a normal person—if you'll permit me to call you 'normal,' and not see it as an insult. I have so little time to spend with my friends anymore, people who want nothing from me other than for me to be myself. It's the most distressing aspect of my job."

He's openly sharing himself with me, and it's amazing. But I can't reciprocate. Virtually anything I say would be a complete fabrication. I don't want to be that person, so I'm thoroughly stuck. I literally don't know what to say.

Worse, by saying nothing, he'll eventually think I'm either stuck up or a crashing bore.

I suspect Archie is one of those people whose personalities is so huge, so all-encompassing, he won't particularly notice how silent I might be by comparison. One such person can fill a room and expound upon their life and everybody wins. Politicians, teachers, actors; they're always on. But I've got to find a way to keep him engaged.

"What made you decide to go into the military?"

"I come from a long line of Butts." He must always use that joke, and yet I smile and suppress a titter. "My grandfather was a soldier in the American Revolution, my uncle in the War of 1812, and another uncle was a General for the CSA. It's in the Butt blood. I had to.

"It was the outbreak of the Spanish-American War that did it for me. I felt an overwhelming duty to serve my country, and to honor my family heritage."

"Did you ever wind up in danger?" I ask.

He smiles. "Rarely. Of course, the Spanish-American war was over in a mere three months. I didn't even have the chance to join the fight in Cuba. So I began in the Philippines. I was there four years. Quartermaster and animal husbandry. That's where I first met Will Taft—he was Governor General in Manila—and that's also when I came to the attention of Theodore Roosevelt."

"What was it like over there?"

"Hot! Fully one-third of our forces were stricken with

malaria. Quite a culture shock, but after four years, I knew it like the back of my own hand."

"Did you manage to escape and have any fun? Get to know the country?"

"Oh, yes. I was secretary for the Army & Navy Club, and we started a fraternal organization, The Military Order of the Carabao. Any excuse to drink gin and tonics. The quinine helps stave off malaria, so we were simply doing a public good. And we'd take grand hikes, bushwhacking through the jungles and visiting all the points of interest. It's a fascinating land when you stop and take the time to drink it all in."

"Someday I hope to see it. I've long wanted to visit Corregidor." *Oops*. That only became important (or even recognized) because of World War II.

I'm delighted that Archie changes the subject.

"You married?" he suddenly asks, focusing on his pork tenderloin and seemingly quite nonchalant.

"Never had the honor, I'm afraid. Just a San Francisco bachelor."

"Neither have I. I've been a D.C. bachelor for so long I figure I should just remain that way. At least until the end of the chapter."

We smile.

Considerable debate exists as to the orientation of one Archibald Butt, as I recall. Archie never married. Lived with a man, an older artist named Frank, and they were famous for throwing amazing parties together. Society women certainly wanted a piece of him, it was well established and clearly warranted. But none caught him.

As he sits before me, the question is far from settled. Ordinarily, my gaydar is pretty good, but there's no such thing as being "out" in 1912—or of even being gay. Not as we understand it nowadays. And the fact that Archibald Butt is a military man and high-ranking member of the President's staff would mean today's equivalent of the highest possible security clearance.

If he has a deep, dark secret, I'll never know it.

So I just decide to drink him in and take him at face value. There's obviously a lot to this man.

Since Theodore Roosevelt is the better-known president to me, I decide to stick to talking about him. "I must admit I've always admired Roosevelt. Not just his policies but as a person, he seems highly engaging."

Read: major stud.

"Theodore Roosevelt is an intense, vibrant man. His mind and body are in constant motion. Mark, it's hard to even keep up with him. His brain causes words to tumble out of him in a cascade. He stuttered as a youth . . . "

Archie laughs out loud for a moment.

"At first, in the presence of my new boss, who happened to be the President of the United States, I could only stand there slack-jawed, unable to comprehend the wall of ideas bursting from him. But I eventually got used to his rhythm, and eventually savored the wisdom he always had to hand.

Colonel Roosevelt—post presidency he prefers to be called "Colonel," I think because he harkens back to his Cuban campaign with such fondness—has come to like me because I seem able to keep up with him: hiking, tennis, swimming in the Potomac. I felt honored each step of the way. He'd telephone me at home to come play tennis at the drop of a hat, rain or shine. We always played doubles, usually with the secretary of state, various senators, or members of the Supreme Court. The whole group eventually became known as the 'Tennis Club.' I'm sure you've heard about it in the press. Major policy decisions—along with no small amount of Washington, D.C. gossip —happened during those games. Fortunately, I was able to keep up, and to listen intently to the goings on.

"But I'd also grown very close to Mrs. Roosevelt and her

daughter Ethyl, before they left in '09," Archie relates, working his meat with his knife and fork.

He's talking full steam in between bites and I'm so fascinated I almost forget to eat.

"While I was still living on I Street, the First Lady would bake mince pies for me. So by way of thanks, I invited her and Ethyl to lunch. It never occurred to me that the president would feel slighted at not being invited as well. He never lunched away from the White House, a fact well known to me, since I'm the one who arranges his schedule in the first place.

"He pronounced that he would come to my house for lunch, too."

I'm impressed. "To your house? The sitting president?"

"None other. My first battle was with my own embarrassment at the blunder. Of course he was more than welcome . . . but suddenly a simple luncheon with lady friends evolved into a full-blown circus. I have no staff. I was on my own, cooking for the President of the United States. Police detectives swarmed all over my house, trampling in the yard, and suddenly all my neighbors were lined up in the street craning to get an eyeful."

"I'd be a wreck. What did you serve?"

"Just pork chops and rice. It was a good lunch, if I may say so. Everyone had a pleasant time. The President stayed over two hours, gazing through my bookcase and making conversation. He only left when I was forced to remind him that he had an appointment with the German Ambassador back at the White House."

Wow. Well, I saw Lady Gaga on a plane once.

"Mrs. Roosevelt was quite taken with my pointer, Duke—and rightly so! He's a good dog. But Duke only speaks Spanish, you see, a hangover from my time in Manila and Havana; yet she took great pride in learning commands and Duke would fall all over himself to please her."

Archie is lit up. He's reminiscing with such fondness, and divulging some mind-blowing information, I'm completely rapt.

"Do you have animals?" he's gracious enough to ask me.

"I do. I have an unfortunately neurotic housecat named Rhoda, and for the past twenty-five years I've been proud steward to an aquatic turtle named Fluffy."

Archie laughs heartily. "How on Earth could a turtle be called 'Fluffy?'"

"Right? Now you know."

He looks tickled. He's looking at me again like he finds me curious, that perhaps I'm far enough outside the box to be an amusement to him. I really hope this is true.

Dessert comes; hot apple pie with ice cream. And brandy.

People are already beginning to file out of the dining saloon, looking as crisp and pompous as ever, yet particularly well-fed.

"Help me count," Archie murmurs, leaning in with a whisper.

"Count what?"

"Women who still wear high collars," he chuckles. "Honestly, they haven't been the style for the better part of a decade, but nevertheless . . . "

He falls silent and straightens in his seat, grinning, as Jake and Letitia Slocombe saunter past, nodding and waving. And although I hadn't picked up on it before, Letitia does, in fact, have a dress with a foreboding, high collar.

"One." He says simply, taking a sip of water. I snicker.

With dinner finished, I figure I'm just going to slink back under my rock again, join the ladies for after-dinner coffee in the next room, but instead he asks: "Would you care to accompany me to the Smoke Room?"

"Certainly!" I respond. I'm beyond delighted.

"We can usually get a round of poker going." His voice

drops to a conspiratorial whisper and he leans more closely to me over the table: "I like nothing more than fleecing these so-called 'Captains of Industry.' They think they rule the world, but they can't hold their liquor."

I laugh. We stand and waddle out, stuffed to the gunnels with fine rich food, and head to the stairs.

We climb the grand staircase three stories up to A Deck and the first-class Smoking Saloon, which is one of the more elegant rooms on the ship: dark woodwork, deep green walls, stained glass windows and a fireplace crackling warmly. It's hard to imagine we're on a ship at all.

I'm dying to get to know more of this man, but it seems I'm going to have to share him in the Smoking Saloon. I'm ready to pout about it until I see with whom.

John Jacob Astor. Even though I'd just met him in passing at dinner, I'm nevertheless faced with sitting at a poker table with him and another man. I'm introduced to Jacques Futrelle, a friend of "J.J." from Boston. He's kinda got a beefy look to him with a tussle of thick dark hair.

Archie ties it all together neatly. He introduces me to Mr. Futrelle first, we shake, and Archie lets loose with the fact that Jacques is a journalist, and in fact, he's got a popular detective book series. "And J.J. here wrote a most remarkable book a few years back. *A Journey in Other Worlds*, life on Earth in the year 2000, have I got it right, J.J.?"

"Indeed you do. That's why I keep you around, Archie. You're among the privileged few who've actually read it. I value that in a man."

I know J.J. Astor is one of the richest men in the world, but I didn't know he was so derpy looking. Hawkish features on his young face. Sharp nose, which, when viewed from the side, causes his face to form a distinct triangle, jutting out. He looks like a cartoon. Of course he's impeccably dressed, suit of the day, buttons and studs, and a flower in his lapel.

Yet I can't help remembering, once reading that his mother, the venerable "Mrs. Astor" of New York, was so staunch and so high up the ass-crack of New York's Society of 400 that she would quite literally refuse to speak to anyone not of her class. Particularly those trailer-trash Vanderbilts.

And yet her son seems to deem it possible that I may converse with him.

As such, I volunteer to say, "Mr. Astor, your books sounds fascinating. I'd love to read what life could be like in the year 2000."

He smiles, modestly. "I'm sure it's out of print now, but essentially I pictured a world with a global telephone network, solar power, and life on other worlds. I spared no expense at poking fun at world hegemony and a Europe felled by socialism.

"Heavens. We're all writers," says Jacques Futrelle. "Archie here is also the consummate newspaperman."

"Don't rub it in, J.J.," Archie pleads in mock hurt. He turns to me. "Before the Army, I started out as a correspondent. Still get the opportunity to file a story or two, but not nearly as often as I'd like."

We sit, yet don't immediately break out the deck of cards waiting on our table; politesse evidently calls for genial chat before the business of playing. We are at a table near the fireplace, and a steward takes our orders. I don't care if it's girlie, I'm in it for some Grand Marnier. It's deftly served in a fierce, crystal, stemmed glass.

I light my pipe, my companions—can't call them my contemporaries—each fire up cigars.

"What sort of business you in, Mr. Baldwin?" J.J. asks of me. Can I call him J.J.? I seriously doubt it.

"Lumber. Not much to talk about there; after some years I've come to the realization that invoices may not be quite so interesting after all."

Fortunately, I get a chuckle out of J.J. for that. He says, "Manhattan real estate is also a bit of a bore as well. It would be a damn-sight easier if we could just fell some of those clumsy old buildings as readily as we could trees."

Astor then seems to angle in on Archie for inside dirt on the Taft Administration and upcoming election. When Archie becomes vague, Astor doubles down and asks after some appropriations bill in the Congress and, as you'd expect, Archie doesn't bite. But Astor's cool. He's a master capitalist and, most assuredly, a greedy bastard. Yet, to have achieved his station in life, he's obviously imbued with infinite finesse.

"By the way, the Colonel sends his regards," J.J. purrs confidently. "I know he counts you among his most stalwart supporters." He's obviously goading Archie and it has a profound effect. Archie looks almost stricken for a moment, as his face does that thing again.

But Archie recovers quickly. "Astor . . . *Astor* . . . let's see now —is that with one 'S' or two?"

My eyes dart up in alarm. But J.J. merely giggles fondly, as if it's an old joke between them.

"Meanwhile I hear you're playing quite a lot of poker with Mr. Taft," he chides Archie.

"Mostly bridge, every evening. But we've been known to sneak out past the secret service to get a poker game going down to Senator Crane's place in Dupont Circle. Half the fun is eluding the security detail. Our dear Mr. Taft in no way possesses a poker face. Any time he has a good hand he simply cannot stifle his glee. It's devilishly hard for us to not just mercilessly clean him out. Mrs. Taft hates that he dares play for money, so we hide it in the scullery budget lest she get wind of it."

Jacques Futrelle asks Archie if he isn't, by chance, from Georgia?

"I most assuredly am. Augusta. Are you a Georgian as well?"

"Indeed. But, like so many of us, in order to make my way in my field, I migrated to New York and eventually Boston. Followed the scent of money. But home will always be the South."

"That's certainly true, isn't it?" Archie replies with a near wistful look upon his countenance.

The men casually banter political conversation back and forth, on topics I don't understand, yet a certain "reciprocity" seems to play a frustrating political role in Taft's legacy, along with electoral delegate counts and the brash behavior of the Colonel, Theodore Roosevelt. Among his many talents, the man seems to delight in grabbing an incredible amount of public bandwidth.

But it's time to play cards. The first few hands are played amid light conversation and with low antes; they are obviously just a warm-up.

Conversation quickly falls to the wayside and serious playing begins.

My poker skills are moderate at best, but I have plenty of cash and we each ante a guinea. I keep my bets modest, and strike out most times but at one point I have three aces and am faced off with J.J. Astor. I call his £3 and raise him another three. He calls my three and raises me another three. I'm looking into his eyes, trying to gauge if he's bluffing. But all I see are the steely eyes of a business tycoon and, although he seems to be enjoying himself, he lets nothing show.

He wouldn't, would he? He's used to dealing with hundreds of millions without breaking a sweat.

I call him at £9. A huge sum of money. He was bluffing after all; he only has a pair of kings. I excitedly pocket my winnings and keep playing with my remaining cash.

Whew. Let's not do that again, shall we?

Archie and J. J. Astor, in between hands, crack inside jokes about the military, the insanity of military command, the numb-headed plodding way of going about things. They speak of people I obviously don't know and engage in manly gossip. "General Bell talks so much that he gets on peoples' nerves. He always seems to be talking for the benefit of someone in the adjoining room." And on some other major politician: "One of his mental legs is shorter than the other, so any time he tries to make a point, he invariably circles right back around to it, time and time again."

We play for about an hour and a half. I keep the rest of my bids ridiculously low. The gentlemen of the table seem to have enough tact to realize I'm not imbued with great wealth, and thus take it easy on me out of kindness. The brandy and Grand Marnier are flowing freely. I've lost track of how much I've had, but on top of the wine, I can tell I'm pretty well squiffed.

All the while, the three men are amiable and kind and are treating me as an equal. It's totally blowing my mind.

After more hands than I can possibly count, Archie says he's had enough and that he's going for a stroll on the Boat Deck. He asks me if I wouldn't mind taking a walk with him. I'm more than happy to, and surprised he didn't ask J.J. Maybe they're not *that* close? More likely it would somehow be socially inappropriate.

We take our leave of Messrs. Astor and Futrelle, shaking hands, and they both say they hope to see me again, which, even though I know they're just being polite, feels like a great honor.

I figured I'd be completely alone on this ship and instead, I've landed on a social gold mine. I'm frankly over the moon about it.

Up the grand staircase to the next deck, across the parquet to small doors, pointed aft against the wind and in my drunken state I realize I'm just following Archie like he's the Pied Piper. I'm completely mesmerized by him.

It's cool and damp out, a shock after the warmth of the Smoking Saloon. But it feels good.

On the broad, impressive boat deck, one's attention is immediately brought to the four brilliantly lit stacks soaring to the night sky. They're held in place by thick metal cables all around, the cables anchored to the deck in odd places, slanting up. The passage of wind causes each cable to hum, softly. I observe one man walk too close to one and get his hat knocked soundly off, his head most likely scraped.

The ship is aglow with incandescent bulbs, spotlights aimed up at the stacks. And yet, if I look out to sea, there's nothing to focus upon. It is a wall of blackness. Archie and I approach the rail and look down, seeing the waves and slip-stream bubbling past, lit by so many portholes, the ship gliding strong and imperious over the shiny sea with a hiss.

Being on any ship is grand, epic, heady, and exciting. That this particular one happens to be the RMS *Titanic* has me giddy with awe.

Seriously wondering what we'll talk about. And why he's choosing to hang with me. But I accept it. Own it. Still drunk; that'll help.

"When we get to New York, I guess you'll just take a train down to Washington, DC?"

"Yep."

"Cool. What did you do in Rome?" I ask.

"Very little, by design. My only official duty was to deliver a letter to the Vatican from the President. It wasn't to be an official visit, as obviously that would have various constituents in a fine feathered fluff. But I was all uniformed up and escorted through several impossibly lush apartments and left my missive with a functionary in a silly hat. It was . . . interesting."

"And your brother? Where in London is he?"

"Bloomsbury, by the British Museum. He also has a house in Maidstone. Do you like England?"

"I have a love-hate relationship with it," I decide it's safe to say. "I stayed there for a full summer a few years ago. The people can be cranky at first, until you get to know them. Then they're simply wonderful. The weather is horrible, and the food . . .

"Do you know the old observation—I don't know who made it up," (or if it would even apply in 1912) "that 'Heaven is where the government is English, the cooks are French, the police are German, and the lovers are Italian. And hell is where the cooks are English, the police are French, the lovers are German, and the government is Italian.'"

Archie chuckles genuinely; I can't believe he's never heard it before. If he has, he's being polite.

"As you heard me say, I'm from Georgia. Have you been?"

"Sadly, I haven't seen much of the South. At least not yet. I hear it's charming and the people are kind."

"Oh, they are! It's hard to describe, but being from the South means something to a man. It sticks with you."

"So you grew up in Georgia in . . . the 1870s? Did you just play in the dirt with the chickens or what?"

He laughs. "Pretty much. We certainly were poor enough. I can eat dirt with the best of them. Georgia dirt is delectable, savory; bar none the finest dirt on Earth. Good for your bowels." We laugh.

He continues, "We didn't have much in the way of means when I grew up, so it was a stroke of great fortune that I could go to college in Tennessee. My mother worked as librarian while I was there. Many good times, and friends long held."

Meanwhile I grew up in the 1970s, with *The Partridge Family* and fish sticks and a Ford Country Squire station wagon, so once again I'm stuck in the quandary of having nothing to share with him. I can't even say I'm from Seattle; hell, I don't think there were but five hundred settlers in Seattle back in the 1870s. So I have to steer clear.

I despise the tissue of lies I must spin for this man.

But he freely continues; not seeming to wish to build himself, but because he apparently finds it important that I know: "I started out in journalism, wrote for several newspapers. I correspond constantly with my sister-in-law Clara. If I didn't have the chance to compose my thoughts on paper on a regular basis, I think that I would go quite mad. Yet one of the few things I don't like about my current position is that it doesn't lend itself to any substantive writing."

"I actually worked at a local magazine in San Francisco for a time," I decide to venture.

And this much is true. Most of this, to Archie, I cannot accurately say, but it gives me an edge, something honest I can share (at least in edited form) with this man.

"Excellent. What did you do there?"

"I mostly paid the bills and swept the floors, but eventually moved up into writing book reviews and did a general interest column towards the end. The enterprise folded, as so many do."

"What was the magazine's focus?"

Bearded men with their penises out.

"General San Francisco lifestyle and culture—long before the fires, of course."

"Ah. It's an amazing feeling, seeing something you've written in print, isn't it?" Archie asks, warmly.

"Yes! I'd go to a book shop and pick up a copy of the magazine just to read my own words in print. Even found a mistake or two, or saw something I wish I'd worded differently, but enjoyed the feeling. I'd love to make the jump into writing novels—actually it is my ultimate dream—but it seems too hard for me yet. Just haven't gotten the knack of plots and characters."

"Well, by all means, stick to it. It comes easier with practice. It helps to have a world of real-life experiences under your belt as well, so don't be surprised if it all starts to come to you, even in later years. I wrote a short novel myself once."

"What's it called?"

"*Both Sides of the Shield*. I'm told there are still a few copies to be found. On a free afternoon I stopped by the Washington Public Library and, much as yourself, found my book on the shelf. It had even been checked out by a person. Once. They apparently returned it on time; other than that I have no idea if they ever actually read the damned thing." He smiles, a disarming, enchanting grin.

"There doesn't seem to be much you haven't done in life," I venture.

"On the whole, I'd have to say I've been extraordinarily blessed with good fortune, from eating Georgia dirt to White House dinners of state. And I can play all the golf I want. President Taft insists." He smiles.

He's looking at me in an amused way. He's intrigued. By what, I cannot say. I suppose I must seem different to him, and while we can all agree that's certainly the case, he has no idea by how much.

"I can't figure out why you're not married," I say. "You're an . . . agreeable sort of man."

He smiles again, and looks down. If he's blushing, A) I can't see in the gloom; and B) I seriously doubt that he is.

"It's never too late."

"I can see you now," I decide to tease him a little. "With some blushing nineteen-year-old named Prudence, who curtseys and does needlepoint."

"Hah! I'd need a more vibrant female in my life than that, I think. She'd have to be educated and willing to stand her ground. But if she can bake mince pies, I won't be opposed to an occasional . . . curtsey . . . now and again." He wiggles his eyebrows in a lascivious fashion, and I'm suddenly seeing lewd variations on a standard curtsey move through his head.

Nasty fothermucker.

We're facing each other, looking into each other's eyes and none of the tension I felt before in the dining saloon is here now. He's a real person. Archie. And for reasons unknown, despite my cloak of mystery, he seems to like me.

Yet since nothing's liable to happen here, like . . . ever, I break the mood and wander down the rail a bit, to take a picture of Archibald Butt on the deck of the *Titanic*. He's turned to the side again, leaning against the rail, staring into the inky blackness.

One thing I've always adored about iPhones is their uncanny facility for taking exceptional, low-light pictures. Archie's just looking off to sea in a dreamy way and I've captured it for myself.

I walk back, phone slithered silently into my front pocket.

We're face to face at the rail again. A few others stroll the decks, almost to a body wearing dark cloaks and hats against the night sea air, and just we smile at each other. I take the time to learn his face a bit more, still unaccustomed to seeing it in color and in 3D.

I'm going to be heartbroken to leave him tomorrow to his fate. But I don't want to push, overstep, or be a bore. I feel I should extricate.

I tell him, "I'll be at the breakfast table, tomorrow at 8:00 a.m.; it will be nice to see you."

"Excellent plan." He hesitates, wobbly a little bit—we've both had an awful lot to drink— and says, "Good night, Mr. Baldwin," and staggers off alone toward the door back inside.

I stand alone for quite a while, wondering what just happened.

Did I just dismiss him? And did he obediently comply?

Still soaking up the ship in all its glory, in the cool wind, I look up at the brightly lit funnels, hear the sea whooshing in complaint as *Titanic* forces herself through it, kicking up spray. I feel the slight dip in the deck as she crests a small wave.

After a while, I reluctantly go back to my cabin and snap on the light—someone had switched it off.

The mystery is solved when I see that my bed's been turned down, and laying atop the pillow is an ornate, freshly printed *Titanic Passenger List*. I page through it and, with a small start, see my name duly typed among all the others. And I realize, with a clench in my stomach, that I am thus now installed in the history books.

I probably wasn't supposed to do that.

Well. I take off those dank clothes I've been wearing all day and go to bed, my head spinning from all the Grand Marnier, spinning from my interactions with Archie. I take out my £9 won from John Jacob frikkin' *Astor* and place it on the desk.

I set my phone alarm. I don't want to miss breakfast.

38

Thursday, April 11, 1912

Sencha, my favorite alarm, wakes me up at 7:30. Uuugghh. I'm hungover. Again. My mouth is dry, but I grab my phone in the darkness of my cabin and look at my picture of Archie leaning with his arms against the rail and wish I could send it to Dropbox right now. I'm going to have a print made and frame it on my wall at home, that's what I'm going do. I'd almost tattoo it to my chest if I could.

It is pitch black in my cabin, lit only by the screen of my phone, so I switch on the brass lamp over my bed.

I have to put that damned suit back on. Nothing for it. I make my way down the corridor to the Gents', splashing warm water on my face. There is but one communal towel hung on the rod, eww, so I leave with water dripping from my beard.

Titanic is now sailing to the northwest, from the coast of France to the edge of Ireland for her final stop.

I don't have a lot of time left aboard, but I can already tell I wish to selfishly spend each moment I can with Archie, drawing him out, experiencing him, memorizing him.

At the table I order a good English breakfast of ham and eggs with baked beans and tomato and start on my bitter coffee.

History does not know this, but the coffee on the *Titanic* sucked.

Archie comes walking in but stops for a brief discussion with the dining steward. Then he comes my way and looms over the table in a pinstriped men's suit, a long narrow jacket and funny collar that's just a skinny slit at the throat with a vibrantly colored red necktie.

He's got bags under his eyes; he looks like he had a rough night. But he's here.

He looks shy. A little unsure of himself, which only makes him cuter.

"Good morning, Mark," he says, and even though it's silly, I stand and shake his hand.

We sit down.

"Did you sleep well?" I ask.

"Eventually," he replies. "I had rather a bit too much to drink last night."

"Me, too. Still, I wouldn't change anything."

He looks me in the eye. "Nor would I."

Archie orders eggs, kippers, toast and coffee.

"Why are you wearing the same clothes?" he asks me.

"This is all I have," I answer. "I didn't have time to bring anything else. I was in a hurry to sail on *Titanic*."

I go on: "The sad truth is I'm getting off at Queenstown this afternoon."

"No . . . "

"Yes. I got a telegram last night from my father. It seems I overlooked something important in London and he's demanding that I go back and put it right. If I muck it up, I'll never hear the end of it."

Archie actually looks a little disappointed.

"So the fact of the matter is," I continue, "I won't be making this crossing after all. I'll have to head home on a later ship."

"Well, damn," Archie says, plinking his coffee cup down onto its saucer firmly. "What time do we leave Queenstown?"

"One-thirty," I reply.

"That's a pity," he says, and seems to mean it.

"What is there to do between now and lunch?" I ask.

"I could always stay in my cabin and work," Archie says, "but that wouldn't be very stimulating. And I'm meant to be resting from work. How would you feel about a game of squash? It's the best cure for a hangover."

"I've never played it before. You'd have to teach me," I respond.

"I can do that. I used to be a squash instructor in earlier days."

I've never liked sports of any kind; I'm going to have to really fake it here. I'm sure the man will run circles around me and I shall embarrass myself greatly. I halfheartedly go to the gym back home, so I doubt I'm in appreciably solid cardio condition. But I'll be damned if I won't at least try.

Our food comes; we partake.

Archie looks up and says, "I've become aware that I've been blathering on about myself this entire time, which is flagrantly rude, and not socially acceptable in the least. Tell me about yourself." It's like a command, but a pleasant one. "What do you want out of life?"

"Well, the first thing I want out of life is to get out from under my father."

Lying again . . .

"It's not that he's bad; it's just that he's no bleedin' good."

Archie laughs. "Ah. I think P. G. Wodehouse said that."

And we laugh yet again.

"Is he insufferable?" Archie asks.

"Damned near. Nothing's ever good enough. I suspect he feels slighted that he was never able to become a magnate in the lumber industry. We have a few solid clients, a few solid foresters to keep us in good supply . . . "

Lie upon lie upon lie.

"But he's without humor, and I seem to be a perennial disappointment to him."

"I hear most fathers are like that. I take it your offices are in San Francisco?"

"Yes, in the South of Market area. I like living in the city, but it's expensive, and the weather's always cold. I look over to the East Bay simmering in the afternoon sun, while San Francisco is shivering under fog, and long for warmer climes. Yet living out that way would be dull, and I'd be at the mercy of ferry boats every day just getting myself to work."

"What would you do if you weren't working for your father?"

"As I mentioned last night, I really wish I could write. And we all know what an absolute gold mine that is," I say with a smile. Which Archie returns.

"I majored in economics," I decide to tell him. "But that seems to make the universe think I should either become a professor, or only just be some sort of bookkeeper, as I am now. There's got to be more."

"Have you considered going back to school? I hear Stanford is superlative."

"I'd love to. Wouldn't know what in. Is there a master's program for drinking scotch?"

Archie laughs. "There sure ought to be. In any case, you're clearly a bright man, I can see that your mind is constantly in motion. I hope you find ways to harness that."

Yes, my mind is constantly in motion. To most people that just makes me seem weird and evasive. I'm delighted that Archie seems to see past this. I find myself relaxing even more.

Our breakfast is over, and the stewards seem to swoop and clear as if they're in a hurry to see us gone.

"Well," Archie states, "we should see about getting some squash in. If we can find the damned courts on this boat."

"I think they're down forward, on F-Deck."

"On what?"

"F-Deck."

He glares at me in mock indignation, his arched brow ever more pronounced. "F-Deck you too, sir," he says.

It's just silly enough to be funny.

We head down to find the squash courts—turns out they're one floor down, on G-Deck—only to be told there's a wait. We can have a slot at 10 a.m.

We take one of the three elevator cages up to A-Deck and scope out some deck chairs on the port side, where the daylight is.

The term "posh" is actually an anagram for the English concept of fine sailing: Port Out, Starboard Home, to catch any available sunshine while at sea. And we make use of it. The sun is out between fluffy clouds and, although quite bracing, we're protected from the wind by a run of windows. We sit and digest breakfast and wait for our slot. A deck steward immediately shows up with his hand out; Archie produces eight shillings for the both of us, the steward writes our names on little cards, inserts them in a brass holder aback our headrests and these deck chairs are now ours.

They will be ours *forever*.

Without prompting, Archie tells me more of himself. Difficult to explain, but I really get the impression that he's more intent that I should know him, as opposed to merely showing off.

"I'd volunteered as a lieutenant in the Army, and, with the Spanish-American War being just mopped up, it was decided

I'd be stationed in the Philippines where fighting was still going strong.

"They assigned me to a certain ship through the Suez, but I was anxious to get there, to get in the fight. I found I could arrive much faster through San Francisco, but that meant I'd be taking charge of over 550 horses and mules. I'm well versed in animal husbandry, so I leapt at the chance, and I'm glad I did.

"I was supposed to lay the creatures over in Honolulu. The practice at the time was to never attempt to take horses on long sea voyages without resting them somewhere along the way. Which, as you can instantly see, constitutes both a delay and a significant expense. The more I learned of the proposed conditions in Honolulu—they were going to charge an arm and a leg for it, and sources told me that the facilities were seriously below par—the more it seemed to me that, with certain modifications, it was perfectly acceptable to plow straight through.

"So I made the decision to sail the animals straight to Manila without stopping, against policy and against established procedure. Could have been court-martialed for it. But I landed them in Manila a week early, without losing a single animal.

"Wow," I quietly reply.

"I was quite relieved," says Archie. "And straight-through sailing has since become a standard practice."

"How long were you in the Philippines?"

He continues: "Four years. They took me from volunteer to a commissioned officer within a year—with back pay, which was damned white of them. While I was there, I wrote several papers on animal husbandry in tropical climates. Some of the rules are different, but frankly most of it is simply common sense for someone who grew up in Georgia. Gets hot there in the summers as well. Some of my work was evidently appreciated by Theodore Roosevelt, given his extreme fondness for 'horse flesh . . . '" (he emphasizes the phrase with a knowing smile) "which is how I first came to his attention.

“A mere five months after William Taft was installed as Governor General of the Philippines, the guerrilla factions laid down their arms and made overtures of peace. The war was over.

“The people of the Philippines are a wonderful, passionate lot. They were treated poorly by the Spanish and saw us as simply yet another occupying force. Taft did an amazing job for the people there, helping to establish a constitution and a democratic form of government. He threw all his resources into education, made English the official language and it was all to the good. Which, yet again, proves what an upstanding man Will Taft is. Of course he has his detractors, those opposed to what they call Dollar Diplomacy.’

“I made fast friendships in Manila that I maintain to this day.”

I’m checking Archie out again. Handsome suit, handsome self, natty, smart, shipshape. Flower in his buttonhole, which I don't know how he gets while at sea. I like how his moustache doesn’t go past the corners of his mouth, making it bristly and trim and very . . . controlled. Orderly. Prompt.

But despite that facial hair discipline, he lights up when he talks. I like listening. I’m hungry for his mind, his ideas, his thoughts. He’s a bit of an ubermensch, I realize just then. He’s been everywhere, he’s done everything and seems to have laughed the whole way. I still worry that I’m boring him to tears.

“You must find me incomparably dull,” I muse, looking off.

He thwacks my leg with the back of his knuckles. “Not at all. On the contrary, there’s something about you I find acceptable. And when that happens, I just follow my gut.”

He continues:

“Most people have an obvious angle, an agenda. They

openly try to get at the President's ear, through me. It becomes tiresome. Among your other charms, you don't do that. I suspect you're also someone who can instantly see through the dross straight away. People like you are rare, and valuable. Some of your disinterest may also derive from being a Westerner. You Californians don't seem even remotely interested in the goings-on of Washington. I find it refreshing and, frankly, rather charming.

"You'd be amazed at what we have to contend with. We get death threats almost daily; people sneaking onto the White House grounds . . . and the press! They never stop. They even try to write about me, a mere silent functionary. I sure wish they wouldn't. I was never in it for recognition or fame, I'd prefer they leave me out of it.

"Since I'm commonly seen merely as a gateway to presidential access, it leaves me feeling entirely disposable and without worth—if I let it. I have to really fight to keep it in perspective and to not take it personally."

"Wow, Archie, I can't picture you ever seeing yourself as a non-worthwhile person. You're quite the opposite."

I watch his face cautiously, as he could regard what I just said as an extremely poor manipulation, an unworthy attempt at flattery. In truth, I mean every word. And apparently it came through in my voice, because he accepts my praise with a terse nod and genuine smile.

This man is whipping up every one of my senses; visual, auditory—olfactory, from his cigars and slate-like *eau de cologne* —brain swirling with ideas and wonderment. And I've barely scratched the surface.

Oblivious to the emotional dishrag I'm becoming in his hands, Archie merely adds more words, paints more pictures.

"The White House is overrun with demands from various charities, fundraisers, donation drives. Some genuinely serve a decent purpose, but many are simply pious do-gooders using charity as a means of social or political recognition in plain sight.

"It was during one of these that gave me what, so far, is my favorite incident in all my years at the White House. It was back in the Roosevelt administration. A tea was being held on the White House lawn, a benefit charity for Fallen Women in Washington, DC.

"Which was fine, until . . . they kept falling down."

"Huh?"

"During the speeches. And in front of the grandstand, amid all that bunting, a woman would stand, and proceed to . . . fall down. Right on the grass. As a fallen woman, she would boldly, brazenly just . . . fall. Bloomers and hoops, legs in the air, she'd cry out: "Oh, no, for I have fallen!'

"First one did it, to disconcerted giggling among the spectators, then another one would do likewise. Suddenly we had a cavalcade of 'fallen women' rolling about the White House lawn, bemoaning their fate in society, legs kicking in the air.

"Poor Mrs. Roosevelt was apoplectic."

I'm openly grinning . . .

"The President, when he heard the commotion and saw what was happening from his office, was furious. He stomped out onto the lawn with his arms up, ready to inveigh upon the situation, but somehow, they got the better of him, and he finally found the humor in it. I'm not sure Mrs. Roosevelt ever recovered . . . but you may not be surprised to learn that particular event was never held again."

We laugh.

I'm not used to thinking people from the olden days as having a sense of humor, but this is friggin' hysterical. I grin for a good long while after that.

At the appointed time, we head back down to G-Deck, and prepare to commence our workout. It appears we just strip down and play in our woolen pants and undershirts.

In the two-story, white-painted room, odd that one feels sensorily deprived and alone on a ship crowded with people. Since it's never before been used, it's clean and free of scuff marks.

I don't know the first thing about squash. Archie has to teach me, and it's a challenge. He's a total jock, and I am not, so in addition to having to learn the game, I have my work cut out just to keep up with him.

The game is incredibly fast-paced, and we quickly work up a sweat, chasing and swatting that tiny ball back and forth. Occasionally the deck cants slightly beneath our feet. I worry about keeping my breakfast down. I'm not very good at the game, but Archie is kind and patient with me, gives me plenty of encouragement, teaches me to keep my eye on the ball. We do that for half an hour until our time slot is up. I'm glad it's over.

We go to the Turkish baths, just down the corridor a little way. That's £2 each. Steep! Archie pays, without so much as a mention. It's so beautiful inside. They have the cooling room, the uber-fancy Moorish one, then a temperate room which is also lush, a dry sauna and a steam room. At the dressing cubicles we're given shorts and a towel and of course I'm checking him out in his trunks. 'Bout like you'd expect. No rippling anything and pale skin. To him I must certainly seem the same. I catch him looking once or twice. We move from climate to climate, showering in between and talking about various, inconsequential things.

I have to leave soon, and I'm going to be damned sad to do so. What could I ask him? What could I tell him?

Then, freshly dressed, me in my increasingly un-fresh clothes, we head up to the smoking room for pipe (me) and cigar (Archie.)

We talk more about writing. He promises to take a look at my writing and gives me his business card.

I look at his address on the little card and feel it again in my belly, like a swift kick to the gut.

The main dining saloon won't finish serving lunch before I need to leave, so we go to the Café Parisien, with all that fake ivy, dripping from trellises, and wicker chairs.

From the Café, you can see out the large windows. Ireland is visible in the near distance as we make our way towards the harbor of Cobh. Seeing green land moving past *Titanic's* windows is odd. I realize I'm one of the few people on Earth who will ever enjoy the sight.

Lunch is beef tongue sandwiches. I wasn't sure I wanted the likes of that but find it's not bad. I pretend it to be a mere liverwurst. The Major orders us a bottle of champagne. Veuve Clicquot, one of the best. I'm glad. It means he's still willing to be himself with me.

It isn't long before he launches again: "Since I was in charge of the horses, Roosevelt wanted a new one. His old beloved favorite, Roswell, was getting long in the tooth. I searched high and low, and finally picked out a suitable horse in Philadelphia. Had it brought by train to the Capital. I felt I'd done my level best, rode it myself several times, and thought I'd found the perfect mount.

"The very first time the President took him out riding, the horse reared up and dumped the Colonel, ass-over-teakettle, right into Rock Creek. I watched in horror, certain I was going to lose my job on the spot. I was still brand new then, it was one of my original tasks, and I was stricken with the knowledge that I had failed spectacularly.

"But, as always in the face of a setback, Roosevelt was in a good humor about it. He even laughed. He calmly walked over, clamped a soaking wet arm ostentatiously over my shoulders and calmly said, 'Try again, Archie.'

"I was eventually able to find another horse in Virginia soon thereafter and they've been inseparable ever since."

"I would have freaked," I say, and instantly realize he won't quite understand my use of the term. But he seems to.

I also wonder what they did with the ill-tempered horse. They're Republicans, so they probably just shot it.

"Although President Taft will still occasionally go riding, I can't help but remember what Mr. Roosevelt muttered to me about him: that Taft, attempting to ride, would be perilous to the nation and a damned cruelty to the horse."

He smiles when he says this. He downs his glass of Veuve.

I'm laughing out loud. A pinpoint of hot warmth that has been spreading in my belly, quickly flash-radiates outward, bending me into an entirely new emotional shape.

I adore this man.

And never have I ever been able to say that before. About anyone.

My mouth is hanging open, I guess, because Archie has a curious expression on his face as he addresses me kindly: "You're quite certain you have to leave us this afternoon?"

"Oh, I'm sure all right," I hear myself say. My ears are ringing.

The ship is slowing down, making its last stop. I only have a few minutes.

The champagne is hitting me hard. My head is spinning but in a nice way. In a way where everything sounds like a good idea and the world is rosy. I try not to think about what's going to happen. Maybe it won't? This ship is too real, too solid. It can't sink. It's too big for that. It has too much invested in it. It's no longer some vague abstract out of the mists of ancient time. I am within it, right now, drinking champagne. What's more, Archie is in it, and there will be no way for him to escape.

Seeing the *Titanic* is an absolute dream come true, an impossible magic gift given me by the universe and by David.

But finding Archie was a curveball I didn't see coming.

My god, the universe is a sick motherfucker.

I've waited forty-nine years to feel this way. Doesn't matter if he doesn't love me back—doesn't matter in the slightest. My triumph is centered on feeling love for the first time. It's right here in the pit of my belly and the palm of my hand. I'm looking out the window at Ireland and I am in love, a condition I dismissed years ago as a made-up piece of fluff designed to sell cosmetics and movies.

But here at the end, I find it. Of course it would come at the end. The end of my time with Archie, the end of this bottle of Veuve; the end of this too-new ship, and . . .

That's when the inevitable yang to my yin seizes me in its grasp. It comes at the end of Archie's life. And he has no idea.

It's time for me to go, to take my newfound secret feelings of love and run far away.

Mid-discovery, still cooing in my blanket of amorous warmth, I'm once again having to erect steel walls in my brain to keep away the horror and harm that shall be visited upon this wonderful man in a few days' time. I can't go there. I can't allow it inside my head. So while one part of me wants to soak up as much of him as I can these few remaining minutes, the other part wants to flee in terror. My emotional balance is going rapidly off-axis, and I can only down more champagne to quiet my nerves.

Suddenly, lunch is over. The champagne is gone.

Fortunately, Archie, who is aware of none of this, saves me with a kindly suggestion.

"Would you care to see my stateroom real quick before you leave?" His face is flushed, and I don't know if it's the champagne or not.

"I'd be happy to," I say, flooded with relief. "I need to stop by my cabin and collect a few belongings."

"Excellent. I'm in B-38, port side."

"Just give me two shakes."

So I leave first. Hurriedly, I go up the staircase and I say goodbye to A-15, taking more pictures even though I've taken the same ones before, twice already. Suddenly my mind sees my cabin flooded with icy green salt water with seaweed on my bed.

I finger the cloth again; it is dry and clean.

I'm at Archie's door a moment later. I haven't got much time, but I want this brief additional glimpse of the man, and I'm further delighted to see that Archie has procured another bottle of Veuve Clicquot and two glasses. He stands aside and I enter his domain.

He's right, his stateroom is a little unusual. It's an "L" shaped room; it wraps around cabin number B-40, with the porthole at the end of a long hallway, serving no apparent purpose other than to allow daylight inside. It is larger than A-15, and obviously more expensive since it has a porthole. The single bunk is high-up like mine, to the left, and a small sofa to the right. No bathroom either. We sit on the settee as the ship finally powers down completely and becomes silent. The sofa is a golden silk damask, smooth and cool under my fingertips; expensive and luscious.

Water absolutely ruins silk.

Archie kicks off his shoes and I smell the leather and maybe even a little whiff of his socks.

We have more champagne; I'm practically gulping mine down.

He toasts me. "It's been grand getting to know you, I hope you'll look me up if you're ever in Washington. You'd be welcome to stay, I've always got plenty of room."

I'm flushed and drunk, like it's not really happening, lazing there on the sofa, the cool silk of the fabric.

I've got to go, but my head is swimming and I'm on the couch with my boyhood hero and I decide to take a brief, stolen moment. I close my eyes. I listen to the sounds of the quiet ship, footfalls in the companionway. Archie's out. He's snoring softly, just next to me, and I listen to it: air, moving freely in and out of his lungs. It sounds warm and delicate.

I drowse, soaking up the sounds. I feel bliss. This moment in time, this snapshot of a world that does not yet know pain.

§

My body jerks at a heavy sound. Is it in my mind? A far off, baritone whistle, strong but muffled. Close and familiar, but certainly none of my concern . . .

I snap to.

Shit! What time is it?

I run over to the stateroom window, instantly calmed by the same view of the Irish countryside, the timeless buildings of Queenstown off to the left; green, everything green.

We haven't sailed yet.

Archie's awake now.

"Mark, you better twenty-three-skidoo if you want to get ashore!"

He's up, I'm up. We shake hands hastily, something I wish was protracted and pregnant, but it's not. I almost hug him, but that wouldn't do.

"I gotta go!" I bark, and Archie sees me to the door and says, "Good luck, look me up!"' and I tear off down the companionway in a very undignified fashion, almost knocking a woman in ruffles and flounce over, and she says something very unladylike in American English and I head for the stairs, my shoes sliding on that tile.

The B-Deck grand entrance doors are locked. Black.

Then I remember the entrance down on D-Deck. The one I used before? Hello? Duh. I tear down the forward staircase two floors, to that departure lobby and . . . those doors are closed, too. No one's there. I'm flummoxed and going into a panic. A steward is casually passing by, though, and I'm huffing and practically yelling, "How do I get off? I need to get off!"

"Aft, sir. Second Class gangway. E-Deck. If the boat hasn't yet shoved away."

Shit. I've got the whole length of the ship and down a deck to navigate and I don't even know how you do that right now. I tear towards the rear end of the ship, straight into the first-class Dining Saloon. That steward is calling something after me, but I can't hear. Whatever it is can't be important.

The dining saloon is still filled with luncheon people and here's me running like a madman, aft, only to come up dead against the kitchens. They span the entire width of the ship.

There's no way out.

"Oi. Can't go in there, sir." A steward has an enormous silver tray of salads hoisted at his shoulder.

"Fuck me. Where's E-Deck aft?" I'm imploring him.

"See here, mate! That sort of language is not . . . " He's boiling mad at my use of the word.

"Sir, please! I *have* to get ashore!"

He sucks in a calming breath, like he needs to count to ten before continuing. "Head forward to the stairs, go down one deck, then you'll find your way aft." He says it begrudgingly, still hefting his tray and looking about to lecture me on my language in the presence of ladies. But I'm already off, sprinting.

Back to the forward staircase, down to E-Deck, then it's a straight shot, two city blocks long, to the gangway at the aft staircase. I'm full-on running.

I come tearing into the foyer as the steel door is pulled to, blotting out the luscious daylight, feeling as if it's cutting off my air circulation. Huge steel rods are slammed home with finality and I'm still screaming along the deck.

"Hey!" I yell.

I come sliding up in my shoes to a stop and two White Star Line officers and several crewmen are standing there.

"I need to get off!"

"Oi, mate, don't we all," mutters one of the lackeys under his breath. The others cackle. An officer gives him a sharp look, but I'm beyond caring.

"No." I'm huffing, out of breath. "I got a cable . . . I have to get off the ship!"

"Caun't do that, sir," one of the officers goes, his arm out to block me.

"Please!" I'm sounding frantic and very, very gay.

"The tender is long away, sir. It's done."

I look at him, his smugness, his crisp officious bearing. I'm about to protest further but he deigns to add, "There's two thousand aboard want to get to New York on time, see? Now, go set about getting yourself a nice cuppa and be good about it, sir. We don't want any trouble."

I just stare at him, heaving for breath. His gaze is cold and bored. Unmovable.

I'm trapped. No way out. Next stop is New York, and they won't even get that part right.

The men are unconcerned and resume completing their tasks. I'm not even in their thoughts anymore as they turn their backs and busy themselves.

I take a moment, still gasping for air, standing there, wondering what my options are.

Apparently, I have none. As he said, "It's done."

I slink away, suddenly unable to bear the sight of those men.

Fear's quite squarely back. That new, rancid ooze begins to ferment in my belly once more. This time the fear takes an interesting twist: It turns into savage anger. I suddenly have a surging desire to slug someone in the gut. Further along the thought path comes the realization that the person I wish to slug . . . is me.

How could I have been so goddamned stupid?

Eventually I move away from the gangway doors, and up the grand elegant staircase. Instead of being pleasing and fancy and lovely, it looks wretched to me. Evil. I picture it warped, sagging, rotten, too abysmally deep for even the most blind and ugly deepwater fish to play about the filigree.

This very section of the ship, so beautifully wrought and lovingly turned, will slam into the seabed at over forty miles an hour, all banged up. In *Titanic's* final resting place, two and a half miles down, the water pressure is something like 6,500 pounds per square inch. Enough to compress a human body to the size of a most unhappy egg.

Told you. I've read about this my whole life.

All this beauty, all this finery . . . wrecked. All of *me*, not particularly possessing of beauty or finery but I, apparently, am to be dead. As this finery rots, so too shall my remains.

I might actually be dead soon.

My ears are ringing, my pulse hammering, bile rises in my throat and, for a moment, I'm back in an air raid shelter being smothered.

You still have cancer, too. Don't forget that, sweetie.

It deepens. Panic now comes. Unbidden, out of control, fear amplified into senseless terror.

I just start walking. I'm dimly aware that the engines have fired up, making their *pockitty pockitty* sound, powerful and strong, as if in a hurry to hie themselves to their eternal fate.

I simply walk around in circles. I seem to be in the second-class portion of the ship with literally nowhere to go. I'm spun up into a frenzy of unthinking, heart pounding panic, dimly aware that my fellow passengers are looking at me in keen discomfort. I must present the appearance of a mad man to them. It's certainly how I appear to myself.

Eventually, after an indeterminate amount of time, some of my basic senses reassert. I am breathing—if hyperventilating. I am walking. The ringing in my ears is less and I'm now consciously aware of my racing heartbeat.

Failing anything else to do, I make my way to the after deck in a complete daze. A crowd of third-class passengers is there. This is their territory, mostly Irish, standing in awed silence as their beloved homeland slides away forever over the horizon.

Many tears are shed by them. Mine own eyes are dry because I'm not entirely certain I have even so much as blinked in the past twenty minutes. A man playing some form of bagpipes honks out a dirge and people are openly weeping. I'm just numb with shock.

Always one to fuck things up, I've just fucked the most fucking fuck of my fucking life. Fear has been supplanted by the deepest self-loathing I have ever known.

How could I have been so stupid?

It must be well over an hour that I stand at that rail in the wind. Ireland has disappeared from view. It is only the sea and sky now. That's all we have left to us. I was blithely OK with it because I'd never seen them with my own eyes. It wasn't real, just a highly decorative abstraction.

I've been crassly zipping in and out of the misery of others like some mad tourist, dancing with disaster, feeling charming and dashing and being all "look at me, I'm Mister History over here . . . "

I suddenly feel like this whole time I've been the sort of person who would take selfies at a murder scene.

It just got real. *Titanic*'s death toll will be 1,503 souls. 1,504, if you include me. I'm on the guest list now.

I've come a hell of a long way just to find out that time is not a toy after all.

I'm frozen in shame and dread. But like all things emotional, you can't hold on to any one thing for too long, neither joy nor anguish. I cycle into some other state of agony, one that at least allows me to return to my thoughts and focus on the here and now once more.

Separate Your Hazards.

Because of my annoying, encyclopedic knowledge of this stupid ship, I know of a possible way off. One of the lifeboats, number seven, will be the first one launched and have only twenty-eight people in it, both men and women. It leaves before the urgency starts, when no one wants to get into the boats.

So far as I can tell right now, it may be my only chance. After that, like the man said, it's done. There will be no way off this ship.

Eventually I just slow-walk my shattered self back to my cabin. It's still mine, I paid full passage.

I lay on my bunk and stare at nothing. My heart continues to race.

Alternating between hope for that first lifeboat and utter horror that it's still all going to happen, that nearly two-thirds of these people are going to die, and all this will be smashed, I just untether my emotions and let them do what they're going to do. They're out of my hands.

Maybe this is why, in old movies, they'd often give a hysterical woman a hard slap across the face in an attempt to turn fear into anger. As I surf the deepest fears I've ever known, I suddenly wonder if maybe we should bring it back into immediate practice. I could use a good slap just now. To get outside of my own head.

I know far too much about this impending disaster than is strictly healthy for a normal person. It's not helping me right now. Unless it can? I *do* know all about it—I'm the only one here who does. Can I somehow stop it? Could I do that?

The collision with the iceberg comes down to three things: They don't see it in time, and then First Officer William Murdoch turns left and reverses the engines.

Sounds simple, but a huge number of variables come into play. Any slight change to that would have produced a different outcome. The whole thing almost never happened.

But it did happen. It's going to happen, this Sunday night. Could I stop these things? How could I be on the bridge barking orders? It just isn't possible.

Not even David could tell me what would happen if I messed up the timeline on such a huge scale. These people are *supposed* to die, as far as history is concerned. It's hardly my job to mess with the universe just to save my bony ass.

"These people" were just some vague thought up to this point. But now I've seen them. I've gone and fallen head over heels in love with one of them.

And he's still right here, alive, in his cabin and, if I'm any judge, drinking that exquisite Veuve Clicquot without me and that, at least, is something I can fix right now.

Within seconds I'm rapping on B-38 with my knuckles.

Archie opens the door and breaks into broad laughter.

"Oh, Mark!" He thinks it's funny.

I do not.

But there's plenty of champagne left for me. He invites me back inside warmly. He's still in stocking feet and now has his shirt sleeves rolled up.

"How much trouble will you be in with your father?" he asks, handing me a bubbling glass.

"A lot. This won't go over well. I'm not sure what excuse to give him," I manage to croak out in an uneven voice. I can't bring myself to look him in the eye.

"Cheer up, it's not that bad."

I down my glass of Veuve in one go. Archie invites me to sit once more on the settee.

"I'm sure the purser's office can give you timetables and get you back to London as soon as possible. Meanwhile you're just going to have to languish in utter luxury with the rest of us, waited on hand and foot for a few extra days. Men have endured far worse."

"I know you're right, but I might need to pout for a while."

"Fair enough. What did your father want you to do in London, anyway?"

Lie: "He needed some earnest money on a shipment; said they'd chisel out if they didn't have actual cash on the line."

"Well, that part, at least, is sound, sorry to say. You want to go back on deck? We might as well, right?"

"Sure. I could use the air."

I'm once again simply following Archie blindly.

Up on deck, a few tiny sun breaks are visible far off; so being out in our deck chairs is fine. We're offered wool tartan blankets that are heavy and soft, and cups of bouillon by the stewards.

Archie's right, I am in the lap of luxury. For now. I choose to let that much in. I'll have plenty of time to get my fuss on about my predicament in the coming days.

I need to distract myself. So I ask Archie to tell me about more of him. I know it'll help me focus. I ask, "Are your parents still with you?"

"Alas, no. My father died when I was fourteen, and I lost my mother three and a half years ago. We were awfully close, she and I."

"I'm so very sorry."

"Thank you. The loss of my mother was a shocking counterpoint to such a successful few years in Washington. It's been the hardest lesson of my life, moving on without her."

I ask, "Do you still talk to her?"

"What?"

"When everything's quiet. Do you still speak to her in your mind?"

He looks at me funny, almost blushing, but also in slight wonderment. "Yes. Yes, I must confess that I do."

"That's good. I think it's healthy."

"My brother's wife, Clara, and I correspond a great deal now; nearly every day. It in no way replaces the presence of my mother in my life, yet the act of composing words, and sending them to a cogent female relative seems to greatly help. I was never one to keep a journal. I find it pompous. But writing my trials and triumphs to a beloved family member serves me well."

"What was your mother's name?"

"Pamela. Boggs."

"Pamela!" I fairly bark, my face is probably lighting up like a dolt.

"Yes?"

"Oh, sorry, it's just that I recently got to know a wonderful woman by that name, on an earlier trip to London. Only for ten days but she was a pure delight. I'm so startled to hear your mother shares the name."

He breaks into a rather salacious grin. "Did you have an affair with her?"

My stomach sinks. I get confused. A douse of cold water pours over my fledgling hopes for Archie's orientation. But I quickly let it go. I'm not actually hoping for anything here, I just want him to be himself with me.

I take a deep breath and remind myself that straight men aren't so bad, once you get used to having them around.

"But lo; the opposite, if there can be such a thing. When I met her she was nine months pregnant. In fact, I was there for the birth of her baby girl."

"You're having me on."

"No, we were stuck . . . "—lie—" . . . our motor car broke down and she went into labor. It was only the two of us there."

"That's incredible."

"It was an amazing experience. I've been designated Auntie, and it is a mantle I shall bear with pride."

He laughs. Auntie is pretty gay and he doesn't seem fluffed by it.

"Losing your father at fourteen," I say. "That had to have been completely devastating."

"It was. It was quite sudden. We're a large family. I have two older and one younger brother, and a sister. So that's five of us."

"Wow. Big family."

"Georgia. What can I say? Anyway, my father apparently had a weakened heart that none of us suspected. It was sudden and it was . . . so utterly final. Our extended family swooped in to help my overwhelmed mother, but I must say with clarity that the woman stood up to the challenge and never wavered, no matter what agony she must have held in her own heart. She was strong. And determined.

"We had to move to a smaller house, saying goodbye to my childhood home and all its memories. As my older brothers came of age, they found work and sent money home to us, and my mother eventually became a librarian.

"It's a miracle that I was afforded a scholarship to attend college in Tennessee. And my mother, devoted as she was, moved with me and became staff librarian at the school during my time there. Ah, I can't tell you how grounding it is to be away at school and yet have your faithful loving mother always available to hand. She kept me reading, far beyond my normal coursework, and we'd share books and ideas till the wee hours of the morning."

"Sounds like a nice, safe space. Like going away to college without the drama of leaving home. It's like you lucked out."

"I think you're right. I was a vibrantly freckled redhead in those days, graced not only with the last name of 'Butt,' but also with my mommy in tow with me at school. As such my classmates attempted a regimen of extreme torment upon me. But as I had learned to fight early in life, I put an end to that in short order.

"I studied journalism, but my mother ardently wished that I'd go into the seminary."

"Seriously?"

"Oh, yes. I very nearly did. But I begged off from the idea, as journalism and a bourgeoning fascination with the military came to the fore. I eventually had to break it to my mother that my direction had changed. True to her nature, she took it stoically and vowed to love and support me on whichever path I chose.

"She was endlessly proud of me being at the White House. I wrote her every day. She, a diehard Southern Democrat, chided me for working for a passel of Republicans. But it was all in good fun.

"After I lost her in October of '08, I continued writing to Clara, and it's been a godsend for me. I must admit that I'm still writing to my mother as much as I am to Clara."

We sit in silence for a while, then he asks me, "Mark, what's your mother like?"

"Oh, she's wonderful. As you were with yours, she and I are close. She has little truck with my father, and I can't fault her for that. We can speak of things as adults and she's very smart. She got a university degree, knows politics, and is a Democrat too. As am I."

"If I were forced to choose," Archie says, "between being a Republican or Democrat, I'd have a hard time toeing the line. I was taught to distrust Republicans, but since Roosevelt and Taft are such fine upstanding men—truly, in their hearts—it has led me to believe they're perhaps not so bad as all that."

Just wait, pumpkin. Someday you'll know.

"By the way," Archie asks me, "what's your take on giving the women the right to vote?"

I practically gulp, realizing that Archie has never lived in a world where women can participate in their own democracy.

"It's so unthinkable to me that women shouldn't be allowed

to vote that I find it preposterous. Women absolutely deserve the right to vote."

Finally. I get to issue a true, declarative sentence to this man.

He nods in quick agreement. "At no point do I question the judgement and viability of the fairer sex. Women are fierce thinkers. But when you add the temperance issue . . . things tend to get murky, damned quick."

"What's the correlation?"

"Well, surely you're aware that it's not just your Southern Baptists crying for a prohibition on alcohol. The women of this country have long had a hand in wishing it were so as well. To be fair, I can't blame them . . . running a household and caring for children while their men get roaring drunk . . . spending all their money and becoming either useless, or absolute beasts at home. It's natural for women to wish that influence in their life minimized.

"So the prevailing belief is, the minute women get the right to vote, we're going to see prohibition on a national scale. Men are quaking in their boots. Vast is the number of establishment thinkers, high in the American political system, who become apoplectic and furious at the very idea of the suffragette movement."

This has never occurred to me before. And Archie's right: women voting and Prohibition do occur at almost the same time. But I'm pretty sure the Noble Experiment was passed a year or two before the first American woman could cast a ballot. I feel untethered at the idea of women being ineligible to vote simply because of their gender. It's mind-blowing and not OK.

Meanwhile, I find I'm alternating between fascination with Archie and overwhelming panic.

I can't spend every last second in existential horror. Human brains just don't go that way. Instead I phase in and out. I'll be listening to Archie and suddenly my eyes glaze over, and my stomach drops in my innards and I fugue out. So far, Archie hasn't noticed, but the swings are liable to become greater each time. I can only imagine I'll finally give over to complete, unbridled terror the closer we get to Sunday night.

Mostly I'm still here and present, and appreciating my companion. Archie'd brought a book with him, so he falls silent and reads in his chair.

I lean back and snooze in mine. Years of meditation help me disconnect my brain from the horror under the surface of my mind, and I float free under that luscious wool blanket. Archie's right; I am, for now, in the lap of luxury. I let go of the rumbling panic that seems to be squeezing my pancreas, and settle in for a snooze, hearing the whoosh of the sea and clunky shoes of fellow passengers ambling the soft wood deck, back and forth without end.

Later, we each take to our own cabins to "dress" for dinner. Which for me, obviously, means doing nothing at all. I must look positively skank.

§

We meet in the seating area outside the Dining Saloon and walk together into the restaurant, Archie stunningly turned out in yet another fresh suit and me in my raggedy-ass same clothes. I ask him if this bothers him and he says, "Hell, no, I still think it's hilarious!"

I wonder if he's worried about being seen too much with me, since all eyes seem to be on him at every step and he's got an image to uphold. People talk. The rich and powerful gossip just as much as everyone else.

After we're seated at our tiny table, Captain Edward "Ted" E.J. Smith enters the dining saloon in his dress whites, gleaming buttons and epaulets and marches straight to our table. I'm on my feet, instantly erect. Archie also stands but in a much more leisurely, confident way.

"Archie!" Captain Smith has his hand out. "Nice to have you back with us."

"Thank you, Captain. Delighted to be here. You should have seen that old Italian bucket I went over on. It was a disgrace. Oh, Captain, this is Mark Baldwin, from San Francisco. I've been boring him until his ears bleed. So much so, I fear he may require medical intervention long before we reach New York."

Captain Smith smiles.

I put out my hand and grasp the warm, meaty, scratchy hand of the captain of the *Titanic*. His eyes are gray-blue, sea-seasoned, craggy, with crow's feet. Hair and beard a snowy white, and rugged handsomeness just as I'd seen in pictures my whole life.

"Captain? Pleasure to be here."

"Glad to have you."

He turns to Archie. "I hope we'll get the chance to catch up." They both agree that they shall, and the Captain heads over to his table and awaiting guests.

"You know him?" I manage to stutter as we are once again seated.

"I've sailed with him a few times. On the *Baltic*. He's an enormously successful senior captain. He's happily ensconced with the privilege of launching each of the White Star Line's newest ships. Last year was the *Olympic*. Next year, he'll bring out the *Gigantic*."

"That's fascinating."

"These days, a sea captain is as much a social director as an established seaman. I'm sure he reads the passenger lists ahead of time, so he knows who to butter up. I try not to let it go to my head. Actually, I'll be dining at the Captain's Table tomorrow night. Would you care to accompany me?"

"I'd love to. But wouldn't that mean I'm displacing someone?"

"I'll speak to the purser. I'm sure arrangements can be made." Archie says it in a way that makes the issue seem settled and final.

Dinner is excellent. Lamb, rice, cold cucumber soup, Archie doesn't seem to be making good on his threat to stick to salads, and I'm glad. We have more of the '98 Margaux and I let him talk about his childhood.

"So why did your mother wish you to go to the seminary? What exactly would that have entailed?"

"Well, being Southern Protestants, it would have led my way either to the clergy or an academic position."

"Are you devout?"

"Yes. Quite."

"Oh."

"I take it you're not?" Archie asks.

"Like all humans, I crave a spiritual connection to the universe. There's definitely forces greater to us that are unseen. Do you believe in Karma?"

"I know of it, yes."

"While I don't believe in Karma per se I have decided to live my life as if it were completely true. I wish my interactions to be above reproach. Although I don't believe in sin, specifically, my personal Ten Commandments would begin with 'do no harm,' and to never undermine someone else trying to make their way in this world. That, to me is outright sin."

So is lying.

"But where does that leave you on the subject of Christianity?" he replies.

"Well," I gulp some wine. I don't want to piss him off, yet

this is one of the few times where he's getting genuine, unfiltered me.

"I've taken a good long look at Christianity, and to me it feels like a house where all the furniture is too small."

"Oh."

"Does that bother you?"

"A little."

"Sorry."

"Don't be! Heavens, if we all believed the same thing this world would be dull and overly sanctimonious. You asked if I'm devout. In most respects I am. But I'm not what you would call pious, and hope never to be."

He takes his own gulp of wine, as if to prove his point.

He's sexy. Looking at the man, I have absolutely no illusions that he's gotten his wick wet on more than one occasion out there, without the bounds of matrimony. And I respect him for that.

"I have a story," I begin.

And it'll be entirely true. I'll just have to factor for the time differential.

"A good friend of mine is a train driver for the London Underground. A few years back he had an incident that . . . well . . . it either proves there is a god or proves that there is not. I still can't decide."

"What happened?"

"He was driving Central Line stock, one of the newer trains, and he was pulling into Bank. That station is sharply curved; it forms a sort of arc, so the train cars are at odd angles when they are at rest against the platform, leaving gaps.

"As he was pulling into the station, he spotted something ahead on the tracks in the dark. The closer he got, he realized it was the form of a human body."

"Good lord," Archie mutters.

"Well, there's more. Half of it was on one side of the track, and the other half was . . . somewhat removed a small distance hence. He had mere seconds to choose to slam on the emergency brakes—which would guarantee many of his passengers would be injured. But, in those bare few seconds, he realized the damage had been done. The poor soul was already rent in two and there was nothing for it. So he brought the train to a normal stop, signaled the platform guard and they took the train out of service and cleared the station.

"The subsequent investigation revealed a mind-reeling set of factors.

"The dead man, in his apparent sixties, was so blind drunk at three o'clock on a Tuesday afternoon, that several passengers reported seeing him staggering and lurching around the platform. And that platform was curved, creating uneven edges when the trains parked. Also, the train ahead was one of the older Central Line stock. They're not even in service anymore. The spaces between the carriages, on that model of train, had no protective cladding on the outside, as opposed to the newer stock that do.

"So with just the right amount of gin, with a train old enough to matter and just the right bend in the platform, at that precise location and time should appear a man drunk enough to fall through the exposed opening to the tracks below.

"The train just ahead of my friends' was the one that did it. The man was beneath the undercarriage, hopefully passed out, and he was cloven in two by the metal wheels."

"My God," Archie says in a hushed way.

"When I think of all the factors that had to be present to create just this particular accident, in just this particular way, at just that particular time, it completely boggles my mind. The odds were astronomical. And yet it happened."

"Is your driver friend all right?"

"He seems to be. They gave him a day off. He knows he didn't cause the incident, he's merely the one who discovered it.

"But that's why I don't know if it proves there's a god—or proves there isn't. Things happen. They don't make sense. I guess it's all just to say . . . " and I suddenly feel horrible saying it to *this* man, in *this* dining room, on *this* ship, "when it's your time, it's your time. Game over.

"Which is why, although I'm prone to worrying and fussing over every little detail of my life, every inconvenience, it's all out of our hands anyway. We've been given the gift of living. I believe it is our responsibility to enjoy it. It's one of my hardest lessons so far."

And as soon as I say it, I wonder if I'm just full of shit and even capable of such lofty goals myself. I'm certainly on deck for it right now.

Archie speaks. "Well, for me that just dovetails into the belief that there *is* a god, one whose ways we've long accepted as mysterious. But I agree that we've been given the gift of life and we must cherish it, lest we actually offend the gift that God has allowed us to enjoy."

"Fair enough. Besides. My mantra has always been: you get back what you put forth into the universe—minus 40 percent for friction."

Archie laughs.

We clink wine glasses again in a toast.

"Wanna go gamble later?" He says it all cute.

"Ch-yeah!"

We still have a few morsels of dessert to get through. We're taking our time, despite the promise of cards when we're done.

As per usual, he's talking about work again. He's already expounding on current events, delegate counts, state dinners. The First Lady, Nellie Taft, is clearly very dear to him. She sounds like a sweet woman. Archie tells me how odd it is to see his longtime friend, William Howard Taft, that mountain of a man, suddenly in the Oval Office and in charge of all domain. How he's exactly the same man he always was, yet the strain on him is visible: the tightness of his jaw, shoulders up, economy of words. Oh, he'll always put on a brave face. But being bridled with such awesome responsibility changes a man. How could it not?

"I'm usually required to sit in on all but the most sensitive affairs of state. Ambassadorial visits, trade agreements, caucuses, Chinese legation, the Germans, the French, the Catholic Archdiocese . . . "

"Do you participate?"

"Heavens, no. I am to stand at erect attention in full uniform, even in the vicious heat of summer, and not make a sound. But I'm relied upon to help remember every nuance, every detail, to be discussed later. Both Roosevelt and Taft have frankly asked my opinion on very delicate matters of state. It's awe inspiring, and it's exhausting."

I look at him again. How cute he is, his little bit of red hair and dimpled chin and moustache and those green droopy eyes and quizzical brow. So much going on in that adorable head of his.

No wonder the icons and scions aboard ship want to pick his brains. He's in. He's the real thing.

"I'm blathering again. I apologize." He looks down and actually means what he says. He's embarrassed, like he's doing something wrong.

"Archie, let's have a minimum of pretending. Let's make like I'm not really from 1912 but some far-flung other place where people talk about their true feelings all the time—too much, in fact. I know little about people who don't air their laundry in public or speak personal feelings or complain or say what they really mean. Keeping it all inside, maintaining a stiff upper lip; propriety society and joculiety—Yes, I know that's not a word, but either way, let's not do that. You be you, and I'll be me."

"Good lord. You really are from California, aren't you?"

"Yes. Furthermore, I won't have the slightest idea how to act around all this, so apologies ahead of time if I stick my foot in it."

Without even meaning to, I put my hand out and upon his woolen jacketed arm and give him a squeeze. Back then, men could show affection a lot more than they could in later decades. But still, I don't want to scare him.

We've left the table and are making our way back up to A-Deck and the Smoke Room.

For the first time in my adult life, I'm not in it for the nookie. I'm not looking to get into the man's pants. It's uncharted territory for me, to be sure. I like him too much to try anything so stupid and vulgar. I want to catalogue him, learn all that is learnable, and to make him comfortable and happy. He's down to three days left in life. I want it to be as serene and wonderful as possible. If I can learn and remember him, then he won't be as dead as he otherwise would be. He can live within me. I'll make room for him in my head and carry him around in the twenty-first century. I'll speak to him in my mind and show him things. I'll know the sound of his voice and the dreams in his heart.

I am unused to this sensation. Wonderment offsetting utter terror—two polar opposites—are swirling in and out of my brain.

We're still making our way upstairs but walking close and talking quiet.

"Who are the biggest thorns in the President's side?" I ask.

"Elihu Root! And . . . " Archie leans in so close to my ear that I can feel his moustache tickle. He whispers very quietly, "Vice President Sherman. They are at complete odds." In a more conversational tone he continues, "And of course Pinchot and Ballinger. I interact with those men often. I realize they have their passions too, just different from mine, different from the president's. Do you think less of me when I say I think they're misguided?"

He's still going strong as we amble into the Smoking Room. We take a table for two and the steward brings me a Grand Marnier without even asking, which is quite nice.

Archie just keeps going. "White House dinners are huge affairs, and I'm in charge of the footmen, staff, butlers, president's secretary, Nellie's secretary, the White House chef. Seating arrangements! I was born to be in battle, now I'm saddled with prickly seating arrangements. No matter what we do, someone always manages to get offended. It's just a sad fact of life for me.

"We often have to usher up to 5,000 people through a receiving line with the President and First Lady. I must announce their names, which are first whispered to me, and by God, sometimes I just don't hear right. I mangled a Czech count and his wife's name so bad—if looks could kill!—but what a tortured language that is.

"We try to configure White House dinners at ten dollars a head, not counting wine. So budget becomes a major concern as well, as it all comes directly out of the president's salary. They have to be planned carefully . . . "

"Directly out of the *president's* salary?" I'm shocked.

"Certainly. You don't expect the taxpayers to foot the bill?"

"Yeah, I do . . . huh."

"All upkeep and maintenance of the White House must come from the President's own income, including the china. Some presidents barely scrape by."

We're at a quiet table for two, talking softly, yet people keep glancing our way, getting a glimpse of Archie.

But we're chummy already. He's opening up, layer after layer, like a quivering rosebud of information, and I am rabid for it.

"I have a good friend in Alice Longworth; she's Roosevelt's

eldest daughter. You've probably seen it in the newspapers how she brazenly insists on smoking cigarettes in public—it's completely scandalous. She utterly feeds on it. That's just how Alice is. She's brilliant, one of the smartest women I know, but has always been a complete rebel. Her father famously once said, 'I can tend to the running of the country or I can tend to the running of Alice. I cannot, however, do both.'

"We've had a running water fight for the better part of a year, Alice and I. I fear I started it.

"After work one night, in an insufferably crabby mood, I'd promised to stop by one of her parties. Normally they're quite gay, but I had a lot on my mind . . . Anyway, a particular gentleman, whom I shall not name, was haranguing me for being the 'president's pet' in front of everyone. I don't know what came over me but I lost my composure entirely. And proceeded to dump a full bottle of soda water over his head.

"Shut 'im right up, but I'd inadvertently given Alice a thorough soaking as well. She was seated on the divan just below, directly in the line of fire. She was half-livid, half-energized, in an almost frightening way—with that Rooseveltian glow in her eyes I know so well. She roared promises of revenge but was half laughing and the room as a whole erupted in laughter and the tension of the moment was fortunately reduced.

"Nevertheless, I went home quickly after that and was readying for bed upstairs but made sure all the doors and windows were locked. It wasn't long before I heard the unmistakable sounds of women's heels on the gravel in my garden. Alice and two of her man friends were skulking about the bushes in the dark with buckets of water, thinking I'd be so foolish as to leave my doors and windows open. I wasn't.

"I was still in a perfectly vile mood. I filled a mop bucket with tap water upstairs and calmly poured it down upon them.

"Mark, she howled in the darkness! She vowed ultimate revenge, and by God, she'll have it. Some day in my future, I must prepare to be thoroughly soaked through to the skin when I least expect it."

I smile wanly at the image.

After several conversations along similar veins, each tale alone would be a week's worth of material on *TMZ*, I ask Archie, rather anti-climactically, if he wants to see my stateroom. He says yes. Mine's not nearly as nice as his; it has no porthole, no little couch.

We go and simply hop up on the bed together.

We play with turning out the light, since the blackness is so complete. I reflect that the room should get used to being in the dark. It's going to spend a lot of time thus starting Monday morning.

Archie's sitting at the head of my bunk where the reading lamp is, and he begins to spin yet another tale.

"Things in the White House have taken a rather unusual turn of late," he begins. He's speaking softly.

"Yes?"

"I have wound up inextricably involved in the housekeeping staff. They come to me with their lives, their woes, their petty squabbles. I encouraged it. I will not have them bothering Mrs. Taft with their troubles, she takes everything so personally, has a heart of gold, and frankly, enough on her mind without having to worry about the running of the house as a whole. So they come to me. Well. We're having a rather unique problem on the upper floors.

"I will only tell this to you in the dark," he says, and I'm wondering WTF.

He switches off the lamp and we're in complete blackness.

"Everyone is convinced there is a ghost among us, haunting the White House. Three maids have had fainting fits in the past six months."

"Really?" My voice is quiet in the dark. I'm trying to decide if he's just playing a game with me.

"Yes. Several people, while alone on the upper floors, have reported a definite tapping sensation on their shoulders. Yet when they turn around, they're quite alone in the room."

Since I'm deprived of any visual cues on Archie's face, I must rely on his voice. And he seems to be speaking the honest truth.

"The most stalwart and unmovable of all is Mrs. Taft's personal maid, a Miss Marsh . . . hell, I don't even think I can recall her first name—I've got to overcome the fault of never remembering names unless I particularly like the owner—anyway, this Miss Marsh chidingly dismissed all of these tales as being perfectly ridiculous, until one day she rounded a corner and came upon a young boy. He was approximately fourteen years old with wildly disheveled blond hair, in an old blue sailor suit. As she stood there blinking, he shimmered and vanished. She fainted dead away."

"Whoa," I mutter softly. Being in the dark really helps move his narrative forward. I've got goosebumps.

"The staff have become so rattled that I finally brought it up with the President and he nearly bust a gut. He declared he won't have such a spectacle become known to the public. There'd be no end to it in the press."

"Do you personally believe it?" I ask, still trying to determine his level of sincerity.

"I'm not sure I disbelieve it. I'm working with people who experienced what they consider to be a definite, supernatural phenomenon, and they're refusing to go alone into the upper floors of the White House."

I think I know why Archie wanted the lights out. From what I know of the man he is not given to flights of fancy. Spectres and the supernatural don't mesh with the pragmatic Archie Butt I have come to know. But he's surrounded by people who do believe it, to the extent that it's interfering with his job. He has to be allowing it on some level, even if he doesn't understand it.

His voice is steady, calm, with a hint of exasperation. "There's a lot we don't know about the afterlife and the spirit world. But for heaven's sake we need calm in the house. I keep meaning to research the archives, to see if one such fourteen-year-old boy ever lived at—or died in—the White House. But I scarcely have the time.

"Do you believe in ghosts?" Archie asks me. I decide to be frank.

"I think I do. But I don't believe they're particularly strong. Spirits can be so alive as to leave traces of themselves behind. Like tendrils, caught in the fabric of time. Echoes. I believe in echoes but not much more than that. I've felt a few lingering presences that had me in goosebumps. Whatever it was, it was subtle, nuanced, and vague. It was never a threat, but seemed, for the most part, that it wanted simply to be felt by someone still alive, still tethered to the world.

"But, Archie, I also have to tell you: I attended the death of a few friends. My hand was actually on a friend's heart as it took its final beat."

This was Jeff, the guy who died of lymphoma after only three months, destroyed by chemo.

"And I've never seen nor felt anything so enchanting as a spirit leaving the body. They were simply alive one moment and gone the next. It was a biological event, nothing more. I try to carve out time to recall the people in my life who have died. Because ghosts or not, they are present when they are in our thoughts."

"That's a very kind thing to say, Mark," Archie says in a soft, reverent voice.

Suddenly the light snaps on and Archie's face is zooming right at me in a horrid, toothy grimace, his eyes wide, and he growls, "*Raaawr*!"

"*God*! Dammit! Jesus Christ, Archie . . . " I stammer, having half-slithered off the bunk.

He laughs first, and finally I do, too.

Archie goes on. "But the ghost in the White House is truly an issue right now. I was being genuine when I told you. It's a calamity. The staff are completely on edge. While I was at the Vatican, I should have asked their fee for an exorcism."

We both smile.

"Meanwhile, there's certainly not a lot to do around here," I say.

"Got that right. Five, six days, nothing will ever make it any shorter."

"We could have a séance, try to summon the White House ghost," I offer.

"I have a better idea." He hops down from the bunk in his natty suit and turns the light out once more.

Blackness. Complete.

"Very slowly, in your head, count out to twenty. And when you're done, see if you can figure out where I am."

Sounds silly. Maybe actually flat-out lame. But I figure to myself, these people have never had television or internet—only prior generations from which to learn ways of amusing themselves on their own. And I'm on their turf now.

I count to twenty, slowly.

Periodically I feel Archie brush past, trying to psyche me out. I try to catch his whiff of cigar long past, or the totty water of the day, but in the airless, stuffy vault of A-15 my sense of smell is not going to help.

He's silent, too. Maybe he learned it in the Army. I can't even hear him breathing.

I've finished my count. I am quite blind, even with eyes wide open. I reach out in your standard Frankenstein fashion and begin waving around, trying to find this decidedly odd man in the darkness.

He's not on the bunk, not by the door. I'm stumbling around, grinning despite how lame this would seem to people back home, and cover a good deal of my cabin, groping high and low, before my fingertips make contact with a man's heavily dressed belly next to the wardrobe.

The exhale from his nostrils, that almost-giggle sound, signals the end of his turn.

"Now, you go. I shall remain here and count twenty."

And thus I stash myself away, crouched next to the desk. He finds me within fifteen seconds.

We do it a few more times. It's somewhat amusing. But we finally put the light back on and sit on the bunk once more.

Conversation, for the first time since we met, seems to be on the wane.

But bless his heart, he seems reluctant to leave, to head back to his own stateroom alone. I cannot bring myself to make any kind of actual play on him—it wouldn't be right. Yet I don't know when I've ever liked someone more.

He finally takes his leave of me, lingering in my doorway.

"G'night, Mark."

And he's gone down the corridor and I shut my door, alone in this space that will soon rot in darkness.

39

Friday, April 12, 1912

We meet again at the breakfast table. He's already seated when I arrive, in yet another fresh suit, this one brown. I notice that when I see him, my innards perk up. My nervousness goes to the side.

We each order cereal and fruit and coffee.

"I really ought to make use of the gymnasium," he says. "I'm in poor fighting condition right now. Fortunately, Taft enjoys brisk walks, and I always accompany him, so that helps. And we play more golf than you can shake a stick at. I can always tell his frame of mind or what's bothering him by how he plays a round of golf. I have to work hard at not trouncing him, because if he catches me sloughing, he'll yell at me and throw his clubs."

"I'm not much in good shape, either, although walking San Francisco's hills is a pretty good workout."

"Do you golf?"

"Haven't yet. But I'm still young, right?"

"Right."

"So I figure I have plenty of time to pick it up in my golden years."

Archie says, "According to public opinion, I'm near death."

That gets my attention. I look up at him. "Huh?"

"President Taft tends to fall asleep in meetings, to the point he'll actually snuffle and snort. It's my job to nudge him awake, or to cough, loudly. The problem is, I cough so much that people openly speculate in the press that I'm a consumptive." He shrugs, like, what can ya do?

As we eat, Archie relates yet another tale about Theodore Roosevelt, one of going on a long hike in Rock Creek Park in Washington, DC, scaling cliffs and swimming, fully clothed, in the river on a hot, rainy day.

"The president dismissed the carriage and secret service detail, and we set out, just the two of us, climbing cliffs and swimming in the creek. At one point, he began climbing a cliff over the river and, of course, I had no choice but to follow, lest he think me a coward. Halfway up, the president got stuck, lost his grip, and plummeted straight down, back into the river with all his clothes on. He very nearly hit his head on an outcropping of rock, and would have, had he not had the good sense to push himself free of it on the way down. He came up laughing.

"He's always laughing. The more dangerous something is, the more hilarious he finds it. He made it up the cliff on the next try and sat waiting for me to follow.

"Mark, it was harrowing! I got stuck in the same place he did. I could move neither up nor down for the longest time, and I began to tremble, all over—I was frankly wobbling, and I thought my fingers would rip loose from their sockets. I was about to admit defeat when suddenly I saw a way up, possibly. It didn't look promising, but I had no choice. I managed to climb up and join him on top of the rock. He clapped me on the back.

"It was then that he told me the most profound of things. He said, 'Archie, I don't know what I would do if I didn't have you to play with. You do all I like to do, and yet your advice is always so clear and direct that sometimes I feel that I am imposing on you.'"

"Wow." I'm surprised and awed.

"If I die, I somehow wish at least that sentiment be known about me. I consider it my highest honor."

I let his words hang in the air for as long as they deserve. History should know this about Archie.

Eventually, though, I decide to ask Archie a question that's been on my mind: "What would the Washington establishment do if they wound up with a president who broke all the rules of propriety, openly did shady financial dealings, broke the constitution at every turn and destroyed all international agreements with punitive tariffs and out-and-out insults?"

"You're not suggesting either Taft, Roosevelt—or even Woodrow Wilson—would do such things?"

"No, it's just a hypothetical. Some day we might get a president who really is that bad. What should Washington do?"

"Well, I'm by no means a scholar of it—you should ask Henry Cabot Lodge. He'd know. If you come to Washington, I'll introduce you. But I'd think there would be enough systems in place to rein someone like that in, and quickly."

Archie is so adorable.

He asks me to tell him what happened the morning of the earthquake and fire in San Francisco, so I do. In every detail. He's rapt, and I feel glad that I can capture his attention with an actual tale, one that isn't another of my bullshit stories. I tell him freely of Ben Wade, and, while I don't include the naughty stuff, I leave him with the impression that manly camaraderie was shared. I even tell him about Iris in the Barbary Coast.

"I steered clear of 'The Coast' while I was there," Archie says. "They make it sound as if every individual to ever set foot in the place will be instantly robbed, beaten, drugged, shanghaied and murdered—without exception, to every last man, end of story."

"I've heard that too! I always thought, why would anyone go there? The stories, while essentially true in some form, must be overblown. If nothing else, it would be extremely bad for business."

Archie laughs.

"So yes, I have always avoided the place," I add. "But after the fires, they've really been clearing it out. It's becoming more of a tourist attraction now."

After breakfast, Archie finally does paperwork in his cabin and I have a bath slot at 10:30.

A male attendant fusses to make sure I have clean towels, and I enjoy the white clawfoot tub and warm water and filmy White Star Line bar of soap with a nice, lineny smell. I slosh the water around a bit, spilling some onto the deck to see where it goes. It runs down little holes around the outer edge of the floor.

Feeling fresh, I go down and see that the stories are true: There really was a coal fire aboard *Titanic*.

Long-held unproven rumors were that a fire had been burning in a starboard bunker since before *Titanic* left Southampton. I sneak in, through a door, and down a white-painted metal staircase, and find myself on "Scotland Road," the crew passage that runs the entire length of E-Deck. I'm certain to be chased out at any second, but I dog a hatch and just manage to see the evidence of a large fire: black streaks, ambient smoke, intense heat. I'm drinking in the scene with my eyes, almost ready to get my phone out for a picture, when I'm suddenly, and quite literally, scruffed at my collar by a delectably large seaman.

"Oi. Passengers aren't allowed 'ere!" he growls.

"Sorry, I was looking for the Turkish Baths," I stammer in a pathetic way. He's not even buying it. He gruffly points me to the staircase and tells me to keep moving forward.

So the long and short of it is, it's true. There apparently was a fire.

The problem is, the fire will have weakened the hull, right on the starboard side, exactly the part that gets sliced open in the collision. I mourn that, if I survive, I can't just call Robert Ballard or James Cameron and go, "Guys, guess *what*?"

I amble back up the companionway, musing on the So Very Many Things that go wrong in the sinking of the *Titanic*.

Just like my friend and his train horror: Things both simple and silly, major and catastrophic, will all converge in disaster.

The biggest problem is the most famous: The *Titanic* doesn't have enough lifeboats for everyone. They have as many as are required by present law but only enough to accommodate about half the humans aboard.

Upon sighting the iceberg, First Officer Murdoch turns the ship to the left and slams the engines in reverse. Well. *Titanic* has three propellers, a smaller one in the center, and two bigger ones to either side. The center engine doesn't go in reverse. Yet the center engine, paradoxically, controls the rudder—which also is found to be far too small for a ship this size. Bottom line is, when he slams the engines in reverse, he unwittingly robs *Titanic* of its ability to steer.

So there's that.

The rivets they used in building *Titanic* were perhaps industry standard but not nearly as tough as they could have been. When the ice cracks the side of the ship, already weakened by the coal fire, many rivets just pop out, leaving cleanly-sliced openings between hull plates.

The "unsinkable" nickname for the *Titanic* comes from the relatively recent invention of watertight compartments. Several could be flooded, and the ship would remain afloat. Great innovation, but here again, in the case of *Titanic*, poorly executed. They don't extend nearly high enough, and they aren't sealed at the top. Water will just flow from one compartment over to the next as the ship settles lower in the sea.

Ice warnings will not be flatly ignored—but neither will they be taken quite as seriously as they should.

The ship's binoculars, needed for the lookouts, happen at this very moment to be locked in a cabinet—and someone forgot to bring the key when we left Southampton.

On Sunday night, the sea will be shockingly calm: no waves at all, no moon. No way to see the iceberg until it is too late.

There is even the story, I don't know if it's true, of the sailor in charge of checking the ocean's temperature to look for the presence of ice. It's seriously low tech: You put a bucket on a rope and dunk it and take the water's temperature. Unfortunately, *Titanic* is so big that the rope isn't long enough to reach the ocean from the Boat Deck. So, rather than climbing to a lower deck, the guy reportedly just fills the bucket with the ship's tap water and logs its temperature for the report.

Titanic is doomed. Too many things go wrong all at once.

The disaster will shock the world almost to the degree of 9/11. It's a cold slap in the face to a civilization long complacent and proud of their technological superiority, confident that nature has successfully been dominated by Man. *Titanic* will become a vivid wake-up call. A glacial reminder that, in the end, nature bats last.

None of this will matter to me if I am to die. I cannot ignore the possibility, if I can't get a seat on that first lifeboat. Boat number seven is just outside the gymnasium on the starboard side of the Boat Deck. I go up and check. It's right there, looking like all the others, wrapped under tarps and ignored by all.

How am I going to do this?

I feel like a coward. It burns.

§

ARCHIE and I spend time reading together. *Titanic* has a decent book library. I stumble upon a copy of *Peter Pan*—it's right at about my level of concentration by this time. I spy a book called *The Ballad of the White House* and show it to Archie. He grimaces and says, "No thank you," and picks something entirely different.

We play squash again, Friday afternoon, and I'm getting a little bit better at it, but my lack of physical stamina frustrates me. I say as much to Archie.

His response is yet more encouragement and soothing words. He's as protective of my feelings as he is proficient in the game.

We're at sea. We don't have much to do. More sitting around and talking.

At our deck chairs, Archie tells me of his recently completed fifty-eight-day trip across America, stumping for and with William H. Taft for the 1912 election.

"We covered 15,000 miles by rail, spending forty-four nights on trains, traveling through twenty-eight states. Bad food, little sleep."

"Do you have your own rail cars?"

"Yes. Three. The president's personal car, and two others for staff. They're fairly well appointed, but they're always at the back of the train. Sometimes we were whipped around so badly on poorly worn freight track that one could practically get seasick. It's a major trick of logistics to find trains going where we want to go, so that we can latch onto them and keep to our schedule. I'm so glad such is not my responsibility. I think I'd have gone insane.

"The end result was speech after speech, in town after town, in halls, or simply off the back of the train. People surge, trying to grasp the president's hand, and when they can't reach him, they grasp mine instead. Hundreds—thousands—all day. All told, he spoke to approximately three million Americans.

"On more than a few occasions, people would openly yell, 'Hey, fatty!' at the president. He heard it. He'd put on a brave face, but I know it hurt him deeply. I can't believe Americans could grow so ill-mannered as that."

§

GETTING ready for dinner at the Captain's Table tonight, Archie dresses me up in his own, rich clothes. "I'm fond of dressing well," he says. "I have seven trunks with me in the hold; I asked for this to be brought out. I think it should cover our bases quite well."

He lets me paw through his stuff, and I'm like a girl squealing at a Barney's rummage sale. We're pretty much bang-on the same size.

The trunk, like the ones I saw at the hotel so many days ago, is epic: silk-lined, leather, drawers, fold out bits and wooden hangers, and everything smells of wool and cedar and heliotrope and . . . of Archie. You don't just wash wool, and he's been on the road for six weeks, so strictly speaking I'm in little gay heaven. He smells like skunk and cigars.

Mostly hidden behind the trunk, I strip to my altogether and select some beautiful pieces: striped, wool, gray gaberdine trousers, a white dress shirt, freshly laundered somewhere along the way, starched so well that it makes a rustling sound when I unfold it from the drawer.

He's having as much fun as I am, but he looks quizzically at my socks from Ross which need no garters, and which, unfortunately, are dirty enough that they're starting to develop the telltale Corn Nuts™ smell of too many days on repeat. He decides they simply won't do. He sits me down and takes them off me. On bended knee, he slides his garters up my legs. I feel his fingers on my bare skin, warm and rough, and I'm almost in danger of sprouting wood, but I manage to keep it parked. The leather of the garters feels cold and uncomfortable against my shins, and the socks he hooks onto the garters, although freshly laundered, feel scratchy and annoying.

He's about to offer me a pair of shoes, and that's when he notices that he's got seriously tiny feet compared to mine. It's comical. Or maybe a little embarrassing. He may or may not be aware of the relative coefficient on foot size.

He then proudly produces a pair of spats! I try to protest—it's just a bridge too far. But he insists. White cotton covers atop my shoes. They almost don't work, owing to the smallness of size, but he pronounces them viable, with tiny pearl buttons, which he takes upon himself to fasten for me, still on bended knee. The do serve in that they hide my shoes' many visible shortcomings.

Vest and coat, silk-lined, serious quality. Tie. Flower in buttonhole.

I'm in.

I'm totally going commando in another man's fatigues. I can feel my tackle resting on stitched seams, dangling loose in there.

Overall, the fit is just shy of amazing. All this stuff has been tailored and is exceedingly rich in quality. I feel awash in his smells.

Standing face to face, he examines me critically for a

moment, head cocked to one side, and suddenly tries to part my bristly short hair in the middle, like his. When it doesn't work, he licks out some spit on his thumbs and tries to go back in. I duck slightly and giggle and say, "Stop it." We both laugh.

At 7:00 p.m., Archie and I strike out from his cabin. I'm thinking I'm all that as I fairly swagger down the corridor, bursting with pride. We're surrounded by other well-dressed first-class passengers, graciously descending the grand staircase slowly, with pomp afforded to station, and for the first time I don't feel like I stick out like a sore thumb. Right now I look like I belong, and I like it.

We enter the Grand Dining Saloon to find E.J. Smith waiting at his table. I can't believe I'm so close to him. I shake his hand once more. He has spots on his hands, which feel rough and warm. Silvery white beard. I gaze into his droopy, icy eyes. He has a kind, ready smile.

Twelve people, including the captain, are to be seated at the table tonight. Me and Archie; the Astors; J. Bruce Ismay, Chairman and Managing Director of the White Star Line; Thomas Andrews, the man who actually designed and built *Titanic*; Doctor O'Loughlin, the ship's surgeon and apparent good friend of the captain; Isidor Straus, owner of Macy's department store, and his wife, Ida; and finally, a Mr. and Mrs. Charles Hays—it's mentioned that he heads a railroad in Ohio. His wife, Clara, is prim and has a small mouth.

The women are dressed to the nines. Flowing, floor-length gowns, shoulders under puffed tulle or otherwise daringly exposed, in what must be a newish and shocking style. The women of first class seem to have three general hairstyles: Modified Gibson Girl; bangs with long trailing hair, brushed to an elegant sheen; or curls, braids and ringlets, all trussed up with jewel-encrusted clasps.

Mrs. Straus' hair is of the long variety, proudly gray, as coloring it would be but a flashy and gauche fad.

I greet each in turn, having already met the Astors, yet J.J. shakes my hand enthusiastically and says "Say, if it isn't the man who stole £9 off me at a poker table. We'll have to have a rematch."

I beam with pride.

J. Bruce Ismay is handsome with a cute, bristly moustache. We exchange pleasantries, I tell him how happy I am to be aboard. We shake hands.

He will be saved the night of the disaster, amid deep scorn. People will call him a damned coward until the end of his days and as our eyes briefly meet, I wonder if I will I feel the same about myself. Anyway, I don't have much to say to dear Bruce, although he seems personable enough.

We take our seats.

I'm at the captain's left, and Archie is at the captain's right, across the table from me. That means Archie is the guest of honor and, in a shocking turn, that makes me the second-place guest of honor—and that bothers me a little. I wonder who I displaced? I feel bad about that . . . but wouldn't change it for the world.

Thomas Andrews is seated to my left. He's a kindly man, perhaps a bit nondescript. I struggle to sort out the reams of inquiries I'd make of him. He literally designed all we see around us. As such, sitting between him and Captain Smith, I'm like a puppy with two peters. I have so many questions!

The featured main course is to be chateaubriand, and nearly everyone at the table opts for it. Bottles of delicious red wine are strategically placed around us, and I, being me, immediately make use of one.

Archie clears his throat ostentatiously and catches my eye. He tugs at his tight shirt collar and nods his head slightly in the direction of Mrs. Hays. Casually, I glance over.

She's wearing a deliciously high collar. We snicker at each

other across the table and he flashes his fingers up in a vee. *Two.*

Captain E.J. Smith: Just sitting next to him is freaking me out. I sneak a few sidelong glances at the man. One thing he's got going is his gray beard is perfectly trimmed, but his moustache is longer, it fairly bursts from his face and swoops out to either side. I've always wanted to do my own that way, and here I am examining the possibility on E.J. Smith himself. Mostly, I recognize I can't get away with a moustache like that. I don't have the genetic predisposition.

Smith is chatting with Archie. They talk about some other journey they'd shared on a different White Star Line ship. But eventually, being polite, and the consummate host among his other attributes, E.J. Smith, Captain of the *Titanic*, turns his attention to me.

"How about you, Mr. Baldwin? What business are you in?"

I know he's not really interested, he's just being polite. So I politely issue my lumber declaration and then decide to help him out by turning the conversation towards something about which he may have a slight degree of interest: boats.

"You took the *Olympic* out, didn't you, sir?"

"Aye. It was to much fanfare. This is an entirely new class of ship. Sailed her several times, but since the bit about the *Hawke,* I've been rather tied up in meetings, stuck on dry land much more than I'd care to be."

I'm quite surprised he brought the topic up, and in such a casual manner.

"The harbor pilot was still aboard the *Olympic* at the time, wasn't he?"

"He was. So the whole investigation has been largely procedural. Of course, the White Star Line was slightly displeased. *Olympic* was laid up for eight weeks. In fact, the launch of *Titanic* was delayed twice. They swapped propellers with the *Olympic* to get her back in service as fast as they could. Steamship companies rather dislike having their brand-new flagship out of service," he says, with suitably English dryness. It's a massive understatement if ever there was one. It was a major fuster, and I hope Bruce Ismay isn't eavesdropping from his place a few seats down.

What happened was this: The brand new *Olympic*, on only her fifth voyage, got bunged up with a British naval vessel in the Solent, right outside Southampton where we were the other day. It happened six months ago, with Captain Smith in command. *Olympic* was heading to Cherbourg, just as we did, and in the crowded waters off the Isle of Wight, the *Hawke* tried to pass the *Olympic*. But, inexplicably, the *Hawke* veered left and plowed right into the *Olympic*'s side, creating a forty-foot gash. Water began flooding the brand-new superliner. Watertight doors were ordered closed, and E.J. was fixing to ground her in a mud bar—literally ready to drive the four-block-long ship right up onto the beach if it were necessary to save lives.

It wasn't necessary. In this case, the watertight compartments performed as they should. They were able to limp back to Southampton and get everyone off to safety. But the *Olympic* was out of commission for eight weeks—which further delayed the maiden voyage of *Titanic*, since they kept bogarting parts off her to get the *Olympic* back into service.

So, in a further twist of fate, if the *Hawke* incident hadn't happened, *Titanic* probably never would have struck the iceberg. She would have sailed earlier and not been in the wrong place at the wrong time.

Just like the encounter with the *New York* on Wednesday.

It all gets increasingly surreal.

The British Naval tribunal found *Olympic* entirely at fault, which is complete rubbish; E.J. Smith is in the middle of that. Still going on. He must be tense. Yet he certainly appears at ease, even with his boss's boss's boss at the table with him.

I venture to mention, "I've always loved ships, and the sea. But being away from home must get awfully tiresome."

"Oh, you get used to it. Being at sea, I am home. As I've accrued sufficient seniority, my accommodations have become altogether enjoyable." He, with the slightest nod of his head, indicates the grandeur of the surrounding dining room and gives an amiable smile. He's right. It's not bad.

Another thing that confuses me is how people here bandy about the name *Titanic* with such ease. It's either an afterthought or with a bit of proud reverence. To us, of course, the name is synonymous with death and doom and tragedy for all time. Just one of those things I notice at the table.

"When did you first go to sea?"

Our appetizers are swooped in. The Captain and I are both enjoying orange caviar on toast points.

"1867. I was seventeen. A square-rigged packet named the *Senator Weber*."

"So you learned the ropes? Flew sheets? Spiralled yardarms?"

He laughs fondly in remembrance. "Oh, yes. All of it. Despite appearances, I was quite spry in my youth. It's a laborious process, learning the ropes. Sailors are a bawdy, angry lot. You're not going to get away with slouching or making a silly mistake. They'll thrash you. It was agonizing, grueling work. I don't know at my present age and ability if I could handle it.

"But my first voyage took me to Hong Kong, San Francisco, and Peru. I knew then that I had it in my blood."

"I bet you've encountered some seriously rough seas."

"Oh, heavens, yes. Even on larger ships. A few years back, on the *Cedric*, it took us nine days of ceaseless pounding and crashing to make our way across the Atlantic. We lost a seaman over the side—there was no saving him. Sometimes the decks would seem practically vertical, and then plummet, only to crash yet again, the entire ship shuddering violently. Everyone had to be confined to their cabins. And mind you, the *Cedric* is a 700-foot vessel. Yes, it can indeed become quite exciting. And uncomfortable."

"I had a near similar experience in '08," Archie interjects. I'd been so busy with the captain I wasn't sure he was listening to us. "Six days of agony. We were thrashed around so! Everybody lost a good deal of weight that week," he smiles cutely.

My caviar mocks me for a moment in my mouth, as I picture the gawd awful nature of the thing, knowing even a ship this size can be tossed so violently as to make one lose the will to live.

But E.J. Smith seems content to keep talking to me directly, and I'm hungry for it. "I had to learn navigation, devilishly incomprehensible at first, but I had it under my belt by the time I was twenty. Made captain by age twenty-one."

"Permit me to say, that's inspiring. I mean, from the forecastle of a wooden sailing ship to commander of the *Titanic* is wholly remarkable." I subtly toast him with my wineglass, but he merely nods. He blushes.

I make E.J. blush a little bit. Something I never imagined in my wildest dreams.

He simply remarks off-handedly, "It just takes hard work and dogged determination. I enjoy a challenge, always have."

"How much coal does a ship like *Titanic* burn?"

"Six-and-a-half tons."

"Per crossing?"

"Yes."

"Good God. That's an enormous amount. It's almost obscene. And I'm sure it's not supplied free of charge to the company."

E.J. laughs hard at that, indicating quite the opposite.

He adds, "Well, these engines are far more efficient than their predecessors. I'm sure even further advancements are well on the way. Someday soon we'll be burning oil instead of coal."

"Is it true that *Titanic's* center engine won't go into reverse?"

"You seem to know a lot about her," E.J. muses, dipping his fork in sauce.

"I've studied a bit about it, and the *Olympic*," I admit. "Your first ship was the *Celtic*, wasn't it, sir?"

"Actually, the first vessel I commanded was the *Lizzie Fennell*; a three-masted wooden cargo ship, a mere 175 feet long. I was captain of her for three years. But in Liverpool I began to see the early steamers of the White Star Line, enormous steel ships with glistening trim and smokestacks, carrying passengers rather than cargo; twice and three times the size of the *Lizzie Fennell*. I felt it was for me. I was hired as fourth mate aboard the *Celtic*. Quite a step down from my own command, but it was well worth it. I knew I had to put in my time. My first actual steamship command was the *Baltic*."

"Do you ever wonder what happened to your first ship, the *Lizzie Fennell*?" I ask.

"She caught fire and burned. They had to abandon her in the North Atlantic." He sighs. "I was many years aboard her, learning all about her shapes, her sounds, her ropes, the noises she made . . . up in smoke."

To know a ship that well, and to know it later burned and sank. It's sad. And a strange omen here. I once again look around the dining room, even though I've got it memorized by now, and try to acknowledge the ultimate truth: Everything ends. But for something as grand as this, and only four days old, an abrupt end is deeply unjust.

Like poking him with a stick, I flat out ask the captain of the *Titanic* if he worries about icebergs.

"We have lookouts around the clock keeping watch," he says simply. "I cannot imagine any condition which would cause a modern ship to founder. Shipbuilding has gone beyond that." He's looking me in the good eye, smiling. He believes what he's saying.

Thomas Andrews, *Titanic's* shipbuilder, seated to my left, has been listening in somewhat, perhaps having tired of Clara Hays on his other side.

He tells me, "We build strong ships these days, Mr. Baldwin. It's quite exciting. Of course, I'm highly biased." He smiles.

I can't help but gush. "Mr. Andrews, I'm so amazed to be here. The ship is stunning. How do you manage to conjure up an entire ship in your mind?"

"I'm allowed to let my imagination run wild. I enjoy it immensely. Yet it does get very stressful at times. Everything has to be on time and on budget. The North Atlantic passenger trade is the most lucrative—and competitive—market on Earth. No expense is spared, and I'm honored to have a hand in it all. Every steamship company aims to be the fastest, the most luxurious. Visions of bilge pumps, expansion joints and potted palms fill my head, even in my dreams. I am but as a child, given leave to play with incredibly expensive toys."

Gentle laughter comes from the other end of the table. It seems to be involved in a completely different conversation. I hope I'm not being rude, having secretive discussions with these men to the exclusion of the rest of the table, but I can hardly contain myself.

Stewards deftly swoop in with a cold consommé and the clattering of spoons on fine china begins.

Still speaking to Mr. Andrews, I go on (and on and on): "I saw some photographs of the *Olympic*'s keel being laid at Belfast. The sheer size is incomprehensible. So massive . . . would it be fair to say it's the length of three football fields? I can't believe you have it all in your head. And that it can come to fruition without the slightest error. And all without computers."

Oops. Wine.

"Oh, every draftsman has a computer," Thomas Andrews tells me confidently. He pulls an object out of the breast pocket of his dinner jacket, and upon the table does he place a slide rule. I don't think I've ever seen one before.

"Well, there ya go."

"You never know what will happen when you first launch a vessel this size into the water. Ideas on paper become years on the drafting boards. Thousands of workers and ungodly amounts of steel later, you've got a nearly thousand-foot, eleven story behemoth on your hands. All you can do then is grease 'er up, give 'er a shove, and hope for the best."

We all laugh.

"After she's afloat, it takes a year to fit her out." Andrews waves about the dining room slightly with his wineglass in his hand. "All the appointments, brightwork, electricity, and plumbing. Although massive in scale, in essence, you simply repeat the same process, strut by strut, cabin by cabin, until suddenly you have a ship at long last. At which time you're immediately called upon to go and build a bigger one. It is seemingly without end, but I consider myself one of the luckiest men in the world." His eyes are aglow with pride.

Thomas Andrews won't survive the catastrophe. He dies, leaving a wife and two-year-old daughter at home.

Archie's been talking to Madeleine Astor on his right. She looks sufficiently charmed by him, as everyone is. I catch the words "Narragansett" and "*The Mayflower*," evidently Will Taft's private yacht.

E.J. Smith and Mr. Andrews get into a lively discussion, with me stuck in the middle, about steam pressure, engine torque and our current speed, which is twenty-two knots. They talk about going faster, trying to beat speed records. But they both agree there's nothing to be served by arriving in New York too early. We apparently wouldn't be allowed to dock ahead of schedule and would just have to drop anchor in the harbor and wait. And E.J. mentions he'd rather not stress his new engines unduly, and to no apparent purpose. By now, I notice J. Bruce

Ismay, two seats down, is finally craning to overhear the discussion.

The chateaubriand arrives and the table falls somewhat silent as we enjoy the main course. As people finish, and their plates are swept away, conversation becomes general, primarily about news, politics, and the economy. Mr. Straus, owner of Macy's, doesn't seem to have much to say, but it becomes apparent that he served in the New York State Legislature for a time. The railroader, Mr. Hays, is a touch more conversant and avid on a political point or two. Running railroads is an intricate business. It sounds damned interesting.

Dr. O'Laughlin has been silent but has the ruddy complexion of a good drinker. He seems content.

I, of course, have nothing to add, and don't even try.

But Archie steals the table. He cracks several jokes, and the group roars with laughter. He describes the endless political and social wrangling in Washington.

"There is no one like a well-trained society dame of Washington to know the right place to insert a knife." He laments the endless parade of soulless parties, whose only aim is to accumulate a body count for the newspapers, thus validating their political worth for all to see. Partygoers' names sprinkled with coerced minor officials, " . . . along with the names of all the other guests they chloroformed to get there. Most are dry as dust, the women a sea of tiaras, dog collars and stomachers."

Several at table beg to hear the tale of his ride to Warrenton. And since I have no clue what that means, I'm sufficiently pulled away from Thomas Andrews to hear the story.

"Well, as you know, Colonel Roosevelt is a daredevil of the highest order. He never stops—even when he clearly should."

Light nervous chuckle all-round the table, and I check Archie's face against an apparent slamming of his former boss. He's as poised as ever.

"It was just a few months before the end of his term, in 1909.

He'd gotten into his mustachioed head that we should break all *horse-flesh* records," (he again eyes me lasciviously when he says 'horse-flesh' and I feel myself blush once more) "by riding ninety-four miles in one day. I'm sure none of you would ever attempt more than forty miles at a time on horseback, no matter how many mounts you're given to switch off.

"We lit out from the White House at four in the morning for the ride to Warrenton, Virginia—and back. The wind was cutting. Of course it had to be winter. Why attempt such a thing on a fine summer's day? The roads were rutted and frozen mud, so the going was slow and treacherous. We started on our own horses, good steeds that we'd trust with our very lives. But once we got to Fairfax it was time to switch horses.

"I'd phoned ahead and told the gents at Fort Myer we'd need several changes of horses, but I didn't say who it was for. If I had, it would have turned into a media frenzy and drawn undue attention. Yet, lacking that information, they simply tossed out the most worthless rides they could be bothered with letting loose, and in this, they exceeded our wildest expectations. The horses were complete rubbish.

"Mine was vicious. He kept trying to bite me, and when I had to dismount to check the President's saddle, it took me a good fifteen minutes to get back astride the beast once again, he'd plunge and buck so."

But Archie describes how the men kept to their schedule, the President made speeches at Warrenton, and then they began the long journey back to the White House in a blinding snowstorm.

"By the time we regained Washington again, the sleet and snow had us blinded and frozen. To this day I think the sight of Edith Roosevelt, waiting for us in the open front doorway of the White House, bathed in golden light, dresses whipped by the wind, was the keenest sight I've ever beheld. By the time the President dismounted his horse, his glasses were completely caked with snow and his face had frozen over. He looked for all the world like Santa Claus.

"Mrs. Roosevelt handed us juleps and lined us up beside the fire and I was able to relax for the first time in fifteen hours. But we did it: A record ninety-four miles on horseback and no digits lost to frostbite—or to ill-mannered horses.

"Of course, I couldn't sit properly in a chair for a good number of days after that."

The assembled guests titter in light laughter and a smattering of applause sprinkles the table. I steal a glance at E.J. Smith, and he seems suitably enraptured but visibly glad his life involves the sea rather than horses that bite.

Archie's always in a good mood. How does he do that? It's wrong . . . but it's cute.

We end with the cheese course. I'm so stuffed, I can hardly eat anymore. But I love cheese. I have Stilton with grapes and biscuits with a glass of port, a chèvre, and some Morbier.

Dinner breaks, I thank Captain Smith and Thomas Andrews for their indulgence, and they of course utter, "Not at all," but I'm sure I just represent another annoying passenger to them.

Having over-eaten and drunk even more than usual, Archie suggests he and I go up to the Boat Deck.

I'm worn out, liquored up, full, still in Archie's clothes, following him blindly.

By now I'm getting used to being on the ship, and when I'm good, I'm good. Soaking up the loveliness of the opulent steamship, the clothes, the wine, the cheese; it's epic. It's why I'm here. I guess I feel like, in a way, I'm getting away with something extra, since I'm allowed to enjoy far more of it than I was strictly ever meant to.

But then I remember why, and the price that I must pay in the end, and I slide back into horror, ghastly shock, trembling, nausea.

It is bleak.

Sitting in that fool lifeboat like a loser, a coward: That's really bothering me. Assuming I'm lucky enough to make it work, what'll I look like? A fag in a boat while 1,500 people around me are going to freeze to death and drown? Do I really want to be that person?

Archie will lose all respect for me, just the way the world will lose respect for J. Bruce Ismay.

If I live, it will be in deep, deep shame.

It's Friday night, April 12, 1912. We're on the famous *Titanic*. Not only have we dined at the captain's table, not only have I gotten to know E.J. Smith really well, and picked Thomas Andrews' brains about his masterpieces, but I'm also wearing Archie's clothes and they feel so good, so smooth. They smell like him. So I smell like him.

Back on the Boat Deck, it's downright chilly now.

But I'm getting weird again. My stomach is clenching. And it's no ordinary fuss; I know those. This is impending terror. And it's sliding, unbidden, to the fore. For some reason, right now, I'm spitting nails at how much I have to withhold from Archie, the one human who is my anchor right now. He's literally holding me together and I've given him nothing but lies and half-truths.

We say little.

"It's cold. Come to my cabin and warm up," Major Archibald Willingham Butt suggests to me.

Along the corridor on Archie's deck he knocks on the deck steward's door and orders a bottle of scotch and two glasses. The man says, "Yes sir, right away."

We're in his cabin on the sofa when the steward shows up with a bottle of scotch and we're drunk enough already and don't have a lick of sense between the two of us.

"Mark, why are you always so distracted?"

"Hmm?"

"You seem to be in a funk about something."

You got that right.

"I think it's time we do something about it."

I'm wondering what the hell he means when he walks over to his bunk and starts stripping the bed of its linens. He wads them up in a careless pile, then moves to his great trunk, and before I can lend a hand or even figure out what he's up to, he pushes it across the carpeted deck toward the bunk, and thereupon, before my wondering eyes, commences to build a fort.

He tosses his pillow on the deck and commands, simply, "Soldier, assume your position in your billet. That's an order."

I'm baffled but snicker anyway. The man is certifiable. I duck in. The comparative darkness and snugness is a thing, and feels immediately cozy. He follows me in with the bottle of scotch and thus we sit, in the fort on the floor, legs crossed Indian-style.

"What's on your mind, soldier?" he asks it kindly.

Sound, in here, is muffled, close.

I don't know what I can tell him. I have been, I'm sure, an impregnable wall of mystery to him this whole time. He's spilled his guts to me, and I haven't been able to repay him in kind. I'm still surprised he hasn't just dismissed me as aloof and boring long ago.

I've been rude, even though there's a damned good reason for it. Maybe I decide to go with it?

"I guess you can tell, there's a certain reticence with me."

"To put it mildly."

"Shall I tell you why?"

"Uh-huh." He hands me a glass full of scotch, which spills, creating a big blotch on the rug.

Oh no! The rug!

"Remember how E.J. was talking about his first ship? Ropes and wood and sails and nothing but the stars to guide you?"

"Yes. It was fascinating."

"Well, 1874. Compare that to *Titanic*. Right now we're four stories above the surface of the ocean, riding along at twenty-five miles per hour, with electric lights and a Marconi wireless that has us in contact with the outside world. Technology brought this. Applied human invention. Would you be willing to assume that such advances will continue to be wrought?"

"I'd say that's definitely a fair assumption."

"Good. Because I am the product of such advances. My being here is a result of such. In fact, it is a technology so new and dangerous that I'm one of the very first. And I wanted to be here, on this ship."

He's looking a little suspicious now. "Why did you want to be here on *Titanic*?"

"Oh, the *Titanic* will become a terribly famous vessel. I've been given the most amazing gift. A friend of mine named David invented the ability to . . . "—here's the part that is going to be impossible for him to swallow. It's a damned good job we're drunk, I could never get away with this sober.

" . . . to travel back in time."

I say it. And wait.

And examine Archie's face, wondering which emotion shall take him first.

Mirth. He breaks in to a broad, albeit somewhat confused and crooked grin.

"Well, I do enjoy your ability to keep me entertained . . . "

Shit. Now what?

"I figured that might be your response." The whole thing is in danger of sputtering miserably until I get an ingenious idea: I fish my iPhone out of the front pocket of the trousers I'm wearing—Archie's trousers. The screen lights up, achingly, lovingly familiar to me. The phone scans my face and unlocks, and I hand it to Archie.

He accepts it skeptically, but his eyes are bugging out ever so much. His face is bathed in the phone's artificial light inside the fort.

"What is it?"

"Well, primarily, it's a telephone." I reach over, leaning into him, smelling him, and boink my finger on the little bright green square and my array of voicemail messages is displayed —most of which are from "Mom." I push the phone icon, and displayed—perhaps very undramatically—is the keypad. Not informationally rich, but nevertheless, here we are.

"This is the keypad. You press the numbers you want to dial."

"Will it work?"

"Naw. It requires an entire global network to be in place, one such that won't exist for quite a long time. J.J. Astor was right in his book: There *will* be a global telephone network in place someday. And we don't even have to pay long distance charges anymore.

"Speaking of invention, though," I flip up the display with my finger, swiping it away and revealing my home screen. "This started as a telephone, but people kept inventing so many other ways for the device to be used, people rarely bother to talk on the phone anymore. It's considered an annoyance. It can be used for all sorts of things. They are, frankly, quite addictive."

I push the camera button and snap a picture of him, sitting there in his fort with his mouth open in shock. I show it to him. It's amazingly cute, by the way . . .

"With the network in place, I could send this photo to my friends, to your friends; I could publish it in the *New York Times* with the push of a button."

I'm losing him. Not surprisingly.

"This is my bank account, the book I'm reading, and any number of puzzles and games. Oh, and music! I have over 1,500 songs. My automobile has speakers, and the phone connects directly to it when I get in and start the motor. So my songs play for me while I drive."

He's stumbling in his cognitive battle. I'm seeing complete confusion on his face and it's adorable. I'm going faster and faster, really getting into it. He's getting left further and further behind.

"Where do you keep the music?"

I've handed the phone back to him, he's hefting it and looking at it and with his forefinger pokes the icon for Google Maps.

"The music is stored inside."

"*Inside*? *This*?" He hefts it again, looks at the underside in complete disbelief.

"Yeah. Like I said, applied technology. Things built upon other things, ideas growing upon ideas, leapfrogging over each other. Mostly to make money. That's still the main focus for mankind."

I press iTunes and "shuffle" and suddenly the phone loudly pronounces:

Uhh! Where the hell my phone?

Where the hell my phone?

Huh?

How I'm posta git home?

Archie drops the phone to the carpet in shock. I laugh, and silence Lizzo.

"Sorry. Musical tastes will go through a few astonishing iterations. We have a saying: "Ya just gotta go with the flow.'"

He smiles wanly.

I guess I need to know why I've told him all this and what my game plan is. At this point I have not made an overt move on him, and don't believe I ever will. I certainly can't indicate I'm here because the ship is going to meet with disaster. That would be rude and hurtful and serve no earthly purpose.

"Where are you from?" He asks, suspicion creeping into his voice and his eyes harden slightly.

"San Francisco, as advertised. That part was entirely true. The year, for me, is 2019."

"Two thousand nineteen," he repeats it reverently, in a hushed, amazed tone, staring down at the carpet without focus. "Have you been to the moon?" he asks, eyes darting up to mine in slight hopefulness.

I suppress a laugh. "No. A few people have; it's frightfully expensive to accomplish, and there's nothing there. No air to breathe. Just rocks. But the photographs they have taken, looking back down at Earth, are astonishing. They really give you a sense that we're all just living together on a beautiful big blue ball."

"Why are you telling me this?"

"Because virtually everything I've said to you until now has been a complete fabrication. You have shared yourself with me for days, and I drink up your every word and all I can repay you with is lies and deceit? I think far too much of you, Archie, to treat you like that. And the only way I can fix it is to tell you the truth. So that you can know the real me. I'm sorry I haven't been honest with you."

He seems a little taken aback. I have just openly professed a degree of "like" for him. That's not cool, although, truth be told, it's gone way past "like" by now.

"I'm not in lumber. I'm an economics columnist for periodicals that haven't been invented yet. My father is alive, but we don't speak. Haven't seen him in about eighteen years, although everything I said about my mother is one hundred percent true. She's a brick.

"I wasn't raised in the 1870s. I was raised in the 1970s. I have had to lie to you ever since I met you and I despise it. It's not fair to you. So, I guess, this is the only way."

I pour a lot more scotch in his glass.

"Well, I'm sorry, for one thing, to hear about your father. As you know, I was robbed of my father at a young age."

By God, Archie is a kind man: Of all the things I've just dumped into his brain, he chooses to pick up on the very one which would provide me with the most comfort, disregarding his own consternation entirely. It's pure, unfettered class.

I need to keep going, however. "You probably want to ask all manner of questions, what happens in the future. And this is all so new, there are no rules yet. But it's a good bet that I shouldn't spoil things for you. It's a very unnatural situation, and I've learned that time is an alive and textured thing. It's so impossible. We don't know if it's damaging as a whole. There's an old saw about if you went back in time and killed your grandfather, you'd never be born; therefore, it would be impossible for you to go back in time and kill your grandfather.

"Changing people's destiny, altering their outcomes . . . we don't know what it'll do, but it's almost guaranteed to be a zero-sum game. So I can't do that. I can only tell you I think you're pretty swell."

I let him digest this. It's a lot. If I hadn't had the phone to show him, there's no way I could have made any of it stick. But a quick game of Angry Birds keeps him on the right track.

"Well. At least now I understand your hesitancy," he says reassuringly. Kindly.

But I'm not done. Maybe because I'm drunk, I don't know, but I decide to shed the last of my mystery once and for all.

"I know a man in San Francisco who works on ships, rides a motorcycle, yet confided to me that his predilection is towards the male humans, as opposed to the female. Have you ever met men like that?"

I'm watching his face carefully. Iron jaw? Or is it always like that?

"I, too, have known such men," he says. "Even in the Army, which you may think of as surprising, but nevertheless I have.

It never particularly bothered me. To each his own, I say. But it certainly isn't discussed in society."

He's distant. Not freaking, more like guarded. Not going to divulge.

"Well, that's how it is with me. I am one such person. I hope you don't mind."

There. It is said.

Instead of obliging him to answer, I simply keep going. "San Francisco became a safe place for people like me to live openly. In some part, due to the Barbary Coast. New York is much the same way."

Archie is good enough to further the conversation: "A good friend of mine in Washington is thus. We've talked about it. The way I see it, that to which a person is attracted seems innate, unique to that person. I see no reason why people should be penalized over it, although society would have something to say about it, clearly. There's always the question of propriety."

"In the future it becomes far more accepted and mainstream, although the highest levels of government are still a little taboo. And Hollywood . . . "

"Hollywood? What's that?"

"Oh . . . anyway. That's the last of my story. I wanted you to know the real me, no holds barred, omitting nothing. Finally."

Except the knowledge that you're going to be dead in forty-eight hours.

"Where, in time, have you traveled?" he asks. Is he anxious to dodge the penis issue? I'll just have to parse that out later.

"My first trip back was to San Francisco in the 1970s, a wild, politically charged time. Oh, yeah . . . I didn't lie about the 1906 earthquake and fires in San Francisco. I really was there. I traveled to see it, by way of my friend's Machine. I really wanted to get to know the 'real' San Francisco, to see what was lost. It was very important to me. That's where I met Ben and experienced the entire catastrophe.

"And then I went to London in 1940 to . . . " Sigh. Can't say boo about that. "Well, that's where I met the wonderful woman named Pamela, and she had her baby Sloane while I was there.

"Then I came here. Because the *Titanic* is so famous.

"My friend assures me that this whole concept of traveling through time is dangerous. Unhealthy to the user in the extreme, so it's not something I'll be doing much more of. And the technology, if it became commonplace, would be devastating. People are idiots. Untold damage would occur.

"So I'm just here, now, and . . . " getting a little braver in my tone, "just damned happy to get to know ya."

He soaks it all in, but he's drooping. We're looped. Even a diehard drinker such as myself has limits, and I know I exceeded mine long ago. Both our heads are full of outlandish concepts, our veins are full of peaty scotch, and there is such a thing as too much information, after all.

"You're sleepy. You should go to bed," I tell the confused man.

He stumbles drunkenly as he climbs clear of the fort and, fully clothed, sprawls across his bed and passes the hell out. I don't have much strength to move either but manage to slither along the deck and grab the seat cushions from the settee to form a bed for myself.

I sleep on the floor in my fort, wearing Archie's clothes.

There's a definite rocking of the ship at this point in its journey, the motion of the ocean. It's soothing. And thus I fall asleep, drunk again, being rocked side to side, the sound of Archie snoring softly, and "Where the Hell My Phone" thoroughly stuck on replay in my brain.

40

Saturday, April 13, 1912

Ouch. My head.

I come to awareness in my fort, couch cushions long since shoved aside by my tossing and turning. I'm a restless sleeper at the best of times, and when I'm liquored up, I'm told I thrash like a maniac. I'm thus stiff and sore from sleeping on the unyielding carpeted deck of *Titanic*.

I sit up and quickly file a mental damage report:

- How bad is this hangover going to be?
- What did I tell Archie last night?
- I'm still going to die, aren't I?

It hurts, but I climb out from the fort. Daylight is streaming through the porthole. Archie's gone.

The cabin's a mess, with clothes strewn everywhere, and an embarrassing stain is on the carpet. I'm momentarily confused.

Hangover doesn't seem to be nearly as bad as it ought to. I'm not strictly well, but I am functioning.

In the night I told Archie I'm a time traveler from the future and that I prefer men. No idea what that'll turn into as the day progresses. None.

Yes, I might die tomorrow. But I'm just not going to go there right now. My immediate concern is why is he gone, and the certainty that I really have to pee.

Making sure my clothes (Archie's clothes) are presentable, I step into my shoes and head for the cabin door—only to have it burst open, producing one Archibald Butt in the flesh, apparently in no better shape than I am.

"Oh, Mark. I was just down the hall. How you feeling?"

He looks wan, but normal. His voice is strong. He doesn't appear to be fussed.

"I might need the better part of the morning to reassert, but I'm certainly no stranger to that. I need to use the loo."

"Certainly." He steps aside and I go take care of that, splashing tap water on my face for a good few moments, the shock of it helps bring my systems back online. The water from the *Titanic's* faucet is ice cold right now. Gee. What might cause that?

Despite trying to banish the thought, I nevertheless recognize I still might die.

Back at Archie's cabin, with no idea what to say, I simply set about clearing the fort, tidying the place up. He assists, wordlessly.

"We should eat. Food will definitely help," I decide to suggest.

"Right-o," he says chipperly. "It's after ten, I think. They keep changing the ship's clocks back an hour a day to line up with New York, so I never actually know if I'm coming or going."

Without even thinking, I produce my phone. It says it's 11:14, but I hadn't changed it yet. so it should actually, in fact, be 10:14. Archie's looking at the phone with an expression akin to disappointment. "I thought I'd hallucinated all you told me."

I look him in the eyes. Those green, close-together eyes. It would be a lot easier on him if I hadn't divulged the overwhelming truth to him, but I did it. I have to own it. Right now, I feel selfish, that my need to come clean with him would be at a painful expense to his brain that I now fully regret.

"I'm afraid it's all still true."

His voice doesn't change, in either surprise or disappointment. He merely changes the subject: "So . . . we can get food in the à la carte restaurant, and I hear greasy sausage and coffee will be the best thing for us right now. Regardless of our individual points of origin."

Was that bitchy? I don't think so. At least he's handing me a fresh one of his shirts to use, a kind overture.

We set out for the B-Deck restaurant, saying little, just brushing past others in the corridors. Archie pays the 6s3d for the both of us and we get some coffee into our systems and it feels good.

He seems in no hurry to revisit the enormity of the information shared last night, so we talk about the immediacy of our morning.

"What would you like to do today?" He asks it freshly, as if today really were just another grand day to be greeted with open arms.

"I wanna see the bridge." I'm being facetious, but in truth I'd kill for it.

"OK," he says simply.

And I think two things: He's patronizing me; and people really do say "OK," even as far back as 1912. It's such an odd term to have pervaded our lexicon.

Bent on normalcy of conversation, Archie mentions he's sad he'll have missed the famed blossoming of Washington's cherry trees this year, which comes the first week of April. They originated from the mayor of Tokyo as a personal gift to Nellie Taft just two years ago. Archie tells me he took her by carriage to see them their first spring in bloom and Nellie simply clapped her hands in delight.

"It's both wondrous and miraculous that they took to root so well and have flourished. If they'd up and died it would have been a major international incident. I wonder if I'll even get to see them next year. For all I know, I may no longer be employed in Washington." He sighs and sips his coffee. "I don't know that I mind changing jobs, I just abhor the uncertainty."

But we're skirting an issue. We have to touch on last night.

"How are you feeling about what I divulged last night?" Just going to dive in and ask.

"I'm mightily confused. I awoke, and, amid my headache, was the certainty that you were just having me on. But when you pulled that contraption out of my own trousers, well, that hope was lost."

"Archie, in a way I'm terribly sorry I burdened you with it. As I said, I had my reasons. I wanted to be truthful to you. But now that I'm post-scotch, I'm realizing it was also really unfair."

He remains the gentleman. He gives a wave with his hand. "Don't give it a second thought, Mark. I'm a big boy. I can handle things. But I must confess to being deeply overwhelmed. I have so many questions!"

"Which, of course, I absolutely cannot answer for you."

"I know. I recognize that. But I can't lie: I'm so rabid to know who wins this blasted, accursed, annoying election, so that I may know which way to jump and where my life will go . . . You know, and you can't tell me." He's not complaining, but there's real emotion in his voice.

I rather wish I wasn't looking him in the eye just now, because he locks his upon mine, and I see genuine pain and it's all my fault for bringing it to him.

"I'm so sorry, Archie. If I told you, then your behavior would change, even if you weren't aware of it. Ripples would form and dynamics would shift, unseen, and . . . this whole technology is so new and unprecedented, we have no idea what will happen if we change the past. David, my friend who invented this, warned me that mucking up the timeline could have disastrous consequences."

"I understand. Fully. For example, if General Lee had approached the Battle of Gettysburg even slightly differently, the South might have won the war and the world would be a vastly different place right now. I see it." He breaks eye contact, and, true to his nature, is bravely accepting the oddity. He's not going to whine about it.

"By the way," he looks around furtively, to make sure we're not being overheard by others, "how the hell do you get back to your own time? When does it happen, and by what device?"

"The return is automatic. It's built in at the beginning. I chose to be here for ten days, so at the close of that, I shall simply vanish."

"Is it an odd sensation?"

"Extremely! I tend to fall over and have to fight the urge to vomit. It's all apparently very bad for one physically. So I can't plan on doing this more than a few times."

"Then I'm grateful you chose one of them to come play with me."

Awwwww!

"Is there anything interesting you can tell me about the future?"

"Well, in general, I can tell you it will not be free from warfare, but also, there shall be long periods of peace and wonderful prosperity. Money continues to be the root of all evil, and human behavior can be both fair and foul, just as it is now. People will fall in love and make babies and it all moves forward.

"Words are different. For example, if I told you I got a new router on Amazon and watched *Big Bang* on Hulu, you'd know the words but not their meaning."

He's looking at me like he knows the words but not their meaning.

"I think I can safely give you a fun specific. In my day, they've developed automobiles that can completely drive themselves. It's still experimental, but they have a far lower accident rate than those piloted by humans. And the holy grail, that of a flying car, finally seems to be close on the horizon."

I knew he'd be up in that and I was right. He's grinning like an excited little kid.

"I really enjoy driving," I go on to say. "I don't want to have to give it up. But someday soon it'll probably become illegal to drive one's own car, as it will be patently more dangerous to everyone else. The insurance companies will eventually step in and put a stop to it."

Archie offers a painful smirk. "I see that insurance companies will retain their charming sense of humor throughout the centuries. That's a comfort. Have you flown in an aeroplane?" He asks suddenly, like it's a fantastic idea.

I chuckle. "Yes, many, many times. It's quite common now. I mean, for us."

"I was once offered the chance to go up in a 'plane, with a British stunt aviator. It would have been my ultimate dream. But my dear boss Mr. Taft immediately tut-tutted the idea. He discouraged it as a needless hazard to my person. I was peeved. One of the only times I've been truly out of sorts with the man. Later, as I thought about it, I think his real concern was that it would just be too ostentatious and would send the wrong public message."

His eyes gleam. "Oh, but how I would have loved the experience. Is there a sensation to it? To flying? Do you feel it in your bosom?" His hands are up, fingers extended. "The fact that you're freely untethered from Earth, soaring into the skies?"

He looks positively beatific.

"Well . . . "

Sorry folks, the Wi-Fi and entertainment aren't working, we're gonna try and reboot the system. Thanks for your patience.

"Almost."

The other matter, regarding men who like other men, I'm not even going to go near. Possibly never. And I'm just going to have to be "OK" with that.

Breakfast is over, and I'm certainly feeling like I'm on much stronger footing now. I decide to play it cool and give Archie some room. I tell him I'm going to do some paperwork in my cabin, and suggest we grab a light bite to eat later, at 1:30, in the Palm Court. He agrees.

So after a few hours locked in complete fuss in my stateroom, rotating through endless emotional horrors and hopes, I bound forth wearing an amalgam of Archie's and my own clothes.

The Palm Court, back of A-Deck, is nearly a religious experience. I thought the height of glamor was the Smoke Room, but this here's the living end. Pillars, fancy alcoves, carvings in gold, potted palms, everything is elegant and prissy. Archie meets me there promptly at 1:30 and as we're seated, he announces, simply, "We have an appointment with the Captain on the bridge this afternoon. At our convenience."

"Really? Archie, that's incredible!"

It's extremely rare that civilians are allowed anywhere near the bridge of a ship at sea—particularly on a British ship, which is nothing but rules and bureaucracy—but Archie's got serious pull. Wow.

Our food is, of course, superlative. Cucumber sandwiches and tea with bikkies.

I can hardly eat, I'm so excited. I was only supposed to be on *Titanic* for twenty-four hours, speaking to no one, and slinking away into obscurity. Instead, the universe is piling on more and more pilf. I feel like I'm sitting atop an enormous mound of gold coins and rubied goblets muttering *precious . . . precious . . .*

The cost of all this may very well be my life, but I'm in it for now. For the next few moments, I am emboldened to my fate and gagging to see the bridge.

I find it hard not to swagger as we go up to the Boat Deck and proudly swing open the gate to the Officer's Promenade, ignoring the "KEEP OUT" sign with impunity. And then we close it behind us. To keep "people" away.

We saunter into the foremost part of the bridge. It's over 104 feet wide when you count the overhanging wings on either side. Several officers are there, suddenly looking ready to pounce at unannounced civilians. Fortunately, E.J. himself appears and greets us warmly.

"Welcome, gentlemen." He introduces us to the men in this front, wide part. It consists of a large ship's wheel, wooden with the peg handles all the way round, and engine telegraphs: large ringer stanchions for the engines, made of shining brass, with a lever that signals various commands to the engine room: Ahead Full, Slow Reverse, Station-Keeping. Only a couple of men are standing as lookouts; no one's at the wheel. Which confuses me for a moment.

The bridge actually consists of two rooms. The very front is the navigation bridge, open to the elements at either side. Inside and just behind is the actual wheelhouse. This is enclosed and heated. Men are stationed about at pieces of navigational equipment and controls, and here a smaller ship's wheel is manned by a sailor in suitable garb.

In here, the nerve center of the ship, we're presented a series of men and names I shall never retain. Except for one particularly handsome bloke with an iron jaw who's introduced as Fourth Officer Henry Wilde. We like him.

I gaze around to take it all in as quickly as I can, and smell the linseed oil and pipe smoke and cigar smoke and coffee and farts while examining the control board for the ship's watertight doors. A hallway directly down the centerline of the ship leads back, E.J. tells us, to the chart room, Captain's quarters, the Marconi room and all the other officer's berths and lavatory.

Envious of the man who gets to steer the ship, which, for hours on end, means simply standing on a wooden pallet and pointing the vessel in a straight line. Despite the awesome power he holds in his hands, it must get frightfully dull.

I ask if I may approach the wheel, and with a nod from the Captain, I do so. I step to just one side of it and gaze out at the open blue.

I'm at dead center. My view forward is a run of windows, and far forward, 180 feet away, is the prow of the *Titanic*. Cables from the forepeak arc straight up to a steel mast just in front of the bridge, partially blocking the view.

Out the broad windows, there is nothing but open ocean as far as the eye can see. I lean in and I let my jacketed arm touch the *Titanic's* wheel. Just for a moment, I press lightly against it.

Before us lays a vast emptiness of ocean. I stand high above the surface of the water, the forepeak bursting its way across the empty Atlantic. Blue sea meets cloudy blue sky, and it is devoid of any object. It's empty. Vast. There's nothing to run into appreciably larger than an errant champagne cork for hundreds of miles in any direction.

And yet they manage to hit something, after all?

Finally, I get it. Why no one seems particularly concerned about icebergs. The chances are one in a million, bordering on the ridiculous.

I gaze at the simple controls. Wheel, compass; it's fairly simple and low-tech. The commuter, a simple level detector that shows if the ship is listing, indicates we do have a six-degree list to port. I enquire.

"Coal consumption, Mr. Baldwin," E.J. Smith assures me.

"We've consumed a good measure of the 6,000 tons of coal I mentioned to you. When the bunkers on one side have become more empty than the other, we simply begin taking from the other side. Plus, we're also subject to the wind component. We're somewhat tacking into the breeze right now. *Titanic* presents a sizable profile. She'll lean a fair bit, even in a modest wind."

I ask if it's all right to take a run to the loo, and go. I get to pee where they pee. Down that most private of corridors to the "officer's head," trying not to peer into open doorways but of course I do. I sneak the quickest of glances into the Marconi wireless room, a staccato series of electric blips play endlessly; Morse Code, their only way to communicate.

Back forward again, I find Archie and E.J. engrossed in conversation about some sort of drama on an earlier crossing aboard the *Baltic*. Jewels went missing, a man was lost overboard, and then some horrific kerfuffle at U.S. Customs in New York. The American officials were on an absolute tear and went through everybody, including the crew. An apparent journey from hell.

I listen, yet also marvel at what I see around me. All this carefully forged steel; the masts, funnels, well-decks and port holes—none of it was ever built to be beautiful or particularly stylish in form, it all comes from a basic need to cross the Atlantic as speedily and luxuriously as possible. It's not art, it's economics. And yet it is inherently handsome in its own way. A bygone era, tough as nails and beautiful.

Captain Smith leads us out to the starboard bridge wing and we just stand, the three of us, looking back along the Boat Deck at the superstructure of the grandest vessel in the world, her four stacks, children in heavy clothes playing games along the fresh pine decking.

E.J. is obviously proud of *Titanic*. His smile is one of heavy satisfaction. After such a long life at sea, he's earned it.

§

Before dinner we go to a concert held in the first-class Lounge. The passengers, all well-dressed, listen attentively, heads cocked to one side or staring vacantly, enjoying the strains of lively Bach pieces and Handel bits. I recognize some of the music, but most just have the vague sound of classical music: pleasant, yet kind of all the same. The musicians are excellent. I watch how effortlessly they play, as if simply born to it.

It's a gentle diversion on such a long voyage, so free of drama or even anything to actually do with oneself.

Dinner again in the Dining Saloon. Archie finally bails and gets the salad he'd promised. But he's in a fine feather; any semblance of a hangover seems to be long gone.

"I haven't actually bothered to ask if you've spent time in D.C. yourself," he asks me. "See how self-absorbed I can be?"

"You're not! And I have indeed been to Washington. It's an amazing city. I stayed in an apartment off Dupont Circle."

I have to remind myself that there would be no Metro, no Vietnam Memorial. In fact, if memory serves, by 1912, they were only just trying to decide where to place the Lincoln Memorial.

"Your descriptions of Washington society last night at the Captain's Table weren't particularly encouraging," I say. "Sounds like a tough place to keep friends."

"Oh, but I do. I've got loads. Washington is sort of a nexus point for the East Coast, so everyone eventually passes through, whether on business or simply as a result of geography. My house is always open to overnight friends and Army mates. I manage a few successful parties a year.

"My New Year's Eve parties, always on January 2nd, have

become legendary. Three hundred people. My first one was in '09, and I was quite taken aback when, running around greeting my guests, I came face to face with Will Taft standing in my front room. He just wandered in and seemed keenly uncomfortable for all that. I've held the party every year since then, but that's the only occasion when the president—then president-elect—showed up.

"Just this February, I had Mr. Taft to my house for lunch on a Tuesday, and baseballer Ty Cobb the very next day, on Wednesday. I had much more fun with Ty Cobb, but to be fair, the president is my boss, so I will simply attribute it to that.

"What's Ty Cobb like?"

"He's hysterical. A good humor, and a blasted pleasant fellow to have around. A manly man, if ever there was one, and quite spry, too."

I hope they got nasty with each other.

Our various courses are served and consumed. No wine. Neither of us are quite ready to go there just yet. But dinner consists of potted shrimps, vichyssoise, and roast beef with potatoes and succotash. I don't often get to interface with succotash, much to my lament. Mostly I just like using the word.

"I lived at the White House for most of last summer," Archie tells me. "At first, I was honored and proud as a peacock, but as the summer wore on, it became an actual bore. I couldn't have any of my friends over. It was like being on duty the entire time. I had a big four-poster bed, and that was nice, but a disappointing amount of street noise can always be heard on my side of the mansion. And, of course, being so blasted hot, there was no such thing as shutting a window against it. I was so glad to get back home, but it wasn't long before the president and I headed out on our dreaded two-month political tour.

"Home is where the heart is. Home is good," Archie proclaims satisfactorily.

"Right?" I reply.

We finish up our meal and head to the Smoke Room, Archie waving to the Wideners and Astors, me just nodding. I feel like I'm not socially placed high enough to be waving at these people.

I finally brave some Grand Marnier in the Smoking Room. The first sip seems somewhat revolting to me, given my over-indulgence last night, but after a few sips, I'm back in. I'm smoking my pipe like mad and I love it.

This time we're joined by several men: Jacques Futrelle, Mr. Widener, and Mr. Guggenheim. Once again, they're talking about "reciprocity," and an unnerving situation in Mexico. Apparently, Mexico has had a dictator, a coup, guerrilla fighting, Americans getting kidnapped and killed, American economic interests are under serious threat, and thousands of U.S. troops are stationed on the border at El Paso. It's been a tense stand-off for months.

True to form, Archie will comment on only what seems to be established fact, and at any attempts at inside scoops—the mood of Taft regarding these matters—he remains calmly and politely mum. He speaks of living in Mexico City for three years, as secretary to Ambassador Matt Ransom in 1895. I didn't know this. I'd love to ask questions. More accurately, it explains why he seems to speak Spanish so well.

Tariffs seem to be a huge deal. The men all discuss them heatedly, and I get the impression that the imposition of trade tariffs with other nations forms the substantial bulk of the U.S. government's overall federal budget. There is no such thing as income tax yet. While I've long known these things in textbook terms, it's still odd to ponder, in real life, how much things have changed.

Obviously, I have nothing to contribute, and after learning even more than I ever thought my brain could hold, I kind of want to go away.

I'm getting upset again. It's all back, crushing me. Making it hard for me to breathe.

Eventually I decide I have to excuse myself, shaking hands with everyone, including Archie and taking my leave, making it clear that I'll be in my stateroom. I'm full-on hoping that Archie should want to come and find me. But in truth, I hardly think he will.

I head to my cabin alone in full fuss, my anguish firing on all thrusters.

I lay in bed fully clothed and wait. I don't know what for. To die? For Archie to come hug me?

Fear comes again as I lie there. And for perhaps the first time, I'm able to recognize that a full life of worry and fuss, which is all I ever do, is nothing compared to actual, real fear. It's like I've only recently met it for the first time. And I don't care for it. I don't know what to do with it. It cuts me. It hurts. Make it go away.

By laying in my bunk the normal way, my feet point toward the back of the ship and my head toward the front, I'm positioned and moving exactly as if I'm on a gurney being wheeled into some sterile, tiled theater of doom.

I wish I didn't already know that this section of the ship will land upright, two miles down; this room will survive the impact more or less uninjured. Oh, it'll be plenty full of water, but it will remain like this, frozen in utter darkness. My mattress will probably break loose, float off and willow down somewhere over there by the desk, sheets slithering around like shrouds.

All wood and fabric will quickly rot. The steel of the walls, always cool to the touch even now, will burl with rust, dissolving. By the end of the 21st century, *Titanic*, this room—this metal wall upon which I'm rapping my knuckles right now—will finally dissolve into paste.

Titanic, in stately operation for precisely four days, will have a childish tantrum, shake loose her frail creators, and fling herself to the seabed in a huff, where she will then spend the next two hundred years slowly surrendering until nothing remains but basic chemical compounds.

And I came along for the ride.

Emotions too big to handle or describe fight for supremacy in my brain. I'm just a helpless bystander at this point. I've reached the point where all I can do is tell the warring constituents in my brain to go ahead and duke it out amongst themselves. Lymphoma even tries to sneak in and join the fight, but I manage to, temporarily at least, tell it to go to hell.

So I manage to reassert myself once more. The mechanisms of fear and worry are winding down, but they're taking me with them. I haven't much left with which to fight.

I think of Archie, how fun he is, how he bears the weight of things that would buckle me in a New York minute. He's always smiling, always upbeat, always quick with a joke.

Is there any way I can get him to get into lifeboat number seven with me?

I put a good think on that, but he's a famous person who is supposed to die. Saving Archie would constitute messing with the timeline in an overt way. I'm not sure I dare. Moreover, there's no way in hell he'd get into that lifeboat when women and children need saving. He wouldn't do it. I'm more certain of that than I am any other thing right now.

An hour goes by. An hour and a half. I phase in and out of horror.

Just when I think I might be able to get some sleep after all, I hear a light tapping on my stateroom door. It's Archie.

I let him in, and we sit and talk. He'd obviously slipped back into the ways of alcohol himself. He exudes the smell of Courvoisier. He hops up onto my bunk.

"Talking with those men was interminable. I wish I could have fled as readily as you. I haven't told you quite how serious it is for me back home, what's waiting for me back in Washington. A few weeks ago, Alice Longworth pulled me aside and gave me a private message, direct from her father, the Colonel: 'Alice, when you get the opportunity, tell Archie from me to get out of his present job. And not to wait for the convention or election but do it soon.'

"Alice, in her own words to me, said 'Archie, get out from under this edifice before the crash comes.'"

Archie's looking quite pained just now. I'd pat his hand if I could.

I lay down on my bunk, squished up against the wall, and in a surprise move, Archie lays down beside me. There's hardly any room, we're completely scrunched in and I feel his body next to mine.

But he keeps talking, as I knew he would, and I'm glad to lie prone and listen.

"It's weighing on me fiercely. But I've subsequently come to realize that I would not ask to be relieved from President Taft now if my whole life depended on it. My devotion to Colonel Roosevelt is as strong as it was the day he left office, but this man, Taft, has been too fond of me for the past three years for me to just throw him over right now. And, worse, having it said all over the country that another Roosevelt man, reading the writing on the wall, has abandoned the sinking ship. Or some other mixed metaphor."

I gulp. That's the worst metaphor imaginable.

I feel his pain. It's tremendous. All things being equal, if he were to somehow live, it sounds to me like he'd do well to stay put with President Taft. I know I can use my words to put him at short-term ease. I have the power, and I believe he will value my input.

"It sounds to me like staying put would be the appropriate thing," I say. "I mean, you're there, you're fair; go for it and be proud. Bloom where you're planted."

"'Bloom where you're planted . . . ' I like that."

We're staring up at the ceiling. I can't see his expression, but I feel him relaxing.

"Well. I just wanted to tell you that's what's up with me, occupying my mind. And blast! Everyone on this ship is eyeing me sideways, wondering which way I'll jump. I guess I'm a little tired of it all. Taft's own doctor has pulled me aside several times and said he fails to understand why I haven't simply cracked up under the strain. Everyone, it seems, is placing bets as to when I'll finally buckle.

"Frankly, Taft may well lose re-election. I believe he is a wonderful president, but there is no room in his heart for the vagaries of politics. He simply cannot and will not play the game. Well, it's all game. He's simply too earnest for it. The public has been crying out for the Colonel, but the more he goes out and stumps his speeches, the more he comes off as a radical, a socialist, a demagogue, sounding almost like a dangerous cult preacher.

"I've just got to get through the next year. Then I can get my life back on track, step free of this mad whirlwind. Maybe I'll go back to the Army. They'd be glad to have me; they've openly said as much, several times."

It's too much. Archie's problems would overwhelm most people. His concerns involve the actual White House—his woes are epic in scale.

Even though the bunk barely accommodates two humans and we're already squished together, I roll to my left and hug him close with my right arm. I'm about to tear up. This powerful man hurts and has nowhere to run and I want to punch the world for hurting him.

I just grab him and hold him, and, for reasons I'll never understand, he lets me. He goes limp, and sighs, and in that sigh I hear the slightest catch. He is a mere "hic" from tears himself.

He quickly falls asleep in my arms and I hold him as he dozes, as the ship hastens toward its doom.

I feel his clothed body, warm against mine, heavy with sleep. He's gone and dreaming of happy things. His tiny little feet sort of paddle in his sleep.

An errant tidbit of knowledge dances through my brain, unbidden, unformed—and is gone.

What was it?

My curiosity gets the better of me and I go searching through the contours of my mind, replaying my last few thoughts in order to recall what that information was.

It comes. I remember now: They never find Archie's body.

This body. Asleep in my arms. His hair tonic smells like orange blossom on my pillow.

I want to stay awake to memorialize this for all eternity, but it isn't long before I lose the battle. I'm ripped from being present in the moment by sleep, which whisks me away to another place, proving how nothing can be permanent.

I hate it. It's the way of all things, but I'm not ready to accept it.

41

Sunday, April 14, 1912

Consciousness never hurt so bad. My ugliest day is upon me, slamming into me like a freight train, gripping mind body and soul in a dark, cold grasp.

The ship—and Archie—and I—will die tonight.

We're still inextricably wrapped up on the tiny bunk in our heavy clothes, one of my sleeves is half off, yanking at my collar under the inert weight of the man beside me. I can scarcely breathe.

The lamp is still on, but with no window, I can't tell what time it is. Is it even morning yet? With my free hand I manage to fish out my phone, upside down. It says 9:40 a.m., which means ship's time will be 8:40.

I don't want to wake him up. By now we're pretty comfortable together, but I suddenly remember it was once said Ernest Hemingway killed—or nearly killed—a man for making an overt pass at him. What shall be the reaction of this Army Major?

Whatever. I need to breathe again and my arm has completely fallen asleep.

"Archie?"

My voice has a catch in it, as it often does in the morning.

"Archie?"

He stirs, the redheaded nature of his self, hair all messed up, oil making it stick in all the wrong positions. He comes to and sits up.

"Uh," he mutters.

I'm finally free to adjust my shirt and catch a decent breath. My arm, long asleep under his weight, begins tingling and zinging madly with fresh blood flow. Archie swings his legs over the edge of the bunk and sits, hands on each side, weight on his arms, hunched over. He looks confused and sleepy, with a crease etched on his cheek from the folds of my clothes.

"I think I must have dozed," he says simply and rubs his hands on his face. "What time is it?"

"It says just after 8:40 a.m."

We make our way down to the Dining Saloon for breakfast, Archie in a new suit, having stopped by his cabin, and I in my same old one once more. People are starting to notice and take nervous second glances at me.

Archie brightly informs me that this evening the both of us are invited to a special dinner in the à la carte restaurant, hosted by the Wideners tonight. "It's an evening to toast and celebrate Captain Smith, with champagne and food and all the trimmings. It should be quite gay."

He's smiling and speaking lightly and I can tell I'll need things to occupy my psyche as this evening progresses, so I eagerly give my assent. I can't help but wonder if the scion of Philadelphia society really wants me to be there—I've got no social standing beyond my association with Major Butt. But if I am to be considered an associate of Major Butt, I'll gladly take it. I'll take it all the way to the bank.

"Excellent," he says. "It's all settled. Meanwhile, there's to be a Sunday service right here at 10:30 this morning. Would you care to join me?"

"Sure. It'll be a thing."

It's something to do. E.J. will be there. It will be culturally relevant and perhaps a spiritual handhold for my tired, time-weary self who is clearly starting to wig now that we've approached the actual day of disaster.

Archie seems to be too tired to spend much time talking, and I'm clearly setting myself up for the ultimate fuss of my forty-nine-year existence. Breakfast is much in silence.

They shoo us from the Dining Saloon rather harshly this morning, as it all needs to be torn apart and set up for the service in barely a half hour.

We wait in the entrance lobby outside. Many people are milling about, preparing to get their God on, and Archie and I stand so the women may sit in the few chairs. He chats amiably with the Wideners about what the weather should be like in New York. I choose to remain quiet and attempt to smile, which I'm sure must appear more closely to bowel strain than a pleasant Sunday greeting.

At 10:30, we go back into the Dining Saloon. Chairs are suitably placed, and the great sideboard is awash with blooms. There's a lectern and E.J. Smith leads us in several hymns. I feel like one of those fallen women suddenly faced with church, but Archie's really into it. He sings well. I do not. I struggle to keep up, kind of going "mum mum mum."

The service itself is generic enough that I, in my heightened state, can't really even track it.

For reasons I cannot quite fathom, I draw strength from the number of women seated around me. For, among all this, I know that most of the first-class women will survive. Even if I don't.

Archie does more paperwork in his cabin and I nervously wander the ship taking pictures. I no longer care what people think of my phone, they aren't going to live anyway. I run into the Slocombes again. They seem to be getting on well with another couple. Out on the open deck, Jake has wrapped his jacket over his wife's shoulders in the chill, and I finally get to check out his backside. Better than I'd hoped. Funny how that mechanism still manages to function in my brain when precious few other faculties remain.

Lunch again, more rich and expensive food. I'm feeling fat. I almost join Archie in the salad routine but figure on eating well my last day on Earth. Only it sticks in my gorge, an unwelcome reminder that human bodies can die.

For a while we sit on deck chairs on the sunny side of the Boat Deck, reading and enjoying the cool bright sunshine. It's not very warm at all, we're under our heavy White Star Line blankets.

Listening to Archie will help. "You were in Cuba, too, right?"

"I was. They only gave me three hours' notice. A coup took place in August of '06, destabilizing the Cuban situation yet again. Several assassinations took place, and Will Taft, as Secretary of State, rushed to Havana to start negotiations and bring the two sides to the table. It was mostly successful, but it was still decided that it would be in the best interests of all if the U.S. would send troops in to lend stability and to enforce the terms of the treaty.

"I got down there first. Rather than sail with everyone else from Norfolk, I took a train to Key West, hired a boat and managed to set up the quartermaster depot in record time, before the arrival of the troops.

"Wasn't much in the way of action. We mostly built roads

and aided the newly formed government. Technically we were there as an occupational force, but they elected their own leader in the fall of 1908 and organized their own military, and we left them in pretty good hands. That's when I came back to Washington and got tapped by Roosevelt to be his aide. I was able to renew my acquaintance with Will Taft while in Havana."

Certainly a more engaging tale than who's going out with whom, and what's on sale at Costco—my normal range of conversation back home. It helps clear my mind.

Maybe someday I'll finally make it to Cuba. Or not.

By now, as you can tell, I'm starting to lose my shit. What was earlier an intermittent terror begins to take true root in my belly. A panic, a claustrophobia, a desire to run . . . yes, run! Somewhere, anywhere.

But there's nowhere to go. The sizable *Titanic* suddenly feels tremendously small and confining to me. We're all alone out here on an endless ocean. The engines throb, the horrid black smoke belches from the stacks, people wander aimlessly in their heavy and ridiculous 1912 clothes, blithely unaware and I'm freaking out.

I keep pacing the Boat Deck. I find I'm circling the general area around lifeboat number seven, as if I need to keep it in my sights at all times, as if I'll somehow forget how to find it, like what happens so often in dreams.

Archie is my only anchor right now, but I'm unable to make conversation, I'm unable to hear him. His mouth moves, sound comes out, but it makes no sense.

"Mark, what on earth is wrong with you?"

"Oh . . . nothing."

"Well, something's clearly on your mind." He sounds a little frustrated with me right now, but then I see something else slide over his face.

The fact that I'm here is beginning to suggest to his keen mind that something's up. If I can't get my shit together, he's going to be able to add two and two and draw conclusions. I'm sure I have less of a poker face than Will Taft, and it's starting to seep through. He's becoming ever so slightly rattled.

Suddenly it becomes my job to protect him. I'm shocked to realize I have that power. I draw upon this new energy source and turn myself around, for Archie's sake.

I want him comfortable and happy for as long as I have it within me to do so.

The smile I flash at him could easily come out fake and horrifying, but by putting my stomach into it, I seem to get it over the hump. It has an obvious effect. The furrow in Archie's brow eases noticeably, and I ask him to describe a typical day in the White House for me.

It's like flipping a switch. He's on again and in his element, that of the consummate raconteur. He happily launches into the minutiae of his daily life at the seat of American power, Will Taft's secretary, Nellie Taft's secretary, paperwork, functionaries, guest lists and budget items.

I just let him go on, listening intently with a lot of eye contact. I've just played him, on purpose, but for the lofty goal of soothing his soul.

After some time, having assured myself he's once again happily Archie, I leave him for a while to take another long walk. Trudging seems to help, back and forth in front of lifeboat number seven. The late-afternoon sky is clear and it's fully sunny, but there is no warmth.

In my cabin I get ready for dinner. I make sure I have all I'll need in case I get through this: my credit cards, room card to the Ritz—it looks completely alien to me right now—some cash, my passport and phone.

I hope I don't have to find out how water-resistant an iPhone 11 is in real life.

I'm unspeakably nervous, nudging toward low-grade terror. I know the events of tonight backwards and forwards, but I've never had to factor myself into the equation. Now it's become personal.

Somehow—I don't know how—as I leave my cabin for the last time, I tell myself to saddle up. I even say it out loud. Cold fear, which I've always managed to sidestep in life, can theoretically be harnessed as an energizing force. So I try it on for size. I am a time traveler. I have an event to get through and I need to keep my wits about me.

This feeling lasts about as long as it takes me to walk to the à la carte restaurant on B-Deck. One look at Archie, facing away from me, standing in conversation with his peers, and my bravado starts to crumble once more.

I greet Archie as off-handedly as I can and try to not look him in the eye as he introduces me to yet another sea of people, glittering in jewels and nursing champagne cocktails.

The party begins as all do; everyone milling about making social connections and conversing about the speed and luxury of the *Titanic*, with snippets of business conversations thrown in. In 1912 one doesn't discuss business or financial matters in front of women, so I catch the merest abbreviated topics before more elegant first-class females wander over in satin pumps and tiaras to check up on their spouses.

Captain Smith is mingling in his best dress whites, looking dapper and elegant and yet as comfortable at the attention being thrown his way as if he were in his pajamas fielding Father's Day greetings. I stare at him perhaps longer than I should; his decades-long career has led him to this apex moment, and he's as if born to it, with grace and no small amount of glee.

I'm not up to having anything to drink right now, I make do with seltzer and remain cautiously alone—although when E.J. Smith passes by and warmly greets me by name I feel my insides melt. I flash him my warmest and most genuine smile.

Any slight glistening in my eyes will probably be chalked-up to joyous gratitude at the honor.

They're not. But no one here will ever know.

I surround myself with women as tactfully as I can, just to be clear of substantive conversation. I'm unable to track the merest shred of discourse. I'm peppered with the usual polite questions by the fine ladies of first class: "Where did you attend school?" "What does your family do?" "Any relation to the Baltimore Baldwins?"

On the surface it's all above reproach, and seems to be genuine interest in my story. But I suspect deep down each query is an attempt to scratch the surface and show me up to be a nameless rube.

Archie is unreachable to me right now across the room and I use my remaining psychological tools to remain present in proper social intercourse with this sea of women.

Finally, to my great relief, seatings begin and the wait staff gears toward getting everyone seated and dinner started. I'm resigned to dining in a sea of strangers when Archie, in a way that touches me greatly, breaks free and steers me to a quiet table for two.

"How did you hold up under the Spanish Inquisition?" he asks, smilingly.

"I told them of my peerage in Dorset; and how the Baldwin Castle, Gropsholm Manor, is frightfully draughty this season..."

Archie laughs. 'That'll keep 'em happy until they start asking around. Which I assure you, they will."

While the astonishing fare currently being served two decks down in the main Dining Saloon is sure to be top notch, what we're faced with here is simply wonderful.

After perusing our menu cards, printed fresh this morning, we each select oysters, cream of barley soup, filet mignon, cold asparagus salad, and Waldorf pudding for dessert.

I'm delighted until my brain takes sick charge of the situation:

This is to be Archie's last meal.

When the realization hits me, any last attempt at mastery over fear evaporates.

I guess this is what it's like to become quietly hysterical and to go into negative panic. How very interesting.

I watch myself become unresponsive, sliding into a fugue state, and all I can think is it would make a fascinating article someday. Too bad I won't be around to write it.

I can't bear to look directly at Archie. My heart is hammering in my throat and I know my face and ears are red. And it's alarming him. He's gazing at me with concern, trying to engage me in polite conversation, but he's also kind of eying me with a certain degree of disgust right now.

Sullen silence hangs over the table. I can't help it. I'm out.

Food comes; I go through the motions of consuming it. But it's all for show.

Nowhere in history is there a precedent to know a fellow human being right in front of you, breathing, trying to make small talk, fine dining, is going to be dead in a few hours. He's savoring his food, and it will never be digested.

We're not built for this. I'm all alone and out on a limb and stretching the bounds of human emotion, and, let's face it, my emotions aren't too sound to begin with. I want to run away, but there's nowhere to go.

And I still must maintain for Archie's sake. I owe it to him. He deserves the best I have to give.

So I turn to the only thing I know that'll help me. I signal the steward and order a double scotch with ice.

Bad idea, but it'll work.

Yet when it comes there's just one dying ice cube in it. They're British, right? Long standing battle for Americans traveling in England is their insouciant lack of ice in beverages. It drives Americans crazy, and makes me almost mad enough to bark out loud. Here I am fussing about an ice cube and—believe me—the irony is in no way lost on me.

But slowly I begin to reassert as the alcohol moves in and gives me strength. That's what it does. That's why I like it. Much to my detriment, but that hardly matters anymore.

I'm able thus to return to the present with Archie at our little dinner table. I'm able to listen to him talk about parties and events and golf. Golf, golf, golf. We normalize a little bit, then.

After dinner, Archie has to go to the men's room and I follow him. I refuse to let him out of my sight.

I smell asparagus in his pee from the next urinal and almost start to blubber.

Once more to the Smoking Room in front of the fireplace, Charles Hays is nearby with two other men, talking loudly about how "the *Titanic* is a superlative vessel, yet the trend to playing fast and loose with larger and larger ships will end in disaster one day." I actually overhear him say that. Tonight of all nights.

I'm basically in a stupor. I feel like I'm going to lose my mind. I have massive amounts of Grand Marnier; it helps a bit, but I have to keep my wits about me. *What wits? I'm losing them.*

I listen to Archie talk, all those ideas and plans and *life* . . .

Mr. Weidener joins us, and I have to fight to remain civil. He seems to take pleasure in informing Archie that he's just received a wireless: Roosevelt won the Pennsylvania primary today, a massive win over Taft.

Archie looks stricken.

I become quietly hammered as the clock ticks on. I'm not proud of this, but after the slushy phase of alcohol, for me comes a window of clarity of thought. I'm drunk, but in command at last. I'm in the zone, and it's the only state I can think to arrange that will allow me to get through the next few hours.

Engaging in banal conversations with powerful men, I surf the limits of my alcohol window, careful to stay within bounds but numb enough to function at all.

Time's up.

It's 11:30 p.m. My heart rate surging, I break into the conversation and ask the Major if he'd accompany me to the Boat Deck for a moment. He looks a little irked at the interruption, but I also see concern on his face. By now he's surely tipped off that something might be about to happen. Despite my best efforts, I'm totally throwing out sparks, both janky and wrong.

He comes with me up the steps, those solid, wooden steps, lovingly edged in polished brass, and out to the starboard rail. Outside the gymnasium, right behind lifeboat number seven.

"I need to tell you something."

"What is it, Mark? What's wrong?"

"I . . . don't want to keep you from your friends, I just wanted to thank you for spending time with me. It means a lot, and I think you're an amazing man." I'm getting brave. I look into his soft eyes, memorizing that adorable face, the reddish moustache, the dimple. His perennially quizzical expression.

"Why? Are you leaving us?" he jokes—then snaps into acute alarm as a realization strikes him. He probably thinks I'm about to jump off the ship and kill myself, mid-ocean. I've certainly been messy enough all day to do exactly that.

"Say! What's going on?" He's openly concerned. He even positions himself slightly between me and the *Titanic*'s rail as a safeguard.

"Will you wait with me here? Just for a few minutes?" I ask.

"Of course, but what's this all about? Are you all right?"

"I'll be fine in a few minutes."

When we see the iceberg, I suspect Archie's military brain will become activated. He'll probably handle it all significantly better than I will. Meanwhile I'll be thrown back into disaster mode once more, back onto my emotional skids. I'll go from bystander to participant, with all the glorious emotions that come with it. That I'll lose my shit at some point in front of Archie suddenly becomes my greatest concern for a moment.

It's a cold, dark, clear night with a blaze of stars overhead. We can see forward; the wind is such that my eyes tear up and I keep blinking. I keep my own watch out for the iceberg. Stupid, I know, but I have to be there. I have to see it. Archie needs to see it.

And he'll finally know why I'm here.

I look up to the crow's nest, ninety-five feet up on the forward mast. Two men, Frederick Fleet and Reginald Lee, are up there, with no binoculars—they're still locked in a cabinet. I can't see them, but I know they are there. History knows they are there. Captain Smith has just retired for the night—he'll be a few feet away from us right now in the crew quarters just forward of where we're standing. His windows are right over there; a single lamp is burning. He's probably in bed, reading, scratching his balls, having a nice little something to drink.

11:35. It is about to happen. I still can't see anything. My heart is pounding like mad. Archie is standing quite near me at the rail, we're as far forward as you can go on the first-class Promenade. No one else is nearby. Immediately before us is the gate to the Officer's Promenade. This time, when its actually important, we're not allowed in.

11:38. They should be able to see it by now.

I hear the clang of the bell then and know it is happening. Frederick Fleet would be on the telephone to the bridge. History recorded the conversation:

"What do you see?"

"Iceberg, right ahead!"

"Thank you."

And the phone was summarily hung up.

Suddenly I can hear some shouting from the bridge and the clang of the telegraphs: The dreaded order to reverse engines.

I feel a slight change in the ship. I doubt Archie even notices. The pitch of the engines changes. By now the huge main engine will be powering down, and the One and Three engines slammed into reverse. Cavitating—meaning the water around them is in such turmoil the enormous propellers aren't even able to gain purchase in the water. The ship is now virtually rudderless.

Slowly we turn to the left. Agonizingly slowly.

Then I do see it. An unassuming hunk of ice appears ahead, about sixty feet tall and black as night. We are headed for it, the bow swinging leisurely to port. I watch transfixed as the distance closes between us and it at an alarming rate. We are turning, slowly. After what seems like ages, the turn becomes more significant and the iceberg moves somewhat to the right. The closer it comes the more it looks like we're going to miss it. But I know what is about to happen below the waterline: A huge barb of ice is jutting out, ready to slice us open like an orange. Just when it gets to us—and it really feels like we're going to miss it—impact is felt.

The railing shudders under our hands and a scraping sound is heard. Just as quickly the iceberg races by us at twenty-five miles an hour. It's so close! I almost feel like I could have touched it.

"My God," says Archie.

As the iceberg sails past, I know that Murdoch is making hard-to-port call, trying to turn around the berg to protect the propellers. But it is too late for that. The damage is done.

More clanging of the telegraph bells: "All Stop."

By now E.J. Smith will have dashed to the bridge, just ten yards from where we stand, demanding a report from Murdoch.

I'll always wonder what words they exchange. They are lost to history but could only have been seriously intense.

"Close all watertight compartments" is ordered, this much we know. The ship falls silent as the engines are cut. A few gentlemen come out on deck.

"What is it?" someone asks.

"Looked like an iceberg," Archie says.

"We must have just glanced it," the man says. "Wasn't much of a collision. Well. I'm going back inside to my drink."

After a few moments, an unimaginable sound returns. *Titanic's* engines, all three, have been ordered one-quarter ahead. They're trying to keep going.

This will actually force more water in, at a faster rate.

Perhaps fifteen minutes go by. I'm glued to my spot, the closest I can get to the unfolding emergency. And Archie is standing at my side, physically leaning into me, whether aware of it or not. Any doubts about my presence here must surely be gone from his mind now.

I know what would be happening on the bridge: Damage reports are coming in. Water is pouring through multiple gashes in the hull, filling the very compartments I looked down into my first day aboard. An ungodly amount of water. Cold, ice cold, green. Heavy. Merciless.

Bruce J. Ismay and Thomas Andrews walk past us on their way to the bridge, in nervous consternation, Mr. Andrews carrying a giant roll of ship's plans under his arm.

After a few minutes, the engines shut down once more. For good. *Titanic* is still slicing through the water but slowing. We'll go at least a quarter of a mile before she finally comes to a standstill.

"Archie, tonight's going to end badly," I tell him finally. "This is why I've been so upset all day." I look him in his eyes, and I wait for the realization to dawn over his features.

"This is why I'm here. It's why my failure to get off at Queenstown had me so upset."

He nods. "Bad?" he asks.

"Worst in maritime history," I say matter-of-factly.

I don't add anything else. I just watch him absorb what I've said.

"Do you want me to stay with you?" I ask. And I mean it.

"Do you know of a way off the ship?" he asks, his voice breaking just a little bit.

"I do. This lifeboat right here. It will be the first to leave and there will be room on it for both of us."

"I . . . I don't think I could do that," he says.

"It will have empty seats."

"My God, *why*?"

"People don't believe anything bad is going to happen. They think the ship will be all right. It won't. As we begin to sink, they'll fill up the boats, but by then it will be too late."

Archie nods again. "You have a chance to save yourself. You should take it."

"I don't want to if you won't come with me. There isn't enough room in the other lifeboats for everyone. We have a shot with this one! Will you take it with me?"

"No, Mark, I won't. It wouldn't be right."

Damn! I knew he'd say that.

"But I find it difficult to understand why any lifeboat would be dispatched with empty seats. Surely that's not the right thing to do if we're in as grave a difficulty as you say . . . "

Obviously, I've read ahead: Thomas Andrews does his calculations and informs E.J. that the ship will likely sink in one hour—maybe ninety minutes at the outside. And it takes a good hour to launch twenty boats, assuming everything goes smoothly. A panic would only cripple their efforts and waste valuable time. E.J.'s thinking will be that it is more important to get the boats safely in the water, within the allotted time, so they could be used to rescue people off the sinking ship.

It is a judgement call. And, if E.J. were to survive, he'd be raked over the coals about it for the end of his days.

But he doesn't survive.

In any case, the point is moot since the lifeboat capacity can only accept roughly half the souls on board. Hundreds will die either way. There's nothing for it. They just didn't consider a total loss of sea frame a viable possibility. It's one of the reasons the *Titanic* disaster will shake the world: It serves as a cruel and stark reminder that Man has gotten way too confident in his mastery over nature.

I don't want to leave Archie behind. Suddenly I feel like such a coward! A pathetic queen. A snake. If only he'd get over himself and get in the damned lifeboat! But Archie shall be Archie, through to the end. How do I reconcile this? How do I salvage self, dignity . . . and Archie? At least one of these three things shall perish tonight—perhaps all will be extinguished.

My inner turmoil is lavish. I'm losing the ability to think on any rational level.

For a while, though, nothing seems to happen. Most people are still warmly in bed. Those who are awake mill around, bemused. Something interesting is happening. They'll want it to evolve into an interesting tale to always have on hand.

The biggest notable difference is that the engines have, at last, gone silent.

By midnight, twenty minutes after the collision, the ship is already tilting to the right and nosing forward and down.

42

Monday, April 15, 1912

Sea water is now gushing into the ship's boiler rooms. If it should come into contact with a hot boiler, the result will be a massive explosion. And *Titanic* has twenty-nine of them, each a ticking time bomb. So the dampers have to be closed, and thousands of pounds of steam let out through the stacks immediately.

It is beyond loud—a cacophony. It is impossible to speak and be heard. Suddenly the calm air is rent with sound, and it goes on for twenty long minutes. Passengers who had begun to gather on the Boat Deck quickly go back inside to escape the horrid noise.

It has the desired effect. No explosions occur. But any illusion that this is just a drill effectively ends. The ship is stopped cold in the water, her engines bled dry and cold. It would take twelve hours to fire them back up again, but that command will never come.

At 12:05 E.J. orders the lifeboats swung out and passengers mustered to the Boat Deck.

Stewards ship-wide begin banging on stateroom doors, rousing passengers, telling them to be on deck with their lifebelts. On the Boat Deck, sailors, seamen, and officers start unwrapping the canvas covers off the boats and getting them ready to be swung out. Crowds form to watch. It's all just so interesting, new people showing up every moment, bewildered, chilly, carrying—rather than wearing—their lifebelts, but only a few moments of genial amusement are afforded. Passenger after passenger comes out, hears the unbearable sound coming from the stacks, turns right around and goes back inside and downstairs.

I encounter the Slocombes and their new friends and encourage them to get in a lifeboat when the time comes. Jake seems unconvinced.

It's about 12:30 when the venting finally stops. It had the benefit of clearing the decks so the crew could prep the lifeboats unimpeded. Now that the noise is gone, crowds are gathering once more. It's shockingly quiet now. Just murmured, confused conversation and seamen shouting orders at each other, and the squeaking and clanking of ropes and gear.

Archie and I are still on the starboard side, and the officers and men, now granted silence from the boilers, are trying to coax women and children into lifeboat number seven.

It's not going well. Something's obviously wrong with the ship, but it's still six stories down to the surface of the water. It's cold. It's dark. The *Titanic* is an enormous, brand new, magnificent machine, fully lit with the heat on, the cocktail bars open and a band somewhere playing bright music. It's impossible at this point to recognize that the ship has, in fact, been mortally wounded. The general mood seems to be that the whole thing is preposterous.

So there are few takers for a while. Archie and I stand,

watching, while people mill about, officers cajole, a few women get into the boat, but as yet no one is taking it seriously. I look toward the bow and see Captain Smith pacing on the bridge wing in an exasperated fashion.

Lifeboat number seven is just in front of me. All I have to do is to leave Archibald Butt behind to his death, walk ten paces, and have a seat among a smattering of waiting women.

And for the life of me I can't do it.

My brain squelches into unchartered chaos. Suddenly I'm not processing any rational thought.

Something snaps. First the fear comes back. The gripping absoluteness of it . . . Just like it did in the shelter, lymphoma happily joins the chorus. The once-again feeling that my body shall simply explode where it stands courses through me. This is far beyond anything so charming as a panic attack. This is utter terror.

I let it play for a moment—nay, I have no choice but to surrender to it entirely. But somehow, it only takes me for a short time. Fear more highly attenuated than I have ever known seizes me in its grasp, then climaxes, peaks, and crashes me down into the state in which I, eventually, find myself now.

Which is one of complete resignation. I've had it.

Until David gave me time travel, my life was a waste of time. Unfulfilled, empty, drunk, alone and a case of cancer thrown in for good measure. Then I callously, laughingly, threw myself in the middle of riots, earthquake, fires, and bombings, thinking they'd shake me from my malaise.

Instead, I'm quite neatly, emotionally collapsing.

You're not supposed to do that, and now I know why. I'm losing it.

Fuck it. All of it. I've got nothing at home but "my bearded men who don't love me," as Pamela Jarvis put it, and a cratered career. And a horrible, painful death lurking in my immediate future anyway. Archie's going to die now and I'm not sure I want to go on any longer.

The idea of my gay ass in that lifeboat suddenly enrages me. How dare I? Am I really that pathetic? I suddenly know that doing so would completely cancel out my time with Archie. He'd go to his death knowing I'm a coward. And I'd go on living with a kind of shame I don't think I can bear.

Apparently, I've already decided: it's not gonna happen.

I wouldn't mind dying. Not really. I hear the water's cold; like knives stabbing at you, but once you're in, you just surrender and you don't feel anything anymore. It will serve as its own anesthetic, something that suddenly strikes me as appropriate and calming. I think it is meant to be.

I'm just tired. Tired of Clarence and all his ilk; tired of trying. Whatever it is, it's not working.

What do I care that a man born in 1865 thinks less of me for getting into a rowboat?

But I do. I really do. I'd jump into the cold, black sea now if it would mean his approval. I can't leave him here to die alone. He's so alive, so full of hope. The goddamned President of the United States is waiting for Archie to come home and be his friend and golf buddy again.

Me? I got nothing. A city full of acquaintances and a cat who pees.

Whatever. I'm done. Fuck it.

My body hasn't moved from where I've been standing, yet my will to live has gone elsewhere in its entirety. And yet I feel absolutely calm. Relieved, actually. It's OK that I just want this all to end.

It's OK.

I rejoin Archie, who I'm sure has been lost in his own thoughts—I can't presume to know what they are—but he's an Army Man and a brave soul. Now, maybe, I am too.

I suddenly find it exhilarating. "Looks like it's you and me, kid."

"Huh?" says Archie.

"We're in this together."

"Wait. Do you have a way off this ship or don't you?"

"I do. But I'm not going to take it if you don't."

"You can't be serious. Mark, if you have a way off you have to go. I'll not have you stay here for my sake. By God, I'll physically chuck you into that lifeboat if I have to." He's growling at me, and knows he'd be perfectly capable of accomplishing it.

"Too late. They're lowering it. I'm not on it. No other boat would let me on now. It's you and me, like I said."

Lifeboat number seven is indeed, at this very moment, squeaking on its ropes right below us, jerking unsteadily down, its few occupants huddled and confused and ashamed.

"Mark, that was damned foolish." He sounds genuinely pissed, an emotion I've never observed in him.

"Whatever." I'm slipping into my home dialect. "This whole thing, in modern army parlance, is going Tango Uniform. Let's just get this over with. When the time comes, I'll tell you what we should probably do. Until then, we can't do a damned thing but watch."

The deck becomes crowded with people not necessarily in a rush to abandon ship, but mostly to see what the hell's going on.

Rockets start shooting up from the bridge wing. They're startling, and beautiful, too; but they alter the mood of the passengers precipitously. To even the most obtuse individual, the situation is taking a much more serious tone, and a palpable tension is beginning to mount.

Music had been issuing from somewhere inside the ship, but eventually the eight musicians, chairs and all, set themselves up on the Boat Deck and resume playing airs, just as history has always told us.

More people are climbing into boats (in our case, numbers one and three), officers coaxing and goading, and for the next forty-five minutes or so I follow Archie as he goes from boat to boat on the starboard side, helping women—and a few men—into the rescue craft. Archie is grandly helping women in epic gowns and cloaks against the chill, trussed up in lifebelts that seem to be little more than cork covered in gray canvas.

"That's all right, ladies, I've got you. You'll be fine. We'll get all this figured out and have you back in your cabins in no time."

Few actually believe him, but his words have a calming effect. The men are there watching in shocked silence.

Couple after couple says goodbye to each other in their own way, each with their comparative grasp of the enormity of the situation. Some are devastated, heartbroken, and in tears as they rip themselves apart for the final time, saying "goodbye." They're the ones who know.

Most are simply confused, banal; certain they'll see each other again soon once the difficulty has been sorted out.

By 1:00 a.m., we're a fair bit lower in the water and still a few lifeboats remain, mostly further aft in the second-class section of the Boat Deck. I stand at the open space that once held number seven. There's no railing. It's a straight shot down, only about three stories now.

The predominant sound is hushed conversation and the squeaking of winches, cranes, and davits. Accompanied by ragtime music.

"Mark," Archie says suddenly, "would you go to my cabin and bring up heavy coats for us? They're in the trunk."

"Yeah, that's probably a good idea. I'll be right back."

So off I head, through the doors and over to the grand staircase, fighting the outbound traffic. Everyone's moving up. I'm the only fool struggling to go down, two levels to Archie's door.

To do this I must deliberately get much closer to the

swirling water and I don't like the idea. I don't try to look down the stairwell, I just proceed to B-38 and everything, aside from the worsening angle of the decks, seems normal.

Once inside his stateroom I get a coat for each of us, and look around the cabin, just briefly, and sigh. A lot happened in B-38. Our scotch stain remains stubbornly visible on the brand-new carpet.

Atop the wardrobe are two life jackets. I snatch them as well. Fat lot of good they'll do.

Back at the Grand Staircase, this time I take the trouble to look down the open well to one side and immediately wish I hadn't. Angry green water is swirling just below. C-Deck is filling with sea water, and it's all lit by submerged lightbulbs, still burning brightly. It's horrifying.

I back away in revulsion.

When I find Archie, he insists on giving me the heavier of the two coats. I tell him no and take the lighter one. I then put on a life preserver and offer one to Archie. He declines it, as I suspected he would. I toss it aside for someone else to use.

I go over to observe the port side and find an altogether different scene. For reasons unknown, the deck on this side is mobbed with people and it's far more unruly. On our side, left-over men are being put into open seats. Here no such undertaking is allowed. When they run out of women and children the boats are dispatched with open seats and that's that.

It's getting ugly.

And most of these people are just first-class passengers. Second class has full access to the Boat Deck a bit further aft, but the teaming masses of third class, below decks, are, by and large still there. Sailors were supposed to open the gangway doors and put those people into the lifeboats with empty seats, but history will reveal that no one actually does.

I go back to our side and see the boats down in the water, oars out but nowhere to go. The angle of the ship is getting worse. We're definitely going down by the head, and all the lights are still on, even below the waterline, which is weird and against all the known rules of electricity.

Archie is determined to just work his way aft, into the second-class section of the Boat Deck, to assist with the loading there. And I follow, saying nothing. The music is further away, but the surface of the sea is getting closer and the mood far more tense. But it isn't long before we run out of lifeboats to load.

We're surrounded by people who now, suddenly, have nowhere to go.

By now it's 2:00 a.m. *Titanic* has about twenty minutes left, and it's becoming readily apparent to all. The only lifeboats remaining are four collapsible craft lashed upside down on the roof of the officer's quarters up front. Crewmen are working to extricate them and none of it seems to be going well.

Ships don't sink in silence. I didn't know how loudly it would complain at surrendering to the sea. The old girl and her billions of contents protest in constant pops and groans, the tinkle of dying crystal goblets.

I decide to give Archie the final low-down.

"OK, Archie; by now you know why this ship is famous. The events of this evening have been studied and broken down, bit by bit, for generations. Here's what's going to happen: As the bow goes down, the stern will rise until finally the stresses become too great, and the ship will break completely in two. Right back there. This end, the front, will be gone."

His eyes bug out as he looks back at the stern, examines the still brightly lit stacks and mobs of people, and imagines the scene. His face shows only confusion. How can metal, crafted into a vessel as solid as this, simply snap in half?

"But the back end will still float?"

"Only for a few moments. It will become almost completely vertical," I'm demonstrating with my hand and arm, "and then plunge to the bottom. Almost all humans still aboard will be in that back section, on deck, suddenly with nothing to cling to. I think it's really important that we not be among them.

"We should remain out here in the middle, ready to jump with the first section. But that only means we'll be going into the water earlier than mostly everyone else, and I'm not going to lie to you: It won't be good."

"All right."

"Try to get atop any wreckage you can and limit your exposure to the sea water as much as possible. It'll kill you in twenty minutes. And the nearest rescue ship is still two hours away at least."

"Yes, sir."

We spend the remaining time unceremoniously chucking deckchairs from the Boat Deck into the Atlantic, now only a few feet below us. We get a good thirty of them over the starboard rail, during which time a small part of my mind seizes on the fact that I am now literally rearranging deck chairs on the *Titanic*. Some float away, most just hang around in a tangle, bobbing a little.

Archie, after several glances in the direction of the bridge, says he wishes to check in with the captain, to see if he can be of help in any further way. I see no reason not to. I'm just mentally operating on low candle power right now.

We make our way forward. Men are still working the collapsibles free, and now that the ship is so low in the water, the work becomes frantic—and, as a result, visibly less effective. Squabbles and arguments are breaking out. Heavy ropes are tangled and nothing's getting accomplished in the chaos.

The sea is almost level with the bridge. The prow is completely gone—only the cables stick up out of the water to signify that it still exists.

The Officer's Promenade gates are open, and we just walk onto the bridge to find Captain E.J. Smith talking to a man, who, startlingly, is standing there in his underwear. Long boxer shorts, socks and garters, and wife-beater shirt. Fourth Officer Henry Wilde is lounging off to one side, smoking a cigarette, watching with what looks like bored detachment.

Underwear Guy is saying he's about to go into the water but he's going to have a drink first, to guard against the chill.

Archie interrupts.

"Captain Smith, sir, will any attempt be made to bring those boats back to the gangway doors and continue loading passengers? By the looks of it, most lifeboats are half-empty, even now."

Smith looks as in command as ever, but issues the death knell to hundreds of people, as of a single body, in his reply.

"Major Butt, I appreciate your concern, but if the boats get too close to the ship now, they'll become hopelessly swamped with a surge of people. Many more lives will be lost. We can't risk endangering the lives already in the rafts. Additionally, most are far out of hearing range now. We have no means of calling them back."

That's his answer. I don't agree with it, and history won't, either. Neither does Archie, judging by the look of disgust on his face.

"Well, sir, I came to say what I felt I needed to say." His jaw is a stern line of tension. Years of serving army lieutenants and presidents prevents him from speaking out of turn, but nothing in protocol can ultimately waive a seething contempt beneath the surface.

"Thank you, Major Butt. Soon it'll be every man for himself." Captain Smith sounds resigned. It is done.

Underwear Guy stubbornly re-inserts himself into the conversation. "There isn't much time left. Won't you take a drink with me, Captain?" he asks.

For a brief moment I find myself once again at the controls of the ship. Nobody cares now. I gaze forward to a sea that reaches very nearly to the windows. The front of the ship is simply gone. It's like a horror show, immediately close at hand. Nature is reclaiming the massive vessel, a masterpiece of man's creation.

Titanic is only four days old and has just been totaled.

The side-commuter indicates a 28 degree down angle and steepening, and that's just not good. Water will ooze over the floors of the bridge before long. It's coming.

The brass engine telegraph, now set to its forever new position, simply says *STOP*.

Captain Smith has agreed to have a drink. The four of us, one in underwear, walk the short distance to E.J.'s stateroom. It is his sanctum. A space too new to soften into the funk of the man occupying it, as yet sterile and without tendrils of memories or the scent of a man. Books sit on shelves with fiddles to keep them in place. There are charts, art, statues and a lamp sweetly burning, yet everything is sloping at an angle, making it macabre and wrong.

E.J. hefts a nearly full decanter of brandy and pours out four stemmed crystal glasses and we each take one and toast. Not a word is said; none would be even remotely adequate. I look into the eyes of each, the heart-stopping, beautiful blue of E.J.'s, the brown confused eyes of Underwear Guy, and the familiar pools that are Archie's, which I have come to know so well.

One swallow burns, and the brandy is gone. I want the whole bottle for myself and very nearly grab it. Why would anyone undergo this sober? But everyone's playing it cool, even now.

We simply put the glasses neatly back down where they belong, as if we don't want to leave a mess for the cabin steward, and march back out to the bridge.

Saying nothing, Underwear Man swan dives into the water off the port wing and is never seen again.

We shake hands with E.J. Smith. I glance into those eyes once more and, just like with Ben so long ago, wish I hadn't. I see a proud, powerful man reduced to pain and utter shock.

"Godspeed, Mr. Baldwin," he tells me, releases my hand, and turns back to the shattered remains of his command.

Moving aft again, even a little bit, is a palpable relief. One wants to move away from the waterline instinctively, and, to that end, most of the remaining passengers are quickly making their way back uphill. Some remain by the canvas collapsible boats still being wrestled into position. But this entire section of the ship is sinking, canting forward rapidly now, the water perilously close.

"We've got about fifteen minutes, I guess," I say to Archie. He simply nods in acknowledgement.

We quickly move back along the Boat Deck, away from the sinking bridge, the water following us fast enough to observe but slow enough to easily outpace.

The band stopped but has taken a new position further aft and has resumed playing ragtime.

I can't believe I'm still on this ship. I should have been long gone by now. I look out and see lifeboats, nearly empty, floating, maddeningly, a few dozen yards away. I see fur and jewels and the privileges of class sneaking off in the night at the expense of every man, woman, and child left on this vessel.

But then I remember my decision and why I made it.

I'm ready for death. I'm ready for the cold.

We stand at the starboard rail, wide open vistas now that the lifeboats are gone. The slanting deck is quite empty and clear. We look forward. The bridge is beginning to dip. For some reason I think of the fire logs in the Smoke Room fireplace, wondering if they haven't yet rolled out and down the carpet by this point.

The ship wasn't built to withstand such stresses. We can hear groaning and snapping in the hull.

Archie gives me a long look and takes my hand in his.

It's what I'd always wanted, simply holding hands with this man. Yet instead of feeling new and daring, the sensation is one of old, familiar calm. As if it's ever been thus.

We hold hands as the water rises. The bridge, sixty feet ahead of us, is dipping into the sea. As we watch, E.J. Smith, in full uniform and captain's hat firmly rooted upon his head, is waist deep in water lit from below. He walks to the starboard bridge wing and hoists himself up on the rail. With the ease of a casual bather, he lowers himself into the freezing sea and, arm over arm, swims a few yards clear of his vessel. He then gazes back at the masterpiece of the White Star Line, the pinnacle of Man's achievements over the seas, and, even at this distance, the shock and horror on his face are clear.

His command is dying. As captain, the responsibility is his.

He lifts his arms and plummets beneath the surface of the water. I don't see him come back up, for this is the moment where my feet, and Archie's, have met the sea.

Such cold as I have never known oozes into my shoes and starts rising inexorably up my shins.

If it has to be this cold then fuck everything. It is terrible.

We quickly scramble further back, uphill, away from the rushing water. I stop us at the entrance to the Grand Staircase. We're clear of the rising water again, momentarily, but I seriously doubt we should go any further aft. I don't want us to be too close to where the ship will snap in two.

I turn to Archie. We're still holding hands. I can't read his expression, it's one of plain shock and resignation. His jaw is tight.

The bridge is now totally submerged. Three of those canvas boats they've been wrestling with are below the water, including all who were fighting them. One collapsible boat is bobbing properly on the sea, ringed with wet and shivering sailors. The other boats then bubble up in various states of unreadiness, on their sides or upside down. A knot of people is now in the water scrambling to grab hold of them, their faces white and shocked. As water floods the interior front part of the ship, it is turbulent and surging. People are being tossed and pulled, thrashing.

The pace of events, almost languid up until this point, speeds up to a rapid blur that can barely register on the mind.

As the ship brazenly tips forward, a sound like gunshots rings out. The metal hawsers keeping the foremost funnel attached to the deck snap. The water swirling at the base exerts too much pressure and it collapses. The massive stack bends and rolls over to port, almost in slow motion. Mostly empty metal, it is nevertheless an enormous, heavy thing, and many humans are extinguished beneath it.

The ship's final plunge begins. That which makes a ship a ship has now been wiped clean from the *Titanic's* balance books.

To this end, the angle of the deck increases even further, and Archie and I, his right hand in my left, begin skidding inexorably in our clacky fancy shoes toward the water. It hardly matters, because the water is rushing up on its own to meet us in a frothy swirl.

With nothing to stop us, we're in. The *Titanic* is slithering away from beneath our feet.

It's so cold I'm burning. No human can withstand it. It's ungodly. My clothes feel like hot oil clinging to me, Archie's hand tightens in mine as *Titanic's* lights wink out. A roar of complaint issues from the crowd as everyone says "oh!" in unison. The lights flicker back on once, feebly, seemingly the color red, and then go out for good. Crashes and explosions are occurring to the left of us in the great ship, massive breaking of glass and gushing of water and . . .

Major Archibald Butt slips out of my life and back onto the

faded page of my childhood history book. I don't even see it happen. It's too fast, too violent.

One moment we're thrashing in painful, turbulent water, hands still locked, and in the next, the windows leading to the Grand Staircase have given way and a tsunami of water is now gushing into that part of the ship.

Because Archie is closer and without a life vest, he is instantaneously sucked into it. He never calls out, he is simply ended.

He is gone.

This particular wave subsides. I get pulled under the surface completely for a brief moment, but because of my life belt I simply pop back up, burning with cold, trying to process everything around me, gasping for air. But my body feels locked in a vice. I try to move my extremities a little, to generate warmth, but . . . I can't. I cannot move my body. I'm hanging by the neck from my cork life vest, it's choking me, and I'm huffing ghastly jagged breaths, unable to move.

I try to focus on Archie, as if the powers of my erratic mind can somehow reach him, save him, tell him to hold on . . . to let him know that I'm still here.

I'm still here, Archie! I haven't left you!

But I'm robbed of all that by what happens next.

The too-heavy stern, now almost entirely out of the water, begins to crack *Titanic* open. Slowly at first, a sick moaning of tortured metal groans long and loud. The structural integrity of the iron giant has bent beyond reckoning. Water is now freely pouring into it and the front half of the ship begins to angle straight down.

I prepare to die. I don't know that I regret my decision. It's all the same to me right now.

I swivel slightly to visually take in what remains of the ship. The bow section is no longer visible. It's gone, fully submerged and pointing straight down, yet apparently, stubbornly connected to the larger stern section by unknown tissues of steel. This causes the stern to rise straight up. It's huge, just in front of me. I'm only about ten yards away by now. People are everywhere along the structure, hanging onto anything they can. Hundreds more are thrashing in the water and screaming for help.

Then the steel tissue snaps, and the front section of the ship begins its journey to the ocean floor.

Archie!

He'll be dozens of feet underwater now, somewhere inside the most beautiful of the ship's appointments, sinking into complete, frozen, airless blackness. His lungs will have surely collapsed. The sweet, slight sound of air flowing in and out of his nose that lulled me to sleep one day is forever choked to silence.

Yet I am riveted by my view of the stern of *Titanic*. It has now become a building, thirty stories tall, vertical in the water, a black silhouette visible only by starlight.

It freezes a moment, as if having second thoughts. Untold hundreds of people are clinging to it, yet many lose their grip and crash to the water from obscene heights. The distance is so far to fall that they land further away from the wreckage than I am right now, and despite my best efforts, my mind stubbornly insists on comparing it to people leaping from the World Trade Center. The horror is the same, but this is real. It's actually happening.

Things end. And that time is now.

The stern section quickly begins to subside. Slowly at first, then picking up speed as air rushes out and water floods in. With a deliberate sort of grace, the great length of it leisurely slides into the water until the back rail snicks beneath the waves.

The cries of 1,500 people, helpless in ice cold water, has been likened to the roar of Tiger's Stadium after a home run hit. It's loud and horrifying. I'm in a sea of people thrashing and screaming, grasping for small bits of wreckage while nothing larger than a deck chair exists for hundreds of miles.

Something bangs my head from behind, *hard*. I'm mad. It hurts! I consider losing consciousness for a mere second, but recognition snaps me to.

An upside-down collapsible lifeboat, left over from the roof of the officer's quarters, is floating the wrong way and it's that which just bumped me in the head. It is strewn with people hanging on, draped over the top like upon a beached whale. I grab onto the edge of it and hold on for dear life. Everyone else is hanging on to it too. People are swimming up to it and being pushed away. I'm holding on too tight to dare push anyone off.

I will never know how I manage to climb up atop the boat. It's patently beyond my strength level, but I've scrambled up and quickly turn to help others. You *have* to get them out of the water. It's too cold. The night air feels like an icy slap on my soaking, heavy clothes. Everyone's thrashing and trying to climb up, but soon the boat is at more than capacity. We're all standing on its back in a clump, clasping at each other. There's no more space, and I'm suddenly horrified to realize I'm taking up room that should have been filled by another person.

I've just killed someone. I've taken one square foot on the back of this lifeboat from another man who was originally supposed to survive. Who? Jack Thayer? Harold Bride? Who did I just consign to a watery grave?

I'm not supposed to be here, and I've just displaced someone who was meant to live.

Very near to throwing myself back in the water to undo the damage I have just done to history, in a useless fit of anger I savagely wrestle myself out of that life preserver, greatly upsetting those clinging to me. I throw it in the water and am relieved at least to see a woman clutch at it hopefully.

It's time for me to off myself, to restore the universe to its proper shape.

And I can't fucking do it!

I'm ready to jump. My body already craves that icy water once more, the cold anesthesia it will ultimately provide . . . and I can't do it.

A faint-hearted chickenshit who only found bravery in the past few moments of his life has once again relapsed back into the state of cowardice.

I retch. I draw air into my lungs with greater reluctance than I have ever known.

If Archie were here, I'd jump. But he's gone, and I'm still here, simply because I'm not strong enough to face death after all.

I turn my face away from the edge. I am physically weak and morally devoid of character. And such shall be my designation as long as my life goes on.

I've just straight-up fucked with the universe. I can't even imagine what my punishment shall be.

The inverted canvas boat provides only a curved, soft surface, slippery and treacherous. We're all along its back, as many as will fit, with dozens of people in the water clinging to the rim, and others, clinging to them, like ants forming a chain.

With *Titanic* gone, time stops. The thrashing in the water becomes less. The main lifeboats—some of which are still virtually empty—are off in the distance. All that's left are the people flailing in the water around us. People are floating on whatever they can, but being in virtual ice water, they don't last long. One by one, the flailing stops. The people hanging off the collapsible begin to slip beneath the waves. They're not even shivering anymore. The reflex is stopped.

Suddenly, worse by far than the screams a few moments ago, there is quiet. Countless human voices are cut to stillness. The silence is so horrifying, it signifies an awful truth so relentless and evil I find myself wishing for the screams again.

It's nearly pitch black, despite the night sky being a canvas of stars, a huge dome of pinpricks of light. Roughly thirty of us are standing on the back of that overturned lifeboat, balancing, shivering, holding onto each other for the perception of warmth, although the bodies I grasp feel as cold as death.

We're freezing. We all have wet clothes. But we can't complain, not to the universe or to each other, for at least we're not in the water.

My brain has ceased to function. It is just another useless extremity, numbed by the cold.

The Cunard Line ship *Carpathia* is the closest one. They're steaming to our rescue at top speed, but they're still an hour and a half away at the very least. We're resigned to a long night balancing on the back of that lifeboat.

Yet the boat itself is slowly sinking. Whatever air is keeping us buoyant is oozing out and the boat is settling lower and lower in the water. Soon we're in the sea up to our ankles, then to our knees, and that's when we begin to lose people. The water had been perfectly calm till now, but a swell soon comes up, bringing waves, and we have to balance to keep our equilibrium. The people—almost all men—line up and face forward and lean against the swell, trying to keep us upright on the back of the boat.

But people lose their footing and fall back into the water, and no one has the strength to help.

Finally, two of the *Titanic's* regular lifeboats row alongside us. They have tiny lights on poles, and we're led off the sinking collapsible one by one, with the use of great oars. It's harrowing. More than one person lands in the sea but is hastily fished out by the warmer and fresher people in the regular boat.

When it's my turn, I ungracefully yaw my leg out and land, smacking my balls resolutely on the gunwale. But I'm so numb I'm scarcely aware of it. I turn to help the person behind me, who, I'm no judge, but in the dark I feel certain that it's Harold Bride, one of the Marconi operators.

At least him I didn't kill . . .

We get situated in our new boat. A few extra blankets are put upon us. Just to sit down in comparative dry is a wonder. We wouldn't have lasted long otherwise.

So we sit. And wait. Not a word is uttered.

Eventually, after a lifetime of ardent shivering, the lights of a ship can be seen—just a tiny spark from our south. At first it seems simply one of the stars of the heavens. Suddenly, though, it becomes distinguishable as an oceangoing vessel, impossibly small, and forever away.

It's still an hour off. That's the scale of things. That's how alone we are.

The emotion that washes over me upon sighting the other ship cannot be explained: hope and disgust, emotional opposites, claw at each other in the ruined temple of my psyche.

We wait as the light grows brighter, the ship draws nearer. Even once it's recognizable as a ship, it takes forever to get close. It's a small steamer with one smokestack.

Finally, the Cunard Line's *Carpathia* draws alongside, and lights are shone down upon the scattering of boats. We're shivering, many are soaked through to the skin with iced-over wet clothes. But help is here at last.

It takes four hours to unload all the people from the lifeboats, almost all of whom are first- and second-class women. The men stayed behind on *Titanic* and were killed. J.J. Astor, Guggenheim, Captain Smith, Thomas Andrews, Mr. Hays, Mr. Straus, Dr. O'Laughlin. Major Archibald Butt.

Up a ladder, almost impossible for me in my condition. I'm mobbed the minute I squish my shoes upon the deck of the *Carpathia*. A fresh heavy blanket is thrown over my shoulders and a cup of tepid broth thrust at me by a stewardess. I'm dimly aware she's in a crisp, clean, white uniform, but beyond that I can't focus on anything.

It's silent. No one is saying a word. An outstretched arm

directs me over to some deckchairs where other *Titanic* survivors are sodden and seated, looking down at the deck to a body. All shocked, bereft. All draped in Cunard Line blankets.

They have a system going. In small batches we're led below decks. Our names are taken down. I give my own name. I am a paying passenger, history be damned.

I can't look any of the survivors in the eye. I feel like too great a coward.

We're in a lounge of the *Carpathia*, a cheaper knock-off of the grandeur of a great liner, yet there is an oriental carpet, carvings on the walls, potted palms.

A collection had been taken up and piles of *Carpathia*'s passenger clothes are stacked on tables and a steward hands us garments based roughly on our size; none too clean, but dry. Behind a makeshift blanket screen, I shuffle and fumble to get out of my wet things.

Now that warmth is returning, I begin shivering like I never thought a body could. I'm frankly gyrating. I lose all muscle control. I can't undo my own buttons. Thawing out, I'm dripping on the rug.

It's nearly impossible to coordinate my movements in such a state, but I finally manage to pull off my soggy clothes and let them drop to the deck. I put some new ones on. No knickers, but striped wool trousers and a blue work shirt—I can smell the sweat of the man it belonged to, like I'm in the worst Goodwill changing room ever known. Yet I'm glad for it just the same.

Still shivering manically, I pull my sodden cash, Archie's business card, my streaked and runny *Titanic* ticket, credit cards, soaked passport, and dead iPhone out of my old trouser pockets.

I doubt that my iPhone will have survived, but I shall keep it anyway. Maybe someday I can get the contents back out but probably not. What do you tell the facially pierced person at the Genius Bar?

I put my old clothes in the bin provided but remember with a shock that the overcoat belongs to Archie and I want it. I want it forever. I grab it and they try to take it away and I won't let them.

Others amble with me as we're shepherded through the lounge to yet another lounge, ostensibly for the ladies, as it's pink. Tables are set and other survivors are beginning to eat. The crew of the *Carpathia* are smart—they're not lavishing us with heavy food, just soup, tea, and cakes. I can't taste any of it, and I'm still gyrating so bad the soup sloshes off my spoon before it reaches my mouth like an invalid.

Always just around various corners are the *Carpathia's* regular passengers, craning for a look at us.

When I'm alone in a toilet cubicle, somewhat more in control of my faculties, I pull out my phone and try to power it back on. The damn thing works! I'm stunned. God bless Apple for finally deciding to make them marginally waterproof.

Their voyage from New York to Gibraltar already sufficiently disrupted, the passengers on *Carpathia* double up in their cabins to make room for the roughly 700 people off the *Titanic*. I'm given the option of a shared stateroom but turn it down. A deck chair and a blanket is all I deserve.

It's what Archie would have done.

I was ready to die. In a way I did die; but then I took the coward's way out. I'm heavy with disgust. I know I took someone's place, but the fight to survive kicked in and was stronger than I was. Why couldn't I have just swum away and quietly drowned?

My guilt consumes me.

I'm in shock that I was willing to die, amazed that I'm not already dead, and panicked that I soon will be if this ship doesn't dock in New York before midnight, April 18th.

I'll die all over again.

I have to get off the *Carpathia* and onto dry land before my ten days run out and I Snap Back. It would be a cosmic joke if I came all this way only to plop back into the open North Atlantic of my own accord.

Carpathia takes aboard the *Titanic*'s lifeboats and at about 11:00 a.m. turns tail and heads back to New York. I feel some relief to be on my way but ever more sorrow at steaming away from the remains of Archie. My overly vivid imagination wants to crowd my mind with visions of the state of his remains, but I take surprisingly harsh control of myself and forbid it. I delete the mental file. Forever.

We're battered, but we're safe. We're heading for land . . .

Until we're not.

After only a short while we're completely stopped, trapped in a field of ice. They've seen first-hand what ice can do and they're not going to take any chances. The *Carpathia's* engines shut down, and yup: I'm right back into panic again.

I'm so tired of my emotions! Do I want to die or do I want to live? I honestly can't tell. The universe is batting me around without mercy and all I can do is shut down.

43

Tuesday, April 16, 1912

I remember nothing of the rest of that day. Most of it was spent sleeping fitfully on a hard deck chair on the *Carpathia's* starboard side, sheltered beneath the overhanging deck above, with enough blankets to keep my corporeal form within standard temperature norms. A chill wind has been up, though, and my face remains perennially cold.

I don't care.

At some point early in the morning, the *Carpathia* has at least floated free of the ice field and is once again steaming for New York.

But that isn't all.

As the day progresses, after I'd managed some food in the pink room and returned to my deck chair, heavy squalls and storm-tossed seas come up, cutting down our speed once again. The ship pitches like mad. Every jolt slams my bones back down onto the wood of the deck chair and I just roll on one side and heave my food upon the deck. So is nearly everyone else. I just yell it out. By God, it would almost be cathartic but for the smell.

Stewards come by with buckets of water periodically, swishing everything over to the drains under the railings, they themselves barely able to stand on the roiling, canting deck.

Still, I don't care.

I'm occasionally looked in on by a nurse or stewardess or steward, offered all the broth I'd like. I eventually take some and it helps.

Looking out over the rail, the sea is now green and frothed with white foam, massive rain showers are loud and violent. Sometimes I get wet. The wind is of that marine variety, barely over freezing, sodden with moisture and stripping away any heat it finds.

Why would anyone go to sea? Ever?

But what unsettles me the most is that we've slowed to a virtual crawl. The ship is making barely any headway, once again drawing me nearer to my Let Go Point. We're not going anywhere fast.

Fine. Whatever.

By nightfall, although the decks are still heaving, the rain and wind are less, and although we're not going appreciably faster toward New York than we were before, I become brave enough to return to the pink room for a light meal.

I'm surrounded by women. At the Sunday service aboard *Titanic,* I found the presence of the fairer sex calming. Now it is a source of burning shame. I make no eye contact; I don't really attempt to recognize any faces. Most of them are overflow *Carpathia* people. I learn to spot who's well-dressed (*Carpathia*) and who's not (*Titanic*). I can't look at the women in lesser clothes, for I know that I am here at the expense of their beloved husbands.

I doubt very much they want to look at me, either.

Back on the deckchair, wrapped like a swaddled infant, I just cross my arms over my chest, lay my head back, close my eyes . . . and wait.

44

Wednesday, April 17, 1912

I guess I slept. A lot. I wake to sunshine and a calm, flat, blue sea.

Carpathia is chugging along nicely now, at what I assume is her normal pace, albeit visibly slower than that of a *Titanic* class of ship.

At least we're on our way, and I am no longer in constant danger of vomiting.

I spend most of my time in my deck chair, staring out at the water. I can hardly manage to think of Archie, and when I do, I am overcome with strong, oily emotions: grief and anger and guilt and unspeakable sadness. If he were here, he'd comfort me with a joke, but he's not here.

I somehow can't believe he's dead—even though he's been dead my whole life.

All that time I spent memorizing his words and features, I

now wish I could—not delete, I never want to delete them—but just put them on a mental thumb drive and stick it in a drawer somewhere for much, much later.

Right now I just can't go there.

Now that the sea has settled down, an uncomfortable number of passengers are always walking past, standing around, staring, congregating. All conversations are hushed and respectful, but the crowding presence is getting on my nerves.

Brunch in the pink room, back to the deck chair.

Finally, at early afternoon—I have no idea what time it is, I'm not going to even touch my iPhone right now; the battery is super low, and it could still just kack without warning—it's time for me to climb off my deck chair and attempt to move around.

I decide to go for a walk.

This is a tiny ship, only four public decks. I've been camped out on the second one from the top. The *Carpathia's* Boat Deck is above me but virtually inaccessible due to the number of *Titanic's* lifeboats stacked in every available space. It is for this reason there are so many people everywhere else. The *Carpathia* is woefully overloaded right now.

Although, I muse glumly, at least now they have enough lifeboats for everyone. There's a first.

It is with unspeakable joy that I encounter Jake and Letitia Slocombe in a cramped companionway. They got off *Titanic* in a lifeboat with nary a scratch. As we obnoxiously block foot traffic, I tell them an abbreviated version of my tale. As I begin speaking, I realize it's the first time in about two days that I've attempted to use my voice. I start out a little squeaky and gravelly, which I'm sure is adding to the traumatic nature of the tale of *Titanic* going down from under us, the death of Archie, and about the collapsible boat. Letitia is nearly stricken by my account. Tears are in her eyes.

I'm just so happy they're alive. Like I said, I'd studied survivor lists but never actually committed them to memory, so it's just as well that I was wrong.

I ask after the couple they were hanging with and they get quiet. They never made it off.

We part ways in the corridor. I'm sure I'll see them again, but as I walk away, I review the mental picture of Letitia just now in her borrowed clothes.

High collar . . .

I see Madeleine Astor, but we merely nod, shocked and embarrassed. It would be highly inappropriate for me to offer condolences, or to ask after her well-being. But she gives me a knowing smile that, true to her class, is richly packed with unspoken emotion and reassurance.

At dinner in the pink room later, I am joined by none other than Margaret Brown. She recognizes me from the Dining Saloon on *Titanic* and asks how I am holding up. We enjoy a consommé with bread and she, unlike anyone else thus far, seems willing to have a normal conversation. And damned if I'm not flooded with relief.

Not wasting time with pleasantries, she boldly places her hand over mine and looks me right in the eye: "You know there wasn't a man, woman or child who didn't absolutely love Archie Butt. He had the ears of presidents. Had your ear too, I could tell. He really liked you."

Bitch. You want me to cry? Right now? Shit . . .

But I quickly rein in my emotions and thank her for her kind words.

"Archie was an amazing man," I manage to say, somehow keeping my voice even. "I just wish I'd acted differently, though. That I'd made a difference . . . I guess I feel like I took the coward's way out."

Margaret Brown's response yanks me back and pulls me in an entirely new direction. "Get a hold of yourself, Mark. You went down with the goddamned ship. In what way does that make you a coward?" She looks borderline impatient with me. "I simply fail to understand that. You know," she's looking down, slathering a piece of bread with a heavy knife-full of butter. "We have a saying out in Colorado. 'Get off the cross. We need the wood.'"

Although that's as old as dirt, I almost let out with a completely unbidden guffaw at the dinner table. People look at me sharply, tut-tutting at mirth during such a time.

"Face it, Mark. Life's gonna throw you all manner of horse-shit. I'd encourage you to not take things personally. That's what gets people into trouble. How you cope with said horse-shit is the only thing you can change, and it makes every bit of difference. You can wallow or you can get back up and keep going—the world don't give a damn which way you jump. You're on your own. Frankly, you have to be man enough. And I suspect you are. But I think you haven't quite tapped into it just yet. Just something to think about."

1912 people, so far as I've seen, don't talk about their feelings. Nor do they swear thus. But Margaret Brown seems unbothered by such conventions. I think I'm going to like her.

"It's just . . . this is the sort of thing that happens to someone else," I murmur.

"Honey, ain't that the truth? But the way I see it, I've been dirt poor. I've been rich. I've seen death and loss and horse-hockey-high pretention, and none of it matters a lick. You live out in San Francisco, is that right?"

I nod.

"Well, you got through that, didn't you? I suspect you're a bit of a scrapper underneath. Maybe someday you'll own up to it and learn to take the bull by the horns. Give yourself twenty years and see if you don't get what I mean.

"In the meantime, do yourself a favor and don't bother wrestling with the devil right now. Sit quiet. Let him get bored with his little handiwork here, and for him to move on. When he's finally got his back turned then you'll be able to look all this square in the eye."

It's an interesting take.

Roast beef is served, and my stomach feels stronger than it has in days. We continue chatting but without the previous intensity. She tells me of her husband and life out west, general rollicking tales of good times and bad. I don't interrupt. I let her tales spill over me and find sublime comfort in them.

We part after dessert—some messy profiteroles and coffee that hits just the right spot—and Margaret Brown takes her leave of me.

"I hope we'll see each other again, Mark. Come see me in Denver if you're ever out that way."

And she's gone, waddling in her borrowed clothes, looking for other people to pepper with her unique cheer on life.

After dinner a well-dressed man, hence an obvious *Carpathia* passenger, comes over and tries to chat me up in a friendly, supportive way. But it quickly becomes apparent that he's some kind of reporter, and hungry for a scoop. What at first seemed a kindly approach quickly turns unctuous and greedy. And I almost fall for it for a sec. But once onto him I clam up quick. Even though I could tell him more than is known by any human on this planet—every detail, facts that won't be revealed for another sixty years—it's not my place. Not going to happen. They'll have to learn, without any further intervention from me, the absolute truth of this clusterfuck.

I'm given a bath slot later that evening. I will have to stick with the clothes I've already been given, but the slightly-sticky, salty ocean sheen I've been wearing on my skin for nearly three days gets to go away now. Even though water is what got us into this mess, this time it is warm and safely contained in a tub. It is once again my friend. It feels wonderful. For a few precious moments I am free from the sensation of cold that has dogged various parts of my body for so long.

Soon thereafter I am back at my deck chair. Archie's cashmere coat, carefully hung around the headrest, is finally drying out, but looking bedraggled as cashmere will do after a salt soaking. It doesn't smell like him. It smells like wet dog.

45

Thursday, April 18, 1912

I can barely endure this day.

I'm awake early. Clouds are gathering. Breakfast interlude in the pink room is with yet more strangers, and we're gradually becoming slightly more conversational. Some *Carpathia* people are at my table with their children, and one of the boys is named Archie. When I hear that I practically spit out my mush. He's a cute kid, about three years old with curly black hair and big blue eyes and rosy cheeks, wearing a sailor suit, and he looks up at me like I'm a rock star. His sister Gabby is shy and only whispers to her mother, who harshly corrects her and tells her to speak up.

After yet another excruciatingly long day of featureless sea travel, heavy rains begin as darkness falls.

People are up, pacing, craning for a first glimpse of land. We pass the Nantucket Light Ship, visible only as blobs of illumination, and soon the lights of Long Island appear in the mists.

They named it appropriately: It takes forever to steam down the length of it, well over three hours. I can't even manage to detect the Rockaways in the dark. Finally, off in the distance, a brightly lit Coney Island twinkles into view. It would certainly be empty of people with all this rain, but the brilliance of it floods my stomach with warm goo.

§

LONG AFTER WE pass the Verrazano Narrows-With-No-Bridge, I see a tiny Statue of Liberty, lit up in the distance, shrouded by sheets of drizzle. It would be a lovely and emotional image, but I'm beyond actually cataloguing my feelings.

Then the ship comes to a complete stop. A harbor pilot must be brought aboard to guide *Carpathia* in. My stomach is back in knots again.

We power back up.

With me running out of time, I become alarmed that we'll have to stop at Ellis Island first to unload the steerage passengers. It will take *hours* . . .

Fortunately, I soothe myself off that particular emotional ledge: The *Carpathia* was outbound from America. She has no undocumented inbound immigrants, and the number of steerage passengers rescued off *Titanic* is too pitiful and few to require the services of Ellis Island.

Let it go, I tell myself through clenched teeth. *God, please, just let it go.*

Doesn't help. I'm practically hopping from foot to foot.

At 8:00 p.m. we stop at Pier 58, the White Star Line terminus, whereupon they spend a vital precious hour merely to offload the *Titanic's* lifeboats. At an empty dock.

What a stupid, useless gesture! I'm severely pressed for time, yet it's like Cunard derives a slow, delicate pleasure in saying to their rival company: *Hey. White Star. Here's your shit. You can pay us later*.

Finally, my Snap Back time drawing ever nearer, we eventually pull back out into the Hudson and tie up at Cunard Line's Pier 54 so that, at long last, final debarkations can take place.

It's taking ridiculously forever, and I am freaking out.

Although I suppose I'd survive falling into the Hudson River in December 2019, I'd really rather not.

I almost shove my way off the *Carpathia*. There are injured people who obviously deserve to go first. Then they appear to sort by economic rank. The well-monied are escorted off, both *Titanic* and *Carpathia* passengers, then the lesser first-class guests, including me. It's taking forever and I'm stomping to get off the ship and onto the crowded dock below.

Finally it's my turn to disembark, with less than an hour to spare.

I'm corralled into the first-class lane, waiting for Customs clearance. It's an annoyance, but now that I'm safe and on solid ground I manage to slow my heart rate and try to be present for the proceedings. I'm already going to be throwing off enough alien vibes that any Customs officer would be massively on edge about me.

I'm questioned briefly by Customs agents and let through. No one off *Titanic* has any sort of passport, and in fact I don't see any being thrust back and forth, so I assume they just aren't generally yet a thing yet in 1912. And if they are, practically no one will have thought to retain theirs in the disaster.

Out of Customs, I am a free man in New York. I made it alive. But at what cost?

I'm never going to be the same again, I know this to be true.

Forty thousand people are waiting outside Pier 58. Loved ones, relatives, and spectators crowd the Cunard dock to hear the latest news. The *Carpathia*, it will later be learned, had been ordered into radio silence by the powers that be—namely, Bruce Ismay. No details or confirmations were sent. The world knew of the disaster but could only hold its collective breath and wait for the *Carpathia* to eventually reach dry land. Speculation was rampant. Sources claimed all hands were lost, while others claimed *Titanic* was being safely towed to New York.

When the *Carpathia* finally docks and only 700 of the 2,200 souls come forth, the immense crowd turns silent in shock. People are crying everywhere. I just make my way through the throng, brushing past those who openly sob.

There's nowhere for me to go. I Snap Back in an hour—an hour! That's how close I came. I can't believe the universe would have made such an exception for me. It makes me sick.

I basically just wait with the crowd inside the building, out of the rain.

As my time approaches, I make my way out to 11th Avenue and trudge to the north in the rain, away from people for when I Snap Back, wearing clothes from who knows who. I have on Archie's wool coat, dried out on *Carpathia* but getting wet all over again.

The time comes. I flash forward 107 years to 2019 in a whoosh, dizzy, sick and on the sidewalk, hugging the wall of a building.

PART IX

2019 - NEW YORK

46

Thursday, December 5, 2019

It's early December in New York and it is chilly. About forty degrees with a chance of snow. You can tell by the milky whiteness of the sky. It's noon.

Standing against an abandoned building, weeds growing out the cracks in the sidewalk, I take out my phone and gingerly power it back on.

Still works. Battery's at 8 percent.

I text David: "I'm back."

"How's Ireland?"

"I'm in NYC."

"WTAF?!"

"Didn't get off in time. Whole disaster, almost died."

"Shit! Call me!"

So I dial his number and standing on the street, shivering, quickly give him a summation, warning him that my battery is almost dead.

"Jesus. Do you need anything?"

"No, I think I'm good. I still have my credit cards, they just got wet. I'm assuming they still work. I'll just take a cab over to JFK and fly back to London to get The Machine."

"OK. Call me when you have some juice and a chance to settle down. And Mark? Welcome home."

We end the connection, and I don't have to wait long to see an empty cab coming down the West Side Highway. I hail it and climb in.

The cabbie is hysterically happy that he gets a fare to Kennedy. His name is Negasi, from Ethiopia. He wants to talk; he hates what Uber is doing to the taxi industry . . .

I can seriously not go there. I answer in general terms and single syllables and just look out the window, not really listening. Not really registering the modern New York visible to me. More than uninteresting, it feels patently unreal.

Traffic is stuck in the Queens-Midtown Tunnel. I roll down my window but the air is heavy with exhaust.

Since I can't risk firing up Expedia on my phone, I just have Negasi drop me off at Terminal Two, and I'll try my hand at the ticket counter with Delta.

Agent Brenda, in blouse and scarf—tied in a knot and over to one side—takes my Visa card and tries to find me a seat to Heathrow. She's visibly at Red Alert that an oddly-dressed bearded man is buying a last-minute, one-way ticket with no luggage, at an actual airport ticket counter, and not over the internet like a normal person. She overly examines my warped and still somewhat wet U. S. passport. I swear she looks ready to sniff it for traces of C-4. And my insides melt with relief that I had decided, at the last minute, to bring that passport with me at all. Had I not, I would be completely buggered.

I manage to soothe Brenda back down a little bit, since I'm just a California Dude after all. There's a flight in three and a half hours, and they have a few coach middle seats left.

A 757. A whimper. And at a price just shy of extortion.

I take my leave of Brenda, hopefully having charmed her well enough to keep her hand off the hotline to Homeland Security, and make my way to TSA.

I don't get any grief at security. There's zero line and the guy's friendly. He says, "Hey, bro, you dressed like my granddaddy."

As I move into the modern airport terminal and feel myself sketching back into my own, proper timeframe, it all seems a surreal blur. I grab a sandwich, a Red Bull, a USB cube and cable, and once seated among the endless rows of The Black Chairs of the American Airport, plug in my phone and quietly zone out.

I could handle Facebook right now about as well as I could a colonoscopy, and while I hope a few work-related emails are waiting for me, I just can't go there.

Modern people are noticeably overweight and poorly dressed. No thought is given to flair, status, art, or beauty. We've become a loud, frumpy lot. Instead of giggling at the presence of a high collar, I'd be overjoyed to see any sort of collar at all.

At long last they call my section. I'm sure I smell plenty funky, wedged into my tiny seat wearing odd 1912 clothes that are not only 107 years out of date but unwashed hand-me-downs as well. I feel like explaining to my seat mates that the body odor they may detect is not actually mine, but that of someone who's dead; that it's not my fault.

I consume many scotches on the plane, and twice almost light my pipe without thinking.

The five-day ocean journey to London is now only six and a half hours. Of course, in coach it feels somewhat more interminable, spoilt as we have become.

I pay for inflight Wi-Fi and have plenty of juice in my phone once more.

I can't bear to look at Archie's pictures directly. Not yet. But I pull up a few articles related to the loss of the *Titanic*, mostly hoping my name does not appear among them, and I find something that nearly ends me.

William Howard Taft wrote of Archie: "He conducted himself with a singleness of purpose and to the happiness and comfort of the President, who was his chief. To many fine qualities he added loyalty, and when he became one of my family he was as a son or a brother."

The article goes on to describe Archie's memorial service in Washington, some weeks after the disaster. Taft rose to the lectern to speak of his friend and aide but could only get a few words out before his emotions overcame him. He stopped.

The President of the United States, Governor General of the Philippines, Supreme Commander of American Expeditionary Forces in Cuba, and future Chief Justice of the United States Supreme Court broke openly into tears and was unable to continue speaking.

He left the podium.

That was Archie Butt.

I lean back in my coach middle seat and close my eyes and fight tears of my own. I hic once. A few tears spill openly down my face and manage to get as far as my beard. I wipe them on the scratchy cocktail napkin with Delta Airlines and Diet Coke logos on it, wad it up, and shove it into the seat back pocket.

I snooze the snooze of the long-haul economy class passenger. I empty my mind of thought and simply exist, untethered from the Earth.

To borrow a hackneyed phrase: I'm flying.

47

Friday, December 6, 2019

We land in London and I don't want to be here. Not even a little bit. But I have to rescue David's Machine from my room at the Ritz and deliver it back home to San Francisco. It's a rather valuable piece of equipment.

The weather is uncharacteristically nice—particularly for December—which helps buoy my mood somewhat. I breeze through Customs, make the ridiculously long walk to the Heathrow Express train to Paddington, then catch a cab to the Ritz.

I key into my room. The icy salt water of the North Atlantic didn't demagnetize it, which surprises me. Despite the Do Not Disturb sign on my door, they'd cleaned my room anyway. The Machine is sitting right where I left it, my 2019 clothes and iPhone charger laying on the bed. Pamela's sweater is still in the drawer. I get undressed and take a long shower, at once eager for—and yet obliquely uncomfortable with—the warm water playing upon my skin.

With a heavy heart, I look at my pictures of Archie. But I don't cry. I'm still too shook.

Here's The Machine. I could go back and get him. But I know that would be impossible. I could Appear into his life at an earlier time, but that seems wrong. I'd have to introduce myself to him all over again and he's completely wrapped up in his career. Where would I fit in his life?

I wouldn't.

I just curl into a ball on the bed and stare for an hour.

Of no mind to remain in England any longer than necessary, I take a cab right back to Heathrow to go home.

By the time the taxi is fighting its way through the Talgarth Roundabout, I can only stare at the dull scene as it always appears, forever under gray skies: Fuller's London Pride brewery across from the gleaming Porsche dealership, cars trying to cut each other off around the circle to no perceivable purpose.

I can feel my mind again tripping up in turmoil. I'd just as soon it wouldn't.

Time travel sounded too good to be true. Now it feels like a horrible thing to me. I made my choices, insouciantly, foolishly, and am destroyed by them. Why didn't I just pick that quiet weekend in 1928?

I had to see all these disasters, not realizing I'd be a victim of them as well.

I don't like that word, "victim." I refuse to succumb to the concept.

Our current culture seems to be obsessed with everyone being the victim of something—it's as if we, collectively, seek victimhood as a path to enlightenment, to status, or to some sort of power. As if there's a prize to be won.

It's bullshit. There are no prizes for getting whacked by

circumstance—particularly when it's self-inflicted. It just makes you hurt all over and distrust all you see.

I now carry the pain of these events. It's like I've been cutting myself with a knife on purpose, all while trying to look fabulous to an audience . . . an audience of . . . no one.

I feel like I'm losing my mind.

Talking to a therapist would help. But nobody would believe me. Time travel is still impossible to the world at large, so a therapist would just think I had some sort of psychosis. They wouldn't hear me. They'd probably remand me to some sort of custody—if they even have that anymore. Sometimes it feels like they don't.

That makes me feel awful, and alone. I hurt all over. I want to go home and heal.

Finally we pull up to the DFS Freight Terminal, somewhat removed from the central section of Heathrow Airport, on an industrial back street that I find myself tickled to see is called Faggs Road. Little-boy humor is about all I can handle right now.

I have the taxi wait as I drop The Machine off to be shipped back home. It's only a short wait. David is thorough in all things: Pre-paid, bill of lading, hazmat certificate—everything is in order, and I'm soon back in the cab and dropped off at Terminal 5.

I'm deeply thankful the cabbie is in no mood to talk during the hour we spend together.

My return British Airways business class ticket to San Francisco was open-ended; again, kudos to David for his smarts. I'm through passport control, security search, and arrive at the gate to one minor disappointment. The aircraft is being downgraded to a 777-300 instead of an Airbus A380.

Before all this, I'd have been devastated. But now I'm just lucky to be alive. I manage to keep it in perspective. Business class is good whatever plane you're on, and this would very much be in the purview of a “first-world problem.” I decide to treat it as such.

I attack my inflight meal with vigor, enjoying a scotch and many glasses of red wine before rolling over in my pod and trying to get some sleep.

I’m half expecting us to crash. I keep seeing the world in terms of disasters.

But as usual, when flying westbound over Greenland and upper Canada, sleep doesn’t add up to much. I’m awake.

So I fish out my laptop and start writing. It’s painful, but I have to get these things off my mind. I simply review the days I spent, more or less in order, to the best of my recollection. I don’t speak of emotional reactions or deep feelings. Just the facts. I can always fill in the blanks later, should I ever feel strong enough to do so.

Eleven hours later, I’m back in Northern California.

The sun is shining, except for the ever-present fog oozing over the hills toward SFO. Daly City will surely be lost in it, cold, empty and boring, all its houses constructed together in wan, pastel blocks.

I’ve only been away six days. It seems flatly impossible. Weeks have gone by for me. Weeks of horror and friendships, death and destruction—and a brand-new baby girl.

Once outside Customs, I consider taking BART. It would be financially responsible, but I am beyond such things and call a Lyft instead.

My apartment strikes me as alien and uninspired in the extreme. It’s familiar. All is as it should be. Rhoda is even mildly curious to see me. David had been checking in on her and she seems no worse for wear. I pass by Fluffy in her tank—it’s in need of a good clean, but she’s pleased as punch to paddle over, even more so when I shake out some food pellets for her.

There’s something quite off in the refrigerator. I tend to that and unpack my few things: my 1940s clothes and *Carpathia* hand-me-downs and Edgar's sweater.

Huge pile of bills, most past due, a humiliatingly small number of emails, and I don't know how I'll ever find the strength to focus on my work projects again. I'm wrung out.

How do I incorporate all I've just experienced without cracking up?

I wander up to David's apartment. He gives me a great big hug and I sit on his couch and tell him the entire tale, omitting nothing. He listens in stunned silence. I can't have a therapist, so this will have to do.

Scotch. I have scotch.

"My God," is all David can say.

Maybe he's starting to get a glimmer of the human equation in his overly-scienced brain after all.

I go out that night, jet-lagged and janked. I fall to my chicken panang curry and a good stiff sweet jolt of Thai iced tea with a passion.

Thursday night at the Edge is populated with people. I know most of them and say "hi" with quick hugs but otherwise barely speak to anyone. People seem able to make only general small talk, endlessly droning on about local politics and how awful Trump is and what a soulless shell San Francisco has become of late.

Without realizing it, I become impossibly hammered.

I walk back to my apartment visibly weaving, trying to walk a straight line, which just makes me weave even more.

Seriously uncool.

I go to bed alone, amid bed spins, yet, despite my haze, I detect a hot new shot of piss from Rhoda at the bottom of my nightstand.

PART X

2020 - SAN FRANCISCO

48

Thursday, January 9, 2020

2020 is going to be a great year! I feel clean.

Although I am still riddled with emotional scars—and although I cannot tell another living soul aside from David Meisenhoelder—by putting one foot in front of the other and simply living from one breath to the next, I somehow, slowly, begin to reassert.

The damage to my poor self will manifest at odd moments, often while trying to have normal conversations with people. I turn angry at the banality of content. I wish to grab people by the t-shirt and scream: *"Don't you know how unimportant all this is?!"*

Not only do I now have PTSD, I have it for three separate traumatic events, any one of which would be enough to cause what I now face: the shakes, night sweats, waking up in cold terror, sudden panic attacks. These may never go away, and I just have to simply accept them as my new normal. I assume they will gradually subside on their own. They'd better. I have no options in terms of actual self-care.

The knowledge that, out there in the north Atlantic, lies a *Titanic* deckchair with my name on it ought to be worth a lifetime of bragging rights. But the cold truth is I can never tell a soul. I doubt by the time Benny Goodman's "Sing, Sing, Sing!" hit the charts in 1936 that deckchair would have been anything more than an off-color bit of muck, reduced to rot.

When I first got to San Francisco in 1990, I was distracted to the point of being a pest by a particular man called Joe. I was twenty, he was in his late fifties, and I was so into him . . . I pestered him and pursued him and would have openly danced in front of him if I thought it would get me his phone number. The age differential served only to excite me. It was against him I measured all my crushes over the years, never having gotten more than the merest nod from him, ever.

Saw him in line at Molly Stone's yesterday, first time in—what, fifteen years? I heard he'd been living down in Redwood City or some such tomfoolery, partnered and out of view. And suddenly yesterday there he was, right in front of me. All his allure, all the DNA I coaxed out of my body on his behalf . . . and what I saw before me was an old man. He didn't need a walker yet but was clearly headed that way, head craning forward from his shoulders. His hands trembled, it took him three-times the normal pace to enter his PIN number on the card reader, and he hobbled off never having seen me.

I know only that death takes everyone in its grasp and I am missing some serious point here on Earth. David's Machine has elevated me to some ungodly Advanced Placement learning course, but I do not know what it is that I cannot figure out. Only that I can't see anything clearly, other than the visceral impression that people die.

Is that really all we have in common with each other?

I go for walks a lot. I tried to limit my alcohol use for a while but that quickly went out the window. It always does.

Even went to a pot dispensary to see if a good indica would help, but as has always been the case, it does little but make me feel cold and sad. I found it impossible to write my next article, due in a week; pot just numbs the motor functions of my brain and leaves me stupid.

My next lymphoma PET scan isn't until February, so I have time to ignore that for all I'm worth. Time travel is like free days added to my vacation allotment in violation of all the rules and it's deliciously yummy and maybe I'm cheating the devil. I'm OK with that.

New Year's Eve was spent at the Lone Star Saloon, with lots of acquaintances and beer and I smooched a few fellas—one real good. I counted it as one of the first normal nights of my new, scarred life.

David even tried to get frisky with me the other night. On his couch, in his sweatpants, he began to present the appearance of male arousal. He's quite formidable in that aspect of his person, and, for a brief moment I thought about it. Truth be told, it probably would have done me a world of good.

But I broke the mood.

"Oh, please. Last time I went down it was the actual fucking *Titanic*. Now you tryna come at me with that tired old thing? What the hell is wrong with you?"

He just laughed it off and went to get us another drink. I knew he wouldn't take it as a serious rebuff, that's just not how he rolls. I long ago developed a brash, in-your-face savagery with him that is completely outside my norm yet always works with David. He expects—and frankly gets off on—being given a hard time.

But tears suddenly welled up in me. I just got flip and ruined a moment. I let an opportunity for intimacy (yes, there's a powerful intimacy to that, don't let anyone ever tell you otherwise) escape from my grasp. My sass mouth thoroughly slammed the door on him. The moment was over.

I walked home unthinkingly. No thoughts at all.

My mind has finally been shocked into obedient silence. It's a first. It's somewhat peaceful, but I know better than to trust it. A brain like mine turning suddenly quiet probably just means it's up to something. Something bad.

In general, one thing has become quite clear: I have got to get my work life back on track.

With a vigor I haven't felt in years, I completely redesign my website, run ads, update my CV, and start emailing potential clients. I've always known what to do and how to do it, but for a long time I let the most crucial elements of wage earning wind down into apathy.

That ends now.

If I'm to be stuck in San Francisco, I can at least take steps to have money in my pocket once more. My days of whine and poses are over.

After a week of fervent work toward that aim—and in fact, getting promising nibbles—with a glimmer of hope, I remember that Sloane Jarvis is still alive and living close by. I could go see her .

What do I say? That I knew her mother? I'm only forty-nine years old, how could this be?

Yet I must do it. It will help me.

I cyber stalk her a little bit. She's at the Sequoia Retirement Community in Walnut Creek.

I call the main number and enquire after a Sloane Jarvis Norbury.

"Sir, we don't disclose the names of our residents."

"I understand. Well, I'm a correspondent, working on a piece. If it's all right, could you forward a message to her letting her know I seek to interview people who, as children, lived in London during World War II?"

I schmooze. Eventually seem to make headway with Asunción on the phone.

"Please forward my message to her. It would really help me out."

Asunción's not entirely convinced even now, but says she'll take down my message and see that it gets sent to any appropriate persons.

That just leaves me to wait.

Two days go by before a 925 area code shows up on my caller ID, and I thrill a bit, hoping it may be she.

It is. "I'm Mrs. Norbury, returning your call."

And I realize I've never actually heard the woman's voice, beyond the wailing of a two-day-old infant. She sounds hale and cogent.

"Thank you so much for calling me back, Mrs. Norbury. I really appreciate it." And I launch into my spiel: "I'm a journalist, studying the effects of the Blitz on the people of London, and I understand you were there?"

She laughs, kindly but with a hint of pity.

"I was there, yes, but at an extremely young age."

"I've only just returned from London last week. I took a good hard look at some of the bombing sights, such as they exist today. I visited the Churchill war rooms. It's a subject that keenly fascinates me. And you were actually in England during the war?"

"Yes. I was born in a Tube station in London during an air raid in 1940."

"In a Tube station? That's incredible. I'm interviewing anyone who still remembers it. Mostly, I'm focused on how rationing ultimately affected the youth of that era."

"Ah, *that* I remember, all too well. The rationing . . . it went on for years." She laughs a little. She has a bit of an accent still. "I remember the day I got my very own, brand new gingham dress. I was over the moon. I honestly believed I was Princess for a Week."

I chuckle lightly over the phone. She seems nice.

"I have to be in Concord tomorrow for meetings. Would it be all right if I stopped by and visited with you for a moment? I promise not to take up too much of your time."

"Well, I suppose so. As I said, I don't remember much of those years, I was only five when the war ended. But I'd be more than happy to help in any way I can."

I feel good that I'll get to see Sloane Jarvis again.

Today is when I get in my SUV and drive out to Walnut Creek.

I'm nervous. Why am I nervous? About a baby I held in my arms? Whose umbilical cord I personally cut?

We meet safely in the lounge of the Sequoia Retirement Home yet must begin on a somewhat formal and cautious footing.

Sloane is hardly elderly, these days 80 is the new 60. She's just been playing tennis.

I see the resemblance right away. That chin and nose, ostensibly Edgar's, and Pamela's eyes, wide-set and blue.

"Thank you for seeing me," I begin.

"Certainly, Mr. Baldwin." She's looking at me in an odd way. "Have we met?"

Uh . . . I don't know how to answer this. As a two-day-old, there's no way she'd recognize me, no human brain has that power. Yet she's still looking at me quizzically for some seconds. Until she snaps to and smiles bashfully.

"Forgive me, Mr. Baldwin, I do believe I was staring at you just now. That was rude. I'm sure it's nothing."

"Oh, that's fine. Maybe we knew each other in a past life?"

She giggles.

"Oh, and please, call me Mark."

"Mark?" She comes up a bit short at the sound of my name.

"My mother always said that was her favorite name for a man. In fact, it's what I named my eldest son."

I gaze over at Sloane in amazement. Does that mean what I think it means?

I wrestle my thoughts back toward our intended conversation as we seat ourselves in the lounge. "So what do you remember of the war?"

"Precious little, I'm afraid. We lived in a rooming house—those were my earliest memories—my mother and me.

"Tell me about your parents."

"My mother worked in a munitions factory and my father was a pilot in the RAF. Father was killed in action when I was three. That would have been in 1943."

Oh. Damn.

"I'm so sorry. Do you remember him?"

"Barely. It was a big deal when he came to visit. I still have an impression of him in my mind; of course, I don't know how much of that is real or how much are blanks that I filled in with my own childish yearnings for something lost. I just remember how devastated my mother was, and knowing I could do nothing to console her."

"I'm so sorry to hear. Do you remember the other people in the rooming house?"

"Indirectly. They came and went. Apparently, the house itself was bombed and we lived in shelters when I was a baby. Then the house was rebuilt at the end and we moved back in. Those were my earliest memories, there in that house. I shared a room with my mother until a few years after the war, then we moved in with my grandparents in Essex. My grandmother was very mean, I didn't like her. My mother worked various jobs, day and night, until she met my step-father."

"So she remarried?"

"Yes. To a man named Cecil Hayden. An actor. Oh, Grandmother was furious! Even as a child I sensed the scorn she had for that man. He and I got along well, but it turns out Grandmother was right: Mother abruptly left Mr. Hayden in 1956. Packed me up and carried me to California. My mother always said she wanted to live in San Francisco, so we came here. To her, San Francisco was like some beacon on a hill. She always vowed she would come. And what my mother wanted, she invariably got."

Yep. Sounds like Pamela.

"Mother married for a third time in 1960, here in California. To a good man, named Terry Johnson. They remained together until his death in the late '80s. And then my mother died in 1999."

End of the line. Pamela died at the age of 82.

Cecil Hayden! So he survived on the roof that day after all. I'll never know about Rodger—a huge gap remains in the story. Still, I'm able to connect many more dots than I ever thought possible. Full circle.

I'm sure Cecil never gave up his love of women, that much seems clear.

I find myself wiping my right hand on the leg of my Levi's even now, remembering it being sticky on a rooftop somewhere, in some before-time.

Sloane shares more on the war, her earliest memories: rationing, blackouts, shelters, buzz bombs. The Germans tried bombing London again later in the war with V2 rockets, fired directly from Germany. You never knew where they would hit, and they were devastating.

I feel the formality and cautiousness between two strangers slowly slip to one side. Sloane seems like a fascinating woman, and apparently finds me agreeable to talk to. She's vivacious and polite, putting me at ease.

She is a lady.

She volunteers that she married a man named Norbury in

1966, a good solid English name in his own right, and they had three children: Mark, Susan, and Ryan.

"I separated from my husband years ago, but my children are among the good ones of this world. They still manage to be close to their dear old mother whenever their schedules permit."

Someone approaches us in the lobby of the Sequoia, an attractive man about fifty-two years old, blond with a blond beard, a little chubby in all the right places with blue eyes and a cute smile. I can see some of his grandmother in him. He's wearing a Lone Star t-shirt, which can only mean one thing: like me—and despite their mountain of foibles—Mark prefers the company of men and isn't concerned about advertising it. I feel myself instantly at ease, and more than a little intrigued.

"Speaking of! Mr. Baldwin, I'd like you to meet my son. His name is Mark, too. Isn't that a coincidence?"

I shake hands with him, stealing a chance at eye contact. He's sexy. Blond and gingery, with blond eyebrows, a perennial weakness for me. Soft bluish eyes, irises nearly to gray; irises that are busy with delicate strands and intricate patterns I'd love to learn by heart.

"I go to the Lone Star sometimes," I volunteer to him. "I've never seen you there before."

"I live out in Castro Valley. So I'm only in the city for work, then I just usually turn tail and head home."

The three of us chat then about general things such as the weather. But I don't want to cut into Mark's time with his mother—I heard all I came to hear and learned more than I ever dreamed. My head is still spinning over the connections I've just made.

I'm thrilled to have met Sloane as an eighty-year-old woman.

I give each my business card, thanking Sloane very much for her time and lingering with Mark a few extra moments.

Mark makes sure to hand me his card, too. “Call or email me, anytime. It might be fun to hang out.”

“I’d like that,” I say, and we make more, smiling eye contact and shake hands once again.

I take my leave then, hoping to see Sloane again and definitely wanting to see more of Mark.

He’s predominantly English: Jarvis one side and Norbury on the other. As I drive through the MacArthur Maze and toward the Bay Bridge, I wonder if I’ll be given leave to discover just which part of Mark might be crooked after all.

for Archie

Thanks for reading! If you've a mind to, kindly leave a review on my Amaon page. Reader reviews are, literally, our bread and butter.

A Quarter Past - Book II is on its way soon and I think it's going to be a pretty good read. The JFK assassination, the moon landing, the stock market crash of 1929—followed by a gentle, calming trip to Nazi Germany in 1936. On the *Hindenburg*. Still working on a title, *Mark Fights Like a Girl* is coming out a little too fresh.

ACKNOWLEDGMENTS

Fluffy the turtle and Rhoda-the-cat-who-pees are entirely true. They're here right now and say 'hi.' I'm lucky to have a great mom, Mary (a.k.a Mildred), who not only read this thing, but read it twice. That's a lot to ask of anyone. Rod Hagan so graciously volunteering as a beta reader, pretty much saved my bacon. No less than nine errors, missed by my proofreader, were caught by him. I am eternally grateful. I find it doubly amusing that he's also my yoga instructor. I dedicate all future chaturanga dandasanas to him. Heidi, my neighbor, who encouraged me to make the jump to fiction. George my brick my rock. Thank you for being you. Tish: All of this came at the expense of a wee cat at my side. Because of you she is not allowed on my keyboard and hence flies into a complete frustrated rage, daily. Hissing and biting. She knows I love my keyboard more than her and it eats her alive. For hate's sake, she spits her last breath at thee. Thanks also to the Titanic Historical Society and Encyclopedia Titanica. And to James Cameron, only because I talked to him on a plane once and he told me I was pretty.